Praise for *The Court of the Air*

"Hunt has packed the story full of intriguing gimmicks. . . . The 'steammen' and their refreshingly tender machine culture are affecting and original." —*Publishers Weekly*

"A curious part-future blend of aerostats, mechanical computers, psychic powers, self-willed steam-powered robots, Elder Gods, talking superweapons, and more . . . Harry Potter mugs H. P. Lovecraft and L. Ron Hubbard explains it all." —*Kirkus Reviews*

"An adventure tale in the grand old style, full of mystery, magic, and skulduggery, as well as riveting bouts of gun- and sword play." —*BookPage*

"Endlessly inventive and as intricately plotted as George R. R. Martin's *A Song of Fire and Ice*, *The Court of the Air* is a tale no reader should miss." —*Grasping for the Wind*

"An ultrasupersonic speed Dickens fantasy thriller . . . Put on your seat belts for a frenetic cat-and-mouse encounter that includes some nasty paranormal adversaries as this is an exciting tale of two orphans trying to save the world from those who want Armageddon now." —*SFRevu*

D0377060

The
Court of the Air

Stephen Hunt

TOR®
fantasy

A TOM DOHERTY ASSOCIATES BOOK
NEW YORK

This is a work of fiction. All the characters, organizations, and events portrayed in this book are either products of the author's imagination or are used fictitiously.

THE COURT OF THE AIR

Copyright © 2007 by Stephen Hunt

First published in Great Britain by HarperVoyager, an imprint of Harper-Collins Publishers.

A Tor Book
Published by Tom Doherty Associates, LLC
175 Fifth Avenue
New York, NY 10010

www.tor-forge.com

Tor® is a registered trademark of Tom Doherty Associates, LLC.

ISBN-13: 978-0-7653-6022-9
ISBN-10: 0-7653-6022-5

First U.S. Edition: June 2008
First U.S. Mass Market Edition: April 2009

Printed in the United States of America

0 9 8 7 6 5 4 3 2 1

Thanks where thanks are due.
You know who you are.

Chapter One

Molly Templar sat dejected by the loading platform of the Handsome Lane laundry. An empty cart bore testament to the full tub of clothes inside, bubbling away. At least Molly tried to imagine what dejected would feel like, and scrunched her freckled face to match the mood. In the end though, it was one of the other poorhouse girls, Rachael, who came to fetch her, not the Beadle, so Molly's player-like mastery of 'dejected' went unappreciated.

Damson Snell, the mistress of the laundry, came out to see who had turned up, and looked disappointed that it was just another Sun Gate workhouse girl. 'The Beadle too busy to see the quality of the idle scruffs he's forcing on my business, then?'

'His apologies, miss,' said Rachael. 'He is otherwise engaged.'

'Well, you tell him from me, I got no room for workers as slack as this one.' Snell pointed to Molly. 'You know what I caught her doing?'

'No miss.' Although Rachael's tone suggested she might have an inkling.

'Reading!' Damson Snell's face went red with incredulity.

1

'Some gent had left a thruppence novel in the pocket of his coat and she—' her finger stabbed at Molly '—was only bloody reading it. And when I bangs her one, she cheeks me back. A fine little madam and no mistake. You tell the Beadle we runs a place of work here, not a library. When we wants a lady of letters, I'll send for an articled clerk, not some Sun Gate scruff.'

Rachael nodded with her best impression of contrite under-standing and led Molly away before the laundry owner could extend her tirade.

'A fine lesson in business from her,' said Molly, when they were out of earshot. 'She who slips the Beadle twenty shillings a month and gets her labour free from the poorhouse. Her lesson in economics forgot to include a fair wage for those who have nothing to sell but their labour.'

Rachael sighed. 'You're turning into a right little Carlist, Molly. I'm surprised you weren't turned out for trying to organize a worker's combination. That thruppence novel in the gent's pocket wasn't a copy of *Community and the Commons*, was it?'

'From one of her customers?' Molly snorted. 'No, it was a naval tale. The jolly aerostat *Affray* and its hunt for the submarine pirate Samson Dark.'

Rachael nodded. The Kingdom of Jackals was awash with writers from the publishing concerns along Dock Yard, sniffing out heroes, bandits, highwaymen and privateers to fill the pages of pocket news sheets like *The Middlesteel Illustrated News* and the cheap penny dreadfuls, fact and fiction blended into cut-price serials to hook the readers. The more imagina-tive stories even plundered legend, culling gods from the dark days before the citizens of Jackals embraced the Circlist medi-tations; writing devils like the wolftakers onto the pages of their tales, fiends sent to kidnap the wicked and terrify the immoral with their black cloaks and sharp teeth.

Viewed from the workhouse, the stories were bright distractions, an impossible distance from the children's lives of grind and hunger. Molly wanted those stories to be true, that if only somewhere there might be bright ballrooms and handsome officers on prancing horses. But the hard-bitten streak of realism in her realized that Samson Dark had probably been a violent old soak, with a murderous temper and a taste for cargoes he was too lazy, idle and stupid to earn himself. Far from fighting a glorious battle, the jolly airship *Affray* had probably blundered across the pirate fleet feeding innocent sailors to the fish, then held position over Dark's underwater vessel while they tumbled fire-fins into her masts and deck, leaving the burning pirates to the mercy of the ocean and the slipsharps. Days later some hack from Dock Yard would have chanced across the drunken aerostat crew in a tavern, and for the price of a keg of blackstrap, teased out an embellished tale of glory and hand-to-hand combat. Then the hack would have further embroidered the yarn for his editors on the penny dreadfuls and Dock Street imprints like the Torley Smith press.

'Have I been blown to the Beadle yet?' asked Molly, her concerns returning to the present.

'As if you wouldn't have been,' said Rachael. 'Though not by me – I'm no blower. This *is* the fourth job you've been chucked from in as many months. He was going to find out somehow.'

Molly teased her red hair nervously. 'Was the Beadle angry?'

'That's one word for it.'

'Well, what can he do?' asked Molly.

'You're a fool, Molly Templar,' said her companion, seeing the flash of defiance in Molly's eyes. 'What haven't they done to you? The strap? Administrative punishment, more days on than off? Short rations? And still you ask for more.'

'I'm out of it soon enough.'

'You've still got a year to go before your ward papers expire and you get the vote,' said Rachael. 'That's a long time to have the Beadle pissed off at you.'

'One more year, then I'm out of here.'

'To what?' asked Rachael. 'You think an orphan scruff like you or me is going to end up nobbing it up in grand society? Being waited on with partridge pie and the finest claret? You don't settle to a living soon and you'll end up running with the flash mob on the street, dipping wallets, then the crushers will have you and it'll be a transportation hulk to the Concorzian colonies for our young Damson Molly Templar.'

'I don't want to end up back there.' Molly flipped a thumb in the direction of the Handsome Lane laundry.

'Nobody wants to end up there, Molly girl. But if it puts food in your tummy and a roof over your head, it's better than starving.'

'Well, I'm being starved by a gradual process in the poor-house, or by a quick one out of it,' said Molly. 'If only . . .'

Rachael took Molly's hand. 'I know. I miss the damson too. And if wishes were shillings we'd all be living like princesses.'

There was only one damson for the orphans. Damson Darnay had been the head of the Sun Gate poorhouse before the Beadle; four years now since her heart attack. A reformer, she had argued that the rich financial district of Middlesteel could afford a model poorhouse on its doorstep. A house where the children were taught to read and write, where the mindless make-work of the poorhouse was replaced by an education and a good Circlist upbringing.

It was a vicar from the Circlean church who had taken away her shroud-wrapped body on the back of a wagon one cold morning, and the Beadle who turned up to take her place. In the pocket of the local merchants, the cost of their keep was now defrayed by placement in local businesses. Ward apprenticeships to prepare the grateful orphans for their necessary adult living.

It was strange how the children's placements never included perching behind a warm desk in one of the fancy new pneumatic buildings along Gate Street, or an articled clerk's position along Sun Lane. Sewer-scrapers, yes. Laundry jobs that would see your nails fall out from constant dipping in chemical bleach. Positions in dimly lit workshops and mill works, hunched over a loom or cutting engine, splashed by metal and losing a finger a year.

Small for her age, Molly had spent her own twelfth and thirteenth years as a vent girl, climbing the dark airshafts of the Middlesteel pneumatics with a brush, unclogging the dust and stack smoke. That was before the Blimber Watts tower breach. Fifty storeys high, Blimber Watts had been a pioneering design for its time, able to house thousands of clerks, marble atriums and even a sun garden inside its rubberized and canvas skin. But the draughtsmen had got the stress calculations wrong and the water walls had burst, sending the pneumatic structure tumbling down into the clogged streets.

Molly had been in the vents on the thirty-eighth floor when the tower lost cohesion, coming down even faster than it had gone up. Clawing in darkness at the deflating walls as her stomach turned in freefall; a smashing impact, then lying trapped for five days between two leaking water cells, licking at the walls for the stale, dirty liquid. Throwing up in terror, her voice a knife-slicing croak screaming and screaming for help.

She had lost hope of being rescued, lying in the embrace of a pressing crush of rubber. Then she sensed the steamman worker cutting through the building's remains above her. Molly knew she possessed an unnatural affinity for the mechanical race, the polished boiler hearts and intricate mechanisms of cogs and silicate prisms calling out to her to be examined, turned over in her fingers, assembled into intricate patterns. She had screwed her eyes shut and willed the worker to hear her thoughts – here, here, down HERE.

Minutes later the silent steamman had peeled back a foot-thick strip of rubber, letting a flood of impossibly bright daylight come gushing in. It stood there silently, an iron statue, until Molly noticed its voicebox had been removed. A gentle nod of its head and the steamman was moving off, as if bloodied, blackened girls crawling out of the ground were an everyday occurrence for the creature of the metal.

How the Beadle had cursed and beaten her to try to get her back into the vents. But the only time she had tried, two other vent girls had to be sent in to drag her trembling, mute form out of the passages.

'Come on,' said Rachael. 'Let's take the turn down Blackglass Lane; they were putting on a march across Grumblebank when I came to fetch you.'

'The King?' said Molly.

'Better than that, girl. The Special Guard.'

Despite the trouble that was waiting for her back at the workhouse for another job lost, Molly smiled. Everyone loved the Special Guard. Their extreme powers. The handsome cut of their uniform. Days spent at the muscle pits to whet the curves of their athletic build.

The two girls cut across a series of old rookeries, bent and puddled with garbage filth, before emerging on one of the broad clean avenues that ran parallel to Sun Street itself. There, a crowd of eager onlookers were thronging the street, a line of crushers from the local police precinct holding the press back, dark bandoleers of gleaming crystal bullets criss-crossed over their black constable's uniforms.

Back down the thoroughfare a column of the Special Guard moved with their trademark sweeping leg march, high boots whip-cracking on the road in unison. The ground seemed to vibrate with their approach.

'There's your guardsmen,' said Molly.

'And there's your king,' added Rachael.

His Majesty King Julius, eighth monarch of the Throne Restored and King of the Jackelians, sat on a cushioned red seat in an open coach and four, staring sadly back at the curious crowds.

Molly gestured at Crown Prince Alpheus sitting to the king's side, hardly any older than either of the poorhouse girls. 'He doesn't look happy.'

'Why should he be, when his father's got the waterman's sickness? His pappy won't see out another two years as monarch, then the boy's for the knife.'

Molly nodded. The King's robes had been subtly tailored to accentuate the fact that both of his arms had been surgically removed, and in time the young prince would no doubt be dragged bawling to the bone-cutter's table by his Special Guard jailers.

It had been ever thus, since Isambard Kirkhill strode across the land in a sea of blood and pistol smoke to assert parliament's right of supremacy at the head of the new pattern army. No monarch shall ever raise his arms against his people again.

Five hundred years since the civil war and the House of Guardians were still adhering to the strictures of Isambard Kirkhill, old sabre-side as his enemies had nicknamed him. There was the weekly march to Parliament Square from the palace – the latter little more than an empty marble jail now. The symbolic unchaining of the king's iron face-gag, then the king would bend down on one knee and assert the House of

7

Guardians' right to rule for the people. These days his only witnesses were a few uninterested spectators, a handful of curious foreign visitors and the long line of silent statues of Guardian Electors past.

'Look,' said Molly, pointing behind the carriage. 'Captain Flare.'

Rachael pushed at the costermongers and fish-stall hawkers in front of her to get a better look.

'It is him. Molly, will you look at those muscles? He could crush a regiment of Cassarabian sand riders between them thighs.'

Molly knew that Rachael favoured the lewder penny dreadfuls, adventures that featured the action between the silks of dune-swept harems as much as the ring of sabre steel across a battlefield. But it was true. The commander of the Special Guard was impossibly handsome. None of the penny dreadfuls' cover illustrations had ever done him justice. Captain Flare's cloak drifted behind him like a thing alive, a dancing shadow, his piercing blue eyes sweeping the crowd, making them feel he was staring straight at each of them alone. A flash of light glinted off the captain's restraining neck torc, blinding Molly for a second.

'Hooray the Guard!' An almost hysterical scream from one of the crowd, and as if it were a trigger, the entire multitude took up the shout, cheering and stamping along the broadways. Someone in the crowd started singing 'Lion of Jackals' and soon half the avenue had joined in the bawdy patriotic lyrics.

Molly stood next to Rachael, cheering, a swell of pride rising in her chest. Hooray the Guard indeed. Between the Royal Aerostatical Navy ruling the sky and the powerful and heroic Special Guard on the ground, demolishing any enemy that dared to threaten Jackals, the kingdom was the most powerful force on the continent.

Other nations would have used that power to build an empire, bully their neighbours into subservience. But not Jackals. Their people suffered no rule of mad kings, power-hungry caliphs or rapacious senators. The quiet, peaceful Jackelians had pulled the teeth of their own would-be overlords and had prospered for centuries – trading, building, and quietly, doggedly innovating. If a Jackelian had a town garden to potter around in, or a village field to snatch a quick afternoon game of four-poles in, their empire was complete.

Other nations had dictator kings, political assassinations, and the heart-tugging wail of starving children and barren fields lying fallow while peasant armies slaughtered each other at the whim of local warlords. Jackals let its over-ambitious fools argue and wag fingers at each other across the House of Guardians.

Other nations had dark gods and wild-eyed prophets that demanded obedience, child mutilation, slavery, and poverty for the people while wealth flowed to an all-powerful priest class. Jackals had its deity-free Circlist philosophy, gentle meditations and a wide network of oratories. A Circlist parson might drop round and request a quick brew of caffeel, but never call for the beating heart of a family's firstborn to be ripped out of its chest.

Every few decades a foreign power would mistake the Jackelians' quiet taste for the rule of law for the absence of ambition. Would mistake a content and isolationist bent for a weak and decadent society. Would come to the conclusion that a nation of shopkeepers might better be put to serving what they had built, made and grown to warriors and bullies. Many enemies had made the assumption that *prefers not to fight* equates to *can't fight and won't fight*. All had been punished severely for it. Slow to rouse, once they were, their foes discovered Jackals was no nation full of bumbling storekeepers,

9

greedy mill owners and stupid farm boys. They found a pit of lions, a people with a hard, unruly thuggish streak and no tolerance for bullies – either foreign or raised on Jackals' own acres. Of course, being the only nation on Earth to possess a supply of celgas had never harmed the kingdom's standing. Jackals' unique aerial navy was truly the envy of the world, a floating wall of death standing ready to guarantee her ancient freedoms.

'Better a knave in Jackals than a prince in Quatérshift' went the popular drinking song, and right now, caught up in the wild jingoistic crowd, Molly's heart followed the sentiment. Then she remembered the Beadle waiting for her back at the poorhouse with his stinging cane and her heart briefly sank. Her spirit quickly returned; she found her resolve stiffened as she remembered one of Damson Darnay's history lessons. Each of them was a gem to be treasured in her now miserable life, but one in particular she recalled with fond clarity, even now, years after the death of the woman who had been like a mother to her.

The lesson had taken the form of a centuries-old letter – a horrified report to the then King of Quatérshift from his ambassador in Jackals, generations before Jackals' civil war, when most of the continent still suffered under the heel of absolutist regimes. The monarch of the old throne of Jackals had been attending a play at the theatre when the mob took against the performance, booing the actors off the stage, then, noticing the King in the royal box, stoning him too. The stunned Quatérshiftian had described to his own monarch the unbelievable sight of the King's militia fighting a rearguard action down the street as the rioting mob chased the portly Jackelian ruler away from the burning theatre. How alien to that bewildered ambassador, from a land where compliant serfs would be beaten to death for failing to address a noble with respect. But how true to the Jackelian character.

Molly had taken that lesson to heart. She might be an orphan, brought up by an uncaring state, but she would brook no bullying, and she was equal in the eyes of the law to any poorhouse official or Middlesteel laundry owner.

Now, if only the Beadle could see things that way.

The head of the Sun Gate workhouse had an office increasingly at odds with the rest of the poorhouse's shabby buildings, from his shining teak writing desk, through to the rich carpets and the obligatory oil painting of the current First Guardian, Hoggstone, hung behind it all. After Molly realized the Beadle did not seem inclined immediately, to start screaming a tirade of abuse at her, the second thing she noticed was the calm presence of the elegant lady seated on his chaise longue. Smart. Quality. Too richly dressed for any inspector of schools. Molly eyed the Beadle suspiciously.

'Now Molly,' began the Beadle, his lazy con-man's eyes blinking. 'Sit down here and I will introduce you to our guest.'

Molly prepared her best barrack-room lawyer's face. 'Yes, sir.'

'Molly, this is Damson Emma Fairborn, one of Sun Gate's most prominent employers.'

The lady smiled at Molly, pushing back at the curl of her blonde bob, streaked by age with a spray of platinum silver now. 'Hello Molly. And do you have a last name?'

'Templar,' said the Beadle, 'for the—'

The lady crooked a finger in what might have been displeasure and amazingly the Beadle fell silent.

'Molly, I am sure you can speak for yourself . . .'

'For the Lump Street temple, where the Aldermen found me abandoned, wrapped in a silk swaddle,' Molly said.

11

'Silk?' smiled Damson Fairborn. 'Your mother must have been a lady of some standing to have thrown good silk away. A dalliance with the downstairs staff, or perhaps an affair?'

Molly grimaced.

'But of course, I am sure you have dwelt on the identity of your parents at some length. There is not much else to occupy the mind in a place like this, after all.'

A sudden shocking thought gripped Molly, but the lady shook her head. 'No, Molly. I am not she; although I suppose I am of an age where you could be my daughter.'

The Beadle harrumphed. 'I should warn you, Molly has something of a temper, damson. Or should I say temperament.'

'To match her wild red hair, perhaps?' smiled the lady. 'And who would not, stuck in this damp place? Denied fine clothes, good wine, the company of gallants and a polite hand of whist? I am quite sure I would not find my temperament improved one whit if our positions were reversed.'

The Beadle glared at Molly, then looked at the lady. 'I don't—'

'I believe I have heard enough from you, Beadle,' said Emma Fairborn. 'Now then, Molly. Would you do me the favour of bringing me that book over there?'

Molly saw the leather-bound volume she was pointing to on one of the higher of the Beadle's bookshelves. She shrugged, walked over to the shelf and slid the book out. She blew the dust off the top. Pristine. Some work of philosophy kept for impressing visitors with the weight of the Beadle's intellect. Then she walked over to where the lady was sitting and passed the work across.

Damson Fairborn gently held Molly's hand for a second before turning it over and examining it like a gypsy palm reader. 'Thank you, Molly. I am so glad that your tenure in the employ of that Snell woman was brief. Your hands are far too nice to be ruined by bleach.' She placed the book down beside her. 'And you have a good sense of balance for someone with your height. A shade over five and a half feet I would say.'

Molly nodded.

'My dear, you have no idea how many pretty girls I meet who clump around like shire horses at a country fair, or waddle like a duck with the bad fortune to have been dressed in a lead corset. I think I can work with you. Tell me, Molly, have you enjoyed your time here at the house?'

'I have found it . . . somewhat wearisome, damson,' Molly replied.

She seemed amused. 'Indeed, have you? You have quite an erudite turn of phrase for someone raised between these walls.'

'The last director here was a Circlist, Damson Fairborn,' said the Beadle. 'She had the children in classes well past the statutory age, flouting the Relief of the Poor Act.'

'A mind is the hardest thing to improve and the easiest thing to waste,' said the lady. 'And you, Molly. You have received no salary for these labours, I presume?'

'No, damson,' Molly answered. 'It all goes to the Sun Gate Board of the Poor.'

Damson Fairborn nodded in understanding. 'Yes, I am sure I would be amazed at how expensive the ward's Victualling Board can buy in the cheapest kitchen slops. Still—' she looked directly at the Beadle '—I am sure the suppliers have their overheads.'

The Beadle positively squirmed behind his writing desk.

'Well, my dear.' Damson Fairborn adjusted the short silk-print wrap draped around her jacket's shoulders. 'You will do. I think I can pay you a handsome stipend once the poor board's monthly fees have been accounted for.'

Molly was shocked. If there was an employer who was paying the poorhouse's dole and adding on an extra salary for the boarders, it was a first for the Sun Gate workhouse. The whole rotten idea of the poorhouse was as a source of cheap labour for the ward.

'She's an orphan, mind,' reminded the Beadle. 'She reaches her maturity in a year and then she's a voter. I can only transfer her ward papers to you for twelve months.'

The lady smiled. 'I think after a year with me our young lady's tastes will be expensive enough that she won't wish to return to working for your Handsome Lane concerns.'

Molly followed her new employer out onto the street, leaving the dank Sun Gate workhouse to the Beadle and his minions. The lady had a private cab waiting for her, the horses and carriage as jet-black as the livery of the squat, bullet-headed retainer standing beside them.

'Damson Fairborn,' Molly coughed politely as the manservant swung open the cab door.

'Yes, my dear.'

Molly indicated the high prison-like walls of the poorhouse behind them. 'This isn't the usual recruiting ground for a domestic'

Her new employer looked surprised. 'Why, Molly, I don't intend you for an undermaid or a scullery girl. I thought you might have recognized my name.'

'Your name?'

'Lady Fairborn, Molly. As in my establishment: Fairborn and Jarndyce.'

Molly's blood turned cold.

'Of course,' the lady winked at her heavily muscled retainer, 'Lord Jarndyce is sadly no longer with us. Isn't that so, Alfred?'

'A right shame, milady,' replied the retainer. 'Choked on a piece of lobster shell during supper, it was said.'

'Yes, Alfred. That was really rather careless of him. One of the very few occurrences of good living proving harmful to one's constitution, I should imagine.'

Molly's eyes were still wide with shock. 'But Fairborn and Jarndyce is—'

'A bawdyhouse, my dear. And I, not to place too delicate a sensibility on it, am widely known as the Queen of the Whores.'

The retainer stepped behind Molly, cutting off her escape route down the street.

'And you, Molly. I think you shall do very nicely indeed as one of my girls.'

Back in the Beadle's office the Observer faded into the reality of the poorhouse. She was allowed only one intervention, and it had been one of her best. Small. As it had to be. Hardly an intercession at all.

Originally the Beadle had been intending to rent Molly's ward papers to the large abattoir over on Cringly Corner; but that reality path would have seen Molly returned, dismissed for insubordination, and back in the poorhouse within six weeks. Which would not have been at all beneficial for the Observer and her designs.

It had been so easy to nudge the Beadle's brain a degree to the side, letting the new plan form in his imagination. Harder to push Emma Fairborn's steel trap of a mind, but still well within the Observer's intervention tolerances. The Beadle was sitting behind his desk now, working out how much graft was due in by the end of the week.

The Observer made sure everything was tidy and accounted for in the man's treacle-thick chemical soup of a mind. Something, a sixth sense perhaps, made the Beadle scratch the nape of his neck and stare directly at where the Observer was standing. She increased the strength of her infiltration of his optic nerve, erasing even her background presence, comforting the small monkey brain back into a state of ease. Silver and gold, think about the money. The Beadle shuffled his papers into a neat stack and locked them away in his drawer. It was going to be a good take again this week.

The Observer sighed and faded back out of reality. Sadly, the Beadle was not going to live long enough to purchase that twelfth cottage by the coast to add to his burgeoning property empire. She could have saved him. But then there were some interventions the Observer was glad she was not required to make.

Chapter Two

The aerostat field at Hundred Locks was slowly filling up with passengers awaiting the *Lady Hawklight*'s arrival. Oliver checked his trouser pocket. The description of his uncle's guest still lay crumpled in there.

'Oliver.' A voice diverted his attention away from his uncle's errand – Thaddius. A boy he had known from school. When Oliver had still been allowed to attend school, of course.

In the way of the young everywhere, the lad's nickname was Slim, because he was anything but. The portly Thaddius had about as many friends in Hundred Locks as Oliver. At least, as many friends as Oliver had been left with, after the word had spread about what he really was . . . or might become.

'Tail spotting?' asked Oliver.

'Tail spotting,' confirmed Thaddius, his portly cheeks spreading in a grin. He showed Oliver his open book, neatly criss-crossed by a pencilled grid. 'See, I got the *Lady Darkmoor*'s tail code last week. She normally operates on the Medfolk-to-Calgness run, but the merchant fleet are introducing the new Guardian Cunningham class in the south, so some of the uplander airships are being reallocated here now.'

Oliver nodded out of politeness. Thaddius was desperate to join the Royal Aerostatical Navy but his family had too little money to purchase him a commission, and just a little too much to countenance him ever signing up as a humble jack cloudie. Poor fat Thaddius was going to follow the family trade and become a butcher with his father and brothers, spending his evenings at the field, wistfully watching the graceful airship hulls sailing in and out. Dreaming of what might have been. And soon too. There were only three months to go before Thaddius and his classmates left the gates of the local state school for the last time.

'Fieldsmen to the line,' cried one of the green-uniformed airship officers and a burly gang of navvies took position, making a cigar-shaped outline on the grass. A pair of large dray horses walked to the nose of the formation to stand alongside the field's tractor-like steamman; ready to provide the heavy muscle. The steamman hardly looked up to the job. His name was Rustpivot, and he had been a worker at the field when Oliver's Uncle Titus was a boy. As large as two wagons, his boiler belly was bordered by six spiked wheels. Despite his advanced years, the steamman could still reach out with any of his four arms to tow an aerostat back into lift position.

'Those with passage booked, please make sure you have your tickets to hand,' called an official.

Oliver sighed. Travel.

Thaddius looked at him and read his mind. 'They can't keep you registered forever, Oliver. They've either got to pass you, or, well, you know. . .' his voice trailed off.

'They're never going to pass me,' Oliver spat. 'They enjoy keeping me prisoner here too much.'

Thaddius fell quiet. The woes of his approaching family apprenticeship were put into perspective for him, set against the alternative prospects faced by his companion on the airship field. Remaining an outcast. Marked out. Gossiped about. Unable to travel further than was allowed by the state's requirement that he sign on every week. Thaddius gave him a long look of sympathy, then left for the airship hangar to join the gang of tail spotters waiting by the doors.

From the south the wheezing heave and fall of a quartet of expansion engines hushed the noise of the waiting crowd. The airship rose out of the forest behind the field, the top half of her hull painted merchantman green, the bottom half a bright checkerboard of yellow and black squares.

The *Lady Hawklight* dipped her nose and sailors threw open hatches along the side of the gondola, casting down lines weighted with lead heads towards the ground. The fieldsmen caught these and the airship's massive envelope was dragged towards the docking tower, the aerostat's nose pulled with a loud hollow clank into her capture ring. Now she was fixed, the lines from the aerostat were wound into pulleys and the airship was drawn down to her hover-side position ten feet above the field.

The docking tower sat on a single iron rail. If the airship's plan of flight included a berth for the night, both tower and ship would eventually be drawn back into the hangar at the far end of the field where Thaddius and the other children eagerly waited. Disembarkation stairs were pushed up to the gondola doors and wagons carrying ballast water and precious cylinders of celgas drew up on her starboard side.

The usual pool of passengers with business in Hundred Locks began to disembark. Half the travellers were foreigners from outside the Kingdom of Jackals, the white togas from the city-states of the Catosian League clashing with the brightly multi-coloured ponchos of the Holy Kikkosico Empire. Neither country allowed Jackelian airships to overfly their lands, suspicious of the Kingdom's monopoly on air travel and the opportunities for reconnaissance it provided. The foreigners would travel by canal navigation to the head of Toby Fall Rise, and from there return home by schooner and ferry across the Sepia Sea.

There were archaeologists in the group too, from one of the eight great universities, easily conspicuous by the leather cases they carried, filled with fine tools that they would not want to risk to the movements and shifts of the cargo hold. They were still arguing over whether the colossal dike that overshadowed the town was a natural freak of nature or some feat of an ancient civilisation.

Oliver put his hands into his pockets for warmth, and finding the note, suddenly remembered the reason for his visit to the aerostat field. His uncle's guest!

Most of the arrivals had already dispersed. The queue of passengers boarding the *Lady Hawklight* thinned to a few late arrivals. Out on the field the local boys had set up a game of four-poles, the amateur fast-bowling watched with amused detachment by the officers from the aerostat as they waited for the airship to take on her full load of celgas and ballast water.

A peddler was hawking to the remaining passengers from the Holy Kikkosico Empire, a smoke-filled glass bottle hanging on his chest, offering six breaths of mumblesmoke for a ha'penny. The ranks of barouche-and-fours had emptied too, the small horse-drawn coaches taking any willing travellers through the small crowded town and up to the Hundred Locks canal navigation from which the settlement took its name.

Among the stragglers stood one man who fitted the crumpled description Oliver's uncle had dashed out that morning from his desk. He was thin, a touch under Oliver's height of six foot, and also possessed a shock of dark blond hair cut short and ragged. What the description had omitted were the dark iron glasses that rested across the bridge of his nose. Cheap milled fare, they had never graced the exclusive shelves of any optician back in the capital.

Oliver was well used to guiding visitors from the field and across to his uncle's home at Seventy Star Hall, but they were normally well-to-do merchants like Titus Brooks himself. His warehouse in Shipman Town swelled with barrels of empire wine, city-state contraptions and – it was rumoured – brandy still smuggled through Quatérshift, a trade legal for hundreds of years but now forbidden in both Quatérshift and Jackals since the end of the Two-Year War.

The man Oliver was staring at looked more like the cheaply dressed clerk of a parish council. Oliver walked over to him. 'Mister Stave?'

'Harry,' said the man, extending his hand to Oliver. 'Harry Stave. The last time I was called mister anything was—' he looked at Oliver and thought better of the tale '—well, a long time ago, let's say. Just call me Harry.'

'My uncle is expecting you, Harry.' Oliver pointed towards the town.

'I don't doubt he is, old stick. But my luggage, such as it is, is still coming off the *Lady Hawklight*.'

A cushion of hemp netting was assembled underneath the gondola's cargo hatch, set up to take the royal mail sacks, scarlet with their KoJ seal, a lion resting underneath the portcullis of the House of Guardians. A steamman was pulling a trolley away from the airship's shadow, piled high with crates, packages and travel chests.

'You're not exactly travelling light.'

'Just the one,' said Harry, lifting off a battered ivory-handled travel box. 'And there we are.'

Each of the visitor's words was carefully nuanced, as if Harry were polishing each vowel before saying it. They belied the otherwise rough appearance of the man. Oliver offered to take the case, but Harry shook his head. 'You work for Titus?'

'He's my uncle. I suppose I do.'

'Ah, well then.' Harry stopped to look at Oliver as they left the field. 'Young Master Brooks. Perhaps I should have recognized you. Although there's not much about the babe that I see in the man.'

That made Oliver start. 'You knew my parents?'

'That I did, Oliver. My trade sometimes put me in the path of your father and mother. You were nearly sick on me once, as a swaddling. Do you remember either of them?'

'No. Not at all.' Oliver could not keep the pain out of his voice. 'My uncle. He doesn't talk about them.'

'It's as hard to lose a brother as a father, old stick,' said Harry, gently. Seeing the effect the conversation was having on Oliver, he stopped. 'Let's not talk of it either, then. We'll allow those who have moved along the Circle to rest in their new lives.'

Oliver wondered if his uncle's visitor knew he was registered. Probably. If he had known his parents, he would have heard the stories of what had happened to them. And to Oliver. If it bothered Harry, he did not show it.

They were in town now. Seventy Star Hall lay beyond Hundred Locks proper, nestled at the foot of the hills that led up to the Toby Fall Rise. A dog tied to a post outside the fish market was barking as dockers down from Shipman Town arrived to find evening lodgings at the inns and drinking houses, their heavy steel-capped boots clattering against the cobblestones.

The talk of his parents had lowered Oliver's mood. So this was to be the map of his life, then. Allowed no proper trade or apprenticeship. Signing onto the county registration book once a week. Shunned by most of the townspeople. Running small errands for his uncle to keep him busy and out from under his relative's feet. Unable to leave the parish boundaries without being declared rogue and hunted down. Denied those simple freedoms that even the fox in the burrow or the swallow in the tree took for granted. An object of pity, perhaps; charity, on his uncle's part; aversion from those who were once his friends and fellows.

With those bleak reflections they reached Seventy Star Hall to be met on the doorstep by the maid of all works, Damson Griggs. She took in Harry Stave – his battered travel case and cheap clothes – and wrinkled her nose in disapproval, as if Oliver were a cat returning with a dead mouse for her pantry.

Damson Griggs was a fierce old bird, and whether it was the prospect of working with the damson, or being in the same house as a registered boy such as Oliver, she was now the only full-time member of housekeeping staff at Seventy Star Hall. Any other house of similar size in Hundred Locks would have at least five or six staff keeping the place. But Titus Brooks was something of a lonely, anti-social figure, so perhaps it suited him to keep the arrangement that way. Damson Griggs regarded the town's superstitious fear of Oliver as stuff and nonsense. She had known the boy since a pup, and if there was an ounce of feymist in him, it had not manifested itself in front of her these last eleven years.

Oliver might have been of the same opinion himself, but then he had never told his uncle or their housekeeper about his cold, dark dreams.

'What wicked wind has blown you to our doorstep, Harold Stave?' asked the damson.

'Harry, please, Damson Griggs,' said their visitor.

'Well then, I suppose I had better be about locking up the master's brandy cabinet if you are to be staying with us. Unless you have finished with your dirty boozing and lusting across the length and breadth of Jackals – and a good many other nations besides, I don't wonder.'

'Now who's been impugning my reputation in such a manner?' asked Harry, scratching at his blond mop of hair. 'There's not a drop of the old falling-down water passed my lips these two weeks, Damson Griggs.'

'Your manners were too coarse for the navy to keep you.' Damson Griggs wagged a sausage-sized finger at the man. 'And they'll keep you no better under this roof either.'

Despite her admonishments, she opened the door wider for Harry to enter, taking his thin summer travel cloak and hanging it on one of the bullhorn-shaped hooks in the hallway. Wide and white-tiled, the hallway was still filled with bright clean light. By late afternoon the sun would be behind Toby Fall Rise and the north end of Hundred Locks would live up to its name – Shadowside – as the shade from the dike fell across their house. Then the damson would bustle around, lighting the oil lamps filled with fatty blood from the massive slip-sharps netted in the Sepia Sea and slaughtered above them in Shipman Town.

'Thank you kindly, damson,' said Harry. He winked at Oliver.

A noise came from upstairs. Titus Brooks was still in his study, an onion-shaped dome in which the previous occupant – a retired naval officer – had installed a telescope. Now only the brass mountings remained in the centre of the room, the telescope itself having been removed when he died and sold off by his sons and daughters.

Damson Griggs disappeared with the guest, coming back down the staircase alone. 'You pay heed to my words, Oliver Brooks. Stay away from that man. He's a bad sort.'

'Is he a sailor, Damson Griggs?' Oliver asked.

'The only airship he flies in is the *Lady Trouble*,' spat the housekeeper.

'He was a sailor, though? You said. . .'

'You just mind what I have to say now, young Master Brooks. The only action that jack ever saw was the watering down of an honest sailor's rum ration. Harry Stave used to work for the Navy Victualling Board before you were even born, buying in victuals, celgas and other supplies for the RAN. He knows your uncle from his contracts with the Board. But Mister Stave was discharged. Caught with his hand deep in the till, no doubt.'

'And he works for Uncle Titus now?'

'No, young master. He most certainly does not. He works for himself, just as much as he always did.'

'So what trade does he keep that would bring him here?'

'A good question indeed. And if you ask him direct I doubt you'll get an honest answer. Some old toot about buying cheap and selling for a little more is as like what you would hear.'

Oliver stared up the stairs towards his uncle's study.

'No, young Master Brooks, you had better give that man a wide berth. Your neck is too valuable to me to see it ending up dancing for the hangman's crowds outside the walls of Bonegate. And if you keep company with that rascal for too long, you'll be heading down the path of criminality, of that I am certain.'

There was no tweaking Damson Griggs's nose when she took against someone, so Oliver just nodded in agreement. From where he was standing, the path of criminality had more to recommend it than an errand boy's apprenticeship granted out of pity and familial kinship for a dead brother.

'Out from under my feet now with your questions, young Master Brooks,' commanded the damson. 'Millwards delivered our pantry stock this morning and I have a pie to bake for supper. An extra large one, if that rascal upstairs with your uncle intends to stay the night.'

Returning to Seventy Star Hall from the crystalgrid operators' at twilight's last gleaming with a leather satchel full of Middlesteel punch-card messages for his uncle – prices from the financial houses of Gate Street and stock movements from the exchange at Sun Lane – Oliver was worn out from walking.

Damson Griggs had returned to her cottage in town, leaving his pie and cold boiled potatoes covered by a plate in the kitchen. From the two empty wineglasses, red with the dregs of a bottle of claret, Oliver guessed that his uncle and their guest had eaten already. He walked to the top of the staircase and saw that a light was still showing under the door of his uncle's study, the muffled sound of conversation inside.

Damson Griggs's words of warning came to his mind. Why was this interloper of uncertain provenance visiting his uncle? Was Uncle Titus stooping to involve himself in some scheme of a dubious nature? Oliver was not a financier from some fancy address in the capital's Sun Gate district, but his uncle's business affairs seemed sound enough from his limited vantage point.

Oliver crept back down to the ground floor and lifted a key from under the stairs, then quietly unlocked the door to the drawing room. Inside, the fireplace's flue ran upwards through to the study, opening into a grill above, the only source of warmth for the study during the cold winter nights at Hundred Locks. As Oliver had discovered, where heat carries upward, the sounds of conversation echo downward. Oliver placed his ear to the opening. Outside, the first evening stars were appearing. Before midnight, all seventy stars the grey limestone house was named after would be visible. His uncle and his guest's voices were not raised and Oliver had to strain to catch snippets of the conversation.

'Trouble – counting on a commo plan – compromised—' His uncle.

'If it is – think they – hostile service – learn—' The disreputable Stave.

'This time – up to – in the black—'

Oliver leant forward as much as he dared. There was a familiar tapping. His uncle clearing his mumbleweed pipe on the side of his desk.

'Will they be coming—' Harry Stave.

'Our friends in the east?' Uncle Titus.

The East? Oliver's eyes widened. The Holy Empire of Kikkosico lay northeast. And directly east lay Quatérshift – but no friends there. Not since the Two-Year War.

In defeat, the Commonshare of Quatérshift had completely sealed its land border, hexing up a cursewall between the two nations; to deter any of her own compatriots who developed a yearning to leave Quatérshift's revolution-racked land, as well as putting off military incursions by the Jackelians. There was no official trade with the shifties, although smugglers still landed cargoes of brandy along the coast, where moonrakers could evade the attentions of officers from the customs house. Like all the children in Hundred Locks, Oliver had been severely warned never to stray into the hinterlands east of the town, where only the shadows of patrolling aerostats and the odd garrison of redcoats and border foot lay dotted across the wind-blighted moors.

'A dirty game—' Harry Stave.

'Already – in the wind—' Uncle Titus. There was a rasp as a chair was pulled back. 'Two of my people dead—'

Dead! Oliver caught his breath. What foul business had Harry Stave involved his uncle in? Was their warehouse in

Shipman Town concealing casks of untaxed brandy? Had officers from the customs house been murdered on some small rocky harbour in the mountains above?

A sudden realization struck Oliver. His uncle had never revealed the full extent of his business dealings to him. Oliver ran errands and gleaned what he could, learning piecemeal from the occasional tale of which factor could be trusted to deal fairly, which clipper captain might be tempted to skim a cargo. Only his uncle was at the centre – none of his staff. Even Oliver could see the interests of those in the warehouse never stretched – or were allowed to stretch – further than Shipman Town's wharves. Was this more than a cautious nature? Or did the left hand's ignorance of the right hand's dealings stem from the need to keep Uncle Titus from dangling on the wrong end of a hangman's rope outside Bonegate gaol?

There was more scraping of chairs from upstairs and Oliver silently slid the drawing room door shut, then climbed into his bed on the ground floor. Damson Griggs had the measure of Harry Stave, it seemed. But just how deep did his uncle's involvement go? Oliver felt the sting of shame as his immediate reaction to the thought of his uncle being thrown into prison was not concern for his sole surviving relative, but worry for his *own* fate. His uncle had already risked exile from what passed for polite society at Hundred Locks for keeping a registered boy under his roof, but no, the unworthy Oliver Brooks was more concerned about what might happen to his own neck.

If Uncle Titus were incarcerated, he would be left with no chance of employment at Hundred Locks, no future save the cold unwelcoming gates of the local Poor Board. He shivered at the thought. The county of Lightshire's poor and down on their luck had enough problems of their own; a registered boy being thrown into their midst might be the final straw. How much easier to arrange a small accident at night? A pillow slipped over his face and the unwelcome interloper smothered out of the poorhouse inhabitants' lives.

His grey future, ensnared between the invisible walls of his prison-in-exile at Hundred Locks, was growing smaller and smaller as he drifted off into an uneasy sleep.

Chapter Three

Surveillant Forty-six nudged the telescope a touch to the left with the foot pedal. It took a couple of seconds for the transaction engine to balance the array of mirrors, the image in the rubber face-glove losing focus before returning to sharpness with a clack – clack – clack. From the corner of his eye, Surveillant Forty-six could see the other surveillants riding the cantilevered brass tubes, cushioned red seats attached underneath the large cannon shapes of the telescopes.

The scopes followed the arc of the monitorarium, curving around the inside wall of the sphere. A gantry and rail ran behind their telescopes, monitors in grey court-issue great-coats treading the iron plates. You could almost see the chill in the monitorarium – no heat that might interfere with the operation of the viewings.

'Your report please.' It was Monitor Eighty-one. She was always brusque and efficient. The wires in his earphones looped back to the gantry, to a voice trumpet where Eighty-one was bending down to speak.

The monitor was one of the new batch, fresh out of training, one of the ones who thought that relaying reports *through*, was the same as reporting *to*. He harrumphed. She lacked even the slight worldsinger craft the surveillants practised. Kicking her feet along the gantry in her fur-lined boots to prevent frostbite, unable to heat her body with her mind. Wearing one of the surveillant's own leather skins would see her frozen to death in a telescope sling before the end of her first watch. Unable even to modify her blood after sampling one of the many potions the surveillants took to stay awake and focused, weeks at a shift.

'This unit is still pulling slightly to the left,' complained Surveillant Forty-six. 'I thought a mechomancer had taken the telescope up to the maintenance level.'

'Stop your whining,' hissed the monitor. 'This is a priority observation – someone could be listening. It might be for the old lady herself. You lose the plot on this job and there'll be bloody analysts crawling all over us. Just give me your report.'

The surveillant held his tongue. Priority it may be, but not high enough to get his scope pulled out of the monitorarium and into the maintenance schedule, it seemed. 'Target's aerostat arrived at the Hundred Locks field as scheduled. Target was escorted to the contact's house, as anticipated. Target has remained there for the last seven hours. Do you have any analyst predictions or instructions?'

'There is an eighty-seven per cent chance the target will remain in the house for the next sixteen hours. Maintain surveillance.'

The surveillant sighed. 'Preparing for night-time sighting.' He pulled a drinking tube from the telescope, supping at the orange gloop that dribbled out. The potion warmed his skull as sparks fireworked across his eyes; the brew's night vision would last until sunrise. As the liquid coursed through his body, he reached inside himself with one of the worldsinger magics, rendering the potion inert before it struck his liver, where the strange brew would have ruptured that organ into a broiled stew.

He gazed back into the rubber mask and centred the view on the smokeless chimney of Seventy Star Hall. True to form, the scope slid to the left. He cursed the bureaucrats of the Court. Silently.

Chapter Four

It was hard to predict when the Whisperer would come to Oliver in his dreams. Sometimes he could go for weeks without a visitation – other times the Whisperer might come four nights in a row.

Oliver was in a large palace somewhere, his uncle, Damson Griggs and others running through the corridors, trying to find a missing chair. The chair was important, obviously. Oliver knew it was a dream because he had never met the King, and the not-so-merry monarch said if they could only find the chair, parliament might agree to sow his arms back on. Then the Whisperer pushed through into the dream.

'Oliver, I can see you. Can you see me?'

'I can't see you, Whisperer, go away.'

'Then you can, Oliver,' hissed the misshapen form that had appeared before him. 'I can connect with you. I can connect with almost all of our kind.'

'I'm not like you, Whisperer,' said Oliver.

'No. I realize that, Oliver. You are the best of us. I have waited a lifetime or more for you to arrive. The others think they're perfect, the ones who aren't locked up in here with my friends and me. But they haven't met you, Oliver. If they had they wouldn't be so proud, so vain, so content with themselves and their powers.'

Oliver knew they kept the Whisperer locked somewhere dark, deep beneath the earth. Chained in by hexes and curse-walls and powerful worldsinger gates. His ugly lumpen face was beyond description, a wreckage of human flesh. When the Whisperer had been born, his terrified parents must have run a league in the opposite direction.

'Can't you get out of my mind?' pleaded Oliver. 'Get out of my life?'

'You are my life, Oliver,' hissed the creature. 'You and the others I contact. Do you think my own life is worth the living? They keep me in the dark, Oliver, alone in a cell hardly tall enough to stand up in so I can't rush the warders when they remember to check I'm still here. The rats visit me, Oliver. Drawn by my smell and waste. I break my teeth on their bones, sometimes, when the warders forget to feed me.'

Oliver felt sick. 'And what do they taste like?'

The Whisperer laughed, a sound like air escaping from an expansion engine. 'What do they taste like, Oliver? Like chicken, Oliver, like the finest roast chicken. I borrowed the taste from your mind. I hope you don't mind. I have so few reference points.'

Oliver gagged and the Whisperer danced a mad little jig in front of him. 'I try not to eat the food they give me, Oliver. They put potions in it, to soften my brain and keep me tired, sleepy.'

In the dream palace the King had appeared again, but he took one look at the Whisperer and turned smartly around.

'How sad, Oliver. Even the phantoms in a dream find me repulsive. Remind me. This time, is it me dreaming of you, or is it you dreaming of me?'

'What does it matter?' Oliver shouted. 'Leave my mind alone.'

'Your time is coming, my perfect friend,' said the Whisperer. 'You are about to find out what a flexible and surprising thing life is. And when you do, you might be very glad of me crawling around in your skull. Yes, you might be very glad indeed.'

'I am rather sure I won't be,' said Oliver.

'Don't make your mind up quite so fast, Oliver. Things have already started moving. Your curious visitor, Harry Stave. What do you think of him, boy? Bit of a dark horse, perhaps. Bit of a bludger and a broadsman?'

'I don't—'

'Shhhh,' hushed the Whisperer. 'You're going to get woken up in a couple of seconds.'

He was.

It was an early start to sign on the county registration book, and as always, Oliver found himself outside the Hundred Locks police station in time to see the prisoners from the night before marched away from the cells, across to the magistrate's small office along Rayner's Street. Among the usual string of tavern brawlers were a handful of Quatérshiftian refugees: two men and a single woman – possibly their sister.

Their clothes were ruined and Oliver guessed they had escaped across the sea, circumventing the cursewall along the border with Jackals. One of the men was shaking uncontrollably, his compatriots stunned into a shocked silence. What tales had they been told by the Commonshare's propaganda committee? That Quatérshift had won the Two-Year War? That Jackals was now a model of Carlist right-practice? That Jackals had suffered a famine too, after replacing its farmers with Committees of Agrarian Equalization and marching its educated yeomen into a Gideon's Collar – the steam-driven killing machines which now filled the Commonshare's city squares?

Whatever the lies, they had not been enough to keep these three from escaping the great terror in Quatérshift. Since the Commonshare's worldsingers had laid the cursewall, there had been so few refugees making it alive to Jackals that magistrates now granted the shifties automatic political asylum. One of the many émigré charities would be called in to help. After all, there were now more Quatérshiftian nobles sloshing around Jackals than there were back in the homeland – the lucky ones who had flooded out with their gold before the cursewall was raised. The less fortunate quality were still in Commonshare camps waiting on a piece of paper with a red number scrawled across it . . . followed by an iron bolt fired through the neck.

As the line of prisoners disappeared down the street, Oliver knocked on the station door and entered.

'Oliver.' Sergeant Cudban glanced back from locking the door to the cells. 'That time of the week already?'

'I'm afraid so,' said Oliver.

'Come on in laddie, don't stand on ceremony. Your wee conjurer is already around the back. Would you like a nice cup of caffeel? Young Wattle's just brewed up.'

Oliver nodded. Sergeant Cudban was a brusque, straightforward uplander, and he had little patience for the worldsingers and even less for the superior manners of Oliver's personal tormentor, Edwin Pullinger, the county's Inspector Royal from the State Department of Feymist.

'A busy night?' Oliver asked.

'Aye, the usual. Although I did have the parson in here yesterday. Somebody's been stuffing political pamphlets inside the book of Circlelaw.'

'Pamphlets,' laughed Oliver.

'You should have seen the man's face. The highlights of *Community and the Commons*, it was. I don't think the parson had ever read it before and the thought of Carlists in the pews of his good Circlist church had him in a right tizzy.'

Oliver shrugged. 'For that matter, I don't think I've ever read it either.'

The sergeant winked at Oliver. 'I'll slip you a copy later then, compatriot. Never sat well with me, laddie, burning books. Them's the sort of larks foreigners get up to, not us Jackelians. Benjamin Carl hasn't been seen alive since eighty-one anyway, and to my mind, since the uprising was crushed most of his revolutionaries have been baking bread and milling steel for the last fifteen years.'

'And printing pamphlets,' Oliver added slyly.

Sergeant Cudban pinned up a reward on the wall, an illustration of a highwayman and a modest reward staring down on them. 'Grumbles, laddie. Everyone's got grumbles. You happy, laddie? Being dragged in here to sign on every week at the pleasure of that purple-robed prat? And do you think I'm happy? Three wee constables to keep the parliament's law in Hundred Locks while Shipman Town above has ten times that number. What do they do all day – interview cod? Arrest gulls? And send their beered-up sailors down here to break each other's heads in my taverns.'

Constable Wattle poked his face around the door. 'Inspector Pullinger wants to know why he's being kept waiting.'

'See, laddie. Grumbles.' The sergeant turned to his constable. 'The Department of Feymist would not like the answer to that question, young Wattle.'

Oliver was ushered into the office. Cudban unobtrusively took up position underneath the station's weapons rack, cleaning the cutlasses in the top row and oiling the walnut-stocked rifles below. Listening all the while. It was not unknown for the Department to resort to worldsinger mind tricks to get results – but it would not happen while old Cudban was in charge of policing the Hundred Locks Township.

The oily sorcerer had a new arrival sitting by his side, another Department of Feymist worldsinger, though not much older than Oliver. An acolyte. Pullinger rubbed his brow where a tattoo of four small purple flowers shone – the mark of his rank among the worldsingers.

Edwin Pullinger turned the register on the writing desk around and pushed it towards Oliver. 'Your official signature, Mister Brooks. My colleague here will be counter-signing for the Department.'

Oliver picked up the stylus and dipped its nib in the inkpot. 'Planning to retire, Inspector Pullinger?'

'Not any time soon, young Master Brooks,' Pullinger replied. He took out a small snuffbox of purpletwist and, measuring a pinch on the back of his hand, sniffed at the rare pollen. Addictive when inhaled, it also enhanced the power of a worldsinger. The acolyte produced a flat green crystal, tracing a line of truth sigils in the air over it.

Resigned, Oliver placed his right hand on the truth crystal while Pullinger commenced the ritual questioning.

'Have you manifested any of the following powers of feymist abomination? Telekinesis, the power of flight, abnormal strength, mental control over animals, invisibility, the power to generate heat or flame. . .' Pullinger ran through the exhaustive list.

'I haven't,' said Oliver, when the sorcerer finished at last. 'Have you?'

Sergeant Cudban snorted with amusement at the answer.

Pullinger leant forward. 'If I had, young Master Brooks, it would have been as the result of the disciplined study of the worldsong and mastery of my own natural abilities over the bones of the world.'

'Naturally.'

'And that is precisely the point,' said Pullinger. 'By nature. Naturally. I could take the most talentless clodhopping constable in this station and with enough time and diligence teach him to tap leylines and move objects around using the worldsong.' To demonstrate his point, the pen rose from Oliver's hand and floated in the air to the worldsinger.

'Don't bother on my account,' muttered Sergeant Cudban.

Pullinger leaned back in his chair, addressing his acolyte. 'Young Master Brooks, as you can see, is my greatest challenge. An enigma. How much exposure to the feymist does it take on average for an abomination to occur?'

'Anything from two minutes to an hour,' answered the acolyte.

'Correct,' said Pullinger. 'You can be sleeping soundly in your bed when a feymist rises from the soil, and the first you will know of it is when your body begins to change in the morning.'

The boy nodded.

'Two minutes,' Pullinger repeated. 'Yet young Brooks' aerostat crashed into the very feymist curtain itself when he was just one year old. And he was found wandering out, alone, the sole survivor, four years later. Four years exposed to the feymist. Too young to feed himself. And when he resurfaces – no feybreed powers, no abominations, no memory of what happened to him behind the curtain.'

'Perhaps I was raised by wolves,' said Oliver.

'Have you remembered anything of your time behind the feymist curtain since our last meeting?'

'No,' lied Oliver. As usual the truth crystal was not alerted by his reply.

'Have you had any dreams you would class as unusual?'

'No,' lied Oliver, the Whisperer's hiss in his ears.

'Have you had any mental conversations with relatives you believe might be dead?'

'No,' said Oliver. 'Although if I did, I really wouldn't mind.'

Pullinger clearly did not believe a word of it. Four years exposed to the feymist and no resulting abominations. It was unheard of, an impossibility. Oliver had become his life's work. His obsession.

'I know you are hiding something, boy,' said the worldsinger. 'You may pass the crystal but you are not telling me everything, I can feel it in my gut.'

'Been staying at the Three Bells, have you?' muttered the sergeant. 'We'll have to do something about the state of their kitchen.'

Pullinger ignored the jibes. 'What do you have to fear, Oliver? You are normal physically. You wouldn't end up with the broken gibbering things at Hawklam Asylum, I can promise you that.'

'I would serve.'

'Yes, Oliver. You would serve. In the Special Guard your powers would be put to the service of the people. You would be a hero, Oliver. No longer something unknown, to be feared and loathed. But a champion of the state – protecting your countrymen from our enemies abroad and at home.'

'With a torc around my neck,' said Oliver. 'Controlled by someone like you.'

'For all our powers, Oliver, the order is still human. Trusted to contain those who clearly are not. The torc is our insurance in case a feybreed goes rogue . . . or insane. How many fey are ever executed by torc? None so far this year.'

Oliver shook his head. 'I'm more human than your friends in the Department of Feymist.'

'I know you think you have been treated badly, Oliver. But that's the self-centred perspective of a young man who has seen nothing of life or the world. This is for your safety – and ours. You have not seen the things we have in the Department. You could go fey one night and wake up in the morning with as much in common with us as you have with the insects in your garden. You could decide to turn your uncle's body inside out just to see what it looks like. You could walk through Hundred Locks setting people alight with your mind just to hear the difference in their screams. I have seen that happen, boy.'

'I would never do that.'

'People fear the feymist, Oliver. They fear it when whatever is behind the curtain seeps its poison across Jackals, changing its victims. They fear an abomination that hasn't been tested and submitted to the people's control.'

'But I am normal,' Oliver nearly shouted. 'I'm the same as the rest of you.'

'You can't be the same, Oliver. Not after four years inside the feymist curtain. You are the only one who has been inside and lived to return.'

'I don't remember those years.'

'What life is it here for you, Oliver? Your neighbours and friends terrified of your torcless neck, terrified you'll wake up one day fey and rogue. Show me what you really are and let me conscript you into the Special Guard.'

'Hundred Locks is my home.'

'It's your prison, Oliver. You would be happier among your own kind. Captain Flare would welcome you into the legion like a brother. Bonefire and the other champions of the guard would make you into a hero.'

Oliver remained silent.

'The common herd worship the Guard, Oliver. There

wouldn't be a tavern in the kingdom you couldn't walk into and have Jackelians falling over themselves to stand you a drink. And the women, Oliver. You haven't seen how the women drool over the Special Guard; hang on their every word. You would have Dock Street writers penning your adventures in the legion into myth. All that, and what do you have here?'

'My freedom,' said Oliver, quietly.

'A curious sort of freedom,' said the sorcerer. 'And it has come very cheap for you, so far. But the day may not be far off when you find the price of it rises.'

'I am normal,' Oliver protested, the words sounding hollow even as he said them. 'Normal.'

Pullinger and his Department stooge made ready to leave. 'You'll slip one day, Oliver. Lose control and reveal yourself. When you do, we'll be there to bind you. Or *stop* you.'

Sergeant Cudban shook his head as the two sorcerers left. A row of polished cutlasses and rifles lay on the table in front of him. 'I admire your spirit, laddie. But are you doing yourself any favours?'

'You think I should give him what he wants?'

Cudban shrugged. 'I de nae know if there's an ounce of fey in your bones, laddie, but that four years inside the feymist curtain is a life sentence as far as they're concerned. They'll keep you on the county register till your hair is silver and you're walking with a stick. It's no life for you.'

'It's not fair.'

'I knew a Ham Yard detective, laddie; once he took it into his head that you were guilty, you might as well confess to the doomsman and take a shorter sentence, innocent or no. Either way they'd take you.'

'Even if I'm not fey?'

'Especially if you're nae, laddie. Just tell them that old

Isambard Kirkhill is sending you messages from beyond the grave – let them put a suicide torc around your neck and stick you in the Special Guard. He wasn't lying about that. They live like Guardians down in Middlesteel. A bit of light duty protecting the people from the King. Let the heavy crushers like Captain Flare do any real fighting that parliament orders your way. I'll be reading in *The Middlesteel Illustrated* about what a fine young champion of the state you are before midwinter.'

But Oliver was not thinking about the Special Guard. He was thinking about Hawklam Asylum; the sibilant venom-words of the Whisperer; what it would be like to be ensnared for the rest of his years in a dark airless cell next door to the inhuman dream walker.

Maybe it was a sixth sense – something within him finally fulfilling the Department of Feymist's expectations – but Oliver knew something was wrong the moment he opened the back door to Seventy Star Hall. Everything in the lumber-room was as it should be, the jumble of rakes, earthenware pots and old garden boots, the dusty cloth-covered round table.

Despite this, the hairs stood up on Oliver's neck, a deep sense that things were no longer as they ought to be. Cautiously he left the garden door ajar rather than clunking it shut, and peered into the kitchen. Damson Griggs lay face down on the kitchen tiles, her blank eyes staring lifeless across the pooling blood. There was a small wood-handled knife from the kitchen drawer embedded in the back of her head. The practical, protective Damson Griggs, the old lady who did not have a single bad bone in her body; snuffed out with the casualness of a garden beetle flattened under a boot.

Oliver choked back a sob. He felt faint, like his soul was being drawn into the sky, his body lifted in the updraft of the death. Then his raw animal instinct for survival kicked in and he was back in the kitchen. Had Damson Griggs come in the back way too, surprising some cracksman stealing the house's silver plate? Where was his uncle?

Oliver felt a wave of panic rising in his stomach. His uncle should be home; why had he not heard the damson's cries? He slipped a large knife out of the sharpening block by the porcelain basin, briefly comforted by its heft. Someone coughed outside the kitchen. Oliver tried not to slip on the blood – impossibly brown when it surely should have been red – and he went to look through the crack of the door to the hallway.

There was a man he did not recognize – no, two of them – rifling quickly through the hall's letters cabinet. They wore black clothes of a cut Oliver had never seen before. Where was his uncle? Oliver gripped the knife tighter, willing himself to move – when a hand clamped over his mouth and his knife arm was seized in a vice-like grip.

It was Harry Stave.

<Oliver>

The voice was in his skull, their guest's lips still sealed grimly shut.

<Don't make a sound, Oliver. There are others in the house. Killers. Move your mouth without speaking. I'll lip-read.>

'How are you doing this?' Oliver silently mouthed. 'Are you a worldsinger? Where's my uncle?'

<Titus was in the house when I left this morning. Mind echo's a worldsinger technique, but you'll not find any purple tattoos on me, old stick.>

'Who are they?' Oliver mouthed. 'What are they doing here?'

<The who is something I would dearly like to know myself. And the what is too complicated a tale for right now.>

'Are they armed?' Oliver mouthed.

<Miracle if they're bleeding not. I need you to run back to the crushers, Oliver, bring back as many constables as you can.>

'But you. . .'

<There's a chance Titus might still be alive upstairs. I'm staying. I'll fight if I have to, run if it comes to it. Now GO!>

Oliver arrived back at the police station lathered in sweat, his heart hammering inside his chest. Please let the station be manned. Hitting the door latch, he burst in, startling Sergeant Cudban.

'Sergeant,' Oliver panted. 'Damson Griggs is dead, killers still in the house.'

Then Oliver noticed the two smartly dressed men on the other side of the room. 'Well, sergeant. It's as I was just telling you. It appears my words were prophetic.'

Cudban nodded at the two men. 'Brigadier Morgan and Captain Bates from Ham Yard, Oliver.'

'And it's no great feat of detection on my part to name the leader of the killers,' said the man Cudban had identified as a brigadier.

'Harry Stave,' said the one called Bates.

Oliver's eyes went wide. 'But he's still—'

'Harry Stave slipped the scaffold outside Bonegate fifteen years back,' said the brigadier. 'And he's been leaving a trail of corpses across Jackals ever since.'

'You've had a lucky escape, laddie,' said Cudban. 'Him and his gang of cut-throats are still at your house?'

Oliver groaned. Uncle Titus. His uncle was at the mercy of a gang of thugs and tricksters. And he had abandoned him to his fate back at Seventy Star Hall. Oliver glanced at the warrant that Cudban was holding, an illustration of Harry Stave looking out at him below a line of blood-code sigils, information that could only be read by a transaction engine, then the warrant's script. The red lettering leapt out at Oliver. Harry Stave. Escaped execution from Bonegate prison, 1560. A long list of aliases underneath. Two oversized initials at the foot of the page: C.I. – crown immunity if handed in dead.

Cudban pulled a rifle down from the wall rack, broke the gun and carefully slipped a glass charge into its breach. 'He got Damson Griggs then, laddie? Murdering wee jigger. Well, he won't be getting close to the noose this time, not even if he gives himself up.'

'But he let me go,' said Oliver. 'He could have killed me too.'

'Ego,' said the captain from Ham Yard. 'Not much good leaving a trail of villainy in your wake if the penny dreadfuls blame it on a rival crew.'

The brigadier lifted a cutlass off the table. 'Your other constables?'

'One's at the airship field, the other man's out towards the dike and the Hundred Locks navigation,' spat Cudban. 'By the time I round them up, Stave and his crew could be halfway to Hamblefolk.'

'Not good,' said the brigadier.

'I told the county we're running short-handed here,' said Cudban. 'Maybe they'll listen now we've finally had a killing.'

'No,' said the brigadier. 'I meant not good for you.'

He thrust the cutlass up and into Cudban's stomach, twisting it as the sergeant stumbled back, a line of blood spilling from his mouth as he gurgled his last breath. At the same time, Bates's arm snaked around Oliver's neck and a fist punched him in the spine, collapsing the boy to his knees.

'It's a terrible thing,' said Morgan, watching Cudban's death throes with a solemn gravitas. 'when a young man goes fey, killing everyone in his home.'

His colleague was pressing down on Oliver like a mountain. 'Then murdering his registration officer.'

Oliver thrashed on the floor but couldn't find the purchase to struggle free. The brigadier slipped a thread-thin noose from under his coat. 'Then the boy hangs himself from a beam in the station-house for the shame of it.'

The noose looped over, cutting into Oliver's neck.

'How long, would you wager, captain?' asked Morgan.

'With his weight?' said Bates. 'Three minutes.'

'Not long enough,' said Morgan. 'I'd have the boy down as a six-minute thrasher, choking and kicking all the way.'

'Nah. Too skinny.'

'A guinea on it, then, captain?'

'Done, you old rascal.'

Oliver was hauled to his feet and a chair scraped close, the noose thread tossed over a beam.

'Come on, son,' grinned the brigadier. 'You do your best and last four minutes for me.'

As if in a dream, Oliver's chair was kicked out from underneath him, the cord of his noose biting tight – as if someone was pouring molten metal down his throat. Feet kicking and flogging the air, he tried to scream with pain but could find no voice to do it. Then the floor was slowly rising up to slap into him – were the gates of the underworld opening up underneath his shoes?

<Roll under the table.>

A rifle crack and the brigadier was tossed across the room in a haze of blood, the pistol he was reaching for suspended in the air. The other Ham Yard detective was fumbling for something underneath his coat, but Harry Stave was not waiting to reload Cudban's rifle. Wheels of darkness spun across Oliver's confused eyes. Harry Stave was moving like a whiplash across the room – surely nobody could move that fast? The cord must have starved his brain of air.

Bates doubled up as Harry pushed the long rifle's butt into

his stomach, then one step forward and the captain was twisting in the air, a snap as his neck cracked, limp body flopping back down onto the ground.

Coughing, Oliver pulled at the cord still circled tight around his neck. He looked up and saw the knife quivering in the wall, where it had struck after cutting his noose.

'Uncle Titus?' Oliver hacked.

Harry Stave shook his head sadly.

'Oh Circle.' The enormity of what had happened began to sink in. Three fresh corpses at his feet. Cudban dead. Damson Griggs. His uncle. 'They tried to kill me.'

'You were just an excuse, old stick. A convenient registered boy to blame the killings on. It was Titus and me they wanted.'

'But they were police?'

Harry Stave kicked Bates's body. 'Maybe. But if they were, they weren't the kind of crushers you'll find cluttering up Ham Yard.'

Stave raised a finger to his lips as Oliver tried to speak. 'I killed two back at Seventy Star Hall, Oliver. Two here. Questions later. We have to leave now.'

Everything was upside down. The police were killing people. A murderer was protecting him. Everyone he had half a care for in Hundred Locks was gone. As if he were sleepwalking, Oliver left the police station, closing the door on a huddle of sprawled corpses.

Closing the door on his entire life.

Chapter Five

Molly's lessons with Damson Darnay in the poorhouse had never been as intensive as the month of training Lady Emma Fairborn and her tutors supervised. Lessons in etiquette conducted in empty rooms the size of warehouses, only the silent black-clad presence of the house whippers blocking the door for company. Protocol, balance, poise, how to walk, talk, think. The difference between a thrust and a parry – more than you might think. The difference between the various factions in the House of Guardians: Heartlanders, Purists, Levellers, Roarers, and Circleans – less than you might think.

Not yet allowed to roam the large mansion and its high-walled grounds – including a small boating lake – Molly was confined to a room shared with one of the other girls. An old hand bawdy girl called Justine. An air of expectation and menace hung in the air. Of what would happen to her if she failed to please a tutor, stumbled in front of one of the cold-eyed instructors of dance, philosophy or comportment.

'We're not a ha'penny tumble around the back of Hulk Square,' explained Lady Fairborn with a tone of contempt in

her voice when Molly had balked at the need to master yet
more current affairs. 'Of the clients who step through the
doors of Fairborn and Jarndyce, those that do not directly
decide the fate of Jackals will own title to significant parts of
its lands and commerce.'

Molly exhaled in frustration.

'Come, my dear,' said Lady Fairborn. 'Don't play coy with
me. I know what it's like to be brought up in the poorhouse.
You think that if you give your body to a boy or a girl, that
is all there is to pleasuring them. But that is barely a tenth
of being a good lover.' She tapped her head. 'The rest is what
occurs within this organ.'

Molly started. 'You were born in a—'

'I can't speak for where I was born, Molly. And that is
largely irrelevant to where one intends to end up. But yes,
like you I was raised in the orphanage wing of a Middlesteel
workhouse. Not behind your well-kept walls at Sun Gate,
mind, but down in the Jangles, among the city's rookeries,
sewage and human cast-offs.'

'But you have a title. . .' said Molly.

Fairborn laughed. 'Oh Molly, the most successful whores
you'll find in Middlesteel are down on the floor of the House
of Guardians. Which makes my title one of the cheapest
purchased in Jackals.'

Molly seemed lost in thought.

'Your education here, Molly, is not just about facts and
where on the table to locate the soupspoon. It's about seeing
the world as it really is. Lifting the veils of hypocrisy and the
lies we tell ourselves to get through the day. You still believe
that working here will prove distasteful? An honest answer
if you please. . .'

Molly nodded.

'That's because you have been sold a tissue of lies designed to chain you, Molly. Keep you unquestioning in your place, a compliant female and an obedient worker. Your beauty, your raw attraction for men, is a weapon. Use it well and you can achieve as much as I have. Some would have you believe that I am a victim, Molly. But when clients walk through my door, they are nothing but sheep to be shorn of their skin and their wealth. The bargains we strike here are as much an economic transaction as any that occur at a society ball or in front of a Circlist altar.

'The genial pensmen of Dock Street might steal their small amusements by writing my activities into the pages of the penny sheets as the Queen of the Whores, but the only difference between myself and a merchant's daughter being hawked at a coming-out ball is that I get to name my own price.' The lady leant over and kissed Molly, her tongue brushing lightly against the girl's. 'And unlike those respectable married ladies of Middlesteel, I find greater opportunity for repeat sales.'

'But what about love?' Molly questioned.

'The greatest lie of them all,' Fairborn retorted. 'A biological itch telling you it's time you started churning out tiny copies of yourself. Weakening your body and ravaging your beauty. Trust me on this; if there was ever a handsome prince waiting for either of us on a horse, he took a wrong turn somewhere. Love is like winter flu, Molly. It soon fades after the season. Better you learn to master it, package it, label it with a price and start building a future for yourself with it.'

The time had come for Molly to be introduced to her first client. A training patron, as it was euphemistically known, to orientate her in the trade of bawdy girl to the capital's quality. Justine sat behind Molly on the red velvet bed, combing her hair.

'You've nothing to worry about, Molly. I've seen your jack and he's a regular gentleman, dapper as a dandy and old too – his beard is as silver as this here comb.'

Molly's voice dripped with sarcasm. 'Sell him to me some more.'

'Not one of our usuals, but he must have come highly recommended to be here. Besides, an old one is best for the hey-jiggerty. He'll only last a couple of minutes.'

Molly shook her head. 'I can't do this.'

'You've got no choice, Molly. You bail out and you'll be transferred to housekeeping duties, right up until you go hard down some stairs or get crushed by a falling cabinet. The only way you'll get out of here is by paying off your contract.' The girl handed Molly a square of green-coloured gum. 'Chew this, it'll take the edge off.'

Molly gnawed suspiciously at the square. It was almost tasteless, the consistency of wet clay. 'What is it?'

'Leaaf,' said Justine.

Molly nearly choked. 'That must have cost a guardian's ransom!'

'Seventy sovereigns an ounce and the scaffold if you're caught with it. One of the perks for the girls here. How old do you think I am?'

'A couple of years older than me. Eighteen maybe?'

'Thirty-six,' said Justine proudly. 'They say there's caliphs in Cassarabia five hundred years old or more – and they'll give you the death sentence too, if they catch you smuggling leaaf across the desert and over the border. Not all our patrons are on the right side of the law, Molly.'

Molly rubbed the clay-like substance between her fingers. Lifelast was its street name. How the life-extending substance was made or grown nobody knew, and the mages of Cassarabia had never indicated whether it came from a rare plant or was something grown in the slave wombs alongside their twisted biologicks.

'I could have bought out my contract sixteen years ago,' said Justine. 'But once you've had money, it's hard to go back to having nothing. Lot harder than having stayed poor and never known the difference. And you can't buy a brick of leaaf across the counter at Gattie and Pierce.'

A small brass bell jingled and a moment later a large house whipper opened the door.

'This way, sir,' said Justine, beckoning the client in. She went to take his cane, but the man waved her away. He looked to Molly's mind like an old artist, his forked silver beard arriving at two sharp points just above a fussily folded cravat.

'I'll take a moment to catch my breath, if I may,' said the man. 'This place has more stairs than the Museum of Natural Philosophy.'

There was a slight accent to his voice. Not one Molly could place.

'As you asked, this is the new girl, sir,' said Justine. 'Although I believe you haven't been acquainted with any of our other ladies before?'

'Usually my free hours run to tending the orchids in my hothouse or listening to a well performed piece of chamber music,' said the man. 'But I believe this is just the girl for me.'

Justine made to go. 'Just ring the bell pull when you're finished, sir. I or one of the other ladies will escort you out down a private passage. No risk of accidentally bumping into another of our gentlemen that way.'

'Yes, I can see how that would be embarrassing,' said the old man. 'Although I would prefer it if you would stay a while with Molly and myself.'

'If you would like an extra lady, sir, I can arrange that—'

she stopped puzzled. 'But I told you this girl was called Magdalene. . .'

'You misunderstand me, my dear. I do not require an extra girl,' said the old man. A steel blade snicked out of his cane as he slashed it across Justine's throat. 'I require one less witness to have seen my face.'

Choking on her own blood, Justine stumbled and fell dying towards the green felt bell pull, the one they were to use if a patron ever turned violent. The door exploded open and the house whipper was in the room, a police-issue lead cosh in his ham-sized fist. Molly did not wait to see the bruiser closing on the old man; she was rolling off the velvet sheets, eyes darting around for an exit. The sash window had bars across it; the door was open but blocked by the two men; then her eyes fell on the cold fireplace. She had done smaller vents. Before the Blimber Watts tower breach. The memory of the last time she had crawled through a small space hit her. How could she go back to that?

There was a hacking noise from the whipper. One of his arms had been severed below the elbow, blood fountaining from the stump. The old man's cane had split into two blades and they traced a strange almost hypnotic dance in front of the shocked bawdyhouse enforcer.

Maybe it was the rush of leaaf into her system, maybe it was the realization that she was surely going to die in the next few seconds, but Molly was into the fireplace and up the chimneystack as fast as a fox to its warren. The cold weight of the darkness seemed to slip past her, the air sucking her up, her feet defying gravity as they shimmied weightless from brick to brick, her fingers almost too fat now for the child-sized sweep's holes. Was that a disappointed tutting below her at the fireplace opening? How long before the old man retraced his steps outside and found her again?

Air, cold, evening. She was on top of the roof, two storeys up. She recognized the skyline – western Sun Gate; one of the big mansions with its own wooded gardens. She slid down the iron drainpipe, each breath a wheeze and with the super-human speed she had found the grounds flowed past her body. She vaulted fences, raced around a miniature lake; bang bang her hands slapped the wall. She glanced back – the wall was twice as tall as she was. She couldn't have jumped that. It had to be the leaaf.

Who in the Circle's name had that old man been? No, that was the wrong question. He was a topper – as clear as day, he was one of the kingdom's professional killers for hire. An assassin. The right question was, why had he come into her room? Was Molly the target? Surely not. Damson Snell and her tub-load of ruined laundry were not about to lay good guineas to see young Molly Templar sliced in half. Had he killed someone in one of the other rooms and wanted to make a clean sweep? But neither she nor Justine had heard or seen a thing that night. And he had known Molly's name when he should not have – and said something about witnesses. Perhaps Justine had been a witness to something she could not be allowed to live to repeat and Molly was the bystander. Surely the killing had not been intended for *her*?

Molly could not testify to any crime except the Beadle's hand out for bribes, and he had taken care of her in his own rotten style by selling her ward papers to Fairborn and Jarndyce. Yet the killer had known her name. Asked for her specifically. That was an expensive way to end a cheap life.

She was back at the Sun Gate workhouse. Her feet had led her subconsciously to her sad excuse for a home. The hall lantern was off. Everyone would be asleep. She entered the poorhouse with trepidation. Would the Beadle believe her story? With a trail of corpses left behind in Lady Fairborn's establishment the head of the poorhouse would have no choice. Perhaps Lady Fairborn would cut her losses and throw her out as a Jonah. She had not brought any more luck to the bawdyhouse than she had to the Blimber Watts tower.

The large double doors to the entrance hall had been left ajar slightly and there was no sign of anyone sitting on the night chair. If the Beadle caught whichever boy or girl it was that had sloped off night duty, they would be for it and no mistake. She turned left and down the rickety wooden stairs to the girls' dormitory in the basement.

Strange. It was not past ten yet, only an hour after house curfew; there should have been some cheap tallow candles burning, the orphans reading penny dreadfuls, talking, eating fruit lifted from Magnet Market's throwaway bins. The room was pitch black, no skylights to the street above. Molly reached for one of the matches and lit a candle.

Cheap plywood bed frames lay overturned, hemp blankets scattered across the floor. Not just blankets. Molly stood over one of the bundles on the floor, hardly daring to flip the huddle over. She did. Rachael's cold dead eyes stared back at her.

'Rachael.' Molly prodded her. 'Rachael, wake up!'

She would not be waking.

Who had done this? The world had gone mad. Toppers breaking into bawdy shops. The same senseless slaughter at the Sun Gate poorhouse.

'Molly.' A voice sounded from the linen chest. Something moved under the blankets. It was Ver'fey, the craynarbian girl. She was wounded, one of the orange shell-plates of her crab-like armour shattered above the shoulder.

'Ver'fey! Your shoulder. . .' Molly ran to her. 'For the love of the Circle, what happened here?'

'Men,' coughed the craynarbian. 'They came dressed as

crushers from the ninth precinct, but they were no constables, I knew at once.'

She should know. Half of Middlesteel's police force was craynarbian; their tough exo-skeletons made them natural soldiers and keepers of parliament's peace.

'They did this?'

'They were looking for you, Molly.'

'Me?'

Ver'fey sat down on the chest, exhausted. 'Rachael told them that the Beadle had sent you off somewhere, but he wouldn't tell any of the rest of us where you were. Just said you'd finally got the job you deserved. One of the men thought Rachael was lying and started laying into her with his Sleeping Henry. They just beat her to death in front of us. We tried to stop them; that was when they gave me this.' She pointed to her broken shoulder plate.

'Where are all the others?' Molly looked around the dormitory.

'Took them,' sobbed the craynarbian. 'Took them all. The boys too.'

'Why?' said Molly. 'What would they want with us?'

'Better you ask what they wanted with you, Molly. It was you they were after. What have you done, Molly?'

'Nothing that the rest of you weren't up to,' spat Molly. 'None of this makes any sense.'

'Perhaps it's your family?'

'What family?' said Molly. 'You are my bleeding family.'

'Your blood family,' said Ver'fey. 'Perhaps they're rich. Rich and powerful enough to hire a gang of toppers. Some father who's just found out he has an unwanted bastard and is out to simplify the act of inheritance.'

Molly grimaced. Simplifying the act of inheritance was Jackelian slang for leaving an unwanted child on the poorhouse doorstep. Ver'fey's theory had the ring of truth to it. She had never once felt wanted in her life, but this was preposterous. Perhaps her mother had abandoned her at Sun Gate out of love after all, out of fear of what might happen to her if her father found out he had sired a bastard

'Come on old shell.' Molly helped Ver'fey out of her hiding place. 'They've cleared off. Best we do likewise, before someone comes back.'

'You could come with me to Shell Town,' said Ver'fey. 'Hide out.'

'Unless you can fix me up with armour and an extra pair of arms, I'm going to stick out like a sore thumb in Shell Town. You'd be in danger every minute I was with you.'

'But where can you go?' asked Ver'fey.

'The Beadle always said I'd end up running with the flash mob. Reckon I'll prove him right and disappear into the undercity – try to reach Grimhope and the outlaws.'

'That's too dangerous, Molly,' said Ver'fey. 'Do you even know how to get into the undercity?'

'I do,' said Molly. 'Don't you remember when Rachael was working for the atmospheric authority?'

'Yes! Guardian Rathbone station.'

Guardian Rathbone station was the main terminus on the atmospheric network for Sun Gate's workers. Thousands of clerks and clackers rode the tube capsules in through the tunnels every day, large steam engines labouring to create the airless vacuum the trains traversed.

'There are entrances to the undercity in the atmospheric. Rachael was always going on about them. It'll be safer than going in through the sewers.'

Ver'fey agreed. There were plenty of things in Middlesteel's sewers, but none you would want to run into on your own. The city's sewer scrapers only went inside armed in teams of five or six. 'Please, Molly, you come with me to Shell Town. It's no life for you in the undercity. There's nothing down there but junkers, rebels and the flash mob. If some criminal doesn't do for you, the political police will – they're always pumping dirt-gas down into the tunnels to cull outlaws.'

Molly shook her head and knelt down beside Rachael's body. 'She was always the sensible one, our Rachael. Settle down to a nice safe job. Keep your nose clean. Don't answer back.'

Ver'fey tried to pull Molly away. 'You're right, we should go now.'

'Look where it got her, Ver-Ver. Bloody dead in this rotting dung heap of a home.'

'Please, Molly.'

Molly picked up a candle and threw it into a pile of penny dreadfuls, the cheap paper catching light immediately. Flames jumped across the hemp blankets, crackling like a roasting pig.

'A warrior's pyre, for you, Rachael, and when I find the filthy glocker scum that did this to you – to us – I'll burn them too and everything they hold dear. I swear it.'

Ver'fey trembled nervously on her feet. 'Molly! Oh Molly, what have you done?'

'Let it burn,' said Molly, suddenly weary. She led Ver'fey back out of the dormitory before the flames took the rickety wooden stairs. 'Let it all burn to the bloody ground.'

First Guardian Hoggstone tapped his shoe impatiently against the large porcelain vase standing by his writing desk, scenes of triumph from the civil war rendered delicately in obsidian blue. The weekly meeting with King Julius was a tiresome formality, little more than a cover for the chance to be updated by the commander of the Special Guard. Still, parliament held to its ancient forms. Two worldsingers stood silently flanking the door to the First Guardian's office. Hoggstone smiled to himself. The Special Guard watched the King. The worldsingers watched the Special Guard. He watched the worldsingers. And who watched the First Guardian? Why, the electorate of course. That anonymous amorphous herd; that howling mob in waiting. Captain Flare came into the room. Without the King, but with the pup, Crown Prince Alpheus, in tow instead.

'Julius?' asked Hoggstone in a sharp voice.

'Waterman's sickness again,' answered the captain. 'He won't be leaving the palace for at least a week.'

Hoggstone sighed and looked at the pup. It always made him nervous, seeing an almost crowned monarch with his arms still attached to his body.

'Why, sir, is the boy not wearing his face mask?'

'Asthma,' said Captain Flare. 'In the heat he chokes sometimes.'

'I hate the mask,' complained the prince. 'The iron rubs my ears until they bleed.'

Hoggstone sighed again. 'We'll find you some royal whore, pup, for you to breed us the next king on. Then I'll try and convince the house not to teach it to talk. Waste of bloody time having you able to say anything except parrot the vows of affirmation once a week.'

'I hate you!'

Hoggstone rose up and drove a ham-sized fist into the prince's stomach. The boy doubled up on the floor and the First Guardian kicked him in the head. 'As it should be, Your Highness. Now shut up, or we'll take your arms off early, cover them in gold plate and show them next to your father's down in the People's Hall.'

Flare lifted the gagging, gasping boy up and put him down on a chair. 'Was that necessary, First Guardian?'

'It was to me,' said Hoggstone. The shepherd, that's what they called Captain Flare behind his back. That's what he had been, a herd boy, when a feymist had risen on the moors, turning Flare into a feybreed, giving him the kind of physical strength that demigods from classical history only dreamt about. But the man was soft, a useful fool protecting his new flock. The people. Yes. Everything for the people.

'We're not as modern as the Commonshare, sir,' said Hoggstone. 'Running all our nobles through a Gideon's Collar. We still have to rely on a bit of shoe leather and a stout Jackelian foot every now and then.'

'It's putting the Jackelian boot in that you want to talk about?' asked Flare. 'The Carlists?'

'I don't even know if we can call the people we're facing Carlists any more,' said Hoggstone. 'The local mob seems to have moved beyond the normal communityist platitudes our compatriots in Quatérshift have been mouthing of late.'

'You suspect something?'

'There's trouble being stirred in the streets. Too much and too widely spread for it to be anything other than organized.'

'That's what the House of Guardians' Executive Investigations Arm is for,' said Flare.

'The g-men have been cracking the usual skulls, netting the usual suspects. Whatever's happening out there on the streets, the old-time Carlists are as afraid of it as we are. Their leaders have been disappearing, at least, all the ones who have been opposing the new generation of rabble-rousers. The river police have been pulling the corpses of Carlist committeemen out of the Gambleflowers for a year now.'

'You have a target in mind for the Special Guard?'

Hoggstone sounded frustrated. 'This isn't a Cassarabian bandit sheikh or a royalist pirate flotilla you can smash for the state – this needs subtlety.'

'I can rip plate metal apart with my bare hands,' Flare pointed out. 'Rifle charges bounce off me and my skin can blunt a fencing foil. I am not sure the Special Guard can do subtlety.'

'But there are others who can,' said Hoggstone.

Flare's eyes narrowed. 'You are talking of the fey in Hawklam Asylum.'

One of the worldsingers flanking the door moved forward. 'First Guardian!'

'Stand back.' Hoggstone's voice was raised. 'Damn your eyes, I do know how the order feel about the things we have contained in Hawklam.'

'They are there for a reason,' said the worldsinger. 'The abominations they have endured have twisted the creatures' minds far more than their bodies. Those things have as much left in common with beings such as ourselves as we do with an infestation of loft-rot beetles, and, given the chance, they would treat us much the same.'

'It is their minds which interest me. We do not need many – just a couple with the talent to root out the core of the enemy in our midst.'

'Soul-sniffers,' gasped the worldsinger. 'You believe the order would release soul-sniffers into the world.'

'The people would not like it,' advised Flare.

'I am the people, sir!' Hoggstone roared. 'The voice of the people, for the people. And I will not let the people fall under the spell of a horde of communityist rabble-rousers. I will not have the talent and prosperity of this nation run through a Gideon's Collar like so much mince through a sausage grinder. I will not!' Hoggstone slammed his writing desk and thrust a finger towards Captain Flare. 'You think that if the people see the misshapen human wreckage in Hawklam Asylum the mob might stop worshipping the ground the Guard walk on.

Start associating your guardsmen with feybreed abominations rather than the latest damn issue of *The Middlesteel Illustrated* with a stonecutting of your face grinning on the cover.'

'It is possible,' Flare acknowledged.

'The art of leadership is knowing when the mob's applause has become a self-destructive echo,' said Hoggstone. 'If the choice is the veil being pulled off your perfect persona or the state collapsing into anarchy and mayhem, I'll choose the former over the latter. But do not worry, we shall keep the feybreed on a short leash and run them only at night. After all, it does not do to scare the voters.'

'We will need to fashion special torc suits for them,' said the worldsinger. 'And organize teams to make sure the abominations don't slip them.'

Hoggstone gestured wearily. 'Do it, then. We need to know who is behind the unrest and when they intend to act, when they intend to take advantage of their mischief.'

'As you will.'

'As the people will, sir. And for the Circle's sake, put the gag back on the royal pup before you leave the House. I don't want *The Middlesteel Illustrated* running a story on him being seen naked within parliament's walls.'

Chapter Six

Ver'fey tapped Molly with one of her manipulator limbs, the short one under her big bone-sword arm. 'Molly, we're being followed.'

The craynarbian had never seen a creeper or vine in Liongeli, but she still had her jungle senses.

'From where?'

'As we turned off Watercourse Avenue.'

Molly swore to herself. They *had* set watchers outside the poorhouse then. Damn her family. It was one thing to know from your earliest years you had never been wanted, cast out like the previous night's garbage. It was quite another to have your own blood trying to tidy up loose ends by slitting your throat. 'How many?'

'Two men.'

Molly pondered their options. 'If it is me they want and they've clocked me, their numbers won't stay at two for long. The gang that did for Rachael and the house will be swarming over Sun Gate.'

Ver'fey gestured off the street with her bone-sword. 'We could play alley-dodge, then slice them good.'

Molly shook her head. 'You're a game bird, Ver-Ver, but the two of us are no match for a crew of professional toppers. End of the street, you jump left for Shell Town, I'll cut right and lose them in the Angel's Crust.'

Ver'fey made a noise of disgust. Like all her kind, she would only be seen dead in a jinn house – quite literally. The only effects the pink-coloured drink had on craynarbians were to make them vomit and to slow their hearts to a dangerously low palpitation.

'Luck to us,' said Ver'fey.

'You blooming well look after yourself, Ver-Ver,' said Molly.

They got to the end of the street and Molly lunged right and up Shambles Lane, the sound of Ver'fey's heavy, shell-covered body clattering the opposite way fading as she found the narrow corridors of the Pinchfield rookeries. The Angel's Crust was up the Shambles and on the left, a three-storey temple to Middlesteel's sinners; the low-rent equivalent of Fairborn and Jarndyce. Two floors of drunken loutish revelry with bedrooms on the third floor, where women with low necklines and even lower morals plied Middlesteel's oldest trade.

As she sprinted for the bright yellow light of the place, Molly caught a glimpse of two shadows racing after her. Even as she cursed, part of her was glad they had left Ver'fey to escape; the craynarbian girl could move fast over a short distance, but her armour made her a poor bet for a marathon chase. This was confirmation. Someone wanted Molly dead. Very badly indeed.

Molly hurdled a clump of collapsed snoring drinkers and hurtled through the doorless entrance. She blundered into a drinker, spraying jinn over the sawdust on the floor.

'Crushers,' Molly yelled like a banshee. 'Get out – it's a raid. Ham Street bawdy.'

The ground floor erupted in confusion as chairs wrenched back and the surge for the exits started. If there was an honest man or woman drinking or conducting business in the Angel's Crust, they were here by mistake. Like many of the girls at the Sun Gate workhouse, Molly had earned pennies in the evening moonlighting as a watch girl at the Angel.

A pistol charge rang out by the door and something pinged off one of the roof beams, followed by a swell of uproar and even more confusion. Her two pursuers were in the taproom and Molly dived low, riding and hiding in the panicked flow of the crowd. One of the barkeeps shoved past her clutching an old black blunderbuss. She went under the bar and darted through to the cellar, racing around walls of piled oak jinn barrels, each burned with the red marque of its Cassarabian exporter.

Thank the Circle. The old staff chute was still there, behind a tattered cloth curtain. Their backdoor if a rival flash mob decided to move in on the Angel. Molly was careful to leave the cloth in place as she shoved off down the short slide, landing in a puddle of grimy water and rotting bottle corks at the foot of the tumbledown rookeries beyond.

The maze of corridors changed all the time as the inhabitants added new doorways or closed off collapsed tenements. Little chance of them catching her now. She navigated the claustrophobic streets towards the back end of the Guardian Rathbone atmospheric. Molly smelt it before she saw it; two columns of large stacks pouring dark coal smoke into the sky, keeping the atmospheric's tunnels in vacuum.

Guardian Rathbone station was a castle of white marble stained black with soot, arched domes of glass and girders crisscrossing the passenger concourse. It was thought to be one of the most magnificent stations on the atmospheric – rivalling

Guardian Fairfax station out by the palace, perhaps even Guardian Kelvin station across from the House of Guardians. It would be dangerous now, though; too late for Molly to work the mob of Sun Gate clerks going home as camouflage; just a few revellers belatedly leaving the respectable cafes and salons along Goldhair Park.

Three steammen were cleaning the concourse, collecting rubbish and polishing the mosaic of the Battle of Clawfoot Moor, the scene of parliament's final victory in the civil war. Molly had to get out of here fast. The atmospheric was too obvious an escape route. She checked her money. A penny short of the cheapest journey on the atmospheric. Damn. If she had realized earlier she could have dipped someone's wallet back at the Angel's Crust.

At the end of the station two figures in dark jackets walked onto the concourse. Molly danced into the shadow cast by one of the steammen, an iron skip on short stubby legs. No chance now to vault the ticket rail and make a dash for the underground platforms – the two bruisers would clock her. Of course, they might be innocent, watchmen for one of the Sun Gate towers. Sneaking a peek over the iron box, Molly saw they had split up and were drifting through the sparse queue of passengers, sweeping the hall in a precise pattern. Not so innocent, then.

She went over the side of the iron skip, sliding into sacks of litter. The head of the steamman swivelled around to regard her. 'Ho, little softbody. What are you doing in my collection of gewgaws?'

'Quietly with your speaking tube,' Molly pleaded. 'Two men are searching for me. They mean me harm.'

An iron eye-cover blinked over the steamman's vision glass in surprise. 'Harm, you say? That will not do.'

'They'll do for me, unless you quiet down.'

The volume of the steamman's voicebox dropped to a whisper. 'I believe you are known to me, little softbody.'

'Not in this life,' said Molly. 'There weren't any steammen in the Sun Gate poorhouse.'

The steamman had started moving its eight stubby legs, a wheel at its front directing them, jiggling her across the public space. 'The people of the metal do not abandon our brothers to the workhouse, that is not the way of our kind.'

'I need to get to the undercity. Can you take me down into the atmospheric?'

'There is a high level of physical danger in the undercity,' said the steamman. 'The rules of community are not adhered to below.'

'I know it's an outlaw society,' hissed Molly. 'But I haven't got anywhere else to run to.'

'Crawl under my sacks,' commanded the steamman. 'Your pursuers draw close.'

Molly buried herself under the bags of waste, leaving as small a space to breathe as she dared. She heard a gruff voice asking a passenger if he had seen a missing runaway girl. The thug omitted to mention what Molly was running away from. Then the voice was left behind and the tap, tap, tap of the steamman's legs on the concourse became the only sound she could hear.

Molly angled her face for a better view out of the skip; the metal bars of a door were being hauled into the ceiling and they were passing into a sooty lift of a size to accommodate the large steamman.

'Steelbhalah-Waldo has been watching over you. The ones who wish you harm have been left behind.'

Steelbhalah-Waldo indeed, Molly thought. Her rescuer spoke of the religion of Gear-gi-ju. The steammen worshipped their ancestors and a pantheon of machine-spirits, sacrificing high-grade boiler coke and burning oil from their own valves and gears.

Molly crawled out from under the piled sacks. 'Thank you for your help, old steamer. I think you may have just saved my life.'

'My known name is Slowcogs,' said the steamman. 'You may call me by my known name.'

Molly nodded. Slowcogs' true name would be a blessed serial number known only to himself and the ruler of the machine race, King Steam. That was not for her to know. The old lift started to vibrate as it sank.

'Can you show me the way to the undercity, Slowcogs? The way to Grimhope.'

'The way is known to the people of the metal, young soft-body. But it is a path filled with danger. I hesitate to expose you to such risk.'

'Middlesteel above has become too dangerous for me, Slowcogs. A professional topper has been sent after me and now many of my friends have died because of my presence. There aren't many places left to run to. I'll take the risk of Middlesteel below.'

'So young,' tutted the old machine. 'Why do the master-less warriors of your people seek your destruction?'

'I don't really know,' said Molly. 'I suppose it has something to do with my family. I think one of my kin is trying to remove my rights of inheritance the easy way, by removing me from Middlesteel.'

'That those who share biological property with you should act in such a way is disgraceful. But all may not be as it seems – there are many sorts of inheritance.'

The lift room opened and they were in a large vaulted chamber facing a row of empty iron skips of the type that made up Slowcogs' body. With a wrenching sound – like metal being torn – the front of Slowcogs disengaged from the multi-legged skip, leaving it behind like a tortoise abandoning its shell. The new, smaller Slowcogs was as tall as Molly, running on three iron wheels in tricycle formation. 'Our way lies across the atmospheric platforms. The masterless warriors who seek your life will undoubtedly finish their search above and begin looking for you below.'

'I'll be quick,' Molly promised.

They followed a small gas-lit tunnel, a locked door at the end opening onto Guardian Rathbone station's main switching hall. In the centre of the cavernous circular hall was a series of interconnected turntables shifting windowless atmospheric capsule trains between lines. Large shunting arms terminating in buffers pushed the atmospheric capsules through leather curtains and into the platform tubes. Molly could hear the drone of the passenger crowd boarding the motorless capsules on the other side of the curtain, then the sucking sound as the capsule was shunted through the rubber airlock and into the line's sending valve, before being pressure-sped into the vacuum of the atmospheric.

Slowcogs led Molly across the switching hall on a raised walkway, into a smaller maintenance hall where capsules lay stacked like firewood across the repair bays.

'This is the way to the undercity?' Molly asked.

'First we must consult Redrust,' said Slowcogs. 'He is the station controller and a Gear-gi-ju master. He will know the safest path.'

They climbed a shaky staircase, coming into a hut over-looking the maintenance bay. Sitting inside watching the hall through a grimy window was a steamman with an oversized head, rubber tubes dangling from his metal skull like beaded hair. Redrust's speaking tubes were three small flared trumpets just below his neck.

'Controller,' said Slowcogs, 'I have need of your assistance for this young softbody.'

Redrust's voice echoed out like a wire being scratched across a chalkboard. 'When do we not need the guidance of those that have passed away on the great pattern, Slowcogs?'

'I am in particular need today, controller,' said Molly.

The rubber tubes on his skull jangled as Redrust turned his substantial head to stare at Molly. 'A particular need, so? Much haste in your words. You would do better to wait a while and contemplate your part in the great pattern.'

'Events dictate otherwise, old steamer.'

'So? Let us throw the cogs and see what Gear-gi-ju has to reveal to us this evening, then.'

Slowcogs passed a porcelain cup to the controller, filled with small metalworkings of different sizes. Redrust released a small puddle of dark blood-like oil onto the floor from his valves. Scattering the cogs into the pool, he traced an iron digit through the pile.

'I see a girl, climbing out of the wreckage of a collapsed tower.'

'That would be me,' said Molly.

'I see shadows. Moving through the city. Deaths. A stalker.'

'Lots of people die in Middlesteel,' said Molly.

'I see your desire to travel into the belly of the ground, escaping the perils that snap at your heels,' said Redrust.

'That is my wish, sir,' said Molly.

'I see—' Redrust stopped. 'Ah, so. Great complexity. Many wheels. You did well to bring this softbody to us, Slowcogs.'

'She is known to us,' said Slowcogs.

'Indeed she is. The gears have turned so far already, and now they have turned to this.' The controller looked at Molly. 'What do you see in the cogs, young softbody?'

'I am no Gear-gi-ju master, controller.'

'Nevertheless, look into the cogs; feel the pattern with your mind. Tell me what you see there.'

She knelt to look. The smell of the dark oil made Molly dizzy. 'History. I see history, revolving, turning back into itself.'

Redrust seemed pleased with the answer. 'I have lived many years. Seen generations of softbodies quicken past on your own wheel, filled with hurry and the hasty ambitions of your fastblood kind – but I have never seen one able to read the cogs.'

'Remarkable,' agreed Slowcogs.

'But not without precedent,' said Redrust.

'There's something else you have seen,' said Molly. 'Something you're not telling me. . .'

'That is so,' said Redrust. 'Often that which you do not say means as much as that which you do, and sometimes knowing the future can change it. There are things I will not speak of.'

'You will help me to the undercity then, to Grimhope?' Molly asked.

'Sadly, we will,' the scratched reply sounded from Redrust's voicebox. 'Your path and that of our people are tangled together in some way. I only wish we had a hero to accompany you, a champion. But our steammen knights keep inside the borders of the Steammen Free State, and it would take too long to send for such as they.'

'I shall go, controller,' said Slowcogs. 'It was I that found her.'

'You, Slowcogs?' A soft wheeze escaped from Redrust's boiler heart like a laugh. 'This is a task for young metal. Your design was drafted by King Steam before even my own and I am one of the oldest steammen to serve in the atmospheric.'

'It is as you say, controller. Our paths are bound together by the great pattern.'

'You are a poor excuse for a knight, Slowcogs. But let it be so. Old metal guiding a young softbody. Join with me.'

Slowcogs rolled past Molly and a thin crystal rod extended from the controller, slotting into a hole in Slowcogs' torso. They remained joined for a minute, then Slowcogs disengaged from the crystal arm with a cracking noise.

'Thank you for your wisdom, controller.'

'Thank you for your courage, Slowcogs.'

The old steamman took Molly's hand and they rolled out of the controller's hut.

'What did he share with you?' asked Molly.

'Such knowledge as we possess of the paths and passages of the undercity,' said Slowcogs. 'But the tunnels we must travel change frequently. The outlaws of Grimhope seal caverns off to confuse the political police and the soldiers of Fort Downdirt, and the political police often send in sappers to destroy tunnels. Then there is the stream of earthflow through the ground – the same energies of the leylines that cause floatquakes.'

The mention of the word sent a shiver down Molly's spine. Whole regions of land shattered by the earth's forces, ripped out of the ground and sent spiralling into the air, along with any unfortunates unlucky enough to be on the sundered ground. If those caught on rising land were lucky, the newly formed aerial islands would stabilize at a height low enough for RAN airships to rescue the inhabitants. If they were unlucky, they would rise far out of sight, into the airless night, beyond even the reach of RAN aerostats; their icy graves an occasional cloudy shadow passing over the land beneath.

Geomancy was the first duty of the order of worldsingers, tapping and relieving the lethal forces surging below the ground before they coursed into violence and destroyed large swathes of Jackals.

'Can we get there on foot?' asked Molly, trying to take her mind off the possibility of a floatquake.

'The undercity? We must walk part of the way,' said Slowcogs. 'The first portion of the journey will be through the atmospheric.'

He rolled up to a small felt-lined service capsule, opening a circular door at the flat rear of the metal plate. Inside lay none of the comforts of the passenger tubes – no velvet-cushioned seats or gas lights; just a small wooden bench at the opposite end of the carriage and leather straps on the wall holding bundles of esoteric-looking tools. Slowcogs entered the carriage after Molly, clanging the door shut and spinning a wheel to lock it.

There was a moment's darkness and then a phosphorous strip lit the spine of the capsule with a witching green light.

'Sit,' advised Slowcogs, 'and hold onto the ceiling strap.'

With a jolt the capsule was shunted through the rubber lock of the sending valve; when the flap closed, the other end of the chamber opened and the carrier capsule was on its way. Stilled for a second, the motorless carriage started to accelerate through the airless lead service tunnel as the pressure differential caught it.

Molly had rarely been on the public atmospheric, but the windowless capsule made for a featureless journey, the only variation in their speed the slight deceleration and acceleration as they passed pressure-pumping stations.

After half an hour of near silent travel the service capsule braked to a halt and Slowcogs pulled a mask with goggling eyes out of a crate, attaching it to a brass oxygen cylinder with back-straps dangling from its front. 'There is still vacuum outside. Place this over your face and I will help you strap on the cylinder.'

The small canister felt heavier than it looked and Molly

nearly buckled with the weight of it digging into her back. Slowcogs adjusted the straps and the weight was redistributed, her field of vision shrinking to the view through the mask's two crystal eyepieces. It took a moment or two to get used to the mask – everything appeared further away than it actually was.

When Slowcogs was satisfied she could move and breathe, the steamman equalized pressure with the tunnel outside and they stepped onto a stone platform set inside one of the atmospheric's receiving valves, littered with tunnelling equipment, lead solder and bags of sand. Their platform was lit by the same green light that had illuminated the atmospheric capsule – the tunnel seemed to shine with it. Molly walked past the buffers that had caught the service capsule and ran her hand along the cold wall. The tip of her thumb shone with a green lichen smear.

Slowcogs beckoned Molly along the platform, rolling to a vault-like door in the stone. It opened onto a small room and another door. Pulling a chain hanging from a machine in the corner, Slowcogs moved back towards Molly as the hissing sound made her ears pop.

'You can breathe in here,' Slowcogs said, pulling Molly's air tank off her back. 'The passages of the undercity start beyond this door.'

A weight lifted from Molly's shoulders. 'They'll never find me down here, Slowcogs. We're free.'

'Freedom from rules does not equate to safety,' said Slowcogs. 'With softbodies I have often noted the opposite to be the case.'

Slowcogs pulled back the second door and Molly gasped. A hall lay beyond, stairs leading downwards. It was massive, a vast cathedral of space, columns supporting the ceiling, statues as big as Middlesteel houses in alcoves shadowed by the lichen light.

'I don't understand,' Molly said, overwhelmed by the scale of the space.

'The under-people and outlaws live here now,' said Slowcogs. 'But they did not build this. Thousands of years ago Jackals lay under the rule of the old empire, Chimeca. These ruins are their legacy.'

Chimeca. That was ancient history, but Molly dimly recalled lessons of insect gods, locust priests and human sacrifice. 'I thought the undercity was just an old level of Middlesteel under the sewers that had been built over.'

Slowcogs shook his head. 'No, it was always thus. There was a period of great cold in ancient times and to survive the Chimecans riddled the earth with their cities below the surface. It is said the first steammen Loas date from that age, holy machines.'

Molly stared at bird bats circling near the ceiling, tiny dots of black. 'I always wondered why the political police couldn't just dirt-gas the outlaws. The crushers could lose a whole legion of police militia down here.'

'Only a small fraction of the passages are known to us,' said Slowcogs. 'Much of it now rests collapsed by the ages. What you see runs deep and far. Entire sub-cities have crumbled as the earth has twisted and turned on its journey across the great pattern.'

Molly looked at a large section of wall collapsed over the stairs half a mile down-slope. 'As long as it doesn't cave in while we're here.'

'This exit was chosen by Redrust for both its stability and its remoteness from Grimhope,' said Slowcogs. 'There should not be any sentries here. Only the workers of the atmospheric know of its existence.'

'The outlaw city is still down here?' asked Molly.

'I believe so, in body if not in spirit,' replied Slowcogs. His wheel axles spidered down the stairs, leading them to a much smaller staircase hidden behind one of the statue alcoves. 'This passage heads to the outskirts of the great cavern of the Duitzilopochtli Deeps; Grimhope stands there at the centre of the fungal forest, a day and a night's travel from our present location.'

Molly and Slowcogs descended down the side passage for hours, the light-lichen growing fitfully in places, plunging them into near darkness. Occasionally the stairs deviated into box-like rest chambers; plain bed-slabs carved from the walls. If their journey had been uphill rather than down they would have been glad of the respite. As it was, Slowcogs had already pronounced the fungal forest as their first rest stop. Eventually the path forked in four directions and Slowcogs started to lead them down the passage on the far left.

The exit became a bright dot in the distance two hours later. Molly's legs ached after the effort of tackling the stairs, her calves tight and cramped. She stepped outside the tunnel.

For a moment Molly thought that there must have been some mistake – a trick of gravity – that they had walked back to the surface, the green lichen-light replaced by bright daylight. Her eyes watered after the dim darkness of the side passage. Blinking away tears, she saw she was standing at the foot of a cliff, a rock wall towering away into the mist a thousand feet above them. The fog was suffused with red light and crackled intermittently with raw, lightning-like energies.

Below the mist, stretching as far as she could see, a forest of mushrooms crouched as tall and dense as oak. Many of the fungal growths were ebony-dark, but there were splashes of colour in the forest too, fluted fungal spires with bright mottled markings of scarlet, gold and jade.

'By the Circle,' said Molly. 'It's handsome. It's like there's a sun down here.'

'Observe.' Slowcogs pointed to a gap in the vapour along the cavern's haze-wrapped ceiling. 'Not one sun, but many. Crystals left by the empire of Chimeca's sorcerers. They used the crystal machines much as Jackals uses her worldsingers, to direct and tap the flow of the leylines' earthflow, to stop their underground cities being crushed by the turning of the world. The sparks you see are the violence of the world diverted into light.'

'Shall we press on now?' Molly pointed towards the forest.

'Sleep first,' said Slowcogs. 'We are at the far northern end of the Duitzilopochtli Deeps. The outlaw city has most of its sentries to the south, where the easy entrances from Middlesteel are positioned – the sewer outlets.'

Slowcogs led them along the cliff wall until they came to the façade of an old temple carved into the rock. On one side of the entrance a seated stone figure crouched, human except for an ugly beetle's head. It was matched on the other side by a second seated man-statue, a mammoth spider-head rising from its neck.

'I don't like the feel of this place,' said Molly. 'Not one bit.'

'The old gods lost their power after the fall of Chimeca,' said Slowcogs. 'The temples and forces of ancient Wildcaotyl have no capability here now. It will be better to sleep within these walls. There are prides of pecks living inside the forest.'

Despite her misgivings, Molly accepted the steamman's advice. It was only when she got inside the temple that the wave of tiredness overtook her. Molly shivered. Locust priests had once practised their dark rites down here . . . she could feel it. From what she recalled from her poorhouse lessons, the pantheon of Wildcaotyl gods still lingered over the world like an ugly ancestral memory; each deity more obscene than the last – from lesser gods such as Khemchiuhtlicue Blood-drinker and

Scorehueteotl Stake-burner, right up to Xam-Ku himself, old Father Spider.

It was the middle of the night in Middlesteel above, and she finally fell into a deep dream-filled sleep. Rachael's ghost came to speak to her, warning that Grimhope was no place for a nice Sun Gate girl, telling her that she should find a respectable job as a seamstress. Next the Beadle came; his body still covered in the torture marks of the gang that had stormed the poorhouse. He shouted at Molly that she was headed for the gallows outside Bonegate – until he was decapitated by the refined old assassin from the bawdyhouse, whose cane split into twin sword sticks like a conjurer's trick.

'Where's my father?' Molly demanded of the killer.

'I am your father,' said the assassin. 'And you are such a terrible disappointment to the family. I don't think we can bear your existence any more.'

'You shouldn't be trying to kill me,' said Molly. 'I want to speak to my mother.'

'She died of shame,' said the assassin. 'After you were born.'

'That's not true.'

The topper shoved her to the dirt, pushing her red hair back from the nape of her neck. 'Time to die, Molly Templar.'

'Please,' Molly pleaded. 'I just want to see my mother once before you kill me.'

'Hold still. I'll send you to her now.'

It was Slowcogs that shook her awake, rather than the kiss of cold sabre steel. Molly groaned.

'It is midday in the world above, Molly softbody. Time to move on.'

The first growths in the fungal forest were tall white mushroom trees with multiple cups and red mottling; then the lichen-covered ground grew denser with darker single-cup growths. At times they needed to retrace their steps so Slowcogs could squeeze through the thick forest.

Molly watched a squirrel-like rodent chewing on one of the trunks. 'You could live free out here, Slowcogs. If you didn't mind a diet of mushrooms.'

'Grimhope is safer,' said the steamman. 'Relatively speaking.'

'Is it still like the legends of the Green Man?'

'I doubt if it ever was the place of your tales, Molly soft-body,' said Slowcogs. Then, as if it explained everything, he added, 'It is an outlaw city.'

'They will welcome us there?'

'My people have not updated our knowledge of Grimhope for many years,' said Slowcogs. 'There are few outlaw steammen; although one of our kind does live down here. Silver Onestack. He is a desecration.'

'You mean he is malfunctioning?'

'Which of us does not, with age?' answered Slowcogs. 'No. He is a joining – a creature formed from steamman cadavers at the hands of one of your human mechomancers. His pattern has been violated, the architecture laid down by King Steam tampered with. Three souls of our fallen lay trapped within the corpses that make up his body by Onestack's selfish refusal to deactivate. It is a great dishonour for him.'

Molly remembered her dream of the night before. 'Poor Silver Onestack.'

'So he hides himself away down here in the undercity. But he is still steamman. Word has been sent by the controller – if he is alive I hope he will meet us outside the town.'

'Word?' said Molly. 'Surely there is no crystalgrid network down here?'

Slowcogs pointed towards the ceiling mist, where black dots rode the cavern thermals. 'There are older ways to send a message, young softbody. Trained bird bats with leg clips do as well in the deeps.'

They travelled at a steady pace for the rest of the day, uneventfully except for when one of the mushroom trees rained spores down on them as they passed. Molly's eyes swelled up like the crimson ball from a game of four-poles and she sneezed uncontrollably for another two miles. Apart from the odd spike of earthflow-fed lightning, the bright red light from the crystals high above them never varied or dimmed. It was always day in the Duitzilopochtli Deeps.

By the late afternoon the cavern floor started to slope upwards and the fungal forest began to grow less densely. The presence of fields of stumps in the dirt suggested heavy felling by the inhabitants of the undercity. Before the brow of a hill they came across a field of a different kind, the stone markers and headstones of a graveyard stretching back to the fungal forest.

'This is where Silver Onestack will meet us, if he is still activate,' said Slowcogs. The steamman rolled along a path towards a shrine at the corner of the graveyard. The temple looked as abandoned as the Chimecan structure Molly had slept in the night before, but with none of the half-human, half-insect effigies. She guessed the outlaw city, rather than the ancient fallen empire, had constructed the shrine. Peering inside its gloom, Molly saw a figure squatting on the floor. A steamman, as silent as one of the Guardian's statues in Parliament Square.

'Have you no greeting for us, Silver Onestack?' asked Slowcogs.

Raising itself on a tripod of three pincer-like legs, the large spherical body of the creature rotated, a silver-domed head emerging from an iris on the globe. 'I had hoped no greetings would be necessary, Slowcogs. Did the controller not receive my message?'

'We did not wait for your reply,' said Slowcogs. 'The Gear-gi-ju wheels have been thrown.'

'Then he has read badly, Slowcogs. Grimhope is not the place it once was. Whatever threat this softbody faces in Middlesteel, it is only a fraction of the disorder that now rules down here.'

Slowcogs rolled back. 'I do not understand.'

'Then let me show you,' said Silver Onestack, his three legs scissoring him out of the temple. They reached the top of the hill and stared down into the valley.

Old Chimecan ziggurats lay dotted around the cavern floor overwhelmed by the towers of a human city, smoke rising from workshops and manufactories. It looked like the Jangles in Middlesteel viewed from the top of the hill at Rottonbow.

'Where is the tree town?' asked Slowcogs. 'Where is the palisade and Lake Chalchiuhtlicue?'

'Cut down. Built over. Drained,' said Silver Onestack. 'The Anarchy Council fell three years ago. What is left of its members rests behind you in those plots.'

'You have not reported this,' said Slowcogs, accusingly.

'Rather, I have, but you have not received my messages. The new regime brought flying things with them, all teeth and claws. I lost my whole loft of bird bats within a week. You were lucky the controller's communication got through to me at all. It is the first word from the people of the metal I have received for years.'

'It is strange this has been kept from us,' said Slowcogs. He was clearly not used to the knowledge of something on such a scale having escaped the attention of the steammen's all-knowing network.

'Stranger still that the new regime were instantly able to identify all of the political police's informers down here,' said Silver Onestack. 'Those informers that still live now tell the

Guardians on the surface whatever the new regime wish them to hear.'

Molly stared down at Grimhope, deeply disappointed. She had expected freedom to look different, not like a miniature replica of Middlesteel. But however bad it was, her murderous family would not be able to track her down here.

Silver Onestack passed Molly a green cloak with a large hood. 'Wear this, Molly softbody. And if anyone speaks to you before we get to my lodgings, do not forget to address your reply with compatriot, not sir or damson.'

'They are communityists?' Molly asked.

'Not any more,' said Silver Onestack, looking back at the bone-white gravestones of the Anarchy Council. 'No. Not any more.'

Chapter Seven

If Harry Stave was a typical criminal, then Oliver couldn't understand how the constabulary had not captured him years ago. Since fleeing from the police station at Hundred Locks, all they had done was enter the woods to the south of the town, go into the middle of a clearing, and peg out a strange yellow flag with a black circle in the centre.

'Now what?' Oliver asked, watching the drizzle falling from the sky soak the odd-looking flag.

'We wait,' said Harry Stave.

'For what?'

'For three hours, old stick.' said Harry.

'That's not what I meant.'

'I know.'

Oliver couldn't goad any more out of him. So he shut up and waited. Someone must have discovered the bodies in the police station by now. The corpses at Seventy Star Hall on the other hand could take weeks to be found. Damson Griggs brought everything to the house; she would be noticed missing first by one of the nosy neighbours she was always complaining about. Or perhaps one of Uncle

Titus's businesses would send a runner to see what had happened to their reclusive owner.

Shortly after three hours had passed, a figure appeared on the other side of the clearing, shrouded by the curtain of rain – heavier now.

'Who's that?' Oliver whispered.

'If we're lucky, our ticket out of here,' said Harry.

'Harry!' the figure called.

Harry Stave stayed where he was, sheltered by the tree from the rain. 'Monks! You're not meant to be here. Where's Landless?'

'Reassigned,' said Monks. 'Who's the boy?'

'The whistler's nephew. We need to extract, Monks. We've been rolled up here.'

Oliver was about to ask why his uncle was called the whistler, but Harry signalled him back.

'Did you get to meet the walk-in, Harry?'

'The walk-in didn't show. That's why I put up a signal. A rival crew arrived and nearly did for us. We've been bleeding rolled up, we need to get out now.'

'That's why I'm here, Harry. Come on.'

Stave shut his eyes, not moving. A shadow seemed to separate itself from the criminal, a spectral outline moving forward into the rain and across the clearing. To Oliver's astonishment a similar figure misted out of his own skin, drifting after the Harry-ghost.

<Quiet.> Harry cautioned the boy. <We're masked now under the tree. He can't see us here.>

In the centre of the clearing two thunder cracks exploded, a lick of flame splashing through the apparitions and off into the trees on the left.

'Damn,' said Harry. 'A marksman. I do hate to be proved right.'

They were running back into the forest, the man Monks shouting something after them.

'That was your friend?' Oliver wheezed as they darted through the trees.

'An associate,' said Harry. 'It was a bleeding set-up. My own people.'

Another crack sounded beside them. Whoever it was, they were shooting into the trees blind.

Oliver ducked under a fallen oak. 'You don't sound surprised.'

'Let's just say I had my suspicions.'

Oliver pointed to the north. 'The town's that way I think.'

'Too well covered by now,' said Harry, pushing Oliver on. 'And besides, I never like to go into a place without knowing where the back door is.'

They followed the sodden forest trail to the west, doubling back and switching trails to throw off any pursuit. The breeze lent a cold edge to the run. Since he had found Damson Griggs on the floor of their kitchen, sprinting about Hundred Locks was all Oliver seemed to have done. The shots into the trees had stopped.

'Not coming after us,' panted Oliver.

'Not their style, Oliver,' Harry replied. 'My associates like to keep to the shadows. The minimum of fuss. They were going after an easy kill, not a forced march through half the county's forests.'

They slowed their dash as they began to come across tracks, leaves and twigs scattered across the ground. A horse trail. Oliver tried to locate the sun beyond the trees' canopy. By its position they were into the late afternoon now. Then, against the fast-moving white clouds, he saw *it*. A black globe rising into the sky.

'Look, Harry. I've never seen an airship like that.'

Harry stared upwards. 'Bloody Monks. That was our ride out of here.'

'But there's no expansion engines on it.'

'Don't need them to go up and down, Oliver. Which is pretty much all it does.'

'I don't understand.'

'I'll explain later. For now, let's concentrate on our journey out of here.'

Harry's route led them to what Oliver at first took for a river; then he saw the towpath and realized it was the tail end of the Hundred Locks navigation. If they followed the canal path north they would eventually reach the hundred locks carved into the dike wall of the Toby Fall Rise.

'Keep back under the trees for the moment,' cautioned Harry. 'We need to stay in the black. See the tunnel in the hill? We'll head for there, keeping under the tree line at all times. The towpath goes into the tunnel. We'll get into the channel behind that bush growing down there on the left.'

Harry's precise instructions left Oliver puzzled. 'You think someone might be watching for us?'

'Trust me,' said Harry. 'Someone's always watching. Come on.'

They hugged the forest until the mouth of the canal tunnel was upon them. The bush extended all the way up the hill and pushing past it, Oliver scraped his neck against the sharp twigs that grew between its small orange flowers. It was cool inside the tunnel. Damp too. Harry sat down in front of a navvy's alcove and dangled his feet over the edge of the waterway.

Oliver joined him. 'Now we wait?'

'Clever lad. You'll go far.'

After half an hour the tunnel mouth darkened as the first

of three nearly identical narrowboats entered, a single paddle at the rear of each boat tossing water across the towpath.

'When the middle boat passes,' instructed Harry, 'jump for the cabin.'

Oliver did as he was bid – the narrowness of the tunnel and the slowness of the canal craft making it easy to step through the cloud of smoke and onto the deck. There was a steam-wreathed figure at the back, hand on the tiller, and if the canal man was surprised at the sudden addition of two passengers, he did not show it.

Harry pushed Oliver through the door into a narrow room. It looked like the inside of the gypsy caravans that visited Hundred Locks during the Midwinter Festival. 'Right. We stay here for the rest of the day – don't even think about getting out of the cabin until tomorrow morning.'

Oliver felt a wave of exasperation rise in him towards his enigmatic saviour. 'Why, Harry? You think that strange-looking aerostat is going to be floating around looking for us? That's a pile of horse manure – what's the chances of us being spotted at that distance?'

Harry sighed. 'More than you'd credit, old stick. It's not human eyes you need to worry about. There's watchers up there with transaction engines to assist them; but they can only focus on a single place at a time, and we'll be outside of their sweep area by tomorrow.'

Oliver sat down on a small three-legged stool. 'Harry, that sounds like paranoia.'

'It's only paranoia if they're not out to get you, lad. And judging by our reception back in the woods, they are.'

'But who are *they*?'

Harry sighed again and pulled up a stool. 'Both myself and my associates back in the woods are what are colloquially known as wolftakers.'

Oliver snorted in disbelief. 'Wolftakers? So you're a demon who's come to—'

'—snatch naughty children, Oliver? Every myth has its substance in reality. The tale's just a twisted version of the truth.'

'You're an escaped convict, Harry. I saw the paper on you in the police station.'

'That's true enough,' said Harry. 'Although I would prefer to be known as a free-spirited entrepreneur who ran afoul of the navy's taste for bureaucracy and regulations.'

'So what's this nonsense about wolftakers in the sky? Next you'll be telling me you help Mother White Horse give gifts to the children every Midwinter.'

'Wolftakers are human enough,' said Harry. 'Listen. When Isambard Kirkhill seized power in parliament's name, he had only one fear left – and that was the throne. The navy and army wanted him to become king. Old Isambard had to fight them off with a sabre to stop them making him the new monarch. Then there were our own royalists in exile in Quatérshift plotting a counter-revolution and restoration. Kirkhill knew that if the rule of parliament was to last, it would have to resist both the plots without and the ambitions of its own Guardians within the house.'

'What does this have to do with a children's tale?' Oliver asked.

'Everything,' explained Harry. 'Kirkhill established a court sinister as the last line of defence, a body that was to act as a supreme authority and ultimate guarantor of the rule of the people. But it was to be a court invisible. The House of Guardians knows the Court is there, but they know nothing of its location, its staff, its methods or its workings. If any First Guardian were to start looking at the throne restored with envious eyes, the existence of the Court would give them pause to think.'

'But all the stories about demons?'

'To those that wish ill to Jackals,' said Harry, 'we are demons. A conspiracy of Guardians is plotting a coup and one morning they wake up and their ringleader has disappeared – never seen again. A merchant starts taking Cassarabian gold to smuggle navy celgas across the border and his tent is found empty on the sands. The political police begin taking orders to stitch up the ballot, and one day the Police General's river launch is found adrift empty on the Gambleflowers – no trace of the old sod. That sends a powerful message. We're the ghosts in the machine, Oliver, keeping the game straight and hearts pure. The only thing they know about us is the name Kirkhill gave us – the Court of the Air; the highest bleeding court in the land.'

'But the men who tried to kill us – who killed Uncle Titus?'

'Your uncle was a whistler, Oliver. Part of the Court of the Air's network of agents on the ground. He'd discovered something, something worth killing him for.'

'Uncle Titus?'

'He was one of the best. His people were all over: clipper crew, traders – Cassarabia, Quatérshift, Concorzia, the Catosian League and the Holy Kikkosico Empire, every county in Jackals from Chiltonshire to Ferniethian.'

'All this time,' said Oliver. 'He was never one for talking, but—'

'Part of the job, Oliver. He was recruited by the same man who saved my neck from the drop outside Bonegate, the greatest wolftaker of them all – Titus's brother.'

'But that would mean—'

'Your father, Oliver. He was the wolftaker who trained me in the craft. Took my not insubstantial talents and gave them a purpose beyond diverting navy biscuits to the merchants on Penny Street.'

'If you work for this court,' said Oliver, 'why would they be trying to kill you?'

'It's the old quandary. Who watches the watchmen? I've been coming across little things for a couple of years now, signs that someone in the Court is playing both sides of the field. Your uncle suspected the same thing. When our extraction became an ambush just now, those suspicions became a reality.'

'Extraction?'

'Craft talk. Laying the flag is called putting up a signal. Calling down an aerosphere to lift us out and take us up.'

'The Court lives on an aerostat?'

'Not an airship, Oliver. We've got an entire city up there in the sky now. Higher than any RAN high-lifter can reach, just the skraypers for company.'

'And now they're trying to kill you?'

'Only some of them. They must have spiked poor old Landless and got Monks onto the aerosphere roster in his place. Never did trust Monks; not enough of a thief for my taste. Who to trust now, Oliver? Always a tricky one in the great game at the best of times. Now, let me think. If they're acting in the open then they must have declared me rogue. They couldn't blow an extraction and hope to cover it up. That means regulator-level intervention. Circle, the rot in the Court goes a lot higher than I'd thought.'

'And the phoney police in the station at Hundred Locks?' said Oliver.

'Someone's dogs,' said Harry. 'But not the Court of the Air's. We've got a military arm called the incrementals for the hard slap work. Proper killers. If they had come after us neither of us would be alive to be discussing it now. So, so, who to trust?'

'Can I trust you, Harry?'

'Trust him with your life but not your wallet.' The voice sounded from the narrowboat's doorway. The steam-shrouded steersman from earlier. Rising no higher than Oliver's chest, his earless, whisker-bristled face buried beneath heavy rolls of leathery brown skin, the master of their canal boat was a grasper.

'Armiral, you old rascal.' Harry stood up to greet the grasper. 'Room for a couple of stowaways?'

'Is he a whistler?' Oliver whispered to Harry.

<Armiral? Circle no. He's one of my murky acquaintances. Too valuable to waste on Court business. You might say I've been saving Armiral for a rainy day. You never know when you're going to need to retire from the great game.>

'We're running for the Julking Way navigation,' said the grasper. 'Should reach the outskirts of Turnhouse by tomorrow. You'll be letting me know where we're heading after that?'

'I expect so,' said Harry.

The grasper looked like he was going to say something, then shook his head and went back outside.

'It was stolen naval supplies that paid for the *Chaunting Lay*,' said Harry, winking at Oliver. 'That's the boat we're sitting on. Of course, the payment was somewhat indirect.'

'Someone's got to move those biscuits around,' said Oliver.

'You're a fast lad, Oliver Brooks, and no mistake. Your blood shows through, all right.'

'Father. And all these years I thought he was in the same trade as Uncle Titus.'

'He was,' said Harry. 'In a manner of speaking.'

'Was he a good man?' Oliver asked.

'Good enough for the times we were dealt,' said Harry. 'I won't lie to you Oliver. There was a brutal edge to Phileas Brooks. If he thought you were playing him false or were coming against him direct, he could be a ruthless sort. But he did alright by me, and there was none better among the wolftakers.'

'The things he must have seen,' said Oliver. 'The things he must have done in the service of Jackals. Only to die in an aerostat accident. How utterly pointless.'

'An accident? Perhaps,' said Harry. 'I always had my doubts about that.'

'What? You don't think—'

'They're just suspicions, Oliver. Your airship came down during the start of the not-so-glorious revolution of 1566, quickly followed by the Two-Year War with the Commonshare. The Court of the Air had its hands full making sure Benjamin Carl's committeemen disappeared. Now my capacity in the navy may only have been in the Victualling Board, but I know enough about the job of an airmaster to understand that if you've got an expansion engine fire, you don't plot a course that will take you anywhere near the feymist curtain.'

Oliver's eyes were red. 'And I was the only survivor.'

'The only one that was ever found, old stick. The only one that was ever found. Unless you know different?'

'Not that I remember, Harry.'

'Let's put your memory to the test,' said Harry. 'Titus never got around to telling me what he had discovered; he was waiting for someone from down south to turn up before letting me in on it. But instead we got those two phoney crushers from Ham Yard and the toppers at the hall. I'd say that whoever Titus was expecting to arrive was intercepted by the same crew that tried to do for us and most likely done away with. Any idea who your uncle's visitor could have been?'

Oliver mulled the question over. 'Uncle asked me to meet you at the aerostat field last week, but he didn't mention anything about anybody else arriving. The next airship isn't due at Hundred Locks for four days either.'

'Let's try something else,' said Harry, pushing his glasses back up the bridge of his nose. 'It's like when I talk with my voice inside your skull, except everything flows in the opposite direction. I might be able to pick up clues from your memories.'

'More worldsinger tricks?'

'Of a sort. Although the people that trained us aren't in the order, which wouldn't please the worldsingers one jot if they ever found out. One of the reasons they dislike the fey so much is they don't like the bleeding competition.'

Harry placed his left palm in front of Oliver's forehead and shut his eyes, straining to make contact with the boy's thoughts. Oliver expected to feel something, a tingle, or a pressure, perhaps a headache, but there was nothing.

'Now that's a first,' said Harry. 'I can't establish a lock with you. But you can hear my mind-echo, yes?'

'Like you were talking an inch away from my ear, Harry.'

Oliver thought back to the inactive truth crystal at the police station. Something appeared to be protecting him from worldsinger probing. Was there already something fey, dangerous and defensive developing inside him like a tumour, ready to erupt and twist his body in terrible, unnatural ways? Perhaps old Pullinger had been right all along, Oliver would be better off with a torc around his neck and kept under close observation by the order.

'Damn queer, Oliver. Well, there's some that can resist a glamour; though you're the first I've ever met in the flesh. We'll just have to do this the old-fashioned way. Are there any visitors you can remember arriving for Titus in the last few months?'

'A handful,' said Oliver. 'A skipper back from the Holy

Kikkosico Empire. Runners from the crystalgrid station with tape. The head clerk from uncle's Middlesteel counting house came at the start of the month as usual.'

'Anybody uncommon?'

Oliver racked his brains. 'Back in Barn-month we had an old grasper visit twice. Once at the start of the month, once at the end.'

'Old?' said Harry. 'Older than Armiral here?'

'The spine-hair on his face was white and his cheeks looked like a field of snow, except where he had this mark on his right cheek.'

'A tattoo?' asked Harry.

'No. More like it had been branded there.'

'Armiral.' Harry called the grasper back into the narrow-boat's cabin. 'Get a pencil for the boy. Oliver, draw for us the mark you saw.'

Oliver sketched out a circle with three slanting lines drawn through it.

'What do you think?' Harry asked the grasper boat master.

'Celgas miner from Shadowclock.'

'That's what I thought too,' said Harry.

Armiral leant against the open door to the deck and scratched his heavy-jowled face thoughtfully. 'Each line represents a cave-in survived – few of our people reach three. The one who wore this will be senior, Harry. High warren.'

Oliver remembered the way the visiting grasper had scuttled inside Seventy Star Hall. Like he was glad to trade the space and sky outside for the confines of the hall. 'Uncle Titus didn't have any contracts with the celgas mines. Why would he be meeting a mining combination man?'

'Nobody has contracts directly with Shadowclock, Oliver. The State Victualling Board handles it. The place is practically a closed city – only town with a military governor appointed by parliament instead of an elected mayor. There are plenty of people who've died for the riches under the mountains at Shadowclock. Smugglers, agents from every great power on the continent, gas runners. If Titus found some mischief going on at Shadowclock, then I don't doubt there's some rascals out there who would judge his murder and our deaths a cheap price to keep their transgressions secret.'

'Does your business take you to Shadowclock, Harry?' asked the grasper. 'I can ferry you as far south as the navigation at Ewehead. After that you need special papers to use the mining waterways.'

'I need to make a stop in Turnhouse on the way. When that's done, if you can get us to the county boundary at Medfolk, I'll take us the rest of the way to Shadowclock on foot.'

'Harry,' said the grasper, 'do you really want to go to Shadowclock? The citadel to the north is the largest RAN fortress in Jackals – our old friends might recognize you. And if the navy don't do for you, you've got the mining police, the regular army and a garrison of the Special Guard.'

'Jackals knows how to protect its monopoly on celgas, Armiral. Even from me.'

'So be it,' say the grasper. 'You really do like to live dangerously, Harry Stave.'

'If you're not living on the edge you're taking up too much space, old stick.' Harry saw Oliver's face. 'Don't worry, lad. After what we've been through, a trip to see the celgas mines is going to be a walk in the park.'

Monitor Eighty-one was not expecting to have her duty interrupted in the monitorarium, but she could tell by the way the other monitors had silently cleared a space for the newcomer – busy finding things to do at the far end of the gantry – that the interloper had rank.

'Monitor Eighty-one?'

The monitor nodded. Something inside her, a prudent voice of caution, stopped Eighty-one from asking the newcomer why her skin-tight black leather airsuit was bereft of Court insignia, except for a thin yellow stripe running down each trouser leg.

'I'm interested in your report from Lightshire, Eighty-one. The Hundred Locks incident.'

'Passed to analyst level, now, ma'am,' said the monitor.

'Of course,' said the visitor. 'Nevertheless, I would value your raw impression of events.'

Eighty-one was about to reply when she saw the regulator nervously waiting by the entrance to the great monitorarium – a level green. And they only waited on one person. It was *her*. All the refectory gossip tided over Eighty-one.

She was a lover of Isambard Kirkhill. She was over six-hundred years old. She was a weather witch holding the Court of the Air fixed in the troposphere by the power of her mind alone. She was a leaaf addict. She was a failed revolutionary. She was a shape switcher, rogue fey escaped from Hawklam Asylum. She was . . . standing in front of her; and she was Lady Riddle. Advocate General. Head of the Court of the Air. There was no doubt about that.

'Go on,' said Lady Riddle.

'It was the morning,' said Eighty-one. 'My normal surveillant was off-shift after his telescope had been withdrawn for maintenance.'

'Is that usual?' asked Lady Riddle. 'To withdraw both a telescope and a surveillant midway through an observation?'

Eighty-one thought before answering, a bead of sweat

tickling her eyebrow despite the cold in the massive monitorarium sphere. 'It's not against protocol, ma'am.'

'No,' agreed Lady Riddle. 'Not against that. And what was the report of the *reserve* surveillant using the *spare* telescope from the floating pool?'

'It appears our own wolftaker terminated the local whistler station, then attempted to murder the extraction team and seize their aerosphere. The wolftaker in question has now disappeared. Four surveillants are currently on a high-sweep of the Hundred Locks area.'

'The wolftaker in question is Harry Stave,' said Lady Riddle. 'And good hunting to you because you'll be on high-sweep for the rest of the year.'

'Oh,' said Eighty-one regretting the inanity even as it escaped her lips.

'If you were to flag one element of the extraction, which one would it be?'

Eighty-one sweated under her grey greatcoat. Symbolic logic had been her weakest subject when she was being broken in. 'That the usual pilot on the mission was switched to a different roster.'

'Law of coincidence?' asked Lady Riddle.

'Patterns beat coincidences, ma'am.'

'So they do,' said Lady Riddle. 'Most people would have said the most significant thing in that file was Harry Stave reverting to type.'

'But I am relatively new to all this,' said Eighty-one. 'And perhaps a little slow.'

Lady Riddle's dark southmoor eyes narrowed. 'Far from it. Do me a small favour, my dear. When your colleagues ask what I was talking to you about, tell them it was about the Quatérshift border observation.'

That was a small favour it would be dangerous to withhold.

Eighty-one nodded, but Lady Riddle had already turned and was heading for the regulator-green by the monitorarium entrance. The game, as her old Court instructor used to say, was afoot, and the open space of the monitorarium felt even more frosty than usual.

Chapter Eight

Silver Onestack's lodgings in Grimhope were a set of small rooms above a workshop where Onestack had a trade mending whatever mechanisms and gewgaws came his way. 'They practically expect me to cannibalise my own body parts to fix their junk,' was the only comment Onestack had to make on his outlaw patrons.

Molly remarked on how few people had been on the streets of Grimhope, while those that were out seemed oddly subdued. But Onestack just muttered, 'You will see, Molly softbody, you will see.'

For the next seven days Onestack kept Molly in his workshop, asking her to observe the people who came in, to acclimatize her to the customs and mores of the undercity before braving its streets. Slowcogs, too, for the steamman appeared reluctant to share knowledge through a crystal link as he had done with the controller back in Guardian Rathbone station. Onestack's status as a desecration made him unclean to his people in many ways, it appeared. Slowcogs gave no visible offence, but the steamman's attitude to his unfortunate brother was obvious by the way he spent as much time as possible in any room where Onestack was not, obsessively cleaning the floor and surfaces of the workshop rooms, until there could have been no cleaner habitation in all of Grimhope.

There was a nervousness to Onestack's clientele, as if they hoped not to stick out from the crowd. It was the same beaten look Molly had seen in the eyes of some of the weaker poorhouse children. The ones who had been broken by their circumstances. The urge to fit in, to fade away into the background dance of Middlesteel's streets, becoming an invisible breathing spectre, beyond detection, beyond observation and the pain of punishment tasks, ridicule and anguish. Grimhope – the city of outlaws, freedom and wild revelry – had become the city of subdued toil, where no one looked you in the eye for fear of being detected and singled out.

Even confined within Onestack's lodgings, the noise and smell of Grimhope was ceaseless. The clatter of the manufactories, the smack of punching and cutting machines, the thump of the forest of pipes sucking the smoke away to spew it out in the lower cavern levels. Slowcogs dearly wanted to investigate the nearest mill to discover the nature of their incessant labours, but the cautious Onestack forbade him from leaving the shop; pointing to the gang of chained mill labourers who were sometimes marched down the streets, heads bent under their green cloaks. Soldiers in red cloaks, the new regime's enforcers – nicknamed 'the brilliant men' by Grimhope's citizens – guarded them.

Molly helped in the shop, surprising Silver Onestack by her natural grasp of mechanisms and gadgetry.

'You were never apprenticed to a mechomancer, Molly softbody?' the steamman asked.

Molly laughed. 'In Middlesteel, families pay a master for their children to be apprenticed to a good trade, Silver

Onestack. They don't take the sweepings from the work-house.'

'Would that the mechomancers had proved so discriminating when it comes to experimenting on my own people, Molly softbody.'

Molly had not previously broached Onestack's status as steamman unclean – a desecration. Taking Slowcogs' lead she had ignored it, for fear of breaking some taboo of the metal race. 'Is that why you live down here?'

'I am outside the fold, Molly softbody,' said Onestack. 'King Steam makes use of my vision glass and hearing folds when it suits him, but my pattern is not to any plan laid by the architects royal in the Steammen Free State. Above ground, not a single one of my kind would share boiler-grade coke with me.'

'Were you built in Middlesteel?' asked Molly.

'I was not built, Molly softbody. I was scavenged, cannibalized from the parts of other steammen,' said Silver Onestack. 'Your mechomancers cannot build us, but they still hope to understand our bodies by desecrating the corpses of our fallen. There are steammen souls trapped inside me, blended to make that which I am. I hear them during my thoughtflow, crying, begging me to release them.'

'By dying,' said Molly.

'Yes,' said Onestack. 'By returning to the great pattern. I carry my own ancestors inside me and every step I take is a dishonour to them, but I cannot bear to deactivate. Life is too full, even down here. There is the beauty of the ceiling storms. The satisfaction of making whole that which is broken. The smells of the forest when the spores eject and cover the ground like snowfall. So instead of dying I live down here in the belly of the earth like a coward, showing my face to no brother of the metal, keeping my own company.'

Molly lit the stove in the corner of the room. 'How did the mechomancer get his hands on so many bodies?'

'There was a tower collapse,' said Onestack. 'Blimber Watts, the pneumatics gave way.'

Molly nearly dropped her coal shovel. 'Silver Onestack, I was there! It was a steamman who rescued me from the ruins.'

'Then you understand, Molly softbody.'

'Yes. Yes, I suppose I do.'

'The steamman who rescued you would have been looking for our corpses as well as survivors, to bring peace to our souls before scavengers looted the metal dead. By Steelbhalah-Waldo, we are as brother and sister under our shell. You must see my work, you will understand.'

Molly watched Onestack's tripod legs knife across the floor, then he unlocked a small wooden door behind a curtain. 'Come.'

Silver Onestack led her up a narrow staircase and into a loft room. The room was piled with canvas paintings – all in monochrome – otherworldly scenes of the crystal light falling through the forest, a solitary figure sitting cross-legged under a fluted mushroom. In all the paintings the same figure stood indistinct, lonely: by a window painted from outside, small against the stretch of a building or walking isolated by the shore of a subterranean lake.

Molly ran her fingers over the texture of the paint. 'You always use the same model.'

'She is not a model,' said Silver Onestack. 'I see her in the distance, often. I am not sure who she is. A shade of one of the dead from Blimber Watts, perhaps. Or a ghost image stuck in my vision glass after the softbody mechomancer put me back together.'

'They are beautiful,' said Molly.

'I am the only steamman I have heard of who has ever

painted,' said Silver Onestack. 'If I ever find the courage to deactivate, perhaps these works will survive me. Something of me will be left, that was not stolen from the souls of my pattern kin.'

Molly rested the canvas she was looking at back on the floor. 'It's not cowardly to want to live, Silver Onestack.'

'My life keeps three souls in torment, withheld from the great pattern. I have no illusions about the cost of my own survival.'

'Neither of us seems to be popular with our families, Silver Onestack.'

'Yes,' said the steamman. 'It could not have been easy to be raised without pattern kin inside a poorhouse.'

Molly sighed. 'No, it was not. In Sun Gate we looked out for each other and made as much of a family as we could. But I can't fool myself and say it was the same as having a mother and father who you knew loved you, who would do anything for you. When I walked the streets of Middlesteel there were days when all I would see were fathers and mothers out with their children. Holding hands. Laughing, doing things together. I would always wonder what was the matter with me, not to have that; there must have been something wrong with me to be abandoned. Do you only paint in black and white, old steamer?'

Onestack pointed to his silver-domed head. 'The mechomancer who put me together lacked the skill to do anything else with my sight. I remember from my old bodies what it was like to see in colour, though. I think I sometimes thoughtflow in colour, especially red. Apples are red, aren't they?'

Molly nodded. Silver Onestack opened an iron door to his spherical main body, exposing a maze of crystals, boards, silicate and clockwork mechanisms. 'I went to King Steam and begged him to give me back my sight the way it was before, but he refused. He said the law forbade the people of the metal to deactivate me, but he would not suffer the undead to be given succour or repair.'

Something about the workings seemed out of place to Molly. A wrongness that she could feel inside her as a tangible ache. She reached inside Onestack's open hatch, repositioning boards and switching valve groups.

'Molly softbody, desist,' the steamman protested. 'It is forbidden for those outside the people of the metal to tamper with our bodies.'

'What is this?' demanded Slowcogs, rolling into the loft garret. 'This is an offence in the eyes of Steelbhalah-Waldo. Molly, you must cease this violation immediately.'

Molly withdrew her hands and shut the casing plate. 'Onestack was broken. I could not bear it.'

Onestack's voicebox sounded in amazement. 'The floor is brown! Dried fungus wood. And Molly softbody, your hair is red – as red as any apple. I can see in colour again. By all the saints of the Steamo Loas, you have restored my vision glass to see in colour!'

'How can this be?' Slowcogs asked. 'Molly softbody, you are no mechomancer or draughtsman from the hall of architects.'

'It just looked wrong,' Molly explained. 'My hands knew what to do.'

Silver Onestack spun his head to look at Slowcogs. 'Slowcogs, has Molly softbody read the wheels?'

'In the controller's presence,' said Slowcogs. 'The pattern of Gear-gi-ju was revealed to Redrust.'

'I just knew what to do,' said Molly. 'I have always had an affinity for such things.'

'This is no normal affinity, Molly softbody,' exclaimed Silver Onestack. 'Oh Slowcogs, you fool of an old boiler. To bring this softbody down here, of all places. This nest of villainy and chaos. You should have sent her to King Steam with an escort of steammen knights to guard her precious soul.'

'What are you two old steamers talking about?' said Molly.

Silver Onestack's tripod of legs had collapsed his large spherical body onto the floor. 'What a turning of the pattern this is. A foolish old boiler and a walking corpse to protect her.'

'I can bloody well protect myself,' said Molly. 'It's all I've been doing since I could walk.'

Molly was about to demand an explanation when a fierce banging sounded on their door. Onestack arched up like a spider and opened a skylight to peer down into the street.

'Who is it?' asked Slowcogs, his voicebox volume on low.

'The committeewoman for our street and the others nearby. A political, an informer.'

Other men and women in crimson cloaks were walking up and down the street smashing on doors. 'Rouse yourselves, compatriots,' shouted the woman outside. 'Mandatory loyalty display in the main square. Our district has been selected. It is a glorious day.'

'We must go,' said Onestack. 'The brilliant men will search all the buildings. Any malingerers will be executed.'

Out in the street dozens of locals had spilled out from their quarters, more arriving every minute, green hoods hiding their faces in shadow. The only sound was the dull thump of workshop cutting machines from the next street over.

'Come,' said the committeewoman. 'Come.'

Everywhere they went red-hooded figures were rousting the citizens of Grimhope out from their homes. The woman led them through the subterranean streets to Grimhope's central square, built on a scale to rival Middlesteel's Hope Park – but with the unfinished patina and dust of recent construction hanging over it. Standard bearers holding aloft flags – red fields marked with a gold triangle – marched out to look over the scene. The subdued disposition of the people in the square was replaced by an electric anticipation. More and more towns-people were arriving, until an outlaw host enveloped the granite flagstones.

Molly had to cling onto Slowcogs' iron hand to stop her being separated from the steamman by the crush of the rally. Silver Onestack sat in front of them like a beached slipsharp, his tripod of legs partially retracted inside his body.

'Is he here yet?' one of the crowd asked Molly.

'Who?'

'Tzlayloc,' said the outlaw townsman. 'Who else?'

'There,' called one of the mob. A figure had walked out onto the podium, throwing back his crimson hood. He slowly raised his arms and a hush fell over the crowd.

'My people,' the voice boomed across the open space. 'I look across you all assembled here and I see an army of equals – of brothers and sisters – of compatriots standing with a common purpose.

'Look at the person next to you. There are no mill-owners here. No landlords or kings or guardians. Nobody to call you tenant or subject or slave. And why is that?'

'Because we are equal,' the crowd yelled back.

'Everything here belongs to the commons – to you,' the man called Tzlayloc rumbled. 'And compatriot, everything that is you belongs to the commons.'

The crowd screeched their approval. Molly could not believe the speed at which the rally had turned from an apprehensive flock to a mob running at fever pitch. It was as if a glamour had been cast over the crowd.

'When another man, another woman, gives you the right to vote, says they give you freedom, they are making you a present of that which you already have – that which you were born with. And by so doing they make a grateful slave of you.'

'We are not slaves,' someone yelled back.

'No. No, we are not. Compatriots, we stand together, a perfect commonshare. No poppy taller than the next, stealing the sun, casting their neighbour into the shadow, sucking up the goodness of the earth while letting their neighbour wither and die. Are we equal?'

The crowd roared in near-perfect unison: 'We are!'

'Compatriots, let me show you our heroes of society, those who lead by example.'

At his signal, a man hobbled onto the stage, one of his legs glinting steel in the red subterranean light. 'Many of you know me,' said the newcomer. 'I am Ikey Solomon, once the fastest dipper in Middlesteel. And when the crushers finally came to take me away and transport me to the Concorzian colonies, I ran all the way down to Grimhope.'

The crowd cheered his defiance.

'But I was not equal. I could run from one end of the Deeps to the other in eight hours, and then drink a yard of ale. Not one of you people here today could match me.'

The crowd murmured darkly at his incorrect boasting.

'So I have had my left leg equalized. Look.' He raised the limb from the ground. 'The bones have been fixed with steel pins. I am equal in my speed to you. I am the Commonshare – and you are me. Now when we run, we shall run together, not against each other!'

The crowd went into an apoplexy of delight at Compatriot Solomon's sacrifice.

'Compatriot, you have shown the way,' said Tzlayloc. 'But he is not alone. Step forward, Sister Peggotty.'

A short woman came though the crimson-hooded honour

guard, holding the hand of a boy – no older than nine or ten years in Molly's estimation.

'There are many of you here, who might have once frequented the gambling pits on Stalside,' she began. Laughter sounded from the crowd.

'Those that did would have seen my son play the boards there . . . two jump-stones, chess, round circle's move. In the old days, the pit owners used my son like a magnet to empty the pockets of the desperate and the addicted. They called him a prodigy – able to beat any of you at a game of skill or chance. Exploited him like an angler's lure. But look at him now. . .'

The boy stared uncomprehendingly out at the rally, drool running down the left side of his chin.

'Compatriots, now he has been cured. Equalized. Now he is one of us. By the grace of our own renegade worldsingers his mind has been adjusted. Why, any of you could play him at a game of your choice and beat him as oft as not.'

The mob roared their approval.

'Which of you here will show your devotion?' exclaimed the mother. 'Which of you will show your love for your compatriots?'

A young girl pushed her way past Molly. 'I will! Tzlayloc, take me. I am beautiful and it is nothing but a curse to me. Scar my face with acid from the workshops.'

'No.' A giant of a man rose out of the crowd. 'Tzlayloc, look how strong I am. Make me equal, cut off one of my ugly beef-hooks of an arm.'

'Compatriots.' Tzlayloc waved the supplicants back down. 'Your willingness to join our Commonshare is a credit to you all. But not everyone shares our beliefs. While we live free down here our brothers and sisters still toil under the yoke of Middlesteel's barons of commerce and the false idolatry of a sham ballot every four years. Bring forward the corrupt ones, compatriots.'

The red-cloaked soldiers – the brilliant men – moved forward with two struggling figures in white togas.

'These evil leeches. . .' Tzlayloc's voice echoed off the square's walls. 'These two evil leeches come to visit us from as far away as the city-states of the Catosian League. Why? To benefit from us! To *profit*.'

There was a collective rush of breath from the crowd.

'Please,' one of the Catosian traders begged. 'Last year you needed high-tension boilers from us for your mills, parts and plans for automatics. We brought them to you. For mercy's sake, let me live. I have a family who need me, three girls and a baby boy.'

'Listen to these philosophers,' Tzlayloc mocked. 'To feed their families they would suck our blood. Is that not the excuse of the vampires on the surface? Just a little trade, just a little blood – work for me, not for each other. Work for me, not for the commons. Make me fat. Make me rich. Let me show you a new philosophy, men of Catosia.'

Tzlayloc drew an obsidian-handled knife – the blade sharpened stone. His crimson-hooded retinue dragged the two traders to an altar where they were arched back and strapped thrashing and sobbing to the stone. Tzlayloc thrust aloft the knife.

'In life, you leeched blood from the people you should have cared for. Now, in death, your sacrifice will strengthen the people's sinews and advance their cause. Xam-ku, Father Spider, hear my prayer – let the sacrifice of these two rats caught with their snouts buried in our grain bins swell your power and speed your return. Too long have we laboured under the yoke of slave master and merchant and market without the light of Wildcaotyl to guide us.'

'Look away, Molly softbody,' advised Onestack.

Molly did, but she couldn't shut out the screams echoing from the walls of the square as Tzlayloc carved the traders' beating hearts out of their still living bodies. Tzlayloc held the still pulsing organs above the crowd. 'Xam-ku, feel the nourishment of their souls.'

The crystals in the cavern ceiling came alive with lightning, crimson fire arcing between the stones above them. Down in the square the crowd chanted their saviour's name.

'The old gods of Wildcaotyl have not fed in a long time,' said Slowcogs.

'I can feel their hunger,' said Molly. 'Welling up beneath the ground. The souls spilled are like the taste of meat for a slipsharp that hasn't fed in a thousand years.'

Blood from the two limp bodies was coursing down channels in the stone. 'In death,' Tzlayloc bellowed, 'these two corrupt vampires have made the sacrifice to their companions they were never willing to make in life. Behold, I have found their centre, and it nourishes the commons.'

Molly tried to turn away from the scene, but the press of the chanting mob was too fierce.

'Our compatriots in Quatérshift feed such as they into the Gideon's Collar, but in their admirable drive for efficiency, they have forgotten the wisdom of our ancestors. Wasting good souls which could be dedicated to Xam-ku,' said Tzlayloc. 'Yet in Middlesteel above, the streets still throng with the oppressors of the people, the enemy inside our walls, withholding paradise from the hands of the starving, the propertyless and desperate. Shall we make a land of equals? Shall we free the people?'

'Yes!' the crowd roared.

'Shall we pull the selfish bloodsuckers down into the gutter and thrash them until the streets of Middlesteel run red with their blood?'

'Yes, yes, yes!' the crowd howled.

'Now you see,' whispered Silver Onestack. 'Now you see why you were wrong to come here. Grimhope has died. This rotting carcass of a city is all that is left of the legend.'

Slowcogs bowed his head. 'Forgive me, Silver Onestack. I did not know.'

'No,' said Molly. 'This is not your fault, Slowcogs. I was meant to come here. I have seen this madness before, or something like it.'

Slowcogs' head sunk in shame. 'There is a song in your blood, Molly softbody, and the memory of your cells points the way you must travel.'

But where have I seen this before? Molly asked herself as they drifted away from the square. *Where?*

Molly and the two steammen had only just arrived back at Onestack's lodgings when the political organizer who had dragged them to the rally appeared at the door. She banged on the front of the workshop. 'Token day, compatriot metal, token day.'

Silver Onestack opened the door. 'Enter, compatriot softbody.'

'Such a gathering, compatriot metal. Such a show of equality. The day is coming when the dogs on the surface will whine under the weight of our boots, surely it is.'

'Surely,' Silver Onestack mouthed.

'Your ledger, compatriot.'

Onestack led the way into the room at the back of the workshop, picked up a dusty book of accounts and handed it to the woman, saying nothing as she leafed through the last few pages. 'Excellent, compatriot metal. The communal share is now set at ninety per cent. The state will receive its share now.'

'So much?' said Onestack. 'I have two assistants now. The girl must eat. We need boiler-grade coke.'

'Careful what you say, compatriot metal,' warned the woman. 'Those words smack of shirking and defeatism. Your talent with matters mechanical has kept your position on the reserved list, but the mills are hungry for labour too.'

'My apologies, compatriot softbody,' said Onestack. 'Perhaps you could put a word in for us with the committee of supplies for two extra food chits.'

The woman's tone softened as Slowcogs handed over a bag of coins. 'I know your contribution to the commons is hard, compatriot metal. But the struggle always is. Your gift to the cause is helping us forge hammers of freedom to strike down the tyrants and leeches.'

'We'll eat well when the tyrants are struck down,' said Molly.

The woman failed to notice the sarcasm in Molly's tone. 'You're not old enough to remember the famine of Sixty-six, young compatriot. I lost my husband at Haggswood Field when the crushers charged us. My young ones died of hunger when I was locked away in Bonegate for breach of the riot act, nobody in my lodgings with the food or the inclination to feed them. Everything I ever valued and loved was taken away from me by the quality of Middlesteel. All except my freedom. One day we'll see the light of the surface again, compatriot, and the day will be ours.'

'I doubt it,' said a green-hooded figure coming down the stairs leading up to Onestack's loft.

'What! How did you get into my workshop?' Onestack demanded of the intruder.

The figure leant on a cane and Molly felt a sinking feeling strike her stomach.

'Perhaps you forgot to lock your door?' said the figure

removing his hood. It was *him*. The refined old killer from Fairborn and Jarndyce; somehow the topper had caught up with Molly, even down here in Grimhope. 'But then one imagines the concept of a propertyless state rather negates the need for locks, would you not agree, compatriot?'

'Which district are you from?' spat the political. 'And who are you to question the word of the revolution?'

'Why the district of Vauxtion,' said the old gentleman. 'And once I carried a marshal's baton. So I do hope you will forgive my small observation that the earnestness of your hod carriers is not going to prove much of a shield against navy fin-bombs falling from a Jackelian airship.'

'What are you rambling about, old goat?' said the woman. 'There is no Vauxtion district in Grimhope.'

'I see, damson, that your knowledge of geography is as tired as your rhetoric. Vauxtion is – or should I say, was – a province of Quatérshift. No doubt it bears a drearier label now. Area twelve of the Commonshare, or a similarly tedious designation. Something of a personal inconvenience for myself, given that I bear the title of the Count of Vauxtion.'

'An *aristo*!'

He placed his cane on the workshop counter and was walking slowly towards the woman. 'Indeed, an aristocrat. Although rest assured, your Carlist colleagues in my land have done their best to rid themselves of my kind. I saw my retainers, wife, children and grandchildren marched into a Gideon's Collar by a mob of your self-righteous compatriots.'

The political at last recognized the old man's air of menace and broke for the front room. As she did so a pepperbox-nozzled gas pistol appeared in the count's hand, and as quick as it did, the woman was collapsing to the floor within a cloud of vapour.

'A tip for you, damson,' said the count, standing over

the corpse. 'The best way to evade famine is not to seize the breadbasket of the continent, leave her fields unharvested for two years of revolution, then fire a bolt through the neck of every disfavoured soul who knows anything about agriculture.'

Slowcogs powered towards the old assassin from behind, wheels spinning over the fungus-wood boards. In one smooth movement Count Vauxtion knelt and drew a double-barrelled harpoon gun from his back, the black claw smashing into Slowcogs' mid-body. Sidestepping, the count watched Slowcogs trundle to a stop by the workshop door, hissing steam from his punctured boiler heart soaking the floor.

Molly was immediately by Slowcogs' side as the count covered her with his gas gun.

'I am sorry, Molly softbody,' wheezed Slowcogs. 'I have failed you.'

'No, Slowcogs,' said Molly, tears welling in her eyes. 'This is my fault. I led us down here.'

'Oh, *please*.' Count Vauxtion threw a set of rusty Gear-gi-ju wheels on the floor. 'You might as well blame Guardian Rathbone station's controller. Do you know how difficult it is to torture a steamman mystic? They can shut down their pain centres at will. I had to find a specialist to break your friend down to a state where he was willing to tell me where to find you.'

'You softbody barbarian,' cursed Silver Onestack. 'May the Steamo Loas blight you for your evil.'

Count Vauxtion casually shot one of Onestack's legs off with the remaining barrel of his harpoon weapon. With only two sides left on Onestack's tripod the ponderous steamman bowled over, beached in his own workshop. He tried to stand, slipped, then lost consciousness, his valves overwhelmed by the pain.

'Hardly a barbarian,' Count Vauxtion said to the immobile

steamman. 'The controller described you as a mad old boiler scratching art with peck blood and fungus water, but he lacked the sensitivity or the reference points to adequately describe your works. They are magnificent, steamman. As one artist to another, I shall leave you your arms and sight. Call it a professional courtesy. I have taken the liberty of taking one of your miniatures as payment; the scene of the girl against the canyon wall.'

Molly took a step towards the stairs, but the gas gun was instantly pointing at her. A rubber pipe from its handle dangled like a cobra from the count's sleeve. 'Please, Molly. My commission requires you to be delivered alive. And there are no chimney stacks in Grimhope for you to shin up.'

'Alive!' Molly spat. 'An invitation to supper would have been cheaper.'

'Not to mislead you, my sweet. I have the feeling my present patron will not be leaving you in that state for long.'

'You tell my stepfather to go to hell.'

'Stepfather?' The count seemed amused. 'Perhaps, although I doubt it. My current patron prefers to hold to his anonymity, so I can't speak as to his motives or cause. Not that it really matters. I do not participate in causes any more. I spent most of my life following that course and all it bought me was a cemetery full of friends, family and fallen comrades.'

'Let me help Slowcogs,' Molly implored.

The count shook his head. 'You are too slippery a catch, my dear. And I aimed for your friend's boiler. Put your hood on and say your goodbyes. Bear in mind anyone you try to warn on our journey out of Grimhope will be dead before you close your beautiful lips, as will you. My patron will pay more for you alive, but dead will do almost as well.'

Molly tried to reach out to the steamman as the count pushed her towards the door. 'Slowcogs.'

'Follow your pattern, Molly softbody,' whispered the dying metal creature. 'Wherever it may take you.'

Standing outside, Molly tried to punch the topper. 'You've bloody killed him.'

'I led twenty thousand of my own soldiers to the slaughter at Morango,' said the count. 'And I loved them. One more, one less – just a number, Damson Templar, just another number in a forgotten ledger no one is numerate enough to read anymore.'

Producing a key, the count locked the door to the workshop. In the street a fat man approached them, puffing. 'Is compatriot metal not in?'

'The excitement of the rally was too much for him, compatriot,' said the count. 'He is taking the rest of the day off.'

'But there's a broken extraction belt at mill twenty! What shall I tell my committeeman?'

'Tell him?' the count, said. 'Tell him that compatriot metal is currently putting a couple of his legs up for a while.'

Getting into Grimhope with a well-known boiler like Silver Onestack had been relatively simple. The crimson-hooded guards blocking their path showed that leaving with Count Vauxtion was not going to be so easy.

'Papers of travel, compatriot,' said one of the soldiers.

'There have been reports of a pride of pecks attacking the farms,' said the count. 'Productivity will suffer. The committee demands answers.'

'Pecks are always dragging off spore hands, compatriot. We'd have more luck farming the black-furred little buggers instead. But it's your papers of travel I need to see if you want to go on a picnic with bright eyes here.'

'But of course,' said the count. He reached inside his cloak as an explosion lifted the roof off a mill in the bottom of the valley.

'Sweet Tuitzilopochtli!'

'Stay here,' the sergeant shouted at one of the men. 'The rest of you with me. It could be counter-revolutionaries from the Anarchy Council.'

Count Vauxtion smiled at the remaining guard. 'And where would any good revolution be without its counter-revolutionaries?'

'You stay put, compatriot,' scowled the guard. 'Until we've sorted out what's happening in town you ain't going nowhere.'

'Hardly very fraternal, compatriot,' said the count, bending down to pick something up from the cavern floor. 'As for the mill, I think you'll find someone rather carelessly turned the water system off on one of the boilers. See here, a worm.'

'Do I look like I bleeding care?'

Molly tried to pull away, but the count pushed her back. 'It's a matter of philosophical niceties, compatriot. My own personal form of equalization, although where I come from it's called a vendetta.' Vauxtion's hand shot up and a blast of gas spurted into the guard's face. The brilliant man collapsed to the ground as if an axe had felled him and the count tossed the worm contemptuously on his body. 'See, compatriot. I have made you equal to both my family and these toiling gardeners of the soil. May the worms enjoy the meal.'

'You murderous old goat,' Molly shouted. 'You don't care who you kill.'

The count waved his gas gun in the direction of the fungal forest. 'Quite the opposite, my sweet. Shall we go for our picnic?'

'I—' Molly flinched back as a boot came down from the sky, flashing past her cheek, and sending the count sprawling over the corpse of the dead guard. The breath whooshed out of her as an arm rammed her spine, encircling her, tossing her into the air and onto a wicker floor. She gazed up stunned into a craynarbian face.

'Ver'fey!'

'I told you it was her,' said Ver'fey.

Standing behind the craynarbian was a large woman, the sleeves of her shirt cut short, massive tanned arms jutting out. The same arms that had just seized Molly and lifted her from the ground. She looked oddly familiar.

Molly rolled off her back and onto her feet. She was in a wicker gondola hardly larger than a boat; above her was a sausage-shaped canvas. A miniature aerostat. Beyond the woman a man stood holding the tiller of a pivot-mounted expansion engine. Molly swayed for a second, dazed, and looked back towards the ground.

Count Vauxtion was a small dot on the edge of the fungal forest.

'Molly.' The craynarbian steadied her human friend. 'Are you hurt?'

'Back,' said Molly. 'I need to get back to Grimhope.'

'You're joking, kid,' said the woman with the muscled arms. 'Those asylum rejects would shoot us down as soon as look at us.'

'I have friends down there,' protested Molly.

'Then make new ones, because we're heading for the surface.'

'Ver'fey,' said Molly, 'in Circle's name what are you doing here? Can't you tell her to put us down on the ground?'

Ver'fey shook her armoured skull, pointing to the man tending the expansion engine. 'I told him where to find you, Molly, and I said I would come along to help them identify you.'

She turned to face the engine man, his thin hair whipping in the backdraft from the propeller.

'My apologies, Molly,' he said. 'We have risked too much to find you to risk losing you back in Grimhope.'

'A thank you would be nice, kid,' added the woman. 'I doubt if the count's intentions towards you were any more altruistic than they normally are.'

'You know him?' said Molly. 'Who are you people?'

'We've run into each other before, kid, the count and myself. Normally at high speed.'

'Don't you recognize her, Molly?' asked Ver'fey. 'From the books at Sun Gate?'

Of course – the penny dreadful cover illustrations. A tanned woman with gorilla-sized arms sweeping across a ravine in a Liongeli jungle, clutching a massive purple gem stolen from a temple.

'Amelia Harsh,' said Molly.

'Professor Harsh,' corrected the woman.

'What are you doing down here?'

'The best I can, kid. But if you mean why are we pulling your scrawny frame out of Grimhope, you can talk to the money.' She pointed to the man by the expansion engine.

'Money?'

Professor Harsh shrugged. 'Poking around the ruins of Chimeca doesn't come cheap. This boat might be theirs, but what the university pays me doesn't cover half of my work.'

'Why are we here, Molly?' said the money, sadly, 'Because someone in Middlesteel is offering a fortune for your body – alive preferred, but dead perfectly acceptable.'

Chapter Nine

Analyst Ninety-one pretended not to have noticed the newcomer standing outside the door to Lady Riddle's office. She casually shuffled the punch cards for the afternoon's transaction engine load as Analyst Two-eighty slotted them into a pneumatic tube container.

'It is him,' said Two-eighty, her voice low.

'I thought he would be taller,' whispered Ninety-one. But she didn't sound disappointed.

It was the signature tweed cap that really settled it. He looked like he might have just walked in from a day's grouse shooting on some green limestone pile in the uplands.

'Eyes front and centre,' ordered Regulator Nine as she walked past the processing station. They busied themselves as the regulator went up to *him*.

'Lord Wildrake, the Advocate General will see you now.'

Shutting the door on the calculation hall, the regulator ushered the visitor into a private chamber, a vista of thick armoured crystal glass overlooking the still sky-reaches of the troposphere. It was always calm here, so high; the Court of the Air floating far above the storm systems and the worries of the Jackelians below. He stood a moment, watching the smaller aerostats patrolling beyond the tethered spheres and globes. Razor-finned and tipped with long pulse barbs, their exclusive purpose was to drive off any skraypers that floated too close to the city.

He took off his cloak and hung it on a hook next to the marble head of Isambard Kirkhill, then clicked his heels to announce his presence to Lady Riddle.

At the other end of the room, the light and the space of the office offset the ebony skin of the Advocate General perfectly. No doubt as was intended.

'Take a seat,' said Lady Riddle.

Wildrake shook his head and with a small jump, grabbed hold of one of the message ducts running across the ceiling. He began to do chin lifts on the pipe, the ripples of his muscles raw agony after his morning workout.

Lady Riddle swore to herself. His addiction to the damn drug was getting worse. 'How much shine are you taking now, Wildrake?'

'Just enough to keep me hard,' said Wildrake. 'To keep me solid. Talk to your sawbones in pharmacology, they keep me supplied.'

There was theoretically no upper limit to how much muscle an abuser could put on while chewing shine, the drug obtained from guard units of the city-states, where whole elite regiments warped themselves into living bull-women.

'Tell me about the *RAN Bellerophon*, Wildrake.'

Lord Wildrake talked quickly, trying to get each sentence out between the blaze of pain in his arms. 'I tracked down what was left of her to the dunes outside Dazbah under their camouflage nets. Full marks to the analysts involved for that prediction.'

'Go on,' said Lady Riddle.

'One of the officers had been turned; they were holding his

family prisoner and blackmailed him into putting the airship off course. Then he arranged for it to land on the other side of the Cassarabian border with a buoyancy leak. The local tribesmen took it from there.'

'Our cloudies?'

'Most of them were poisoned by something the traitor had put in their grog ration. I managed to free a couple of the survivors. The women in the crew had already been passed to the caliph's biologick breeders by the time I arrived, I fear to say.'

'Too bold,' said Lady Riddle. 'They are becoming far too bold. Something will need to be done about Cassarabia before long.'

'The airship's celgas has been siphoned off to a facility outside Dazbah,' said Lord Wildrake. 'They were using the wombs of our female ratings to try to witch up an organic substitute for celgas.'

'The surveillant watch said you destroyed the place.'

'They haven't made any more progress on making their airship gas less flammable,' said Wildrake. 'You might say I just turned up the heat on the situation.'

'If they don't like it, they should have stayed out of our kitchen, Wildrake.'

'My thoughts exactly, Advocate General.'

'Now that the caliph has had his fingers burnt, I have a new job for you, Wildrake.'

'I thought you might.' Wildrake's skin had taken on a healthy red sheen, the shine-induced sweat filling the room with a scent like cinnamon. 'Another one of our airships is missing?'

'Not an airship,' said Lady Riddle. 'A man. Wolf Twelve has gone rogue.'

'Harold?' said Wildrake, allowing his body to hang from

the message duct for a minute. 'Well, well. Naughty old Harold Stave. So it's set a wolftaker to catch a wolftaker.'

'Precisely,' said Lady Riddle. 'I understand you have some history with him, beyond your naval service, I mean. Will that be a problem?'

'Moving barrels of ballast water around Jackals doesn't exactly count as naval service in my estimation, ma'am,' said Lord Wildrake.

'But of all those captured it was only yourself and Harry Stave who survived the camp at Flavstar,' Lady Riddle pointed out. 'Along with that rich boy, the freelancer.'

'Six months' hospitality courtesy of the Commonshare's Committee of Public Security took its toll on the team. It was something of a miracle any of us lived through it.'

Lady Riddle sat back. It was after his time in the camp that Wildrake had started taking shine. Bulking up; as if the wolf-taker could swell his muscles large enough that no Commonshare torturer could ever reach him again. 'After your escape, I recall there was a difference of opinion as to whose error led to the operation in Quatérshift being rolled up.'

'No doubt in *my* mind as to whose fault it was, Advocate General. Harold Stave is a chancer, an accident waiting to happen. Not a gentleman at all.'

'The latter may be true, but given the wake of destruction you leave behind you, Wildrake, I hardly think you are in a position to lecture.'

Wildrake gasped with the pain of the exercise. 'I suspect, ma'am, it may be my previous disagreement with Wolf Twelve that has led you to drop this proposition into my lap. Consider myself stimulated. The circumstances will make for a rather interesting hunt.'

'You have the field then,' said Lady Riddle. 'And Wildrake. . .'

'Ma'am?'

'Enough of him back alive to be interrogated by one of our truth hexers, if you please.'

'Best efforts, Advocate General,' said Wildrake, dropping to the floor, feeling the glorious pain in his aching arms. 'Best efforts.'

Oliver stood in the cobbled streets outside Bonegate prison, the crowds lining up by the thousand to see him hang. Hawkers were selling trays of rotten fruit, some of which was already lashing past the scaffold. It was normally considered more fun to let the condemned prisoners feel the drop, then pelt them with garbage as they danced the Bonegate quadrille.

Inspector Pullinger raised his hands and a hush fell over the expectant mob. 'For breaking of a crown registration order, for breach of registration boundary lines, for failure to submit to the Department of Feymist's articles under statute six of the Feybreed Control Act, for the most foul deed of premeditated murder on three counts, Oliver Brooks is sentenced to death by hanging.'

The crowd cheered and clapped as a Circlist vicar stepped forward to administer the rites of conversion. She spoke the litany quietly, so that only Oliver and the others on the gallows platform could hear the words. 'Troubled souls in this life, may your essence return to the one sea of consciousness, so that as the Circle turns, you are returned to this good earth in a happier vessel.'

The vicar spun in horror as the misshapen form of the Whisperer pulled himself up onto the gallows. 'New vessel? Nothing wrong with the old one.'

Guards were running away screaming, the crowd falling back in a stampede.

'See, wherever I want to sit, I can always find a space.'

'Whisperer,' Oliver groaned.

'Stress dreams, Oliver?' said the Whisperer. 'I can go closer to home for them. Always someone new being introduced back at my place. Worldsinger guards with their funny ways and their scalpels, potions and rubber gloves.'

Oliver struggled to untie the noose around his neck. 'Thank the Circle, I thought this was real. I really did.'

'A little realer every day, Oliver,' hissed the Whisperer. 'If they catch you, this *is* your future. A cell next to mine buried under the earth in Hawklam is the premium option for you now. I warned you about Harry Stave, did I not?'

'My family's dead, Whisperer. They killed my uncle. Killed Damson Griggs. They tried to kill me too.'

The Whisperer stroked Oliver's back as he sliced the dream noose with a bony appendage, part teeth and part arm-bone. 'See how similar we're becoming, Oliver. My family died too. My father strangled my mother for giving birth to me, and I haunted his putrid dreams until he climbed a windmill at Hazlebank and threw himself off it.'

'You're mad,' said Oliver. 'We're nothing alike.'

'You think I am mad?' hissed the Whisperer, giggling. 'You should see the things they're releasing from the asylum, Oliver. Soul-sniffers. Special torcs to contain them – more like suits of armour than torcs. In the asylum we used to call them the wild bunch, and wild they are.'

Oliver looked out over Bonegate Square. It was empty now. 'What are you doing here, Whisperer?'

'So little gratitude, Oliver. I am taking care of business. For the both of us. A dream here, a dream there, not just the fey either – normals too.'

Oliver tried to avoid looking directly at the misshapen thing. 'I didn't know you could do that.'

'The feymist curtain has been in Jackals for over a thousand years, Oliver. Seeping its essence into the fields and the moors and the forests. The worldsingers won't admit it, but there's a bit of fey in all of us now.' He laughed. 'More in some than others though, eh?'

'I haven't started to change yet.'

'Pah,' spat the Whisperer. 'Dreams are about the truth, Oliver. They are a door through which denial is rarely allowed admittance. Ask yourself this question: why does your mind, your perfect mind which can slew off worldsinger truth-hexing and mind-walking like water off a duck's feathers, why does it still allow me entry into your dreams?'

'I—' Oliver had not anticipated the question.

'Think on it, Oliver. I like it in here, Oliver – your mind is by far the best. Lovely detail. Perfect clarity. It isn't as easy to make contact with the normals. But I have been bearing up, Oliver. I've been minding the shop for the both of us. The places I've been – even steammen minds; like wading through a stream of broken glass, riding one of the metal's thoughtflows.'

'And in your travels,' said Oliver, 'have you found anything more practical than obscure warnings about Harry Stave?'

'Oh, I'm warming to Harry,' said the Whisperer. 'He's a son of a bitch, and damned if I know if he's our son of a bitch yet, but right now he's the only game in town as far as young Master Brooks is concerned.'

'How comforting.'

'You've got a few surprises in store for you, Oliver. For me too. There's someone else out there, or something. Leaving little traces behind in people's minds. She thinks I don't know about her, but I am powerful, Oliver. That's why they buried me so deep beneath the earth. No special torc suit for me.' The Whisperer's normally sibilant voice had risen to a screech, the background reality of the tenements surrounding Bonegate wavering under the lashing fury of his temper. 'No fun and games with the wild bunch for the poor old Whisperer. No midnight walks through Middlesteel's wide boulevards for me. No moonlight. No cold evening air!'

'Stop it,' Oliver shouted. 'My mind!'

Fading away, the dream storm died down as the Whisperer collapsed sobbing on the gallows platform. 'I'm not predictable, Oliver. That's why they fear me, that's why they've got me surrounded by a dozen interlocking cursewalls, that's why they use a trained hound to drag the drugged slop they feed me into my cell.'

Oliver watched rapt with a mixture of fascination, horror and pity as the Whisperer started to pull himself across the platform, his club-footed shuffle becoming a rhythm from his childhood only he could hear. 'Do a little dance, do a little dance.'

'What will you do, Whisperer,' said Oliver, 'if they catch me and the doomsman stretches my neck at the gallows?'

'Don't say that, Oliver,' the Whisperer hissed. 'The memory of last night's roast beef is still so fresh in your skull. So clear. Ah, now I see what you're trying to do. Distracting me the way you'd dangle string in front of a kitten.'

'That beef sure tasted good though,' said Oliver, sitting down on the edge of the hangman's platform.

The Whisperer arranged himself alongside Oliver. It was difficult to tell if the feybreed had a sitting position or not. 'I could almost bear my prison, Oliver, if it was not for the Special Guard. All the beautiful people, all the pretty-pretty boys and girls, eating the best, their fey gifts trotted out on call for the state. Like a basket of pampered, indulged pets. I used to visit their dreams, Oliver, in the early days. But now it's just a little more than I can take.'

'They wanted me to join the legion,' said Oliver. 'To put a worldsinger's control torc around my neck.'

'Pretty cat needs a collar,' said the Whisperer. 'You think my father didn't promise that for me when he hauled me to Middlesteel on the back of his cart? I trade messages for all the prisoners trapped in Hawklam Asylum, like a one-fey crystalgrid network. There's hardly a soul penned in here that wasn't expecting the finest steak and long lazy days of muscle-pit oil massages. You'd be surprised how normal-looking some of the condemned are down here. But if your powers can't be turned on and off like a tap on a jinn barrel . . .'

The dreamscape started to fade. Oliver was waking up.

'I'll mind the shop, Oliver Brooks,' said the Whisperer, once more back in his underground cell. 'You just mind yourself with that devious jigger, Harry Stave.'

'You need the hat,' said Harry. 'Trust me.'

The *Chaunting Lay* was moored four miles from Turnhouse, tied up outside a tavern at the back end of crown parkland – like everything else in Jackals, in the king's name but belonging to the people. Coaches and fours were scattered across the grass, families from the town with checkerboard picnic blankets enjoying the Circleday afternoon.

'Why do I need it, Harry?' said Oliver, adjusting the cap. 'I thought you said the all-seeing eye in the sky would have its attention elsewhere.'

Harry winked at the boy. 'A little paranoia is never unhealthy.'

Oliver looked around the busy tavern yard, canteen tables crowded with navvies from the waterway clearance board. There had not been a crown park in the Hundred Locks district – the nearest one was in Beggarsmead, far outside the distance of his registration order. That was well and truly shot to pieces now.

'Lots of people here,' said Oliver. 'How are we going to find your man?'

'Not a man, Oliver. A woman. And crowds are good, lots of movement and extraneous detail – like a good cloth cap – to keep a surveillant and their transaction engine on their toes.'

They found their lady sitting on a stool outside a covered box-wagon, the kind normally found at country fairs hawking baldness remedies of a dubious provenance. She had a bottle of jinn on her left side and balls of wool piled on the right. She was carefully knitting a child-sized sweater.

'Mother,' said Harry, as she looked up. 'More grandchildren on the way?'

'She's your mother?' Oliver looked in disbelief at the grizzled old woman.

The old woman jabbed a knitting needle towards Oliver. 'If you're looking for the mare that birthed Harry Stave, you can just look on, dearie. My children are all married off and in respectable trades.'

'Oliver, this is Damson Loade,' said Harry. 'Mother to her friends.'

She chuckled and took a swig of the jinn through a largely toothless mouth. 'On account of a lucky strike I made, mining silver in the colonies.'

Oliver made a little bow. 'Mother Loade.'

'You're a little cleaner than this reprobate's usual travelling companions,' said Mother.

'A fine one to talk you are,' said Harry. 'You forgot to mention the reason you were in Concorzia was by way of a transportation hulk.'

'Details,' said the old woman. 'The doomsman may have given me the boat, but a little silver buys a lot of forgiveness in Jackals. Enough to set up in business with Mister Locke as master gunsmiths to the nobility of Middlesteel and the twenty counties.'

'Loade and Locke,' said Oliver. 'I used to see your details advertised at the back of my uncle's copies of *Field and Fern*.'

'A privilege for which Dock Street charges handsomely, dearie,' said Mother. 'Now then, Harry. I don't normally do house calls, not least because that chinless wonder of a partner of mine is liable to have lost the deeds to the shop at the gaming tables by the time I get back.'

'Sorry, Mother,' said Harry. 'I'm in a bit of bother.'

'When aren't you, boy?' said Mother. 'She picked up a folded copy of *The Middlesteel Illustrated News* from behind her stool. 'Page twelve, towards the bottom.'

Harry leafed through the newspaper. 'Hundred Locks slay-ings most foul as feybreed child and escaped felon murder constables and family guardians.'

'What!' Oliver choked. 'They're saying *we* killed them. What about the bodies of the toppers at the hall?'

'Strangely absent,' said Harry, 'from this story. But then the Court's got as many editors on the payroll as Dock Street has.'

'I picked up a more detailed summary from my drop,' said Mother. 'You're on the disavowed list, Harry. They say you've gone rogue. Every whistler from here to Loch Granmorgan is on orders to turn you in.'

'Mother, this is horse manure,' said Harry. 'Someone in the Court's been turned, but it isn't me.'

'You're a rascal, Harry,' said Mother. 'But I believe you. Not because you're a straight die, but because I don't see how you could possibly turn a coin out of this mess.'

'Nice to know you have such faith in me,' said Harry. 'Did the drop say which wolftakers you're to give assistance to?'

Mother nodded. 'Wolf Seven.'

'Jamie bleeding Wildrake. I don't know whether to be flat-tered or insulted. Someone up there has got a sense of humour.'

'Stay off the big crown roads, Harry,' said Mother. 'The crushers have got blood machines set up at some of the toll cottages, they're testing for you. Ham Yard is like a wasp's nest with a burning rag stuffed down it.'

'Those two jokers back at Hundred Locks were real policemen?' said Harry. 'That's a turn up for the books. I had them pegged as toppers with counterfeit inspector brass. What's the world coming to when you can't trust a crusher?'

'Complicates things,' said Mother.

'Yes it does,' Harry agreed. 'The blood machines won't do Ham Yard any good though. My records were given a right old hocus when I joined the Court. My blood code on the census belongs to a poulterer called Jeremiah Flintwinch who died of syphilis twenty years back.'

Mother jerked a thumb in Oliver's direction. 'And his blood code? You can leave the boy with me, Harry. Safer for the both of you.'

'I do have a name,' Oliver protested.

'And a good one at that,' said Harry. 'The station that got rolled up was run by Titus Brooks. Mother, meet Oliver Brooks, as in the son of Phileas.'

'Phileas Brooks,' said Mother. 'Now there's a name to conjure with. Bloody Circle, dearie, that's a lot to live up to.'

'There seems to be no shortage of people in the kingdom aiming to make sure I don't,' said Oliver.

The old woman got up and stretched her arms, 'I can see it now, Harry. Like listening to Phileas's ghost talking. Well, boy, let's see if old Beth can help you even the odds a little. Now, where's that useless beanpole of an assistant of mine?'

As if on cue a young apprentice turned up with a tray of hams wrapped in wax paper.

'Creakle, I told you to lay in victuals, not to buy the store.'

'Of course, damson. Sorry, damson. I was delayed by the crowds from the county fair.'

'Delayed by a tot of Puttenland cider, by the looks of you, Creakle. Now open the door to the wagon, we've got clients to attend to.'

'Very good, damson.'

Inside the wagon a workbench and counter had been squeezed in between dozens of tiny cupboards. It was just large enough to accommodate the four of them at the same time, Mother sitting down while the others stood.

'Alright,' Mother said. 'Harry, your pleasure?'

'Something discreet, small enough to fit under a coat, but large enough to pack a punch. Not a long-arm, but it might need range.'

'And young Master Brooks?'

Harry looked at Oliver. 'Did Titus ever take you out hunting or the like?'

Oliver shook his head. 'We didn't have any guns at Seventy Star Hall. Uncle used to say that a man's mind was his best weapon. Guns just give you a false bravery – make you behave stupidly.'

'He didn't like them, Oliver,' said Harry. 'But never confuse disliking fighting with not being able to fight. He kept a pistol in a secret compartment in his desk. Much good that it did him in the end.'

'That old Tennyson and Bounder?' said Mother. 'You'd have better luck spitting at an enemy. He should have let me make him a proper pistol. Circle knows, I made the offer often enough.'

'We all get sentimental about things, Mother,' said Harry. 'They were all the go when I was a boy.'

'Oh, sir,' said Mother's apprentice. 'When you were a boy? Leaaf addict were you, sir? Oh, a Tennyson and Bounder, they belong behind the glass in a museum.'

Harry looked at the young assistant with a glimmer of irritation in his eyes. 'You like guns, old stick?'

'Oh, sir. I do. All sorts. Duelling pistols, gas guns, mail-coach pieces. Special commissions for navy officers, long-arms for the gamekeeper, but I have a particular fondness for ladies' weapons sir. Nice delicate pieces, sir. The sort of thing you can tuck into a purse or under a skirt.'

Mother rolled her eyes at Harry. 'We apprenticed Creakle as an arrangement of a debt with one of Locke's gambling companions.'

'Well then, apprentice, what would you recommend for my friend here who has never shot before?'

The odd young man moved over to Oliver and started feeling his arm, sizing up his height, weight and balance. 'Never shot, sir? Not often we get a virgin through the doors at Loade and Locke. Something flared I think, sir, something with a bit of heft to make sure it doesn't jerk around. Would you like a bit of heft, sir? No need for customization, just something to get you going, something to set you off, something off the peg.'

He opened one of the drawers, rummaged around, and drew out a black pistol with a bell-ended barrel. 'Our boatsman model, sir. Intended for the salty sea dog, the gentleman of the ocean, where the yaw and pitch of the waves renders accuracy obsolete. Not good for long range, but should you let off your weapon at a close distance, sir, you will find the results are quite devastating.'

Harry signed his approval of the choice for Oliver. 'You need to fire that, Oliver, do me the favour of making sure I'm standing behind you at the time.'

Mother pulled out a couple of drawers and began scattering parts across the work counter – barrels, chambers, hammers, clockwork igniters. She began to run her fingers across the pieces, muttering instructions to her assistant, sending him scuttling off into the dark recesses of the wagon for some part or another. When she was happy with her selection, Mother began assembling the parts, slipping pieces together, sometimes reaching for a set of fine watchmaker's tools. Her old fingers seemed to shrug off age as they danced across the flat surface, adjusting, tinkering, pressing pieces of clockwork against her ear and listening to the whirr and click of each mechanism. The gun began to take shape before Oliver's eyes, a square blocky pistol with a long barrel.

Harry looked on with interest, appreciative of Mother's craft. 'You're using a Catosian breech ejector.'

'Nothing but the best, Harry. Talk while I work. I like to hear chatter. Dig out some charges for young master Brooks.'

Mother's apprentice produced a bag of crystal bullets and passed them across to Harry. 'Did they grow blow-barrel trees in Hundred Locks, Oliver?'

'No. There was talk of setting up an orchard a few years ago, but the voters in the town got the permissions refused. Said it was too dangerous.'

Harry held up a glass shell in front of the oil lamp, gripping it between his thumb and finger. 'A bullet is blown by a glassmaker in pretty much the same way as nature grows the seed-barrels on the tree. Two chambers filled with sap, separated by a thin membrane. Each sap by itself is harmless, but mix the two and you'll lose a hand in the explosion.'

'Someone in Claynark died when they were hit by a seed-barrel from a wild tree. They found the sapling five miles away,' said Oliver.

'A mature tree can blast its seed-barrel up to twenty miles,' said Harry. 'When you trigger your pistol, the hammer mechanism strikes and shatters the weak point in the shell's glass casing, breaks the mixing chamber and ignites the charge.'

'Oh sir,' said the assistant. 'The crack, boom and whine of a bullet, it's like a symphony. Does the young sir know the rules?'

'You press the trigger and nothing happens, Oliver, that's a misfire. Never turn around and show the gun to anyone whose life you value. Hold the gun away from you, break it in the middle like this, then pull the lever on the side to eject the charge,' said Harry. 'If you need to clear a used charge manually, take the rod off the side of the gun and push it out and down the barrel. Never use your hand. Blow-barrel residue can burn through your fingers; that's why the charge is blown crystal, not cast metal. When you're on the field of battle, be careful where you step. A charge that hasn't fired is likely to have been blown too strong in the glassworks, jettisoned with a crack that can shatter when you step on it, taking off your boot – with foot attached.'

'Never skimp on the charges, dearie,' said Mother as she worked. 'You can't afford to buy cheap ones. Shoddy crystal's killed more soldiers than accurate fire ever did. Cheap crystal will shatter in your gun when you don't want it to; you take a wallop against your charge sack and your friends will be scraping pieces of you off the grass for your coffin.'

'Same reason you never walk around with your gun charged. You wait until you're looking trouble in the face, then break the gun and load,' Harry said. 'In polite company, like a shoot or a hunt, you walk around with your gun broken in the middle so everyone knows your weapon is safe.'

Mother held up her nearly assembled pistol to the light. 'It'll take you a while to learn the glassmaker's marks on the charges, dearie. Quick way to tell cheap crystal is to check if one half of the charge has the sap a different colour or not. Natural blow-barrel seed sap is as clear as water, both left chamber and right chamber. A good gun maker will add dye to the liquid on one side or the other. I use red dye on right-chamber sap. Cheap gunsmiths that sell to fools won't spend the extra coin on the dye.'

Harry passed Oliver a crystal charge. There was a hollow in the glass shell, forward of the two explosive sap-filled chambers – packed with dozens of lead balls. 'Your blunderbuss uses these; they're called buckshot charges. Not good on range, but then I haven't got the time to make a marksman of you. You let off that bessy and the charge will spread the shot in front of you. Ain't intended to discriminate, you understand?'

Oliver looked at his bell-barrelled gun. Now he understood what Uncle Titus had meant. The false bravery seeped from the weapon like warmth from a hearth. Next time some bent Ham Yard crusher tried to slip a noose around his neck, he had better come armed with more than a Sleeping Henry and a police cutlass. 'I understand, Harry. No friends in front of me when I fire.'

'Young sir,' said Mother's apprentice. 'You *are* a fast learner. What a magnificent piece you have. Quite the young duellist now, sir.'

Mother passed Harry his newly assembled pistol. He began to check it, looking down the barrel and sizing up its weight in each hand. The old woman looked at Oliver. 'If you ever travel abroad, dearie, you might come across what we in the trade call suicide guns.'

'Suicide guns?'

'Two-barrel guns, tri-barrels, quad-barrels, even accordion guns. Stay clear of them. You load more than one charge in a gun, the first charge goes off and weakens the crystal in the other shells. Each extra shot and the chance of the gun exploding on you rises real fast. My first husband died in Concorzia that way when he was called out packing a tri-barrel. Never could shoot worth a damn anyway.'

Harry placed a hand on Mother's shoulder. 'Mother, you're an artist.'

'I aim to please, Harold Stave. Now dearie, a curio for the son of Phileas Brooks.' Mother stood up and unlocked a drawer on the floor of the caravan. Removing a cloth bundle tied in string, she unwrapped a blunt-looking knife with a dull black handle. It was unremarkable in every way except for an image of a boar's head carved into its end. 'Your father gave this to me as a payment, a while before his aerostat went down. Never did have the heart to sell it after that.'

Oliver felt the heft of the knife. It was unnaturally light, like holding air. 'Thank you, Damson Loade. Why would my father have used this though?'

'I know what you're thinking,' the old lady chuckled. 'Wouldn't cut the string on its wrapping. Pass it back.'

Oliver gave the gunsmith the knife. She took out a heavy block of lead for casting balls, twisted the head of the pommel and pushed the blade through the lead slab like it was soft Fromerset cheese. Clicking the boar's head back into place she laid the knife back on the workbench. 'Phileas got it on one of the continents out east, a hex-blade, folded into shape by whatever passes for worldsinger sorcery out there. Your father could make the blade do things too, change its form and become a sabre or an axe – I never did work out how.'

'As ordinary-seeming as a tanner's knife and as deadly as a slipsharp,' said Harry in admiration. 'The perfect wolftaker's weapon.'

'I really don't have any money to pay for this,' Oliver said.

'There's debts other than those that run to coin,' said Mother, passing Harry a bag of crystal charges. 'And I seem to be repaying most of them today. You need any more supplies?'

'Just enough food to get to Shadowclock,' said Harry.

'Shadowclock! Of course,' Mother tutted. 'When you've

got the crushers in front of you and the wolves of the Court behind you, where better? The most heavily guarded city in the whole of Jackals.'

Harry tucked his pistol under his coat. 'I think it was you who once told me the best place to hide is in the shadow of a police station.'

'Harry dearie, I also spent ten years of my life swapping those same stories with transportees while I was digging out irrigation channels for tenant farmers in the colonies. From here on in, you're not going to find any more whistlers damn fool enough to get themselves disavowed for your sins.'

'You're a saint, Mother.'

'Listen boy, I'd like at least one of the old crew alive enough to put flowers on my grave when I'm under the soil.'

'Mother, you're going to live forever.'

The old gun maker took a generous swig from her jinn bottle. 'No. But ever since my doctor got me off my mumble-weed pipe, it sure feels that way.'

The crystalgrid clerk looked annoyed that someone had arrived at the front desk just as the station was about to go over to its night shift. 'We're closed to the public. Priority state traffic only now. Unless you have a permit you'll need to come back in the morning.'

'Oh, sir, I have, you know,' said the customer. He produced a police inspector's badge from inside his coat, as shiny as it was false. 'You're not going to go off right now, are you sir?'

Resigned, the clerk pulled out a pencil and a message slip. 'It is late, you know. We sent off all the Turnhouse station dispatches four hours ago.'

'I would have come earlier, sir, but I had to wait for my mother to fall asleep.'

As the latecomer filled out the message slip, the clerk glanced back into the transmission hall. Some of the day shift's blue-skinned senders were already going into their hibernation cycle in front of the daughter crystals.

Reading the message, the clerk looked up. 'You know that state traffic is sent free – you don't have to pay tuppence for each word. You can write more if you want. . .'

'Oh no, sir. Length isn't important to me.'

The odd fellow left and the desk clerk pressed the bell for a transcriber. Seconds later a woman poked her head through the door.

'Late one, Ada,' said the man. 'Flash traffic.'

The transcriber read the message on the slip of paper. 'Wolf twelve. Shadowclock. What in Circle's name am I meant to do with that?'

'I reckon it's a tip for a horse at tomorrow's races,' said the clerk. 'Bloke who passed it in was police. The blooming crushers are having a laugh. Just code it and pass it down the line.'

'Do you see what he's written under destination – it's not a town, it's a crystal node.' She passed back the slip the customer had scribbled on.

'What?' The clerk read back the sequence of numbers. 'So it is. Not a mother crystal I recognize, either; do you, Ada? Maybe the crusher worked on the crystalgrid before he became a policeman.'

'The mother crystal won't be in any of the blue books we've got here,' the transcriber sighed. 'I don't even think the inheritance check is validly formed. Look, I don't get paid night rates. I need to get home. I'm just going to send the message down the line exactly as it is; someone on the grid will know what to do with it.'

Someone did.

Chapter Ten

It had taken two hours for the mob outside the royal palace to gather to its full strength and reach the maximum intensity of its natural curve into violence. Now they were finally boiling over. The chants had reached a self-righteous zenith. The lack of response from the thin line of black-uniformed police behind the palace rails, nervously clutching their cutlasses, was making the crowd bolder still. Bold enough to ignore the occasional tripod-mounted grasshopper cannon loaded with gravel and grapeshot, standing behind the police line.

'We're trying to get a magistrate to read the riot act,' said a police major to Captain Flare. 'But she's stuck behind the barricades that have been raised in Gad's Hill.'

'No doubt wedged alongside the heavies,' Flare said.

The major looked miserably out across Palace Square. There were none of the craynarbian Heavy Brigade reinforcements from the Echo Street station he had sent for. Let alone the exomounts from the stables behind Ham Yard.

'It's deuced busy out there on the streets,' said the major. 'The dockworkers' combination withdrew their labour early this morning and the port owners tried to lock them out. Half of the Gambleflowers is up in flames.'

Flare nodded. From the fourth-storey palace window he could already see the storm front brewing. The order of worldsinger's weather witches had been called in to put out Middlesteel's blazing warehouse district. Heavy black clouds were gathering along the river.

'Will you open up on them?' asked Flare.

'They haven't broken through the railings yet,' said the police major. 'We'll hold our fire.'

Of course he would. It might well be the major's head on a pole that was called for on the floor of the House of Guardians if the protest in Palace Square turned into a blood-bath.

'Did somebody say fire?' Flare's two lieutenants in the Special Guard had arrived from the palace barracks along with their worldsinger minder, a four-flower bureaucrat.

'Bonefire, Hardfall.' Flare pointedly ignored the order's man.

'Have we got the nod yet to put this down?' asked Bonefire.

'The House of Guardians isn't in session,' said Flare. 'I sent Cloudsplitter off half an hour ago to locate the First Guardian and secure a cabinet order. If you can find a doomsman out there hiding under a magistrate's bench, please do get them to read the riot act.'

Bonefire gazed out of the throne room's tall windows. 'Look at them down there. The face of reason, the heart of democracy. Bloody hamblins.'

Flare grimaced. He did not like his people using guard argot around the palace. Hamblin Normal was an upland village in Drochney outside the feymist curtain; where a waterfall was rumoured to have the power to cure the fey. Hundreds of families made their pilgrimage there each day, to take the waters and ward off any exposure to the body-warping mist they imagined might have occurred. Flare had always suspected it was a tale concocted by the worldsingers to allow them to net potential feybreed.

Bonefire turned to the captain. 'These are the people the Special Guard protects. What are they worth to you? I'd sooner trust a rabid dog not to gnaw my arm off.'

'There's no such thing as a pretty mob, lieutenant,' said Flare.

Outside, the shouting had got louder. Sections of the mob were trying to pull the railing bars out. The grasshopper guns were being swivelled by their crews to face the sections of the wall that looked likely to fall first.

'The soldiers will fire if they break the fence,' said Hardfall. 'It will be a massacre.'

'There's children in the crowd,' said Flare. 'We can't allow that to happen.'

'You have the order's blessing to intervene,' said the worldsinger. 'If casualties are kept to a minimum.'

Flare looked at the sorcerer with contempt. 'I think it's gone a bit beyond that, don't you?'

'There will be no bloodshed this day!'

Flare turned around. King Julius was out of his sickbed, standing shakily in a bed robe. Crown Prince Alpheus rushed down the corridor after his father.

'Your Majesty,' said Captain Flare. 'You are not well enough to be on your feet.'

'Listen to them down there, captain,' said King Julius. 'It's my head they are baying for. No republic with a king, isn't that the old Carlist cry?'

'It's not a republic they're thinking about right now,' said Flare. 'It's your blood.'

The tired old nobleman collapsed onto his throne. 'I think

I have a little of that to spare, young man, before the waterman's sickness puts me under the soil and I move forward on the Circle. Bring me my mask and open the doors to the main balcony.'

The crown prince was horrified. 'Father! There's no need for you to go, to humiliate yourself. Hoggstone hasn't ordered this.'

'My boy,' said the King. 'Alpheus, it is me that they want.'

'You gutless old fool!' Alpheus shouted. 'Just once why don't you stand up to them? Refuse to do what they want. Walk away from them. Did they cut your courage away when they took off your arms?'

'Alpheus,' said the King, 'our circumstances may be reduced, but our duty is not. Remember the blood that flows in your veins. Our ancestors protected Jackals for nearly a millennium, they helped cast down the dark gods and watched over the people for centuries. We do what we have to, what we *must*. Not what our fancies dictate.'

'I hate you,' shouted the prince. 'And I hate your fairytales. That's your *people* out there, and all they want to do is tear you apart.'

The king had a faraway look in his eyes. 'Bring me my mask.'

Flare sighed. 'Bring the King's gag. Bonefire, Hardfall, cool the mob's appetite for blood a little first.'

Bonefire grinned. 'Twitching time for the hamblins.'

Opening the balcony doors, the wind caught the velvet capes of the two Special Guards. Bonefire raised a fist and cerulean false-fire leapt from his arm, lashing out along the perimeter of the palace railings. Unlike some of the other burners in the Special Guard, Bonefire's ethereal energy did not ignite physical objects, failed to even leave a mark on a victim's skin; but for anyone caught in the witch-light, they felt as if they were burning alive at the stake, a pain more terrible than plunging a hand into a hearth.

Flare had fought to have Bonefire brought into the Special Guard. Originally the political police had illegally apprenticed the boy into their coercement and interrogation section, using his unnatural fey fire to loosen reluctant tongues. He still enjoyed his work.

As the front of the crowd fell back in burning agony, Flare nodded to Hardfall. She moved forward onto the balcony and placed her hands on her head, pressing her skull in her concentration position. Down in the square thousands of protesters began to lift off the ground, boots and shoes thrashing as they paddled desperately against the air. A brief quiet fell as the yells and abuse faded away, a silence broken only by the screams of the protesters still suffering from the after-effects of the guardsman's false-fire.

When the mob had been lifted four feet in the air Hardfall gently lowered them back onto the cobbles. As the stunned mob's feet touched the ground King Julius slowly walked onto the balcony, his royal face-gag strapped on. Some of the protesters – the hardcore Carlists and republicans – ran forward and started throwing fruit and stones up towards the balcony.

Without arms to steady himself, the King was quickly knocked down in the rain of rubbish and debris from the square. The stoning continued; the dazed monarch fell to his knees then slipped down in a huddle under the hail. But it was half-hearted. Hardfall's demonstration of the Special Guard's abilities had broken the spell over the majority of the crowd. They milled around startled, then began to drift off, shaken by their fey protectors' powers. Eager to withdraw before they were treated to a repeat manifestation.

The major had to restrain the crown prince from dragging

his father off the balcony. Tears were running down his face. 'They're killing him, the jiggers. Why do they hate us, why?'

'He's a symbol,' said Captain Flare. 'Just a symbol to them. Nothing more.'

Bonefire walked back into the throne room smiling. He had enjoyed his afternoon's workout. 'Don't worry, boy. The architects planned the distance of the balcony from the square. Just far enough away to land a few licks without maiming His Highness permanently. You'll see, you'll get your turn on the balcony soon enough. Your father won't die from a few empty jinn bottles tossed in his direction, not today.'

Alpheus looked with rage at Bonefire. 'There was a time when the guard protected the King from the enemies of the land, protected the people from mobs and thugs.'

Captain Flare quietly led the crown prince away from the throne room. 'I have heard your father's stories too, Alpheus. Leave him now, I'll bring him inside in a minute after the mob's dregs have had their sport.'

'They were more than stories once, captain,' said Alpheus. 'But now? We're just royal geese being made plump for the Midwinter Festival, a morsel to whet the people's appetite. You can toss the mob my family's bones to pick their teeth with after they've had their fun. My whole life is little more than a fattening cage.'

Flare tapped the silver suicide torc hexed onto his neck and inclined his head towards the crow-like figures of the ever-present worldsingers. 'Your ancestors would have been better served by trusting the fey, Your Highness. If the old kings had put their trust in the Special Guard rather than the order, Kirkhill could have been made to stay a loyal servant of the crown, rather than keeping the crown in a box under the speaker's seat in the House of Guardians.'

'The sorcerers are powerful,' was all Alpheus could say.

'When they choose to be,' said Flare. 'There haven't been any serious floatquakes in Jackals this year, I grant you. But I did not see a cursewall hexed around the palace just now. A five-flower worldsinger could have dispersed that mob as well as any Special Guardsman. But they never seem to place themselves in physical danger unless they have to, do they? Far easier to stir up prejudice against the feybreed, lock away a few twisted unfortunates and pass themselves off as the protectors of Jackals. A position which pays the order handsomely, I assure you.'

'Sometimes I think about killing myself, captain,' said Prince Alpheus. 'Wouldn't that be a fine thing for the people. I could just step out on that balcony and jump over it in front of them all. That's about the only freedom I have left. To decide when to die.'

Flare smiled regretfully. He did not point out how hard it was to commit suicide with no arms on your body, with ranks of worldsingers waiting to paralyse any king or queen who attempted to deprive parliament of its sport.

'Please don't, Alpheus. We both have our cages and our roles to play. Besides, life has a way of surprising you when you least expect it.'

'You, captain?'

The Special Guardsman opened the door to the prince's chamber. 'Once my life was the quiet of the moors. Leading the sheep out to pasture with each sunrise, the four walls of a flint cottage in Pentshire. That was before the mist came and changed me; the things I have seen with the Special Guard are nothing I could have ever imagined chewing mutton and bread on the hills over Wickmoral.'

Flare turned to go, but Alpheus reached out and touched his cloak. 'Captain, please. I think I can bear the stonings, but for Circle's pity, don't let them take my arms off.'

147

'Your Highness, there's many a slip, between a cup and a lip.'

Ver'fey had to hold Molly back from assaulting the aerostat navigator in the small basket.

'Mug-hunters, filthy mug-hunters!'

'Molly.' Ver'fey struggled with her friend. 'They're not after the bounty on your head, really they're not. I wouldn't have led mug-hunters down here if all they wanted was to top you.'

'Let me introduce myself,' said the navigator. 'My name is Silas Nickleby and I *am* interested in the price that is currently on your head among the flash mob. But not, I would point out, for the purpose of collecting your reward for myself or my employer.'

Molly stopped struggling. 'Your employer?'

'Dock Street's finest, Red,' said Professor Harsh, watching the fracas with casual amusement. '*The Middlesteel Illustrated News*.'

'You're a *pensman*?' said Molly. Why would anyone want to write about my life?'

'If we hadn't got to you back there, Molly, your part in my story would have been as the latest in a long line of murders I've been following for the last six months. I take it you've heard of the Pitt Street slayings?'

'Not many people going up Pitt Hill after dark now,' said Molly. 'Of course I've heard about the slayer. The papers have been saying it's some mad Carlist stalker with a grudge against the quality, killing nobs and leaving their bodies in the street with their eyes sliced out.'

'Not just the great and the good,' said Nickleby. 'Although it's mostly the rich that have been the victims of the slayer. And it's not just their eyes that have been taken, Molly. All of the victims have been drained of their blood. Every last drop.'

'You can't think that wicked old goat back there was the slayer?' said Molly. 'He was an aristo himself.'

Professor Harsh laughed. 'The count might slip a knife in your back for a bag of silver crowns, kid, but he doesn't work for thrills. Whatever else you can accuse him of, being cheap is not one of them.'

Nickleby passed the rudder mechanism on the expansion engine to the professor. 'This is my story, Molly. I was one of the first pensmen on the scene of the original Pit Hill murder and I have been covering each new death since. As I've been digging around, I keep on uncovering odd little details, things that point to the murders being more organized than the work of a single lunatic. So I've been keeping my eyes open for the esoteric, trying to find a connection between those being murdered.'

'What's this got to do with me?' said Molly. 'I'm not rich. You want to know who set the count on me, you want to look to my family.'

'That's what Ver'fey first told me when I tracked her down,' said Nickleby. 'And in a way, Molly, it's true – although I don't think there's an inheritance involved. Many of the Pitt Hill Slayer's victims have had red hair and two of the dead were cousins twice removed, which has led me to suspect there might be some family connection involved.'

'It isn't whole families that have been topped,' said Molly. 'It's just the odd nob here and there.'

'Indeed so,' said Nickleby. 'Curious, is it not? Almost as curious as a poorhouse being burned to the ground with a lot of bodies inside that were obviously corpses before the fire even started – and half a mill's-worth more children missing. Then there's the workhouse girl with the kind of price on her head that was last seen when King Reuben was hiding in trees from parliament's men.'

'I don't understand,' said Molly, tears misting in her eyes. 'I never thought I'd say this, but I just want things back the way they were before. I want a nice quiet job in a Handsome Lane laundry, with Circleday off to sit in the people's library.'

'I can't give you that, Molly,' said Nickleby. 'But you're under the newspaper's protection now, and my own. I can give you the best chance you're going to get to find out who is behind the Pitt Hill murders and uncover the person who wants you dead.'

The pensman stuck out his hand and Molly briefly hesitated, then shook it.

Professor Harsh laughed. 'If anyone from his rag comes to you with a piece of paper to sign, you show it to me first, Red. Otherwise you're going to end up badly illustrated on the cover of a penny dreadful surrounded by twenty axe-wielding toppers and with ginger hair as long as a Special Guard cloak.'

Nickleby flexed his arms, a thin imitation of the professor's gorilla-sized muscles. 'Queen of the Sands, as deadly as a viper and as quick as the wind.'

'Poor as a church mouse and refused tenure at seven of the eight great universities,' said Harsh. 'Not much of a story in that.'

Molly left her two rescuers to their banter and stood with Ver'fey, watching the landscape slide by. The first airship flight for both of them. Their pocket aerostat drifted through a series of caverns, some of them empty, some of them covered by the ruins of Chimecan cities, ziggurat buildings overgrown by fungal jungles. They floated up natural chimneys and what might have been air-vents hewn out of the rock, each massive opening taking them a little closer to the surface. After an hour of flight, swaying in the gondola to the rhythm of the airship's single coughing expansion engine, Molly's nose was assailed by the foulest of smells. They were sailing above a sea of dark sludge, sliding like cold russet lava beneath them.

'Break out the heliograph,' said Professor Harsh. 'If our friends don't receive the code they're liable to assume the worst.'

Nickleby levered open a crate and removed a large gas-fed heliograph, firing its lighting mechanism up. Pulling the heliograph's handle back and forth, the pensman started signalling down the cavern. A minute later a series of answering flashes blinked from the shadows at the far end of the cavern. As they drew closer, Molly could make out the outline of a squat stone fortress built into the face of the cavern wall.

Nickleby pointed to the huge pipes on either side of the fortress, pumping out the noxious smelling sludge into the underground sea. 'Fort Downdirt, Molly. The Worshipful Company of Nightsoil Engineers and the last civilized outpost of Jackals down here.'

If anything the stench became worse as they approached the fortress. As their craft got nearer, Molly noticed large ball-mounted cannons were tracking their progress, hoses connecting the guns to tanks of noxious flammable vapours. There were gas-masked figures mounted on tame pecks patrolling the perimeter, long lances tucked behind their saddles. Squatting on top of the walls, bombards loaded with dirt-gas mortar rounds pointed their ugly frogmouths out towards the sea of sewage.

'Are they expecting trouble?' Molly asked.

'War on two fronts,' said Harsh. 'The outlaws of Grimhope would love to back up the city's shit, although the last time they managed that was back in King Jude's reign. Then you've got the sewer scavengers and other misfits in the higher under-city and basement levels who seem to regard Middlesteel's crap like it's a precious resource that's being stolen away from them.'

Their pocket aerostat was drifting towards the stone fortress.

'Don't know why they should be bothered,' said Molly. 'There's always more shit in Middlesteel.'

Harsh passed Molly a line with a lead weight on the end. 'My thoughts precisely. Cast this down when we're about the same height as the buildings. Try not to brain anyone, kid.'

As they were hauled down by a team of engineers, Molly saw that the fortress inhabitants' faces were all concealed by menacing brown gas masks, even the four-armed craynarbians' – names stencilled above their visors alongside little silver stars of rank. Molly was about to leap from the basket when three engineers with large porcelain tanks of flammable vapours and iron-tipped hoses took position around the aerostat. A fourth engineer on a peck wheeled out a blood machine on a cart. The peck was impatiently scratching the floor, its bird-like feet shorn of all its toe claws.

Dismounting from the peck, the engineer stared at Molly through the visor of his gas mask. 'This is the girl you came for?'

Professor Harsh vaulted the airship gondola. 'Scrawny little thing, sergeant. No meat on those arms.'

'No gold statues this time, then, professor?'

'If you find a temple in the Duitzilopochtli Deeps that hasn't been turned over a thousand times by grave robbers, outlaws and scavengers, you be sure and give me first refusal, sergeant.'

The professor pressed her thumb on the needle of the blood machine and waited for the small steam-driven transaction engine to confirm her identity.

'You match your census record, Amelia,' said the engineer officer. 'And you can vouch for your companions?'

'Didn't leave the aerostat once,' said the academic. 'Didn't even touch soil in the Deeps.'

Moving past the engineer, Molly dodged under the peck's vicious beak and looked at the transaction engine on the blood machine. Something about the way its calculation drums were turning whispered to her that it would break down before the end of the month.

The engineer sergeant switched off the machine's boiler. 'There's fey runners down here, girl. Shape switchers. Outlaw worldsingers who can put the glamour on your face too, mould your skin like putty. You can't be too careful.'

Molly gave the engineer her best dumb female smile and when his back was turned, she pushed and clicked the out-of-calibration drum into its offsteam mode. Their maintenance staff would spot the wear on it now, when they came to check the blood machine.

Ver'fey called out to her and Molly saw that the pensman and the professor were entering the fortress; two lines of thick metal doors opening like interlocking dragon's teeth. Inside, a private line on the atmospheric lifted them to the surface in a bare service capsule. The capsule was crowded with the Worshipful Company's engineers, large soldiers with gas masks and unloaded pistols dangling from their belts, the stench of sewer pipes and peck sweat still clinging to them.

They emerged at the foot of the North Downs, low chalk hills that bordered the outskirts of Middlesteel and the Crystsoil Palace. Acres of glass domes and greenhouses covered the sewage treatment fields, masking the smell of the city's swill from the wealthy homes and estates of north Middlesteel; villages until Jackals' capital had devoured them in its spread outwards from the river.

Professor Harsh shook Nickleby's hand; her massive arms making the writer's seem like sticks in comparison. 'I need to wait for them to crate up the stat and send it topside. I trust that *The Illustrated* is good for the finder's fee we agreed?'

'They're paying me, aren't they?' said Nickleby. 'You are still searching for the city then?'

'Going to head out to the mountains in Airney,' said the professor. 'There's a lashlite nest there where I heard the flying lizards have an old legend of a hunting party finding something in the sky. I need to look into it.'

'The university won't be pleased if they find out.'

'That's why it's your money paying for the trip,' said Harsh. She ruffled Molly's hair and slapped Ver'fey's sword arm. 'It's not too late to accept my offer, Ver'fey.'

'I like the feel of Middlesteel's cobbles under my feet too much to join your expedition, damson,' said Ver'fey. 'Besides, Mister Nickleby has already secured me a position on his newspaper.'

'Copy runner?' said Harsh. 'Kid, that's more dangerous than life with me. You'll have runners from the *Star*, *Journal* and *Post* waiting on every corner from Dock Street to your print works to slap you down.'

Ver'fey tapped her shell armour with her sword arm. 'There isn't anyone who knows the lanes and passages like a Sun Gate girl.'

Molly nodded in agreement.

'You change your mind about life in the smoke,' said the professor, 'you can find me through Saint Vine's College.'

Nickleby led the two poorhouse girls through the maze of crystal-covered buildings and accordion pipes that made up Crystsoil Palace – most of the works given to processing expansion-engine gas from the slops and sewage before sending the torrent of waste spewing into the caverns below. The building seemed strangely majestic for the purpose of taking away the capital's waste; white stone walls supported by temple-like columns and scattered openings, statues standing in alcoves.

'Ver'fey, what city was the professor talking about?' asked Molly.

'Ancient Camlantis,' said the craynarbian. 'The professor thinks that it was destroyed in a floatquake and its ruins are still drifting through the sky somewhere.'

Molly laughed. 'And how's she going to get high enough to find out? Train a flock of flying pigs?'

'There speaks the next chairman of the royal academy of science,' said Nickleby.

The three of them gave way to a line of engineers with black sewage poles, then Nickleby pointed to a horseless carriage in the shadow of a building. It was one of the six-wheeled imports from the Catosian League, its high-tension clockwork mechanism far in advance of the crude Jackelian copies that could be seen clattering over the horse dung on Middlesteel's avenues.

'You can afford this?' Molly eyed the pensman suspiciously. 'Do you write for *The Illustrated* or do you own it?'

Nickleby smiled mysteriously. 'I also write, Molly.'

Ver'fey and Molly fitted snugly in the red leather couch behind the driver's seat, a retractable cover behind their heads in case rain fell on the open cab. The carriage started with a thrum and Molly could almost feel the tension of the interlocking springs under their seat. She remembered a cartoon – possibly from Nickleby's own *Illustrated* – of the Guardian who had opposed the introduction of the horseless carriages; the politician being launched from a cloud of exploding clockwork towards the floor of parliament, with the words, 'M'lords, regard my unsafe seat' inked into the speech balloon. But it was mostly the cheap Jackelian imitations that exploded. Mostly.

Nickleby drove them through the handsome boulevards and past the stately houses and crescents of Haggswood. School had just finished and children in matching red and brown uniforms were walking home, some accompanied by nannies in austere black robes and prams just as dark.

Holding the steering wheel between his legs, Nickleby tugged a mumbleweed pipe out of his coat pocket. He opened the door of his cab and banged the pipe on the road's cobbles to empty it. He then proceeded to refill the pipe with grey Concorzian leaves. The pensman lit his pipe as he weaved their horseless carriage between a hansom cab and a milk cart doing its afternoon rounds – the plodding shire horse made skittish by the carriage's thrum as it was overtaken. Molly winced. They must have been pelting along at nearly twenty miles an hour and Nickleby was steering the contraption with his knees!

Very'fey leaned over and whispered, 'He's always doing that.'

The tree-lined streets began to narrow and the residential crescents and their faux-marble facades gave way to Middlesteel proper. At one point, Molly thought she saw smoke rising from the east, wisps of black oily haze between the towering pneumatics of Sun Gate, gulls sweeping up on the thermals.

Her suspicions were confirmed when they came up to a wooden pole suspended across the road from a couple of barriers. Three crushers – two constables and a brigadier – nodded politely. Anyone riding an import from the city-states would warrant extra civility.

'Brigadier,' said Nickleby. 'Has there been an incident along the road?'

'In a manner of speaking, sir. The dockers' combination has been rioting. Four other combinations have come out in support and now there's trouble outside the palace as well as the House of Guardians.' The policeman pointed up the road. A column of craynarbians was trotting down the street three abreast, their thorax shells painted in black. They carried round metal shields, the yellow hedgehog arms of the national police painted in the centre.

Ver'fey stood up and waved. 'The Echo Street Heavy Brigade.'

Molly stared up – the street was briefly eclipsed by the dark shadow of an aerostat. She read the name on the side, the *RAN Resolute*.

'Dear Circle!' Nickleby sounded astonished. 'Parliament's not sitting – who's ordered in the navy?'

One of the constables gazed up perplexed. 'Ham Yard's been in contact with the First Guardian, sir. We received instructions from his country residence through the crystal-grid to bring up army units from Fort Holloden in case they were needed.'

'But Hoggstone wouldn't order in the navy in an election year,' said Nickleby. 'The Purists would be massacred at the polls by the Roarers and Heartlanders.'

Doors were opening along the belly of the massive airship, and metal cages filled with gleaming glass fin-bombs were lowered into view.

'They're clearing for action,' whispered the constable. He obviously could not believe what he was seeing.

'We've never bombed Middlesteel,' said Nickleby. 'Not even during the worst days of the Carlist uprising.'

Everyone in the street had stopped to stare up at the disappearing bulk of the airship. She was heading east, towards the river and the docks.

'Red tips,' said Nickleby.

Molly looked at the writer. Tears were welling in his eyes. 'Red tips?'

'Red tips for firebombs, Molly. Green for dirt-gas. Blue for explosive and shrapnel. I was called up into the navy information section during the Two-Year War. I was there when we flattened Norlay and the Commonshare's other mill towns. I never thought I'd see this again. And never at home.'

A collective gasp rose up from the Middlesteelians in the street as rumbles of man-made thunder echoed in the distance, the ground trembling. The two girls and the pensman held tight as their six-wheeled carriage shuddered. The sound died. A hush fell over the city. Down the street, the disciplined legion of craynarbian crushers still trotted in formation; they had not even broken a step. Molly doubted they would be needed now when they got to the scene of the disturbance.

Nickleby backed the horseless carriage up and headed down a side street.

'Where are we going?' asked Molly.

'Where else when news happens, Molly?' said the pensman. 'We're off to Dock Street.'

Pistols drawn, the first mate and the captain of the red-coated marines on the *RAN Resolute* faced down their bomb-bay crew.

'Back to your posts, damn you,' shouted the first mate.

'They weren't revolutionaries,' said a sailor. 'I didn't even see anyone down there with a pitchfork, let alone a rifle.'

More jack cloudies were crowding up the passage from the lower deck, trying to push past the two officers.

'The skipper had orders,' said the first mate. 'From the House and the Board of the Admiralty.'

'You seen 'em?' yelled a sailor.

'Let's have the orders in writing, then,' demanded another.

'Don't you play the barrack-room lawyer with me, Pemberton,' barked the captain of marines. 'The first one of you jacks that crosses this line is a dead man.'

A sailor waved a wicked-looking fin-bomb loading hook. 'You've only got two pistols, that's enough for two of us.'

'Enough for you, lad,' warned the first mate.

The captain of marines glanced back at one of the nervous redcoats holding the corridor. 'Get the airmaster down here, now!'

Captain Dorian Kemp, airmaster of the Royal Aerostatical Navy vessel *Resolute* lay next to the pistol he had just used to take his own life, what was left of his brains cooling in the wind blowing through an open hatch.

A dwarf with two heads did a little jig near the fallen officer. One of the heads was full-size, the other a shrunken, puppet-like growth. 'Reached into his mind and pop. Reached into his mind and bang.'

His companion looked with pity at the feeble-minded fey creature dancing around the corpse. There but for the path of the Circle went half the Special Guard. 'You've done a fine job, brother. The bombing run's finished. Time to be away.'

'All I had to practise with in my cells was the rats,' giggled the two-headed figure. 'I made them stand up and dance for me. Fighting in battles, my brave rats lining up and attacking each other with stones. Hold the line. Hold the line.'

'No more games with rats, brother. You can make the hamblins do anything now,' said the man, his skin starting to shimmer with witch-light. 'Possess anyone you like.'

'You won't throw me back in my cell, will you?' pleaded the dwarf.

'Of course not,' lied his companion, scooping up the small fey thing. Not until the wild bunch's real job was done at least. There were standards to maintain, after all.

With a spurt of energy the man and his minuscule passenger accelerated out of the airship, contemptuously kicking the hatch shut, before vanishing into the sooty clouds floating up from the ground.

Middlesteel's docks were a single wall of flame, the fires

of the rioting mob burning out of control, now the dark brooding shape floating above them had spilled her deadly cargo.

The twenty-fourth floor of *The Middlesteel Illustrated News* was a riot of staff running past writing desks. The clatter of iron typewriters – hulking machines that translated the fusillade of words onto transaction engine punch cards – a background to the shouts and din across the open floor, drowning out what Nickleby was trying to say to Molly.

'Need a comment from the Admiralty Board.'

'Bodies are coming in to the Circle of Targate hospital, survivors too.'

'There is *no* comment.'

'Printers say they want extra money.'

'Send someone around to the First Skylord's residence. Doorstep him.'

'Pay it.'

'Interviews. Now.'

Through the confusion and hustle a crow-like figure on two crutches swung his corpulent bulk like an obscene pendulum – eyes bright and malicious, surveying the mayhem. It was *him* – no doubt about it, the editor and proprietor of *The Illustrated*. Molly remembered a cartoon of Gabriel Broad shortly after his legs had been broken by the flash mob – pointing a crutch accusingly across the magistrate's court. 'The truth needs no crutch,' scratched next to his mouth in a speech balloon.

'Come you here, boy,' his voice boomed across the room, before continuing towards the figure he had singled out. 'Middlesteel surprised by aerial assault? I am *surprised* when any of you drunken sots show up on time for the morning shift. I would be *surprised* if my wife brought me a glass of warm jinn before tucking me up for the night. When I see one of our own Circle-damned aerostats dropping firebombs on the capital of our great and glorious land, I am not, sir, *surprised*. I am violated. I am jiggered by the enormity of it all. Pull the lead on that subtitle. If I ever see the like of that again on one of my inside pages, I will be *surprising* you by pulling your record of employment from the punch card drawer and feeding it into the fires still burning along the east bank of the river, do you understand?'

Turning from the quivering writer, the editor spotted Nickleby and Molly and swung his way over to them, stabbing his twin crutches into the floor like a duellist's sword blows. 'Found another waif for me to employ, Nickleby? I'll be applying to Greenhall to re-register the paper as a Circlist charity before the week is out.'

Ver'fey had already disappeared with copy on the attack for the printers, but the editor obviously had a good memory for details. Molly and her rescuer followed the old man into his office, large round crystal portholes cut into the walls of the pneumatic structure giving them a good view of the smoke streaming into the air at the other end of the city. When the door was shut the din of the pensmen's pit was instantly cut off; in the silence Molly could hear the soft flow of water shifting through the building's rubber walls.

'Walls have ears, eh?' said the editor. 'So this is the girl? Right now, m'dear, I could get more money for trading your head than I could if I sold *The Illustrated* lock, stock.'

'It's a strange old world,' said Molly.

Broad looked out at the smoke gushing into the sky. 'Indeed it is, m'dear. My paper would be empty most days if it were not.'

'I told you there was more to the Pitt Hill slayings than a lone lunatic,' said Nickleby. 'Molly here is a proof of it, I am sure.'

'We need to find the link,' said the editor. 'What connects this young lady to a bunch of society's finest with their blood leeched out like so much desert butcher's meat?'

'You'll protect me?' said Molly. 'Help me find the truth?'

'Truth has a price,' replied the editor, raising his crutches. 'It extracts a cost from those that stare at it too long, those that seek it too zealously, eh Nickleby?' He looked meaningfully at the journalist. Nickleby shrugged and looked away. 'Well, m'fella here has the best nose for a story of anyone on *The Illustrated*. If someone can help you work out why your dear flame-coloured head is worth a Guardian's ransom, it's Nickleby here. As for protection, where's that fierce bookworm with the amazon-sized arms – isn't she on the payroll?'

'Just for the finder's fee,' said Nickleby. 'She's off to parts foreign now.'

The editor shook his head. 'More grist for the mill for the penny sheets, I don't doubt. Well, I can always pull a couple of whippers from that gang of thieves I pay to guard the print mill and have them follow you about.'

Nickleby shook his head. 'Anonymity is our best defence now, Gabriel. None of the mug-hunters and toppers looking for Molly knows that she is in our care. If you post an armed guard outside my gates, word's going to get back to the flash mob sooner or later. People will start wondering why.'

'So be it,' said the editor. 'That old salt who hangs around your place looks like he might be handy with a Sleeping Henry, eh?'

There was a knock at the door and a breathless runner stumbled in holding out a note. 'The Board of the Admiralty denies that the *Resolute* had orders to even be in Middlesteel, let alone bomb it. They're sending the *RAN Amethyst* and *Upholder* to escort the *Resolute* back to Shadowclock, with orders to bring her down if she resists.'

'By the Lord Harry,' exclaimed Broad. 'A duel over the city. You boy, tell the desk to make ready for a second edition. Nickleby, you did some time on the decks, does the Board's story sound likely to you?'

'An airmaster can be hung for showing initiative with their position in a squadron formation,' said Nickleby. 'A skipper doesn't change the crew's jinn ration without written orders from the Board.'

'Fella must have gone barking mad,' said the editor. 'Boy, boy, send someone down to the taverns where the jack cloudies soak their troubles, get me the name of the skipper of the *Resolute*. Anything about his background – see if this chappie was barking, history of lunacy in the blood, all of that.'

'Dear Circle,' said Nickleby. 'Our own city. I still can't believe it; it's like a dream.'

'Stuff of nightmares more like, eh?' said Broad. 'We'll get to the bottom of this one and have someone's head on the end of a pike for it.'

'By writing about it?' said Molly.

Broad furrowed his brow and picked up an edition of his broadsheet. 'It's easy to mistake this for a couple of sheets of wood pulp, m'dear, but you'd be wrong. This is a weapon. No less than that bloated airship floating above Middlesteel; and this can do a great deal more than burn a district to the ground. It can inflame an entire nation to arms. It can send the people stampeding in one direction or t'other at a polling booth. It can burrow into the heart of the flash mob and turn over the stone of the underworld so everyone can see the worms and maggots crawling through our sewage. It can uproot the stench and sweat of a Stallwood Avenue mill and slap it down inside the comfortable five-storey house of an articled clerk. It can take a selfless act of bravery and make it seem like the grossest foolhardiness – or it can take an idiot and raise him up to strut across the floor of parliament like a peacock.'

'But it extracts its price, Molly,' said Nickleby.

'Not today,' said Broad, pointing to the silhouette of the *Resolute*, still cloaked by waves of black smoke. 'Today the city has paid the bill for us.'

Count Vauxtion swirled the remains of his brandy in the large glass. As they should, the legs of the drink made golden fingers against the side of the crystal. Only three bottles of the 1560 left now. The Carlists had seized the rest of his cellar when the Quatérshiftian nobility found itself overrun during the people's revolution. Drunk in a single evening to fuel the orgy of devastation which saw his chateau razed to the ground, his family arrested, his workers ejected from their cottages and most senseless of all – the grain stores torched. So much of his legacy, his life had gone in that single night.

Ka'oard entered the library, holding a package wrapped in brown paper. 'I hope you are not brooding again, sir.'

Count Vauxtion allowed the craynarbian retainer to take the brandy glass out of his hand. 'I find it hard to focus on the words in the books, old shell. I am not sure if that is a function of my fading sight or the distraction of too many accumulated memories.'

The craynarbian placed the package on the reading table. 'Your beard and my shell are turning white together, sir.'

'Do you remember the hills outside Estreal, Ka'oard? Your shell took a few cracks then.'

'The King's dispute with the Steammen Free State?' said the craynarbian. 'I remember it well, sir. The cavalry made a disastrous charge against the steammen knights. Colonel Weltard died in the saddle, taken down by a flame-gun.'

'He always was a fool. Brave as a sand lion, of course, but a fool,' said the count. 'Had a lovely wife just as fearless as he was. She had a few choice words for the crowd when they took her to the Gideon's Collar, as I recall. Stood on that platform and cursed the mob for ten minutes before the Carlists dragged her into the bolter.'

'At least the colonel was spared the sight of that, sir,' said the craynarbian.

'Yes,' sighed the count. 'What a pair we make, old shell. We should be sitting by a river in Vauxtion, drowning worms with a rod and a cast, watching our grandchildren throw stones at each other.'

'As I recall it was mostly you who threw stones at me, sir,' said the retainer.

'I was a curious lad,' said the count. 'I liked the sound they made as they pinged off your back. Besides, you used to poke me with your damn sword arm when I was given the bunk above yours in the regiment. Pretended you were sleep-walking as I remember it.'

'My sword arm is rather blunt now, sir.'

The count picked up the package he had been brought and began to unwrap the paper. 'It is still sharp enough, I think. This was delivered by a private courier, I presume?'

'Like the others, sir.' The craynarbian took the unwrapped mirror and stepped back. As he did, the surface of the mirror began to shimmer, as if the glass plane was melting in a fire. A shadowed face appeared.

'You have an update for me?' asked the silhouette. 'News of the girl?'

'I tracked her down,' said the count. 'But your requirement that she be delivered alive proved problematic. Dead is so much easier. She was in my custody, but she was liberated by some rivals.'

'Rivals?' said the shadow. 'Old man, I have had no mug-hunters come to the valuer to claim my bounty.'

'Somehow I did not think they would,' said the count. 'It will help me track the girl's new hiding place down if you could explain why you want her. I need to understand the motivations of her rescuers if I am to bring her to ground again.'

'That is not your concern,' echoed the voice. 'You need only find her, then deliver her to the valuer.'

Count Vauxtion shook his head. 'She is just a Sun Gate waif. If you want her dead, simply let her grow up. In three years her liver will be a jinn-raddled mess, in five she will be on her death bed with match-girl lungs or some similar mill-cursed sickness.'

'I retain you solely for your skill as a hunter,' said the shadow. 'I do not require your philosophical musings on the state of Jackelian society. Where in Middlesteel did she escape from your custody?'

'Not in Middlesteel,' said the count. 'Beneath it. She was hiding in Grimhope – quite the quarry, young Molly Templar. Rather admirable. She's showed more spirit and ingenuity than the grudges I am normally called to pay off among the merchants and flash mob lords.'

'Grimhope!' roared the figure in the mirror. 'She was in the city below? Why did you not tell me this?'

'As you so kindly pointed out,' said the count, 'your largesse is dependent solely on the successful capture of the girl. I am not paid to deliver daily notes on my progress to you. Your two-shilling whippers were of no help to me in Sun Gate. When I require a trail of poorhouse corpses for Ham Yard to follow back to me, I will tip off your thugs. Until then, I will follow my usual practice and work alone.'

'Test my patience too far, old soldier, and those men will come for *you*.'

'I was not merely a marshal in the old regime,' said the count. 'I was also first duellist of the court. You would not be the first patron to attempt to renegotiate the terms of our agreement during an engagement. If you have a yearning to send any of your bullyboys to visit me, you had better make sure they are not anyone you wish to see again. I will be returning their ashes to your valuer cremated inside one of my old wine bottles.'

'Bring me the girl,' commanded the shadow. 'Do not let Molly Templar slip away from you again.'

Steam was rising off the surface of the mirror; the worldsinger hex had nearly worked its course. Soon the artefact would be fit only for the scrap heap.

'One last thing,' said the count. 'You are not by any chance the girl's father?'

A deep cackling laughter like a log being consumed by flames sounded from the mirror. Then the glass twisted and sizzled into silence.

'I did not think so,' said the count.

'May I put the mirror down, sir?' asked the craynarbian.

'Of course, old shell. Toss it out the back with the others.'

'You would think the gentleman would have learnt to communicate using this country's excellent crystalgrid network.'

The count picked up the book he had been reading. *The Strategy of the Wars of Unification* by one of the lesser known Kikkosicoan nobles. 'Our patron might have more wealth than a Jackelian mine owner, Ka'oard, but a gentleman I suspect he is not.'

'As you say, sir, as you say.'

'I am so very tired of listening to the locals sing "Lion of Jackals" at the end of every damn play, every damn prom. It is far past time these people lost a war and gained a little humility. I think when we have collected the money from our current patron, we should take a trip out to the colonies. See what the shores of Concorzia have to offer.'

'A little late for a new start, sir?' pointed out the craynarbian.

'I don't know, Ka'oard. Land is cheap out there. Maybe we could buy a manor with a stream. Free the contracts on some young pickpockets and horse thieves who've been given the boat. Watching them farm the land and roll for fish in the water, it might be like the old days.'

'We did not make war on children in the old days, sir,' the craynarbian pointed out. 'We did not hunt young girls.'

'Don't confuse our present reduced circumstances with the field of honour, old friend,' said the count. 'Here in Jackals we are refugees in a land of shopkeepers. This is not war we make here. It is *business*.'

The retainer put the brandy bottle back in the cabinet and locked the glass door. When he turned around he found the old aristocrat was asleep in his chair. Ka'oard placed a blanket over his employer's legs.

'All things considered, sir, I think I preferred war,' he whispered and left.

Chapter Eleven

It had been a week since Oliver and the disreputable Stave had traded the warmth of the narrowboat for the damp ferns and wind-whipped moors that ran across Angelset, from the town of Ewehead to the outskirts of Shadowclock. To avoid the blood machines and the county constabulary they kept off the crown roads and away from the toll cottages, trekking across open countryside.

Little of the land seemed to be under cultivation; the border with Quatérshift was only a few miles to the east. The presence of the cursewall – and the continual eerie whistling as that dark product of the worldsinger arts absorbed the wind – had been enough to empty any of the villages that had not been laid to waste during the Two-Year War. Now at last it felt to Oliver like he was really an outlaw. They avoided human company, keeping to the wilds, always with an eye to the nearest copse, wood or gully – in case the shadow of one of the RAN's small border patrol scouts appeared on the skyline. Even in summer the moorland they crossed seemed like a desolate, blasted place. Freezing nights, soggy mornings and only the occasional wild pony or tail-hawk for company.

When they found streams, they would replenish their canteens and Harry would boil up water to make a stew from the dried meats and bacon that Damson Loade had crammed into their travel packs. She had also given them an earthenware jug of her favourite jinn, corked with a silver stopper in the shape of a bull's head. The most that could be said for the sharp-tasting firewater was that it warmed them briefly, before they turned in at night under the tent that filled up most of Oliver's bag.

Oliver had also kept the edition of the newspaper that revealed the killings at Hundred Locks. When Harry was not looking, he would unwrap the newspaper and stare at the remains of his old life fixed in print, hoping the details would make sense if he just pondered them long enough. The boring repetitive chores, the invisible cage of his registration order, they seemed to belong to someone else now.

The tent that Oliver lugged around was a strange-looking affair, a blocky harlequin patchwork of greens, browns and black. Harry said a transaction engine had turned out the design; specifically fabricated to disrupt the lines an eye would interpret as a man-made object. Up close it was enough to give Oliver a headache just looking at it. Once, he had pointed at one of the ruined villages, now in the shadow of a wood, and suggested they might camp under the shelter of one of the more solid cottages.

Harry just shook his head. 'They're abandoned for a reason, Oliver. Towards the end of the Two-Year War the Commonshare was getting desperate. Their invasion had been beaten back, their large cities had been bombed into rubble by the RAN's aerostats; the human wave attacks by the brigades of the people's army had failed; the Carlist uprising in Jackals had been crushed. So Quatérshift resorted to mage-war. Their worldsingers hexed shells filled with plague spores and earthflow particles drained from the leylines, and they unveiled their secret weapon. Long Tim.'

'Long Tim?'

'After Timlar Prestlon, the mechomancer who created their long cannon. There's one on display outside the barracks of the Frontier Light Horse; steam-driven monsters with a barrel as tall as the offices of a Middlesteel counting house. During the war the Commonshare was shelling most of Angelset from as far away as Perlaise.'

'The war was over eight years before I was born, Harry,' said Oliver. 'The ruins would be safe now, no?'

'The Commonshare was not playing four-poles, Oliver. They didn't load their balls with shrapnel or blow-barrel sap. The devil's potion their worldsingers brewed up made people sick, like being hit by a dozen plagues at once. The earthflow particles caused transmutations on top of it all – like being caught in a feymist, but without the slim chance of survival. During the months it took the order to neutralize their sorcery, tens of thousands of our people died in agony in this county. Some of that filth could still be active down in the ruins.'

'But Jackals won the Two-Year War.'

'For our sins, we did. The Special Guard smashed Long Tim, my people made Timlar disappear and furnished him with a nice warm cell in the Court of the Air, and the fury on the floor of parliament gave the First Guardian the backing he needed to overturn the conduct of war act of 1501. The RAN dirt-gassed the shifties' second city, Reudox. They say the stench of the corpses was so bad that the God-Emperor could smell the carnage across the border in Kikkosico. Parliament sent the First Committee a list of towns and cities that would be gassed from the air, one every two days. Reudox was head of the list. We accepted their armistice the next morning.'

'That's horrible, Harry.'

'As bad as it gets, old stick. But I am a scalpel, not the surgeon, so what do I know? Perhaps the Court could have stopped the war, but we've always been wary of being too hard-slap outside of Jackals; the world's just too big, too complicated for us to act as high sheriff to every ha'penny kingdom and nation out there. When you're faced with mob dynamics, taking the wolf without killing the flock is all but impossible. If our thinkers had spotted the trend early enough, maybe we could have landed Ben Carl a nice contract writing penny dreadfuls for Dock Street. Maybe we could have put *Community and the Commons* on the back shelf of the public library rather than the House of Guardians' suppressed list.'

'If he hadn't written it, someone else would have.'

'Which comes first, the movement or the man, yes?' said Harry. 'You've a fine mind, Oliver. It's been wasted malingering in the shadow of Toby Fall Rise – if we get through this, I'll have to see if I can change your fortunes.'

'Does the Court of the Air take potential feybreed?'

Harry winked at Oliver. 'You'll be surprised at some of the people who turn up on the wolftakers' pay-book. They even took me in.'

So they moved on. Past the destroyed villages and the roads overgrown with knee-high grass and brambles. Avoiding the shadows of aerostats and the silhouettes of red-coated riding officers traversing the hills and valleys. On the seventh night since they'd begun travelling overland Oliver was sleeping fitfully in his blanket roll. Images of Uncle Titus danced before him, puppet strings dangling from the sky where the unseen masters of the Court made him jig and jerk at their whim.

The Whisperer was trying to break through into his dream. Oliver could feel the pressure of the thing's loneliness like a thousand-weight lifting stone from a pugilist's pit pressing on his chest. The dream was not well formed enough for the Whisperer to break through, though; there needed to be substance to his dreamscape for the thing to appear.

'Oliver,' hissed the Whisperer. 'I can't reach you.'

'What did you say?' Oliver shouted into the emptiness.

'She is here; by all that is holy, I can feel her coming.'

'Who, Whisperer?' said Oliver. 'Who is coming?'

'Her! HER. I am water in the ocean before her, spittle in a hurricane. Dear Circle – her perfection – makes me – an animalcule in the stomach – of the universe. So small—'

'You're breaking up, Whisperer,' said Oliver.

'Shadow – in – the – light.' The Whisperer's presence faded to nothingness.

With the press of the cold moorland wind, Oliver awoke. The flap of the tent had come loose. Harry was at the opposite end of the canvas cover, snoring loudly as usual, wrapped up in his bedroll.

The first glimmering of sunrise reached into the sky outside, fingers of orange and purple climbing down to the horizon. Two deer stood a hundred yards from their tent, a doe and a stag, cautiously sniffing the air. They seemed oblivious to the presence of the woman sitting cross-legged in front of them, protected from the chill of the morning by nothing more than a white Catosian-style toga.

Oliver threw on his long-necked wool jumper, pulled up his trousers and went outside. Something about the woman seemed familiar, almost mesmerising. He walked up to face her. 'Who are you?'

'Has it been so long, Oliver, that you have forgotten me?' As the woman spoke, multicoloured lights started to circle in lazy orbits around her head.

'It was you,' said Oliver. 'You who came for me in the land of the feyfolk, beyond the veil.'

One of the lights hummed and the woman smiled at it. 'You see, I told you he would remember our visit.' She turned back to Oliver. 'I had a hard job, Oliver, convincing the people of the fast-time that your place was here, in your own world, with your real family.'

'I asked you if you were a goddess or an angel,' said Oliver.

'And I said to you that if the angel had a hammer, and the hammer had a nail, I might be the nail.'

'I thought it was a dream,' said Oliver. 'You, my time inside the feymist. Everything beyond the veil.'

'The people of the fast-time move to a different beat, Oliver. The rule-set of their existence is beyond the ability of your mind as it exists here to process. I found it difficult myself to construct meaningful enough arguments to have you returned home by them. I hope you don't miss your foster family inside the feymist too much.'

'I hardly remember them now. But considering the life I have had here in Jackals, maybe you should have left me where I was.'

'I promised your real parents I would save you, Oliver,' said the woman, gently. 'I made, well, you might call it a deal, with your father. If I had taken you out of the feymist too soon you would have died of shock. If I had left you beyond the feymist curtain for much longer you would have changed forever and your mind could not have adapted to life in Jackals again.'

Oliver looked back towards the tent where Harry was still sleeping. He knew the agent of the Court would not wake while the woman was here; she could move like a will'o-the-wisp across the face of the world.

'You're the one the Whisperer was talking about.'

She nodded. 'We have been playing a small game of tag, he and I, across the minds of the people of Jackals. Poor twisted Nathaniel Harwood, trapped in his decaying body and trapped in his dirty cell. The feymist curtain is a bridge, Oliver, and it seems every bridge must have its troll hiding underneath.'

'Nathaniel. So that is his real name,' said Oliver. 'I wish you could help him.'

'I am known as an Observer, Oliver, not an interferer. My interventions are discreet – no parting of the seas, no plagues of insects, no famines or resurrections. Free will, Oliver. You make your own heaven or hell here. Do not look to the uncaring sky for salvation, seek it inside yourself.'

'What are you doing in Jackals, then?' asked Oliver.

'Trouble at the mill, young man. There are forces outside the system, unpleasant, foreign elements, that would love to burrow inside our universe, sup on it like parasites feeding on the flesh of a live hen. Not much room in their philosophy for free will, or any kind of will at all. Your people have met the agents of this evil before. In fact, it is better said that it was your kind's belief in them that *created* these agents in the first place. They are called the Wildcaotyl. They are corrupt entities and the evil they serve is beyond the measure of my scale, let alone yours.'

'Then you're here to save us?'

She laughed loudly, as if that was deeply amusing, the funniest thing in the world. 'No, Oliver. I am a nail, a tool. I can batten down the storm shutters, but I cannot divert the storm. I cannot save the village without annihilating it.'

An uneasy feeling crept through Oliver, an insight too terrible to contemplate. 'You're not here to *save* us. You are here to *destroy* us.'

'The rule-set can't be changed from outside, Oliver. We simply will not allow it. Never. If it comes to it, if a corruption takes and spreads, everything will be wiped out, the board cleared of pieces, every piece of matter you have known or have touched, even time itself, will be erased. Nothing to be given over to the enemy – nothing!'

'But we can stop the end of the world,' said Oliver. 'Free will. We can choose.'

'Yes, but your people are always choosing to believe in the wrong thing, Oliver. The Circlist church was good; closer to the truth than your vicars and parsons realize. But the landlord doesn't like her tenants inviting in troublesome guests. You know the sort. Angry types who get above their station, urinating against the walls, trying to grab the freehold and making threats. When the landlord sees that, she draws up an eviction order. And Oliver, trust me on this, your people don't want to find out what life is like living rough on the street.'

'So that's it,' said Oliver. 'My whole life, I've just been a pawn in your game of gods?'

'No, Oliver,' said the Observer. 'You are my knight, and more. And one I am very fond of. You get to choose your own moves – you all do. It would please me greatly if the game could go on forever. But that is rather up to you.'

'You *have* intervened,' said Oliver. 'What do you call our conversation right now? What do you call dragging me back here to Jackals when I was only five years old?'

The woman looked over at a tree, as if she had noticed something that confused her, and the little spheres of light revolving around her seeming to spin faster. Her attention returned to Oliver. 'Only in so much as I can choose to gently correct any imbalances caused by the presence of external forces, the ones who have no place here such as the Wildcaotyl and their masters. Of course, how I choose to paper over the cracks is left to my discretion, Oliver. But we are fast moving beyond the point where a little extra wattle and daub around the edges is going to keep the roof from leaking. It is going to get fundamental very quickly. When that happens, what I want or do not want is going to matter very little indeed. I will be removed, Oliver. No more nails. No more damage limitation. You will be assigned something very dangerous with a very short fuse instead.'

'Are you alright?' asked Oliver. 'You look shaky.'

'I – need to – go, Oliver. Too much resolution. I am not used to operating at this level of detail, constrained in this silly body. I am a big-picture girl – at – heart. The fractal beauty of the branches, splitting into – leaf upon leaf – simplicity from complexity – complexity from simplicity.' She was fading, the thrumming noise of her lights growing more intense.

'Before you go, I know why the feymist curtain is here,' said Oliver. 'Why it appeared a thousand years ago in Jackals, infecting children at random, killing most of the adults it touches.'

'Clever boy.' Tears were running down the woman's face.

'The land beyond the mist, the feyfolk: they won't be destroyed, will they? They're not part of this, not part of our universe. That's why the mist infects some of us – to allow a few of us to survive outside of our world, to escape extinction, for the race of man to continue to exist beyond the curtain. It's an escape tunnel your kind punched directly into the heart of Jackals.'

'Should it come to it, Oliver,' said the Observer, 'you will know when to cut and run. Only the fey can survive beyond the veil. Breeding pairs, Oliver, lead mainly breeding pairs into the mist.'

She was gone and the lash of the dawn wind seemed colder.

Oliver was left with the memory of a scared five-year-old boy, standing alone outside one of the upland villages that clung precariously close to the feymist curtain. Trying to talk to a crowd of villagers who were curious and terrified in equal measure by this child from beyond. He showed them the pendant that the Observer had given him as a talisman, the one with the miniature painting of his birth mother inside.

Not for the first time his old life had ended.

'Order, order,' shouted the speaker, banging her gavel. She had never seen the chamber so full. Guardians who normally only showed up in Middlesteel for lunch at their club once a year were thronging the hall. Opposite her, the doors to the cramped press gallery had been shut and the hyenas of Dock Street were being turned away.

Yesterday's events had even roused Tinfold from his deathbed, the ancient steamman and leader of the Levellers still representing Workbarrows as Guardian despite the failing state of his body.

A brief hush fell over the chamber as Hoggstone took his seat on the front benches, followed by the minister from the Department of War, looking pale at the prospect of what was to come.

'This House calls the minister for the Board of the Royal Aerostatical Navy to read his prepared statement,' announced the speaker.

'Guardians elect,' began the minister. 'I have received the preliminary details from the Admirals of the Blue in the matter of the *RAN Resolute*'s unauthorized bombardment of Middlesteel. These details serve as a preface to the official crown enquiry. Contrary to the sensational speculations of the Dock Street news sheets, at no point was any order issued through the chain of command for the *RAN Resolute* to assault the capital. Its actions in this matter were entirely unrelated to the disgraceful civil disturbances taking place in many sections of the city at this time. A detail underlined by the fact that the list of casualties in the airship's unlawful bombardment include many prominent officers of the Middlesteel constabulary, militia, magistrates, order of worldsingers and fencible regiments attempting to restore order to the capital.'

'Resign!' shouted one of the Guardians on the Heartlander seats, the call taken up in a hiss by many of the parliamentarians.

Flustered, the minister continued. 'The *RAN Resolute* deviated from the Admiralty's written orders to patrol the Medfolk and Shapshire county boundary. The master of the *Resolute* lied to his own officers, falsely claiming that the vessel had received orders to put down an armed Carlist uprising in the capital.'

On the opposition benches Tinfold waved a small yellow flag. The speaker recognized the point of order and the steamman rose to make his argument. 'Perhaps the honourable gentleman of the War Office would care to explain why one of the navy's most experienced airmasters, a veteran of some forty years' service, would bombard one of our cities?'

'Well,' said the minister. 'That is to say, we believe the commander went insane. Briefly.'

There were guffaws from around the chamber. Some of the Guardians on the government bench started to whistle, mimicking the air that frequently escaped from the steamman's malfunctioning boiler. Tinfold ignored their jibes. 'Yes, that is the fragment of this tale I find most troubling. We have rather a lot of warships and rather a lot of airmasters on the payroll. I find myself a little discomfited to realize that any one of them at any time could suddenly take it into their head to overfly one of our cities and fire-bomb it.'

'Actions have been taken.'

The minister was shouted down.

'How convenient that Captain Dorian Kemp took his own life, saving us the cost of his court martial,' said Tinfold.

'My point exactly,' said the minister. 'The taking of one's own life is hardly the act of a sane man.'

'Sanity seems to be a relative term when applied to those who serve in the navy,' retorted Tinfold, producing a copy of *The Middlesteel Sentinel*. 'Although their antics do seem to produce a steady stream of fodder for the cartoonists of Dock Street.'

A large monochrome illustration on the cover of the steamman's paper showed the wide-eyed airmaster of the *Resolute* reading a government act on the command deck of his airship. The bill read: *The Slum Clearance Act of 1596.*

Both sides of the chamber erupted in a tirade of name-calling and hooting. On the chamber floor the footmen of the Master Whip stood ready with their Sleeping Henrys in case any of the benches tried to rush their political rivals. Ex-political police with at least twenty years' service, these lictors were notoriously ready to dispense violence if the Guardians resorted to fisticuffs. Limited editions of old cartoons showing the more notorious riots on the floor of parliament were always in demand among collectors.

One of the shadow ministers from the Middle Circleans

finally lost his temper as an empty mug of caffeel tossed his way shattered by his feet. Rising with a roar he kicked past a footman, sending him toppling over. Beatrice Swoop, the current Master Whip, flicked her cat-o'-nine-tails around the shadow's left leg, upending the politician with a deft jerk upwards. Her footmen jumped on him like hyenas, two of them holding him down while a third laid into him with his Sleeping Henry, coshing him around the face.

The rest of the lictors held the party line, brandishing their bludgeons as the Guardians forgot their shouting match and briefly united to throw papers and heavy parliament bills at the Master Whip's forces.

'Order, ORDER!' screamed the speaker. As the din subsided she waved her red flag of censure. 'The honourable shadow from the Middle Circleans is banned from the House for a period of one week. Will the lictors please remove him to the parliamentary surgeon's office.'

There was a moment's respectful silence as the unconscious politician was dragged away by his feet from the debating chamber. 'The First Guardian has the floor,' ordered the speaker.

Hoggstone stood up behind the leader's table on his side of the chamber. 'Like my honourable friend from the opposition.' He paused to give a little whistle. 'I find myself more than a little disconcerted that a rogue RAN officer can take it into his head to falsify Admiralty orders in front of his crew and attack the heart of our fair land. Of course, unlike my honourable friend and his Leveller colleagues, the Guardians of the Purist party currently hold the majority in parliament and so we are obliged to do more than just stand around letting off steam on the matter.'

Loud calls of approbation rose up from the government benches.

'We have consulted with the Admiralty and Greenhall, and with the assistance of the order of worldsingers, the cabinet has arrived at a plan of action to ensure this terrible tragedy does not reoccur.'

'How?' someone yelled. 'By resigning?'

Ignoring the whispered chant of 'resign, resign, resign', the First Guardian continued. 'The order of worldsingers proposes to test the minds of all airmasters and flag officers of the RAN for signs of both madness and undeclared feymist infections. Until that truth-saying is completed, which the order estimates will take the best part of a month, the bulk of the fleet will remain stationed at their bases around Shadowclock.'

There were murmurs of discontent from the wealthier Guardians, the ones who used their fortunes to help lubricate the franchised voters in their wards.

'This grounding does of course apply only to the high fleet of war. The aerostats of the merchant marine will continue to serve the cargo and passenger routes as normal. This is the proposal the executive puts before this House and I thoroughly recommend it.'

'Point of order,' called the speaker. 'Is there anyone who wishes to challenge this proposal being put before the House?'

Hoggstone glared at his own benches. Only a Guardian from the party in power could challenge a cabinet proposal. Fowler and Dorrit shifted anxiously in their seats but said nothing. Half of Fowler's family had purchased commissions in the navy – as much as the jealous old fool would like to challenge him, he could not intervene without stirring up more trouble for his navy friends. Hoggstone shifted his attention to the Chancellor of the Exchequer and his backbench cronies. Not that the Chancellor would challenge him directly, that would not be four-poles. Guardian Aldwych rose from in front of the treasury faction. Shrewd. An ex-cavalry colonel, he had no love for the jack cloudies in the navy. 'I challenge the proposal.'

'Do you, sir?' boomed Hoggstone.

'I do, sir,' said the Guardian, defiantly.

The Speaker of the House raised her hand. 'The honourable gentleman is facing a challenge from within his own party. Master Whip, will you please clear the floor and issue red rods to the First Guardian and the challenging member.'

A banging cheer echoed across the chamber, the Guardians thumping the benches in anticipation. Hoggstone dipped his hands in the chalk-powder box by the side of the platform used for debating sticks. His opponent theatrically twirled his moustache as he received his red rod from a lictor. Aldwych was a bruiser and a chancer – his ancestors had switched sides from the King to parliament when they saw which way the wind was blowing. Centuries later and the Aldwych heirs were still tacking their sails against the winds of fortune.

How they looked down their noses at Hoggstone, whose father had died of the yellow plague, whose sainted mother had been a common patcher, climbing the pneumatics with nothing but a soldering iron, a bag of rubber seals and the need to feed six hungry children.

'Time to retire, old man,' hissed Aldwych as they faced each other on the platform. 'Time to hand the First Guardianship to someone who'll use it to make Jackals great, not just line their pockets with merchant guineas.'

'Someone like my chancellor, perhaps? When I need m'ledger balanced I'll be sure and come over to the Treasury offices at Greenhall. Until then, sir, I will take counsel from where I see fit.'

Aldwych whipped his red rod across and tried to land a blow on the First Guardian's face. Hoggstone ducked to the side and saw his own blow blocked by his challenger's staff. Just as Hoggstone thought. Aldwych was precise and powerful, but predictable. A typical product of the House Horse Guards. No creativity, no art in his moves. The staff school of Bludgeon, Bludgeon and Trample.

Stamping to try and distract Hoggstone, Aldwych swung his red rod across, then reversed and swung again, repeating the movement in a fusillade of blows.

Too canny to trade windmills with the Guardian, Hoggstone deflected the blows side on – a flat fighting profile the inhabitants of the Middlesteel rookeries called eeling, after the cantankerous eels fished out of the Gambleflowers.

Aldwych was sweating, tiring. Red rod was far heavier than a training staff or a duelling rod. The ancient debating sticks came from an age when parliamentarians still wore mail armour under their gentleman's cloaks. The young buck was slowing now, and Hoggstone feinted, then landed a jab on the Guardian's knee.

Yelping with pain, Aldwych dropped down and Hoggstone crowned his skull with a smashing blow. The challenge was over. Aldwych lay sprawled unconscious on the debating sticks platform.

'The issue has been decided in favour of the First Guardian,' announced the speaker. 'The proposal is now before the House. Those in favour?'

A sea of yellow flags was raised.

'Those against?'

The opposition Guardians contested the proposition, waving their flags. Even lathered in sweat and still panting, Hoggstone could see that he had carried the day. No one in his party had dared oppose him after the Chancellor's play for power had been beaten down, and the Purists still held the numbers after the last election.

'The proposal is carried,' announced the speaker, banging her gavel.

Hoggstone stared up at the press gallery, at the illustrators scribbling furiously away on their pads. He was not a gambling man, but if he had been, the First Guardian would have betted that Dock Street's headlines tomorrow would describe how close he had come to being defeated by a rebellion in his own ranks.

A bit of roughhouse theatre for the pensmen, and the rising death toll from the docks would be safely buried away on the inside pages. But then the hacks did not want the truth. They wanted whatever sold their penny sheets.

Yes. Quite a satisfactory afternoon's work.

Shifting from foot to foot, the red-coated soldiers were trying to keep warm as they waited on the icy moor. Jamie Wildrake looked at them with dissatisfaction. They were the scrapings of Jackals' gutter. While every child – every *gentleman* – aspired to join the Royal Aerostatical Navy, protectors of the realm worshipped by the people, what was left for the regiments of the new pattern army? Occupation of towns left flattened by airship bombardments? Bad rations and the discipline of the strap? No wonder the doomsmen often had to offer criminals the choice of service in lieu of transportation, spilling the human debris of the jails into the Jackelian military.

But convicts were what the wolftaker needed this day, especially red-coated criminals who had been taken in by his false colonel's papers when he had turned up at their poorly manned border garrison.

Wildrake could feel his muscles straining as he lifted one of the granite boulders from the soggy ground. The pressure on his arms was exquisite, each rise of the rock building him up, making his body harder and stronger, little footsteps on the infinite road to perfection. By contrast, the soldiers of the Twelfth Frontier Foot sat on their packsacks and smoked mumbleweed pipes, bodies soft and fleshy, clothed in layers of fat from too many days spent warming themselves by the fire in their hill fort. Watching the rain beat down on the moors while they chewed salted beef and swigged their daily ration of blackstrap. Sending patrols out to check the listening posts to make sure the shifties were not trying to dig surreptitious tunnels under the killing warp of their own cursewall.

Wildrake did not know how the soldiers could bear to exist with those loose rolls of flesh hanging around their bellies and off their arms. Where was their self-respect? Could they not feel the hum and tensions of their sinews calling out to be stressed and pained with exercise? Pain for the lats, pain for the pectorals, pain for the deltoids and hams. Glorious.

He chewed a fresh cud of shine and watched for the wagon coming from the south. It arrived within an hour of the time he had agreed with Tariq. The soldiers looked nervously at the white paint on the box-like caravan being pulled across the wet moorland by a train of six massive shire horses. Their fear intensified when they caught sight of the twin snakes of the surgeon's guild on the side.

'Colonel,' coughed the company's lieutenant. 'That carriage is sporting a plague wagon's livery.'

'A small deception, lieutenant,' said Wildrake. 'To transport a delicate cargo.'

The driver of the wagon dropped down to the soil and grasped Wildrake's arm in the Cassarabian style. 'So my friend, does this prophet-cursed land of infidels ever get to see the sun?'

'The Circle knows better than to waste its light on the head of a sand cur, Tariq.'

'Ha, is that so?' laughed the Cassarabian. 'Well, your gold

will sweeten the scent of my counting room all the same – perhaps it will pay for one of those ridiculous shades you use to keep out the rain. I will sit under it and take caffeel in one of your gardens and invite all my friends to my house to see how fine I am.'

'With a bit of tweed and a decent tailor you can dress up a spaniel as a Jackelian gentleman,' said Wildrake. 'But it still barks.'

The Cassarabian went around to the back of the wagon and took a key to the padlock there, sliding out a chain and throwing open the door. 'I do not need to bark, my friend. I have others to do that for me.'

Two creatures leapt out of the wagon, brown arcs of panther-sized muscle with flat muzzles and wide interlocking fangs, jaws like mill-saws clicking in greedy anticipation. The human eyes buried in their skull-plates flicked over the ranks of the soldiers and the troops fell back terrified.

'Biologicks!' said the lieutenant. 'The church will not suffer their presence in Jackals.'

'Hence the plague wagon,' said Wildrake, as if he were explaining to a child. 'A craftsman needs the right tools, lieutenant.'

'Colonel, those creatures have been grown inside the wombs of slaves,' insisted the officer. 'They are abominations.'

The Cassarabian shook his head. 'Alikar preserve me from the backward mind of the infidel. What else would you expect us to do with wombs blessed on women by the hundred prophets, bake bread in them?'

'Their presence in Jackals is prohibited,' shouted the officer.

'The state makes the law,' said Wildrake. 'And parliament makes the exceptions to that law. We are both servants of that state, lieutenant. Besides, where would a hunt be without its dogs?'

'Those things are not gun hounds,' said the lieutenant. Both the creatures were flat on the ground, growling, sensing the hostility of the officer of light foot.

'They are at least part dog,' said Wildrake, smiling at the things. They stared back at the agent with their wide children's eyes. 'Or is it sand wolf, Tariq?'

'Colonel, I will not allow my company to follow these unholy blendings, they stand against the Circlelaw,' spat the lieutenant.

Wildrake slapped the man on his back. 'You know, a border fort is the last place I would have expected to find a Circlean, lieutenant, among all the shirkers and punishment company men. But I admire a fellow with principles.'

He nodded at Tariq and the Cassarabian spat a command in his desert tongue. Both biologicks sprang forward, tumbling the lieutenant to the grass. He thrashed, rolled and screamed as the man-dog joinings tore him apart.

Wildrake slid his sabre out and waved it like a wand in front of the noses of the terrified soldiers. 'I am afraid I am not terribly conversant with church doctrine, but a little closer to home, I once read section forty-eight of the regimental code, punishment for mutiny on active service. Does anyone else here think the army would be better run along the lines of a Circlean soup kitchen?'

There were no dissenters.

Both the biologicks left the corpse alone as the Cassarabian made a guttural clicking sound, recalling the creatures.

Wildrake kicked the limp body. 'So, what do Circlist principles taste like? Somebody's idea of a joke, posting the fellow to a punishment company.'

One of the beasts gazed at the wolftaker and made a whining noise. It might have been words, but trapped in a canine jaw the human tongue mangled the speech into a bestial whimper.

Wildrake patted the creature on the skull as if he understood. 'You might think Tariq's two hounds here are the unholy product of Cassarabian womb magic, and you would be right. But you need to understand that the state does not condone their use lightly. The prey we are after are two of the most dangerous killers in all of Jackals. One is a criminal who has been on the run from the crushers for over a decade, leaving a trail of dead police and soldiers in his wake. The other is a fey boy who murdered his own family before escaping the torc.'

Dark murmurs started among the ranks of the superstitious soldiers. Feybreed! The colonel did not have any purple tattoos – surely they needed a worldsinger to subdue a killer touched by the mist? Wildrake flourished his crown warrant. The lieutenant had made an excellent stick. Now it was time for the carrot.

'As you can see, there is a very generous bounty on the heads of these two killers. Now that the lieutenant has moved along the Circle, his share of the prize money belongs to *you*. The warrant states dead or alive, but my two hounds here prefer dead – which means less risk for all of us. I have lost some good friends to the hands of these two jiggers, so I will also waive my share of the prize. I want these two assassins eating worms by the end of the day.'

Now the redcoats were happier; they waved their rifles – cheap Brown Jane patterns from Middlesteel's mills – and gave him a half-hearted cheer. Most of them had probably done worse themselves in the rookeries and slums of whatever Jackelian city they had been arrested in – but they read well enough to understand the large sum of money printed on the warrant.

Wildrake passed Tariq a shirt that had come from the boy's room in Hundred Locks. The biologicks sniffed at it and stood trembling with anticipation, the taste of human flesh fresh in their mouths. They were used to hunting slaves across the arid ground of Cassarabia and there was always a good meal at the end of a chase.

Nodding at Tariq, Wildrake brandished his sabre in the air. 'Gentlemen, let the hunt begin.'

Chapter Twelve

Molly stared up at the tower. It was not as tall as one of Sun Gate's counting houses – perhaps only eight storeys – but the way it rose out of the tranquillity of the private garden dominating the topiary below gave it an extra sense of scale. An illuminated clock face crowned the square tower, two massive iron hands keeping time in a stately passage against the yellow light. Something Damson Darnay had once said to Molly back in the poorhouse jumped unbidden to mind. *Even a broken clock is right twice a day.*

'You have rooms here?' asked Molly.

Nickleby pointed his six-wheel horseless carriage into a coach house next door to the tower. 'Tock House is mine, or should I say ours.'

'You're a pensman,' said Molly. 'How in the name of the Circle is this tower yours? Who are you, the part of the Quatérshiftian royal family that didn't hang around for the revolution?'

Nickleby carefully nosed the head of the horseless carriage into a steel dock, then, jumping down, he lit a boiler in the corner of the coach house – the carriage's high tension clockwork whining as its drums were put under pressure by the steam-hissing mechanism, rewinding the engine for its next journey. 'No noble blood in my family's veins, Molly. Unless you consider the blood of poets and theatre players to be noble.'

Molly pointed up at the tower. 'A good opening night paid for that, did it?'

'I thought you were an aficionado of the pulp press, Molly? You must have missed the issues of the penny dreadfuls where my companions and myself found the wreckage of the *Peacock Herne* on the Isla Needless.'

'The King's airship, that was you?'

Nickleby gave a little bow. 'I was covering the expedition for *The Illustrated* – of course, we weren't looking for treasure; a safe passage across the Fire Sea was what the university had paid for.'

'I thought everyone on the expedition died of a curse,' said Molly.

'Tropical disease,' said Nickleby. 'And there were enough of us left alive for parliament to invoke the crown treasure trove laws on the contents of the *Peacock Herne*. But even after the House of Guardians got its snout in the trough, our share of the treasure was enough to pay for a few luxuries.' He lovingly patted the cab of the carriage.

They walked out of the coach house and into the evening air. Tending the lawn were a handful of small iron crabs, busy pulling weeds and cropping grass; Molly nearly tripped over one before she realized what it was. 'There's a steamman slip-thinker here?'

'I told you I lived with a couple of companions. Come on, they should be inside. Aliquot Coppertracks is the reason we survived the Isla Needless. They can die of boiler sickness and crystal rot, but thank the Circle that tropical fever has a hard time with steammen.'

192

Molly tried to pick up one of the metal crabs but the drone sidled out of her reach. Slipthinkers were rare outside of the Steammen Free State; minds so powerful they could diffuse their consciousness among multiple bodies. It was rumoured that even King Steam and his royal architects did not fully understand the detail of their layout, using scavenged plans from the Camlantean age in their construction. Those that did not slide into madness provided the metal race with their greatest shamen and philosophers. She had never even seen a slipthinker, let alone met one.

Inside the tower's hall they were greeted by a bear of a man – at first Molly thought he might be a retainer, but then she spotted the silver trident on his jacket as his voice boomed out. 'So you are back again, Silas Nickleby. And us not knowing if you were dead or trapped a thousand leagues under the earth.'

'It takes more than a pocket aerostat jaunt down to Grimhope to throw out my stars, commodore,' said the pensman. 'This is Molly Templar. She will be our house-guest for a while. Molly, this is Commodore Jared Black – it was his submersible that took us on the little trip I was telling you about.'

'Your stars indeed,' said the commodore, running a hand thoughtfully through his rambling saltpepper beard. 'Lucky for you, but not so lucky for my blessed boat – the poor wrecked *Sprite of the Lake* lying beached on the shores of that swamp at the end of the world.'

'Sunk by age,' whispered Nickleby to Molly. 'It leaked most of the trip. We were lucky we didn't end up roasting like beef on a spit underneath the Fire Sea.'

'Ah, Molly,' said the commodore. 'You are welcome to the hospitality of Tock House. Small recompense has its walls proved for a glorious life lived free on the oceans. Poor old

Blacky. Deprived of his beautiful craft and cheated out of the bulk of his fortune by the swindling bureaucrats of Jackals. Us stumbling around the jungle, half dead of the mortal tropical plague and the only piece of luck that's thrown our way by the Circle is stolen by grasping counting-house men from Greenhall. Let me take you to our kitchen, girl, and I will find us some paltry fare to commiserate the rule of thieves we suffer under while we swap the sad tales of our lives.'

'Time for that later, Jared,' said Nickleby to the submariner. 'I need a hand first with some boxes for Aliquot.'

Molly followed the odd pair back out to the coach house, where they began unloading crates of what looked like old newspapers from a compartment in the back of the horseless carriage. 'You going to burn those on your fire?'

The commodore's face was turning red with the effort of lifting out the heavy crates. 'Burn them, lass? Burn them on the fire of Aliquot Coppertracks' brilliance, perhaps.'

Hefting the crates back to Tock House, the two men loaded them into a dumb waiter, Nickleby pulling a cord to lift the boxes out of sight. Following the pair up a spiral staircase, Molly wished the current owners had gone to the expense of fitting Tock House with a dumb waiter for the building's guests. But, lack of a lifting room aside, the tower had obviously had money lavished on it. The walls were lined with panels of Haslingshire oak, the floors marble and polished starstone, oil-fired chandeliers augmenting the summer light spilling in through stained-glass windows. Rainbow-bright scenes of the King having his arms cut away against a backdrop of columns of soldiers wearing roundhead-style helmets dated the building as at least six hundred years old. Built perhaps by a merchant, bishop or parliamentarian who had been on the winning side of the civil war.

Near the top of the tower they found the crates of newspaper still stacked in the cupboard-sized dumb waiter. Molly helped the pair carry the crates along the carpeted passage to its end, where a door lay slightly ajar. Black kicked the door open with one of his sailor's boots and they lugged the boxes inside.

'More grist for the mill, Aliquot,' announced Nickleby.

They stood inside a hall containing the tower's clock mechanism, the glass of the massive clockface illuminating laboratory tables covered with machinery and chemical stills, smoking glass beakers and coiled tubes filled with bubbling green liquids. The faint smell of sulphur, though, was coming from one of the steammen in the room, a squat creature sitting on two burnished orange tracks, his head a large transparent crystal dome filled with forks of ionised blue energy which seemed to rotate around the inside of his clear skull. There were other smaller steammen in the room, thin iron things the size of ten-year-old children, all identical, with bottle-shaped heads containing a single telescope-like eye. They would be some of the slipthinker's mu-bodies, drones possessed by his intellect.

'And blessed heavy, too,' added the commodore. 'The tree that gave its life for these papers must have been mortal offended by the lumberman's axe. It's been trying to get poor old Black's heart to fail every step of the passage.'

'Newspapers?' said the tracked steamman. 'You have brought me newspapers? Why did you not say so? Place them on the table at once.' Its voicebox had a slight echo, making the steamman sound distracted. As soon as Nickleby and the commodore thumped the crates down, two of the small iron goblins were crawling over them, ripping out old news sheets, their telescope heads scanning the text at a breakneck pace.

Molly picked up a journal out of the box she had carried through. '*Field and Fern*?'

'Ah, lass,' said the commodore. 'Poor old Coppertracks is a slipthinker through and through. He needs new information to process in giant quantities or he starts to act as odd as a dancing hare in Damp-month. The paper is an anchor on his boat, the weight of it keeping that shiny mind of his from rising up out of sight like a village struck by a float-quake. But I don't begrudge him the fortune we spend on subscriptions, for without him, the pensman and me would be as dead as the rest of them on the Isla Needless. There's more cleverness in that fizzing old noggin of his than half the transaction engines in Greenhall.'

'A young softbody,' said Coppertracks, noticing Molly in the confusion of the laboratory for the first time. '*The* young softbody. I know you, yes I do.'

'I am sure I would have remembered meeting a slipthinker,' said Molly, giving a polite little curtsey.

'The memories of the fallen, dear mammal,' said Coppertracks, pointing to a table pushed against the crystal wall of the clockface. On the table was a steamman skull, long cables dangling from the metal like dreadlocks.

'The controller from the atmospheric!' said Molly.

'One of the people of the metal was guided to Redrust's corpse by the Steamo Loas,' said Coppertracks. 'The controller's killers had rolled his body into Old Mother Gambleflowers, hoping the waters of the river would wash over their dark deed, but at least I got to his body before some eel fisherman dredged up his cadaver and tried to sell his components on to a mechomancer.' Coppertracks pointed to the lifeless skull. 'Whatever torturer took him apart tried to erase his silicate boards with electromagnetic force, but they did a poor job of it. I have many partial memories, including Redrust throwing the cogs for you, Molly softbody.'

'He helped me escape to the undercity,' said Molly.

'A kindness which cost him his life,' said Coppertracks. 'Redrust was a powerful mystic, he could ride the Loas with great accuracy.'

'Molly was worried for two of her friends, Aliquot,' explained Nickleby. 'Two of the people of the metal who assisted her down in Grimhope.'

'Indeed, dear mammal,' said Coppertracks. 'I have already thrown the Gear-gi-ju wheels for Slowcogs and Silver Onestack, shed my own oil for the spirits. King Steam will want to receive word of their fate along with the soul board of the controller.'

'They were wounded when I left them,' said Molly. 'Seriously.'

'It is most perplexing,' said Coppertracks. 'The spirits always know when one of the people of the metal has joined them. Yet the cogs I threw could not give a clear answer as to their fate. It is as if they are alive but dead at the same time. That is not something I have ever encountered before. King Steam has more powerful mystics than I at court and I hope one of them will be able to receive a truer reading.'

Molly rubbed her eyes. 'Slowcogs, the controller, my friends at the workhouse, Onestack, everyone who has tried to help me has ended up getting hurt. They have all paid for me.'

'These are strange days, Molly softbody,' said Coppertracks, the lightning storm of his mind flaring up underneath his clear, egg-shaped skull. 'There is confusion in the spirit world – our ancestors and the Steamo Loas do not rest easy. And there are disturbances in the world of information, the subtle suggestion of the hand of forces the like of which we have not encountered before, now at work. You must hold to the knowledge that the controller read your part in this and judged it important enough to give his life to keep you safe.'

'Sweet mercy of the Circle, Aliquot Coppertracks,' said the commodore. 'Do not speak of such wicked things. Let's go down to the kitchen and crack open a bottle of jinn or two to whet our appetite for supper. Let's not talk of strange currents and disturbed spirits. Surely you did not drag our poor diseased bodies out of that hellish jungle just for the three of us to go plunging ourselves into danger back home in Jackals.'

'Molly didn't ask to have a Guardian's ransom placed on her head, Jared,' said Nickleby. 'Any more than the homes down on the docks asked to be firebombed by an aerostat; any more than the victims of the Pitt Hill Slayer asked to be picked up and murdered.'

The commodore scratched at his beard in despair. 'If only we had my blessed boat, we could head out to sea and submerge to safety. You'd have been protected on board the *Sprite of the Lake*, lass, and I could have shown you the wonders of the world's oceans on my darling boat. Steam beds off the Fire Sea, the sunken stone towers of old Lostangels, slipsharps schooling under the Straits of Quat. But her wreckage litters the beach of that cursed isle, while I rot away here in the decadent capital of ancient Jackals.'

Nickleby and the steamman seemed oblivious to the large submariner's inexhaustible well of self-pity. Coppertracks continued his work assembling a bank of strange-looking machinery while his drones devoured the crates of reading material.

The pensman turned by the door. 'Aliquot, I don't think that any of the mug-hunters know yet that young Damson Templar is our guest, but in case they do. . .'

'Mortal Circle,' wheezed the commodore, stumbling after Molly and Nickleby. 'Let us not be waking up that metal monster again. Let it rest safe in its slumber.'

'My dear mammal.' Coppertracks stopped his work and swivelled on one of his tracks. 'That *monster* is little more than an extra arm for me to plug into my body; it is a drone, a mu-body driven by my id . . . to all intents and purposes it *is* me.'

'Ah, Coppertracks,' pleaded the commodore, 'I know your vast intelligence pulls on different bodies like I do a pair of old boots, but that beast you keep in the basement is possessed. It is as wicked as a sand demon.'

'The Steamo Loas only rode it the once and they could have picked any of my bodies,' said Coppertracks. He turned to Nickleby. 'Fire up its boiler for me, Silas softbody. I shall stand sentry outside Tock House tonight.'

Two levels of chambers and junk rooms lay underneath the tower of Tock House. Molly and Nickleby navigated a narrow trail through piled curios and junk. There were globes of the world, many of the continents left a speculative solid yellow for the unknown, oil portraits of Guardians and guild officials, orreries of the twenty planets of the solar system, their celestial motion stilled by rusty clockwork; and more recent additions to the junk – piled daguerreotype prints taken by a real-box.

Unlike the staid upright family shots that graced the windows of fashionable real-box artists, these monochrome prints were of Middlesteel itself. Nagcross Bridge at sunrise, a few lonely milk carts setting out from their depot, the masts of wherries sailing the Gambleflowers rising like trees beyond. The massive bell house of Brute Julius rising out of the House of Guardians, ready to ring each afternoon as parliament began sitting. A child at Cradledon aerostat field, her face wide in wonder at the merchant marine airships poised in a long line down the horizon. Behind the daguerreotype images stood a real-box on its tripod, the sad nose of the lens pointed at the dusty flagstones.

Nickleby saw Molly looking at the card-mounted images. 'They are mine, Molly.'

'I haven't seen anything like them,' said Molly. 'You could make a living just selling them.'

'I did once,' said the pensman. 'As well as writing for *The Illustrated*, I used to take real-box pictures for the newspapers.'

'Used to? What happened?'

'A mixture of the personal and the practical, Molly. I ran out of images I wanted to capture, and then the illustrators' combination lobbied parliament to ban the use of daguerreotypes in printed publications. They said the images could be used in a bawdy and lewd manner and pointed to the sleazier end of Dock Street to make their point. These days the only place I could sell my real-box work would be to the underground press – Carlist flysheets, political pamphlets and issues of *Damsons' Relish*.'

Molly could tell there was something more that Nickleby was not telling her, but they were soon at the end of the chamber and into a second hall, this one filled with furniture and curios left by a previous owner; wooden mannequins wearing armour from foreign lands and earlier times.

Small wonder the present owners had hidden the figures out of sight; it was as if Molly and the pensman stood surrounded by a legion of spectres. There was plate armour from the old royalist army, spiked steel chest-pieces and beaked helmets with holes on either side for rubber gas-mask tubes long since rotted away. There were Cassarabian sand rider uniforms – brittle leather skins with more lace ties than a ball gown and head masks of thin metal gauze capable of filtering a hundred-mile-an-hour desert storm. There were quilted gutta-percha guardsmen jackets from Catosia, ridiculously oversized to accommodate the shine-swelled muscles of their pectorals and latissimus dorsi.

In between the animal skins of a couple of Liongeli tribesmen stood what Molly had first taken for powered duelling armour – towering above its companions – but as Nickleby approached it, Molly realized that there was no manikin underneath. This was one of Coppertracks' spare bodies, the steamman's dark alter ego that had sent the commodore scurrying for the comfort of the pantry. Nickleby slid a couple of bricks of compressed high-grade coke into the steamman's armoured furnace loader and flicked the ignition switch on the oil reservoir.

With a rattle of its iron arms the body started to wake. Four centaur-like legs began to piston the steamman higher, the creature turning its square head to scan them.

'Aliquot, can you hear me?' asked Nickleby.

'Yes,' answered the metal centaur. Filtered through the voicebox of this brute, Coppertracks' consciousness had none of the scholarly inflexions or distracted airs of the slipthinker Molly had met in the tower above. This was a killing machine and nothing else. Two manipulator arms flexed their metal fingers, while above, two long fighting arms – segmented javelins – swung in a testing arc.

'Upstairs, then,' said Nickleby.

'Patrol, guard, protect,' said the steamman.

'Sharparms is a poor conversationalist,' said Nickleby to Molly. 'King Steam would not offend the knights steammen by giving the slipthinkers mu-bodics with minds capable of strategy and war arts – it is Coppertracks' job to supply the brains.'

'Mister Black doesn't like him,' said Molly.

'Submariners are a superstitious lot,' said Nickleby. 'The commodore had a bit of a fright when one of the Loas possessed Sharparms on the Isla Needless. But whether being ridden by the spirits or not, you can rely on Coppertracks' bodies to keep us safe at Tock House.'

* * *

Molly's sleep was not made any easier by the lush depths of her mattress or the round goose-feather pillows scattered across the four-poster bed. Every time she started to fall asleep she woke up with a start, convinced someone was in the room with her. Now it was night she could hear the mechanism of the clock two storeys above, the slow processions of the hands, and every couple of minutes a thud and a clack interrupting the gargle of the tower's water and heating pipes. Cursing herself for a fool, she kicked the blanket off her body and dipped her feet down for her shoes.

There was a bathroom at the end of the corridor; perhaps a glass of water would settle her insomnia. She needed no lantern; the corridor was fitted with miniature chandelier clusters, pressure fed with slipsharp oil and ignited by a clockwork timer. The whole house seemed a faddish monument to machine-time, the clock tower imposing its artificial order on the passage of the day, splitting it neatly into minutes and hours – switching the lights on for darkness and dimming them for dawn.

Yawning, Molly turned and saw a figure at the end of the corridor – it looked like a child. But . . . someone familiar. Her heart turned cold. She *did* know her. She was the girl from Silver Onestack's visions, painted by the steamman across hundreds of canvas illustrations. Had the girl disappeared from Onestack's dreams when Molly fixed the steamman's broken vision plate? Was she looking for a new host to haunt?

A keening moan sounded and it took every ounce of courage Molly possessed not to break and flee screaming. The girl pointed out of the window into the night beyond – the moaning was coming from the garden, not the girl at all. A cough from one of the bedrooms distracted Molly for a second; someone else was waking up in the house. Molly glanced back. The apparition had vanished. Walking forward, she pressed her face against the cold glass, staring down onto the lawn.

Sharparms was standing sentry like a stone lion in front of Tock House, while stumbling across the grass was Nickleby. The pensman was the source of the animal-like cry, his arms raised in supplication to the heavens. In his right hand he held a crystal glass hookah, mumbleweed smoke rising from its mouth pipe like green mist into the cool night air. Following in his wake were two of Coppertracks' iron goblins, the drones trying to convince the journalist to return to the warmth of the house, dragging and clutching at his bed robes.

A hand rested itself on Molly's shoulder and she yelped, jumping back.

'Molly, it is only me,' said the commodore. 'So you've been woken up by the noise too.'

'What's going on down there? Silas is dancing around on the grass, half out of his mind by the looks of it.'

'Leaafed again. That's too bad, poor Silas. A little puff of the weed can settle a person down for the night and ward off bad dreams, but he smokes too blessed much, reaching for oblivion in the southern fashion.'

Nickleby had half collapsed on the grass and Coppertracks' diminutive servants were trying to prop him up, their bird-like iron feet trampling the liquid the hookah had spilled across the lawn. In his horseless carriage, on the pocket aerostat, Molly suddenly realized that the pensman had never seemed to be too far away from his mumbleweed pipe.

'Leaafed for a ha'penny, dead leaafed for two,' said Molly, repeating the old jinn-house adage.

'Ah, Molly,' said Black. 'You don't know what that man has seen. The horrors.'

'You mean the Pitt Street slayings?'

'Not them, lass, though I don't doubt that would turn a

203

person's stomach, those poor dead wretches – no, I mean his days in the war.'

'Against Quatérshift?' said Molly. 'He said he'd been in the navy, but flying an ink blotter – I thought he was writing propaganda for Greenhall or something.'

'He was in the sharp crew, Molly. All the clever-clever types from the eight great universities, the order, the military. Strategy, mind games and black sorcery. Silas was one of the best, a real-box master and a creative thinker. They were running some grand scams, so they were – cracking Commonshare codes with the great machines at Greenhall, writing forged letters to families back in Quatérshift from prisoners that had died at the front. Telling the shifties how well they were being treated in Jackals, what beasts the Committee's officers were – all the atrocities they were forced to commit. Silas was as good at faking daguerreotypes as he was at taking real-box pictures in the first place.

'The sharp crew would fake daguerreotypes of the First Committee throwing banquets with naked bawdy girls on the table as dessert, Dock Street would print them up, and then our aerostats would drop them on the front line. Imagine, lass, if you were a Carlist soldier stuck in the mud at Drinnais while you knew your family were half-starving back in the fields, then you got to see your leaders living high on the hog and pouring wine down each other's naked throats. There wasn't much fight left in the conscript regiments of their brigades by the time the sharp crew had their mortal fun with them.'

Out on the lawn Nickleby had fallen flat on the grass in front of the sphinx-like steamman sentry; Coppertracks' mubodies had no trouble loading his weeping form onto their shoulders and climbing the steps back to the house.

'You should hide his pipe,' said Molly.

'He needs it, lass, to blot out the memories of Reudox.'

'The city we bombed?'

'The city we dirt-gassed, Molly. The sharp crew sent Silas out to Reudox with his real-box. After the attack the airship crew went down in masks and lined up all the shiftie bodies, a nice long line of corpses. Not soldiers or mill workers mind, but the ones who would make for a good daguerreotype picture back on the front line. Children in committee-school uniforms, mothers, babies, and old men clinging onto grandmothers, a good long line of mortal innocents. And then the sharp crew took real-box pictures of them for a series of accordion-folded news sheets, the house number and street name where each body had been found printed underneath. We dropped those pictures of the corpses on top of the people's army and let them pass them to the soldiers who came from Reudox.'

Molly felt sick. 'We did that to the shifties?'

'After the navy dropped the pictures on all the main shiftie cities, the Commonshare folded. Despite all their purges, all their secret police, all their informers, the Carlists would have been fed into a Gideon's Collar if they had let any more of their cities be gassed. The shifties folded and clung to power and poor blessed Silas still tries to smoke away the faces of the dead babies at Reudox.'

'Have you seen any of them?' Molly asked. 'The children I mean. As spectres at Tock House?'

The commodore took a step back. 'Unquiet spirits, lass? Do not speak of such things. Tock House is big enough for us, but not for all the poor ghosts of Reudox. Haven't we suffered enough in this life without having to comfort the poor souls denied passage along the Circle?'

'You haven't seen a ghost in these corridors?'

'There may be ghosts here, lass, but they keep to themselves – and let us leave it at that. Come, Molly, let's help

Aliquot Coppertracks put Silas back to bed and then we will cure our unsettled rest with a warm glass of mulled wine and a slice or two of ham.'

Molly let the commodore lead her downstairs, but she felt a cold shiver as she stepped through the spot where the spectral girl had been standing. She had hoped Tock House was going to be a sanctuary from the people who wanted her dead, but with Silver Onestack's vision following her around and her self-professed protector a half-insane leaafer, the protection of *The Middlesteel Illustrated* and its staff was starting to look distinctly flimsy.

Chapter Thirteen

Oliver stared with horror at his right hand, the wrist swelling up like a black balloon, hair and muscles rippling, more like the limb of a bear now than anything human.

'I told you not to go near any of the ruins,' shouted Harry.

'I thought I heard someone calling,' said Oliver. 'Someone who needed help.'

The disreputable Stave brandished the witch-knife that Mother had gifted to Oliver. 'You're the one who needs help now, lad. Your arm has got to come off below the elbow before it infects your entire body. Mage-war, Oliver, the earth-flow particles are active in your bloodstream – you'll go into shock in three minutes unless I take it off.'

Oliver held the arm out, bubbles of flesh climbing up the limb as he watched. 'Do it now, before it gets to my shoulder.'

'Let's not,' said the Whisperer, 'and say we did anyway.'

Harry started in disgust at the deformed feybreed. 'Circle be jiggered, what the hell are you?'

'Real,' said the Whisperer, passing through the man. 'Which is more than I can say for you.'

Oliver was still yelling as his arm twisted and changed, but the dreamwalker reached out and held it, the limb returning to normal with his touch.

'You're losing your grip on your dreams,' said the Whisperer. 'Come on, Oliver, this is basic stuff.'

'Whisperer. Nathaniel, thank you.'

'Nathaniel is it now, Oliver? You've been charmed by our Lady of the Lights.'

'You were there,' said Oliver. 'Before she appeared to me.'

'She's pure, Oliver. Or perhaps I should say raw – fundamental – even when she's down here slumming with all the sentient bacteria on the skin of the world. Sharing a mind with her, well, I am like a moth trapped in the lantern room of a lighthouse.'

'Yes,' said Oliver. 'She's pure.'

'Snap out of it, boy,' spat the Whisperer. 'She's done a number on you, more than you know.'

'What do you mean, Nathaniel?'

'Nathaniel isn't my name,' hissed the Whisperer, rearing up. 'Nathaniel was a frightened boy who was turned over to the worldsingers by his own father for the price of a couple of jinn bottles. I have better names now – there are tribes of craynarbians in Liongeli who worship me as Ka'mentar, the dream snake. Even the Whisperer is better than that *stupid* hamblin name.'

'I don't care what you want to call yourself, Whisperer, it's all the same to me. What do you mean she's done a number on me?'

The Whisperer scratched at his back with an oddly jointed limb. 'Your memories, Oliver. Your early memories before you came to Hundred Locks to live with your uncle – they were always closed off to me. I thought it must have been some trauma keeping them buried, but it was *her*. Since her visit all the walls inside your mind have come down. I've been dipping into your mind, Oliver, and I've never seen anything like your memories before ... even steammen minds make more sense than that mess, and believe me, I am a connoisseur.'

Oliver felt the skin of his arm, he could feel the hairs, touch the veins; dreams with the Whisperer seemed so real, something about the creature's presence made the imaginings immensely vivid. 'I don't think you can understand their world on this side of the feymist curtain, you have to be there – live with the fast-time people to understand.'

'You know, Oliver, call me a natural pessimist if you will,' said the Whisperer. 'But I have a sneaking suspicion that when the Lady of the Lights was geeing you up to lead all the beautiful people into the sunset across the feymist veil, there was not much scope for the poor old troll to crawl out from under his bridge and join them.'

'I'm sure she didn't mean that,' said Oliver.

'Didn't she?' hissed the Whisperer. 'She is part of the rule-set, Oliver. When some Spencer Street trader complains about weights and measures, wags a finger at Greenhall and complains you can't buck the system, *she's* the system they're talking about. All that *if the angel had a hammer I would be the nail* nonsense. Right now, from where I'm standing, she's rolling about a barrel of slipsharp oil, waving a match and shouting 'fire, fire'. The Circle knows, Oliver, this turn of the wheel hasn't exactly been kind to me – but jigger me, I still like it here. I'm not about to trade life in Jackals for that bad mumbleweed hallucination you call a childhood on the other side of the feymist curtain.'

'We may not have a choice,' said Oliver. 'If our world is destroyed surely it's better some of us live on somewhere else?'

'We're not meant to live there,' insisted the Whisperer, raising a twisted arm with ears instead of fingers at the end of it. 'Just a whiff of that filthy mist does this to more of us than not, those it doesn't kill right off. Your children would not be human – you would not even qualify for membership after a decade more beyond the veil.'

'Life is life,' said Oliver. 'I won't let our people die out.'

'Our people?' hissed the Whisperer, laughing. 'Oh, Oliver, oh, our great saviour. What are you, old man Panquetzaliztli, being visited by the gods and told to dig a warm hall under the mountains before the coldtime sweeps the land? You might be willing to roll over and help stock the Lady of the Lights' menagerie of rare species, but I'm jiggered if I'll lift one of my fate-cursed fingers to help her. Jackals is my country and this world is my home; if the landlord wants to move me on, she'd better send more than some abstraction with a poor attention span and some twinkle-twinkle lights – you understand? She'd better come mob-handed and be ready for a real fight.'

'Nathaniel, Whisperer, you're not thinking.'

'I am thinking, Oliver,' said the Whisperer. 'I am just not trusting. You are waking up, boy. Best you reconsider who's really on your side and what you are prepared to do to win.'

'Whisperer,' called Oliver. But he was being pulled down a tunnel, back to a cold camp on the Angelset moors.

'What do you think, Oliver?' said Harry. 'Take the forest route or keep on over the bog?'

Oliver looked at the oak trees then glanced at the soggy ground of the hills. The shadows between the trees seemed darker than they should, and something about the shape of the trees was wrong. He couldn't put his finger on it, but they did not look like the pine woodland at the foot of Hundred Locks. 'The forest would give us cover. But I don't know, something about it makes my skin crawl.'

'Good instincts, old stick. The cursewall runs through the trees – the canopy of leaves masks its noise. We could be blundering through the forest one minute and dead the next.'

'How close are we to the Commonshare?'

Harry pointed to the east. 'Quatérshift is half a mile that way. The people's paradise, where everything belongs to everybody and no wicked lords trample the common folk of the land. And if you believe that, I'll tell you another.'

'You've been there before?'

'I preferred it before the revolution,' said Harry. 'Less po-faced. Last time I was there they used the words 'Jackelian spy' a lot and didn't seem to appreciate it when I pointed out that they still had a ruling class, it just called itself the First Committee. There's always an authority, Oliver, usually mustered by the ones with the sharpest blades and the fastest rate of fire. Trust me on that. From the perspective of someone who used to be a thief – there's always someone waiting to feel your collar. In Jackals they give you the boat or the drop – in Quatérshift they shove you inside a Gideon's Collar. You can slide a piece of paper between the difference to a poor old jack like me.'

Oliver shifted the weight of his backpack. 'I thought you said you were an entrepreneur.'

'Well, an entrepreneurial thief, perhaps. There I was at the heart of the Victualling Board, all the merchant lords making a fortune supplying the navy, all those cargoes and goods flowing across the land. I wouldn't have been human if I hadn't dipped my fingers in the honey pot a little – just to see what the taste was like, mind.'

Oliver shook his head. 'Must have tasted a lot like the rope at Bonegate.'

'Not my fault, Oliver. Some clever transaction engine worm at the treasury noticed a discrepancy in the books. You know

211

the funny thing, it wasn't even me! The quality that ran the board only had half the staff they were claiming wages for – the rest were phantoms on the books, drawing salaries that just seemed to disappear into thin air. Greenhall sent in truth-sayers, and the quality needed some meat to throw to the dogs to keep their own necks from being stretched. So they put Harry chops on the menu.'

'And my father helped you escape.'

'Wasn't so much an escape, Oliver, as a graduation. The wolftakers might as well rename Bonegate as their finishing school. Normally the Court of the Air just fakes a death in the cells – but there were too many navy jacks and Greenhall types waiting to see me dance the Bonegate jig for the crowds, so I went over the wall. Of course, I would have escaped on my own if push had come to shove. My neck's a little too precious to me to see it stretched for the sins of the penny dippers that sit on the Victualling Board.'

'But you were defrauding them,' said Oliver.

'Spoken like the true nephew of a merchant,' said Harry. 'It's the principle of the thing – you don't let another jack hang for a crime which you committed yourself. The lowest angler in the rookeries, the slipperiest highwayman on the Innverney Road would tell you the same – but that's one fashion that hasn't caught up with the quality yet.'

Oliver pushed on across the wet ground. 'I'm glad they didn't make you catch the drop, Harry.'

'Me too,' said the disreputable Stave, fingering his neck with a shiver. 'Now take the Commonshare over there. What a racket; I wish I'd thought of that one. I'd have got the rope for a few missing bales of aerostat canvas – but you travel a mile over the border and they stole the whole country and convinced everyone in the place to become an accomplice. Masterful. Bleeding masterful.'

They walked on, skirting the forest and then crossing the wet low hills that opened up before them. Oliver was wondering when they would pitch up for lunch when he stubbed his boot against an iron pipe, nearly tumbling over across the boggy ground. Angry with himself for not spotting the metal he gave it a kick. 'Looks like someone's chimney.'

'Not a chimney,' said Harry, pointing along the grass. 'That's a steamman stack.'

Oliver followed the sweep of the wolftaker's hand. Fragments of metal jutted out across the slopes – broken fingers clutching for the heavens, the horns of helmet-like heads, ancient iron bodies smashed open – home now only to frogs and nesting moorhens.

The place looked cold, hard and bleak. 'A graveyard?'

'Of sorts, Oliver. This was a battlefield. We've reached the Drammon Broads – further east is the mouth of the Steammen Free State. The cursewall swings around their territory too; the Commonshare doesn't trust Jackals' oldest ally.'

'Circle's turn, Harry, how many dead are there here?'

'Enough, Oliver. Marshal Adecole marched the Sixth Brigade of the People's Army through the mountains at the start of the Two-Year War. King Steam's knights broke the back of them down here. Most of the trenches have filled in now, but if you dug deep enough, you'd find the bones and rotting shakos of Quatérshift's elite troops – the pieces the foxes haven't dragged away.'

Perhaps the old battlefield had unsettled the disreputable Stave too, because he kept up his commentary like one of the tourist entertainers who haunted the foot of the waterways at Hundred Locks, filling the eerie silence with the life of his voice. The rotting spokes of light artillery wheels, the shattered glass of old cannon charges, rusting harpoons from Commonshare anti-steammen ordinance, lead balls from Free

State pressure repeaters – each picked out as landmarks on the gruesome wartime tour.

After the ranks of buried, mud-drowned corpses fell away, Oliver spotted a splash of red on the side of the hill – out of place, as if someone had spread a gaudy picnic blanket over the gloomy brown slopes. 'That looks fresh.'

'A bizarre enough sight out here, old stick,' agreed Harry. 'Let's take a closer peek.'

As they got nearer Oliver saw that the object was not as uniform as it first appeared. What he had taken for a solid crimson swathe was a patchwork of oblongs stitched together, mostly red, but some with stripes and yellow suns sewn on. They were flags, pieced together by wiry cord – river fisherman's netting by the look of it; the large wave of canvas lying crumpled over a mound.

'What is it, Harry?'

The wolftaker looked towards the east, his lips pursed. 'Let's go, lad.'

'What is it? It looks like flags.'

'You don't need to know – let's just keep going south.'

Oliver took the corner of the canvas and tipped it up. There was a blanket underneath, a huddle of sacks with . . . a field of fungus-like balloons growing out of them. This was a strange way to farm mushrooms. But then Oliver saw the lines of legs, arms, hands, a couple clutching tightly at each other. Dear Circle, that was a baby they were holding between them, its feet as tiny as a doll's – so small and grey he could not even see if it was a boy or a girl. Bile rose in Oliver's throat and before he knew what he was doing his breakfast was vomiting over the grass as he stumbled towards the family to see if any of them were alive.

Harry seized his arm. 'Don't touch them. You can't help them now.'

'They might be alive, they might be.'

'Oliver, no. They've been through the cursewall. Those things growing on them are from the hex – sometimes their hearts give out, sometimes they start sprouting plague spores, sometimes they might age a hundred years or have their blood turn to stone. They were dead the moment their balloon lost height and they blew through the wall.'

'They can't have had a balloon.' Oliver was crying. 'They don't have balloons in Quatérshift.'

'They don't have celgas, Oliver. They don't have aerostats. But take canvas, fire, hot air . . . you have a balloon. Not good enough to get them over the cursewall, but how were they to know? I doubt if there's many engineers left on their side of the wall now.'

Oliver couldn't take his eyes off the human wreckage – bodies that once laughed, cried, walked, lived, now just bags of flesh, no spark of what had made them human. How could it be? One moment something vital with hopes and dreams, the next nothing – compost for a hex-born toadstool.

Oliver sunk to his knees. 'I didn't know.'

'I wish you hadn't had to find out,' said the wolftaker.

'But you knew, Harry.'

'Most of the refugees come by water, Oliver. Can't run a cursewall under the water – over it, but not under it. And yes, I've seen this before. During the worst of the famine years the refugees even tried building a catapult to throw themselves over the wall. It would almost have been funny, if you hadn't seen how thin the bodies were that rained down on Jackals.'

Oliver's throat had dried up. 'Why?'

'Why?' said Harry. 'For the big idea, Oliver. Someone comes up with the big idea – could be religion, could be politics, could be the race you belong to, or your clan, or philosophy, or economics, or your sex or just how many bleeding guineas you got stashed in the counting house. Doesn't matter, because the big idea is always the same – wouldn't it be good if only *everyone* was the same as *me* – if only everyone else thought and acted and worshipped and looked like me, everything would become a paradise on earth.

'But people are too different, too diverse to fit into one way of acting or thinking or looking. And that's where the trouble starts. That's when they show up at your door to make the ones who don't fit vanish, when, frustrated by the lack of progress and your stupidity and plain wrongness at not appreciating the perfection of the big idea, they start trying to shave off the imperfections. Using knives and racks and axe-men and camps and Gideon's Collars. When you see a difference in a person and can find only wickedness in it – you and them – the *them* become fair game, not people anymore but obstacles to the greater good, and it's always open season on the *them*.'

Harry pointed at the bodies huddled in the wreckage. 'That's the true power of evil. You think the people that made those poor jacks' lives so unbearable the only choice that was left to them was to trust their fate to the wind and a bag of cloth; you think they think of themselves as wicked? In their own minds the rulers of the Commonshare are princes on white horses, Oliver, dispensing justice and largesse and making the world a better place. Even as they're tossing burning torches onto the thatched roofs of *them*, even as their boots stamp on the fingers of the children of *them*, in their daydreams the First Committee are heroes, beating down the obstacles to perfection one corpse at a time. Funny thing is, the litany of cant the victors chant over the bodies of the innocent might sound different for each big idea, but you know what, it always sounds like the same jiggering words to me.'

Harry threw the canvas back over the bodies in disgust, covering their empty shells. 'They used flags to make it. That's fitting. More flags in the Commonshare now than blankets.'

'I can still see them,' said Oliver.

'Yes you can. And you will for years. And next time you meet some holy jacks banging on about how the Circle will save you, ask them what their views on the next election are. And when you meet Carlists banging on about how the party will make you free, you ask them what their faith in spirit is. Because the big idea suffers no rival obsessions to confuse its hosts, no dissent, no deviation or heresy from its perfection. You want to know what these poor sods really died for, Oliver? They died for a closed mind too small to hold more than a single truth.'

The wolftaker took out the jug of slipsharp oil and sprinkled black pools of the thick liquid over the crumpled skin of the makeshift balloon. 'Time to burn the flags, I think.'

'I'm sorry,' said Oliver. To the family, to the moor-bitten wind, to no one in particular.

Harry stuck a match and threw it onto the canvas, flames leaping up and crackling across the fabric. 'One day you'll face a trial, Oliver. A difficult task that may seem impossible. A choice you can't confront. When that time comes, you remember these three here on this day. Remember all the details you're going to try so hard to forget. Then you'll know what you need to do.'

'Is that what you do, Harry?'

'Your father told me that, Oliver,' said the wolftaker. 'And he was right too. I've seen so many bodies for so many big ideas. Sometimes it's the only way you can make yourself go on.'

The fire reached across the length of the quilt. At the head of the hill the remaining mist of the day was spreading out towards the sky as smoke billowed and curled around the wreckage of the flimsy vessel. Oliver looked on in amazement. The mist was coalescing into a body. Were the ghosts of the poor dead family returning to visit their own pyre?

'Harry!'

'I see it,' said the wolftaker.

Slowly the mist took shape – a horned warrior in armour – no, not armour – the plate metal was its body . . . a steamman.

'Harry, what in the Circle's name?'

'Steamo Loa,' said Harry. 'One of their gods – an ancestral spirit.'

As they watched, the spectral figure pointed a mailed glove towards the south, its head slowly shaking in warning, then it turned to the east and pointed a hand in the direction of the distant mountains – the Steammen Free State. The meaning was clear.

'It doesn't want us to go to Shadowclock, Harry.'

'Jigger me sideways, now I really have seen everything. Unless there's a worldsinger behind that hill laughing himself silly; but why?'

In answer to the disreputable Stave's question a strange howl rent the air, like a human in pain screaming through the throat of a wolf.

'What was that sound, Harry?'

Harry looked at the mist above the hill – the shape of the steamman now shredding into ribbons in the sky. 'Nothing that should be this far north of the Cassarabian border. Run for the mountains, boy. Fast – NOW.'

Sprinting back through the graveyard of the battlefield, Oliver glanced behind them. Nothing. Just the wreckage of the Quatérshiftian refugees' escape attempt.

'Your blunderbuss,' Harry called across to Oliver. 'The gun, unstrap it and load up.'

Harry was pulling his long pistol out of his pack as he ran, breaking it and slipping in a charge. Oliver's bell-muzzled gun was jouncing along the side of his folded tent – strapped just the way the wolftaker had shown him. One pull of the fastening and the weapon was falling, its wooden handle in his right hand. Thumbing the release as he ran, he broke the gun in the middle so that the barrel was swinging towards the ground on its hinge. The crystal charge felt like ice in his hand, fingers fumbling to push it into the breach. It dropped in perfectly and the blunderbuss clacked shut with a gentle push from the heel of his palm.

Oliver scanned the landscape behind them. 'I can't hear the noise anymore.'

'Close,' puffed Harry. 'Hunting silent.'

Something hammered Oliver into the boggy mud, arcing past and barrelling into the wolftaker; rolling Harry to the ground, a mass of exposed pulsing muscles – as if the creature had allowed its skin and fur to be flayed from its body. Oliver got back to his feet. The creature's paws were smashing the ground and Harry was a blur, using his worldsinger tricks again, dodging the thing's claws even as it had him trapped.

Like the crack of snapping wood something pinged off the rocks to Oliver's right, showering his shoulder with flinty dust. Redcoats stood on the hills where Oliver and Harry had been heading before the spectre's warning, holding long spindly rifles with bayonets fixed on their barrels, barrels that were pointing towards him.

Harry was rolling in the mud with the hunting monster. Even if he had been a marksman, not an amateur with a sailor's boarding gun, Oliver couldn't let a shot off without hitting them both. There was a growl and Oliver looked up at the granite outcrop he had backed into just as the second beast leapt down on him. Oliver screamed as the hunter clawed into his left arm, the weight whamming him down to the watery soil, desperately shoving the blunderbuss into the monster's mouth. It was ripping the naval pattern out of his hand as he triggered the weapon, an explosion of buckshot and thunder ricocheting off the rock – most of it peppering the creature's flank, one of the lead pellets glancing across Oliver's cheek and tearing it open.

Oliver tried to scramble out from under the beast as its wounds momentarily distracted it, but it was too quick, the buckshot a mere inconvenience. Reaching out it cuffed Oliver in the back and sent him sprawling, then lunged forward, snarling. It sounded like it was talking, idiot words mangled by a lolling tongue and razor teeth. 'Eta flug, eta flug.'

Terrified, Oliver met its gaze – the eyes of a human girl, long lashes and blue irises buried in its skull plate looking back at him – angry, angry inhuman rage. Those beautiful eyes blinked in surprise as the ground beneath them disintegrated, boy and beast carried into the air as clods of mud rained down onto the earth. Floatquake or some desperate worldsinger magic called by Harry? But Oliver was tumbling off something, a rusting metal shell rising out of the soil, water pouring out of gashes and hollows.

The startled hunter had rolled off him, leaving Oliver's left arm a furnace of agony, and leapt into the metal sculpture rising out of the mud. It was a corpse, one of the knights steammen, only one battle arm still intact – a pike arm with a rusted brown blade. Metal and muscle joined in a fusion of combat, the panther-sized hunting beast lashing back and forth with its claws, tearing gashes in the zombie's already broken hull. For its part, the steamman corpse was twist-pumping its pike arm into the beast's dense stomach muscles. The only sign of the damage it was doing was the red gore slicking its blade.

The centaur-like steamman fell forward and scooped up the beast with its skeletal manipulator arms. Another corpse was rising from the ground, two-legged and hump-backed, like a jumping rat but with a long metal beak. Soundlessly the iron knight slammed the hunting beast down onto the second steamman corpse's beak, impaling the creature. It let out a reverberating howl so loud it seemed to rattle the heart inside Oliver's chest.

Hearing more human-sounding cries, Oliver looked around to see the redcoats in the distance retreating, falling back in a disciplined skirmish line, the crackle of their rifles breaking against metal bodies uncovering themselves from the hillside. Harry was pulling himself out from under the corpse of the second beast. A headless barrel-sized steamman had pinned the creature to the ground with its pincer-like tripod of legs and the wolftaker was sliding his hunting knife out from the thing's skull.

'There's a caliph across the border,' coughed Harry, 'who is going to be mighty jiggered that his prize hunting cats are feeding the worms in Jackals.'

Behind Oliver the shells of the two steammen who'd saved him were sinking back into the bog, one of the bodies weighted down by a tonne weight of dead meat. 'The Loas, Harry, they're riding the corpses.'

'Well, it'd be rude to turn down good advice freely given,' said Harry, looking at the iron zombies shambling after the company of redcoats. 'And by the looks of it, possibly quite dangerous to boot. Let's go and see what King Steam has to say.'

Harry looked at Oliver's arm, feeling it with the fingers of both his hands. Oliver yelled as the wolftaker applied pressure to the bleeding muscle. 'Make a bandage with your spare shirt. I'll tie a tourniquet above the fang marks. You're going to need to get that sewn and cleaned neater than I can do it.'

'What about Shadowclock, Harry?'

'Shadowclock will still be there after a visit to His Highness in Mechancia,' said Harry, testing the dead corpse of the hunting beast with his boot. It remained lifeless. 'So, who do we know who spends too much time in Cassarabia?'

'The Jackelian ambassador to Bladetenbul?'

'That was a rhetorical question,' replied Harry. He took out a telescope and extended it in the direction of the retreating redcoats. 'There's a white wagon back there, medical corps – plague wagon.' He grinned. 'Bloody plague wagon. That's *old*, Jamie. Let's hoof it boy, before my old chum and his tame womb mage throw any more of the caliph's pets our way.'

Oliver bent down for his blunderbuss. It was intact except for tooth marks on the butt. They left the bones of the hunting beasts to rot with the wreckage of the steammen and the broken divisions of the Commonshare.

Shortly after they had stopped for lunch, the boggy ground hardened up, the low rolling hills replaced by foothills, tall alpine woods and the start of a snow-capped mountain range. They must have crossed into the Free State – there were no mountains Oliver knew of this far east into Jackals. Most of the metal race's villages and cities were up in the crags; this low down the only signs of people were the dried donkey droppings from trading caravans. That and metal rods with long ribbons of a paper-thin cloth fluttering in the breeze, the rainbow colours marking the path deeper into the steammen kingdom.

Maybe it was the icy mountain winds blowing down through the peaks of the Mechancian Spine, but after another hour of walking, pushing towards the steammen capital, Oliver started to shiver. At first it was just a chill and he buttoned up the collar on his coat, but it spread, fingers of cold creeping down across his back. Harry noticed Oliver was falling behind and waited for him to catch up.

'It's like winter here in the mountains, Harry.'

'Winter? You're sweating, Oliver. Let me see your arm.'

Oliver was trembling uncontrollably now. It felt as if just the breeze from the heights was enough to waft him up the slopes, carry him like a leaf spinning into the realm of the steammen. 'I can't raise it, Harry. The bandage has made it heavy, like a block of ice. But it tingles below the shoulder.'

Harry said something, but his voice had faded, then the wolftaker grew very tall – or was it that he was standing over Oliver now? The ground felt firm, almost warm, just the right shape for his body. If he had realized how comfortable it was he would have stopped before. On the slopes the pine trees stood like sentries, tall and clear, parading for his pleasure. 'I've seen some interesting things, Harry. Since I've been free. It would have been boring to spend the rest of my days trapped in Hundred Locks.'

Harry was talking so softly now; he must have lost his voice. This was all very jolly. Oliver laughed. Then the blackness came and swirled him away into the dark.

In the ceiling above the Whisperer the lighting crystal grew brighter, throwing a line of reflections into the puddles of floodwater on the rock floor. So, one of the sorcerers was dropping the interlocking layers of cursewalls, peeling back the invisible barriers of his stone chamber. The black curtain covering the door went transparent. It was Shanks – even under the hex suit, dark, spined and shimmering with multiple worldsinger charms, the Whisperer recognized the current chief of jailers. He had two warders standing behind him with toxin clubs, and a purple-robed worldsinger. Unarmoured. Ah, so, it was *him*.

'Hello Nathaniel,' said the chief of jailers. 'On your feet – or what passes for them. You have a guest who wants to talk to you.'

'Shanks,' hissed the Whisperer. 'You want to come and visit me sometime without that suit? Let's see if those flowers you have tattooed on your face are worth their ink against my powers.'

Shanks turned to the unarmoured worldsinger. 'Careful, sir. He nearly escaped three years ago. He broke the hex on one of the warder's helmets and put her inside a waking dream, then convinced her it was her husband inside the cell and she had to unlock the cursewalls to save his life.'

'I trust the sigils on your suits have been revised since then,' said the worldsinger.

'Don't worry about me and Pullinger, Shanks,' said the Whisperer. 'We know each other from way back. You remember the last time we met, don't you Pullinger? You were an acolyte fey-hunter, listening to your master promise my father how comfortable my life was going to be under the order's protection. No more bad dreams for anyone in the village. No more angry fathers complaining that I'd convinced their daughters I was a blond-haired demigod with a physique like a Special Guardsman.' He laughed at the memory. 'Well, I was young. You use whatever advantages nature's given you.'

'You are no creature of nature, feybreed,' said Pullinger, his features distorted behind the cursewall. 'But you may be in a position to taste a little more freedom than you currently possess.'

'You have my attention,' said the Whisperer.

'Our seers have just returned from a town called Hundred Locks,' said Pullinger. 'Does the name mean anything to you?'

224

'Big dike wall up north – across the bay from the city-states and the Commonshare. My appreciation of Jackelian geography has been, well—' he indicated the walls of the chamber '—somewhat restricted.'

'How odd, then,' said Pullinger, 'that our seers detected the residue of manifestation there; fey manifestation, which they matched to the signature of one of our Hawklam Asylum residents. A continual and abiding presence was how they described it. Centred on a house recently filled with dead bodies – Seventy Star Hall. I suppose that name means nothing to you either?'

'That pollen you sniff,' spat the Whisperer. 'It makes you prone to hallucinations. Communing with the spirits of the earth, hugging trees, all very naturalistic.'

'I will make it simple for you,' said Pullinger. 'There's a boy who I believe you have made contact with across the spirit plane, a boy who now seems to be in league with a rogue worldsinger, self-taught, outside the order and a criminal. If you tell me where they are presently located, I will be able to get the asylum board to move you to a better cell. Real light, real food, a bed – maybe even moved to assistance duties – put your talents to state service and send you outside every now and then.'

'State service,' laughed the Whisperer. 'Hunting down my kind for the Department of Feymist, perhaps? You want answers, dance around an oak circle at night with your dullard friends and ask the trees where they are.'

'It would be better if you co-operated. For all of us.'

'Jigger you, flower-face,' hissed the Whisperer. 'Let me make it simple for *you*. I don't trust a word you or any of your purple-robed friends say. The last time I believed you, you motherless doxy, all it brought me was decades of rat-meat pie and a life-long problem with rising damp. I don't know anything about Hundred Locks or seers or anything that's been going on in the world since you jiggers shoved me down here. Now, are you going to send your pups in to try their luck or are you planning to talk me to death?'

'I told you,' said Shanks, thumping a toxin club into his armoured fist. 'He's as bad as they come. You're not going to get anything from this one by reasoning with it.'

'All right,' said Pullinger irritated. 'I will withdraw and you can try it your way. Your sigils will hold when I raise the cursewall behind you?'

The jailer nodded. 'Things have advanced a bit since you last worked with us, inspector. We only enter with suit hexes personalized to the prisoner's mist-cursed gifts. Give the creature long enough and it could work out a way to bypass them, but there are three of us and it'll have some other . . . distractions to focus on.'

Behind the cursewall the Whisperer raised his body to his full height and spat at the shield. 'Come on Shanks, you think I've got all day? It's been years since I've killed a warder.'

Pullinger had withdrawn down the corridor, raising another cursewall as he backed away. Shanks nodded to the two worldsinger warders and pointed his toxin club at the misshapen inhabitant of cell eight zero nine. 'You've some lumps coming, Nathaniel. Let's see if we can knock you into something a little more pleasing to the eye.'

The inner cursewall fell and the mayhem began.

Chapter Fourteen

Guardian Oswald station was crowded with government functionaries, civil servants and administrators in starched shirts and high collars banded by neckties – the spattering of colours and designs subtle indications of rank and role. Red for transaction engine men, the pyramid and eyes for the Department of Domestic Rule, silver wings for the administrators who worked for Admiralty House. While pushing through the bobbing throng of stove-pipe hats, Molly, the commodore and the steamman slipthinker had to navigate their way out of the atmospheric without getting their legs bruised by the workers' swinging canes.

Like a sea of dancing grasshopper legs the canes of the Greenhall functionaries jabbed and twisted, beating a brisk pattern on the tunnel passageways and concourses of the station. Busy, beat the rap. Important. Business to be done. Information to be processed, meetings to be chaired. Each cane also indicated its owner's political loyalties, the lines of the canes subtly modelled on the debating sticks used by the various wards and parties – from the tapered tips of the Roarers to the flat windmill-style staffs of the Heartlanders.

'Would you look at all the blessed scurrying rodents,' said Commodore Black. 'Nodding politely at each other. Good day to you, damson. Good day to you, sir. A good day every blessed day sitting in their comfortable warm offices, paid for by the robbing of honest fellows like me of the best share of my treasure. Was it any of their well-scrubbed necks that pitted their wits against the traps and creatures of the Isla Needless? Did any of these ink-stained devils have to carry half-dead bodies out of that terrible jungle, Aliquot Coppertracks? They did not, because they were too busy thinking of clever ways to carry away my wealth.'

'It was the crown's treasure, Jared,' said Coppertracks, his broad caterpillar tracks carefully rolling to avoid softbody boots. 'The state's treasure trove laws were legitimately applied.'

'The crown, is it? And how many of those gold bricks and trinkets did poor King Julius end up with, Aliquot Coppertracks? Him with no arms to count it and laid up in his deathbed. No, it was this dirty mob that sucked away my wealth – I must have fair paid for a thousand articled clerks for the next decade. Paid for them to sit around and think of ever more ingenious ways to steal the few crumbs of fortune they left poor Blacky with.'

'Careful, commodore,' whispered Molly, shocked by the man's royalist bent. 'There are parliamentarians here, democrats. You'll find yourself called out.'

'A duel, lass? Grass before breakfast. There's not an ink-soaked courtier in any corridor of Greenhall that can best old Blacky in a game of debating sticks or tickle-my-sabre. Let the black-hearted devils try me, I'll shake them by their wicked boots and see how many of my coins fall out of their thieving pockets.'

Coppertracks' crystal dome crackled in annoyance. 'My

contact here is doing us a favour, commodore softbody. Your thoughts on the rapacious nature of Jackals' bureaucracy would be better left unexpressed.'

Molly was starting to doubt the wisdom of Nickleby's sudden departure to the scene of the latest murder by the Pitt Hill Slayer. A Whineside alderwoman with every last drop of blood sucked out of her, left to swing from the rafters of her apartment in one of the residential towers leaning over the waters of the Gambleflowers. Not only had his diversion meant they had to travel by atmospheric, but the pensman's absence meant she was left alone between the miserable submariner and the detached steamman slipthinker. Molly laughed to herself. *Reduced* to travelling by the atmospheric. A couple of weeks' residence at Tock House, and what in her workhouse days would have been an expensive adventure had been downgraded to transport of last resort after the luxury of her host's horseless carriage.

Oh well, it was debatable whether anyone on Guardian Oswald station's concourse retained a good enough grasp of Jackelian commontongue to appreciate the commodore's royalist slurs. The bureaucrats of Greenhall were notorious for their use of the old pre-Chimecan tongue, Usglish – taking delight in drafting communiqués, minutes and documents in the dead language. Convening meetings where the great and the good could hold forth on matters of state using flowery verbs and tenses that had been brushed aside by thousands of years of history. While the civil servants claimed that Usglish allowed nuances of inflection and semantics that facilitated their work, the real reason was obviously to allow them to run rings around their masters in the House of Guardians – while obfuscating their obligations to the voting public.

Outside the atmospheric station the street was thronged with pedestrians while hansom cabs navigated through the crowds, bringing in senior civil servants across the waterways. Topping up the nearby waters of the Gambleflowers, the complex of palaces, towers and underground transaction halls were constantly supplied by ice barges. But even with the exertion of the cooling pipes, Molly could still feel the residual heat of the giant transaction engines – like walking into an oven. Through the heat-shimmer rising off the cobbled street Molly saw the tall bell tower-like structures running up through the engine steam. There were more than the seven spires from the seven verses of the old children's song now. Greenhall had more mother crystals than any other node on the crystalgrid, the invisible flow of information requiring legions of diminutive blue-skinned senders to process and shape it. Acres of punch cards to be fed into the banks of transaction engines each day, as much the engines' fuel as the coke that fed their boilers.

Molly started to head to one of the open gates where crowds of Jackelians were waiting with chits and half-completed forms – supplicants ready to be fed into the bureaucratic grinder – but Coppertracks clamped his iron fingers around her arm. 'No need to queue, Molly softbody. I have a contact on the inside – this way.'

Coppertracks rolled down Greenhall Avenue, past ranks of stalls serving the eels and dartfish that swarmed around the heat exchangers in the riverbank. The steamman slipthinker led them to a pub opposite one of Greenhall's staff gates, the Jingo Dancer, an engineman's tavern judging by all the sun-aged punch cards shoved behind the window – cheap binary humour and messages swapped between the patrons.

It might have been early morning but the pub was heaving with workers from the night shift. The fashion for cheap imported jinn had yet to catch up with the minions of Greenhall's Data Directorate. Trays of ale were hurried across to the dirt-fingered furnace hands, muscles taut from shovelling coke in the underground engine halls. Bar staff scurried around drum engineers whose beards were braided in the mechomancer fashion; the scene watched in leaaafed detachment by cardsharps sitting in leather chairs while they puffed mumbleweed pipes and chased abstractions in their minds.

The commodore groaned. 'Not him again, the blessed rat – and it's his advice we are to be trusting?'

A slim cardsharp with curly orange hair and a bald spot that had spread out into a monk-like tonsure beckoned them towards a sofa – hanging back from the commodore's reach, as if he suspected the large submariner was about to lay into him.

'This is the filly?' asked the cardsharp, looking Molly over. 'Looks like a Middlesteel girl through and through.'

'Keep your eyes to yourself, engine boy,' said Molly. 'And your hands.'

'Just taking an interest, love,' said the cardsharp. 'No need to take on airs. Coppertracks, you got what we agreed?'

Coppertracks' dome skull lit up the dark corner as he considered his answer. 'If you can arrange the access we require, Binchy softbody.'

'When's old Binchy ever let you down?' said the cardsharp. 'And it hasn't been easy, don't think it has. I've called in favours; lots of friends of friends will be looking the other way this morning.'

The commodore leant in close to the cardsharp. 'Good friends are these, Binchy? Like the same clever fellows who got their hands on my charts for the Fire Sea?'

Binchy flinched back. 'I told you, Jared. I bleeding told you. Those came from ordinance survey charts based on navy salvage from a wrecked empire boat. You think the God-Emperor knows anything about submarine navigation?'

'Just enough to get the *Sprite of the Lake* cooked and wrecked off the wicked shores of the Isla Needless.'

'You got back, didn't you, and a sight wealthier than when you left. You like the sea so bleeding much, Jared, you spend some of your pile on a new boat.'

'Don't act the blessed fool,' said the commodore. 'You know why that would be a bad idea.'

The cardsharp touched the side of his nose. 'A nod is as good as a wink, skipper. Wasn't it old Binchy that came through for you in that little matter as well? Now, given that Coppertracks is somewhat lacking in the old pockets department, I assume that it is you or the filly who is carrying my stuff?'

The commodore nodded and pulled out a thin parcel wrapped in brown paper from underneath his crimson waist-coat. Binchy caressed it, almost as if he was afraid to touch the parcel lest it disappear, then he carefully folded back the paper to reveal five punch cards, black with trim that shone silver in the tavern's gas light. Molly peered across to get a better look. The pinholes had left a tattoo of transaction engine code, tantalizing her. She wanted to run her fingers across the pattern, feel the information, hold the cards.

'This will work – or at least help?' asked Binchy.

'At least help,' said Coppertracks. 'I am a slipthinker, after all.'

'Yes,' said Binchy. 'Clever. Bleeding clever, you are Coppertracks. Your thoughts are all energy and light – mine are just clumsy meat. Like butcher's steak laid out on a slab.'

'Many vessels,' said Coppertracks – one of the steammen race's better known mottos.

'Many vessels,' Binchy sighed. 'Some better made than others. I'll leave now. You follow me in three minutes. Go through the gate opposite, no one will challenge you. I'll meet you inside.'

Molly watched as the press of workers in the pub absorbed the curly-haired weasel. 'He's willing to get dismissed from Greenhall for the price of a few engine cards?'

'Ah, lass, I doubt if old Binchy does much work in Greenhall,' said the commodore. 'He's burrowed in deep, like a tapeworm he is. They'll never turf him out.'

'The transaction engines inside Greenhall are massive, complex,' said Coppertracks. 'System upon system, added to over the ages. Primitive but powerful. The engine men that tend them understand the parts but no longer comprehend the whole, and like any sufficiently complex system, the engines develop parasites and diseases – information sickness. Binchy's wife worked here with him as a cardsharp, but she was infected by one of the parasites – an occupational hazard that the engine men risk.'

'Dear, blessed Becky,' said the commodore. 'A mortal shame, the poor girl lying in bed all day and night, babbling nonsense in binary.'

'Those cards are a cure?' said Molly.

'I fear not,' said Coppertracks. 'The ecosystem of a transaction engine is fixed, Molly softbody. I can cure such a sickness in the drums, boards and switches of a transaction engine, but once an information sickness has jumped across to one of your minds it evolves as fast as I can develop predator maths to remove it. Those cards will give Binchy softbody perhaps a day of lucidity with his life mate. Then she will be overcome by the parasite again, and return to her madness.'

They gave the cardsharp a couple of minutes' lead, then departed the Jingo Dancer and followed the clerks and bureaucrats in through the gate opposite. While the officials pushed small identity punch cards into a turnstile reader, a Greenhall whipper opened a small gate at the side for Molly, Coppertracks and the commodore. Surreptitiously the guard glanced about to make sure that nobody had noticed their passage through the staff entrance, then silently returned to his duties. Binchy had greased the right palms this time.

As was their wont, the mandarins and courtiers of Greenhall had not stinted on their accommodation; acres of interconnected marble floors branched out in front of the three visitors – storey after storey of higher levels rising off the expansive atrium. Greenhall worked with the House of Guardians as assiduously as they had served the kings that had preceded them. No doubt if the Carlists had their way and the boulevards were decorated with the corpses of democrats and merchant lords, the one unchanging constant at the heart of Jackals would be the bureaucrats in this palace of paper and administration. Molly did not doubt that the mandarins of Greenhall would diligently draw up the lists of notables to be fed into the Gideon's Collar if it meant they could keep safe their comfortable positions.

Binchy came out from behind a row of busts on tall granite plinths. He had with him a small handcart piled with forms tied with green ribbon. 'Molly, yes? You push this. Coppertracks you act flash with that head of yours. As for you, skipper—' Binchy tossed the commodore a cane. 'Just look permanently dissatisfied; that should come naturally enough to you. Anyone tries to talk to us, you scowl at them.'

Commodore Black examined the cane. 'A Roarer? I've never voted Roarer in my blessed life.'

'Maybe not, but you look like you could lay about you with that stick good and proper, so Roarer it is.'

The odd-looking party walked through a series of passages and chambers. Molly was amazed nobody challenged them. But then, these corridors did not seem home to any of the bustle she had seen at the mills, tanneries and laundries she had been hawked out to by the poor board at Sun Gate. None of the anxiety of meeting targets and piece-work quotas. The underlying fear that if you got sick, ill or fell behind, or if Jackals' economy entered one of its regular recessions, your cog-like position would prove infinitely exchangeable with other members of the desperate horde of Middlesteel's deserving poor. People walked the corridors of Greenhall as if they were taking a morning constitutional along the topiary gardens of Goldhair Park.

Molly's heart nearly stopped when a craynarbian passed them and nodded a greeting at them. 'Que seog ti nam engine?'

'Ho ton or mal,' replied Binchy.

'That old language,' said Commodore Black as the craynarbian disappeared down the hall. 'Must you lot in here always be blabbering on in it?'

'It has a certain elegance,' said Binchy, 'once you get used to it. Besides, it's the sorcerer's cloak.'

Molly looked at the man. 'Sorcerer's cloak?'

'Same reason that worldsingers wear their purple robes, Molly, same reason magistrates and doomsmen put on their wigs and powder, same reason engine men talk about taking transaction drums offsteam rather than just saying turn them off. Every trade likes to talk up their job with a little mystique and hide its doings with a lot of words that don't do much more than make what is very simple very complex.' Binchy nodded at another passing civil servant. 'Keeps wages up, makes what you do seem bleeding important, and stops your profession from being flooded by Johnny-come-lately types setting up shop in competition just down the street. As for you, Jared, you're a fine one to be lecturing me. You forgot the time you forced me along to the colonies on that iron bucket of yours, you and those salty coves of yours? Hard to port, hard to starboard, down inclination four degrees . . . or is that left, right, up and down? I never heard so much meaningless cant as when I was under the waves with you on the *Sprite of the Lake*.'

A set of sweeping stairs and ramps took them down to a smaller corridor lined in red Jackelian oak wood. There was a doorless lift waiting there, dozens of ivory button pulls indicating the depths to which Greenhall had encroached. Some of the lower floors probably shook when the atmospheric fired past.

'Department of Blood is on this level,' explained Binchy. 'Its transaction engines are down for emergency maintenance this morning – well, that's what the staff have been told anyway. Just some of my people there pretending to be busy.'

'An effective ruse, Binchy softbody,' said Coppertracks.

'Some of the medical people are pretty fair mechomancers in their own right, old steamer,' said Binchy. 'But anyone who knows enough to challenge us received an invitation from the university for a seminar running today on developments in blood cataloguing. You see—' he tapped the side of his head '—forward thinking. The mark of all geniuses.'

Cogs and calculation drums littered the floor of the chamber that Binchy directed them to. Engine men in brown leather aprons were climbing up into the room. Molly peered over the edge of the railed balcony where their ladder emerged. Bank after bank of house-sized transaction engines receded into the distance, some with calculation drums as wide as the jinn barrels in the Angel's Crust, hundreds of them revolving and clacking in the half-light. Engine boys sailed over the subterranean hall on pulleys, grease cans at the ready where bearings had started smoking.

Binchy pointed at the mechanisms and control drums on the floor. 'Hey, I need this bleeding working.'

'Keep your hair on, Bincher,' one of the engine men called back. 'These are the spare parts we pulled from the Bessy ninety-eight over at Prisons and Corrective – you told us to make it look offsteam. Hanging up an out of order sign wasn't going to do it, was it?'

Binchy winked at Coppertracks. 'Initiative, ain't it?' He went over to a panel overlooking the transaction engine pit and pulled a speaking tube out of its copper clip. 'This is the Department of Blood, room five, level one. Stoke up all the furnaces for us, we're going to be running live tests until lunch.'

Replacing the speaking tube on the wall, he walked over to a card puncher where a couple of the brown-aproned engine men were working.

'Bincher, you've got head of department access from here now,' said the taller of the two workers to Binchy. His companion pushed a bank of equipment mounted on rollers around behind their station; Molly prodded the machine – it was full of miniature gears and switches, but on the front facing them stood row after row of tiny square cubes – like an abacus with a thousand too many beads.

'Latest issue,' said the cardsharp, patting the contraption. 'Just coming in from the royal workshops at Exwater this summer.'

Molly rolled one of the square beads between her fingers – each side of the cube was alternating white and black. 'So, this is a substitute for a tape printer? The cubes can be rotated to make patterns – shapes, words, maybe even pictures.'

'Blimey,' exclaimed Binchy. 'You a subscriber to the *Journal of Philosophical Transactions* or something, girl? You can't have seen a Radnedge Rotator before. There's only four of them in all of Greenhall.'

'I've sat in the stalls at the theatre when they've been showing daguerreotype images of explorations and far-off lands,' said Molly. 'This looks like the same thing. But for transaction engines, naturally.'

'Naturally.' Binchy looked suspiciously at the girl. 'Listen, Molly, you get any more ideas like that *before* you see the gear, you come and see the Bincher. I'll introduce you to my friends up in the patent office.'

'Molly softbody seems to have an intuitive talent for such matters,' said Coppertracks.

Binchy looked with interest at Molly. 'Does she now?' He loaded a deck of blank cards into the station's punch machine. Its keyboard was as wide as the piano that Damson Darnay used to play for the children in the workhouse, but far more complex, numbers and alphabetical script supplemented by hundreds of keys painted with the symbolic logic language cardsharps ironically called Simple.

'Let's see what we can see,' said Binchy. 'Molly, you know your citizen number?'

Molly closed her eyes and reeled off the personal twenty-digit code that was drilled into each Jackelian child, Binchy's fingers dancing across the keyboard as she talked.

'Good memory, girl.'

'I had to give it to my employers too,' said Molly. 'I had a *lot* of them.'

'Can't settle to a trade? I was that way myself before my cousin got my engine man apprenticeship sorted.' Binchy passed the serrated card he had typed to Commodore Black. 'Skipper, can you do the honours, please?'

Commodore Black fed the card into the reader and pulled the loading lever. Down in the transaction engine pit the background noise of the rotating drums picked up into a symphony of tapping and cracking, like the sound of a whole forest of trees being snapped apart by a clumsy giant. 'Ah, Binchy. It's just like being back on the *Sprite of the Lake*. Navigating the Fire Sea blind with nothing but the maths of a roll of stolen charts to see us through.'

On the Radnedge Rotator thousands of beads started to flip and turn, revealing a string of pictograms across four columns. 'Not a lot of detail,' said Binchy, translating. 'Standard census gubbins, basically what the poorhouse needed to submit to claim its funding for you. Estimated date of birth, ward ownership claim, state approval of the same, personal details.' He glanced at Molly. 'Jigger me, you weren't joking were you. Is there a mill or workshop in Sun Gate that didn't try and take you on?'

Coppertracks scanned the lines of Simple. 'There is an anomaly in this record. It is my understanding there should be a softbody blood identification attached to the file?'

'There is,' said Binchy, tracing the pictograms. 'It's . . . Circle, it's gone. But it was in there once, look, the surrounding maths has been set up. If it had never been entered that part of the record would be blank.'

'But they took another blood sample from me only last year,' said Molly. 'Pre-registration for my voter franchise. Some cheap penny-cure surgeon – my arm bled for a week. Why would the sample not be in my records?'

Binchy whistled. 'Nora! If we were caught in here we'd get the boat for sure, but *this*, this is altering a record – a capital offence. Some card scythe has written an engine ripper to go into the system and monkey with your files, Molly.'

'That sounds blessed bad,' said Commodore Black.

'Cardsharps write them for excitement or for mischief,' said Binchy. 'Let's do a little nosing about. See if our friend has left a trail.' His fingers dashed across the keyboard, another punch card thumping out a few minutes later. It was loaded up and Binchy nervously tapped his fingers while he waited for the Rotator to catch up with the latest instruction set. New symbols began to flow down the engine bank, a column at a time.

'It looks like the deletion is a side-effect of an illegal search. The engine ripper had to slip in through the back door to escape being noticed by the engine control and it broke the record it was poking for. Someone was doing a hunt for certain blood types and yours was a match.'

'Blood, mortal blood,' said the commodore. 'It always comes back to that. The poor devils left on the streets by the Pitt Hill Slayer as empty husks, and now Nickleby has dragged us into his hare-brained quest for the truth as always. Poor Molly with a thirsty vampire on her trail and me just wanting a few miserable years of peace to enjoy what little life I have left.'

'Your theory may have some merit, Jared softbody,' said Coppertracks. 'Excuse me, if I may.' He rolled up to the keyboard and began to write a new card. Binchy watched with anticipation; the steamman's iron fingers were almost too large for the ivory keys. Molly guessed Coppertracks would normally have used one of his drone bodies for this sort of work – but bringing his entire retinue along to Greenhall would have attracted far too much attention.

Binchy removed the completed card and stared at the hundreds of fine holes Coppertracks had punched. 'Some sort of poke, yes?' He slid the card into the transaction engine's feeder.

'I would like to see how many other files share a similar anomaly to Molly's record,' said Coppertracks. 'This will cross-reference the null field maths and produce a table of matches.'

Symbols started raining down the rotator. Binchy traced the lines of pictograms with a finger, mouthing silently to himself as he translated the Simple. Next door to him, Coppertracks' mind danced with tendrils of energy as the steamman did the same.

The cardsharp's lips pursed and he slumped down on the station's chair. Coppertracks was silent in contemplation.

'What is it?' asked the commodore. 'Aliquot Coppertracks, what has your talent with these blessed thinking contraptions revealed? Don't be silent so, you're scaring the lass.'

'You bleeding tell her,' said Binchy. 'Please.'

'Come on,' Molly demanded. 'Have you found out who my parents are, old steamer?'

'Not that,' said Coppertracks. 'Dear mammal, something else links these records.' The steamman pointed to the rotator board. 'This is the missing blood field. And adjacent to it are the Ham Yard investigation summary notes. Molly softbody, there are over seventy names on this list, and everyone else whose record shares your anomaly has either been murdered or has been reported missing. I still don't know why you are being hunted, but whatever the reason may be, I think you are the last one left alive.'

Deep in the bowels of Greenhall's engine halls something that had been sleeping for over a year roused from its slumber. It checked its own integrity for signs of tampering and found no alterations. Then it moved through the switches and valves, tentatively searching for signs of other watchers. Nothing. So it had successfully remained hidden where it had burrowed in. True emotions were beyond the thing but it noted something akin to self-satisfaction. Not that the presence of the cardsharps' primitive sentinels worried it, those it could handle. It was the other things that moved through the wilds of the system it needed to avoid, breeding and replicating on old transaction engine drums which had been upgraded and replaced, but wisely never quite retired for fear of breaking chains of structure in the legacy systems. These things it feared. Nests of clever malevolent mathematics which would gladly consume it and make it part of their collective.

Now then. Something had tugged it back awake. One of the invisible threads it had spun, tripwires to warn it of possible discovery. One line in particular called out to it. Follow it back. See what was blundering about. Ah, the last active file was being accessed. So, only one left now. Its creator *had* been busy while it slept. A ripple of simulated amusement; it seemed the business of removing the targets had provoked a little curiosity in someone.

The query was good by Jackelian standards, but it still reeked of inelegance – long where it should have been short. Trace the operator function. A head of department – except the head of department had not been recorded entering Greenhall today. Well, it could hardly expect whoever was responsible for this to fly under their true colours, could it – so analyse the pattern signature of the instruction set, match for similar queries, cross-reference back to operator access, re-trace the operator function. An engine man on the payroll, a cardsharp. Copy the staff file, home address, good.

Now there was a second query under the same operator account, but this one had never been composed by a softbody mind, never in a thousand years. Not a line of wasted Simple in the search – elegant, beautiful, like the peal of a perfect bell. Briefly it regretted it could never meet the author of this punch card. A steamman, obviously; and a creature with some style about him too. What a waste it would be to have such an intelligence terminated. The steamman should have kept his olfactory array safely out of its creator's business. Too late for regrets now.

In one of Greenhall's many crystalgrid towers, a hand dipped lazily down into a deck tray and fished out the next card in the queue. It was easy duty, this tower only dealt with automated requests. Flour supplies at Fort Downdirt running low – restock now; automatically coded up by the transaction engines. No need to try and interpret some old woman's shakily written ink-stained birthday greetings to her son like the public station operators had to. Which was just as well for the man. Because if the card runner had translated the cryptic message on the punch card he was handling and tried to report it, his corpse would have been found drifting in the sewage of the Gambleflowers the next day.

Chapter Fifteen

Oliver was at the bottom of a sea. Sometimes he would rise towards the surface and the press of the depths would ease. He would be close enough to the light to hear the voices. A strident tone, someone complaining. *'I'm an architect – not a vet.'*

Then it was gone. At other times he would hear singing. Strange melodies, inhuman but perfect. Not words though. Some sort of code. Then he would sink again into a hall of perfect blackness. It was peaceful, timeless, until a white dot appeared at the end of the hall. It grew bigger, taking form – unpleasant form.

The Whisperer.

'Oliver,' it hissed. 'Can you hear me?'

'This isn't a dream,' said Oliver. 'I'm not dreaming.'

'Focus on me, Oliver. Stay with me, you're in a coma. Your body has nearly died twice in the last week.'

'I feel so light, Nathaniel, like I might float away.'

'You'll float away forever, boy. You've been poisoned. The two slave hunters from Cassarabia had some kind of toxin gland in their teeth – the architects think it originates from a poisonous eel.'

'Architects?'

'You're in the Steammen Free State, the mountains of Mechancia. King Steam's own surgeons are trying to save you.'

'That's nice,' said Oliver. 'Whisperer, you look sick yourself, thinner – those wounds on your side. . .?'

'My food's been off the last few days,' coughed the Whisperer. 'And I walked into a door; but you should see the door.'

Oliver lay down on the hall's infinite floor. 'Let's sleep then. Always better after sleep.'

'Don't sleep,' shouted the Whisperer. 'Oliver, stay with me. You sleep and you're not going to wake up. Your body isn't fighting off the infection well enough – the poison isn't fey, it isn't worldsinger magic, so your body doesn't care, the part of you that's from beyond the feymist curtain doesn't give a damn about a mundane infection.'

'I don't mind,' said Oliver. 'It's time for a rest.'

'Don't care was made to care,' said the Whisperer, grabbing Oliver's arm. 'Well jigger it, you're going to die anyway.'

Something leapt out of the Whisperer's body and into Oliver's arm, as if his limb was being dipped in acid. Screaming, Oliver tried to roll away.

'Does that get the old fey juices flowing, Oliver? Still want to sleep?'

Darkness everywhere, nowhere to run. Oliver tried to struggle free of the Whisperer's grasp, but the creature seized his ankle and another bolt of agony flared like a sun in his leg, muscles bursting and burning.

'This isn't biological, Oliver, just you and me, a little fey horse-play. The kind of japes that got me buried alive in Hawklam Asylum all those years ago.'

Scrambling for freedom, Oliver's body started convulsing,

daggers of pain thrusting in at him from all directions. 'Please! For the love of the Circle . . . the pain, you're killing me.'

'You and me both, Oliver,' the Whisperer laughed. 'In for a ha'penny in for a guinea. Let's see just how much excitement that perfectly formed man-suit you hide in can take, shall we?'

Sinews erupted, flesh smoking, the black hall breaking up as cracks of red pain ran up its ebony walls. Crimson silhouettes poured from Oliver's mouth, angry red traceries of demon-shapes vomiting out from his throat. They swarmed like hornets, twisting around and diving towards his fey assailant. The Whisperer swayed, falling back; part of his arm had vanished, boiling away into steam. 'Took long enough to bloody arrive, didn't you?'

Driving up like magma from a volcano, Oliver rode the pain, higher and higher, his hall of peace falling away as he was propelled into a room of white stone, his back arching, soaked in sweat.

Oliver lay panting on a slab-like table. White. In fact, everything seemed white, pure clean light pouring into the room from a glass ceiling. Snow-frosted mountains outside were the only sign he had not been expelled from hell and gobbed out into heaven. Coughing, Oliver clawed at the mask on his face – a yellow mist-like substance smoked out of it and it tasted like Damson Griggs's carrot broth.

His leg seemed heavy; glancing down, he found what looked like a massive spider sitting on his ankles – the unexpected sight of which made the half-delirious Oliver scream.

'Calm yourself,' said a voice. 'It's only a mu-body.'

A steamman came into view, light gleaming off his polished shell like a dozen star glints. 'You are in the hall of the architects, young softbody – I am what passes for an expert in comparative medicine.'

'This is Mechancia, then?'

'Indeed it is. Your friend carried you in,' said the steamman. 'Lucky to be activate, you are. Your body was infected by the bite of a creature warped by biomancy, your system juices poisoned at a very basic level; similar to crystal blight in my own people. I was in the process of developing a filter to clean your juices when your biology eventually rejected the poison on its own. This is not a capability I was aware your race possessed. Your traders bring me copies of the journals of your Royal Institute – but I have never read of such an advanced case of self-healing.'

Oliver remembered the Whisperer burning his body. He wiped away the sweat that was pouring down into his eyes. 'I had some help.'

The steamman tapped the drone sitting on his leg. 'Indeed you did. There is a test filter inserted in your ankle. I can leave it in – it will dissolve harmlessly in time – or this healer can remove it if you prefer to wait a day.'

'Leave it in,' said Oliver. 'I want to see Harry.'

'Your friend is meeting with the court,' said the architect. 'You must rest.'

Oliver tried to swing himself off the table, but he collapsed back, as weak as a newborn.

'We are at quite an altitude here. Apart from your system-juice poisoning, your softbody biology will require time to adapt to the thinness of air in the city.'

'Please, Architect. . .'

'Architect Goldhead,' said the steamman. 'My skills as a fastblood healer may have previously been limited to journal reading, but even I can see that you need recovery time and nourishment, young softbody. Please to lie down, or with a heavy boiler I will command my drones to bind you to the table.'

247

Oliver's stomach had set to rumbling at the mention of food. 'Nourishment would be very welcome, Architect Goldhead.'

'I have already alerted our embassy staff,' said the architect. 'They have much experience with preparing your food organics in the ways prescribed by fastbloods.'

Meals cooked by a race that could not taste? Well, judging by the sounds coming from his stomach he was not going to complain.

Oliver spent two more days in the surgery of the steamman architect. Not allowed visitors, the only company he kept was that of the voiceless spider-like medical mu-bodies and their master. Oliver would watch the architect's gleaming over-sized gold skull nodding silently in thought as he busied about the room.

He had plenty of time to contemplate the mountain vastness of Mechancia from the large clear windows in the surgery. The city's mist-shrouded buildings rose from the mountains like pearl coral, railing-protected paths twisting around the slopes, wide stairs carved out of stone. At night he could hear high winds rustling a thousand prayer flags, colourful streamers stroked by the wind as chimes made of steammen bones pealed and tinkled to the wind's rhythms.

During the day, Oliver would watch steammen children in their borrowed nursery bodies climb the stairs to open-walled platforms on the peaks opposite the hall of architects. There they would sit in ordered rows and sing in their bizarre machine code, ancient hymns to the Steamo Loas and their ancestors: Steelbhalah-Waldo, Sogbo-Pipes, Legba of the Valves.

Sitting in his bed in the hall Oliver saw things he had only dreamed of while a prisoner of his registration order at

Hundred Locks: processions of steammen mystics dancing and whirling at dusk, the fearsome gun-boxes – house-sized steammen carefully climbing the stair paths on two legs, massive cannons ready to repel any invaders foolish enough to assault this mountain fastness.

On the third day he was judged well enough by the king's surgeon to see Harry. Architect Goldhead led Oliver through the halls and onto a bodiless walking platform waiting outside – its stacks well adapted to the high altitude, leaving a thin ladder of smoke trailing in the cold air as it trotted Oliver and his minder through the steep streets of Mechancia. None of the mountain paths seemed crowded and the walking platform rarely had to sound its whistle, steammen stepping easily out of its way when they saw the transport coming. Mechancian society did not appear as mixed as that of a Jackelian city to Oliver's eyes, but they still passed the occasional craynarbian or Jackelian trader; coal men mostly, wrapped in warm fur coats with trains of mules spilling black coke dust from their heavy panniers. Their jogging transport had to squeeze through many of the narrow streets, white-washed buildings on either side rising as high as the walls of a canyon – red pagoda-style roofs elevated into the drifting ribbons of fog. Steammen at some of the windows waved as they passed.

'Is Harry close?' Oliver asked the architect.

'He is still at the palace,' replied the steamman.

It was freezing in the exposed walking platform and Oliver dug his hands into his fur coat's pockets. No wonder so much of the Steammen Free State's territory consisted of these mountains on the roof of the world – there were few other races in Jackals that would willingly abide in these craggy heights.

Their path broadened away from building-flanked streets, taking them out to a weighty suspension bridge crossing the air to Mechancia's royal citadel. An ivory river of fog flowed underneath the iron bridge. On the other side two shield-stone doors on rollers stood open, protected by a gun-box, its nose a stub-cannon dipped down to smell out threats. A row of steammen knights stood to attention in its shadow, metal centaurs with heads like barb-beaked hunting birds. They might as well have been statues, so still did they stand duty – only the flags on poles clipped to their backs crack-ling and moving in the breeze. Its passage already approved, the walking platform jounced through the opening and into the citadel.

Oliver stared at the large open halls they passed, full of kneeling steammen singing the same machine noise hymns he had heard while he drifted in and out of his fever-wracked consciousness.

'They sing in praise of our ancestors,' announced Architect Goldhead, following the direction of Oliver's gaze. 'It pleases the spirits to hear their achievements and lives honoured by the people. Are not all of our achievements built upon the shoulders of those who have preceded us in the world?'

Oliver remembered the corpses of steammen knights rising out of the mud in Jackals. 'I believe I might owe them a vote of thanks myself.'

'Yes indeed, Oliver softbody. The capital has been abuzz with word of what happened to you and your companion on the border. The last time the Loas intervened in the affairs of fastbloods so directly was . . . well, a very long time ago. I fear it augurs difficult times ahead.'

The words of the Lady of the Lights drifted back to Oliver. *We are fast moving beyond the point where a little extra wattle and daub around the edges is going to keep the roof from leaking.* Oliver said nothing. Did a warm room in Seventy Star Hall and his quiet lonely life of reading books really seem so bad now? Surely boredom was better than having the weight of the world dropped down on his shoulders?

Their walking platform came to a halt by a pair of tall red columns and the architect stepped off the steamman transport – beckoning Oliver to follow him. Beyond the columns was a chilly open hall, its floor a soft golden wood – surely precious material in these harsh rocky climes.

'Your companion and Master Saw are to give a demonstration,' whispered Architect Goldhead, his voicebox at its lowest volume. 'A display of the fighting arts.'

In the middle of the hall stood the disreputable Stave, facing a three-legged steamman with dozens of skeletal arms, many tipped with blades, maces and bludgeons – wrapped in cloth for the sparring match. Young steammen in nursery bodies sat silently at the other end of the hall, curiously waiting to see how this soft-looking animal would match up to one of their own race.

'Master Saw is the Knight Marshal of the Orders Militant,' said the architect. 'To spar with him is a great thing – your friend must have impressed Master Saw at his meetings with the court.'

'Or annoyed him,' said Oliver. 'He probably stole King Steam's crown.'

Architect Goldhead seemed shocked by the suggestion. 'Surely not. It has been whispered that your friend is a worldsinger, that he can fight in witch-time.'

'Watch and see,' said Oliver.

Master Saw tipped his needle-nosed head towards Harry and the wolftaker gave a small bow back. What followed was almost too fast to watch – both man and steamman speeding into a single blur of spinning fury, blows striking out, blocked and returned in a dance fought at a tempo at the edge of human comprehension. The metal soldier fought in a frenetic windmill style, his weapon limbs arcs of destruction. Harry seemed to be using his animal suppleness to bob, kick and punch, giving ground when the steamman advanced – yet hardly seeming to retreat an inch – circling and flowing around the soldier.

After a minute of watching the bout it seemed hardly to be a combat at all – the two contestants so synchronised in their forms it was more like a piece of choreographed dance; more art than violence. Mesmerised by the display, when the peal of a bell sounded, Oliver jolted upright. It was the end of the bout. The young man would have been hard pressed to say afterwards if it had lasted two minutes or thirty. Harry was sweating so much he looked like he had been swimming when he bowed to the steamman, while steam was rising off Master Saw's overworked boiler which glowed red with the additional energy he had been consuming.

Master Saw dipped his helmet-like head. 'The form of water; a good choice when fighting metal.'

'So I was taught, knight marshal. Although fire beats water.'

Master Saw raised his bandaged weapon limbs. 'Even the knights steammen do not use flame weapons in a sparring match.'

Harry Stave spotted Oliver and walked over to where he was standing. 'Lad! You had us bleeding worried for a while. They only let me see you the once and you were in a right old state.'

'It seems your lack of faith in our ability to heal your friend was unfounded,' said Architect Goldhead.

Harry glared at the metal creature and led Oliver to the side of the hall where they could not be overheard. 'I found a human doctor who works on the traders hurt on the mountain paths, landslides and falls, but he was a leaafer – struck off back home without a doubt. I figured you would have a better chance with shiny skull and his friends, once I convinced them you didn't want metal limbs.'

'I'm okay now, Harry.'

'Good lad. I'd rather not have to face your father when I move forward on the Circle and explain to him why I let his son die on the lam with old Harry.'

'Why are we here, Harry? What does King Steam want?'

'Something has got this lot spooked,' said Harry. 'They're hiding it, but not well enough for it to escape notice. I don't doubt their merry monarch knows what's going on. I've seen various officials of the court like old master knife-arms over there, but not King Steam. He's a slipthinker, Oliver. He can move between bodies, control hundreds of them at the same time if he has a care to. I think he's been playing games with me. Steammen keep on coming over to me and striking up conversations – cooks and soldiers and the like. But it's as if they are continuing the same chat. I reckon some of them have been His Majesty.'

Oliver glanced around the hall. So, the king could be any of the steammen; maybe even a couple of them at the same time, watching from different viewpoints.

'I don't think they mean us harm. Not right away at least,' added Harry. 'Otherwise they could have left us back at the border to the mercy of the redcoats and the slave hunters.'

'Can we trust them, Harry?'

'They are Jackals' oldest ally. I don't pretend to understand how their minds work, but until they give us reason to suspect otherwise, I reckon it's safe to give them the benefit of the doubt.'

A courtier approached the pair, rolling forward on a single drum-like wheel. 'Your presence is required by King Steam.'

'About time,' said Harry. 'I've been kicking my heels in your palace for a week.'

'Not you, Harry softbody,' said the courtier. 'It is the other mammal whose presence is required.'

'You are bleeding having a laugh, aren't you?' Harry protested.

'I have my orders and they are quite explicit. I am sure no snub is intended.'

'And I am sure none is taken,' spat Harry. 'Go lad, but watch yourself. King Steam was sitting on his throne when Isambard Kirkhill was pushing our monarch off his; the old steamer is as sly as a box of monkeys.'

Oliver followed the courtier deeper into the royal citadel. The steamman moved at a slow, stately pace, perhaps hoping those they passed would notice his position in the direct service of the monarch. Together they reached their destination. Oliver felt the chill as he entered the new hall; looking up he saw there was no roof. They were standing on a flat bluff carved into the side of the mountain. In the middle of the floor sat a small figure. Shorter than a grasper, it might have been an iron toy, unremarkable except for a more noticeable likeness to humanity than most of the steammen Oliver had seen. Was this King Steam, or was the guiding mind of the metal race trying the same kind of mind games that the wolftaker thought were being played against him?

'King Steam?' said Oliver. 'That is to say, Your Majesty?'

The golden cross-legged figure gave the barest nod of its head. 'Sit, Oliver softbody.'

With no chairs, Oliver followed King Steam's lead and sat opposite him, like a child waiting for school assembly to start – although the steamman did not look like he was about to read a fable from the Circlist book.

'You are not too cold out here, I trust?' asked King Steam. His lips actually *moved* when he spoke – no voicebox.

'I am fine at the moment – Your Highness.'

254

'I like to sit and watch the na-hawks wheel over the mountains,' said King Steam. 'Do you think there is any truth to be revealed in their flight?'

'The truth that comes with a clear mind, perhaps, Your Highness.'

The King nodded. 'Spoken as one, I think, who has done much sitting and staring – as an outsider.'

'It was something of a hobby of mine up until a few months ago,' said Oliver. Had so little time really passed since his old life ended and this new one began?

'You seemed surprised to see me in this body when you entered the hall.'

'I had imagined you – I don't know, as a mountain of machinery, colossal, billowing smoke with thousands of mu-bodies attending your components – all of them you,' said Oliver.

'I have worn many bodies,' said King Steam, 'and been both less and more than you currently see. But I have never, I think, been a mountain. What you have in mind would certainly be impressive to those not of my people. Perhaps we might pile up some old junk to resemble such a thing, and I could hide behind a curtain with a voice amplifier. I would enjoy frightening your ambassador, next time she visits. I fear my own people might laugh, though. For us, less is often more. We prefer great power to come in inconspicuous packages.' He looked meaningfully at Oliver.

'I am not sure I have any great powers, Your Majesty.'

'Please, no modesty,' said King Steam. 'You know the reason I am fond of this body? It was one of my first. It is from an older age, ancient enough to shock your university historians if they had the means to date it. I have seen ages of ice, I have seen ages of fire. I have seen the continents change and change again. I have seen the very laws of physics evolve through phase-transformations – and outside of a few satin-swaddled leaaf users in Cassarabia, I am probably the only creature in the world to see an Observer walking the soil of Jackals and think, oh no, here we go again.'

Oliver looked away.

'Yes, Oliver softbody. I know about the Lady of the Lights. And a few things besides. Steelbhalah-Waldo races through the night like a frightened rabbit, the spirits of Gear-gi-ju tremble and only dare to walk the halls of our ancestors in pairs. And into all this comes a young softbody, with a gentle shove from the universe mother. Curious, do you not think?'

'Curious isn't the word. I wish it wasn't *me*,' said Oliver.

'A perfectly natural reaction,' said King Steam. 'But it is you. To exist, every equal must have an opposite. A smile is nothing without a tear, a pleasure is nothing without a pain. Where there is life there is anti-life. We are threatened Oliver softbody, and you are what we have – well, half of what we have, perhaps.'

'Half?' said Oliver.

'Light and shadow, Oliver softbody. Male and female. Take it from me; it is always best to have some redundancy in the system. You are the scheme of defence – the scheme of offence is somewhere else in Jackals. The Observers are normally subtle . . . but predictable.'

Oliver breathed an uncertain sigh of relief. 'I'm not alone then?'

'Never that, Oliver,' said King Steam. 'Although given your previous life of internal exile inside Jackals I can see why you would feel that way. I am with you, not least because in this matter, we sink or swim together. I just wish I knew *what* you are. I would feel more comfortable. . .'

'I am not sure. You should talk to my friend Harry. He may have more of an idea than he is letting on.'

'You may be right,' said King Steam, his lips moving into an approximation of a smile. 'But I do not trust your friend. Nothing personal, but my country is perhaps unique in being the only state on the continent that does not have a secret police. His colleagues floating in the sky, counting our gun-boxes and planning their perfect society, they make me nervous. They style themselves as shepherds, protecting the flock and slaying wolves. But the life-system needs wolves too, Oliver softbody. Wolves are agents of change, agents of evolution. Change is the only constant we can count on.'

'As one of the sheep he has been protecting, I think I might disagree with you,' said Oliver.

'Well now. Your friend has been – what is the term they use? *Disavowed*. So is he a wolf, or is he a wolftaker? We have been giving him the benefit of the doubt. And I won't say it has not been amusing tweaking his nose while he has been in the capital.'

'I trust him,' said Oliver.

'Trust,' said King Steam. 'The trust of youth. Well, it is only young blood that can survive being changed by the feymist. I am sure the Observer knows what she is doing.'

'Can your people survive?' asked Oliver. 'Beyond the feymist curtain?'

'Not in any form recognizable as that which presently makes us what we are,' said King Steam. 'Much the same as for your kind, Oliver softbody. But we have other . . . avenues of flight open to us, if it comes to it.'

'I'm sorry,' said Oliver.

'Not on my account,' said King Steam. 'I have lived too long and seen too much. But *you* must not let it end. It is a heavy burden to carry, young fastblood, and I only wish I could help you shoulder it – but wishing will not make it so. The darkness of the Wildcaotyl is about to fall. Darkness so perfect and complete it will sweep away everything that supports your people and mine. At any cost, at any price, we must fight it.'

'You said I was the scheme of defence,' said Oliver. 'The scheme of offence. . .?'

'There is an ancient piece of battlefield lore,' said King Steam. 'Sometimes the best defence is a good offence. Your counterpart fares badly. Your presence on the board is still a secret, which is a benefit that is not afforded to the scheme of offence. I could buy Jackals with the price on her head; in fact, I fear that is rather what the servants of the Wildcaotyl intend.'

'Can't you help her?'

'I am afraid I have only just become aware of your counterpart's existence,' said King Steam. 'And frankly, things are not looking good for her. Which reminds, me, it is time.'

On the other side of the hall a door slid open and a large tracked steamman emerged – a glowing crystal crown topping its compound-eyed skull. The small child-like body went silent and Oliver realized that King Steam's focus had shifted to this new body. Two spheres on the steamman's neck vibrated as it boomed: 'More appropriate to the dignity of my role, Oliver softbody?'

'Indeed, Your Majesty.'

A spear of steam hissed into the chilly air from the king's stacks. 'Jump on the front then, young fastblood. I have a function to attend and a council to call.'

'Are you sure Your Majesty?' asked Oliver. 'You wish to have me riding you like the children used to ride old Rustpivot back home?'

'Rustpivot is still working at Hundred Locks? Ha, the old steamer. Oliver softbody, I am quite certain my courtiers will be scandalized. Which is precisely the point.'

Oliver climbed on King Steam's prow and the monarch's tracks rumbled forward, out of the hall and down a spiral ramp hewn out of stone. At the bottom of the ramp two centaur-like steammen knights flanked the monarch and they all thundered through the passages of the mountain, the din of metal hooves resounding down the palace walls. They slowed briefly to cross a busy corridor and a couple of steammen – each with single telescope-like eyes – jumped on the rear of the king's body. For a moment Oliver thought they might be being disrespectful – bumming a lift from the monarch. But then he realized they were attendants, part of the ruler's own slipthinker intelligence.

At the end of the corridor they burst into the throne room and a steamman retainer banged a crystal staff on the polished marble floor. 'His Highness King Steam, protector of the Free State, monarch of the true people, guardian of. . .'

'Enough!' boomed King Steam. 'We are here to honour the fallen, not list the latest titles my courtiers have dreamt up this week. Let the soulkeepers advance.'

The assembly of steammen in the throne room parted – near the front of the crowd Oliver saw Harry standing next to his opponent from the training bout, Master Saw. Out of the cleared passage came a line of skeletal steammen on tripod legs, bearing a sheet littered with the body components of one of the metal creatures. The only recognizable part was a steamman skull, corded cables dangling like dreadlocks from its scalp. The head of the skeletal funeral bearers advanced in front of King Steam.

'Do you bear one of the people?' asked the King.

'We do.'

'Can you commend his name to the people?'

'The controller gave his life for the people,' intoned the

steamman soulkeeper. 'We praise Redrust's true name to Steelbhalah-Waldo.'

The funeral bearers sang in their strange machine voices, a binary hymn that echoed around the throne room. This was the only time the steamman's true name could be revealed to anyone other than the king. During his death rites.

As the metallic chanting died away King Steam swivelled to face the courtiers and citadel officials. 'What are left of our brother's memories have been shared, what are left of his precious components have been dispatched to the chamber of birth. His place of falling is unknown to us, so let his deactivate shell stay not buried, but pass into the furnace of Mount Pistonfuda. Who keeps his soul boards?'

One of the funeral bearers stepped forward holding two crystal panels aloft on a purple cushion. 'I hold his soul.'

'Hold it well,' boomed King Steam, 'when you carry it though the halls of the dead.'

At the end of the throne room a wall began to rise into the ceiling, revealing an open cavern, millions of rows of crystal boards plugged into slots in the cavern face – mile upon mile of steammen dead lit by flickering red arc lights.

'Perhaps there was a little truth to your imaginings of my mountainous form after all,' one of King Steam's mu-bodies whispered to Oliver.

In front of them the steamman funeral bearer began to convulse, his tripod legs shaking and trembling; then the creature stopped, his bearing changing. He seemed to swell and become more erect than the design of his form allowed.

'Which Loa rides this body?' the king demanded.

'Krabinay-Pipes,' cackled the funeral bearer, and seizing the contents of the cushion he took the soul boards and disappeared scampering into the half-light of the steammen hall of the dead.

'Krabinay-Pipes is a crafty fellow,' said King Steam to Oliver. 'But he will find the controller his resting circuit in the hall. Now, where is the voice of Gear-gi-ju?'

A copper-plated steamman emerged from behind a pillar, dipping his skull in a bow. 'Your Majesty.'

'What say you on the matter of our two softbody visitors?'

'We have been casting the cogs for days, Your Majesty. Hundred of seers until we grow faint from lack of oil and the Loas grow irritated from our questioning.'

'As diligent as ever,' said King Steam. 'But in the matter of the old foe, how have the cogs landed?'

'We cannot protect either of the two softbodies after they leave Mechancia,' said the mystic. 'They are safe as long as they remain in the capital. Once they leave, we may take no further part in their immediate affairs. Salvation rests in the young fastblood's power alone, not ours.'

A sinking feeling hit Oliver. No help from Jackals' oldest ally?

'There is more though,' said King Steam. 'Something else. I can sense it behind your words.'

'*One* of the people may offer assistance to these two soft-bodies. One alone.'

'Name him,' ordered the king.

'By your command, Majesty. His name is Steamswipe.'

A gasp of disbelief swept the press of steammen in the throne room. Master Saw stepped forward from the ranks of centaur-like fighters. 'This cannot be, the council of seers is surely mistaken?'

'There is no mistake,' said the mystic. 'Much as we would otherwise, try as we might to find an alternative answer, the cogs only reply with a single name.'

'He is deactivate, he is disgraced,' said Master Saw. 'If it is to be just one, let me go – or one of my knights.'

'It is to be Steamswipe,' said the Gear-gi-ju reader. 'The cogs have spoken.'

The King waved his hand and Master Saw stepped back.

'He would not have been my first choice for a champion,' said one of the King's mu-bodies. Oliver started. The King's ability to inhabit multiple bodies and engage in simultaneous conversation was disconcerting. 'Or even have featured at the bottom of the list.'

Oliver frowned. 'But that steamman said he was deactivate. How can he be dead and help us?'

'The word has many connotations for the people of the metal. Steamswipe's soul boards have not been returned to the ancestors. He sleeps, his higher mental functions held in suspension, as punishment for his crimes.'

Oliver's frown deepened. What kind of defective creature was the King trying to foist on them?

'It was a crime of honour,' said the King's drone, noting Oliver's expression. 'He violated the code steamo of our knights. Cowardice. Steamswipe was one of seven knights we dispatched into the jungles of Liongeli on a vital undertaking for the people. His nerve broke and he abandoned his brothers to die there, choosing to save his own oil at the expense of his duty, his mission and the lives of his fellow warriors.'

'Just the steamman I want watching my own back when things get difficult,' said Oliver.

'The Loas move in their own way,' said King Steam. 'But they know what is at stake – for all of us.'

Oliver shrugged. Well, why not. He already had most of Jackals' constabulary, army and order of worldsingers waiting to push him off the gallows, not to mention the Court of the Air hunting Harry down while the Lady of the Lights' mysterious foe was scouring the land to assassinate him. Why not add an unreliable steamman likely to bolt at the first sight of trouble to their fate-cursed party? It could hardly make things any worse.

High in the ceiling a hatch parted and a claw lowered a limp body to the throne room's polished floor. There were mutterings of discontent from the courtiers and palace officials as architects moved around the warrior, adjusting his machinery, returning him to life. Steamswipe's eyes started to glow, dimly at first, then fiercely – until finally a transparent lid slid down from his brow, protecting his vision. The creature's four arms vibrated as sensation returned to them, two skeletal hands and two fighting arms, one a murderous-looking double-headed hammer.

His head inclined, taking in the King and the surroundings of the royal chamber. 'How long have I been in suspension?'

'A little over two hundred years,' said King Steam.

'Not long enough to atone,' said Steamswipe.

'The winds could grind the mountains of Mechancia to fine sand and still not enough time would have passed for you to atone, Steamswipe,' said the King. 'Nevertheless the cogs have called you. How will you answer?'

'Is there a sword that will accept me?' asked the warrior.

'That remains to be seen,' said King Steam. 'More to the point, will you follow the call of the Steamo Loas? Will you wear the colours of the Free State and follow the code with whatever minor vestige of honour you still possess?'

'If the Loas ride me,' said Steamswipe, 'I shall not refuse the call.'

'Then that is answer enough,' said the King. 'We shall adjourn to the Chamber of Swords and see whether there are also arms that will bend to the will of the Steamo Loas.'

Oliver gripped onto the King's marque of office as the steamman monarch, escort, Steamswipe and – seemingly – half the court, departed the throne room for a stately procession through the mountain stronghold. Some of the sights he saw left Oliver baffled – vast halls with row upon row of steammen seated behind machines, as still as statues and staring into space; forests of glass spheres with arcs of energy leaping and chasing each other across the globes; chasms of grinding clockwork crunching and turning, rolling like an old man's tongue circling a boiled sweet.

Now deep inside the palace, the King led the party into a round room, small enough that most of the courtiers and hangers-on had to remain in the corridor jostling for a better view. There was an opening to another round room beyond, connected to the first in a figure of eight pattern.

'Move forward, knight,' commanded King Steam. Oliver watched the warrior advance into the centre of the next room, the clank of his four legs echoing off the walls.

'There's nothing here,' whispered Oliver.

'Wait and see, young softbody,' cautioned one of the King's mu-bodies. 'The arms choose the champion, just as the times select the steamman.'

In the second room hatches popped open and the white walls slowly began to rotate. Instruments of destruction extended from the open spaces: swords, rifles, maces, things Oliver did not even recognize, all curves and blades – retracting and extending in an oddly delicate dance.

Oliver noticed Master Saw muttering and shaking his head next to the disreputable Stave. The knight commander clearly did not approve of the spirits' choice in this matter, that a convicted coward should defile the chamber of arms with his presence.

'Holy weapons,' said the royal drone. 'Look, Oliver softbody. The Ace of Clubs, once wielded by Trinder Half-track in the war with Kikkosico near seven hundred years ago. And there, Grindbiter – the long gun – capable of tearing the pips off a Quatérshiftian marshal's uniform at close to a mile's range.'

Oliver bit his lip. Steamswipe was pacing nervously in the centre of the room. None of the weapons were stopping. Would the knight be allowed to accompany Oliver if he failed this rite? Or would the master of the orders militant have his way and the centaur-shaped fighter be returned to millennia of suspension?

Steamswipe extended one of his manipulator arms beseechingly towards a curved blade but the weapon was drawn back inside the darkness of the moving wall.

'Stokeslicer,' moaned the warrior. 'By the beard of Zaka of the Cylinders, will no weapon support my claim as a knight?'

'Your voicebox disgraces the chamber with its sound,' said Master Saw. 'Even weapons which you have mastered would sooner stay deactivate rather than feel the iron of your fingers corrupt their grip.'

Whether in response to the knight's plea, the commander's scorn, or the slow procession of its own path, the wall stopped rotating and a single hatch remained open, revealing a snub black package trembling on a metallic stalk.

'Armoury master,' said the King. 'Do you recognize the weapon which offers itself?'

'I do,' replied a steamman. 'It is Lord Wireburn – the Keeper of the Eternal Flame.' Gasps of amazement sounded from the courtiers. The armoury master addressed the crowd. 'The last time this weapon selected a knight is almost beyond the recorded history of the true people, it was—'

'I remember,' said King Steam. 'It was, as you say, a long time ago. Well, it seems we have a champion and the champion has his arms.'

'Your Majesty,' said Steamswipe, giving a small bow before

the King. 'What is to be my penance? Am I to return to the jungle to try and recover what was lost forever?'

'No, Steamswipe,' said the King, pointing to Oliver and Harry. 'You are to accompany these two friends of the people and give aid to them in their journey. Protect their lives as if they were your own.'

Steamswipe turned his vision strip towards Harry and the young man sitting by the King's tracks, the glass of his visor burning red. 'These two – two – hairless monkeys? Your Majesty, say this is not true. By all that is sacred, say that you jest.'

'We have not made you activate to play parlour pranks on you, knight,' rumbled King Steam. 'Your duty is to see that our two softbody friends do not come to harm.'

Steamswipe gazed with contempt at the two visitors. 'Fastbloods – I would sooner trust Adjasou-Rust not to bite my hand than trust another Jackelian to watch over my back.'

'What does he mean, *another*?' Oliver whispered to the king's drone.

The mu-body shook its head with sadness. 'There were two softbody guides on his last venture deep into the darks of Liongeli.'

'So what did they do to Steamswipe?'

'It's not so much what the guides did to him, young softbody,' said King Steam. 'It is what he did to them. Steamswipe staved in the skull of one of the guides with his war hammer, the other he impaled on a spear.'

King Julius's chambers were a shadow of what they had been – only the grand dimensions gave any clue that they once housed the absolute monarch of Jackals, master of an entire nation. Like the man himself they had fallen into a state of disrepair. Julius's hacking cough echoed off the bare walls, a rasping, rattling thing, sounding more alive than its owner now seemed.

Captain Flare stared down at the skeletal form stretched underneath the blanket, the rough wool all that warded off the damp of the chambers. It was summer so no fire burned in the hearth. Parliament had voted on that many years ago: fuel to be expended on the royal person only from the month of Frost-touch onwards – a petty economy that must have given the guardians who voted for it more warmth than it deprived King Julius of. He was barely lucid now, gripped by another bout of waterman's sickness. Each fever reduced him slightly more than the last.

'What's he saying, captain?' asked Prince Alpheus. 'It sounded like something about lice.'

'Not lice,' said the Commander of the Special Guard. 'Alice. Your mother.'

'Mother. Yes. I wish I had met her.'

'The House of Guardians probably wouldn't have allowed it,' said Flare. 'Even if she hadn't been returned to the royal breeding pool, even if she hadn't. . .'

'. . .died of the crinkleskin?' said Alpheus. 'I am always surprised by the number of royals who die of plagues and fevers at the breeding house. I am surprised they are still able to scrape together the blood of a squire's daughter, let alone a duchess, to pair me off with.'

'It's fair to say that medical care has not been a priority over there.'

'It has not been a priority here either,' said Alpheus.

Flare shrugged. 'Waterman's sickness is the perfect illness for our democratic state – it strikes guardians and undermaids with equal ferocity, and once you get it, all the money in Sun Gate can't help you.'

'They say the heat and dryness of Cassarabia helps the afflicted.'

'Perhaps,' said Flare. 'But I don't think parliament trusts the caliphs any more than they do your father.'

'It's odd that I never get sick,' said Alpheus. 'Not even a cold in winter. I obviously don't get that from either my father or mother.'

'Your mother was tough,' said Flare. 'It took the conditions in the royal breeding house to wear her down.'

Alpheus stared down at his father. 'He still remembers her.'

'She was a hard woman to forget, Your Highness.'

A line of Special Guardsmen stood sentry at the far end of the bedchamber, by the light patches on the wall where rich tapestries would have once hung, their silent faces watching the slow death of the King. Flare waved them away and they turned smartly, filing out in a disciplined line. All except Bonefire.

'You can go too,' said Flare.

'I was hoping the pup would lose his nerve – leave the job to a man.'

'Surely not concern for me, Bonefire?' said the prince. 'You just wanted to do the thing yourself.'

'Novelty value,' replied the Special Guardsman. 'It's been a while since anyone let me have my head and I do miss the old days.'

'You could let him do it,' said Captain Flare. 'There's a lot at stake now. There is no going back after this – for any of us. It doesn't have to be *you*.'

'Yes it does, captain. Anyway, what do I have to go back to?' said Alpheus, picking up a pillow. 'A life where I end up like him, tossing fevered in a bed, with no arms to beg for help, no dignity, no freedom, no hope.'

King Julius rasped as the pillow was pushed down on his sweating face by his son, legs shaking at first, then thrashing with a last burst of whatever life, whatever will to live, still

268

subsisted in him. His limbs convulsed and bucked as the contents of his bladder soaked across the plain bed cover. Then the monarch trembled into stillness.

Alpheus removed the pillow. The old man's eyes were wide in shock, his sallow grey skin shining like he had just risen from a bath. 'Be kind to Mother when you see her, Papa.'

Captain Flare put his hand on the prince's shoulder. 'Apart from anything else, Alpheus, the way he was suffering it was a mercy for him to move along the Circle.'

Alpheus swayed, dazed by the enormity of what he had just done. 'If this goes wrong, captain, I ask just one thing. Don't let them make me into him. Kill me first, kill me with your bare hands rather than let them put my arms on display outside the House of Guardians.'

Flare looked grim and said nothing.

'The King is dead,' laughed Bonefire. 'Long live the pup.'

Chapter Sixteen

W hat is it?' asked Molly, tapping the thick glass of the containment vessel. 'It looks like a ball of rock.'

'Here it *is* a ball of rock,' replied Coppertracks, turning across the laboratory at the top of Tock House, his drone bodies moving out of the way in a perfectly synchronized ballet between the machines, tables and instruments crowding the space.

'Ah, Coppertracks, do not make light of that cursed stuff and the problems it caused us – the deaths on the island,' pleaded the commodore.

'Dear mammal, master your fears. It has been inert for all the years since we left the Isla Needless.'

'The rock was anything but inert then,' said Nickleby, his face appearing distorted on the other side of the glass. 'There were creatures made out of this material, Molly, things that attacked out of the stone and rocks. Half the boat's crew had disappeared from our camp by the time we worked out what was stalking us.'

'My poor plucky jacks,' said Commodore Black. 'Billy Top-knot, Sally Gold, old Haggside Peter – there was never a finer

group of tars to draw tanked air beneath the waves. I dug
their graves with my own thin hungry fingers, lass. I threw
the dirt of that terrible place over their cold dead faces.'

Molly stared closer. The black rock glistened under the gas
light of the clock house chamber, little shards of silver and
veins of metal visible through the containment glass. 'A curious
souvenir to keep.'

'The miracle of life, Molly softbody,' said Coppertracks,
passing a tray of crystals to one of his drones. 'Have you
never wondered at how some objects in our universe possess
a vital spark that makes them able to walk, think, feel.
Comprehend and ponder their own place in the scheme of
things – while others – even complex systems such as the
weather or this rock here as it stands at the moment – do
not.'

'Nothing to do with your little contraption outside, then,
Aliquot Coppertracks?' said Nickleby.

Molly glanced to where the pensman was pointing, somewhere in the grounds of Tock House, beyond the orchard and
the topiary garden, but she could see nothing there.

'My scheme continues,' said Coppertracks. Then to Molly,
'Vibrations across the earthflow, my young softbody friend.
We are not the only celestial body to orbit the sun. I believe
there might be existences similar to our own on one or more
of those bodies waiting to communicate with kindred intel-
lects.'

Molly remembered the aeronaut's tales from the penny
dreadfuls – how cold it got when floatquakes sent chunks of
land spinning towards the heavens. How warm the jack
cloudies had to wrap up when they bravely raised their
aerostats in pursuit. How thin the air became as their airships
climbed in search of any survivors clinging onto the floating
earth. Surely nothing could live beyond the sky? They would

271

have to be ice-people, able to survive freezing temperatures – with the humps possessed by desert tribesmen; storing not water but instead holding the very air they needed to breathe. What a story that would make for the penny dreadfuls. Tales featuring strange life beyond the clouds. Perhaps one day there would be a market for celestial fiction in the stationers of Jackals.

'So you squander our few remaining pennies on that blessed thing you're raising in the grounds,' said the commodore. 'An artificial mother crystal, as if there's going to be a crystalgrid operator happily biding their time on one of the moons, waiting to receive an order for cheese from the great Aliquot Coppertracks. Ah well, perhaps there's a couple of moonlight-touched fools walking the streets of Middlesteel who'll pay a few coins to see the thing when you're done . . . to keep the butcher and his debt collectors at bay.'

'My apparatus is not intended as a side-show amusement,' said Coppertracks, angrily. 'Any more than the apparatus which my colleague in the Royal Society has sent over – which I might remind you, commodore softbody, you are meant to be helping me assemble.'

Grumbling, the commodore left to fetch one of the last crates from the corridor's dumb waiter. The slipthinker's tireless mu-bodies were already busying themselves with a pyramid of machinery – sliding copper pistons being greased and fixed in place, glass lenses stacked in frames.

Nickleby lit his mumbleweed pipe and the clock chamber began to fill with sweet-scented smoke, not unpleasant, but too much of it made the bridge of Molly's nose ache – Circle knew what it was doing to the inside of the pensman's body.

'The answer is in front of my face,' said Nickleby from his chair. 'There hasn't been a Pitt Hill slaying in days now. That matches perfectly with what you discovered in Greenhall's records. The price on your head, Molly, reflects the fact that whatever the reason for the death list being drawn up, you are one of the last to be found and targeted for murder.'

'When someone is left on the poorhouse steps they are not meant to be found,' said Molly.

'The unfortunate circumstances of your birth worked in your favour this time, Molly,' said Nickleby. 'I have no doubt that if your mother had kept you, I would already have written up your murder for the crime and law section of *The Illustrated*. So, what else links you with those names on the list?'

'Nothing at all,' wheezed Black, returning with a box of equipment. 'She's a blessed child. A terrible young age to be thrown into the deadly games you involve us in, Silas.'

'You have a point, commodore. Molly is the youngest of all the people on the Pitt Hill Slayer's list of victims. But hardly a child anymore – she is nearly of an age to exercise the franchise.'

'Marking a cross next to the name of some thieving Guardians on a ballot paper is small blessed compensation for being hunted down by a murdering gang of lunatics.'

'There is method here—' said Nickleby '— were we but able to see it.'

For the hundredth time he looked over the list of names which Binchy had copied down following the discovery in Greenhall's engine rooms. The names that were confirmed as Pitt Hill Slayings were marked with a cross. Some of the victims had not been linked to the slayer by the police, too poor to warrant any investigation of substance. There were not that many of those. The majority of the names were from well-to-do families – educated, moneyed. The average age was mid to late thirties, a couple of victims had been in their twenties. Most but not all lived in Middlesteel. Molly was the youngest by far. Both sexes were represented about equally – but the victims were all human – no craynarbians, no steammen or graspers murdered by the Pitt Hill Slayer.

Molly sat down opposite the pensman. 'So what connects these people to me?'

'Nothing that I can see, Molly. You might as well ask what doesn't connect you. In a game of odd one out, you would win every time against the names on this list. I do need to check on some of the people not originally linked to the Pitt Hill killings. I don't have any details on them – one of them might be the link to you. There's a butcher down on Ventry Lane. Ham Yard marked his death as suspicious, but finally chalked it up as an open verdict. How they thought he could have accidentally lost all his blood in his abattoir is beyond me. The crushers must have been waiting for the murderer to paint a sign on the wall saying "The Pitt Hill Slayer struck here".'

'Deduction is a science,' said Coppertracks. 'And it is science which will come to our aid in this matter.'

'Your science is mortal heavy,' puffed Commodore Black, lifting down the last of the boxes. 'If it's not a tonne weight of old journals I'm dragging in here for you to gobble down, it's these strange machines of yours, full of mammoth pipes and fizzing with dark energies.'

Coppertracks moved through the throng of drones, his mu-bodies clambering over the half-assembled machine in the centre of the clock room. 'The scientific method will prove its worth in this case, dear mammal. Lord Hartisburgh has been gracious enough to lend us his latest organic analyser – I would not like to return it to him broken.'

'Well, I wouldn't want to put you in poor standing with your wild friends at the Royal Society now. But could you not tinker with light little gases instead. Or we could convert the whole floor to a telescope for you to study the celestial movements – if you would promise to do it at night and not disturb the well deserved rest of an old submariner.'

'Members of the institute are allowed to use the optics up at Prighty Hill,' said Coppertracks. 'And an installation here would hardly take up less space than this device. Blood, Molly softbody. That is what this dark affair turns on – someone sought out yours and that of all the others on that list. From the million Jackelian names on Greenhall's transaction engine, only yours satisfied the criteria set by your tormentors. This machine will shine the bright light of science on those that seek to stay hidden in the shadows.'

'I don't doubt you, Coppertracks,' said Molly. 'I know all about the scientific method of detection. We managed to collect the entire series of penny sheets with Barclay and the Game Chicken at the poorhouse.'

Nickleby harrumphed. 'Your penny dreadfuls can only begin to hint at the insufferable vanity of the man.'

'You've met Barclay?' Molly was in awe.

'Our paths have crossed,' said the pensman. 'Barclay and his oaf of an associate. I am sure you will find, Molly, the contribution myself and Coppertracks made towards solving the case of the missing abbot was carefully overshadowed by the size of Barclay's ego and the depth of his connections with the Dock Street press. If I have one consolation with this current grisly affair, it is that Barclay and Bird are not being consulted by Ham Yard or any of the victims' families.'

'Is he as rakish as his illustrations?'

'Reality disappoints,' was Nickleby's terse reply as he burrowed with renewed vigour into the names on the list.

Coppertracks' skull threw light off the nearly completed machine as its assembly was finalized. Gold spheres began to rotate on top of the machine as the mu-bodies connected the device's steam stack to a vent at the side of the chamber. What the pensman's far-off neighbours would think if they peered out from their windows and saw the clock tower venting steam the Circle only knew. Molly guessed that with Coppertracks' eccentric interests they had probably seen worse and stranger in their time.

The wooden floor began to vibrate as the device's transaction engine drums started rotating, steam now visible venting outside into the evening. A flight of startled egrets lifted off from the orchard in search of a more tranquil night's rest.

'Molly softbody,' said Coppertracks. 'Your assistance in my exploration is now required.'

Molly looked sceptically at the thing. 'You're sure it's safe?'

'I assure you, Lord Hartisburgh is an expert in his field and this is the very latest thing.'

'He is not a surgeon, though, Coppertracks.'

'Dear mammal, few surgeons could afford such an expense as this machine. Now, please, if you would submit some of your system juices I shall begin the analysis.'

Molly rolled up her sleeve as one of the diminutive drones climbed up on a bench, a syringe clutched in its pincer-like iron hands. 'My system juices are precious to me, Aliquot Coppertracks. It's not oil I can drain into a saucer for you to skim Gear-gi-ju cogs across the floor. Your rich merchant friend's machine looks a little unstable to me.'

'Hardly that,' said Coppertracks, watching his mu-body drawing blood from Molly's arm. 'Its basic design is similar to the blood machines the constabulary use to establish citizen identity when they are sealing a district off for a crime sweep. Your system juices contain a unique biological metric that allows Greenhall to register your birth file. The metric also allows them to estimate your potential for criminal tendencies as well your pre-disposition to plagues – even your latent prospects for worldsinger talents.' Coppertracks fed the blood into a glass container and it started to bubble, then drained away down into the machine.

'Ah well,' said the commodore, looking askance at the analyser as it banged and thumped on the floor. 'At least you showed the sense to borrow the machine from your club. I would hate to see our funds eaten away procuring one of these blessed things for your studies.'

'The Royal Society is not a club,' said the steamman slip-thinker. 'It is a organization for the furtherance of philosophical enquiries of the most fundamental and useful sort. Nobody there sits in leather chairs and puffs away on mumbleweed pipes, I can assure you of that.'

Molly pushed a handful of cotton gauze against the syringe mark on her arm, a tear of blood showing through the fabric. 'A serious kind of place, then.'

'Indeed, young softbody, indeed.'

Behind Coppertracks the device's tape printer began winding out a reel of results with a gentle smacking sound from the print hammers. The interior of the steamman's transparent skull sparked with excitement as he scanned down the tape, then forked angrily in a surge of energy as the implications of what he was reading sunk in.

'Aliquot?' said Nickleby.

'What is it, Coppertracks?' asked Molly.

'My poor young softbody friend. By Zaka of the Cylinders' beard, it is small wonder that they wish you dead.'

'Out with it now,' said Commodore Black. 'Blessed Circle, what have you found with that fool machine of yours?'

Coppertracks dangled the tape from his iron fingers. 'What have I found? Why my dear friends, I believe I have discovered why someone wrote a transaction engine ripper to scour Greenhall's records. I have discovered why so many wealthy corpses have been turning up across Jackals drained of their vital system juices. And I have discovered why young Molly softbody must die!'

It was strange, Captain Flare considered, that the palace – once so opulent that even the ambassadors from Cassarabia would marvel at its giant chandeliers, its hundred Circlist chapels and private topiary gardens – had been reduced to the shell of a prison quite so perfectly. The room the Special Guardsman sat in, going over the arrangements for the coronation, had once seen intricate waltzes, glittering receptions, feasts of eel and river crab from the Gambleflowers and venison from the hunting lodges. Now its bare walls were decorated only by mould, washed off once a month by a staff that had centuries ago been reduced to a handful grudgingly paid for by the functionaries at Greenhall.

It was one of Greenhall's junior administrators who was taking up his time now. The one commodity they were always generous with was their attention when it came to matters of centralised control.

'The royal carriage is being renovated for the progress,' said the civil servant. 'The people will expect to see the prince firmly manacled to the holding cross in each town, fresh face-gags to be supplied at each stopover.'

'With equally fresh fruit to throw at the boy, perhaps?' suggested Flare, only half facetiously.

'The citizens can bring their own rotting food, captain,' said the administrator. 'Now, I understand you have expressed reservations at the length of the royal progress.'

Flare nodded. 'You cannot expect the Special Guard to visit half the towns in Jackals with the field strength your people have suggested. We have other duties to fulfil as well.'

'What could be more important than your ceremonial duties

as warders of the monarchy? The people are looking forward to a good show – there hasn't been a coronation for nearly half a century. Let all our free people enjoy the shock of horror they feel, seeing a nearly crowned king with his arms still attached, reminding them he might yet use those corrupt limbs to snatch back the reins of power and reimpose the tyranny.'

'Warders of the monarchy,' spat Flare. 'Hoggstone just wants an excuse to wine and dine the voters with his state-sponsored circus. Protect the people from the human sheep you keep locked up in the royal breeding house? I would have to go to the history books to find the date of the last act of royalist-inspired violence against anyone in Jackals. You want ticks on the ballot paper, not protection from the prince – the King.'

'Greenhall serves no single party,' said the administrator. 'We serve the people.'

'I am sure that sounds very impressive when you say it in Usglish,' said Flare.

'The people expect a couple of weeks of revels,' retorted the functionary. 'And we, captain, expect you back at the capital by the end of the month. There will be massive crowds vying for a position in Parliament Square, waiting for the surgeon royal to sever the boy's arms and crown him the new king. It will be a glorious occasion, captain. There's hardly an aerostat packet, canal boat passage or coaching billet into Middlesteel left to purchase in the whole of Jackals. I would not want to be the one to report to the House of Guardians any impediment to the start of the carnivals. Good Circle, man, fey powers or no, the people would rip you apart – there would be riots.'

Flare shook his head wearily. 'I predict an early election this year.'

The two Special Guardsmen at the end of the chamber clicked their heels as the doors were flung open, the gust from the corridor catching their scarlet capes and lifting the administrator's papers from the table. It was one of the worldsingers – one of the new acolytes. What was his name? Blundy.

'Captain,' said the worldsinger. 'I have an urgent matter to report.'

Flare looked at the administrator. 'If you would excuse us – it seems the guard has some business other than carnivals to discuss after all.'

'I am sure what the gentleman from the order has to report will also be of interest to Greenhall,' said the administrator.

'This is urgent, captain,' said the worldsinger, approaching the table.

'Oh, very well,' said Flare.

'It is the King, captain.'

'Alpheus?' said Flare.

'No, the old king – Julius. I was on the detail transferring his body to the undertaker at the royal breeding house. The taxidermists from the state museum didn't want a repeat of what happened with Queen Marina's body.'

The civil servant from Greenhall nodded in agreement. The corpse of Julius's predecessor had been intercepted by an excitable mob and thrown into the Gambleflowers, swept away by the tidal pulls and lost to the sea. No body left to stuff and display.

'You have my sympathy,' said Flare. 'But I am sure the smell is nothing a little rosewater won't mask.'

'You don't understand. I was alone with his body. I was bored, curious – and I am still studying for my second flower.'

'Does this conversation have a point, son?' said Flare.

'I thought I would practise a mind-touch summoning.

Memories can last for days after death – it's always good to practise.'

'You practised on the King's corpse?' said the administrator. 'That is disgusting. Dear Circle, do your superiors authorize that sort of thing?'

'No,' said the acolyte, shame-faced. 'They would not approve if they knew. But it is practise – and I know now how the King died.'

'Hardly a secret,' said the administrator. 'Nobody recovers from waterman's sickness.'

'There was one memory left – only one. It was strong enough to last for a week, probably. Prince Alpheus was suffocating his father with a pillow. The sense of betrayal and shock was so strong, I can still taste it.'

'Alpheus murdered his own father?' said the administrator. 'When waterman's sickness was about to kill him off anyway?'

'I know it doesn't make sense,' said the worldsinger. 'But the last memory was so strong. I could not have misread it. The pain in his soul was terrible.'

'It changes nothing,' said Flare. 'Remember the revels, the carnivals, the riots if the people don't get their holiday. The coronation must go ahead as scheduled.'

'It changes everything,' said the administrator. 'However we mate the royal vermin, it seems we just can't breed that streak of wickedness out of them. There are plenty of candidates in the breeding house we can select for the succession – and the people will turn up just as happily to see the murdering little jigger get the rope outside Bonegate as the crown at Parliament Square. The vicious scum were always poisoning each other in the old days. It looks like our dear little prince is reverting to type. But what an opportunity for us, captain. Think of it. We remind the entire state of the moral authority of our rule with a good hanging – and the people still get a new king on the throne for carnival week.'

Flare reached out and snapped the administrator's neck, the crack reverberating across the room. The functionary flopped back in his chair, lifeless head hanging limply to the side. 'Somehow I thought you might say that.'

Across the chamber the worldsinger was stepping back, his legs moving him subconsciously towards the exit. Towards the two Special Guardsmen standing there. 'You killed him!'

'Regrettable,' said Flare. 'But I doubt he'll be missed. Unlike yourself, Blundy. Your disappearance will ring too many bells within the order.'

The worldsinger threw his hand out and chanted a hex, swaying as he tossed the magic towards Flare. Nothing happened, the captain stood still, as tall and immovable as a rock.

'You—'

'Should be burning?' said Flare, tapping his neck torc. 'All those nasty runes and rituals stored inside my torc for a rainy day, ready to tear me inside out? I have seen your kind activate a torc on a feybreed, worldsinger, have you? I still remember the young guardswoman's eye sockets smoking in the snow. You would call her a rogue – but I just saw a frightened girl who bolted from her first taste of battle, sickened by the bodies and the murder. That's a terrible thing to wish on anyone.'

'Only a worldsinger can unlock the hex on a torc.'

'So it's said,' nodded Flare. 'Of course, while we may have the majority of feymist changelings, Jackals is not the only country with people who sing the worldsong.'

One of the guardsmen opened a door and a deformed grasper-sized thing hobbled out, one of the ill-fated inmates of Hawklam Asylum.

'Have you gone insane, captain, where is that thing's hex-suit? Where are its handlers from the order?'

'The plates that bind? Well, Blundy, it must be a laundry day. As for his handlers, let me show you what happened to them. . .'

The worldsinger's head jerked up, blood bubbling out of his nose as the wild creature's mind forced itself into his brain, advancing on him. Both arms of the sorcerer were seized from behind by a guardsman and a hand clamped over his mouth to stop him screaming.

'I like this one,' said the feybreed, caressing the sorcerer's chest and arms. 'Strong. Young too.'

'Mist-brother, you know what must be done,' said Flare.

'You are so good to me, brother.'

With a pop the creature's jaw detached, its chin flowing down to the floor. Then the feybreed clambered up the shaking sorcerer. Blundy, struggling for his life, thrashed and tried to break free of the guardsman restraining him. He did not stand a chance against the fey-born strength of his captor. When the feybreed reached the worldsinger's shoulder, Blundy's head vanished as the thing's lips sucked down over it. Rivers of fey flesh poured down and covered his body. There was a flickering translucence of skin as the two beings merged. The worldsinger fell forward, legs stumbling like a newly born calf finding its feet. Blundy steadied himself against the wall, breathing hard.

'Are you done?' said Flare.

Blundy stroked the nape of his neck, feeling his groin with his other hand. 'Oh yes. This body will last *months*.'

'Long enough,' said Flare. 'Long enough for our purposes.'

Hoggstone followed the spiral staircase down into the depths of Ham Yard, his footsteps echoing up the stairwell. 'This is important, Inspector Reason?'

'The politicals seem to think so, First Guardian. The yard's been turning down their custody transfer requests ever since we caught the man.'

'I know,' said Hoggstone. 'Where do you think the political police's complaints end up?'

Inspector Reason reached out to a bank of switches and beneath them a rank of gas lanterns flared into life, the light revealing stairs corkscrewing down into the distance.

'Your people really should put a lifting room in here,' said Hoggstone.

'The exercise wouldn't have bothered you so much when you were younger, First Guardian.'

'I was stuffing pamphlets through the doors of the Driselwell rookeries then, playing debating sticks with the young bucks from the Levellers.'

The inspector smiled. 'And I was a green-around-the-gills crusher trying to run down dippers and the flash mob.'

'We've both come a long way since Driselwell,' said Hoggstone.

'Yes. That we have, First Guardian. And don't think I'm not grateful for the little nudges you've given my prospects.'

'It's always good to invite the local crusher in for a cup of caffeel, as my mother used to say.'

'She always made it too sweet,' said the inspector. 'Although I don't think anyone ever told her.'

'Cheap jinn burns away your sense of taste. Sweet is all you have left.'

'I'm temperance myself, these days,' said the policeman.

'What did the political police leave out of their report?'

'Most of the credit we took in nabbing him in the first place, I expect. Although to be fair to the g-boys, it was plain luck that we rumbled him.'

'Did he ever run with the rioters at the docks?'

'I dare say some of them used to be his compatriots, once upon a time. But he is not directly involved with the new mob, First Guardian.'

'These new revolutionaries need to be uncovered,' said Hoggstone. 'I will not abide this damnable mystery to fester on my streets, eating away at our authority.'

'Yes,' said the inspector. 'I've seen the reports from my crushers on the gaslight shift – terrified out of their wits by what they think they've seen. Companies of worldsingers and Special Guardsmen herding unmentionable things through the rookeries and the alleys.'

'Nothing to get to Dock Street,' said Hoggstone.

'The news sheets will catch wind of your excursions soon enough if it keeps on,' said the inspector. 'Am I to presume your acceptance of my invite down here means your friends haven't run down any useful information?'

'You would think they were hunting ghosts,' Hoggstone snarled. 'The man you've got. He was a printer?'

'Yes. A small Hoax Square operation – bill stickers for the tonics, supposedly. We raided him on a tip-off he had a side-line in relish, which he did. Crates of real-box smut, enough pictures to keep the Greenhall censorship committee in sitting for weeks. It was probably one of his girls that blew on him – artistic differences and the like.'

Hoggstone held onto the rail at the side of the wall as he walked down the stairwell. 'But you went back to his print house after the blood machine results?'

'Too right, First Guardian. We raided it at night, ripped the place apart just as quietly as we could. That's when we found the other stuff. I have a watch on the place now, to see if anyone else turns up there.'

'You'll be lucky if they do,' said Hoggstone.

'Could be a waste of time, but stranger things have

happened. I dare say the politicals have got the place under observation now too.'

The stairwell finally ended – a single iron door waiting for them. Inspector Reason rapped on the metal and a grill pulled back, then the door swung inward. A grasper in a black police uniform saluted them. 'You've never been down here before, First Guardian?'

Hoggstone shook his head.

'One door in, one door out. Both manned. Plenty of people have done a bunk from Bonegate after we've passed them to the doomsman for sentencing, but nobody has broken out of the yard's cells. Some right old rascals have had the chance too – the Lions Field strangler, Vaughan the highwayman, even science pirates like Newton and Krook.'

In front of them a second constable unbolted the last door revealing a long corridor, cells on both sides with glass doors. Ignoring the other inmates Reason led Hoggstone to a cell at the end – the only cell with an iron door and rubber seals like the cabin on a submariner's boat.

'Turn the noise off,' Reason called to one of the guards. 'And pull the bolts on this one.'

Three cracks echoed off the enclosed space and Reason spun the door wheel. Inside, a figure stood upright, blindfolded and chained to a metal frame.

'The political police would be able to get information out of him a lot quicker,' said Hoggstone.

'Slow but steady, First Guardian,' said the inspector. 'You know the yard doesn't approve of their methods. Matey here has got all his fingernails intact, and I don't need some back-street sorcerer to rip his mind apart either. Besides, if you are strong you can train against the politicals' methods, and if you are weak you'll just say whatever they want to hear in the end. When the yard wants the truth, we just leave them alone with the noise – a day, a week, a month, the noise gets them all in the end.'

Hoggstone glanced around the cell, bare except for the reflecting plates that helped the noise move around the chamber. The sound of devils dancing.

Inspector Reason pulled the blindfold off the prisoner. His wide eyes moved slowly around the room, taking in Hoggstone and the policeman. His gaze was wild, splintered, as if his reality had been fractured and there were other things in the room only he could see. Things he had to move aside to make room for the two visitors.

'What name are you using today? Garrett or Tait?'

The prisoner mumbled something.

'It must be hard choosing,' said Inspector Reason. 'You've been living as Garrett for fourteen years. But your blood records show you to be Tait. Now Garrett was not very respectable, was he? Maybe on the surface he was, but all those boxes of smut you were peddling. That's good for a couple of years in the clink in itself. So tell the gentleman here what your name is.'

'Tait,' said the prisoner. 'It's Tait.'

'But Mister Tait is a combination man,' said the inspector. 'From the coal fields. How did you end up as someone else?'

'Identity. I took Garrett's name. He was dead in the famine – nobody knew.'

'Well now that's a problem,' said Reason. 'Because Tait is still wanted for organizing the mine labour in the Carlist uprising. Garrett gets two years in Bonegate, but Tait – well, he's going to get the rope, isn't he?'

'Tait, I'm Tait.'

'Good,' said the inspector. 'To tell you the truth, Tait, I don't really care about your relish, and as for what you did in the old days? Well, if I were to arrest everyone who stuffed a fuse in a jinn bottle during the uprising, I'd have the lords of commerce lining up outside Ham Yard to complain about the labour shortage. What worries me is the hidden basement under your print room. All those fresh copies of *Community and the Commons* boxed up and ready to distribute. Do you find much of a market for that rubbish these days?'

'Please, let me sleep. I just want to sleep.'

'Then tell me what I want to know, man,' said Hoggstone. 'So we can move you to a cell with a bed. Tell me about the troubles on the street. Were you and your friends at the docks when things got ugly down on the Gambleflowers?'

'Not us,' said the prisoner. 'It's not us.'

'But the rabble rousers call themselves Carlists, man.'

'Not the sort to join my chapter,' said the prisoner. 'Different.'

'How?' Hoggstone demanded.

'They want things. Things from their members. Crazy stuff. Crazy like a hex. People start believing it.'

'I often find the most powerful ideas are like enchantments,' said Hoggstone. 'Who are the organizers, where does their committee meet?'

'Vicious,' said the prisoner. 'They're killing us off. Killing their own.'

'He doesn't know who they are *himself*,' said Inspector Reason. 'The noise would have winkled it out of him if he did.'

'Something this well organized doesn't just spring up from thin air,' said Hoggstone. 'Tait, you might not be familiar with the new Carlist movement, but one of your people must know where this latest brand of revolutionary poison is coming from.'

Tait moaned in pain.

'Tell him the name, Tait,' said Inspector Reason. 'Tell the

gentleman the name you blew for me. Tell him exactly who your relish money was going to. Who you're funding and printing for.'

Tait shook his head.

'Damn your eyes, man, I need that name,' said Hoggstone.

'You lasted three days alone with the noise, before,' said the policeman. 'I've seen a real hard man last five, maybe seven days before they broke. You want to find out if you're a hard man, Tait?'

'Carl. Ben Carl.' The prisoner said the name like a prayer. 'He knows about the new revolutionaries.'

Hoggstone bit his lip. 'Middlesteel's prodigal son? Circle, I thought he was dead for sure! Where has he been hiding all these years?'

'Worth the trip?' said Reason to the First Guardian.

Tait was crying, stung by the shame of how easily betrayal came. 'I only saw him the once, at a meeting. He's scared too. They're hunting for him now as well, the new ones. He's too important to leave in peace.'

The First Guardian turned to Inspector Reason. 'Do you believe the fellow?'

'Three days in here, I do.'

'Keep his works under watch,' said Hoggstone. 'Day and night. The devil take Benjamin Carl. I never thought I'd need an audience with that bloody troublesome philosopher. He must be in his dotage now . . . and still up to his old mischief too.'

Reason gestured towards the prisoner. 'The magistrates? He'll be given the scaffold for sure.'

'I just see a tired old fool who has traded printing one type of dirty book for another. Charge Garrett, not Tait. Do it quietly and put him through my district. I'll see he only gets the boat.'

'Sleep,' Tait moaned.

The inspector checked his pocket watch. 'You'll stop seeing the visions by this evening – then you'll sleep for days.'

'The first days of a fairer nation,' said Hoggstone, quoting the opening dedication of *Community and the Commons*.

The inspector called for his warders to come in and unchain the restraining frame.

'Ben Carl,' said Hoggstone, rolling the name around his mouth. 'Benjamin Carl. Old man, I thought you were dead.'

'I got everything on the list you gave me,' said Awn'bar.

'Nice one,' said Binchy, taking the wicker basket of food from the craynarbian boy. He reached into his pocket and took out a thruppence coin. 'How was Jerps on the Park?'

'Big queue, same as always.' The adolescent mottling on the boy's armoured skull glowed in the sunlight of the corridor. 'The jellied eels looked fresh, so I got you a cup's worth of those too.'

Binchy smiled. 'Good lad. That's my supper sorted then.'

'My matriarch said to ask after Damson B,' said the boy.

'You say thanks to your mam, tell her we're both winning the race.'

'The race?'

'The race of man,' laughed Binchy.

'You haven't got time to show me the cards again, have you?' asked the boy.

He was good too. At an age when most of the Shell Town youngsters were running through the rookeries tossing mud balls at anyone who took offence at their larks, the boy could sniff out a recursive loop in a line of Simple and read the tattoo of a punch card like a born engine man.

Binchy checked the time on the grandfather clock in his

hall. 'Best you get back to your clan, Binchy must be about it. There's always tomorrow.'

'Circleday then,' said the craynarbian boy, sounding disappointed.

They both turned as the tapping of a cane sounded down the tower's corridor. Nobody who lived on his floor as far as Binchy could tell.

'Mister Binchy?' said the dapper old man as he came up to them.

Binchy put the basket of food down on the hall floor. 'You have me at an advantage, sir?'

'Professor Vineis. My office wrote to you, I believe.'

'The alienist? I only got your letter yesterday.' He looked at the boy. 'On your way then, Awn'bar. Tomorrow.'

'Tomorrow,' said the craynarbian, running down the corridor.

The professor rested on his cane. 'They are a fine people, the craynarbians, are they not? I have heard about your wife's unfortunate condition, Mister Binchy, and would like to talk to you about her if I may.'

'Best you come in, then,' said Binchy. 'You're not on the Royal Institute's list? I've consulted with most of them – useless buggers. Engine sickness is beyond their field of expertise. If it struck down guardians and counting-house masters I'd say they'd find it within their field of expertise fast enough.'

'I have been consulting in the city-states for the last few years,' said the professor, taking off his cape.

'Thought your accent had a touch of the exotic to it.' Binchy took the cape and hung it on a hook on the back of the door. 'How did you find me? It's been a while since information sickness appeared in any of the journals I subscribe to.'

'A curious turn of events,' said Count Vauxtion. 'Culminating in a message and a broken mirror.'

Binchy scowled in incomprehension. 'A broken mirror? That's bad luck.'

'Indeed it is,' said Count Vauxtion. 'For someone. Now, Mister Binchy, shall we begin our consultation. . .'

Chapter Seventeen

Oliver looked at the makeshift bandage being wound around Steamswipe's war hammer, then checked outside the stone barn again to make sure they had not been seen ducking inside. The steamman knight looked at the sacking covering up his arm and the panniers loaded on his back with a notable lack of enthusiasm. 'Disguising my status in this way is not honourable – and a single layer of cloth is not an effective ruse.'

Harry continued winding the sacking around the metal limb. 'Would that be your status as a reinstated knight steamman, or your status as a disgraced warrior sentenced to deactivation?'

'Little softbody,' rumbled the knight, 'if I was not under code oath to protect your life, I would break your bones with that which you so clumsily seek to conceal.'

'It is necessary,' said a strange voice.

Oliver looked to where the knight's sacred weapon, Lord Wireburn, lay on a bale of hay. Something about the weapon's voicebox made him uneasy; the sound of all the souls it had dispatched from the world caught within its piercing artificial timbre. Luckily for the Jackelian the weapon spoke rarely.

Steamswipe did not reply to his weapon but it was clear he was willing to defer to the holy relic – without its intervention in the chamber of arms the knight would have been returned back to his eternal dreamless sleep.

'Too bleeding right it's necessary,' said Harry. 'Since I'm the only one in this party who's been to Shadowclock before, let me clue you in on what we'll be facing. Shadowclock is a sealed city – its walls date from the civil war. There are four gates, all manned by redcoats and watched day and night. Inside the city is the entrance to the mines – outside are the largest, best-protected aerostat fields in the kingdom. Anyone coming in or out by road and waterway is searched for contraband.'

'Celgas?' said Oliver.

'Bang on,' said Harry. 'The House of Guardians is paranoid when it comes to the gas mines. As it should be, given they think they're the only source of the gas in the world.'

'But they are,' said Oliver.

Harry tapped the side of his nose. 'Actually, you would be surprised where celgas turns up, old stick. But I digress; the important thing is if you control Shadowclock, you control the navy. And when you control the navy, you control the continent. Everyone knows that, and someone in the city is playing silly buggers. Your uncle was on to something, something that involved that place, and everyone who has had a sniff of it so far has ended up dead.'

'We're still alive, Harry.'

'Not for want of trying, Oliver. If it weren't for this old steamer's kin, those Cassarabian slave hunters back at the border would be chewing our bones. A sad end for a fellow of my talents.'

'Some would say fitting,' said Steamswipe.

'No doubt some would,' said Harry. 'But seeing as how

your ancestors seem to have volunteered your services to this merry outing, how about you devote some of your superior steamman intellect to working out how we are going to get into that city without being rumbled by the army, city constabulary and navy.'

'Haven't you got any of your people in the city, Harry? Wolftakers, or whistlers?'

'None that I can trust,' said Harry. 'Those two sand cats and my old friend Jamie weren't waiting for us because they were taking a picnic on the moors, lad. My network has been compromised. Even if the whistlers in Shadowclock haven't been turned directly, people who want to see you and me disappear will have briefed them. Too risky by far.'

'We can breach their walls at night,' said Steamswipe. 'Stealth will serve us well.'

Harry looked thoughtful. 'Yes, you see as well at night as we do in the day, don't you? It may yet come to that, but if there's no one I can trust in Shadowclock, I can think of at least one that I can't.'

'That is the level of your strategic thinking?' asked Steamswipe.

Harry finished concealing the knight's war arm. 'Keep your friends close and your enemies closer. I think it's time to send a message to the Circle and pray for assistance.'

'A friend you can't trust, Harry?'

'The bonds of friendship dwindle with age, Oliver. But a little blackmail lasts forever.'

Oliver looked at the coal dust on his clothes. The caravan of traders they had joined to sneak out of the Steammen Free State might have gone their own way, but the dust from the dirty mules still clung to his breeches. If he had gone home to Seventy Star Hall looking like this his uncle would have set Damson Griggs on him with a scrubbing brush.

'Your secret police, the cloud-hidden, they will be watching for us?' asked Steamswipe.

'Perhaps,' said Harry. 'But they have to sight us before they can follow us. The Court of the Air might have been compromised, but not everyone up there is bent – I doubt if there's a watch on Shadowclock. Whoever is behind this is killing people who poke their noses into the celgas mines. They're not going to want to draw attention to the city with a full-scale quarter and sweep of the area running day and night for us.'

'Conceal me in the panniers,' said Lord Wireburn. Oliver realized the holy weapon was speaking to him. It took all his strength to heft the thing off the straw and into one of the bags on the side of the steamman. When Steamswipe lifted the weapon it appeared as light as the boatman's gun that Mother Loade had given him.

'You are a strange excuse for a squire,' said Steamswipe.

'You don't look much like old Rustpivot back at Hundred Locks either,' said Oliver. 'Panniers or no. Harry, what about the county constabulary here – are they going to be looking for us?'

'Lightshire is a long way from here, Oliver. Our details will be in the town garrison for certain, but you aren't going to find Ham Yard blood machines at the toll cottages this far south. We'll travel by day from now on, like the respectable Jackelians we are. There's a full moon tonight; too many villages and farms around here for us to be sneaking around – I don't want some farmer taking pot shots at us for poaching or sheep rustling.'

Stave proved correct in his decision to switch to travelling by daylight. Every morning the roads they took filled with people. Drovers herding hundreds of geese to market, young dogs bounding around the honking birds to keep them off the meadows and on the road. Independent traders, carts filled with barrels of supplies and market goods rattled past. Sometimes the three of them stopped and rested in red barn-sized structures by the side of the road, the Lissacks Commons, named after the Guardian who had raised the bill in the house that paid for their construction. Oliver would listen to the hoots of owls and drift into a deep sleep while Harry traded ghost stories with the other travellers and merchants staying in the free accommodation.

The evenings were becoming balmy as high summer arrived, and for a while the cares and worries lifted from Oliver's shoulders. Even Steamswipe seemed to draw barely a second glance as they passed through the rutted tracks of the county's hamlets. Villagers in the gardens seemed more concerned about when the next mail coach would arrive, and Oliver became tired of telling them when the last time was that the cheap ha'penny post had passed him. The mail coaches often overtook them – their drivers showed no inclination to spare the whip on their poor horses. They raced against each other as they had always done, to beat the best times for the stage. It was doubtful if anyone else in Jackals cared. Penny post went by aerostat and urgent letters – where money was no object – could be entrusted to a crystalgrid station.

Occasionally they would be resting underneath the foliage of a shady ash tree when the shadow of an aerostat would pass over them, one of the massive warships heading south to Shadowclock. Harry was curious about the frequency of the airships travelling overhead, until he found the reason from a horseman resting his stallion at one of the Lissacks. The high fleet of war was confined to port after some trouble in the capital. Only the merchant marine was running in and out of the aerostat fields now. This news seemed to trouble Harry although he would not – or could not – say why.

It was in the lee of one of the coaching inns marking the route that they came across a party of rovies with the same wild style as the gypsy caravans that descended on Hundred Locks for the Midwinter Festival. Their horses were sixers from the colonies, the extra pair of legs useful for hauling the double-storey house wagons of the nomadic travellers. Oliver stared up at the house wagons; they were works of art, built like colourful wooden galleons of the land. Many of the rovie clans had fled to Jackals from the plains to the east of Quatérshift during the dying days of the revolution. The state's new masters had targeted the free-spirited people as uncommunityist, selfishly unproductive. Punishment began with the accused being exiled to an organized community – and usually ended when they were finally fed into a Gideon's collar.

Harry decided the gypsies would make excellent cover to travel the remaining miles to Shadowclock and quickly set about befriending their headman at one of the trestles behind the inn. They both laughed and sang drinking songs that sounded lewd even in the incomprehensible tongue the two men were using – possibly a shiftie dialect. A deal was struck and Oliver and Steamswipe found themselves attached to one of the house-boxes. Between the taciturn steamman warrior and the jabbering travellers with their mangled Jackelian, Oliver found himself wishing he were riding up front with Harry. At least his stories made sense. The family chief of Oliver's wagon had a near neckless head the shape of an upside-down potato and a permanently slumped stance. When he was not drunk and insanely happy, he was scowling and scratching at his silver hair while his horses plodded along at an unbroken pace.

Still, the food was good: soft baked hams in a peppery breadcrumb crust washed down with sloe berry wine. It was a surreal experience, swaying as he rested on the back step of the caravan, listening to the sounds of the wheels crunch over the husks and shells blown in from the grain fields. Bathing in the warm sunlight while somewhere out there in Jackals the members of a lethal conspiracy were plotting his demise. This is what it must have been like for the other children at Hundred Locks – unrestricted by a Department of Feymist registration order – packed off during the teachers' rest weeks to stay with relatives in far-off corners of Jackals. Collecting fallen birch wood for the hearth with their cousins, lying down in glades and watching the clouds pull past overhead.

Every now and then another train of horses would overtake Oliver's caravan in the line. He had been surprised to see that one of the caravans was owned by a steamman, the metal creature's limbs tied with ribbons of gaudy fabric as if he had been decorated for a festival. He spoke no language apart from Quatérshiftian, and the only comment Oliver could elicit from Steamswipe was that his fellow steamman was defective in his cognitive functions.

While the taciturn steamman made for an unloquacious travelling companion, his attitude to Oliver had mellowed enough that he was allowed – perhaps even required – to polish the holy relic from the chamber of arms every evening. What sort of weapon Lord Wireburn was, he was still unsure of. Oliver faintly recalled reading one of his uncle's classic texts on warfare, filled with illustrations of regimental squares and inked arrows of manoeuvre. Steammen were meant to favour air pistols that could be connected to their own boilers for pressurisation. Lord Wireburn did not seem to be one of those. Its black shell-like metal sweated a strange dark oil which needed to be wiped clean every day. Oliver had to wash the rags he used for the job after each hour spent cleaning the holy device.

A crackling sound caught Oliver's attention. On the other side of a canopy of oak leaves a fire burned in the open. The travellers had witches with them, beautiful wild women who could twist the flames from the camp fires into dancing comet streamers and wrap the fire around themselves like silk as they leapt lightly around the grass, unhurried by gravity's touch. Their faces were so perfect, their bodies so lithe, that just seeing them was enough to make a heart ache. Harry had already warned him off the rovie women – suggesting that any liaison would likely end in him being stuck with a jealous lover's blade or forced into a hasty traveller's wedding. Oliver doubted if he would have the courage to approach them anyway. The few times that he had tried to show interest in girls at Hundred Locks they had laughed at him, looks of fear and pity curiously intermingled on their faces. The cries of 'fey-boy, fey-boy' from the gangs of his peers when he stumbled across them in the town still stung in his memory, along with the tittering half-whispered conversations when he passed girls of his age. He polished the relic harder. That would not be happening again in the near future. Never again.

Under the shade of the tree, Steamswipe cut the evening air with his martial forms, sweeping and ducking in a slow dance as the sky turned red with sunset.

Oliver sighed. 'Why did you come with us, knight?'

Oliver had meant the question to be rhetorical, and was surprised when the voicebox in Lord Wireburn's barrel vibrated with an answer. 'Because it was necessary.'

Oliver reached for a clean rag. 'You seemed to be one of the few to think so. His own commander wanted him left buried underneath Mechancia.'

'Master Saw has not known fear, he does not understand the knight's crime.'

'Steamswipe has known fear?'

'Steamswipe has faced that which no other steamman dares. In the rotting heart of Liongeli there are a people related to our race – the siltempters. They feed on the life force from our soul boards, they would drink our oil, rip the crystal components from our chest assemblies to wear as necklaces for their perverted rites and not think it too much. Are my barrel manifolds warm?'

'They cool as I wipe this black liquid off,' said Oliver.

'Steamswipe has been to the heart of darkness and faced that which no mind should see without being bent out of shape for eternity. Master Saw has not known fear, but Master Saw has only faced craynarbian tribesmen and Quatérshiftian regiments on the border of the Free State. He does not *know*. That is why I chose the knight.'

'If you understand that,' said Oliver, 'then you also know fear?'

'I understand.'

Oliver looked at the ugly dark weapon cradled on his lap, heavy enough to be uncomfortable even horizontal. 'What in the name of the Circle do you fear, Lord Wireburn?'

'I fear that which I must do, young softbody. And I fear that one day I will come to enjoy it.'

Chapter Eighteen

'What has your analyser uncovered, Aliquot?' asked Nickleby.

'Is it my parents?' said Molly. 'Have you discovered their identity?'

'I am afraid no blood machine is sophisticated enough to do that,' said Coppertracks. 'Although theoretically speaking, with some modifications I am sure I might . . . but I digress. You may see for yourself, Molly softbody. Press your eyes up to the magnification glass.'

Molly placed her face inside the rubber hood on the front of the machine, cold glass staring down onto a pink river filled with the flow of creatures – fragile jelly-like things moving in liquid. 'This is my blood?'

'It is,' said Coppertracks. 'The gas compression acts as a powerful lens, magnifying the view of your system juices a thousand fold. What you see under the glass are the animalcules that constitute your biological cooperative.'

'It looks – odd. Like a river filled with fish and eels.'

'Filled with other things, young softbody. Filled with answers. Look!' Coppertracks turned up the magnification, the machine hissing as the gas cylinders intensified their internal pressure. 'Do you see the smaller organisms in your system juices?'

'What can you see, lass?' Commodore Black moved closer. 'Through that infernal periscope of Aliquot's?'

'Tiny things – with cogs turning, moving through my blood, like the screws on a boat. That's not normal, is it?' A terrible feeling of apprehension seized Molly. Had she been poisoned, was she dying?

Coppertracks held up a wad of tape from the analysing machine. 'Your people have a name for it, young softbody. Popham's Disease. If you needed a transfusion of system juices during a medical operation you would die in agony unless the donor of the juices also suffered from Popham's Disease. This is the missing link, the thing that you share with all the other victims of the Pitt Hill Slayer. This disease was not to be found on your records in Greenhall's transaction engine rooms because the information entity that uncovered your details erased that data. I warrant that every name on the list of victims had the same disease.'

'Why would a rare blood type make Molly a target for murder?' said Nickleby. 'Is there someone important who is ill with the disease – and the slayer wants to wipe out all sources of donor blood?'

'A logical reason if the murderer could not directly make their intended victim deactivate,' said Coppertracks. 'But in this case I think not.'

One of the slipthinker's mu-bodies returned to the clock chamber bearing a leather tome, its cover cracked and brown with age. Coppertracks took the book and rested it carefully on a workbench. He opened it wide and Molly saw that the pages were illuminated in metallic ink – still shining despite the crinkled age of the paper. She had never seen such beautiful illustrations before, delicately rendered raised metal images surrounded by black calligraphy in a language she did not recognize. It made the linework pictures of Jackals' news sheets and penny dreadfuls look like bored scribbling dashed out by amateurs. Something told her that whoever had painstakingly created page after page of this work – surely a life's labour – had not belonged to the race of man.

One of Coppertracks' iron fingers moved over the page and Molly saw what it was he wanted her to see – a rainbow block of what she had first taken for abstract border-work around the edges of the page. The drawings were clusters of the same tiny creatures Coppertracks had pointed out swimming through the internal rivers of her body. Arrows from the script connected to the illustrations, commentary on the creatures no doubt.

'Do you see, Molly softbody? Your council of surgeons classifies Popham's Disease as a disorder of your system juices, but it is not. It is a gift!'

'A gift that would let her die under a sawbones's scalpel,' said the commodore. 'Blessed gifts like that you can keep to yourself.'

Molly calmed the commodore. 'What do you mean a gift?'

'Do you not feel an affinity for mechomancy, Molly softbody? In the engine rooms at Greenhall you divined the purpose of the Radnedge Rotator just by looking at it. Slowcogs and Silver Onestack instinctively followed you through the caverns of the outlaw realm, Redrust the controller gave his life to protect your own after a single reading of the Gear-gi-ju cogs.'

Molly remembered her fingers flickering over Onestack's vision crystals, restoring his sight to colour. 'I can't deny I feel a calling towards your people, a talent for fixing machines – but it's a knack, I've always had it.'

'You have always had it because you have one foot in the world of fastbloods and one foot in the race of steammen, young softbody. Those creatures in your blood are of my people. They are machine life. They are of the metal.'

Molly felt faint – the odd disparity she had always felt in her life, the little differences between her and the other poorhouse children – rushed towards her in a swell of clarity. 'How did they get there, Aliquot Coppertracks?'

'For that,' said the steamman, 'you have to go back to lost books like this, lost history. This tome is from the age following the fall of Chimeca, the first age of freedom following the thawing of the world. Before that, all the kingdoms of the continent – including the lands that would become Jackals – were held under the sway of the Chimecan Empire. They ruled the ruins of the world from their underground holds. You must have seen the ruins of their works in your travels in the world below?'

'Their ziggurats and crystals are still down there,' said Molly. 'In some of the caverns.'

'Their empire's reputation has been diluted by the passage of the millennia,' said Coppertracks. 'But my people still remember something of the ferocity of their rule. They drew power through human sacrifice, blended it with the earthflow streams that are now only tamed by the order of worldsingers. The ruined kingdoms of the surface were little more than slave farms to provide souls for their terrible rites. During the worst years of the long age of cold they ate the meat of their brothers in the Circle, the race of man, graspers, craynarbians, all were food for their table. Half-covered in ice, the broken nations of the over-grounders were helpless to resist the Chimecan legions. Many of the tunnels of the atmospheric are a legacy of their reign; part of an underground transport system that could deploy armies of dark-hearted killers to any part of the continent within days, crushing rebellions and seizing families – sometimes the populations of entire cities – for punishment sacrifices.'

'Then these things in Molly's blood are from their empire?' said Nickleby.

'Quite the opposite, dear mammal,' said Coppertracks. 'When the lands of the surface began to warm, when the cycle of the world turned again to an age of warmth and the ice sheets retreated north, the nations of the over-grounders grew confident again. They began to plot the overthrow of their Chimecan masters. This book tells of a slave of the empire called Vindex, a philosopher and teacher from what are now the city-states of the Catosian League. He discovered a terrible secret. The Chimecans and their dark insect gods of the Wildcaotyl were only too aware of what the rising temperatures on the surface would do to their iron rule and their supply of meat and souls. They were planning something terrible that would solidify their rule – but in the event, their horrific design failed. Vindex escaped and drew to him a band of heroes to oppose the Chimecans' plan of last resort. Under the retreating ice sheets Vindex discovered something, a hatch leading down to an ancient underground station filled with sorcery and machines. Machines which were to change his body, bring him into the realm of metal.'

'He had these things in his blood too?'

'According to this tome and the prayer songs which we still sing for our ancestors, his system juices would have been teeming with the life metal. After he had changed his body, he created seven holy engines to bind the gods of Chimeca to darkness, the seven Hexmachina, and led them in war against the Chimecans and their Wildcaotyl gods.'

Something of what Coppertracks was telling her seemed to resonate with Molly – the horrible dreams she had experienced in the abandoned temple in the caverns below, the feeling of déjà vu.

'Come now, old steamer,' said the commodore. 'Tell me this talk of dark gods and wicked empires is for scholars and archaeologists – what does it have to do with our Molly Templar?'

'Do you not understand? Molly softbody is a descendant of Vindex, which is why her system juices bubble with the very stuff of mechomancy. All those who have died at the hands of the Pitt Hill Slayer are his descendants.'

'But it is only individuals who have been targeted – not families or children,' said Nickleby. 'If you wanted to wipe out such an ancient bloodline you would have to murder thousands of Jackelians today.'

'Popham's Disease is not inherited uniformly,' said Coppertracks. 'Its mechanism is not understood and has baffled your surgeons since its discovery. That is because they look at it as a disease, when it is not. They know that it only manifests itself shortly before or shortly after adolescence, but understand nothing about the random nature of its inheritance.'

'Then this stuff in my blood is there by chance,' said Molly. 'I could have been born the same as everyone else.'

'It is within you not by chance, but by design, Molly softbody. Your gift allows you to communicate with the Hexmachina – to wield the holy engines like a duellist balancing a sword. Not everyone born to the bloodline of Vindex is a natural operator. The gift will only manifest in those with the talent to control the Hexmachina. In those who lack the talent the gift will stay latent, like a chameleon, mimicking the natural animalcules of your system juices so well as to be indistinguishable even under the scrutiny of advanced organic analysers such as this.'

'That is the why of it, then,' said the commodore. 'Poor

Molly, with the unlucky blood of some ancient sage flowing through her veins.'

'But not the whom of it,' said Nickleby. 'Who is it that wants the operators of the Hexmachina dead?'

'The answers to that are not to be found inside this tome,' said the steamman. 'But we already have enough information to conjecture on their motives. Potential operators of the Hexmachina are being eliminated – so the most likely conclusion to be drawn is that someone does not wish the Hexmachina to be operated.'

'Those ancient engines still exist?' asked Molly.

'If our people had the answer to that, the spirit of Steelbhalah-Waldo would sleep easier in the hall of the ancients. Three of the Hexmachina were almost certainly destroyed in the war to overthrow the Chimeca. Two of the remaining four have been lost to us since that time – I have collected as many tales, rumours and legends of what happened to them as there are hours in the day to listen to them. In all probability they have been washed away by the tide of history and the events of the ages.'

'And then there were two,' said Nickleby.

Coppertracks passed the precious tome to one of his mu-bodies, the little drone disappearing with it back to Tock House's library. 'Yes, indeed. One is said to be in Liongeli, broken and near useless, a curio of a hideous race that I must regrettably admit was once distantly related to the steammen. Of them I shall not speak. The other Hexmachina is said to keep to the caverns of the undercity. Scuttling about hidden tunnels and collapsed cities so deep even the grave robbers of Grimhope will not venture there. A solitary ghost haunting the scene of its greatest moment – banishing the gods of the Wildcaotyl to the darkness beyond the walls of the world.'

'What good will it do them to kill me?' said Molly. 'From what you say there will be others who will follow me. Jackals could be filled with children who will develop this disease, this *gift* when they grow older.'

'A most fascinating question, Molly softbody. The last operator – at least for a day, a month, or a year – until other descendants of Vindex with your gift pass through adolescence. And possibly the last Hexmachina too. What mischief can be made in the conjunction of those two facts, I wonder?'

'Nothing good,' said Commodore Black. 'Of that I am mortal sure. With the amount of money they've put on the poor lass's head I am surprised we haven't had half the flash mob in the city knocking at our gates.'

'In this matter, anonymity is our friend,' said Nickleby.

Coppertracks' skull erupted into light, fiercer than Molly had ever seen before. 'Dear mammal, I fear anonymity may have betrayed us. I have just lost contact with all my mu-bodies beyond the woods.'

'An accident?'

'Simultaneously?' The steamman's mu-bodies in the clock room exploded into action, scattering to a dozen synchronised tasks.

'Aliquot Coppertracks, say this is not so,' whined the commodore.

'I fear it is. There are intruders in the grounds. In numbers large enough to destroy a dozen of my mu-bodies in chorus.'

A ball of fear curled inside Molly's stomach. She had found out why her implacable foes were hunting for her. Not for a family inheritance that did not even exist, but for her very blood itself. But now it was too late. Her friends were in danger again . . . and it was all because of her. The hidden enemy were going to do to Tock House what they had done to her family at the Sun Gate poorhouse. She was going to end up on a butcher's table while some history-obsessed maniacs opened up her veins and she became just another name on the Pitt Hill Slayer's tally of victims.

'My beautiful house,' moaned Nickleby. 'I knew this was too good to last.'

Commodore Black raided a storeroom on the side of the clock house chamber and then stumbled out with both arms spilling over with rifles and black leather bandoleers of crystal shells. He saw the look on Molly's face. 'They're from the *Sprite of the Lake*. I never did have the heart to chuck out the blessed things.'

'Circle, commodore, were you piloting a submarine or a man-o'-war?'

'Well now lass, you can be sailing across some rough old coves out there on the oceans.'

Coppertracks' mu-bodies grabbed the weapons out of his arms and dispersed smoothly to positions around Tock House. Black tossed the sling of a eight-barrel monstrosity around his shoulder. Molly had heard the whippers at the Angel's Crust laughing about those things – they had never said anything good about them.

'Commodore, that's a suicide gun!'

'No lass; a suicide gun fires one barrel at a time. This wicked devil empties all eight at once. She's a lucky gun! Mounted on the conning tower of the *Sprite* she was, and many a time I used her beautiful mouth to sweep the decks of a boarding party while we sat recharging the *Sprite*'s air supply.'

Molly jumped as a booming noise echoed up the staircase. Nickleby lay a steadying hand on her shoulder. 'Tock House was built just after the civil war, Molly. Soldiers from both armies laid off and dangerously unemployed on the streets. Why do you think there are no windows on the first two storeys? That was the house's transaction engine triggering the clockwork on the shield above the door.'

'Shield?'

'Twelve inches of layered armour,' said Nickleby. 'The Jackelian Artillery Company would pause before taking our front door down.'

Something pinged off the walls of the tower.

'That was too quiet,' said Nickleby.

Commodore Black risked a quick glance out of the window. 'Toppers, then. Ah, I can see the mufflers on their mortal guns. Real hard men, coming to kill a scared little lass. Come on you dark-hearted jiggers, let's see how you like what old Blacky has got for you!'

A cadre of Middlesteel's professional assassins. Not one, but an army of them. They were all as good as dead. Molly slumped to the floor and pushed her red hair back out of her face. She had brought this on her friends. Better they had caught her on the streets of Sun Gate outside the poorhouse and none of this had happened.

Nickleby lit his mumbleweed pipe and the sweet smell filled the room. He picked a rifle from the commodore's pile and offered it to Molly like he was proffering a plate of cheese at the dinner table.

'I've never used a gun before,' said Molly.

'Lass,' Commodore Black called from his position at the window. 'In ten minutes' time, you are going to have a whole blessed world of experience.'

Oliver noticed that fewer people were passing through the main square of Rattle. The day was wearing on and there was still no sign of the man they were waiting for. Rattle was the last hamlet before Shadowclock, a farmers' market where the drovers could trade their poultry and swine without having to pay the toll on the city road. Their gypsy travelling companions had avoided the main crown highway too, heading south over the hills of the downlands that morning. Paying a levy to the local board of roads held as much attraction to the nomads as swapping their bright wooden caravans for one of Rattle's thatched cottages.

The copper hands of the square's clock reflected the last ember of the sunset from their burnished metal.

'Is your contact likely to answer his summons?' asked Steamswipe.

Harry nodded. 'If he knows what's good for him he will.'

'Can you be sure he'll get the message?' said Oliver.

'I still have a little faith in human nature, old stick,' said Harry. 'And a little more in the purchasing power of the Jackelian shilling I gave that trader for taking him the word.'

Lights were beginning to appear in the windows of Rattle, the smell of slipsharp oil rising from the tavern behind them as the coaching inn's staff lit their own lanterns. Finally a wagon hove into view, creaking at a stately pace, and Harry rose to greet it. Behind the reins sat just about the oldest man Oliver had ever seen – his face fissured with age, part covered by a white beard trimmed into a fork. He was wearing a grey dog collar with the infinity symbol and fish of the Circlist faith on his waistcoat. The man nodded at the disreputable Stave.

'Harold.'

'Reverend,' said Harry.

The preacher cast a languid glance at Oliver and the knight steamman. 'I thought you worked alone.'

'The lad is almost family, reverend. And my friend of the metal . . . well, you could say he is something of a favour.'

The preacher grunted and looked at Steamswipe. 'Those saddlebags would be *his* idea.'

'You would be correct,' said the steamman.

'Saw a fox wearing a hat once,' said the reverend. 'It was still a fox. You can ride alongside us, my dangerous friend. Unless you fancy taking a turn pulling my wagon. Harold, boy, in the back.'

With the nag pulling the cart – nearly as toothless as the churchman – they made a slow arc around the village square, then began trotting down the hamlet's lanes.

'You think I would come, Harold?'

'When you got my message,' said the wolftaker.

'Damn presumptuous of you. But then you always were a chancer.'

'I think I'm on safe enough ground,' said Harry. 'Hallowed ground in fact. We need to get into Shadowclock and I don't have city permission papers this time. We also need a place to hide while I conduct a little business.'

'Has the Court lost its taste for forgery, Harold, or are you running something off the ledger?'

Harry scratched his nose. 'You just worry about blagging us past the gate constables, reverend. Leave keeping the ledger straight to me.'

To Oliver's surprise the Circlist churchman turned the cart away from the main road and into a wood. When they emerged from the press of pine, the high walls of Shadowclock rose before them, a pall of engine smoke hanging over the city. Contained by ramparts sixty feet high the town sat crowded across three hills, tall buildings of Pentshire granite and steep, narrow streets stained with soot. Even though it was late evening Oliver could still hear the muffled thumps and whistles of machinery from the gas mines.

They rolled down the slope towards the city, Steamswipe's red visor gleaming as he scanned the substantial walls for sentries. Counting the towers visible on the highest of the hills, the knight noted every bloated warship docked inside the city, aerostats drifting in and out of view as clouds of smoke from the mines wafted in the still summer air.

Towards the bottom of the slope the reverend's cart rolled past the gates of a graveyard and into a field of head stones, well tended but stained black by their proximity to the city. Two bare-chested graspers with rippling muscles stopped digging a fresh hole to wave at the churchman, then recommenced their labours.

'I wasn't too sure if we were going to find you filling one of your own plots,' said Harry.

'The Circle still has a little work left for me to do here,' said the reverend, 'before the wheel turns for me.'

Tying the cart up in the shadow of a temple the reverend unlocked a door and led them into a cool chamber, the centre of the room filled with a stone sarcophagus, a couple carved out of stone lying serenely in the shadows. Reaching down to the platform of the sarcophagus, the reverend grasped the infinity symbol carved into the marble and twisted it, then stepped aside as the sarcophagus crunched back on rollers.

He waved them down the hole that had been uncovered, yellow lamplight flickering below. They climbed down a ladder and Oliver found himself face to face with more graspers, whiskers twitching as they unpacked the contents of a coffin into the underground passage. Not a cadaver, but bottles of jinn, unlabelled and full of the pink liquid.

Harry scooped one of the bottles up and cracked it open against the wall, emptying it down his throat in one easy movement. 'And here's me thinking the governor was running a dry city.'

The reverend took the bottle off Harry. 'He will be again if you keep consuming the victuals.'

Following the slope of the tunnel for a couple of minutes,

their passage widened into a series of cave-like catacombs and Steamswipe unhunched his back, the low hiss of his boiler the only sound in the cavern. Spared the soot of the engines above ground, the cave walls gleamed white as the churchman's torch passed them.

Harry tapped a pile of barrels as they navigated through the cave tunnels. 'All this money – one day I'll visit and you'll have disappeared. Where's the reverend, I'll ask? Oh, they'll say, he's retired to the colonies. Left a legacy by a nephew. Bought a plantation he did.'

The reverend snorted. 'You know where the money goes, Harold. If you didn't, you'd still be waiting back in Rattle. Not all our coffins are full of contraband. By the Circle, I wish they were.'

The reverend led them through the cold twisting tunnels of the catacombs, passing as many chambers filled with moon-raker's produce as littered with bones – a smuggler's fortune hidden beneath the surface of Shadowclock. The reverend seemed to have moved from preaching against sin to control-ling it inside the city. His Circlist position was the perfect cover. Oliver wondered if the vicar back in Hundred Locks had been helping the moonrakers land illegal cargoes in the bay of the dike too. Perhaps the whole Circlist church in Jackals was a front for the flash mob, the crime barons of Middlesteel all surreptitiously sitting as bishops and prelates.

Surfacing in the basement level of a church, Oliver stepped out of a hidden door in the wall, into a room piled with old pews and a crowd of broken oak-carved gargoyles.

'You can stay in the hospice rooms at the back,' said the preacher to Harry. 'They're not fancy, but I figure for a queer-looking party like yours, it's better than the questions you would get trying to room at an inn or boarding house.'

The reverend went to leave but Harry stopped him. 'There's

someone we need to meet, reverend.' He unfolded a scrap of paper and showed the churchman the scar markings Oliver had drawn back on Harry's narrowboat. 'He'll have a high position in the grasper warren and mining combination. A few years on him.'

The reverend took a seat on an old stone chair from the high Circlist days, thinking. He looked like a monarch from the ancient age of Jackals, a fissured old prophet sitting in judgement. 'You've come a long way for nothing, Harold. I know the man with these warren scars. He's dead. I buried him myself.'

'Dead how, old man?'

'Officially it was a cave-in. Unofficially, well, I've seen my share of rock wounds and what was left of him to bury didn't have them. I would say someone dropped your miner down a very long mineshaft. I didn't hold an open-coffin wake if you know what I mean.'

'He was a combination man,' said Harry. 'High warren! Back when I was last here there would have a been a withdrawal of labour until the crushers found a killer.'

'Yes there would,' said the reverend. 'Five years ago. But things have changed in Shadowclock. There have been an awful lot of cave-ins and gas flares under the three hills – accidents that always seem to kill key members of the brotherhood of gas miners.'

'The combination's done nothing? *You've* done nothing?'

'I'm a tired old man, Harold. On a good day I can just about climb into my cart myself and ride the parish. And the combination's been broken as long as I have.'

'The governor couldn't break an egg in the morning without his valet. What in the Circle's name has happened here while I've been gone?'

'The combination was broken from the inside out, Harold.

Not from the hill, although I'm sure the governor is in on all the merry japes that are being played here. Either that or he is so scared he's looking the other way. The man you were looking for has a son. I'll ask him to come over tomorrow. You can ask him your questions.'

'What does Anna think of all this?' asked Harry.

'She moved along the Circle a couple of years ago,' said the reverend. 'Old age. I buried her out back myself. Elizabeth and the girls left soon after. They got tired of wiping dust from the mines off their dresses, got tired of the engine smoke, maybe they even got tired seeing how little difference I was making here.'

The reverend left to check on the rooms at the back of the church. Harry looked pale and wan. He had been expecting to meet someone different. The old man had changed, deflated.

'The softbody priest,' said Steamswipe. 'You are threatening him with exposure of his smuggling activities?'

'Don't sound so disapproving,' said Harry. 'Sneaking stuff past city customs is the least of it. He was a wicked old fox in his day. Gave the wolftakers the run-around like nobody else in the Court's history.'

'How did a town vicar ever come to warrant the Court's attention,' said Oliver.

'It wasn't the churchman that caught our eye,' said Harry. 'It was someone else entirely. But I reckon that man's dead now. Come on, let's get our packs stowed.'

The reverend's church was built into the narrow terraced streets. Oliver sat on a window seat, carefully cleaning the boatman's gun the way Harry had showed him, with half an eye on the waking city outside. Three storeys below gas miners were changing shift, crowds of graspers wearing dirty gutta-percha capes and gas hoods trudging back home, elephantine breather filters swinging from their faces in a solemn pendulum sway. Normally the graspers would have been quite capable of mining without protection – their own warren cities in the downlands were testament to that. But exposure to celgas caused burns to even their tough hide, so they rode the steam lifts underground in their stifling suits and sweated their labours for Jackals' most precious commodity.

Somewhere out there, obscured by the engine smoke and rock dust of Shadowclock, were the answers. The answers to why his family lay dead in Hundred Locks. The answers to why his name now adorned wanted posters on constables' walls for murders he had not committed. The answers to why momentous events now seemed to swing around the orbit of his small life like drunken dancers around a festival pole.

'You don't look like you're used to doing that, boy.' It was the reverend. For all his years he moved with the silence of a cat. There was something else Oliver found disconcerting. The way the old man's shadow moved sometimes – faster than his age, larger than his bulk. Like it belonged to someone else. 'In fact, you don't look any more comfortable than when you're wiping the gunk off that talking obscenity your steamman friend keeps rolled away.'

Oliver placed a gleaming barrel down on the cloth. 'I've only shot it the once – and if I hit what I was aiming at it was an accident.'

'That I figured. How old are you, son? You look like you should just be finishing off your schooling, not trailing behind a poacher-turned-gamekeeper like Harold Stave.'

Oliver scratched a pattern in the soot on the window. 'I was tossed out of school when they put me on the county registration book.'

'Ah,' said the reverend. 'A bit of wild blood running through the veins, eh? That's too bad. We don't get the mist much in

318

this part of the world. Don't mix well with the earthflow streams and the gas we're sitting on, I reckon. You'll die of black lung and tunnel rot before you choke on a feymist here at Shadowclock.'

'Is that why you stay here?' said Oliver.

'I go where I'm needed, pilgrim,' said the reverend. 'I'm a lifetime too old to fear the mist now, boy. Too old to survive the changes if it got me. Besides, a man has to die of something.'

'You're needed to supply jinn to the miners?'

'That's the mercenary streak you get hanging around Harold Stave speaking, boy,' said the reverend. 'There's more than one sort of crime. As a for instance, Shadowclock doesn't have a board of the poor to help the families here when they fall on hard times. The city's a mining town – if you're not working the governor doesn't want you taking up valuable space that could be filled by someone more able. This is a bad place to get lame, injured or sick in.'

'You sound like a Carlist,' said Oliver.

'That's been noted before,' said the reverend. 'But when you come down to it, there's not much that was written in *Community and the Commons* that wasn't spoken first by one prophet or another in the good book. People are all people have got, boy. We need to look out for each other.'

The truth of what the reverend was doing suddenly settled on Oliver. 'That's why you're running this place like the flash mob! You use the money to help the families that would have gone to the poor board.'

'Keep your voice down, son. The state wouldn't care for it if they knew I had a parallel system of taxation running underneath their noses.'

'And Harry found out about it.'

'That's a polite way of asking is that what he's got over

me,' said the reverend. 'If it was, it would be the best of it. His people might care about the security of this place, but they don't give a damn about skimming the froth off the customs gate. Their attitude to it is the same as mine – people have been drinking and stuffing their pipes for as long as there's been history – someone's going to do it. My way there's fewer hungry children keeping their parents awake at night crying because the stew pot was more water than it was gravy.'

'You sound tired,' said Oliver.

'By damn I am tired, pilgrim. Life at my age is like serving in a war. Everything you ever loved, everyone you knew, has been cut down by the years. I've outlived them all; my wife, my friends, most of my damn enemies too. All I have left is my anger at the foolishness of the world. The unnecessary cruelties, the pomposity and vanity of people who should know better. Most of the time I just want to shake some sense into the world.'

Oliver did not know what to say. Listening to the old man was like hearing the thunder roll at the end of a storm. Their places in the world separated by the gulf of a lifetime. Something about the reverend made him uneasy, but he wasn't sure if it was a hidden darkness in the man or a premonition that he might be seeing echoes of how he would end up seventy years hence.

From down the stairs Oliver heard Steamswipe calling his name. 'I'd better go.'

'Better had, boy.'

When Oliver had gone the reverend checked the stairs then shut the door to the room. He went to the window seat where Oliver had been resting and lifted up the cover. From underneath a jumble of blankets the reverend pulled out a wooden box. Settling his bones into a chair he balanced the box on his legs and toyed with the clasp. What had made him think of it now? He hadn't thought of the box for months, let alone looked at it. Too much talk of the past. No fool like an old fool. Against his better nature he lifted the lid and the light of the box's contents illuminated the crevices of his face. He sighed and put the box away. Then, resting back in the chair, he fell asleep.

It was a light slumber, the slumber of age and weariness. As a child the reverend had laughed when his own grandfather had fallen asleep during the day. It had seemed comical. Now he did the same four or five times a day. His dreams had become pedestrian since Anna had moved along the Circle: he was busying about the church, checking the cushions were still underneath the pews. Then the thing walked in from the street. Surely nothing could have been so badly injured in a tunnel gas flare and lived? It was a gargoyle given flesh.

'By damn,' said the reverend.

'Not quite,' said the Whisperer. 'Although one of us might be damned.'

'What in the name of the Circle are you, my friend?'

'You can think of me as your conscience,' hissed the Whisperer.

'My conscience sure got mean since I last used it.'

'No false modesty now,' said the Whisperer, 'your conscience gets out more than I do. All those secret payments to the widows and the children, the food for the miners with limbs as mangled as mine.'

The dream seemed more vivid than usual. The reverend looked around the church with unnatural clarity. 'My conscience seems very well informed today, sir.'

'I like your mind, old man. It's as still as that graveyard you tend, and has as many secret tunnels buried away beneath it.'

'We all have secrets,' said the reverend, 'and a tale to tell. Behind that flesh of yours, for instance.'

'Ah, but my story is a mere abbreviation in comparison to yours, old man,' said the Whisperer. 'What's to tell? A feymist rising and a sleeping child in the wrong place at the wrong time.'

'The lives of half the Special Guard began that way.'

'You should take a tour of Hawklam Asylum some time, old man. Poke a stick between the bars of the low-risk feybreed with all the other curious ladies and gentleman of Middlesteel. You would see how most of our stories end up.'

'So you are connected to the boy.'

'So I am,' said the Whisperer. 'I've been having a little trouble getting into Oliver's dreams of late. His body's defences seem to be reacting to me as a threat after I had to pour a little unpleasant fey medicine down his throat.'

'Lucky him.'

'Don't be like that, old man. I'm only trying to steer him in the right direction.'

'Yes, but right for who?' said the reverend.

'That sounds a little sanctimonious coming from you, preacher,' hissed the Whisperer. 'You used to redraw the line between right and wrong all the time. Or maybe you've forgotten? The Circlelaw by day, the mask and the black horse by night. Who was ever going to suspect you?'

'The money went to those who needed it,' said the reverend.

'I believe you will find the counting houses and merchants you relieved of all that gold thought they needed it,' said the Whisperer.

'They were wrong.'

'Don't think I disapprove,' said the Whisperer. 'Quite the opposite in fact. You remember when you were given the box, when you found *him* half-dead in your old vicar's church? Now it's time to pass the box on.'

'You're talking about the boy.'

The Whisperer's limbs twitched, but his silence spoke for him.

'Don't you think he's been cursed enough? Given wild blood, chased away from his home in the company of those two killers.'

'It's time to pass the box on, old man. It's time for *him* to ride again.'

'I won't do it to the boy,' said the reverend. 'I've spent the last two decades trying to forget what I was.'

'But you can't, can you, old man? You're like a worldsinger trying to meditate away the urge for another sniff of petal dust. The box calls to you, doesn't it? It sings to be opened, to make you feel alive again – to make the night your cloak and make the wicked suffer under your heel.'

'I will not let him out again,' said the reverend. 'I will not bear the responsibility for it.'

'The responsibility was never yours to give,' said the Whisperer.

'Even if I could, Harold Stave will not let me.'

'Now that's the weasel in you talking,' said the misshapen feybreed. 'Stave knows about you, but he never knew about the box. As far as the Court is concerned the Hood-o'the-marsh died a long time ago. Give Oliver the box. If it's time for *him* to ride, he will.'

'That's an awful thing to wish on a man.'

'He may not live without it,' said the Whisperer. 'You may choose to hide yourself away in the smog of the mines but you have noticed all the odd little things going on in the city, haven't you? The disappearances. The beatings. Out with the old, in with the new.'

'I'm old,' said the reverend, 'but I am not blind yet.'

'Well you don't know the jigging half of it. There's a storm coming and that line from the Circlelaw about where there is pain, ease it, that isn't going to count for a whole lot soon, old fellow. Two ounces of mumbleweed without gate tax isn't going to pay for a pauper's funeral this time. All those hungry eyes of the children you had to bury – the ones that used to visit your nightmares – you better start laying in a fresh stack of small coffins.'

'Get out of my head,' cried the reverend.

'Give him the box.'

'He's feybreed already,' said the reverend. 'Hasn't he got witch powers?'

'They seem a little shy right now,' said the Whisperer, 'and a bit too defensive for my tastes. And as you pointed out, Oliver is just a man. He's been uprooted from everything that's familiar, had what passes for a family cut out from underneath him. He is being hunted to ground like a fox by the order and the crushers for a crime he didn't even commit. If a lifetime of hamblin contempt hadn't made him so anti-social and contained to start with, this would have broken him. You can feel the anger within Oliver, old man. A sea of it. It needs a release. I need *him* released from the box and so does Jackals.'

The reverend crumpled back in his chair, feeling every one of his years. 'I always thought I would die as the Hood-o'the-marsh.'

'You should have burnt the box,' said the Whisperer.

'You don't think I didn't try! I flung it into the furnaces up on the hill. The next morning I found it stored back in my chest under the blankets, waiting for me like a damn dog to be fed. That's what you're asking me to pass on.'

'It'll feed now,' hissed the Whisperer. 'It's time for a banquet.'

Chapter Nineteen

'They're coming,' shouted Nickleby from the window. A volley of silenced shots crackled off the thick walls of Tock House. Molly triggered her rifle and the recoil of the butt smashed painfully against her shoulder. She did not see where her shot landed – it was dark outside and the toppers were wearing uniforms blacker than a stack cleaner's breeches.

'Lean hard into the rifle, lass,' said the commodore. 'Don't give it any room to dance about on you now.'

He rested his monstrous cannon on the open windowsill and fired it down into the grounds, all eight barrels spreading chaos below. Coppertracks' drones ran behind them, taking discharged rifles, breaking them and emptying the shattered crystal charges into stone buckets. One of the mu-bodies passed a reloaded rifle to Molly. Coppertracks stood obscured behind the workbench and the blood machine, lying silent now the servants of his id were helping repel the attack.

'Aliquot,' called the commodore. 'Will you busy yourself over here, we're fighting for our blessed lives.'

Coppertracks did not reply, but from outside the night was

filled with screams. Sharparms was galloping through the darkness spearing toppers with his piston arms. He had waited hidden in the tree line until the assault force had gathered in strength; now he was rampaging through the grounds like the dark conscience of the slipthinker, leaving murder and trampled softbodies in his wake.

'You beautiful, frightful thing,' called the commodore. 'But I'm still glad we've four thick walls between us and you.'

As the toppers tried to assemble to meet the threat Sharparms would crash through the wood, the ghostly chatter of his spear arms moving in and out before he vanished into the tree line, reappearing in their midst from another angle.

Molly, Nickleby and the commodore poured shots down into the distracted assault, spinning bodies around to fall onto the gravel and the carefully tended flowerbeds. Coppertracks came up behind Molly and ushered her to the side as he passed beakers of red fizzing liquid to his mu-bodies. They hurled the chemicals out of the tower's broken clock face, raining them down onto a cluster of toppers who were hefting a battering ram with a blow-barrel sap-filled head towards Tock House's door. Jelly-like fire spread across the party, flames spilling out into the bushes and trees to the side of the coach house.

'Dear Circle, Aliquot,' said Nickleby. 'Careful with my horseless.'

As Sharparms impaled two toppers, one on either arm, a figure stepped out of the bushes behind the steamman, spinning a three-sphere bolas around his head. Unlike the others he was not dressed in black – he looked more like he had been diverted from a dinner engagement at one of the chandelier-lit palaces of food along Goldhair Park. Light from Coppertracks' chemical fire briefly illuminated his face. Molly sucked in her breath. It was him! The old devil from the bawdyhouse, the same jigger who had killed Slowcogs and Silver Onestack. Count Vauxtion. He was like some demon from a Spring-heeled Jack penny ballad. Every time she thought she had escaped him and slunk away into anonymity, he appeared like the calm eye in a cyclone of death.

The count's bolas twisted in slow motion, wrapping itself around Sharparms' hind legs – the steamman dropped the two dead toppers off his spear arms, his helmet-like head turning towards the source of the threat. From the woods one of Coppertracks' other mu-bodies raced towards the warrior – he had nearly reached Sharparms when the explosion leapt out, blowing the diminutive drone back across the gravel. In the clearing smoke Molly saw that both of the steamman's rear legs had been vaporized. Sharparms was trying to use his front two legs to scrabble forward, but the vengeful assassins were on top of him, opening his frayed armour with harpoon-like weapons.

Behind Molly, Coppertracks' body tossed on top of his tracks, moaning as the pain of his warrior drone's death overwhelmed him. Nickleby and the commodore emptied their rifles into the fray, but it was too late. Tock House's steamman guardian lay deactivate in a pool of dark oil, his life force spilled in the warm summer night.

'They're withdrawing,' shouted Molly. It was true, down below the toppers were disappearing back into the trees.

'No, lass,' said Commodore Black. 'The black-hearted devils know we are on our last legs now. They're regrouping.'

True to the submariner's prediction the toppers came back out a few minutes later, odd guns that looked like broomsticks with kegs on their tips strapped to their bodies.

Molly stared. 'What are those things?'

'Get down Molly.' Nickleby pushed her to the floor as one

of the kegs fireworked off its broom and crashed through the shattered clockface. It was pierced with pepper-holes and spun across the floor, filling the chamber with smoke.

'Aliquot,' yelled Nickleby, 'get the girl out of here.'

'My vision glass is impaired,' called the steamman. 'Find my nearest mu-body.'

More of the wooden kegs clattered across the chamber, spinning as gas streamed out. Black was coughing an obscenity, but Molly could not even see him now in the smog. It smelt sickly sweet and stung at her eyes like vinegar – inhaling it was like trying to breathe cotton wool, her throat hacking as her lungs tried to separate air from the foul viscous cloud.

Crawling across the floor, breathing nails, she could not see Nickleby or any of her other friends – her tear-eyed vision was down to a couple of inches inside the mustard thick haze. An explosion shook the tower, followed by a clang as the metal shield door collapsed back with all the weight of a dying slipsharp. Molly's shaking body was enveloped by darkness long before the first grappling hook slashed into the metal frame of the clock face.

'What was in the blanket he gave you?' asked Harry Stave.

'I haven't had the chance to look yet,' said Oliver. 'He said it was a gift. Something he didn't get to use much anymore.'

'He'd spend his time more profitably trying to find the miner we're looking for,' said Harry. 'The old man said he knew the son – how hard can it be to track down a single grasper?'

The reverend appeared at the bottom of the stairs. 'That depends on how hard the grasper in question is trying not to be found, Harold.'

'Good to see your hearing isn't going yet, old man.'

'My sense of hospitality is wearing powerful thin though. So it's lucky for both of us that your miner has just walked into the church. He's waiting out the back with your steamman friend – but 'ware how you tread, this pilgrim is more than a little skittish.'

'About time,' said Harry.

'Come on Harry, he's just an old man,' said Oliver. 'I think he believes he's going to move along the Circle soon.'

'He might be right,' said Harry. 'One way or another.'

In the church hospice the grasper stood nervously, his boots twitching on the floor, although he became slightly calmer when he saw the reverend return.

'This is Mabvoy,' said the reverend. 'His father was the combination man you described.'

'Sit down my friend,' said Harry. 'We're on the same side. The people who murdered your father have been doing their best to kill us off, too.'

'Well pardon me if I don't find that reassuring,' said the grasper. 'I only came here because with the reverend's friends asking around town after me, it was only going to be a matter of time before word got back to *them* that you were looking for me. After that, I'd be as dead as my father . . . and so would you.'

'Your father came to visit us in Hundred Locks,' said Oliver.

'You?' The grasper looked at Oliver as if he was seeing him in the room for the first time.

'My uncle,' said Oliver. 'He came to visit my Uncle Titus.'

'Ah. Yes, he went north a couple of times – said he was telling someone about the problems at the mines. I thought it might be a Greenhall man.'

'He didn't want to tell the authorities here?' asked Harry.

'There's them that did,' said the grasper. 'And them that did weren't seen again. Nothing happens at Shadowclock

329

without a nod from the governor. Everyone knows that. You might as well complain to the highwaymen about the mail coach being robbed. One of the traders that came here told my father that he knew someone who could sort the problems out. It cost him his life.'

'It cost my uncle his life, too,' said Oliver. 'Your killers turned up at Seventy Star Hall and finished us all off. It wasn't much of an existence, but it was mine.'

'Sorry for your family,' said the grasper. He sounded like he meant it.

Harry checked the window. Steamswipe was standing sentry at the wall, his vision plate tracking the workers and families walking up and down the street. Watching for people who might be loitering, repeating their route. Lord Wireburn hung on a clip on his flank, a brooding black presence waiting for murder.

'Tell me about the problems,' said Harry.

The grasper laughed, but there was no humour in it. 'You got all day? It started two or three years ago. There was a wave of young blood coming up through the mining combination. Radicals. Said we were getting the shaft, not the silver mine from the masters. Wanted to demand more money – all the usual things.'

'Your father was high in the warren.'

'He was on the combination committee,' said the grasper. 'They opposed the radicals at first – there was no respect for the elders being shown – that's not the way we do things. But then the radicals bypassed the committee and went direct to the governor, demanded the reforms – and he gave in. Just like that. No withdrawal of labour, no work to rule. He just said yes, as meek as you please.'

Stave made a sound at the back of his throat. Disbelief, but it came out as half a growl.

'I see you know how it works,' said the grasper. 'There's not a penny we earn that hasn't been sweated and fought out of the masters' pockets. There's not a public bath in Shadowclock that hasn't been built on the back of an unlawful public assembly and disorder. But they just ask and the governor gives the radicals it all.'

'That must have caused quite a stir,' said Harry.

'It finished the old committee,' said the grasper. 'After that there was no stopping the radicals. They took over the combination. Strutted around the city like the lords of the town.'

'So how come I don't see a sea of smiling faces coming off each shift down in the streets?' asked Harry.

'Oh, we still get the money,' said the grasper. 'But we get a lot more than that too. Miners started disappearing. Just a few at first, but the ones who vanished were the master guildsmen. Tunnellers, frame layers, engineers. The best the city had. Without them looking after things the gas mines got unsafe powerful fast.' The grasper pulled his shirt open, showing them the burns across his leathery fur. 'Gas flare – killed four of my team. In the old days that kind of seepage would have been detected, sealed and drained. Now, there's barely a worker down the tunnels who knows one end of a cavity-cutter tube from another. The new committee abolished the apprenticeship system – said it encouraged inequitable caste distinctions – now there's so many workers vanished from the city that they're throwing pups down the pits.'

'But that's got to have hit your production quotas,' said Harry. 'The House of Guardians may not care about rock falls in the tunnels, but by the Circle, they do care about the supply of celgas.'

'I heard the governor has been making up the shortfall by running down the reserves,' said the grasper. 'The governor and the combination are working together. You open your mouth to complain and if the combination hands don't beat you along the Circle, the redcoats will pull you from your bed at night and you'll never be seen again.'

'Where are the miners who disappear being taken to?' asked Oliver.

'I bloody well know where the troublemakers go,' said the grasper. 'I went to one of the caverns the combination has declared out of bounds – there's bodies down there, rotting corpses piled as high as houses. Probably my father too if I had the heart to look.'

Oliver felt sick to the stomach. People treated like the scraps from a cleared table, their bodies left to decompose underground without a Circlist burial.

Harry's eyes narrowed. 'Just the troublemakers?'

The grasper nodded. 'The workers are taken away. My sister clerks on the hill and even she doesn't know where they're being taken. They've been told some story about another gas mine that's been discovered and must be kept secret for the state, but that's tunnel-mule manure. Everyone knows celgas is only found underneath Shadowclock.'

'If there is another source of celgas,' said Harry, 'it sure as damn isn't being worked with miners from Shadowclock, old stick. What in the name of the Circle is going on here? None of this makes any sense.'

'Maybe there is another celgas mine, Harry,' said Oliver. 'Isn't that a secret worth killing Uncle Titus for?'

'Perhaps,' said Harry. 'People have killed for a lot less.' But the wolftaker did not sound convinced; he looked at Steamswipe, still standing sentry by the window. 'But I don't think that King Steam is the sort to get all fierced up by a fortune in gas, not even if it had been found squarely underneath the peaks of the Mechancian Spine.

332

Oliver rubbed his eyes; they always seemed to be full of grit since they had come to Shadowclock. A fortune worth killing for – but Harry was right, the riches of a fresh gas strike might spark the avarice of the race of man, but it wasn't enough to vex the Lady of the Lights or produce the grim predictions of King Steam. Jackals was in danger, but the nature of their enemy seemed as elusive as ever.

'Can your sister find out when the authorities intend to ship the next crew of pressed miners out of the city?' Harry asked the grasper.

'I don't want anything to do with you,' said the grasper. 'Just one look at you three maniacs and I know you're trouble. I'm hiding for my life here – the only thing I need to do in Shadowclock is disappear before someone disappears me.'

'Think of your father,' growled Oliver. 'He cared enough about what happened to his people to do something about it.'

The grasper shivered in his chair. 'I'm frightened.'

'I know what that feels like,' said Oliver. 'I've been running for my life every day since I left my home in Hundred Locks. But the people who are after you are not going to forget about you. Wherever you hide, you're going to be going to sleep every night wondering whether you'll wake up with a knife at your throat – or not wake up at all. You don't want to live life like that. It's like dying every day. Think about your father at the bottom of that pile of corpses. You want to pay them back for that? Give them something else to think about ... give them us.'

'Alright,' the grasper crumbled. 'If she can find out when the next aerostat leaves I'll give you the details. It may be a few days. There's not many left here in the trade now worthy of the name brother – the mines are scraping the bottom of the barrel.'

'We'll be here,' said Oliver.

*   *   *

'Sharply done, Oliver,' said Harry, after the grasper had gone.

'He just needed some fire in his belly,' said Oliver. 'You could see the fear in his eyes.'

Harry looked at Oliver. There was something different about the young man he could not quite put his finger on.

'You intend to follow the aerostat back to its home,' said Steamswipe.

'That I do not,' replied Harry. 'I intend to stow away *on* the bloody thing. I spent most of my life arranging for contraband to be sneaked on and off RAN vessels. If I can't get us onto the governor's stat I don't deserve to be hanged as a thief.'

'Then I believe we are as good as on board,' said Steamswipe.

Oliver tossed and turned in the back room of the church. Since the Whisperer had stopped his nighttime visitations, Oliver's dreams had become disjointed and jumbled. Faint, fading things that he woke up struggling even to recall. To make matters worse the whistles and hisses from the mines carried on the wind at night, making it hard to drift off. He was used to the rural stillness of Hundred Locks. Oliver could sleep through a storm blown off the dike wall, but not the clatter of miners' boots as they trampled back from their midnight shift.

He was running through the woods behind Seventy Star Hall, killers from the police and the Court of the Air in pursuit. He could hear Pullinger shouting behind him, promising him leniency if he only turned himself in. Oliver's head was burning, a band of pain constricting tighter and tighter. Please let me live, please let me live, the plea turned over in his mind. As he fled other dreams seemed to mingle with his desperate scrabble to escape – could you have dreams within a dream? – flashing hooves, a black horse slipping through the night with eyes burning demon-bright. Soldiers stood in his way but the horse and rider rode them down, screams as he smashed through a window, standing on top of a roof as thunder and lightning wrapped around his body like a nimbus.

Then he was back in the woods behind his home and the thunder had followed him from the other dream – and the thunder became laughter, deep and hideous, as if every tree in the forest stood possessed by devils. But the laughter was coming from his throat, from him . . . two redcoats emerged from the night and still laughing he broke the first soldier's neck, then grabbed the second man's rifle and rolled back, spinning the redcoat over his head. He turned the rifle around and bayoneted the soldier on the grass. Other soldiers came, but seeing Oliver laughing in the clearing they fled. His shadow moved around him like a cloak – like something alive, stirring to his whim.

'Here's my neck,' Oliver yelled at the retreating soldiers. 'Here is my neck. Waiting for the worldsingers' scaffold, waiting for the caliph's hunting cats, waiting for the Court's justice. But who is to take it?'

He could see them, feel them. Every wicked intention, every sin, little bundles of malevolent sparks fleeing into the darkness, trying so hard to escape, but calling to be snuffed out as they fled.

Where there is evil, the trees whispered.

'Where there is evil,' Oliver repeated like an oath.

He is called.

'He is called.' The pain in his skull intensified and he dropped to the ground, clawing at his burning forehead.

Darkness is your cloak. Fear is your ally. Wickedness is your manna.

Oliver looked around the glade, the mist of pain vanishing, then he filled the forest with his terrible new laughter.

'I ride at night.'

'Oliver,' Harry shook him awake.

'I hear the noise,' said Oliver, half dazed. It took him a moment to realize where he was; perhaps even who he was.

Outside in the street a clatter of marching echoed down the soot-stained cobbles. People from the city were spilling out into the morning to see the sight.

The reverend came into the room and peered out of the window. 'Steammen – an army of them.'

It was true. Outside the church an army of metal creatures stomped in perfect unison, three ranks deep, their boilers pouring dirty black smoke into the air.

'They are not of the people,' said Steamswipe, his fierce vision plate scanning the regiment of marching things. 'They are golem, the clumsy manufacturings of your softbody mechomancers, although I do not doubt the corpses of many of the people informed their architecture.'

Oliver looked closer and saw that Steamswipe was correct. There was none of the uniqueness, none of the life of the citizens of the Steammen Free State in their design. They were peas in a pod, a shambling army of automated undead, transaction engine drums turning in their chests, clumsy welds and rivets sealing their bodies. The fad for steammen produced by companies like Doyce and Clennam had faded decades ago, after the clumsy metal butlers had shown a tendency to pour boiling soup on dinner guests, set fire to drawing rooms and trample over family pets and children. Even the automatics from the workshops of the Catosian League could not begin to approach the simplest of King Steam's subjects. These new creatures were primitive, but still a cut above the servants that had rolled out of Clennam's Middlesteel mills – progress of a sort.

'There's something wrong with them,' said Oliver.

'Everything about them is wrong. They are a violation of the life metal,' said Steamswipe. 'A sacrilegious affront by you damn softbodies cast in mockery of our perfection.'

At the knight's side Lord Wireburn rumbled from his holster, 'They must be *destroyed*.'

'Violation they may be,' said Harry. 'But I would say that Shadowclock has solved its labour shortage.'

'No,' said Oliver. 'Can't you feel it? There are souls inside those things, pieces of human flesh trapped inside the metal. Animals too in some of them. The brains, the hearts of birds and swine. It's hideous.'

Harry stared down at the legion of golems shaking the windowsill. In the street the families of miners stood and gawked at the sight, children running behind the primitive things as if the coronation carnivals had started early. 'A fusion of animal and steamman? Damn but I wouldn't want some mechomancer stuffing my liver inside one of those things.'

Lord Wireburn seethed. 'Nor would our people want your frail meat cooking over our soul boards. This is dark sorcery indeed.'

'Keeper of the Eternal Flame,' said Steamswipe, 'have you heard of such a foul practice before?'

'In ancient times such monstrosities existed,' spat the weapon. 'They were known as metal-fleshers. Fusions of meat and steamman creeping over the ice sheets to murder each other for parts, blood to drink, bones to consume. But they were self-organizing, not like these uniform things, so obviously milled by the race of man.'

Behind them the preacher sat down laughing and lit a pipe.

'What's so funny, old man?' asked Harry.

'Harold, I am only laughing so I don't cry. Just when you get to an age when you think you've seen every horror, every pain we're capable of inflicting on each other, along comes something to shock you out of your dotage. Such baleful ingenuity. You think those things need sleep? Or rest breaks? Gas flares won't slow them down and if there's a cave-in, by the Circle, you can just leave them under the rubble, they'd probably rather die anyway.'

'Shut up, old man,' shouted Harry. 'Get the word to the grasper. There's going to be a shipment of miners out of Shadowclock in the next few nights. The people those things are replacing. I need to know when.'

'Who lit a fire under your tail, Harold?'

'It's the end game, preacher. If the governor is using those things in the mines he has gone well beyond caring if word leaks back to the House of Guardians about the state of affairs in Shadowclock. Why do you think that would be?'

The preacher stood up. 'Because fairly soon it won't matter whether it does or not.'

Down below the sea of clumsy steammen-people hybrids continued to flow past the church.

'It matters to me,' whispered Oliver.

In the Court of the Air's monitorarium, Surveillant Seven's telescope clacked as it swung a degree to the left. A skrayper had momentarily floated into the surveillant's field of vision, blocking her view. Down in the troposphere the massive balloon-like creature was being pursued by a hunt of lash-lites, a dozen of the leathery-winged lizard people riding the thin atmosphere. They were climbing for height, trying to avoid the clawed tentacles dangling underneath the skrayper. There seemed to be a lot of lashlite hunts going on at the moment. Surveillant Seven had counted at least five in the last week.

Admittedly she had been working longer than anyone else realized – her monitorarium logs doctored between shifts to make it look like she had been taking her restoration cycle breaks. Most surveillants could last a week or two without sleep – she had done her first four days without even sipping at the potions in her drinking tube; just using the Court's worldsinger techniques. If she had joined the order on the ground she would have made them come up with a new tattoo scheme to accommodate the number of flowers they would have had to etch on her forehead.

It was no accident *they* had chosen *her* for this duty. She was the best of the best, better perhaps than even her furtive masters realized. She put aside the temptation to watch the lashlites at play and dialled up the power of the telescope, the rubber of the viewing hood disconcertingly cold in the unheated monitorarium. There it was! Exactly what she thought she had glimpsed in her wide sweep before the skrayper had blocked the sight.

A little green pinprick in the night. Increase the resolution again, wait for the Court's transaction engine to catch up with the focus. A pile of powder burning in the darkness, giving off a queer green energy that nearly scorched her eyes. Before the Court's training she could have had her boots standing in that fiery powder and she would not have noticed it burning. Now, at this resolution, it was like staring into the face of the sun.

She noted the location. A church roof in Shadowclock. Her masters would be pleased – although this was one report that would not be passed through the official channel of the monitors. Her testimony would be given verbally, in some distant corner of the Court; a secret within a secret.

The runaway wolftaker had been rumbled. The dangerous, disreputable Harry Stave was being tracked once more and this time the devious jigger would not slip away from her scope.

Prince Alpheus looked at the doctor. Even to his unseasoned eye the man did not seem worthy of the low standard of the Middlesteel College of Surgeons; his hands were shaking so badly that he could barely prepare the syringe.

'If this is a show of concern for my health,' said Prince Alpheus, 'it's rather late.'

Flare watched the greedy eyes of the two Greenhall functionaries who had accompanied the doctor to the palace. They stood like vampires waiting for the vial of royal blood to be handed over.

'It is a security issue,' said the Captain of the Special Guard. 'They want to make sure you have the markers of the house royal in your blood.'

'Given they bred me like a damn spaniel I would think that wasn't in doubt.'

'His Highness is most probably unaware of the Prince Silvar affair,' said one of the Greenhall mandarins. 'Where three royal guardsmen from Quatérshift tried to swap the heir-apparent with a doppelgänger supplied by the caliphs. A failed attempt to create a monarchy in exile and destabilize parliament. That was before the shifties had their own revolution of course.'

'But of course,' said the prince. 'I suppose I can only guess at the warmth of the welcome the Commonshare would extend to me today. But Hoggstone can count his lucky stars, because my unlucky ones have not yet managed to allow me to slip his choke-chain. It is the genuine article you will be dragging through the towns and shires of Jackals.'

'We all but serve,' said the official.

'Yes, but some of you get to keep your arms attached to your body while doing it.'

The doctor withdrew the syringe from the prince's arm and handed the crimson-filled vial to the officials. They slipped it inside a velvet-lined case and then sealed the container shut by pressing Greenhall's arms deep into a bead of hot wax.

'Thank you for your time,' said the more senior functionary, placing the box under his arm. 'Your ratified certificate of royal breeding will be presented to the surgeon before the coronation ceremony culminates in Parliament Square. A quick blood machine test will be repeated there to verify your identity.'

'I may go now?' said the prince.

'Of course,' said the official. 'I am sure you have a full diary.'

'Yes indeed,' said the prince. 'It's a constant effort to fit in all the feasts, dedications and bridge openings in between the stonings.'

'We all but serve,' the two officials chorused, bowed towards Captain Flare and the Special Guardsmen, and departed.

Flare watched Prince Alpheus leave after the two functionaries had been escorted from the palace. Hardfall moved closer to Flarc. It was an oddly intimate gesture, but the Special Guardswoman was wary in case the order was surreptitiously listening in to their conversation in the chamber. Their worldsinger minders had become skittish in the last few days, almost as if they suspected that the normal order of things was not being followed; they would be right of course – but not for any reason they could guess at.

'Greenhall will find out,' said Hardfall. 'After they run the blood machine test.'

'They may not notice,' replied Captain Flare. 'They may not even care if they do. Half a royal is better than picking some non-entity from the royal breeding house to be king. The penny sheets are too used to Alpheus as prince. His face is familiar to the voters.'

'It's the other half of our young princeling that worries me,' said Hardfall, brushing her cape back. Her pistol rode high on her hip, slung provocatively. Not that she needed it with her fey gifts.

'The other half can't be traced back to me,' said Flare. 'Only the mist can make us feybreed – there are no markers in the blood, no gifts that can be passed to our children. If we could breed pure and fey, we would have freed ourselves centuries ago.'

'Yes, I suppose we would have,' said Hardfall. 'And if our blood ran mist-true the order's fey-finders would have noticed years ago that the prince is your son, not King Julius's.'

'Alpheus is a hamblin,' said Flare. 'Whatever else he is, he is normal.'

'For a royal,' said Hardfall. 'But then haven't we all been marked by fate? You will tell him, when all this is over?'

'He'll find out.'

'He might be more cooperative if he knew now.'

'Or he might not,' said Flare. 'He wants his freedom as much as we want ours. I think we can leave it at that for now.'

'As you will, my captain,' said the Special Guardswoman. She watched him leave with sad hungry eyes. 'As you will.'

It was odd. Now that Oliver was packing his knapsack after a week in Shadowclock's church, saying goodbye to the preacher was like a leave-taking from his uncle. It was as if some link existed between them – far more than a few days'

hospitality coerced by the disreputable Stave's blackmail should
have warranted. There were still a few workers outside in the
street, tending the gas mines even in the small hours of the
night. Why not? It was always night in the shafts and channels underground.

'You don't need to stay up so late,' said Oliver. 'It's not as
if you signed on to help us voluntarily.'

'I never get tired at night, boy,' said the reverend. 'It's the
most peaceful time of the day.'

Oliver checked his canteen for water. 'I know what you
mean.' And by the Circle, he did know. Last night he had
only slept two hours and rather than feeling tired, he felt as
though he had rested for a month in one of Middlesteel's
finest hotels. More than that, his bones seemed to vibrate in
the sleeping hours, his blood racing to the call of the moon.
He ached to go outside and feel the beauty of the darkness
on his skin, slip through its cleansing purity. And his dreams
– they had become compressed bolts of images, dense memories of past lives – hundreds of them, all different and all the
same.

The preacher saw Oliver about to strap the boatman's gun
to the side of the pack and reached out to stop him. 'It's time
to open that parcel I gave you.'

'Your book of Circlelaw, it's over here.'

'It's not Circlelaw,' said the reverend. 'I still have some use
for that.'

Oliver unwrapped the case from the faded old blanket and
flipped the box's double latches. As he pulled up the lid a silver
glow illuminated his hands, the lunar light reacting with its
contents like alchemy. Inside a brace of identical silver-plated
pistols, ivory handled, every inch etched with scenes – eagle
wings and duels, warring regiments and the silhouettes of man-
beasts. On the ivory of each handle lay the scrimshaw of a lion

that looked familiar, very nearly the lion from the crest of Jackals. A more primitive form, though, raw and snarling, not pictured in the gracious repose from the nation's coat of arms.

'These were yours?' asked Oliver.

'You might say they have been passed down the family.'

There was a double holster in the top of the case, plain black patent leather. The kind that was meant to be shoulder slung and worn concealed under a greatcoat.

'But then you should leave them to your children,' protested Oliver. 'That's real silver leaf on the metal. They must be worth the contents of a counting-house vault.'

'A long time ago I had hoped my oldest daughter might be interested in them. But it turned out I was wrong,' said the reverend.

Oliver pointed to the old bell-barrelled weapon from Loade and Locke. 'I can just about hit something with that. Surely these are a duellist's guns, meant for a marksman or an officer in one of the regiments.'

'Pick them up,' said the preacher.

Oliver lifted them out of the case – the guns felt warm, comfortable, part of his arm – why had he even entertained any doubts about accepting the gift? They were perfect.

'It's strange,' said Oliver, 'I—'

'The trick,' interrupted the preacher, 'is to know when to pick them up and when to put them down.'

Oliver's hands shook after he placed them back in the case, shook the way he had seen ferrymen shake when they had gone into Hundred Locks' taverns with a thirst that only cheap jinn could quench. He would not reject the gift now. What a fool the preacher's daughter must have been.

'I'm putting them down,' said the preacher, adamantly.

'I won't need the boatsman pattern pistol any more,' said Oliver.

344

'No,' said the reverend. 'But you should keep the knife.'

'I don't remember telling you—'

'You didn't have to,' said the reverend. 'It's a good knife. The kind I wish I had owned many years ago.'

Oliver looked out of the window. The call of the night was stronger than ever before. 'Thank you for everything.'

'Boy, with that wild blood of yours you may be the best of us.'

'I should keep the knife in my boot.'

'That's what I would do,' said the preacher.

Downstairs, the hex Harry had traced in the air was fading away. So, it had not been a waste of time listening in on the old goat. What was the reverend playing at? He was up to some mischief, of that much the wolftaker was certain. Up to now the churchman had kept his end of the bargain, staying in retirement and out of the way in the mining city. As the keeper of so many secrets himself, he hated for the old fool to have something over him. That was not the way he intended the great game to be played – if there was skulduggery to be had in Jackals, far better that it be the hand of the disreputable Stave to be found on the tiller.

Without the breezes of the day to carry away the engine smoke, Shadowclock was subject to the same foul-smelling pea soupers as Middlesteel. Thick engine fogs rose up with the night, reducing the full moon to a smudge of silver behind their haze.

Oliver looked down at the cobbles of the steep streets, his boots moving invisibly below the soup, the damp of the cloud making his socks itch. They could hear patrols along the high walls calling out to each other, see the occasional flicker of a bull's-eye lantern. They were keeping an eye open for night constables or the combination's bullyboys, but the ruffians were saving their vigilance for the city battlements. For all his large bulk, Steamswipe could move near silently, his helmet-like head swivelling, the grill of his voicebox vibrating as he emitted bursts of sound pitched beyond the human ear. The steamman swore he could navigate the fog that way, pick out the combination enforcers and the governor's men. He obviously possessed the talent, as he managed to lead them across the maze of tall deserted streets without coming across anyone else, in twisting turns which always led them up the hill, towards the governor's own aerostat field.

What Oliver did not say to his friends was that he could feel the presence of the enforcers too – could see how well the steamman knight was leading them around the armed patrols. He could feel them all, little candles of wickedness burning in the night. Not just the patrols either – the drunken gang master four streets away beating his wife as she tried to shield their children from his rage; the roof angler who had forced open a skylight and was rummaging around in a darkened room for a key to the locked cabinet, a knife in his belt in case he was disturbed; the governor in his mansion clapping in drunken amusement as his soldiers beat to death one of the miners who had tried to escape the press gang. Each ember of malice smouldering in the darkness.

'Oliver!' Harry helped the boy off his knees. 'Are you ill?'

'I can feel it, Harry.'

'Feel what?'

'The evil. I can feel the evil in them.'

'You're sweating like you've got the pox,' said Harry. 'And talking like you're trying to scare up a crowd for a séance.'

'Less noise. We must go on,' said Steamswipe. 'This night may be the last aerostat run from Shadowclock with miners.'

'I'm fine,' said Oliver. 'The sweat will pass.'

A row of small lights lit up along the side of Lord Wireburn, holstered on the back of the steamman knight. 'It is as if the Loas ride you, Oliver softbody. But I detect no presence here, just the press of great events. Curious.'

'I am here, Keeper of the Eternal Flame,' said Oliver. 'Just me. And Steamswipe is right; this is our last chance to hitch a free ride courtesy of the governor. We go now.'

The aerostat field was at the top of the hill, behind the walls of the governor's mansion. An airship was sitting on the retraction rails in front of a hangar. She was a ship of the merchant marine, no gun ports or fin-bomb hatches to pock her hull. No doubt Thaddius or one of the other boys back at Hundred Locks could reel off her class just from looking at her silhouette. To Oliver she looked just like any of the aerostats that had slid past them in the sky on their journey to Shadowclock. The vessel had been winched in close to the ground, boarding stairs pushed up to her belly gondola.

'It is too open,' said Steamswipe pointing to the box lanterns lined up along the hill. 'Too little cover and too many crew around the hangar.'

Harry rested his spine against the wall. 'I can fix that. We head for the big expansion engine, port at the nose; I can get us in there. If anyone spots us, you use your voice on them.'

'My voice?' said Steamswipe.

'Don't play the innocent with me, old steamer. I saw Master Saw ring a bell from the other side of a practice hall using just his voicebox. You can set a wicked old vibration ringing through our blood, I warrant.'

Harry took the knight's silence for agreement and sat cross-legged, mumbling in the tongue of the worldsingers. As he mumbled the mist swirled around their feet, climbing up the hill and settling over the field. A weather calling. Oliver could feel the tendrils of the worldsong beckoning the fog higher, thicker, the hill thrumming with the power of the land. The fog was so thick already; the currents of earthflow so strong underneath Shadowclock, that the pea souper needed little encouragement to settle higher.

The fey energy inside Oliver bristled at the feel of the worldsong. He could see within himself now, as if a veil had been lifted and the complex springs of his own mist-given powers lay visibly unwinding. It was like watching worms burrow through the corpse of someone he had once loved. Too painful to observe, but too gruesome for him to tear his gaze away. They were a part of him, but an alien part – a part that by rights should not be able to occupy this fleshy sack of meat and water and bones, should not be able to walk in this realm of solid geometries and limited dimensions. They churned within him and Oliver could not believe he had not seen them before. Could not believe that he had actually sat opposite worldsinger fey-finders and inquisitors and had the cheek to protest his humanity.

The fog seemed to be thickening about Oliver's heels faster than the adjacent ground, corkscrewing around his legs – even Harry looked surprised at how quickly the summoning was becoming localized.

'It's alright,' said Oliver. 'I like the fog.'

'We have our cover,' said Steamswipe.

Oliver looked across to the mist-wrapped leviathan of the air. The steamman had not needed to say they also had the element of surprise. Most of the able-bodied workers in Shadowclock were in hiding to avoid being transported on this aerostat. The guards were bargaining on any sane minds avoiding the governor's mansion and their press gangs. As usual, their path was plunging them headfirst into peril.

Steamswipe took five steps back then ran at the wall,

vaulting it with ease. Harry cupped his hand, boosting Oliver up. Once on the top of the wall, Oliver lowered a hand for the disreputable Stave, then the three of them were in the mist. The fog distorted the sounds of the ground crew and their conversations on the other side of the field carried across to the three adventurers as if they stood mere feet away.

'—ballast is loaded.'

'—never seen a smog come down like that.'

'—so he said, talk to the first mate. First mate, says I, it's him who bleeding needs to talk to me.'

Oliver nearly walked into the propeller. Wrought metal blades and an expansion engine assembly as large as a house, its curved lines had been cast by the airship foundry in the image of a giant lion's head, cold steel eyes locked forward, teeth snarling. Harry ducked under the propeller and pulled himself inside the metal housing's mouth, feeding himself to the metal cat.

'There's a maintenance hatch in here,' he whispered.

'I doubt I will fit my magnificent architecture through it,' said Steamswipe. 'I am intended for war, not crawling through the ducts of your flotation vessel like a softbody rodent.'

They waited a couple of minutes and were rewarded by a pop in the aerostat's rigid envelope, then a hatch was lowered down by a hand crank next to the engine. Inside Harry stood in a chamber piled with barrels of expansion-engine gas, glass-lined wood branded with the silhouette of blow-barrel trees, their vapours safely sealed and stored.

'The purser would have checked forward storage this morning,' said Harry, closing the loading ramp behind them. 'We can clear some of these barrels and make a hiding space in case any of the jack cloudies come in here for fuel during the voyage.'

Oliver opened his pack and checked the food was still there.

'You won't need that,' said Harry. 'This isn't a passenger liner, it's a Guardian Smike-class hauler. She hasn't got the range to be exploring the lakes of Liongeli, Oliver. However many miners they're taking out of here, they're taking them as main cargo. And that means a landing somewhere in Jackals.'

'Let us make a concealment position among the barrels,' said Steamswipe. 'I have a feeling it would be a mistake to discharge the Keeper of the Eternal Flame inside this hold.'

Harry looked at the blow-barrel tree silhouette on the barrels. 'Very perceptive. And I will forgo my daily pinch of mumbleweed, given how I remember most skippers' fondness for the strap when they catch a cloudie with a pipe on board.'

Their nest amongst the cargo constructed, the three of them waited an hour before the shouts outside warned them the airship was about to launch. The floor trembled as the vessel was drawn down the launch rail and onto a turntable to match the wind direction. Then the rail claws fell back and Oliver's stomach dropped as the ship began to lift. It became hard to hear each other talk over the rise and fall of the engine's noise – their whispers needed to become shouts. They might arrive at their destination deaf, but at least the racket would make it almost impossible for any sailor passing by to hear them moving about in the fuel store.

Shortly they had stopped rising and it became colder on board. The main gondola and crew compartments might have been heated, but now Oliver understood why – be it summer, autumn or spring – the jack cloudies who had landed at Hundred Locks came into town wearing thick woollen jumpers with roll-necks tied around their striped sailor's vests like belts. Shivering, Oliver and Harry broke open the blanket rolls from their packs and took turns warming their hands on Steamswipe's boiler stack.

Despite the chill and the din Oliver finally managed to drift off to sleep in the early hours of the morning. Harry opened one of his eyes. The young man was breathing deeply, his breath misting the icy air. Steamswipe and his weapon were in their approximation of sleep too, thoughtflow. Leaning over, Harry eased out the wooden case that had been given to Oliver by the reverend in Shadowclock. Checking the narrow corridor outside their fuel store was empty, Harry made his way through the duralumin-framed passage, canvas spheres of celgas brushing his head where he forgot to duck.

At the end of the gantry he opened the wooden door to the small forward head, a simple affair, little more than a seat with a flap opening out to the sky. The disreputable Stave opened the lid of the case. Both pistols were still inside, glinting malevolently. Even without their finely etched scenes, the ivory handles and precious metal plating, the brace would have raised a sack full of clinking guineas in any gunsmith or pawnshop in Jackals. You did not have to be a sorcerer to feel the press of their song, feel the draw of their wicked spangle. Harry shivered, slapped the lid shut, tossed the case into the head and jerked the flush.

As the flap opened, the case tumbled into the sky and Harry watched it disappear into the clouds. It was an expensive hunch, but it was not as if Oliver could have hit the side of a barn with either of those two marksman's pieces.

'Next time, preacher,' Harry whispered to the clouds, 'you can save your bloody gift-giving for Midwinter.'

Captain Stone of the RAN *Heart of Oak* pushed the cutlass hanging from his dress uniform back. The damn thing was always getting under his feet, but it was required dress for tonight. Half the high fleet looked like they had assembled in the ante-room outside the dining gallery of the governor's mansion – the northern fleet, the eastern fleet, even a few stiff blue trousers adorned with the single yellow stripe of the western fleet. It was one of the captains of the west who moved through the press and approached him. Haredale. They had been midshipmen together on the *Skysprite*.

Haredale nodded politely. 'Stone.'

'Haredale.' Captain Stone indicated his fellow officer's hair, shorn to stubble on the side and wedge-high on top. 'Going native?'

'It's all the go in Concorzia,' said the colonial officer. 'Half the fleet officers of the west are sporting 'em.'

'How are affairs abroad?' asked Stone. 'I heard there were some tensions – not just among the natives.'

'The colonials are taking more settlers now, genuine ones as well as the convict labour, heh. They are a damn volatile mob – transportees, the first families and the locals – always scrapping, but nothing the navy can't control. The shadow of a ship of the line always sends 'em scampering for the woods. How is the fleet of the south? I heard you had some trouble down there recently.'

'The *RAN Bellerophon*?' said Stone 'Let's just say there is the story the First Skylord released for the Dock Street pensmen – and there are the rumours from the poor jacks we got back alive. If it was up to me I would close the whole bloody border, but parliament would have every jinn importer in Jackals banging on their door, so that isn't going to happen. These days it's rare for us to take a flotilla out without having to chase off some humpy raiding party coming out of the arids and into the uplands.'

Haredale pushed a finger under his high collar and pulled the cloth loose. 'Which the caliph claims are bandits, of course.'

'Bandits my rear end,' said Stone. 'Too well supplied. Too sophisticated for some tent-dwelling sand shaman. The caliph's hand is over every raid. Mark my words, it won't be long until we have half the upland Guardians calling for us to flatten a few palaces in Bladetenbul and give Cassarabia a bloody nose.'

'As long as it keeps the fleet of the south out of mischief,' said the colonial captain. 'You passed the damn order's tests then?'

'A greater load of stuff and nonsense I have never had to sit through,' growled Stone. 'Half the officers of the blue kicking around the county waiting their turn for a truth hexing. How many feybreed have they turned up in the service? They're tacking against the wind this time.'

'Admiralty House should never have agreed,' said Captain Haredale. 'And it takes the governor of Shadowclock to throw us a do to send us off now the order has had its pleasure. Have you even seen an admiral or skylord back at the citadel since they ordered the high fleet home?'

'There's no danger from the Admiralty Board,' snorted Stone. 'Not unless parliament are worried they might prick someone with a quill. They would have better luck having us cleared by an alienist. The *Bellerophon*'s captain was clearly mad – not a feybreed.'

'Never liked the man,' said the colonial officer. 'Ran an unhappy ship. Too damn keen to resort to the cat, rather than trusting his middies to keep discipline. Not surprised he went out barking.'

'Still,' said Stone, 'dropping fins on Middlesteel. We're fortunate they haven't stuck us with worldsinger political officers like the Special Guard.'

'That would never stand,' said Haredale. 'There's only room for one skipper on a ship. They might as well fit us all with

353

one of those hexed necklaces of theirs and keep us all on a lead.'

At the end of the room two grand doors were swung open by redcoats, revealing a long high table filled with platters of steaming meat and flagons of wine.

'Winds of Thar, there's a spread for you,' said the colonial captain. 'Best we avail ourselves before we get back to our weevil bread and salt jerky, heh?'

The milling officers of the fleet began to move into the larger chamber, failing to notice the thuggish crop of stubble on the faces of the redcoats flanking the entrance, or their badly buttoned tunics.

At the head of the table the governor waited for the officers to take their seats and then the chubby statesman raised a heavy crystal glass. 'Officers of the fleet. I know you sailors normally avoid passing through my city walls due to our sad lack of taverns, but as you can see, my staff have been happy to waive the rules for this evening's entertainment.'

There were some hoots down the table.

'The results from the order have now been reported to the Admiralty and handed into the House of Guardians – sadly, none of you would make celgas miners and so the fleet has reluctantly decided to keep you on!'

That raised more whoops of merriment.

'I think that proves what we all knew all along.' The governor raised a news sheet freshly couriered from the capital. On the front page was an etching of an aerostat captain fainting into the arms of a couple of stripe-shirted aeronauts, an exaggerated figure of a worldsinger thrusting a truth crystal towards the officer and the speech bubble from the sailors bantering: 'Does the feymist carry the skipper away?' – 'No, 'tis the odour of an early election that makes him swoon.'

'It proves, gentlemen, that one bad apple does not spoil the barrel.'

Now the captains cheered.

'So, as a small token of recognition for the service you have done protecting Shadowclock, let me thank our neighbours from the citadel and the aerostat fields to the north in a manner befitting as fine a bunch of jack cloudies as ever crewed a stat – with a raised glass of grog. Shadowclock's celgas may float your vessels – now may our hospitality lift your hearts before you scatter to the four corners of Jackals and her possessions. To the Royal Aerostatical Navy!'

'To the navy!' the table chorused.

Seated in the middle of the table, Captain Stone passed Haredale a plate of boiled ham slices. Plenty of honeyed fat, just the way the Jackelians liked it.

'You not drinking, Stone?'

'Touch of sand belly,' said Captain Stone. 'Ship's surgeon has me on powders. Just a taste of wine, jinn or blackstrap has me retching like a newborn.'

Filling up on water – the apothecary's remedy had made him as dry as the skin of a sand nomad's tent – Stone made his excuses and left in search of the rest room. He cursed his luck; ruing the day he had stepped out of the choking dust and tried that skewered stick of lamb in the shade of the border market.

After his gut had cleared, Stone realized he was sweating. He checked the pocket of his tunic for one of the parcels of powder and swore as he realized he had taken the last one before he left the citadel for the governor's mansion. A bit of cool evening air then, even if it was the fog-shrouded miasma that hung over the hills of Shadowclock. He slipped out of a door and followed the line of a hedge around to the gardens. When a westerly was blowing strong enough to clear the smoke, the view from the hill was said to be the best in the walled city. Now all he could see was a constellation of yellow lamps twinkling through the evening smog in the streets below.

Captain Stone glanced behind him. That was odd. There seemed to be a lot of movement in the dining room, a whole company of red-coated men moving up and down the table. Surely the main course could not have finished so quickly? When the rigid envelope of an aerostat did not bind them to their duty, the officers of the high fleet could stretch a feast into the small hours of the morning. He moved closer to the window.

Inside was a picture of madness. Bodies were littered across the floor, others hanging stiff in their chairs, a few captains of the line crawling across the floor puking their guts out while their faces turned crimson. Moving methodically through the carnage the redcoats had knives out, pulling officers back and slicing their throats. At the head of the table the lumpen governor was gorging on the food, laughing and banging the table as his staff dispatched the fleet as if it were a line of animals at an abattoir.

It took a few seconds for the reality of the insane situation to penetrate Stone's consciousness – seconds which stretched like minutes. Then his mind cleared with the first rush of adrenalin and an animal urge for survival. First the captain of the *Resolute*. Now this lunacy? It seemed that the worldsingers had set their hounds on the wrong trail – they should have left the citadel alone and tried their luck in Shadowclock.

Sliding his dress cutlass clear as he vanished into the garden, Captain Stone said a silent prayer to the souk vendors of Cassarabia. A prayer to a skewer of meat chunks of dubious provenance that had saved his life.

* * *

Oliver woke up early. They were sinking and the air was getting warmer. The rise and fall of the expansion engine had changed pitch too. Steamswipe's unblinking visor met his gaze. He had Lord Wireburn unholstered. Harry was propped up against a barrel of expansion engine gas.

'We're landing?' Oliver said over the racket of the engine.

<We are,> Harry replied using his mind voice. <About thirty miles east of Middlesteel. In Middlemarsh Forest unless I am mistaken.>

'How do you know?'

Harry flipped open a compass. <Destination, bearing and average speed of a fully laden aerostat.>

The engines cut off and for the first time in an age Oliver could hear silence as the vessel hung in the air. With a gentle tug they were being hauled in.

'Her lines are out,' said Harry. 'We'll be secure groundside soon enough.'

'After we land we should send out a scout,' said Steamswipe, 'and observe the lay of the land. You could use the crawl space in the engines as a vantage point.'

'Not for an hour or two I couldn't. Right now that rotor drive is hot enough to fry a side of gammon. But there's another way. I can do a soul walking.'

'You can do that?' asked Oliver. 'I thought it was dangerous. Even my fey-finders from the Department of Feymist couldn't do that and old Pullinger was a four-flower worldsinger.'

'It takes concentration,' said Harry. 'You fill yourself with so much of the earth's power that it can surge and sever the connection between your soul and your body – leaving you a mindless corpse. But I won't travel that far. Just a quick poke about, nearby. A true soul walker could float all the way to Hundred Locks and back.'

357

The disreputable Stave moved his pack to the side of their nest among the barrels of gas and adopted a lotus position. 'No noise now – an interrupted trance and you'll be spoon-feeding me gruel until the crushers catch up with me.'

Oliver sensed the presence of the wolftaker lift from his body, drift through the chamber and slip through the catenary curtain of the aerostat. They waited in the shadows of the hold. An orange light on Lord Wireburn's side had begun blinking. The holy relic was ready for the fight and with a start Oliver realized so was he. Harry shook himself out of the trance.

'What do we face?' asked Steamswipe.

Harry looked pale. 'Give me a moment, old stick.' He made a noise with his throat. 'Circle. My skin feels like it's on fire. All right, we've come down in Middlemarsh Forest. There's an old mine behind us. Hasn't been worked for a long time. Most of the buildings have been abandoned – but the shaft's been cleared and the winch house has been rebuilt. I couldn't go any deeper into the mine, the ground blocks a soul walking.'

'How many foe?'

'There's crushers here – or at least, whippers in police uniform. Much the same thing in my book. Some others hanging around – they've got spore filters on their collars, so I'd say they're from the undercity, Grimhope outlaws. But that's not the worst of it. There's Special Guard here!'

'Almost a worthy foe,' said Steamswipe. He sounded pleased. 'Their natural template has been distorted – their abilities in battle will be surprising.'

Oliver extended his newfound senses, touched the souls of the people on the ground and recoiled from their depravity. Wickedness, *here*, from those that were charged as protectors of Jackals. Could there be a greater treachery?

'They're getting ready to unload the miners from

Shadowclock. The poor devils are in leg irons in the main hold,' said Harry. 'But why an abandoned mine? There's no celgas here.'

'There's evil here,' said Oliver. 'And something else besides. . .'

They both stared at him. 'What do you know about this place, lad?'

'I know how to read, Harry. Before these jiggers stole my life that's all I had to do. This place was in the penny sheets a couple of years back. Three children playing about in a worked-out copper mine found temple statues. Solid gold and gems for eyes. The mine was given to the archaeologists from the eight universities and the county constabulary had to fight off treasure seekers and tomb robbers coming out from the capital, hoping to dig out a fortune.'

'The governor isn't risking his neck at the gallows for gold,' said Harry. 'You can skim far more than the price of a few antiques from the patronage that comes with the governorship of Shadowclock. Whatever their jig here, they need miners to work their claim. Deep mine experience. The statues were from the coldtime?'

'Chimecan, Harry. I think they went on display at the museum in Middlesteel.'

'Okay, here's the lay of the land. We wait for the Shadowclock miners to disembark and then we drop the ramp and head for the trees. There are plenty of people around. Even if we are spotted they're as like to assume we're crew. In the woods we'll set up an observation and see if we can grab one of their people – find out where the miners are ending up and see how easy it's going to be to penetrate this bleeding place.'

Oliver could feel the apprehension of the miners, their fear of the unknown as they descended the main loading ramp, and the hard hearts of the guards watching them. They did not see the miners as people at all, just a means to an end.

It was morning outside. As they lowered the ramp the bright light made Oliver wince after the darkness of the hold. Down. Walk casually – with purpose. Not three scuttling intruders fleeing the shadow of the airship. Crewmen. Then Oliver heard the shout and risked a glance back. There, by the line of resigned workers being ushered into the gates of the old mine. It was the Whisperer! A shambling child-sized feybreed, so distorted by the mist it was hard to see where his limbs began and his torso ended. But it was not the Whisperer's bitter soul inside the fey creature; and this thing wore plated armour – a worldsinger containment suit – metal shells covered in runes and strung tightly together with wire. It was pointing at them and howling like it was caught in the embrace of a torture rack. Pointing straight at Oliver.

From the cover of the trees they were heading for a patrol of redcoats stepped out into the clearing.

'Now we fight,' said Steamswipe.

Oliver's hands burned searing. He looked down and realized that the reverend's gifts had appeared there. Harry stared at the two guns open-mouthed like a man whose life had ended. A shot splintered past them. Steamswipe turned and Lord Wireburn shot out a ball of revolving fire – a miniature sun that slapped into the guards behind them. Seven soldiers were incinerated, a splash of jelly-like fire landing on the nearest guards. Steamswipe fired again. After each shot Lord Wireburn let out a shriek, half an inhalation, half a gagging exhalation, as if the holy weapon was sucking in the life of the deceased.

Both of Oliver's pistols discharged, two attackers were hammered off their feet, then he flicked the guns open, reloading from his bandoleer with a smooth mechanical precision. The disreputable Stave was moving in witch-time, his long-barrelled pistol in his hand. Oliver could follow him now; see the distortion of the bones of the earth as Harry drank in its energy, leylines snaking around his feet, twisting and pulsing. Stave's pistol crackled, the charge smoke momentarily shrouding the perplexed look on his face. Oliver could see from a dozen perspectives simultaneously: aeronauts from the stat climbing back up the ramp, miners fleeing for cover, redcoats in front, the Grimhope outlaws by the mine entrance.

Oliver laughed like a demon, knowing that the sound of it would unnerve them all. The attacking patrol had discharged their rifles and rather than reloading they were closing at a rush with wicked bayonets fixed, screaming in rage and fear. Steamswipe let his own voice be heard, the echo from his voicebox collapsing a redcoat even as the steamman galloped into their company. A machine of death, he swung his hammer arm in fast meticulous arcs, crumpling soft bodies, staving in skulls, trampling down the soldiers under his hooves. They were almost on Oliver now. He raised his left hand and put a lead ball through the face of one of the soldiers, side-stepping a bayonet thrust. He shattered the bayonet owner's knee with a kick – pistol-whipping the back of the soldier's head as the man's bayonet caught in the mud.

Harry was by his side, then gone and just as suddenly back, tripping up the attackers in a blur of boots. Oliver sensed the rifleman taking aim at them from the top of the mine works; saw the barrel sighting on his own spine. Tipping his right arm over his shoulder his uncharged pistol bucked once, the marksman's corpse tumbling off the roof. He had not even looked.

Harry had stopped moving and was looking up at the sky. 'Not bloody now!'

Explosions flowered around them, dirt showering into the

air. A wave of searing heat punched Oliver to the ground and earth plummeted down on him by the spadeful, as if manic diggers tossing clods of mud had surrounded him and were feverishly digging him a grave. He was deaf now – petals of flame erupted all around him in silent fury. Both pistols were still in his hands, solid and reassuring. Half interred beneath the earth Oliver watched as ropes coiled down through the smoke, ladders for vengeful angels in black leather capes and visored hoods with rubber tubes hanging at either side.

Oliver could not see out of their eyes, could not feel their souls – could barely sense their presence at all. Harry's words came back to him. '*We've got a military arm called the incrementals for the hard slap work. Proper killers. If they had come after us neither of us would be alive to be discussing it now.*'

One of them swept him with a mirrored gaze, hardly registering his existence. Not a threat. Then an identical warrior emerged from the smoke, a body slung limply over its shoulder, the victim's trousers and waistcoat torn to shreds by the explosions. The disreputable Stave! The Court of the Air was reclaiming their rogue wolftaker. Both incrementals were heading for a rope ladder emerging from the dark scud of their barrage – a ladder that for all intents and purposes might be reaching to the ceiling of the sky.

Moaning with the pain of the effort, Oliver pulled out the knife from his boot and tried to rise; but a spiked boot kicked it from his hand before he could activate the witch-blade – a third incremental tracking backwards towards the rope. The warrior's hand reached out and a finger wagged slowly backwards and forwards. <Naughty, naughty.>

In his other hand the incremental held a rifle with a barrel as long as a lance, covering Oliver with its muzzle. They were leaving him behind. But then what did they care about a young registered man ripped from his home and tossed into their savage world? Just one more body for the crushers' justice and the doomsman's gallows. Oliver laughed. If he lived through the coming cataclysm, they would care enough. He would make them. The warrior stopped, briefly surprised by the eerie sound of mirth. Then he was at the rope ladder and hauling himself up after the other two incrementals. The ladder began to lift out of sight.

Oliver cursed and retrieved his knife. Bursting through the smoke, Steamswipe came galloping into view, scanned Oliver and glanced up to the occluded sky. He pointed Lord Wireburn up at a firmament hidden by the dark murk of battle. 'It is an aerosphere,' said the holy weapon. 'I have its signature sighted. Forty feet above us.'

'Can you bring it down?' Oliver coughed, getting to his feet.

'I am an annihilator, little softbody, not a birding rifle from a Jackelian gunsmith,' said Lord Wireburn. 'I can destroy it, or I can let it go. It is at seventy feet now.'

'Let it go. Bloody Circle!'

Harry was gone. They would break his mind and then whatever was left of his body would be tossed into a holding cell, to rot next door to all of the other undesirables who had crossed the Court. His friend, his guide had vanished – all that was left was the terrible hunger and evil that had found Oliver in Hundred Locks and stalked him across the face of Jackals. His hope had gone, but there was the wickedness. He could still feel that.

'Reinforcements are coming out of the mine,' said Oliver.

Steamswipe scooped him up with his blood-slicked hammer and his manipulator arm, dropping him onto his back. Across the sundered ground a line of figures broke through the smoke and the burning gorse, black leather cloaks rising in the heat of the fire. The Special Guard and a handful of the Whisperer-like feybreed. As soon as they caught sight of Oliver, the Whisperer-things struck out at his mind, pulses of hateful energy darting at his mentality. At the same time a Special Guardsman raised his arm, pouring cerulean flames at Oliver and his steamman steed. Blue flame licked off an invisible dome surrounding them while Oliver caught the biting darts of the mind assault and twisted them back towards their owners, the Whisperer-things tumbling screaming onto the ground.

'A worldsinger,' cried one of the guardsmen.

'No,' said Captain Flare, emerging from the line. 'He is one of us. Can't you feel his power? He is a brother of the mist.'

Steamswipe surged forward, Lord Wireburn spitting fluidic sun-spheres at the line. Oliver barely held onto the stampeding knight. 'Let me make you brothers to the worms, you damn murdering softbodies. Steelbhalah-Waldo! Steelbhalah-Waldo!'

Oliver scarcely kept up with the scattering line – some speeded up into witch-time blurs, others turned invisible or swelled up into iron-solid mountains of flesh. Several of Lord Wireburn's sun spheres disappeared into swirling rips in the air, others splattered against a wall of circular orange shields which had been conjured in front of the Special Guardsmen. Steamswipe rode down a guardswoman, his hammer upper-cutting another in the chest, lifting the guard high into the air. The steamman had gone into a berserker frenzy; Oliver could feel the purity of his rage, the righteousness of his fury. Attacks lashed out from all four sides but Oliver turned them back, diverted them, slapped each of them down. Fire, ice, darts of porcupine spine, the claw-like attempts to batter inside his mind. Faster and faster they struck.

Oliver caught the presence of the two Grimhope outlaws behind them, crossbows loaded with a weight of bolas. A pistol bucked in Oliver's hand and the ball caught an outlaw in his gut. His compatriot fired and the rotating bolas caught Steamswipe's hind legs, snarling the knight. As the steamman tripped Oliver flew off with all the momentum of the stalled dash. More Grimhopers rushed him from the rear, fey energies licking out from the front. Too close to reload

Oliver pulled out his knife and activated it with a twist, the hilt squirming in his hand as it reacted to its owner's presence. This blade had not been forged by the race of man. It was alive; it recognized the bloodline of Phileas Brooks.

'Sword,' said Oliver and the blade flowed upwards, a hilt curving out from the handle.

He moved through the charge of Grimhope outlaws and they kept running even as their chests separated from their legs in a rain of severed limbs while Oliver swept the witch-blade around in a fencer's dance – the echo of earlier selves following him like a shadow, the ghost of his father among them. A howl of steam sounded behind him and Oliver dropped to one knee, skewering a brute with a trident. Captain Flare was riding Steamswipe's back, one fist pummelling the knight's boiler, the other pinning Lord Wireburn. His friend's stacks were mewling as the source of his steamman strength leaked away. Steamswipe's manipulator arms were twisted back; trying to unseat the Captain of the Special Guard and bring him within range of his hammer arm.

Oliver stepped forward to help Steamswipe but a figure shivered into life in front of him – an old woman in a guardsman's cloak – either she had been invisible or she could throw her body across distances. She struck out and Oliver barely avoided her kick. Disconcerting. Like having to fight old Damson Griggs. His witch-blade flicked out to pierce her torc-bound throat, following its own enchanted curve of raw ruthlessness, but it seethed against a transparent shield of fire that sparked as the blade glanced off it. Oliver danced back, avoiding the discus of energy she was manifesting. He tried to neutralise the shield, but her fey power snaked out beneath his perception.

'Raw power isn't enough, boy,' she said, circling him. 'You need discipline, focus.'

His ears were still ringing from the explosions; her voice sounded like it was being carried through water. 'Let's see if it isn't.' His witch-blade ached in his grip, eager to sink itself through her chest. His pistols sung to be reloaded, a dozen past lives making him dizzy, detailing the hundred ways he could dispatch the old woman.

She sliced a clawed hand at Oliver and he stepped into her grasp, feeling the crackle of her skin, the energy of her fey-twisted soul – amplifying it, feeding it – making the fields glowing around her hands ignite as bright as one of Lord Wireburn's sunbursts. Screaming, she fell back, her two hands ablaze. There was little evil in her soul, only determination and loyalty to her compatriots – an age served in the guard. He ignored the witch-blade's call to carve her head off its neck and turned towards Steamswipe.

Captain Flare had battered the knight into semi-consciousness. Steamswipe's boiler was twisted and deformed and venting steam from a dozen tears, the light of his vision plate a faint red smear behind his visor. Wrathful, Oliver bounded forward, his witch-blade looping out, boiling to sever one of those perfectly muscled arms from the captain's trunk. But the witch-knife flexed off the Special Guardsman's arm, its blade quivering in agony. After centuries of use it had finally sliced into something dense enough to resist its passàge.

Flare closed on him. 'How did the fey-finders miss you, boy? You should have joined the guard years ago.'

Oliver rolled past his grip and thrust the tip of the witch-blade into his knee, the blade distorting and retracting back into its knife-size in protest. 'I prefer my freedom.'

Flare slapped the blade out of his hand, turning to land a punch on Oliver's face. 'Then we have something in common, mist-brother.'

Oliver reached out and dampened the fey energies in the pile-driving jab. But even as a mortal the captain's flesh had been built up by years in the muscle-pits – it was not just for impressing Jackals' citizenry when he escorted the monarch. Oliver fell back reeling. Another Special Guardsman was behind him and Oliver drained the blue fire that erupted towards his back, sinking it into a fold in the air. Then another guardsman appeared through the carnage wrought by the aerosphere, then a third and a fourth. Gravity turned upside down and Oliver cancelled it; the air turned cold enough to freeze solid but he heated it; he deflected a lance of light back into the feybreed mob as he turned away a blow to his spine from Flare. Oliver fired a charge into the empty space where the translucent guardsman was trying to sneak up on him, the broken glass of the shell crunching as he ejected it.

More Whisperer-things broke against his mind, compressing his skull with pain. Oliver severed their mental link, killing them instantly, but in the second it took to twist away their attack Captain Flare landed a kick against his side, not dampened. It was as if someone had collapsed a house around him. He tried to rise but a dozen guardsmen were on top of him, striking with their fists and their boots and their mist-gifted powers.

They hauled him to his feet, beaten and bloody. Steamswipe was behind them, wheezing and broken on the chewed-up ground. Oliver's bruised eyes rolled across the sky. No sign of the aerosphere. Harry had gone, forced to face the Court's justice at last. It was over. Oliver had failed Jackals and the Lady of the Lights, failed to punish his family's killers, failed to honour his father's legacy or even to protect his friends' lives.

'What's it to be, brother?' said Flare.

'I see you,' Oliver roared. 'I see you all. The evil that taints your souls.' He concentrated on the fallen steamman. Lord Wireburn flew from the side of the prone knight and out towards Oliver's hand, only to slap into the grip of a Special Guardsman who shimmered into existence between them. The guardsman reversed the holy weapon and shoved its ebony butt into his face. Then Oliver's thrashing really began.

Chapter Twenty

Someone was standing in front of the light at the end of the tunnel. Molly stepped forward apprehensively. She had no idea how she had got here – although she knew there were things that had happened to her that she should have been able to remember.

The silhouette of the figure beckoned her; as she got nearer it became more detailed. It was a girl. Someone who should be familiar, someone Molly knew, a figure in the corridor of a house at night. Tock House, the name leapt at her. Something had happened at Tock House, the thing she should be able to remember. Confused, she peered closer at the girl – less ghost-like, more solid, but still as silent as a mime.

Molly tried to speak with her voice, but nothing came out. That was not the way to communicate with this apparition of . . . a steamman, Silver Onestack. That name brought more flashes of memory images. But the girl was *her* spectre now, not the steamman's. She fair glowed, giving off warmth that comforted the pain in Molly's heart.

<Is this a perfect moment?> Molly asked, finding the right register to communicate.

The spectre just smiled and pointed at the light.

<For me?>

The girl nodded.

The light grew, enveloping her, freezing her with its clarity. Then it grew dim and she was on a mud floor in a cave-like cell. The hardness of the floor, the stiffness in her bones and the tingling she felt on her skin – this was real.

'Molly,' said Nickleby.

She rolled over. The pensman and Commodore Black were in the cell with her.

'I—' she could not finish her words, choking and coughing.

'Ah, lass,' said the commodore. 'That's it, cough it out. We were dirt-gassed and you the lightest in weight of us all. It was cut mortal thin though, or we would have left our lungs back at Tock House.'

Molly looked around the cell. No beds, a night pan – more for the guards' comfort than theirs, she suspected. Metal bars joined the ceiling to the floor; the back of the room was a slope of rock.

'Where is Aliquot?'

'He wasn't with us when we woke up,' said Nickleby. 'I think he must have slipped past them in the fighting.'

'Aye, either that or gone down with Tock House,' said the commodore. 'Dirt-gas could scrub his crystals. That's the way you take a boat too, when she's on the surface and you want to board her easy. Cut her hull and pump her full of gas, have the sailors running around like rabbits in a warren; then you send down the stoats.'

'He can seal off the air flues to his boiler system, run cold. Coppertracks could last hours without needing air.'

'Perhaps,' said the commodore. 'But it still leaves us here, hanging like hares in the larder. Waiting for our precious necks to be sliced.'

Molly pressed her face to the bars. She thought she had heard the footsteps of someone coming.

'But who is to be doing the slicing?' asked Nickleby.

A voice came down the corridor. 'A good question, to be sure.'

It was Count Vauxtion, a party of black-clad toppers at his heels and a woman, her grey hair tied into buns. Count Vauxtion looked at the woman. 'You can confirm her blood machine record?'

'I can,' she replied. 'She is the genuine article. I am already preparing arrangements to pay your finder's fee.'

'*She* has a name,' spat Molly, pressing her face to the bars. 'Are you the one paying for my head?'

'I am just the assessor, m'dear,' said the woman. 'You would be surprised how many disfigured corpses have been handed in to me from unscrupulous sources who are only too happy to claim the money on your scalp without doing the actual mug-hunting.'

'Blessed hard to come by an honest murderer, then,' said the commodore.

'Quite,' said the woman. 'But the good news is that we both get paid our commission now.' She turned to one of the toppers. 'Unlock the door. If the girl gives you any trouble, kill these two bumpkins. If these two give you any trouble, you can still kill them – but cut off one of the girl's ears first. She doesn't need to hear to be of use to our employer.'

The count turned to an old craynarbian standing behind them and indicated they would depart, but the assessor raised her hand. 'The contract says "to the satisfaction of the patron", Compatriot Vauxtion. I have yet to hear him express that satisfaction.'

'You appear better informed than I, madam,' said the count. 'I was not even certain that the patron was a *him*.'

'Smoke and mirrors, hmm?' said the female assessor. 'Well, allow me to satisfy your curiosity. You will find him a fascinating fellow, I believe.'

The craynarbian retainer leant close and whispered something to Count Vauxtion and he nodded. Molly was prodded in the back by a topper and she and her two companions were led down a corridor past empty cells. At the end of the passage a pair of double iron doors was unchained and opened.

Molly gasped. She had been expecting the basement of some rich lunatic's mansion in Middlesteel – not this. Wide steps sweeping down to a landscape littered with broken ziggurats; the crimson light of Chimecan crystals in the cavern ceiling, painting the landscape in an eternal twilight. Most of the ruins were wild, overgrown with spiked fungus spheres and flat, red cavern grass like a sea of fire. Paths had been cleared through the undergrowth, boxes of equipment piled behind wire fences. On the other side of the ruins she could see a tent city stretched out in ordered rows, the light from human buildings and the hum of industry. She had come full circle.

'The undercity!' said the count.

'Ah, yes, you came down on the private atmospheric line, didn't you?' said the assessor. 'A little deeper than you realized perhaps.'

'The outlaws of Grimhope didn't raise the fortune sitting on my head,' said Molly.

'Obviously not,' said the assessor. 'But we are a long way from Grimhope, m'dear.'

'This is a mortal bad turn,' whined Commodore Black. One of the toppers shoved him to silence with the butt of his carbine and Nickleby had to help him back to his feet.

As they rounded the nearest of the ziggurats Molly passed by a line of shambling steamman walking out from the tent city. Something about the creatures was wrong. She could see it in their zombie-like walk – see it in the unnatural uniformity of the bodies – the metal equivalent of a womb mage's organic breedings.

She got closer and one of the steamman stopped in the line. 'Molly!' the voice grated from a voicebox in the metal skull. 'Molly, is that you?'

Molly stopped. 'I—'

'Molly, it's me. Sainty, from the Sun Gate workhouse.'

Molly studied the poorly riveted machine life. 'But you are. . .'

'They did this to me!' Sainty's voice was hard to understand through the hisses and metallic popping. 'They were looking for you, but they took us away – the ones they didn't murder like Rachael. They peeled us into slices and jammed us into our new bodies. Most of the Sun Gate house is down here. With the others, with the—'

A man wielding a button-encrusted wand strode towards them and the girl who had been Sainty fell down to her metal knees, a fizz of agony whistling from her voicebox. 'No talking among the equalized. Two minutes of pain as punishment.'

One of the toppers grabbed Molly by the arms as she tried to lash at the overseer who moved behind the safety of his column of shambling metal slaves.

'You jigger, leave her alone. It was me that started the talking. What are you doing to her – what have you *done* to my friend?'

'She is serving her purpose,' responded the overseer. 'When you have been equalized you will understand. Now move on or I shall increase this compatriot's punishment level further. And hope that you are not assigned to my brigade after you have undergone the conversion.'

'If she lives long enough to get a new body I believe she will count herself fortunate,' said the assessor.

'Come, lass,' said Commodore Black, watching the guards restraining Nickleby. 'These black-hearted cavern demons are in no mood to show us a drop of mercy. Help your friend as best you can by leaving her be.'

Pushed and shoved by the toppers, the three of them stumbled after the assessor. She led them across the ruined city and into the centre of the overgrown metropolis. They approached the largest of the ziggurats down a cracked boulevard lined by limb-like black stone lamps, light crystals long dead but recently superseded by gas lanterns lashed to their heads by wire ties. Up to the central stairs of the ziggurat. It had not looked so high from street level, but Molly quickly found her legs aching, having to rest at the caprice of their guards' need to pause for a breath.

From the stone-hewn treads she could look down across the entirety of the ruins. To the right there was a yawning pit circled by scaffolding and wooden ramps where the activity of the resurrected Chimecan city seemed to be concentrated, legions of the dull metal bodies of human-steamman hybrids filing down into the darkness, the distant thump of machines and the whistle of steam engines venting pressure to the dance of spinning regulators. Behind them was the wall of the grotto where their cell had been buried, carved figures stretching from the floor to the mist-shrouded ceiling in an extended procession of monstrosities. Bare-breasted warriors from the race of man – both male and female – with dome-like crystal helmets and the folded legs of locusts. Molly saw Count Vauxtion following the course of her gaze; the ancient statues and the new mine works. From the look of curiosity on his face, her implacable hunter obviously had as little idea as the rest of them what was going on down here.

There were guards at the top of the ziggurat, wearing red cloaks and robe-like uniforms. Brilliant men. So the bullyboys of Grimhope were in on this place's forbidding subterranean machinations. She should have expected no less. The assessor moved through the soldiers' ranks and there, seated on a throne, was the dark-haired leader of Grimhope, lord of this broken place.

Molly, the commodore and the pensman were dragged in front of his throne.

'Tzlayloc!'

'Compatriot Templar,' said the rebel lord. 'So much nuisance in the form of one young damson, it hardly seems possible you have put me to this much trouble.'

'You know him?' said Nickleby.

'Silas, he's the King of Grimhope. You pulled me out of his capital in the Duitzilopochtli Deeps.'

'A temporary parting only, it seems,' said Tzlayloc. 'If I had but known you were my guest then . . . but you do not appear so sure, compatriot pensman?'

'I'm a little older than Molly,' said Nickleby. 'Old enough to remember when there was an exemption on real-box pictures being published in the penny sheets. Pictures of the leaders of the Carlist uprising, *Jacob Walwyn*.'

'You have an astute eye,' said Tzlayloc. 'But Walwyn is dead. That naïve student of Benjamin Carl breathed his last during the uprising, his blood running in the gutters alongside the rest of the Carlists when their hearts and methods proved ineffectual to the tasks that history demanded of them. They were soft while their enemy was hard, so they were broken by their own weakness. Believe me, that is not a mistake Tzlayloc intends to make.'

'If you are my patron,' said Count Vauxtion stepping forward, 'and you are satisfied that I have completed my commission, then I shall take my leave. I fear I find Jackelian politics rather tedious.'

'Compatriot Vauxtion, how good to finally see you without the distortion of a mirror crackling between us. Your words wound me. I am sure you follow the politics of your adopted land as closely as you did at home. You have proved a most capable mug-hunter,' said Tzlayloc. 'But then you did come highly recommended.'

'Recommended by whom?'

A figure in a plain blue military tunic weighed down with medals moved out from behind the line of guards, worldsingers at either side, their robes cut in a foreign style. The sword arm of Count Vauxtion's craynarbian retainer rattled in anger at the sight of the broken boxer's nose and brutish features. 'Captain Arinze!'

'*Citizen-Marshal Arinze* now,' retorted the officer. 'But I hardly expect you two to be familiar with the uniforms of the people's army; the cut has been updated quite a bit since you escaped from the Commonshare.'

'Another damn shiftie,' said Molly, her stare moving between the count and the marshal. 'This whole place is filthy with them.'

'Oh, but the count isn't a Quatérshiftian any more, young compatriot,' said the officer. 'He forfeited that right when he fled over our border. You recall your speech to the general command on the night before the last battle and what I advised you then, don't you, count? It seems I chose the winning side after all, old man. And now it is I that carry the marshal's baton while you have been serving under my command in a manner of speaking, given it is the Commonshare's gold that has been paying to assist our compatriots across the border. You've kept your title but lost your country, old man. I hope the bargain has been worth it.'

'While you have kept your uniform but lost everything that once made it worth wearing,' spat the count. 'A bargain which I am sure you feel well made.'

'Well made indeed.' The marshal waved at the soldiers and they lugged forward a chest. 'But let it not be said we are not men of our word. I said the Commonshare would fund our compatriots' activities in Jackals and so we will. Enjoy the money while you can, compatriot; soon it will be as much of an anachronism as your title and the soiled remnants of your estate. A society of equals needs no currency save our devotion to the cause.'

The commodore's eyes widened when he saw the fat bags of guineas lying in the chest. 'Are you blessed fools? What does your monstrous realm want with this needy lass and a weary submariner like poor old Blacky?'

'We require only the good will of our neighbours,' said the Quatérshiftian soldier.

'That is a courteous way of saying it is his payment for a corner of Jackals,' said Tzlayloc. 'Nothing too grand . . . everything from the border south to Comlonney in a sixty-mile strip. That includes an equal share of Shadowclock and the celgas mines of course.'

'You belong in an asylum, Walwyn,' said Nickleby. 'The navy isn't going to sit back and watch the Commonshare lower their cursewall, form up and march across the border. You'll bring down another Reudox on the poor devils' heads. There'll be hundreds of thousands of Quatérshiftian corpses lying dead in their cities as the price for your insane war.'

'You write very well,' said Tzlayloc. 'I have always thought so. With your left hand I believe?'

The pensman's guards seized Nickleby and hauled him forward. 'However, I found your pieces a little too flowery for my taste. Let me show you what I am about to do to Jackals' beloved Royal Aerostatical Navy.' He slid out a sabre from a guard's belt and whipped it down across Nickleby's left arm, the severed hand tumbling out to land at the marshal's feet. 'Difficult to concentrate isn't it,' said Tzlayloc as the pensman screamed, clutching his bloody stump. 'Of course, to make my point properly I should have cut off your head, but then there wouldn't be enough left of you to undergo the equalization.'

He pointed at the fiery pit behind them and the guards dragged Nickleby towards it, thrusting the bleeding remains of his arm into the coals. The pensman was unconscious by the time his wrist had been cauterized.

Tzlayloc caressed Molly's cheek as she swore at the rebel leader. 'Don't worry, Compatriot Templar. He shall have a new metal hand soon enough.'

'Have you horrendous swine no blessed compassion?' shouted Commodore Black.

'My compassion is for the people suffering under the tyranny above ground,' said Tzlayloc. 'Not war criminals and propagandists from the old regime. I see you are shocked, commodore. I know all about you and your friends – we have plenty of brothers and sisters in the engine rooms of Greenhall. And you must have done worse in your time as a science pirate, Samson Dark!'

Molly looked in confusion at the commodore.

'You're touched in the head,' said the commodore. 'I don't know what you're talking about.'

'I will admit, your fake blood code and the new face your back-street worldsinger gave you had our compatriots in Greenhall puzzled, Captain Dark. But Greenhall is not the only institution to track the ancient bloodlines.' He beckoned with a finger and a figure dressed like a Jackelian country squire came forward, his waistcoat bulging tight over a muscular chest. 'I believe you know our compatriot from the Court of the Air.'

Commodore Black flew at the figure in a frenzy, but the

target of his fury became a blur, tripping the submariner and allowing the guards to seize his arms and restrain the bear of a man.

'Wildrake,' yelled the commodore, struggling, 'stand these beasts down and let's you and me get to it.'

'You have become flabby, captain,' said Jamie Wildrake. 'Your pectorals are a disgrace to a fighting man. But you are to be congratulated on the length of time you have had to let them go to ruin. Fourteen years and the Court were convinced you had died with the rest of your fleet on the island.'

'Commodore,' said Molly, 'what in the Circle's name is he talking about?'

'Commodore is it now?' said the wolftaker. 'Such a lowly title for the Duke of Ferniethian. You have been hobnobbing with the last of the Jackelian aristocracy, little street girl. The royalist buccaneers had been a thorn in our side since the end of the civil war. But until Dark came along they were disorganized, breeding like sea snakes in their ancient stolen boats. Samson Dark united the squabbling émigré families and moulded them into a formidable menace to the trading routes.'

'It took your filthy treachery to sink us,' said the commodore. 'There wasn't a Jackelian skipper fit to tilt a sea lance against us.'

'You can't betray a cause you don't believe in,' said Wildrake. 'As our present masters of Jackals are about to discover.'

'You're a crusher?' said Molly. 'And you're working with these jiggers?'

'He's the worst of all crushers,' said Commodore Black. 'There's a whole nest of them in the sky, watching us like we are blessed ants, reaching down to stamp us out when they see us scurrying the wrong way.'

'Then you should applaud what I am about to achieve,

Dark,' said the wolftaker. 'What your nobles in exile couldn't accomplish in five hundred years of futile raids and a trail of plundered burning merchantmen. No more parliament – the corrupt legacy of Kirkhill torn to pieces.'

'There is no finer compatriot in all of Jackals,' said Marshal Arinze, stroking Wildrake's back as if the wolftaker were his child. 'A true son of the revolution, a shining example of how a brother can have his eyes opened by the truth and renounce the uncommunityist tenets of his birth. Just look how solid his body is now. He is a sword of right-thought, a blade for us to plunge into the heart of the people's enemy.'

'You traitorous bloody jigger,' hollered Molly. 'Your perfect neck is going to end up swinging on the end of a rope at Bonegate.'

Marshal Arinze backhanded Molly's face, slapping her to the ground. 'I wish I had the opportunity to find you a place in one of our camps, girl, open your eyes to the truth of Carlism – you who were born with so little, you who should have been a natural soldier in our cause. But you have another way to serve.'

'I won't serve you. You and your shiftie friends are going to be slaughtered,' said Molly. 'The moment you come across the border our people will bury your whole dirty army, just like we always do.'

Tzlayloc laughed along with the marshal, sweeping his arm down to the ravine where his legions were toiling. 'But our neighbours from Quatérshift won't be coming *over* the border to aid us, Compatriot Templar. They will be coming *under* it. This city isn't the only secret the ancient shades of Wildcaotyl have shared with me. They have led me to the deepest atmospheric tunnel routes, half ruined and collapsed with age, but nothing that a dedicated force toiling for their freedom, striving for an equal society, could not clear. Your tyranny of shopkeepers and mill masters is about to tumble before the truth of the revolution, Compatriot Templar. In a few days I will have a brigade of the people's army ready to march onto Middlesteel's own doorstep. This time the events of the age will not find us wanting. We are not the lenient philosophers and sentimental combination families that fell to Jackals' guns fifteen years ago. We have a purity of purpose.'

Molly was trembling. It sounded mad, but her heart told her that the decades-long bloodbath in Quatérshift was about to be exported to her home. The old empire's atmospheric lines – they must have cleared near two hundred miles of tunnels to get to the border with the Commonshare.

'Search within yourself, young compatriot. You know it is true. And once we have purged the RAN of its patrician leeches we will unleash our eager jack cloudies on the rest of the continent. The complacent mechomancers of the city-states, that fat godhead in Kikkosico, King Steam's cold intelligence, all will be overthrown by our new army of light. We will sweep away the antiquated kingdoms of this land and replace them with our perfect new union.'

Molly kicked the chest of money, rattling the bags of coins inside. 'Why have you been hunting me, Tzlayloc? I haven't got a place in your sullied new land.'

'That's the beauty of it, compatriot,' said Tzlayloc. 'Everyone has an equal place in it – but you, my dear compatriot, you have been marked for a special place in our new order. No false modesty now. We found the ruins of a blood analyser in your new lodgings and I know all about your little visit to raid the memory of the Greenhall engine rooms. I think you understand well enough what you are now.'

Behind Molly the count's retainer was filling an old army pack with the bags of Jackelian guineas.

'Compatriot Vauxtion,' said Tzlayloc. 'Before you depart,

I took the liberty of cancelling your steamer berth for Concorzia. Your services are going to prove exceptionally useful for me in the coming months. There are going to be many people that need hunting down – Guardians, the lords commercial and Circlist council members. The colonies could not begin to appreciate a killer with your unique talents.'

Vauxtion did not look happy, thought Molly. But if he had any doubts the tight-lipped assassin was wise enough not to express them in front of Tzlayloc.

'There's an illness inside you, Tzlayloc,' said Molly. 'I don't need the blood of some ancient fighter running through my veins to see it either. You're one sick scurf.'

'Such valuable blood it is too,' said Tzlayloc. He pressed a stone sphere in his throne's arm and part of the floor began to crunch back, folding as a dais rose up into the artificial crystal light of the cavern. On top of the dais sat a slab-like black cross, a stone surface veined with a network of silver channels. The head of the cross expanded bulb-like into a hollow gem bigger than any jewel Molly had seen before – its crystal walls filled with bubbling blood. Blood that seemed alive, tentacles of it lashing against the walls, struggling to rise up before splashing back down formless into the crimson sea.

Fear held Molly in place, a terror so complete she was paralysed. This gem was all that remained of her distant kinsmen and women; the victims of the Pitt Hill Slayer, their souls and blood intermingled in a tortured scarlet sea of despair.

'I have a throne for you,' said Tzlayloc. 'By my side you will become the sainted mother of our cause, Compatriot Templar.'

'Leave her be, you jigging abominations,' shouted the commodore. 'Lass, lass your poor unlucky blood.'

Tzlayloc laughed. 'Take this fat idiot of an aristocrat and his war criminal friend back to their cell. Have them both measured for the blessing of equalization. I see no reason why a duke should not toil alongside our brothers and sisters in the armament mills. But do not fret for my young sister's blood, compatriot duke. She is the last of her kind. Unlike her kith and kin I do not require her carcass to be drained.'

'What do you require?' asked Molly, her throat drying up.

'Your agony, young compatriot. I need your pain to be milked for as long as I can make you last. Your pain will set us all free.'

Oliver's head cleared to a familiar buzzing, the hum of darting spheres of radiance, miniature stars of intelligence circling *her* orbit. The Lady of the Lights. He glanced around. His surroundings had frozen – Steamswipe lying nearby shattered on the dirt floor, two men he did not recognize sitting forlornly on their side of the iron bars keeping Oliver and Steamswipe prisoner. Time had stopped, insects frozen in mid-flight around one of the men's wounds.

'Oliver,' said the Observer. 'Oh my Oliver, what are you doing here? This is not the path you were to follow. Who will lead your people to safety now? You must survive the end of all this, we need you. Your way has become critically fused with the failure of the yin, the way of offence.'

'I never liked being the fall-back plan,' growled Oliver. 'It looks like your favourite knight is exercising that much vaunted free will you claim to value so much.'

'What is the matter with you, Oliver? There is something else inside you. I can feel it. Your pattern has become corrupted.'

'Life is full of surprises, isn't it, *mother*,' said Oliver. 'If you want to stock a breeding zoo to assuage your guilt over writing

383

us off, find someone else to do it. I'll die fighting here before I set a foot through the feymist curtain again. I belong to the race of man and this realm is my home. I have had enough of running and hiding to last me a lifetime. No more!'

'So, you've worked it out then?' sighed the Observer.

'Yes. Your "deal" with my father,' said Oliver.

'I needed to experience your existence from your people's perspective,' said the Observer. 'So I left what you might call a shadow of myself here – an echo of that which I am. A mortal shadow. A little too mortal, as it transpired, carrying the urges and passions of your flesh. Things did not end well for her, did they?'

'You've seemed to make the most of your mistakes, mother,' said Oliver, bitterly.

Oliver knew he should be feeling something for this goddess, some connection; but, oddly, he felt only a void inside his soul. Was it the pistols anaesthetizing him? No. Even if they had never found him, he knew he would feel exactly the same. It was like discovering you had been sired by the gusts of the north wind. You could feel love for a person. But for a concept? What could you ever hope to feel towards a concept?

'Oliver,' pleaded the Observer, the desperation evident even on her ethereal face. 'You're dooming your kind. You are their last hope for survival. I need your kind to survive, I need *you* to survive.'

'Then you should have left a sacred young boy in the realm of the fast-time people,' said Oliver, 'and never have taken me to Jackals.'

'It's not too late, child. You're in the hands of the enemy's servants now and this position is doomed. Soon the last barriers of containment will fall and the enemy will arrive. The Wildcaotyl will want to invite in far worse things. They will want to recommence their terrible scheme to subvert this realm. When that happens the forces that stand behind me will commence the erasure of everything that supports your existence. You can still lead any fey that will follow you to safety.'

'You do what you feel you have to. Just know that when you try, it won't only be the darkness beyond the walls of the world you'll be facing,' said Oliver.

'This isn't you,' said the Observer. Her body was starting to vibrate, shaking in and out of focus. This was not the smooth fading of recall Oliver had witnessed before. She was changing, her spheres of light pulsing in alarm. She reached out to her lights imploringly. 'Stop them – I still have time – I must—'

Her form grew larger, changing, a chrysalis becoming a butterfly. Even her lights were mutating, shifting from bright spheres to malevolent clusters of spikes that rotated around their new master in rapid loops. It was like the shadow of a bear given life. No features, just a black mass of biped-shaped darkness. A single red eye like a line slashed across its head turned to look at Oliver and take in the cell, its senses flowing over Oliver and stretching out across thousands of miles in the shavings of a second.

'You're it, are you?' said the Shadow Bear. 'She's had a thousand damn years and you are the best she could cobble together. It's a wonder I wasn't called in earlier.'

The Observer's words out on the cold moors echoed in Oliver's mind. *I will be removed, Oliver. No more nails. No more damage limitation. You will be assigned something very dangerous with a very short fuse instead.*

'The fuse, I presume?' said Oliver.

The Shadow Bear glared around the cell, but its gaze was extending across nations. 'What a bloody mess. You haven't looked after the shop at all, have you?'

Oliver laughed, the strangeness of the sound echoing around the frozen timescape. 'What in Circle's name do you know about living in real life?'

'That's new,' said the Shadow Bear. 'No wonder you spooked her into calling me in, but it's not nearly enough to save you. Personally speaking, if it was me, I would scurry away down that rat tunnel she laid the last time there was trouble here.' It pointed an angry finger at Oliver. 'I was made for this. After you smears of water and meat have royally rogered up, I might even hold off from bringing this place down, just so I can tarry a little with the enemy. It has been a bloody age since I had some fun.'

Oliver thrust his face to within an inch of the featureless silhouette of the Shadow Bear. 'Best you start burning then, short little fuse. I would imagine you have a lot of things to do.'

The Shadow Bear shook its head in disgust. 'Man, did she ever go native.'

It vanished like it had never been and time became fluid again.

There were moments when the pain became so intense that it did not even hurt, when the burning fire eating away at Molly's skin grew hot enough for her suffering to transcend the capacity of her nerves to signal their agony. Those brief interludes of cold calm were disrupted when the cross of stone she was strapped to sensed her ascension and shifted the pattern of pain, making it a line of dancing impaling spikes or the crushing grip of a mountain squeezing her down. It was so clever, the ebony slab. It could sense when her mind was about to shut down and splinter into schizophrenic shards to isolate her from the torrent of suffering. Seconds before her mind collapsed the cross would suddenly turn itself off, leaving her senses drifting in the warm cavern air, nothing to watch but the play of Chimecan lantern crystals as they dimmed and flared with the surges of earthflow.

'It is said that it can become addictive,' said Tzlayloc. How long had he been standing there, watching her writhe and yell? 'Such a clever artifice from the coldtime. The stone is as much a surgeon as it is a torturer; it can keep you alive for years, breaking you and then mending you. The beauty of it is that it's all in the mind. It's like a microcosm of life – giving you a little pain, holding out the promise of a little pleasure – or at least a respite from your grief.'

It was difficult for Molly to focus, even when the cross-shaped slab was waiting for her to recover. She tried not to bite her tongue as she replied, 'What do you want? I'll give it to you, just let me off this.'

'This isn't what I *want*,' said Tzlayloc, the man who had once been Jacob Walwyn. 'Please do not think that. But it is *necessary*. You are the last operator, Compatriot Templar. What you feel is what the Hexmachina feels – there are no other operators for it to draw upon, for it to distribute its senses among. When I torture you, I torture it.'

'I haven't even met the Hexmachina,' sobbed Molly.

'Oh, but I think you have.' Tzlayloc stroked the crystal walls of the gem behind Molly, the blood of her family amplifying her suffering as a lens focuses light. 'Like the rest of your distant relatives. I wager you see things at night, in dreams. A young child perhaps?'

Her ghost – the young spirit at Tock House – was the Hexmachina?

'I have seen it in dreams myself,' said Tzlayloc. 'And its real body too, glimpses of it scuttling about the tunnels. I went deep, Compatriot Templar, after the uprising. Even Grimhope was no protection for Jacob Walwyn, with mug-hunters and outlaws willing to risk the free city to turn me in for the bounty on my head. I went further and deeper than any since the fall of Chimeca. Crawling through rubble falls and shinning down air stacks, past the bones of tomb robbers, past the dust and armour of Chimecan legionnaires who had stayed at their posts to the bitter end.'

'I drank from underground lakes that haven't been seen for a millennium, ate the mushrooms the old empire grew to save their people from starvation. Even the wild stock the locust priests kept for themselves. Some of their machines are still breathing down there, living machines made of meat, some of the same sorcery which survives weakly diluted over in the dunes of Cassarabia.'

Molly screamed as the slab decided her body was fit enough for another burst of agony.

'I am sorry, compatriot,' said Tzlayloc, 'but you are the key. Can't you feel it? Xam-ku is almost with us now and Toxicatl, all the shadows of Wildcaotyl. Your agony is unstitching the prison your ancestor and his ill-advised creations sealed them in. Soon the Hexmachina will be able to stand it no more and will be drawn here to try to save you – and we shall tear it to pieces.'

She could see the outlines of the old ones etched in the air, their hungry mandibles clicking in anticipation, awakening memories of ancient clashes against the filthy powerful parasites. Seven holy machines and a band of desperate warriors from every race on the continent locked in a deadly battle to win their freedom. The old evil was back, but its presence was not yet permanent. It would take the Hexmachina's destruction and the feast of souls the leader of Grimhope was planning to consolidate its hold. Hearts tossed into the pyres of Chimecan rites; for what need did the equalized have of beating meat in their chests? Equals required no passion for jealousy, no striving for betterment, no hope to feed their dreams. Their mean was set for them and fixed in their brave new bodies for Tzlayloc's brave new world.

Molly's spine arched on the slab, her cries carrying across the ruined city. 'You can't trust the old ones,' she managed through clenched teeth.

'They are a force, nothing more,' said Tzlayloc. 'Our belief is their manna, our devotion their sustenance. As a gale drives a windmill so we shall harness the Wildcaotyl as the tailwind behind our cause. It is an eminently practical arrangement. They gorge on our souls and there are so many souls for them above ground that will not be missed. Counting-house masters, mill overseers, emperors and every other uncommunityist vampire who has been feeding on the people since the wheel of history began turning. Turnabout is fair play, is it not? They have gnawed at our sinews for long enough. Now it is our turn to make a meal out of them.'

'Don't – do – it,' Molly begged.

'Think of it, Molly Templar. Our compatriots in Quatérshift have been running the unproductive leeches of their land through Gideon's Collars for a decade and producing nothing more than compost for their farms. But with the gods of Wildcaotyl melded with the revolution there is nothing that we will not be able to achieve – no enemy we cannot cut down. We shall create a perfect reign of equality that will last for all eternity.'

Molly screamed as she burned. 'Please!'

Tears rolled down Tzlayloc's face. 'I shall make you a saint, Molly. I shall raise temples to you, the poor street girl who gave her life to seal our perfect world. Your suffering is worth that, is it not, surely you must want to help us?'

Her pain drowned out the rest of his words.

*   *   *

Count Vauxtion sat as he had done for the last hour, in his chair with the chest of money in front of him. A bag of Jackelian guineas had been lined up in neat piles across the shine of his varnished tabletop and the count reduced one column of coins, building up another and then repeating the exercise . . . a game of chess without end.

'I believe you have the means to retire now, sir,' said Ka'oard.

'Yes,' said the count. 'Although I suspect we will find a paucity of berths available in the direction of Concorzia if we should try the stats or the paddle steamers.'

'Perhaps one of the old tall ship skippers, sir. Or a tramp submarine boat. And they do not yet control Jackals. There are the ferries to the city-states and the Holy Empire. If it came to it, my clan connections could no doubt secure us safe passage through the worst of Liongeli. If we got to one of the Saltless Sea ports along Crayorocco we might sail out to Thar. I have always wondered what it might be like to travel to the east, sir. And I doubt if they will be watching the jinn road south.'

'Cassarabia?' the count started laughing. 'An old man sitting on an adobe roof in the shade of a palm tree, chewing leaaf and trying to remember what it was like to drink wine without the taste of sand in it. This is not about Tzlayloc's continued patronage, old shell. This is about the application of power. But his people are only watching me. You can still go to the colonies, there's no point both of us rotting here while this place falls apart.'

'I do not believe I would care for that, sir,' said the cray-narbian. 'I have grown rather fond of this silly bumbling nation. They have the power to overrun the whole continent, but they would rather potter about their gardens cutting their hedges into fanciful shapes, slap each other with debating sticks and stop every hour to brew a pot of caffeel. Jackals deserves better than what happened to the old place, don't you think? Besides, sir, without you things would appear rather dull.'

'Well then,' said the count. 'I am a good hunter but I fear I will make for rather poor prey. So what is to be done?'

The craynarbian retainer proffered a tray. 'I don't think this is a matter of power at all, sir.'

Count Vauxtion stopped building his tower of coins. 'Then what – ah, I see, you kept it after all.' He picked up a polished thin blade from the tray. Ka'oard watched his master's eyes sparkle as he handled the fencing sabre. The command to throw the blade away thirty years ago was the only order on a battlefield the old retainer had ever disobeyed.

'I believe, sir,' said the craynarbian, 'that this is a matter of honour.'

On top of the ziggurat the rulers of Grimhope trembled and wished they were any place except here. They had never seen Tzlayloc in such a murderous fury.

'Why?' he screamed at them, pointing at the limp sweat-covered figure secured to the Chimecan torture slab. 'Why does the Hexmachina not come? She has been on the slab for two days. Her agony has been exquisite – but I see no Hexmachina!'

There was a nervous shuffling among the locust priests. They had embraced the old religion with gusto, their minds filled with the power of the ancient texts that Tzlayloc had brought back from his strange odyssey to the underworld. But now some of them were wishing for the relative anonymity of an equalized shell that their compatriots had enjoyed.

'Compatriot Templar is not the last operator,' said one of them. 'It is the only explanation.'

'We always knew there was a danger of this,' piped up one of the priests at the front.

Tzlayloc stabbed a finger at the red-robed figure that had spoken. 'You are the guardians of the new order, the shepherds of equality – and this is the best counsel you can offer!'

'It is a matter of probabilities,' said one who had been an engine man at Greenhall. 'A new descendant of Vindex with the talent to control the Hexmachina has emerged, or they might have been here all the time with their blood code unrecorded. Some of the distant parishes are tardy with their registrations.'

'But the operators always come here,' shrieked Tzlayloc. 'Always! Drawn by the last of those infernal machines. Wake your transaction engine pet up; set it on the Greenhall records again. If there is a new operator you will find them. I need their blood and I need their pain.'

'What of this one?' said the locust priest, pointing at Molly. 'We can drain her blood for the vat.'

Tzlayloc hit the locust priest in the face, knocking him to the ground. 'Fool of a shepherd. Look at her; she is perfect – abandoned by the tyranny, a ward of the poorhouse, brave and beautiful. She has more fight in her than a dozen brilliant men. If there is another operator they will most likely be of the same ilk as the other catches of the Pitt Hill teams – burghers, councillors, silks and the indolent brood of the oppressors. Would you have us raise statues to some young martyred quality worth ten thousand guineas a year?' He caressed Molly's soaking red locks. 'No, she is perfect. Throw her back in the cells, give her food and let her recover. We shall decide which operator feeds the vat and which gets the cross after we uncover the identity of the new talent.'

The locust priest Tzlayloc had admonished grovelled at the leader's feet. 'Let me lead a force into the tunnels to track down the Hexmachina, Compatriot Tzlayloc. Let me find the filthy device and destroy it for the cause.'

'No,' said the rebel king. 'Perhaps I have been too hard on you, compatriot shepherd. You have read from the texts I recovered, but you have no idea of the cunning of the Hexmachina, how deep it swims now, whispering murmurs of affection to the molten dirt. It scampers through tunnels so deep the crystals that controlled the earthflow have long since melted there. You have no conception of the heat down below and there are other dangers besides lava surges. Just hearing the echoes of the Hexmachina muttering to itself would drive you mad. No mug-hunter, topper or soldier of the cause could hunt the ferocious thing.'

He placed a kindly hand on the kneeling priest's head. 'No. We shall have to bait our trap again. I cannot afford to waste the lives of those loyal to the cause.' Tzlayloc drew out an obsidian dagger and sliced the priest's throat. 'Not when the guarantors of the revolution hunger for the souls of those too foolish to lead the people to freedom.'

With almost indecent eagerness the other locust priests fell upon their brother, holding him down while Tzlayloc carved the heart out of his chest. 'Xam-ku, Toxicatl,' he called. 'Cruatolatl and Bruaxochima.'

As the crystals in the ceiling flared, black outlines of man-insects appeared fleetingly, the locust priests echoing the shouts of Tzlayloc in the excitement of the offering. The King of Grimhope pointed to the coals. 'Fry the heart quickly. It loses its taste if it is left in the air too long.'

Two soldiers dragged the carcass of the lifeless locust priest down the steps of the ziggurat and along the wide subterranean boulevard. In the shadows of one of the buildings something watched and hissed to itself in two voices.

'Another body. The old ones are stronger now.'

393

'We can help, she said—'

'—not yet time.'

'We must time it right.'

'So we must. Shhhh.'

It slunk back into the shadows, whispering to itself.

Molly woke up in the cell. It seemed inappropriate that after enduring so much pain for so long her body could now seem fresh, alive and unmarked. The commodore came over to her. 'Ah, lass, I feared they might have driven you insane with their unholy tortures.'

'Commodore; or should I call you Samson?'

'Let that old name rest,' said the commodore. 'It has brought its line nothing but misery. In another world where Isambard Kirkhill never made his mischief I would have been proud to bear my noble title and partake of the luxuries that would have been mine. But in this world it's better to be poor old Blacky, rather than an outlaw by a wicked accident of birth.'

She looked over at Nickleby who was asleep, sweating. He did not look well, clutching his bloody stump of an arm. There were two others in the cell. A large fierce-looking steamman and a boy with tattered clothing – perhaps a year older than her.

'Who are they?'

'Two bad turns, that's for sure,' said the commodore. 'Our jailers swear he is feybreed and have posted Special Guards down the corridor to make sure he doesn't escape. I think he's been touched by the moonlight – but you should hear his blessed laugh. It's like a demon cackling and he sits there and talks to himself sometimes.' Black pointed to an open cell opposite their own; there was an ugly black gun-like thing and a rusty old knife sealed inside a crystal case, and a brace of more normal-looking pistols next door to it. The blade of the knife seemed to be writhing and twisting like a snake. 'That dark gun is alive. Sometimes the boy and the steamman call out to it and you can just hear it answer back from under the glass. The boy's friend is a vicious one for sure, not like our gentle old Coppertracks. Stay well clear of that hammer, lass, or he'll split your pretty skull.'

Molly peered through the bars, trying to look down the walkway. She could not see anything. 'Guardsmen. They should be smashing this bloody place up.'

'They're helping that devil of a revolutionary, Molly. No chance for us now, lass. Nickleby and me are to be measured up for metal suits in an hour. By tomorrow night we'll both be fit for naught but mu-bodies for poor old Coppertracks. Clunking around these infernal caverns like metal ghosts, toiling like slaves for Tzlayloc and his mortal evil schemes.'

Molly hugged the submariner. 'I'm sorry, commodore. This is my fault. You tried to help me and now you are both going to end up like Sainty and the rest of the Sun Gate workhouse.'

'No tears for Blacky, now,' said the commodore. 'My stars have seen me cheating death since the day I was born on my ancient old boat. Better I perish down here than get thrown into the royal breeding house as a prize heifer expected to serve parliament's cruel pleasure.'

Molly went over towards the four-legged steamman.

'Leave him alone,' said Oliver. 'He's in no mood to be a spectacle to a Middlesteel street urchin.'

'Who are you?' retorted Molly. 'His mother? He's in pain.'

'Let me suffer,' groaned Steamswipe. 'I have failed the duty charged to me by King Steam for a second time. This fate is all I deserve.'

'You are drawing too much power for your body-to-weight profile,' said Molly, scooping up a handful of mud from the floor and shaping it over the rents in his stack. 'And you are no good to King Steam lying here on the floor feeling sorry for yourself.'

Steamswipe breathed a sigh of relief, the red light behind his visor growing brighter. Molly popped a hatch in his belly armour and started to work on the steamman knight's innards, her fingers pushing cogs back in place, adjusting boards and pulling out broken components.

'You're *her*,' said Oliver. 'You're the plan of offence.'

'Quiet,' said Molly. 'How can I work with you twittering on?'

Marching boots sounded down the corridor and Molly closed the hatch, hiding what she had been doing with her body.

Captain Flare appeared outside their cell, a boy by his side, the only one in the captain's retinue not in a guardsman's uniform. He looked familiar to Oliver, the subject of a hundred vicious caricatures by the penny sheets' illustrators.

'Dear Circle,' said Molly. 'Prince Alpheus!'

Oliver stood up. 'Have you come to gloat? You couldn't have taken me without half the guard at your back.'

'Perhaps,' said the captain. He held up a sheaf of papers. 'I have your registration records, Oliver Brooks. The worldsingers did not know what you are and neither did Tzlayloc's killers. You're not a wolftaker; I have confirmation of that from the horse's mouth. You seem to have wandered into all this by accident.'

'When your friends murdered my family it was not an accident.'

'It was the Court of the Air's own people who did that. At least, the ones loyal to Tzlayloc.'

'Why are you here, guardsman?' said Molly. 'You're meant to be protecting us.'

'I'm here to make an offer,' said the captain. 'As to the rest of it, I doubt you would understand, Damson Templar.'

'I'm not interested,' said Oliver.

'You haven't heard my offer yet,' said Captain Flare.

'They all sound the same after a while,' said Oliver. 'You've come to offer me the same thing that the worldsingers used to every week I was dragged into a police station to sign the county register.'

'But with one significant difference.' Flare tapped the torc around his neck. 'The Commonshare's worldsingers have removed the hex. The Special Guard are free – no more executions on the order's whims, no more campaigns foisted upon us by the House of Guardians. We are free!'

'Is that all?' said Oliver. 'You sold out cheap.'

'Don't be asinine, Oliver. We get our own grant of land. Judging by your choice of travelling companion you obviously came by the Steammen Free State. Why not the Feybreed Free State as well? We receive the southern uplands for our part in this. No one wants to live that near the feymist curtain anyway. We shall offer our children to it – we shall found a city of the fey. Free fey.'

'I hope you are not planning to have families,' said Oliver. 'What we've got isn't the winter fever. You can't pass immunity down a bloodline. The mist's changes to your children's bodies will kill eight out of ten you leave to the curtain.'

'We shall learn, Oliver. We know nothing about the feymist – you are living proof of that. You spent your entire childhood inside the curtain. You can teach us how to survive.'

'You're a fool, captain,' said Oliver. 'Do you think your allies intend to allow the south of Jackals to become the feybreeding capital of the world? They'll use you to help smash the kingdom then show you the inside of a Gideon's Collar the moment you are of no use to them.'

'You could not defeat us,' said Captain Flare. 'And neither will they. We have fought for our freedom and we shall fight to keep it. Whomever we have to.'

'Enjoy the illusion of it while you can, guardsman. I have seen inside the souls of those you call compatriot and they are rotten to the core.'

'So much power and it's all going to go to waste,' said Flare. 'The order should never have kept you at Hundred Locks. You should have been with us from the start. Now you are going to compound their error by dying down here. The wolftaker wants to bring in some of his associates to rip your mind to shreds, to see how many of his crooked friends you uncovered on the way to tracking us all down here. If you come with me as a Special Guardsman, Wildrake will have no choice but to content himself with your steamman attendant.'

'If the price of my freedom is the subjugation of everyone else in Jackals, you can bloody keep it,' said Oliver.

By the captain's side the young prince stared at Commodore Black. 'Why do you gawp at me so, old man?'

'Ah, lad, we are related you and I. When Isambard Kirkhill rolled the rightful king off the throne, one of my great grandmothers many generations back was married to the King's brother. In another world you would have been my nephew and I the Duke of Ferniethian.'

'But it is this world I find myself in,' said Prince Alpheus. 'Shortly to gain the crown and lose my arms in the process.'

'The House of Guardians' wicked bargain for your pauper's throne,' said the commodore. 'Dear lad, what in the Circle's turn are you doing in this nest of monsters and villains?'

'It is not only my jailers in the Special Guard who long to be free,' said Prince Alpheus. 'I do to boot – and so I shall be. Every notable in Jackals is swamping Middlesteel at this instant, waiting for the surgeon royal to raise my blood-spattered arms in Parliament Square like a flag up its pole. But my new compatriots are going to give the mob quite a different spectacle.'

'Lad, they're our people. Our fight is with parliament. Circle knows, I have suffered at their hands too, hunted down by the kingdom's warships and aerostats, seen my brave friends, *your* family, slaughtered at the whim of turncoats and traitors. But our cause is to rule for the people, not over them. Otherwise we might as well take all the empty estates royal and turn them into mills stuffed with children earning a penny a day and run for election as Guardians.'

'I wish you had met my father, Duke of Ferniethian,' said Alpheus. 'I think you would have become fast friends. Your cause is finished. The mob is an empty beast that would rather hurl jinn bottles at us every time a game of four-poles is rained off. They take guardsmen like Captain Flare here—' the prince touched the captain's arm '—the finest man I know, and put him on a leash that becomes a hangman's rope if he pulls away too hard. There's nothing and nobody in Jackals I have a care to rule for. When the war is over, I shall ask them for your life, duke. But that is all I shall do.'

The prince and the guardsman left the prisoners to their fate, their footsteps echoing down the passage. Commodore Black sat down and sobbed. 'So that is our cause then. A fool of a boy raised in an empty marble cage who has forgotten his duty. And us to be turned into metal slaves or tortured until death becomes a blessed relief.'

'Don't worry,' said Oliver. 'We're not going to live that long. They think they're riding a tiger, but the reality is that the tiger is riding them.'

'My, but you're a cheerful one,' said Molly. She closed the panel on Steamswipe's belly. 'There you are old steamer. You're running at a level where you can cope with your broken stack. You won't be able to smash down fortress walls and lift aerostats any more, but I wouldn't want to stand in front of your hammer all the same.'

'Truly the Loas ride you, young softbody,' said Steamswipe, raising his centaur-like body on his armoured legs slowly, testing the weight. 'You heal our race as if you were tutored inside the hall of the architects.'

'Molly,' coughed Nickleby from the floor. 'Commodore, for the love of the Circle will one of you get my pipe out from my pocket.'

Oliver was nearest, so he pulled the battered wooden pipe out and filled it with mumbleweed while the pensman's friends checked his left arm, bandaged with green cloth torn from his jacket.

'So you have your story now,' said Commodore Black. 'The mystery of the Pitt Hill slayings. But the devils won't be letting you out to Dock Street to write it.'

The pensman held up his mangled left arm. 'Well, I never was much good at writing with my right hand.'

Molly grimaced as she saw the bloody stump Tzlayloc had made of her friend's limb.

Nickleby looked at Oliver and Steamswipe. 'I thought I had dreamed you, thought I was going to wake up back at Tock House.'

Oliver flicked the flywheel on the side of the pipe and sparked the weed into life. 'You know, ever since I left Hundred Locks I have been waking up every day feeling the same way.'

Nickleby lay back in relief as the smoke started to lift out of the pipe's head.

'If you are a son of the mist, northern boy, how about you turn your fey nature on these bars,' said Molly. 'Melt them or walk through them or something.'

Oliver glared at her. 'I'm the shield, not the sword. That's your job. There's Special Guard by the door – and I know you can feel the other things out there – the ancient ones.'

The commodore shook his head in despair. 'Dear Circle, is it not enough that we are trapped down here without a mortal drop of jinn to warm our hearts, must we have terrible spirits to contend with too?'

'Dear Circle is right,' said Nickleby. 'Jackals has had a millennium following the Circlelaw, a millennium prospering without the passion of gods to bend our knee to. Tzlayloc will return us to an age of Chimecan darkness.'

'At least we are together,' said the commodore. 'Molly, it was your ancestor who crowned the first king of Jackals and until the civil war, it was my family that protected the realm from the return of monsters such as these. Our fates have led us here. We have done our mortal best and there is no shame in that.'

'Someone is coming,' said Oliver.

'I can't hear anything,' said Molly.

'I wasn't using my ears.'

Flanked by two Special Guardsmen and diminutive in comparison, Count Vauxtion stood in front of the bars of the cell.

Molly spat at the bars. 'I thought you would be spending your mug-hunting bounty by now, count.'

Count Vauxtion held up a sheaf of paper. 'More work for the wicked. My benefactor has been very generous with his patronage. I dare say we will catch most of the splendidly distinguished names on this list when Middlesteel falls. Tzlayloc has his ancient atmospheric tunnel cleared now. The Third Brigade is arriving through it as we speak.'

Nickleby groaned. The Commonshare's Third Brigade, their shock troops. As the revolution in Quatérshift had raged the

401

communityists had emptied the jails and conscripted political prisoners, murderers, rapists, thieves. The Third Brigade was where the worst of the devils had ended up, their name synonymous with the greatest excesses of a brutal civil war. They were demons in uniform.

'You're a true topper, count,' said Molly. 'A real piece of work.'

'I am truly sorry, my dear. It gives me no pleasure to do this.' He indicated the lock on the cell and one of the Special Guardsmen pushed back his cloak to reach for the keys. 'The locust priests request your company upstairs for another of their holy services. Say goodbye to your companions, Molly. The war criminal and the sailor will be among the legions of the equalized when you return . . . and there are some truth hexers who want to pick through the minds of the boy and the steamman.' He smiled coldly at Oliver. 'If Molly survives the priests' blessings, she may want to wipe the drool away from what is left of you.'

Oliver knew what was coming. The pressure on his hands increased, the weight of holding an anvil no one could see. With a click the door swung open and the hulking Special Guardsmen moved into position to cover the exit. The tallest of the two looked down in disbelief as a spot of blood appeared on his uniform, the sword pushing out of his chest. Oliver cut the second guardsman's connection to the mist as the count slid his sabre out of the first and turning decapitated the other guard with a stroke so fast it barely registered. The others had not even noticed the brace of ornate duelling guns that had appeared in Oliver's hands.

'I doubt we can afford your rates,' said Nickleby to the count.

Count Vauxtion wiped the gore off his blade and reassembled the sword cane.

'I had two sons once. They paid for you.'

'That's it?' said Molly. 'You spent all that time tracking me down for them and you're switching sides just like that?'

'I choose who I work for,' said the count. 'And I choose which commissions I accept. I warned Tzlayloc once that he would be well advised not to try and change the terms of my contract halfway through the job. He has, and now at least one of us is going to be very unhappy with that decision.'

'Let's be away, now,' said the commodore. 'Before these devils realize you have seen the error of your ways. We can toast your change of heart back at Tock House if your wicked crew of toppers have left any bottles in my cellar.'

'I wasn't lying about the Third Brigade,' said Count Vauxtion. 'And the walls of your folly aren't thick enough to resist shot and cannon.'

'You have not freed us to rescue us,' said Steamswipe, leaving the cell and smashing the glass case where Lord Wireburn lay trapped.

'About time,' grumbled the holy weapon.

'You need our swords,' said Steamswipe, tossing Oliver's witch-blade back to him. 'I have faced your softbody nation on the field of honour often enough to recognize your cunning.'

'You have a long memory if you can remember staring north from the Steamman Free State and seeing any field other than killing ones in Quatérshift.' The count sketched a map into the dirt of the floor with his cane. 'This is the mine works on the floor of the cavern, this is the Jackelian terminus for the atmospheric line – under vacuum now. And this is the chamber where they store the blasting casks of blow-barrel sap, enough barrels to put a dent in a mountain. If we ignite it we can bury the entire invasion force in the tunnel under a thousand tonnes of rubble.'

'They are your countrymen,' said Nickleby.

'I'm a Jackelian now,' said the count. He held up the sabre and the long knife he had hidden inside his sword cane. 'These are my debating sticks, don't you know?'

Oliver loaded both his pistols. 'Let us go and discuss politics with Tzlayloc then.'

Molly saw that the count had produced the gas gun she had seen him use in Grimhope, while the commodore and Nickleby liberated pistols out of the dead guardsmen's holsters. Count Vauxtion led them across the lost city, the gas gun pressed into Molly's back, Oliver suggesting paths through the dark overgrown buildings that avoided the Special Guardsmen and twisted fey things. Molly and her two companions from Tock House played the roles of mistreated prisoners to perfection, aided by the prop of Nickleby's blackened stump of an arm. When brilliant men and the Commonshare's skirmishers challenged them, the count flourished the letters of passage from Tzlayloc; that and the assassin's menacing manner were enough to get them to the edge of the mine.

Bright engineers' lanterns augmented the Chimecan crystals' twilight inside the pit, the same style of lamps Oliver had seen in Shadowclock's tall streets. The stink of badly vented steam-engine smoke and the bash of equipment rose from the pit. Metal legions of the equalized laboured below. They sang the outlawed songs of the uprising with their scratchy voiceboxes, the once-organic population of Grimhope and pressed miners of Shadowclock both toiling under the supervision of brilliant men.

On the pit's sides the rickety scaffolding and ladders were being upgraded, replaced with reinforced ramps, strong enough to support the columns, cannon and sea of boots of the Third Brigade. The group had almost reached the floor of the pit when a shout sounded from the cavern above. Marshal Arinze.

'Compatriot Vauxtion,' shouted the officer. 'Our Jackelian brothers want the girl back on the cross. Why are you down there?'

'Keep moving to the bottom of the ramp,' whispered the count, then shouted back up: 'Tzlayloc wants the girl to see her companions undergo equalization in the conversion mills. He believes it will help amplify Compatriot Templar's suffering on the pain device.'

'Splendid,' the marshal called down. 'Now why don't you explain to me how they are going to equalize that brute of a steamman warrior you have with you?'

He said something to his troopers and they began slipping crystal charges out of their bandoliers and unslinging their rifles. Upheaval erupted across the pit floor, shots crackling down as Steamswipe returned fire, rotating sunbursts searing the walls with plasma light. Equalized workers milled around, trying to work out where and why the sudden explosion of violence had interrupted their toil. A number of the press-ganged compatriots shuffled towards the ramps, trying to use the confusion as cover to escape; their overseers frantically worked their discipline rods and the equalized workers tumbled to the ground in anguish.

'Behind you,' warned Molly as a wave of loyalist equalized shambled towards Steamswipe brandishing picks and pressure cutters. The steamman knight sang to Lord Wireburn in machine tongue and the holy relic poured forth a jet of blue fire, Steamswipe spraying the line from left to right and back again. Screams from the human-machine hybrids died as their voiceboxes exploded in the unearthly fire, a shower of molten metal and charcoaled flesh raining back on the advancing children of the revolution.

Lord Wireburn was smoking in the knight's manipulator arms, the dark oil which slicked his surface fully burnt off.

'Suffer not these abominations to live, Steamswipe. Eradicate every last one of the filthy outrages.'

'Close quarters,' barked Count Vauxtion. Their rear was being rushed by a mob of overseers, unarmed except for their discipline rods. Nickleby and the commodore were frantically reloading from their stolen bandoliers as Oliver raised both pistols and discharged them at the scaffolding joins. High above soldiers plunged into the air as a section of the ramp gave way, an explosion of iron pipes and dust rolling out into their attackers. Both blades from Vauxtion's cane were in his hands as he stepped lightly through the sudden dust storm, flicking his sabre and long knife like butterfly wings, cutting throats and slitting sinews.

Tucked in Oliver's belt the witch-blade shivered with delight; here was an enemy it could engage without the pain of trying to penetrate fey-twisted muscle. Oliver stepped forward and was engulfed by the cloud of rock dust, the witch-blade grown sword long. He moved with a stamping, twisting gait, the hilt of the witch-blade grasped with both hands, sweeping up, sweeping down, a single cut through a body each time. Oliver could hardly see his attackers' faces; they were merely shadows in the dust, their angry bellows cut off as they went down. The part of him that had not died at Hundred Locks was glad he couldn't see the look of contorted astonishment on their faces as the witch-blade sucked the life from them.

He could see the expression of horror on Molly's face though, as the dust cleared and he and the count stood among a sea of fallen brilliant men, three blades slicked with gore. Somehow her disgust mattered to him more than it should.

'An ancient fighting style,' said the count. 'I was not aware it was even taught any more.'

Oliver dipped down and wiped the blood off his witch-blade onto a corpse's jacket. A slippery blade is a dangerous blade; the words arrived in his mind as if from his father. Steamswipe galloped for the tunnel that Vauxtion had sketched out for them, Oliver and the count taking the rear as their three companions sprinted in the shielded lee of the steamman's hull, round shot pinging off his armour.

Someone was shouting at them from above as they reached the shelter of the tunnel mouth, a woman's voice. It was the assessor; her livid words mangled by the row of kneeling Quatérshiftian scouts discharging their rifles. Vauxtion stuck out his hand and Oliver tossed him one of his pistols, the count falling to one knee and turning sideways, gun bucking once. The assessor fell forward lifeless onto the rank of soldiers, spilling one of the troopers into the pit mouth.

'Remind me to tell Ka'oard to engage a new agent.'

Tunnels split out in front of them in all directions and they pushed past bewildered workers – equalized and human – following the count's lead. Molly added to the confusion, shouting warnings of raids by the crushers and tunnel collapses, floatquakes and failing Chimecan roof crystals. Tremors ran through the floor of the mine system, lending authenticity to her warnings.

'An atmospheric capsule,' said the commodore. 'The blessed shifties are coming through. If we don't bring the tunnels down soon we'll be facing a brigade full of the rascals down here with us.'

Count Vauxtion pulled a spherical detonator cap from his pocket. 'Be cautious, there will be guards outside the blasting store.'

Oliver frowned. He could not detect any soldiers around the corner. Steamswipe rounded the corner of the tunnel to find a steel door blocking their passage.

'There is nobody here.'

'So much the better,' said the commodore. 'Let's set your

blessed charge and be away from here before it does its lethal work.'

Steamswipe lifted Lord Wireburn and hosed the locked door with blue fire, melting the barrier with the precision of a Middlesteel watchmaker. Pushing into the blasting chamber's cavernous interior they halted. It was empty. Four solitary glass-gilded barrels lay piled in the centre, an equalized worker about to load one into a two-wheeled handcart.

'Where are they?' shouted the count. 'Where's the blasting store?'

'Compatriot,' grated the equalized worker, 'this *is* the blasting store.'

'The blow-barrel casks,' said Vauxtion. 'This chamber was piled high with blow-barrel casks yesterday evening.'

'They have been shipped back to mill twelve,' said the worker, the calculation drums in his chest turning hesitantly as he tried to summon the words. 'The glass blowers have been out of sap for charge manufacture for days. The mine-works committee said you did not need the barrels in here any more, time for bullets they said.'

Commodore Black kicked the handcart over. 'Our stars. Our unlucky stars.'

'Soldiers,' said Oliver. 'Coming into the tunnels after us. We cannot afford to be dead-ended in this chamber.'

'Tell me we can get out of here,' Molly said to the count.

'I was not planning to die down here,' said Count Vauxtion, slipping the detonator sphere back in his pocket. 'This complex is a termite mound, there's tunnels all around us and the higher ones connect to the old copper mine above. There are airshafts that come out in Middlemarsh Forest.'

'With our mortal luck the Third Brigade will have parked their ammunition train over them,' said the commodore.

They dared the mine passages again, passing equalized gangs

blissfully unaware of anything except the hollows in the rock that they were working on and the equipment they were dragging behind them, ignorance which turned to panic when the Commonshare's skirmishers darted through the corridors in pursuit of the intruders.

Steamswipe overturned three wagons of rubble waiting to be pulled out on a rail. An instant blockade. A tongue of cyan flame licked out from Lord Wireburn, sending the soldiers behind them scattering. Molly ducked her head into a side passage and then tried another opening down the tunnel. 'One leads up, one leads down.'

Bullets cracked past as Nickleby tried to reload his pistol one-handed. 'I can hold them here.'

'With me by your side,' said Steamswipe, loosing another burst of flame. 'I could slay the entire army of the Commonshare in these tunnels and I would not think it too much.'

Molly pushed the commodore down the tunnel towards Oliver. 'I'm not leaving anyone here. We can smash the ladders in the shaft behind us, the shifties don't know these tunnels any better than us.'

'He has a point,' said the count. 'If a couple of us stay and hold the tunnel—'

Molly heard the glass sphere as it rolled down the corridor towards them, two hues of liquid capped by a clockwork head rotating in towards the crystal. Someone shouted 'grenade' and Steamswipe cast himself on top of the crystal explosive, the detonation lashing the steamman warrior into the wall of the tunnel, lifting everyone else off their feet. The burning knight crumpled into the wooden tunnel support, snapping the stay as an avalanche of rock rained down around them.

Oliver got to his feet. Blood was pouring from his head

where a rock had glanced off it. Commodore Black rose out of the haze of rock powder. 'Sweet mercy!'

They had been cut off from the others by the rock fall. There was a small chink of light from the lanterns on the other side of the cave-in – their side had fallen into darkness.

'We're here,' Oliver shouted through the small crevice.

On the other side of the rock fall Nickleby and Count Vauxtion picked themselves up from under the layer of tunnel wreckage and shouted back. Steamswipe's head and chest were visible; the rest of his body lay trapped under a huge rock. The ceiling had collapsed in front of them too; the barks of the Commonshare skirmishers muffled beyond their pocket of tunnel.

'Lass!' shouted the commodore. 'Molly! Is Molly with you, Silas?'

'She's not here.'

Commodore Black stared at the mass of rock. 'Sweet Circle. Molly, Molly!'

Oliver pulled the submariner away from the rock fall as he frenziedly tried to pull at the rubble and rocks. 'I can't sense her under there, commodore. I can feel the Third Brigade passing through in the atmospheric capsules below us, but I can't sense Molly.'

'Lad, she might be unconscious under there. Trapped in a pocket of air.'

'She could be, but better if she isn't. A company of miners with blasting barrels and drills would take a day to shift this. If she woke under there and she wasn't dead. . .'

'Oh lass, my poor lass.'

Nickleby placed his face near the fissure in the rock fall. 'We are trapped in here. Steamswipe is pinned down and near deactivate. The tunnel fall at the other end is lighter.

We might be able to dig out that way although I suspect we are going to find half the Third Brigade waiting for us.'

'I doubt they have waived the brigade's rules on prisoners since I faced them with the remains of the royalist army,' said the count. 'Soldiers who accept a surrender are to feed the prisoners out of their own allocation of rations.'

'There is another way,' rumbled Lord Wireburn from the tunnel floor.

Count Vauxtion picked up the holy weapon. 'What do you mean?'

'I contain within my shell the stuff of anti-life, a grain of a primordial energy superior in explosive force to a forest of blow-barrel trees. I can lower the walls of containment to this power and release my life force in a single burst.'

The commodore climbed up the rock fall to speak through the gap. 'Silas, you'll not survive that. Dear Circle you can't leave old Blacky and the lad down here on our own, scrabbling about in the dark like rats in a trap.'

'Get away, Jared,' called Nickleby through the cranny. 'As far and as fast as you can. We're going to bring down the roof on the Third Brigade after all.'

'No Silas,' wheezed the commodore.

Oliver pulled at the submariner's jacket. 'We have to climb as high as possible.'

'You tell Broad,' shouted the pensman. 'You tell him when they publish the story on the Pitt Hill murders that I want the by-line. It's not to go to anyone else. It's my damn story.'

'I'll tell him,' promised the commodore, as he and Oliver scrambled along the passage and into the darkness. 'And you'll get the whole blessed front page too.'

Nickleby passed his pipe over to Count Vauxtion to re-light. 'Do you smoke?'

'I prefer brandy,' said the count. 'But you can't raise a decent vintage in Jackals. You lack the soil.'

'Yes,' said Nickleby. 'I remember the brandies that used to come over from Quatérshift. Haven't seen one in years. No flask on me, I'm afraid. Not even jinn.'

Red sigils had appeared on Lord Wireburn's oily surface, sweeping down in a circular pattern like a clock. A hum of static was streaming from Steamswipe's voicebox, as if the life of the old warrior was leaking out into the stale air of the cave-in.

'That sounds like a tune,' said Count Vauxtion.

'He is approaching deactivation,' said Lord Wireburn. 'He is singing to the Steamo Loas. Calling their blessing. He remembers only the low-level languages now; too much of him has been destroyed. He has asked me to apologize to you for not being able to sing a little in your tongue. So you also might know their blessing.'

'How long do we have left?' asked Nickleby.

'Three minutes perhaps,' said Lord Wireburn. 'The barriers I am bypassing are not intended to be lowered lightly. It is only the wisdom of my dotage that allows me to override the constraints of my architecture.'

From the other side of the light rock fall came the sound of rubble being removed. Count Vauxtion pulled his delicate sabre from his cane and rested it on his knees.

'I doubt if they will get through in time,' said Nickleby.

'I shall keep my sabre to hand in case,' said Count Vauxtion. 'Some of the Third Brigade are no doubt talented diggers, the number of ditches they had to shovel while convicts. . .'

'Of course,' said Nickleby. 'Well, I with my pipe and you with your sabre. I would say we are both content.'

* * *

Outside in the mine pit a vortex had formed, a tornado of black energy whirling around and sucking Commonshare soldiers, brilliant men and equalized into its maw. Hands clung desperately to the side of the excavation, as tools, rocks and clothes were pulled up towards the putrid-smelling whirlwind.

A terrified soldier ran towards Marshal Arinze, his rifle forgotten, shouting appeals to the sun god that the Commonshare had long since banned. He pushed past the officer and lifted into the air as Arinze shot him in the back. 'Stay at your posts, compatriot soldiers. Hold to them fast.'

By the officer's side two of his worldsingers tried an invocation but a coil of darkness whiplashed out from the pit; piercing their foreheads; and they collapsed back, steam boiling from a tiny hole in each of their skulls.

Tzlayloc appeared and the marshal grabbed at him. 'Compatriot, my people are being slaughtered in there.'

Tzlayloc laughed, pointing to the whirlwind speeding up. 'You have such little faith in the cause. Your soldiers are not dying, they are being saved – they are feeding the Wildcaotyl.'

As he spoke the whirlwind exploded towards the cavern roof, six separate storms of insects darting and twisting around each other. The citizens of Grimhope and their allies covered their ears as a hideous chattering filled the cavern, drowning out the terrified screams of the troops below.

Each cloud looped around and plunged down into the excavation, heading for a single tunnel. Miners and their masters broiled as the stream of insect-shaped energy swept down the chambers and towards the source of the force that was being revealed below ground. At the rock fall the Wildcaotyl were hurled back. A wall of translucent silver outlines was standing sentry beyond the frantically digging soldiers and miners – the Steamo Loas safeguarding their chosen champion. The Wildcaotyl apparitions hissed in rage through tarantula-like

413

fangs. These thin vapours of steammen deities were lesser spirits; they could devour the knight's death guard, but not in the few seconds they sensed was left on Lord Wireburn's flickering display.

Turning as one, the Wildcaotyl poured down the airshafts and found the rubber curtain of the atmospheric terminus. Beating through the station valves they splattered against the walls, mile after mile of the vacuum-filled transport tunnel sprayed with a trembling skin of unholy energy. Then they waited, ignoring the whisper of atmospheric capsules speeding past.

Stones tumbled down from the rock fall exposing a small triangle of space between two boulders.

'What can you see?' a voice sounded on the other side of the obstruction.

Count Vauxtion smashed his fist into the nose that pressed itself up to the space, shaking his hand in pain as the soldier on the other side of the caved-in rock fell back.

'You should have impaled him with your sabre,' said Nickleby.

'There speaks a true jack cloudie,' said the count. 'Warfare is more than pushing fin-bombs out of an aerostat bay. Sometimes it feels good to close with the enemy with nothing but your bare hands. It is a matter of honour.'

'Yes,' said Nickleby. A line of pale lifeless faces looked up at him accusingly from a dead street, the cards with the names of the places the corpses had been discovered hung around their necks. 'A matter of honour.'

Shouts of anger sounded on the other side of the rock and the thud-thud of the engineers and soldiers clearing away the fall grew louder.

The pensman glanced down at Lord Wireburn cradled in

his arms – the crimson light flickering across his face as the sigils rotated around. Would the holy relic be able to fire now if the Third Brigade engineers broke through? He doubted it.

'What say you?' Vauxtion called out through the gap. 'What say you of honour, my compatriots, my countrymen? Is there any honour still left in our beautiful home, or has it been crushed under the boots of the Third Brigade? Has honour yet to be allocated by committee 4302, or was the last of it marched into a Gideon's Collar to pass away under the blow of a steel spike?'

The muzzle of a gun pushed through the gap and Vauxtion seized it, striking the weapon back into its owner's face before pulling the rifle through into their chamber. He caressed the ugly black gun's lines, checking the crystal charge loaded into its barrel. A look of disappointment settled on the count's face. 'Functional, at best. A tool for intimidating farmers and menacing bakers' boys. There is more workshop artistry in a Jackelian redcoat's Brown Jane, more craftsmanship in a lady's purse gun.'

Vauxtion tilted the rifle through the gap and discharged it, the retort of the charge echoing around the small space like thunder. Nickleby coughed and waved the pungent smoke away with his mumbleweed pipe. The count tossed the empty gun contemptuously onto the floor.

'I do apologize,' said the count.

'I think nothing of it,' said Nickleby. He drew a deep breath on the pipe. 'These are rather difficult times.'

'Quite. You realize that when the bludgers on the other side of the rock were my soldiers, we never would have been squirming around under the dirt like thieves digging into your basement. We would have marched across the border in the same old way, marched like men, then battled your new pattern army with our king's military trinity: cavalry, infantry and artillery. By the glory of the sun and all that is holy we would have fought like *devils*.'

'And we would have seen you off in the same old way,' said Nickleby. 'With the red-coated scrapings of the gutter, the threat of the lash on their back and the promise of a large tot of jinn when it was all over.'

Vauxtion smiled and nodded, then turned his attention back to the rocks tumbling down on their side of the divide.

The pensman heard the scraping of an iron manipulator hand behind him.

'Ni.c.kle.by, h.ear m.y wo.r.d_s.'

It was Steamswipe, half-crushed, half-decapitated. Somehow the knight had managed to regain enough of his functions to communicate in the higher languages.

'We a.r.e a.ll c.lo.se to d.e.ac.ti.v_atio.n. The K.eep.er of th.e Et_e.rn.al Fla_me w.ill cle.an.s.e u.s all. Y.ou m.u_st sing. S_ing t.o p.lea.se th.e Loas.'

'I am afraid I wouldn't be much good at the hymns of your people, old steamer,' said Nickleby. 'I simply don't have the voicebox for it.'

'T_he.n yo.u m.ust in.to.n.e the ma.nt.ra of y.our k_in_d. O.ur ti.me i.s at an e_n_d.'

The pensman shrugged.

'Oh, please no,' said Vauxtion.

On the other side of the rock face the troopers and engineers halted their clearance work.

'What's that sound? Do you hear it?'

'They are singing,' replied one of the equalized workers. 'They are singing "Lion of Jackals".'

The whole cavern shuddered, as if the world had bounced the lost underground city a foot into the air. Crystals embedded in the cavern ceiling shattered, raining down the dust of ancient machinery onto the shakos of the Commonshare's skirmishers. Equalized revolutionaries briefly halted then continued to the schedule of their work rota as if nothing had happened. Tzlayloc extended a hand down to Marshal Arinze and the soldier picked himself up.

'The Third Brigade is here compatriot marshal. The revolution has arrived in Jackals.'

Commodore Black stared down the shaft they had just scaled. It had collapsed, filled in by an avalanche following the quake. A minute earlier and they would have been inside there.

'The tunnels still stand,' said Oliver. 'I can feel the troops in their atmospheric carriages. Murderers and killers. Thousands of them.'

'Silas? Your friends?'

Oliver shook his head.

'Silas Nickleby, you dear blessed fool,' wept the commodore. 'Silas and Molly, both dead. All for nothing, all for nothing. I warned him what would happen. You heard me tell him. The scrapes that old goat got me into. What am I going to do without the impetuous fool? An army of the worst slayers in history nipping away at our heels. There's nobody left, lad, just us. What have we got left?'

Oliver's shadow swelled in the dirty tunnel like a living thing, his brace of pistols glowing with a light not cast by the tunnel lanterns. He lifted the bandolier of crystal charges off Black's shoulder. 'Forty bullets.'

Chapter Twenty-One

Brigadier-general Shepperton stared up at the lone aerostat floating over Fulven Fields on the outskirts of Middlesteel. 'What is Admiralty House playing at? We can't move into position without cover from the navy – I don't know what's the matter with our bally aerostats today. Where are those damn loafers from signals?'

Major Wellesley turned on his skittish sixer, the horse unsettled by the ranks of shining metal bodies taking to the field in the low hills opposite; they had no smell and the horses of the riding officers had been spooked all morning. 'Sir, none of our scouts have managed to locate a crystalgrid station that wasn't fired last night by the Carlists.'

The major glanced up at the aerostat. It was an old Guardian Prester class, due to be decommissioned at the royal armoury and manned mostly by retired RAN types and a handful of enthusiast volunteers from the Middlesteel chapter of the Lighter than Air Society. A bunch of tail spotters in the fin-bomb room. Wellesley shuddered and prayed that they would remember which army below stood on their side.

A riding officer galloped at full tilt from the north, reining in at the last moment in front of the staff officer's table. 'Brigadier-general, sir, Admiralty House is burning. Spoke to one of the staff there, said some of the Admiralty Board were feybreed, fey wearing the bodies of the Sky Lords. Quite a to-do in the city, sir, shifties everywhere, barricades and Carlists manning them. Makes getting about rather tiresome.'

'Where's your hat, man?'

'Shot off, sir.'

'Draw a new one from the commissionaire,' ordered the brigadier-general. I won't have my boys looking unkempt, what what. Jack cloudies have let us down badly this time, ships of the line sitting around Shadowclock like a school of useless bally skraypers. There'll be questions asked in the House.'

Wellesley winced. They had already told the brigadier-general twice that the House of Guardians had fallen early on in the Commonshare's assault. It was pure luck the Middlesteel Rifles had been out of their barracks when the nighttime attack had begun.

'Sir,' said Major Wellesley, pointing to the neat lines of their troops. 'Now we have confirmation that the RAN won't be operating in support, might I suggest we look at our dispositions again?'

'You may not, sir,' said the brigadier-general. 'The new pattern army has not lost a battle since it was formed by Isambard Kirkhill. Our order of battle has been tried and tested over centuries by some of the finest military minds produced by Jackals.'

Wellesley shifted irritably in his saddle. 'With respect, sir, our current disposition is intended to involve close coordination with the high fleet. We have a single aerostat – our

419

formation requires at least a squadron of the line. These fellows are not the colonial farm boys we saw off last year.'

'Shifties, major,' said the brigadier-general. 'Shifties and a criminal rabble of Carlists. They will come at us in the same old way and we shall beat them off in the same old way. This is not the time to dabble with new thinking, major. I do not require more than a single aerostat to see off a bunch of damn shifties and a mob of traitors who have crawled out of the undercity.'

Wellesley started to reply, but seeing the look on the brigadier-general's face thought better of it. This was turning into a nightmare. From the moment they had received word that Fort Downdirt had been overrun to sighting the Quatérshiftian lines being dug in outside the capital.

The brigadier-general turned to the riding officer who had just come in. 'You sir, lieutenant I-have-no-hat-sir. Ride over to the other side of the column and bring me one of the worldsingers. I want to know what feybreed are doing running around Admiralty House. And will someone please find me the Special Guard.'

'There, sir,' pointed a staff officer. Blazing through the sky like a comet, the Special Guardsman sailed in a lazy arc over the battlefield, overflying the Commonshare's columns of troops and rows of cannon, before twisting off to head towards the Jackelian forces. With a shock of wind that nearly lifted off their shakos and tricorn hats the Special Guardsman halted above the ground in front of their map-littered folding table.

'About bally time,' said the brigadier-general. 'Did you not receive the written orders I sent Captain Flare?'

'We did,' said the guardsman.

'Then, sir, perhaps you would be kind enough to tell me where in the Circle's name the guards' companies are today?'

Passing a letter to the brigadier-general the guardsman saluted then sped off into the sky, looping back towards the capital. Brigadier-general Shepperton read the note, holding onto it for far longer than it should have taken to digest the message. Then he handed it up to Wellesley on his horse.

Major Wellesley read it for the benefit of the staff. 'The guard will not fight for you. The guard will not fight against you. This is a hamblin war. Let us see how well Jackals fares without our intervention. Flare.'

'Can they do that?' piped up an officer.

From the left flank the riding officer returned with a worldsinger, his purple robes almost the same shade as the brigadier-general's fuming cheeks. 'You man! There's a mutiny in the guards – what have you fellows in the order been doing about it?'

'I have had reports, brigadier-general,' said the worldsinger. 'Sendings.'

'I'm not interested in how much of that damn wizard's snuff you've had up your nose, man, or if you've been playing chess on the spirit plane with the god-emperor of Kikkosico. Facts, sir, I need facts.'

'The torcs on their neck do not respond, the control hex is there but it no longer works. Brigadier-general, the order no longer has command over the Special Guard.'

'The Circle you say!' swore the brigadier-general. 'This is most irregular, wouldn't you say?'

Grass spurted up in front of them as cannons in the enemy line opened fire.

'I do believe that was purposefully aimed at us,' shouted the brigadier-general.

'Bad form,' agreed one of the general staff.

Major Wellesley kicked his horse towards his men below. He rode so fast that he did not notice that the cloud drifting towards Jackals' last remaining aerostat was not rain but a swarm of insect-like outlines.

The battle for Middlesteel had begun.

When she woke up the ceiling was moving, a sea of black rock sliding down and away from her. A stretcher-like affair of old mining stays and canvas lashed together by cable supported her stiff back. Things looked wrong. She was only seeing out of one eye. Her hand touched her face, feeling the swollen cheek blocking her right eye's sight – and shouted in agony.

'Molly,' said a voice, 'Are you conscious?' The roof's motion halted, plunging her stomach into nausea.

Molly's good eye managed to catch sight of what had been dragging her: some kind of steamman – but it looked badly formed, hull plates were missing and exposed machinery twisted and turned through open spaces, an unholy rattling coming from the thing's belly.

'Is this the undercity? Where are my friends?'

'They are dead, we think, Molly softbody,' said the steamman. 'There was an explosion, very large, most of the mine came down. But the enemy was protecting the atmospheric – we survived in the maintenance tube.'

'We?' Molly looked around. None of her companions were with her. Dead? Nickleby and the commodore, the warrior from Mechancia and his strange fey friend, even her deadly nemesis from Quatérshift. No. No. But her last memory came back to her. The steamman knight throwing himself on top of the crystal grenade that had been tossed towards them – the explosion – the ground opening up beneath her feet, falling as an avalanche of rock pelted her sides. Then nothing. Her friends really were murdered. She was alone again, everyone who tried to protect her cut down. No wonder her mother had abandoned her on the steps of Sun Gate; she had obviously had a premonition of what her fate would be if she tried to look after her cursed child.

She might have been crying for hours before she felt one of the pincers of the steamman adjusting the torn fabric that had been pulled over her.

'Molly,' said the steamman. 'Molly softbody, do you not recognize us?'

Her tears burnt like fire on her bruised cheek. 'Have we met?'

'We never thought we would see you again, Molly softbody. After Grimhope, the repair room.'

'Repair—' she looked at the steamman, the shape of the hull pieces and the timbre of the voicebox. Some of the parts so familiar. But how?

'It was straightforward, Molly softbody. The Hexmachina came to us and showed us how to join our bodies. Silver Onestack did not care, as he was already a desecration. But Slowcogs did not want to live that way, until the girl from the paintings opened his vision plate. Showed him the routes that would be travelled by the world if we did not combine. *What would happen to you, Molly softbody.*'

'Dear sweet Circle,' said Molly, reaching out to feel the warm metal of the steamman. 'Slowcogs, Silver Onestack, you repaired yourself.'

'We are joined, young softbody, fused by the will of the Hexmachina. We have violated the law of the Steamo Loas, cannibalized our own flesh, but she is of a higher order and we would do it again. *Do it again to save you, Molly.*'

'I would not have asked you to do this,' said Molly.

'We know.' The ruined steamman began to pull at the stretcher again. 'And that is why we must.'

Molly felt a wave of gratitude towards the brave ramshackle steammen who had suffered so much on her account. 'Circle's turn, thank you. . .'

'. . .Silver Slowstack. Both of us have been stripped of our true names now, but this is our chosen common designation.'

'Slowstack, where can we go? Jackals is being invaded, the undercity has fallen to the same evil. There's nowhere safe for us to run to. When they sense I am still alive they will come after me again.'

'*She* is approaching, Molly softbody. Warmed by the oceans of lava no longer, she climbs towards us and we must venture down to convene with her. The Hexmachina, Molly. She needs an operator. She needs you!'

Outside the palace the sounds of fighting had grown sporadic. There were still fires burning across the city, but most of them were the result of the surprise attack the previous night – crystalgrid stations taken offline, grenades tossed through the windows of police stations, the barracks of the Sixth Foot and the Guardian Horse Guards stormed.

It was a novel experience for Prince Alpheus to stand on the balcony and watch the city without having to endure a shower of rotten fruit and stones from the street. In the square below rows of people knelt facing the palace, a strange keening sound humming in their throats. It had started snowing last night and flurries of white flakes were still falling on the people in the square. Middlesteel was used to fogs from the mills and the dirty miasma of industry, but snow in the heart of summer?

Bonefire came out onto the balcony and looked over Captain Flare's shoulder at the crowds. 'What's a man to do to get some sleep around here? Who the hell are they – that's a Circlist mantra, isn't it?'

'They've been chanting for nearly an hour,' said Prince Alpheus. 'The first ones arrived from the morning congregations before the shifties started shutting down the churches. They were crying for help, begging at the gates for the Special Guard to come out of their barracks.'

Bonefire pointed to the cart of purple-robed bodies piled by the gate. It was amazing that there were still worldsingers in Jackals who thought that the suicide torcs on the guards' necks actually worked. 'Let them go to the order and beg for help. See if their hamblin magicians can beat off the shifties without the guards' assistance.'

'They're not chanting for you,' said the prince to Bonefire. 'They're chanting for me.'

'You!' Bonefire laughed.

'The old legend,' said Captain Flare. 'The sleeping kings. When Jackals is threatened the first kings will waken from underneath the hills of Elmorgan.'

Bonefire started laughing so hard tears rolled down his face. 'The pup? The pup is going to save them? Oh that's good.' He stretched his arm out and fired a volley of blue pain-fire towards the chanting crowd. 'Chant louder, you filthy hamblin jiggers. I can't hear you.'

Flare slapped his arm down. 'That's enough, Bonefire.'

'What do you care? Let them dance a little before we leave this bloody prison.'

At one end of the square a line of equalized soldiers appeared, metal shoulders covered in snow. Marching forward they surrounded the chanting Jackelians in a corner of the square, beating to death with a flurry of iron fists any that tried to flee past their lines. Carts loaded with large wooden boxes were pulled into the centre of the square, blue-uniformed Commonshare troops unloading them into the space that had been cleared.

A shiftie officer stood on one of the wagons, a Commonshare worldsinger by his side, amplifying his voice as it filled the square. 'By order of the First Committee of the Commonshare of Jackals, any gathering of three individuals or more not licensed by prior arrangement with the First Committee shall be classified as counter-revolutionary activity. Secondly, by order of the First Committee of the Commonshare of Jackals, the Circlist philosophy has been classified as an uncommunityist activity and is henceforth banned. The punishment for violation of either of these two rulings of the people is excommunication from the commonality and fellowship of the state.'

People trapped behind the line of equalized troops cried out in fear and anger until the more vocal complainants were beaten down with sabres and rifle butts. Most of them had read enough in the Middlesteel penny sheets about the early days of the revolution across the border in Quatérshift to recognize the euphemism used by the Carlists when they shoved members of the old regime through a Gideon's Collar. Excommunication from the commonality and fellowship of the state.

Bonefire watched the erection of the massive meat-processing machine in the centre of the square in fascination. 'They'll let us go down and watch, you think?'

'Those are Jackelians,' said Prince Alpheus. 'They are our people.'

'We are your people now, pup. *They* are hamblins. I can go down and get them to throw a few jinn bottles up at you if you need reminding.'

'Come on, Alpheus,' said Flare. 'We need to check the stores for when we travel south.'

'Let the pup stay,' called the Special Guardsman as they left. 'I used to watch them give jiggers the rope outside Bonegate when I was a lad. It never did me any harm.'

Outside, the Commonshare's military engineers raised the

frame of the Gideon's Collar with the ease that comes only from practice.

Damson Davenport peered out of the door's peephole at the Quatérshiftian soldiers. They banged harder. She opened the door and they cuffed it aside before she could take it off its chain, breaking the lock and seizing her while a line of soldiers ran into the rookery's hall.

'We're not quality on this street, young man,' said Damson Davenport. 'I work in the jinn house over on Sling Street, not the palace of bleeding Greenhall.'

'Quiet, old woman,' said the soldier, pulling her out towards a gypsy-sized caravan drawn by a train of four horses, a mobile blood machine pouring steam into the sky. The rumours were true, then. In the street the Jackelians were being herded into one of two groups guarded by metal-fleshers. Her neighbour Mister Kenwigs had told her that those metal things used to belong to the race of man once, but that did not seem likely.

They took a sample of her blood and then made her wait for the results. What were they testing for? The wagon was not large enough to contain the records of everyone in Middlesteel. It had to be the new required-citizen register – guardians and silks and famous Jackelians. Nobody on this street would be on that list. If only they did not find the girl. Shouts sounded from inside the rookery and Damson Davenport's worst fears were realized. Poor Cru'brin. Everyone in the crumbling tenement had known the young craynarbian from when she was an infant. It did not take long for them to drag her out, still wearing the tattered red uniform of the Sixth Foot. Better she had been slaughtered with the rest of her company or had disappeared into Shell Town. Hiding with her mother had been madness.

A tall officer appeared by the wagon. The craynarbian's captor jumped up and hastily saluted him. 'Marshal Arinze.'

The marshal ignored them and walked up to the struggling deserter, followed by another soldier, his blue uniform cropped at the side to display his muscled arms. There was a boy who loved himself, tutted Damson Davenport. Too many days down the muscle pits with a mirror in his back pocket.

'Harbouring enemy troops,' said Marshal Arinze. He called to the soldiers pulling the weeping people into the street. 'Compatriot sergeant, burn this building down. There shall be no relief given to the enemies of the people.'

Swearing at the marshal, young Cru'brin tried to break free of the leather straps binding her sword arm. The troops struggled to hold her.

'Compatriot marshal, if I may. . .'

'Compatriot Colonel Wildrake?'

'Let me show these counter-revolutionary criminals the power of the Commonshare, the superiority of our forces.'

Arinze rubbed the colonel's arm with a worried look on his face. 'You do not need to continually prove your loyalty to the revolution, compatriot colonel. You have advanced our cause in Jackals more than any brother save Tzlayloc himself.'

'Look at her, compatriot marshal, her scrawny shell. What kind of muscles can she have under that armour? My lats are falling towards the corpulent without a test worthy of the name.'

Arinze sighed. 'Hold the burning, sergeant. You, compatriot private of the Sixth Foot. You shall have a chance to prove the worth of this decadent city of yours. You see before you a gladiator of the Third Brigade. If you can beat him in a match I will spare your entire street from punishment.'

A space was cleared for the craynarbian deserter and Colonel Wildrake, the marshal momentarily distracted as his soldiers dragged a man with a red beard up towards the commanding officer's entourage.

'You've got the wrong man!' he shouted. 'I've done nothing. I just row a boat on the estuary. I ferry people up and down the Gambleflowers, that's all.'

'Compatriot Meagles,' said one of the soldiers. 'Secretary of the Middlesteel Four-poles Union. His blood code is confirmed by the required-citizen register.'

'The Union is a proscribed organization,' said the marshal. 'You have been encouraging uncommunityist tendencies among the people. *Unproductive* tendencies. The people must labour to advance their cause, ñot spend their days as idlers tossing balls of leather at pieces of wood on the grass.'

'It's just a bit of a lark,' begged the boatman. 'We always go to the inn afterwards for beer and jinn. Please, you can come too, you and all of your soldiers.'

Arinze slapped him to stop the blubbing, then raised his voice for the benefit of the Jackelians being rounded up in the street. 'Four-poles is *banned*, debating sticks is *banned*, summerpole dancing is *banned*, the singing of "Lion of Jackals" is *banned*, membership of political parties is *banned*. You shall work hard in the service of the people as equals and the community will serve you each well in return.'

One of Arinze's troops indicated the boatman. 'Processing group thirteen?'

'A Gideon's Collar is too good for him. A visible example must be set. Take Compatriot Meagles to the boulevard at Rollfield and hang him from one of the lamps alongside the corpses from the House of Guardians.'

In front of the rookery Wildrake had stripped down to his trousers, and the soldiers who had been oiling his muscles stepped back. It was freezing in the street and Wildrake rubbed his biceps as the bite of the cold wind dug in. He nodded at

the troops holding the craynarbian and they released her into
the shadow of the street. She was at the height of her youthful
vigour, sword arm sharp enough to slice a sapling oak in half,
but still looking scrawny on her meagre army rations. Not
that you could judge, of course – craynarbian muscle groups
worked in different ways, and she was at least strong enough
to march with one hundred pounds of shell underneath her
infantry knapsack.

Her manipulator and sword arms sprang open and Wildrake
pivoted on a single leg, slamming his boot into her left knee.
It crunched and she howled. Low tolerance for pain – all that
armour they carried – they were simply not used to it. The
turncoat Jackelian could almost see the rote drill moves the
Sixth Foot had instilled in her. She was not even worth moving
into witch-time for. Wildrake grinned as he ducked under her
slashing sword arm, slipping behind her and circling her with
his arm.

His muscles bulged underneath his skin, swelling with the
force he was applying to her thorax. Better than bench-pressing
ninety pounds in a muscle pit; the agony was electric. Her
shell started to crack, his biceps burning crimson in the cold.
The Third Brigade troops looked on in amazement. They had
faced craynarbians on the border with Liongeli, but they had
never seen the likes of this. There was a sound like a squeaky
floorboard being stood on, then a crack as he burst her chest
armour. Pieces of shell were sticking out of Wildrake's bleeding
arms but he stood over the gurgling Jackelian soldier, roaring
with the thrill of victory as the Quatérshiftian troops cheered
his feat of strength.

Damson Davenport turned away in horror – then she realized that the technician by the blood machine was addressing
her.

'It's your lucky day, compatriot. You're not on the list. Mill duty – you're assigned to the cannon works being put up over at Workbarrows.'

She took the numbered chit he handed her. 'Your queue number. For equalization. Next.'

Damson Davenport watched the laughing troops leaping over Cru'brin's corpse and tossing burning torches into her rookery. She suspected the falling sleet would put the flames out before the fire cart ever showed up now.

A cry went up among the soldiers – 'Remember Reudox! Remember Reudox!'

People were still inside the tenement and the Third Brigade opened fire on the poorly dressed Jackelians as they tried to flee the burning building. A few men and women jumped out of windows on the second storey, some clutching young children. The metal zombies in the street surrounded them where they landed, thrashing the burning bodies with their metal arms until they stopped moving.

The head of the Four-poles Union, Meagles, was being dragged down the street, his feet trailing two furrows in the snow, still yelling that the shifties had the wrong man, his cries drowned now by the screams of those trapped inside the damson's old home.

'Oh dear, oh dear.' She shivered, pulling her shawl tight. Part of her wanted to go up to the metal things, to the soldiers of the Third Brigade, and beg them to stop. Tell them that they *were* the people of Middlesteel. No different from any of the soldiers, but for an accident of geography and birth. No different from them, their mothers, their sisters, their friends. That they could all be compatriots together if they just tried a little harder. But she knew what would happen if she did, and she discovered that as often as she had thought her pains and aches would one day be over with the long march of her old years, she still wanted to live just a little longer. It did not seem like cowardice at all, just common sense.

A thought occurred to Damson Davenport, the kind of random silly thing that the mind throws up to distract itself from a scene too repulsive, too atrocious to observe.

'Excuse me, what is equalization?'

Tzlayloc smelt the cold fresh air of the House of Guardians' quad with satisfaction. Once he had dreamed of being elected to this place, of erasing the grinding poverty of Middlesteel, of changing things. The shattered plinths where statues of Isambard Kirkhill and other famous parliamentarians had once stood certainly bore testimony to his desire for the latter. It was a pity that Hoggstone had not been captured when they surrounded the palace of democracy. Now every lamp-post in Parliament Square was occupied by a Guardian swinging on the end of a noose, his committee would have to consider doing things the Quatérshiftian way and running the First Guardian through a Gideon's Collar when they arrested him.

Everyone had to move with the times, as the sacks being piled in front of the altar constructed in the centre of the quad testified. Tzlayloc stopped an equalized worker with blood from a sack leaking down the dull metal surface of his – or her – perfect new body. The earlier metal-flesher models had retained traces of the compatriot's gender in the voicebox assembly. An inequality his mechomancers and flesh mages had paid for. It was amazing how advanced their hexes and mechanisms had become after he had sacrificed a few of them.

'Where is this sack from, compatriot?'

'Equalization mill of victory nine, compatriot,' buzzed the outlaw metal-flesher.

Tzlayloc dipped a hand in the sack: hearts, hundreds of

them, but so few were still beating. Some of them had been removed almost a day ago. They would be fresher once the equalization mills above ground were completed. Right now they were relying on the few factories of liberation they had raised around Grimhope. 'Splendid. Throw them on the altar fires, compatriot. Incinerate the last vestiges of the sins of difference. Now you are free. Free of greed and lust and pride – free of the master's yoke and all the mills you labour in shall belong to you!'

The equalized outlaw grovelled at Tzlayloc's feet. 'Bless you, Compatriot Tzlayloc. A thousand blessings upon you.'

Tears rolled down Tzlayloc's cheeks. 'On your feet, brother. You need grovel to no one now. You are who I do this for. Your words mean more to me than I can express.'

He looked at the ring of locust priests shepherding the fumes from the pyre into the air. Tzlayloc could see the darting insect outlines circling the column of smoke. Stronger now, more powerful every hour. They were the perfect allies. Staunch, unstoppable and dedicated, each willing to die without hesitation so that their brothers behind them might advance forward.

He raised a hand and called to all who would hear. 'I see a perfect world, compatriots. A world where we run not against each other as competitors, but together, as friends – as brothers and sisters. Each of us equal. Each of us perfect.'

The equalized were slower to chant his name now than they had been when they wore their old unequal forms, but slowly the mantra rose to fill the quad. Tzlayloc nodded, hiding his disappointment. They had only just begun, after all. Their understanding of the equalization process would develop with practice, would advance further still when the Steammen Free State was absorbed into the Union of Commonshares which Quatérshift and Jackals planned. The mean would be raised. Every year there would be an equality more prosperous, more shining. Every year they would move forward. Together. Always together.

Tzlayloc helped the worker to his – or her – feet, and helped to carry the heavy sack of bleeding organs across to the flames. 'I wish I could burn my filthy unequal form away, compatriot. But the Wildcaotyl requires the soiled mantle of flesh to work through, not the perfect symmetry of your flawless beautiful body.'

'The people understand your sacrifice, Compatriot Tzlayloc,' said the worker, tumbling the hearts into the fire. 'You who lead the flock must sacrifice most of all.'

Tzlayloc noted the courtiers and their military escort standing at the other end of the quad. More work. Even sleeping just a couple of hours a night and relying on the Wildcaotyl to purify this weak dirty body, the demands on his time seemed only to expand. But he would prove equal to the task. He had to. Tzlayloc picked a blackened heart off the pyre and chewed at it. 'The people will nourish me, compatriot. As they always do.'

He went over to the courtiers and they parted as he walked onto what had once been the floor of the House of Guardians. The benches had been ripped out to feed the pyre in the centre of the palace of parliament. In their place was a wide round table where all could sit as equals. Of course, Tzlayloc could not claim credit for that idea. Had not one of the first kings come up with something similar?

Both of the locust priests he had dispatched had returned from their errands. So much the better. He looked at the one who had once been an engine man. 'The Greenhall records?'

'They were trying to overload the boilers when we took Greenhall, Compatriot Tzlayloc; destroy the engine rooms.

But my card daemon had got into the pressure controls and was frustrating their efforts.'

Tzlayloc drummed the table in anger. Greenhall functionaries making decisions without authorization from the House of Guardians? Someone had picked a dangerous time to develop a sense of initiative.

'You have done well, brother. We could not control Jackals without controlling the transaction engines.' He turned expectantly to the locust priest newly returned from the atmospheric tunnels.

'The summoning went as planned, Compatriot Tzlayloc, and your intuition proved correct. The Wildcaotyl could only scent the echo of three souls in the ruins – the steamman warrior, the war criminal Nickleby and the traitor Vauxtion. There is no sign of Compatriot Molly Templar, the feybreed or the duke of Ferniethian.'

'The last two are an irrelevance,' said Tzlayloc. 'Flare and his twisted friends are the only ones who will mourn the fey boy, and our fat duke and his family have been on the run for six generations – we could hang him outside Bonegate and his oily body would slip off the rope.'

'But Compatriot Templar. . .'

'Yes. My beautiful, brave little girl. On the run again, and no count of Quatérshift to track her down for our cause this time. I should have expected no less of her.' He turned back to the old engine room hand. 'Your search for the second operator?'

'With all the resources of Greenhall at my disposal the search was a lot easier than hiding my pet in the drums the first time around. This blood code has only been registered recently. I believe you will understand why when you see the name.' He passed a folded punch card to Tzlayloc. Tzlayloc read the name of the second operator, the recipient of the foul Hexmachina's blood curse.

The locust priest had expected Tzlayloc to fall about laughing as he had done himself at the irony of the name, but instead the leader of the First Committee placed the card gently on the table. 'Oh, Molly. My darling sainted Molly Templar. Now I am going to have to do away with you, you foolish girl. You have lost your place in the pantheon of the people.'

'I have the names of Compatriot Vauxtion's associates,' said the locust priest. 'Some of them are no doubt competent enough in their trade.'

Tzlayloc smiled. 'Compatriot Templar is no longer running *from* us. I fear she is running *towards* something now. The Wildcaotyl has fed well in the last few days – let us try a new type of hunt.'

He waved at the guards and his soldiers marched in with six men. He recognized the oldest of the six from the illustrations that had dotted Middlesteel's walls during the reign of the Whineside Strangler. The criminal had done well to survive Bonegate all these years. He sported red welts around his neck where they had tried to hang him three times. How foolish was that rite of Jackelian justice. Survive the rope three times and have your death sentence overturned. Tzlayloc tutted and indicated the six should be escorted outside to the quad. The three-hangings rule was inappropriate in the age of the Gideon's Collar. Nobody ever got a second chance at the collar.

'They said we was to join the Third Brigade,' spat the Whineside Strangler.

'That pleasure is reserved for your compatriots back in Bonegate,' said Tzlayloc. 'I have duties a little more deserving of you and your colleagues' special talents.'

'As long as we don't go back to the gate,' said the killer.

'You will never see the cell walls of a prison again.'

Above the mountain of smouldering hearts the cloud of smoke had begun to be shaped by the locust priests' chanting, tendrils reaching out like the mandibles of an insect. Unnerved by the display of dark sorcery, the six men shuffled uneasily, the cloud swaying hypnotically in front of their faces. Then, as if the cloud had made a decision, spears of smoke darted up the six convicts' nostrils, flowing into their skulls, draining all the smoke from the pyre as the men stumbled around, mouths open in the rictus of a silent scream.

Tzlayloc looked on in appreciation. The six's bull-like bodies had survived the hell of life sentences in Bonegate and now they swelled still further under the power of the Wildcaotyl, frames expanding, clothes rippling and tearing while their muscles bulged out at aberrant angles, as if fragments of broken bricks had started rising out of their skin.

The Whineside Strangler turned to Tzlayloc, his irises swirling black with the smoke that had filled his skull. 'I am remade.'

'So you are. You know what you must do.'

'The Hexmachina must not find an operator. If the fissures are sealed, I – we – they will dissipate. The operator must die.'

'Yes,' said Tzlayloc sadly. 'Molly Templar must die. For the sake of the people get to her well before she reaches that filthy machine. Get to her before you in turn become the prey.'

Looking at the pile of burning hearts, the Whineside Strangler was gripped by a terrible hunger, unlike any of the pangs his old self had felt in Bonegate. 'That is not enough nourishment.'

'There will be more,' said Tzlayloc. 'We have only begun emancipating the people from their old unequal flesh. And there will be sacrifices too – not all of the old regime are dangling on lamps in the square outside. I have our priests looking at converting a Gideon's Collar – replacing the bolt with an obsidian blade and adding a claw which can tear out a heart while it is still beating.'

'I distrust them. Machines,' hissed the Strangler.

'That is understandable, but we live in a brave new world now. These machines will work for us. It takes a locust priest half an hour to feed you the single soul of an unproductive. When we have a collar converted we can feed you a hundred or more in an hour.'

The Strangler flexed his fingers, looking at the way the nails had extended into talons. 'Flesh is reliable. It can be controlled. Always so much flesh here. Breeding, multiplying.'

Tzlayloc smiled. The Wildcaotyl were primitive, primordial, almost child-like. Harnessing them was like harnessing the power of the land itself. He had become the ultimate worldsinger, tapping a force that made the unreliable currents of earthflow look as ephemeral as morning dew. The Wildcaotyl had nourished the Chimecans for a thousand years and now they would become the foundation stone for a global union of commonshares. He picked up the punch card from Greenhall. A single name. If it had been anyone else. If only Compatriot Templar had not fled, rejecting the destiny he had planned for her. Tzlayloc crumpled the paper. There were some things even the forces of the revolution could not control.

Undetected by Tzlayloc or his allies, the Shadow Bear stood in the corner of the chamber seething – but not about the unholy amount of energy he was having to draw down to remain in stealth in the presence of the enemy. It was the name coded on the card. That name was outside the order of things by such a wide degree, his predecessor might as well have left him a note that said 'unauthorised intervention: sorry'.

It was unthinkable. They were the rule-set. Rules did not break themselves. Down that road madness lay. Yet there it was, the name on the card. The Observer could not have known how things were going to develop down here to the level of detail necessary to make an unauthorized intervention of such delicacy. She could not have known he would have to wait now, investigate the threads of this, could she? There was all his fun thrown out of the window. A little beating for the enemy well out of sight, then he would have got to close this place down and remove all evidence of playtime with the Wildcaotyl and the greater darkness they wanted to invite into reality. Tearing the wings off insects was such fun too.

He began the process of erasure.

Hell. They were all going to die anyway.

Chapter Twenty-Two

Commodore Black had been maudlin ever since Oliver had turned them back from the walls of Tock House. 'Has it come to this, then? A company of Commonshare oafs billeted in my fine house. Draining my cellar and packing everything of value in their knapsacks for their journey home.'

'They were waiting for us,' said Oliver. 'Tzlayloc will have our blood codes posted with every patrol in Middlesteel.'

'Ah, lad, do not say that. Let's make a run for the coast and leave Jackals to Tzlayloc and his cohorts.'

Oliver shook his head. There was no distance far enough to make them safe if Jackals fell to the Wildcaotyl. So they had crept past the outside privy and into the back yard of the only house in the capital where Oliver imagined he might receive a half-friendly welcome. He tried the back door. Locked.

'Let me pass, lad. I have a small talent with locks.' The commodore picked up an old nail nearly covered over by the snow and started to lever it gently into the door's mechanism. 'Listen to the canny tumblers clicking, this is a better lock than the door it stands in, Oliver.'

'Not a talent that I would imagine comes in useful often on an underwater boat?'

'Poor old Blacky, pursued for his family name with nothing but a gallows or a cell in the royal breeding house waiting for him. You would acquire a knack for picking locks too if you were in my sea boots.'

With a clack the door opened into a darkened room. The whole place looked deserted, just the smell of blow-barrel sap and gun oil to welcome them.

'Step forward,' said a voice. 'Run and I'll cut you down.'

'Mother?' said Oliver. 'It's me, Oliver Brooks. Phileas's son.'

A small oil lamp lit up with a strike of its igniter. Mother Loade was sitting in an armchair with a barrel-sized gun pointing at them – the same kind of pressure repeater he had seen the steammen knights carrying around Mechancia. No range, but deadly this close.

'Where's Harold, boy.'

Oliver pointed a finger to the ceiling. 'Snatched.'

She tutted. 'So naughty Harold's luck finally ran out. Not that it matters much now.'

'We tried out front first, Mother. Your shop sign's down and the windows are boarded up. If I hadn't seen your adverts in the back of *Field and Fern* I wouldn't have been able to find your place.'

'Why do you think that is, boy? My useless husband ran for the coast when the shifties showed up and my apprentices have all disappeared. Right now all my trade is good for is a place on a production line in an armaments workshop.'

Oliver flicked his eyes enquiringly towards the ceiling.

'I got a penny note from my son before the crystalgrid went down. One word. Bedtime. Do you know what that means, boy?'

'Blessed Circle,' said the commodore. 'Oliver, this damson

you have brought old Blacky to in our hour of need, she's not what I think she is, is she? This damson's with the Court, isn't she?'

Mother Loade looked at the commodore. 'You, I don't know.'

'Run silent, run deep. That's what your little crystalgrid message means. Like a boat being hunted by a Jackelian aerostat. Except this time around it's the shifties doing the hunting. And all the wolftakers and whistlers doing the hiding.'

Her eyes narrowed. 'That's just a little bit more than you should know. Are you trade?'

'Ah lass, poor old Blacky is no player in the vicious games run by you and your friends. He's only the poor fox, hunted down without mercy by the wolftakers for the unhappy accident of his birth.'

'Well dearie, now there's three of us that don't want to be questioned at a barricade or checkpoint—' she stopped as she saw Oliver taking off his coat, eyes widening at the brace of pistols holstered at his side.

'I kept your knife,' said Oliver.

'Sweet Circle,' she whispered. 'They really exist.' She extended a hand and Oliver passed one of the pistols over. Mother Loade held the gun, her hand trembling as she marvelled at the silver engraving, the carefully rendered lions of Jackals, their malevolent patina.

'I never thought I would see one of these.' She looked up at Oliver. 'I can't protect you now, boy. Not for your father's memory. They'll come for you, eventually.'

Oliver took back the pistol and slid it into the holster. 'Harry didn't know about these, did he?'

'He's not a weaponsmith,' said Mother. 'And he never did have much time for legends. But the Court of the Air has weaponsmiths, boy. From places you wouldn't even believe. They will understand, they will know. They always do.'

'They have other things to occupy them right now,' said Oliver.

From the front door a banging sounded, Mother jumping in her chair. Oliver extended his senses and his heart sank, a shiftie officer and a company of the metal-fleshers stood in the street. Commodore Black peered through a crack in the boarded-up window. 'Blessed troops in the passage behind the shop too.'

Mother waved at the rifles racked on the shelves. 'Who would have thought the Carlists read *Field and Fern* too? We're blown. What do you think the punishment for possession of a private armoury is?'

Oliver slid two glass charges from his bandolier. 'I don't believe the new courts will favour transportation.'

'Already tried that.' Mother Loade walked down the corridor, trailing an accordion-like pipe from her steamman gun back to her pressure stove. 'I'm too old for this nonsense.'

'Open up,' commanded the voice from outside the door. 'In the name of the Jackelian Commonshare.'

'Don't worry dearie,' shouted Mother Loade. Her giant steamman weapon began to whistle like a kettle. 'I'm about to open up for you.'

She pushed a lever up on the weapon and it screeched with a noise like a saw blade tearing through a log. The door shattered in half, covering Oliver, the commodore and Mother in a back-blast of splinters. Mother kicked away the two halves of the door hanging from its frame. When she pushed the lever back on the gun there was a rain of metal balls from the weapon's canister as the gun's gravity feed kicked in, reloading.

The officer had been thrown to the other side of the street, his blue uniform turned into a mess of crimson rags.

'Welcome to Middlesteel, dearie.' She turned to the equalized revolutionaries and hefted up the pressure repeater. 'And as for you lot, you're a bloody disgrace.'

'Mother, no!'

Oliver dragged the commodore back into the shelter of the shop as she triggered the heavy weapon, the storm of pellets hosing across the metal-fleshers; the revolutionaries were thrown back, death by a thousand cuts as balls ruptured iron and pierced their buried organs, the blizzard of ricochets cracking windows in the street and raising clouds of brick dust. The sawing noise cut off. Mother was lying face down in the street and Oliver ran over to her. Rolled her over. She was bleeding from a hundred ricochet wounds, her eyes fighting to stay open. 'I'll tell your father when I see him, dearie, before I move along the Circle.'

'I know you will.' He could barely hear her. She raised a liver-spotted hand to rest on Oliver's pistol, the gun seeming to feed her the energy she needed for one last whisper. 'Don't trust them – Oliver. Never – trust – the – Court of – the Air.'

She was gone. He lowered her down, her back staining the snow red. Black shouted a warning. The troops from around the back of the shop had found their way to the front of the street. Oliver heard whistles. They sounded like crushers, but he doubted any constables from Ham House would be responding to the call.

Oliver staggered back towards the shop. Commodore Black wanted Mother's gun, but first he had to prize it away from her dead fingers. He dragged the pressure repeater and its pipe back through the doorway. Equalized revolutionaries with pikes trotted down the street towards them, following their Quatérshiftian officers.

'Sorry, lad,' said the commodore. 'I think this is our last stand.'

Oliver sighed. Mother would keep glass-lined casks of blow-barrel sap in her cellar next door to the tools of the glass blower's trade. They could blow them, follow Steamswipe's example and take a street's worth of the jiggers with them.

'I'm sorry too, commodore. We should have run for the coast, hidden among the crowds of refugees.' Oliver felt tired, like he could sleep for a thousand years. In a few minutes he would have an eternity of peace.

'None of the would have, could have, should have now, lad. They've chased you down for your fey blood as they've chased old Blacky down for the royal claret that runs through my veins. Let's sell it to them blessed dear.'

The witch-blade was in Oliver's fist, extending out like a lizard's tongue, feeding him shadow memories of his father facing a hunting team of toppers. Commodore Black rested the smoking pressure repeater on the shop's counter and covered the entrance. The battle cries of the enemy were getting nearer. Oliver checked both his pistols were loaded, the heat from the steamman gun warming his face.

Harry Stave was in a Court cell, what was left of his mind ripped to shreds by the wolftakers' truth hexing. Steamswipe and Lord Wireburn were walking the halls of the Steamo Loas. Oliver could almost feel their shades standing beside him.

'I'll see you soon.'

The enemy was upon them, filling the passage, breaking down the boarded windows of Loade and Locke's establishment.

'Send us the Third Brigade,' Oliver shouted above the saw-scream of the commodore's gun. 'Send them all.'

Molly and Slowstack were almost across the bridge, a swaying line of glass bricks threaded together with silver cable, the transparent crossing giving them an all too apparent view of the chasm below. It was so hot this far down in the earth, lava running in streams and lakes, bubbling rivers filling the corridors with choking fumes. Once these hidden holds had echoed to the boots of the masters of an underworld empire that covered the entire continent, but the Chimecans had faded long ago. Now only their crystals remained, their sorceries still sucking the power of the earthflow and filling the world they had created with an eerie, inconstant light.

The vision struck Molly without warning, Slowstack grabbing her as she stumbled against the hand cable.

'Do you see her?' asked the steamman.

'I see her,' confirmed Molly. The ghostly figure of the small girl stood at the far end of the crystal bridge.

<*They* come,> said the Hexmachina.

Molly pulled herself along the bridge, the figure receding as she drew closer. 'I can hear you.'

<I am speaking through your blood, Molly. I draw closer to you as you draw closer to me. You vibrate with my essence.>

'We found Molly softbody,' said Slowstack. 'We pulled her into the deep atmospheric tunnels, into the protection envelope of the enemy's own aura to survive the blast.'

<You are both clever and brave, Silver Slowstack. But I must ask more of you. *They* come. The Wildcaotyl ride six hunters from the race of man. They do not wish me to join with an operator. They ride to slay you.>

Molly reached Slowstack on the other side of the canyon and the steamman cut the cable supporting the bridge with one of his manipulator claws, the crystal bricks tumbling into the chasm below and flaring as they rained down onto the lava. 'Let them ride the air.'

<The cities of the coldtime have many passages, Silver Slowstack,> said the Hexmachina. <Many ways to reach you.>

'Are you close?' asked Molly.

<Closer every hour. My lover the Earth has been helping me. I no longer ride her caress in the centre of the world; her liquid heart of fire has carried me through many levels of her body, pumping me towards you at ever-greater velocity. I come for you, Molly, but still the enemy will reach you before I do.>

'I can feel you in my blood,' said Molly. 'The nearer we get to each other. I can feel my body changing. I can feel the earth's heartbeat, the thoughts of the world.'

<The earth *is* alive, Molly. Her warmth and passion have kept me for these many centuries, kept me where all my friends and kin have fallen. She loves us yet, as we scar her skin and consume her resources, she loves us yet, as we steal her power and draw songs of sorcery from her leylines. She cared for us even as the Chimecans burrowed into her core like worms through an apple, as they desecrated her rocks with the blood of your own kind, even as your minds and souls fashioned wicked gods that sealed her skin in a prison of ice.>

Molly felt ashamed.

<You grow stronger as you near me, Molly. Together we are invincible, the sword of Vindex. In the enemy's desperation they will do anything to prevent this. The six who hunt you have split into three pairs, chasing the echoes of your soul I have scattered throughout the undercity.>

'They come as agents of Xam-ku,' said Slowstack. 'They come as agents of the ancient ones.'

<Not Xam-ku. Not yet. The great powers of the Wildcaotyl are still trapped beyond the walls of the world waiting for my death and the feast of souls Tzlayloc plans to offer them. Only the shadows of Wildcaotyl have squeezed through to walk Middlesteel. These things that hunt you are lesser powers, tiny death beetles which clean the skin of the old gods.'

'Powerful enough,' said Molly.

<Yes, Molly. Quite powerful enough. They are wicked creatures, and they are riding the foulest and strongest of your kind.>

'We followed you in our dreams,' said the steamman, 'when we were Silver Onestack, and we will follow you now.'

<Then follow my trail, dear loyal friend of the metal. Molly, you must RUN, as fast and as long as you can. Run to preserve your existence and the hopes of the world.'

They did. As if the gates of hell had opened behind them.

There came a new sound over the tearing-wood shriek of the commodore's steamman weapon, like the crash of the sea at Ship Town, loud enough to be heard over the cyclone of ricocheting balls smattering against the corridor. Black took his finger off the trigger and a single remaining ball rolled down around the inside of the drum on top of the gun. Shouts from outside – the Quatérshiftian officers who had been only too glad to let the equalized Jackelian revolutionaries clog up the shop corridor with their corpses.

'Do you hear it lad?'

Oliver vaulted the broken counter of Loade and Locke's sales room. 'People, commodore. A sea of people.'

Outside the shiftie company was running down the street. Middlesteel's equalized revolutionaries had their pikes raised ready to skewer the wave of attackers coming towards them. The two sides met in a flurry of debating sticks and pike heads. The metal-fleshers were slower than their unequalized adversaries, but the panels of their new shells took quite a beating before their remaining organs burst and they stumbled and fell.

Black watched the ferocious assault with admiration. 'I never thought I would be so glad to see a pack of blessed parliamentarians.'

Two styles of debating stick beat aside the pikes and smashed in metal-flesher skulls – the street fighters of the Roarers and the Young Purist movement had joined forces! It was a fight to the death, no quarter asked for or given and numbers were not on the revolutionaries' side. Soon the street was littered with iron bodies jerking in the snow, calculation drums banging while what blood still cycled around their gutta-percha tubes leaked onto the ground.

The Jackelian street fighters moved like a well-oiled machine, dragging the equalized bodies out of sight into the rookeries' alleyways, the Quatérshiftian dead stripped of uniforms and weapons then tossed aside like garbage. A girl ran up to the window of the shop and dipped a brush into a bucket of red paint, daubing the windows and walls with a line of upside down Vs.

'The lion's teeth,' said a large man walking up to Oliver and the commodore. 'The Lion of Jackals. Mister Locke?'

The commodore shook his head. Oliver pointed to Mother's body in the snow. 'Locke's gone. Damson Loade is dead.'

The man motioned to the street fighters and they hauled the equalized corpses blocking the shop's corridor out of the way, returning with arms full of rifles and pistols and rolling glass-lined casks of blow-barrel sap.

'I see she took a few of them with her when she moved along the Circle; a true patriot. You, sir, you were putting up a rare old fight too. We could hear the battle from the other end of Whineside. Are you Heartlanders?'

'I'm more of an independent thinking man,' said Black.

Oliver looked at the large man, his boxer's nose and thinning hair. No wonder he looked familiar. 'You're the First Guardian!'

'Politics in Jackals are not what they used to be,' said Hoggstone.

Cries came from the rooftop; a lookout had climbed one of the chimneystacks. 'Cavalry, cavalry.'

Bearing away the contents of Mother's weapons warehouse, the street fighters streamed down the lanes, the entire force melting away. Oliver had once seen a torrent of black rodents running past bales of cargo after a lamp was lit in his uncle's Ship Town warehouse, an army of rats evaporating in front of his eyes. These fighters were faster.

The girl who had sounded the alarm slid down a drainpipe. 'Exomounts, riding in from the north.'

'They must have got to the stables at Ham Yard before the hands could poison them,' said Hoggstone. He looked at the commodore and Oliver. 'Can independents alley dodge?'

Black nodded. 'With the best of them.'

Oliver could hear the roll of the charge getting nearer as they fled into the passages of the rookeries. He had once seen an exomount being taken to stud in Kikkosico, the narrow boat shaking as the cage rocked with the violence of the animal. They were taken off their craynarbian sedatives before being ridden. Too slow off the herbal soporific and they were groggy and sluggish in battle, too fast and they would as like throw their rider and devour them. The timing was critical. Oliver hoped the steeds had only just been released, but the hail of claws across the street cobbles told him otherwise.

Hoggstone ran well for someone whose gut had been trained on the finest cuisine Middlesteel could serve for the last few years. The passages narrowed, some so tapered the snow had not yet had a chance to drift in and settle, broken walls leading underneath pipes and lines of washing hanging out above them.

A howling echoed around the rookery streets.

'Their lancers can't squeeze through these passages,' said Hoggstone, using his metal-tipped debating stick to push over a pyramid of wood piled for someone's stove. 'And those metal cans they are shoving people into don't see so well in the gloom of the runs.'

'Infantry,' said Oliver. 'Third Brigade ahead.'

'The shifties don't come into the lanes,' said Hoggstone. 'Too many ambush points.'

The clatter of boots ahead made his words a lie.

'The lad has a talent for sniffing out trouble, Hoggstone,' said the commodore.

They retreated and took a side passage, increasing their speed to as much of a sprint as they could manage through the dirty streets. They ran up some wooden steps and along a street composed of rickety gantries, open doors leading into tenement halls. Hardly anybody was out – with armed revolutionaries and Quatérshiftian troops prowling the streets the population of Middlesteel were hunkering down in their homes. They heard the sounds of carousing down one alley. A jinn house – still open and some of the rookery denizens drinking the place dry while their currency still had value. Before the Commonshare of Jackals emulated its neighbour to the east and made the production, transport and sale of liquid stimulants illegal for their part in undermining community production quotas.

Hoggstone stopped, catching his breath for a second. 'They know where we are. Every time we reach one of the streets that leads out of the lanes they are waiting for us.'

Oliver nodded. This was a game of chess and the shiftie pieces were being moved with a preternatural clarity. If it weren't for his forewarnings of the soldiers' positions they would have walked into a dozen traps already. Commodore Black shaded his eyes against the sun peering out from behind clouds pregnant with snow, scanning the strip of sky above the narrow street. 'There!'

Oliver gazed where the commodore was pointing and saw three triangles of white material turning below the clouds. 'That's not an aerostat, commodore.'

'It's a blessed sail rider, lad. Look at him flashing his helioplate to his friends on the ground. Shiftie vessels would sometimes float them up above their decks if they thought they were being hunted by our boats.'

Oliver broke one of his pistols and slipped out a crystal charge, pushing it into the gun and closing it.

'You won't hit him from here, man,' said Hoggstone. 'The best rifleman in the regiments would be hard pressed to clip the sail with a long gun, let alone hit the rider.'

The clockwork of the hammer mechanism hummed as Oliver tightened his finger around the trigger, shadow images fleeting through his mind; a horse mounting a sand dune in the far distance, its rider spilling off as he fired; a woman sprinting across ice sheets bobbing in a frozen ocean, no more than a far-off silver dot glinting in the sunlight, a single shot lifting her corpse into the glacial waters. Oliver blinked away the waking dreams. 'Then you had best be quiet, First Guardian.'

He rested the pistol on his left arm, the crack of the glass shell followed by an explosion that echoed off peeling posters for a drink that had not been sold in Middlesteel for a decade. High above a grey dot separated from the sail and plunged towards the ground, the riderless kite deforming and drifting up like a hawk climbing for height.

'Hard to control one of those things,' said Oliver. 'When you're not harnessed to it.'

'Well I'll be jiggered,' exclaimed Hoggstone, as Oliver ejected the broken glass charge onto the dirt of the lane. 'You, sir, are quite the shootist.'

'There are patrols all over the area now,' said Oliver. 'Our friend in the sky has done his job.'

'I know a way,' said the lookout girl. 'You follow me.'

Dashing through the tenement halls, the girl found her three charges hard-pressed to keep up with her youthful, eclectic running style, kicking off walls and flowing over fences. Their way became gloomier, down into the cellar levels, passages that were notoriously unsafe. Most were boarded up, others abandoned and empty since the centuries of long Jackelian winters had given way to a milder climate. Deeper still and the stench of sewage rose like bad eggs, making Oliver's stomach turn.

They ducked through an iron pipe and came out onto a ledge. In front of them brown water cascaded over a steep set of stone steps, a channel below carrying a fast-moving river of rubbish. At the opposite end of the ledge a spiral of rusting stairs led down to a narrow barge moored in the dirty channel. To the barge's rear a single barrel spilled a tangle of gutta-percha tubes into the liquid like the tentacles of a squid.

'A blessed gas harvester's wherry,' said the commodore.

'That's it skipper,' said the girl. 'My old ma raised me on the harvesters. Gas burns brighter than oil, don't you know, for the library of a gentleman or a lady.'

'You were apprenticed in the trade?' asked Hoggstone. 'You know your way around the sewage canals?'

'I could ride them all the way down to Grimhope if I had a mind to.'

'I believe the other side of Whineside will do fine,' said Hoggstone.

The girl started a small expansion engine not much bigger than a kettle and two paddles on the side started to rotate, burning the same gases the wherry harvested. Black cast off and the flat boat pushed through the river of sludge, riding the flow into the foetid darkness. Hoggstone stood on the prow clutching his debating stick, a brooding ferryman awaiting his toll.

'You could have run,' said Oliver to the First Guardian. 'Left for the Catosian League. Tried to mobilize the army from the counties.'

'I was born in a patcher's room on the side of a Spouthall pneumatic and I intend to die in a mansion in Sun Gate. As far as I'm concerned the Third Brigade are just a bunch of shifties passing through on the grand tour.'

'They'll never stop hunting you.'

Hoggstone looked at Oliver and the commodore. 'And who in the Circle's name are you two? You shoot like a devil and pick fights with as many companies of the Third Brigade as they can send at you. Are you deserters from one of the special regiments, duellists, toppers for the flash mob – or just a couple of lunatics escaped from an asylum when the city fell?'

'Ah now,' said the commodore. 'That's a long and cruel tale in the telling. I'm just an honest fellow whose hopes for a little mortal rest in his autumn years have been spoiled by the wilful tides of fortune.'

'In my experience honest men do not normally insist upon their virtue. And you, sir, the shootist. You do not wear the tattoos of a worldsinger, and the way you led us around the patrols in the lanes – that speaks of a little wild blood in your veins.'

'My ankles seem to be soaking in the same wilful tide as that of the commodore,' said Oliver. 'They have killed everyone who meant anything to me. So now I am going to kill *them* – the shifties, the revolution, their filthy ancient gods. All of them. I am going to hold their heads under the tide and see how long it takes for them to drown.'

'I believe I was right on m'first impression,' said Hoggstone. 'You two are escaped lunatics.'

Oliver followed the passage of the prow-mounted gas lamp's beam, the low roof above their heads opening up into the curve of a large stone pipe. 'I can feel the wickedness in their souls.'

'I had a similar talent. I used to be able to feel their votes in my pocket,' said Hoggstone. He glanced around. 'This is an old atmospheric. One of the narrow-bore tunnels from the royalist years.'

They drifted out of the tunnel into the remains of a station, the iron bolts on the wall the only sign there had once been a vacuum seal here. Their guide steered the harvester's wherry alongside a makeshift ladder nailed to the platform drop.

'End of the line, skipper,' said the girl. Commodore Black helped her tie the boat up. Hoggstone pulled his heavy bulk up the ladder, tossing his debating stick onto the dusty platform with a rattle. Oliver climbed up as the First Guardian wiped the grime off a mosaic of bricks, bright colours dulled by age.

'Sceptre,' said Hoggstone. 'Sceptre station. This place has been off the atmospheric line for five hundred years or more.'

'Lass,' said the commodore. 'You've sailed us too far. If I remember this place from the old maps, we are across the river, on the south side of the Gambleflowers. The old summer palace by the hill.'

'No skipper,' said the girl. She walked up to an iron door and began spinning a wheel to open it; the metal did not part like it had last been used when an absolute monarch sat on the throne of Jackals. 'I have carried you just as far as you needed to go.'

Oliver sensed them too late, reached for his belt guns. A line of men walked out, pistols and longbows aimed at the arrivals on the platform. From the middle of the fighters an old man in a wheelchair pushed himself out. 'First Guardian, I understand you have been dying to meet me.'

'Benjamin Carl,' hissed Hoggstone. 'Damn your eyes, sir, damn you to hell.'

'You first, I think,' said the father of Carlism. 'Floating through the sewers with all the rest of the Purist garbage, you've found your true constituency at last, Hoggstone. Damson and sirs . . . welcome, welcome to the revolution.'

Captain Flare looked at the guardsman who had come back from the quartermaster's office, passing the requisitions list across – half the items crossed out – for Bonefire to read. 'How can there be only half the grain we requested?'

'Commander, have you seen what it's like in the city?' replied the guardsman. 'Nobody is going to work any more in case they get seized by the brilliant men and passed over for equalization – Circle, nobody is sure if it's even *legal* to work. The canals are frozen, the crops are under snow and the Third Brigade has been looting anything in Middlesteel that isn't nailed down. We're lucky we got what we did.'

'We need supplies for the journey south,' said Bonefire, 'and more besides while we build our new city.'

'Quartermaster's people said we should wait. Greenhall are assigning navvies to break the ice on the waterways – when the Second and Seventh Brigades cross over the border the shifties will be able to help with the work. The Commonshare are working to lower the cursewall; they thought it would be straightforward to take it down, but when they tried to drop it they found the worldsingers who raised the wall have been purged, so now they're trying to solve their own hexes from the spell books.'

'That could take months,' said Flare. 'Where is the aerostat they promised us?'

'Problems there too,' replied the guardsman. 'There's a vessel we can use but we're trying to scare up a merchant crew to fly her.'

'Merchant? What about the navy, the jack cloudies?'

'Seems the mutiny at Shadowclock didn't go as well as was hoped, commander. The fleet had been half-purged, but someone slipped word to the navigators and pilots. When the citadel fell the deck officers had vanished – Tzlayloc's people have been running aeronauts through the Gideon's Collar trying to get the survivors to collaborate.'

Flare shook his head in frustration. 'No doubt inspiring the same loyalty we felt towards the order. These idiots couldn't organize a harvest-merrie, let alone a revolution. This is no way to overthrow a tyranny! Where is the Third Brigade liaison?'

Bonefire indicated the scene below the chamber's window. 'Someone at the Brigade must have heard you.'

Down below, Marshal Arinze's retinue followed the leader of the Third Brigade as he swept imperiously past the shadow of the Gideon's Collar set up in the palace square. Captain Flare got to his feet as the Marshal came through the door, his pet wolftaker in tow wearing a plain blue Quatérshiftian brigade tunic.

'Marshal, I had no idea you were personally involved with the quartermaster's office.'

Arinze took the supply orders, looked at them, then passed them contemptuously back to a staff officer. 'Hardly, compatriot captain. Your store requisitions have been put on hold.'

'On hold?' said Bonefire, his tone less than respectful.

Arinze ignored the mere guardsman and addressed his comments to the captain. 'Things are not moving as fast as they should be, compatriot captain. Middlesteel is ours but elsewhere in Jackals the forces of tyranny are organizing against us. We have not yet managed to float the RAN and our scouts report that some of the survivors from Fulven Fields are organizing Jackals' regiments along the southern frontier.'

'That is not our concern,' said Flare. 'Lower the cursewall; bring more troops across on the atmospheric; chase off the gunboats in the Sepia Sea and land soldiers in the north. It is not my job to teach your forces how to campaign.'

'The First Committee of Jackals believes it is your concern,' said Marshal Arinze. 'If you want to claim your territory you will have to earn it.'

Flare pointed an irate finger at Arinze. '*Claim!* We are not applicants at the board of the poor, Marshal. The Fey Free State is ours. We have a deal with Tzlayloc; we have worked with him, not for him. The Special Guard is not yet an arm of the brilliant men and the Middlesteelians you have been slaughtering may be hamblins, but they are still citizens of Jackals.'

Arinze snapped his fingers and was handed a sheaf of rolled papers. 'All revolutions come with a butcher's bill attached, compatriot captain. It's time you got your hands dirty. Here are your orders from the First Committee.'

Flare tore off the wax seal and scanned the papers. 'March on the uplands under the command of the second company of the Third Brigade. Is this a joke? We had a deal, Arinze. We would mutiny when they ordered us into action against you, but we told you we would not fight against our own regiments. We ensured the RAN would be docked in harbour when you attacked. We made sure every Guardian, every commercial lord and person of quality in Jackals would be in Middlesteel for the coronation when you arrived. Without the Special Guard the remnants of your army would be limping its way back to Quatérshift pulling shards of fin-bomb crystal out of their uniforms.'

'No plan of battle survives contact with the enemy, compatriot captain. Times have changed. The deal has changed.'

'Jigger you!' shouted Bonefire. 'You dirty hamblin, you want a change of deal? Let's see how you enjoy my terms. . .'

Fire lashed out from the guardsman's fist, bathing the Marshal in wraithlike light. Arinze dropped to the floor of the palace screaming in distress. Flare pushed the arm of the Special Guardsman towards the ceiling, dragging Bonefire away kicking from the Quatérshiftian officer.

'Let's see if Tzlayloc and his committee men want to renegotiate when I rip your skull off and toss it to them in a sack, you shiftie scum,' shouted Bonefire.

Arinze got to his feet. 'Striking an officer of the Third Brigade is a capital offence, compatriot guardsman.'

'I'm not in your army, shiftie. I barely even belong to the race of man anymore.'

'Execute him!' shouted Arinze.

Behind the marshal two worldsingers stepped out of his retinue and circled Bonefire chanting. The Special Guardsman started to laugh, but his expression turned to shock as his body started folding in on itself, caught in an invisible press. Around his neck the hexes on the silver torc glowed, the fire of their brilliance sucking in air and whistling around his body like a kettle coming to the boil. The Special Guardsman's arms and legs made popping noises, crushed under their own weight, red slashes hurtling across his skin as veins exploded. Bonefire twisted like a corkscrew, held erect in a hidden field before them as his muscles were crushed beyond use. The two worldsingers stopped their chanting and the bloody mess that was left flopped to the palace flagstones with a sickening slap.

Flare's hand had unconsciously moved to the torc around his neck. 'You—'

'It took a long time for our worldsingers to unlock the

hexes on your little necklaces,' said Marshal Arinze. 'I am told it took a dedicated team three years to solve them. Another two years to leave them in place but neutralize the trigger. Do you really think we went to all that trouble to leave a military force as powerful as the Special Guard in the field unchecked? We did not neutralize the hexes, compatriot captain, we *modified* them.'

Flare stumbled back. 'What have I done, what have I done?'

'Do not worry, compatriot captain, you shall have your territory in the south. After you have fought for it – after you have earned it. You will like serving as part of the Third Brigade. We are not prudes like Compatriot Tzlayloc and his First Committee with their funny little ways. Nobody in the Commonshare of Quatérshift will be lining up to have their bodies changed in your flesh mills. We are proud of our bodies – they must be kept strong to serve the revolution.' Arinze ran his hands down Major Wildrake's chest. 'Your guardsmen have been blessed with power and that power will serve us very well. You shall breed your city of fey-born, and your children will become the shock troops of the revolution.'

'We are free,' said Flare, as if repeating it would make it true.

'There is no greater freedom than service to the community,' said Arinze. 'And service as the guardians of the cause has its rewards. Circlist prigs do not command us; we do not hang our soldiers for taking women, we do not hang them for stealing poultry from the henhouse of an enemy peasant. For hard men to be asked to do hard things in the name of the people, to inflict terror on the enemy, they must be kept as sharp as the sabres they carry.'

'It must be difficult for you, Flare,' said Major Wildrake. 'I am a Jackelian too, I understand. But these people recognize the nature of our race. They opened my eyes to the principles of community, showed me how soft and weak I had become – how decadent Jackals had become.'

'Sometimes it takes one not born in the Commonshare to see its true beauty,' said Marshal Arinze. 'Now, where is the King who missed his crown – where is the pup?'

'Alpheus?' said Flare. 'What do you want with him?'

'For my part, nothing. Tzlayloc wants him.'

Flare's voice sounded on edge. 'Prince Alpheus helped the revolution, he helped ensure everyone was in Middlesteel when you needed them there.'

'And now *Compatriot* Alpheus is to serve the revolution again.'

'How is he to serve it?' Captain Flare demanded.

Arinze motioned a party of worldsingers and soldiers to search the palace. 'A question better put to Chairman Tzlayloc. Like I said, your countrymen do have their funny little ways.'

'Deals change,' mumbled Flare. His guardsmen eyed the worldsingers among the shiftie troops with unconcealed loathing. That strange fey boy they had captured had been eerily prophetic – in the end they had only swapped one set of masters for another.

Molly had never run so far or so fast before – even Slowstack's inexhaustible body had trouble keeping pace with her. There was a strange hum in her legs; a pain that only the exertion of running seemed to cancel. The very stuff of her blood fizzed with her increasing proximity to the Hexmachina, and the closer she got the more her body was changed. She could feel the pain of the earth now, the tunnels and cities of Chimeca like scar tissue over an old wound; the hex-engraved crystals that powered their cities were leeches, sapping the world's energy. Below ground the leylines had become veins of enormous energy, the rock and the magma teeming with tiny life

– earthflow: a world's weight of it – the soul of the earth, breathing, sighing, pained by the coarse manipulations which the old gods were weaving through the gaps in the wall of reality.

And there was something else she could sense – on the surface, not underground – something pure and deadly stalking the earth. It was well hidden, but, however hard it screened itself, to the earth the entity's invisible passage was like the tip of a knife teased across her sensitive skin. Molly was becoming a butterfly, but her body, her chrysalis, was still there to remind her of the urges of the race of man. She realized she was starving. Without thinking she changed course, led herself and Slowstack out of the tunnel they were following – an old micro-atmospheric connecting the estate of a Chimecan priest lord to one of their cities – and through a crevice in the wall into a cavern.

Above them buildings grew down from the ceiling like stalactites, tiered inverted ziggurats. Stone streets divided the cavern floor, raised, and – apart from the cracks of age and ceiling falls – so well preserved that it was easy to think the Chimecans had just left the city a couple of minutes ago. Fields of swaying stalks with bulbous heads grew in the shadows of the raised streets, a clear crystal pyramid in the centre of each field flaring up as lightning forks exchanged between their tips and the ceiling crystals above; energy drawn from the earthflow and dispersed by the pyramid structures to the crops.

Molly sprinted along one of the empty streets towards the pit-like fields. 'Food, Slowstack, a whole cavern of it.'

The steamman accelerated to keep up, his tracks crunching the dusty flagstones. 'Molly softbody, you must not feed from this.'

She waved at the pits, the tall crops shivering as they sucked energy from the pyramids. 'The crops have been waiting here for a thousand years. Nobody is here to stop us.'

'Use your senses, Molly softbody. Touch the stalks with your mind, feel all of the crop's essence, not just its surface.'

She did as the steamman bid and recoiled in disgust, fighting to keep from gagging. Her hunger had vanished.

'If you fed from this crop you would end up like Tzlayloc, Molly softbody, mad and consumed with a terrible unending hunger. When the coldtime came, the states that would become the empire of Chimeca fed their masses with the most abundant resource their flesh mages had to draw upon.'

'People,' said Molly. 'Sweet Circle, those crops used to be people.'

'It was simple to change their pattern using the empire's dark sorceries,' said Slowstack. 'There were millions on the surface who would have died from the cold anyway. The imperial legions took the seed crop as tribute from the nations of the surface.'

She could see it now. Legs, arms and body fused into a single stalk, the indentations on the bulb where a face used to be, their essence blended with moss and lichen so they could divide and be fruitful. For a hundred generations this harvest of people-plants had grown in the artificial light of a fallen empire, fed by the life force of the rotating world. The people-plants were not just the descendants of her race, either. Some of the fields had been graspers, lashlites and craynarbians; the Chimecans needed variety in their diet. No wonder the Hexmachina had abandoned the contemptible race of man to warm her body in the core of the earth.

'These plants may be unfit to consume, Molly softbody, but the water that feeds them will be drawn from the fallen empire's holds under the seabed, purified by miles of filter glass. We need to replenish our boiler system, as do you.'

The steamman led them down the raised street to a ramp cut into the stone. Molly did not want to enter the field pit, but her thirst got the better of her. Row upon row of the fleshy plants lay formed up in front of her, the green skin of their stalks felted in a light covering of fur, the bulbs crowned in a husk that had looked like an acorn shell from a distance, but appeared like a matted crust of human hair now that she was closer.

Slowstack discovered the reservoir mouth feeding the irrigation channels, a statue in the shape of a swollen beetle. He opened his panel and drained as much water from the emerald beetle carving as his tanks would allow. Molly had been relying on his boiler for her water, so now she took the opportunity to slake her thirst. The liquid was as cold and as pure as any water she had tasted above ground – a cut above what came out of the taps in the public baths of Middlesteel for sure. Her feet crunched on something on the ground; Molly bent down to examine it. There was a scent on the husks. Where had she smelt that musk before?

'Slowstack. . .'

The steamman shifted his attention from the flow of water and towards Molly.

'Slowstack, if we are alone down here, why are there dried husks broken up next to the water supply?'

'We fear there is no reassuring answer to that question, Molly softbody. Let us leave as quickly as we can.'

Slowstack was halfway up the ramp of the harvest pit when a bolt of energy cut past his torso and ricocheted off a pyramid in the next field over, the dispersion mechanism singing in anger and burning the people-stalks nearby with a storm of lightning. At the other end of the cavern two figures were leaping down stairs leading from the inverted ziggurats, their bodies glowing with a black radiation, radiant with the hideous glory of the Wildcaotyl. Their hunters!

'The crevice,' called Slowstack, his voicebox tinny at its maximum volume. 'Back to the tunnel.'

'No, Slowstack.' Molly pulled the steamman back down the ramp. 'If you trust me, old steamer, then follow me now.'

She sprinted along the walls of the pit then ducked through the irrigation channel, submerging herself below the surface of the cold water.

'Molly softbody, have you taken leave of your senses?'

She climbed out of the channel, her clothes soaking. 'Through the plants and out of the cavern at the other side.'

'That is the longest route out of the chamber.'

She grabbed his manipulator hand. 'I know.'

Her feet tingled as they plunged into the harvest, the energy feeding the people-plants through the soil grid trickling up into her legs, making her calf muscles prickle and twitch. Stalks sprang back from the steamman's tracks, the bulbs swaying in mute agony above her head as the two of them carved an impromptu path through the crops. They lost sight of the pit walls and the raised streets, but Molly trusted Slowstack's metal-born navigation sense to keep their path true.

To their left the bulbs of the plants erupted in a shower of fleshy pulp as an ebony bolt from one of their pursuer's glowing fists expended its violence. The two convicts were firing blind and the Chimecan crops were absorbing the worst of it.

'I'm going to hold you down, girl,' shouted one of the hunters, his voice still faint in the distance. 'Push you in the dirt while I chew pieces of your flesh off.'

Another bolt sent a cloud of stalk heads flying into the air.

'Faster, Molly softbody.' Slowstack's vision plate was flaring as the nearby pyramid's energy disturbed his own mechanisms.

'You keep on shouting,' muttered Molly to their pursuers. 'Work yourself up into a nice hot sweat.'

The crops fell back. They had reached the far side of the plantation pit. Slowstack seized Molly and with a sudden burst of acceleration mounted the slope of the pit and sent them into the air over the raised roadway, landing with a crunch of protest on the street as his track-treads cycled in fury. Molly glanced back towards the plantation. The pair of convicts were two-thirds of the way across the harvest pit, oblivious to the vectors of swaying crops arrowing in on their position.

'Molly softbody, we—'

'Wait a second,' said Molly, brushing the water from her dripping red hair.

A clamour rose from the crops, a clucking of rattle-like clicks, followed by a storm of white furred bodies leaping towards the men.

'Wild pecks,' said Slowstack, his head tracking the hunting cries of the lizard mammals.

Attracted by the blood frenzy more packs of the albino creatures were pulling themselves from the neighbouring harvest pits and drumming the flagstones with the wicked-looking claws on their right feet. They were clever, cleverer than the outlaws of Grimhope had realized. Molly could feel the waves of information contained in that drumming. These packs nested in the tunnels, near-blind, but all too aware of the value of the crop of meat tended by the Chimecan automatics. Nothing must be allowed to intrude on their rightful territory.

In the plantation they had climbed out of, a shockwave of energy blasted out, setting the crops burning, the bulb heads exploding in the heat. One of the hunters had fallen, the forces of his Wildcaotyl possession scything out in his death throes.

The other would be snowed under by the albino killers before long.

In the heat of the deep caverns Molly's clothes were going to dry out quickly. She would be sweating again too, soon. 'Let's press on, Slowstack.'

Chapter Twenty-Three

Prince Alpheus was dragged shouting to the cross and strapped onto the cold stone. 'Leave my arms alone, we had a deal – I helped you jiggers.'

'And so you shall help us again,' said Tzlayloc. 'And you need not worry about us removing your arms, compatriot. Symbolic gestures were needed when the old regime required the passions of the mob to be diverted. I have more direct ways of controlling their fervour.'

The prince tried to turn his head to look at the crystal full of bubbling blood. 'What's that? What are you doing?'

'It is a lens to amplify your nerve endings. Now be silent, lest you wear yourself out. You will need all of your strength soon. As it is, I suspect you will not last as long as my darling girl.'

'You said you would set me free!'

'I did, didn't I?' said Tzlayloc. 'And by a strange twist of irony, compatriot, it is you who will set the people free with your blood.'

'I am not a royal any more,' sobbed Alpheus. 'I abdicate – I told you I would. You can have the throne. I just want to go to the Fey Free State.'

'It is not your royal blood which I require,' said Tzlayloc. 'How curious that Greenhall has no record of there ever having been a joining between the House of Vindex and your line, and more curious still that no one with the blood curse ever surfaced in the royal breeding house before. Still, that is what comes of letting you filthy vermin interbreed without proper supervision.'

'What blood curse? I am not under any curse. Let me go, please, for Circle's sake.'

'The symbolism of your place in history shall be different,' said Tzlayloc. 'Not a valorous angel of the proletariat giving her life for the cause. Instead, the last peg of tyranny who needed to be dragged down to seal our courageous new realm.'

The locust priests finished securing Alpheus to the stone cross and nodded to the Chairman of the First Committee.

'I want to leave the palace,' screamed Alpheus. 'I want to leave Middlesteel.'

'You are not in Middlesteel any more, compatriot. When we are finished we'll find you a suitable place at the museum, stuffed, next door to an example of a mill owner. The last King of Jackals, uncrowned.'

'Please, you promised—'

Tzlayloc looked at the locust priests. 'By all means stop his whining. My head is starting to ache with it.'

The priests traced sigils on the activation glass and Alpheus's howling filled the subterranean chamber.

'That's better.'

Behind the prince the blood of the last of the operators boiled in fury, joining him in his agony. Tzlayloc nodded in satisfaction. Somewhere below, that filthy machine would be writhing in suffering too. Even if poor Molly Templar had not yet given her life to the cause, there were only two operators for the Hexmachina to distribute its essence between.

One fleeing for her life, the other having his life crushed out of him.

His smugness turned to dissatisfaction as he caught a glimpse of himself in the reflection of the blood crystal. He was getting corpulent. He looked at the locust priests and noticed for the first time that so were they. It was all the run-offs from the equalization mills; that and the harvest of hearts from the new Gideon's Collars. With so many offerings to the Wildcaotyl it was hard to resist sampling some of the nourishment. For a moment the consideration that it was an inequality for him and the shepherds of the faith to have so much briefly suggested itself to Tzlayloc, but then the thought passed. Theirs was a heavy vocation with heavy demands – their bodies needed a heavy fuel to keep them in the condition that the revolution required of them. It was strange, though, how the more he ate the hungrier he became. He would have the Chimecan device moved to Parliament Square, into the light, Tzlayloc decided. He would feel better when he could watch the agony of the last monarch of Jackals from the windows of the House of Guardians.

Alpheus's scream changed pitch as the machine sought to surprise him with its ingenuity, varying the play of torture across his body. Tzlayloc ruffled the prince's hair. So short, so lank and dreary compared to Compatriot Templar's long fiery tresses. Everyone was doing his and her bit. Everyone had a purpose in the new order. Even a filthy royalist.

Relieved of their weapons, Oliver, Hoggstone and Commodore Black sat in a chamber made surprisingly homely given its location in a long-abandoned atmospheric station. Only the presence of the outlaws armed with old rifles and crossbows pointing at them gave away the fact that they were not sitting in a gentleman's library.

Benjamin Carl wheeled himself into the room and navigated his wheelchair up to a table adorned with an old double-headed brass oil lamp. His head shone in the light, a slight silver tonsure all that was left of the ageing revolutionary's hair.

'Now then, fellow,' said the commodore. 'Do you plan to torture us? I see no wicked thumbscrews on your table.'

'Torture? I used to regard having to listen to Hoggstone's Purist friends campaign from the stump as torture. No, I thought we might have a nice pot of caffeel. Damson Barbary, if you would be mother.'

The girl who had betrayed them ducked out of the library, returning with a steaming porcelain pot and four cups.

'Time has been kind to you, Carl,' said Hoggstone. 'For someone I believed was dead up to a couple of weeks ago. Apart from the bath chair. . .'

Benjamin Carl slapped the iron spokes of his wheels. 'Age didn't put me in here, First Guardian. Some rogues more or less on your side of the political debate abducted me. I had to jump from a round black aerostat and the landing was not kind to me.'

'The secret court? And here's me thinking they were an old politician's tale spun to keep me on the straight and narrow. You always did have a devil's luck, Carl.'

'They're real enough.' The old revolutionary indicated the walls of his domain. 'And you're sharing my luck now, First Guardian. You in your pauper's rags smelling of garbage, while the Third Brigade strut around Middlesteel's avenues in parade formation.'

'The Commonshare are your children, Carl. Does your heart swell with pride when you see what they have accomplished?'

Benjamin Carl swivelled his chair to pull out a book from one of the shelves. '*Community and the Commons*, a first edition. Priceless on the black market since you banned it.' He hurled the book at Hoggstone. 'You tell me, you Purist cretin, you tell me where it says in here that we should set up camps to steal children and raise them away from their parents, that we should line up the people of a nation in the shadow of a Gideon's Collar, that one state should invade another, that we should employ a mob of ruffians to kick down doors and drag people to flesh mills. You find where I wrote that!'

Hoggstone picked up the book and waved it back at Benjamin Carl. 'The words might not be in there, Carl, but that's what it takes to impose your perfect beehive of a society on people who are born on their own, die on their own and live their lives by the one and one.'

'We may be born on our own into the world, Purist, but there's no immutable law of nature that connects a piece of land or strings a birthright to a swaddling. We are born into a world that belongs to all of us equally.'

'That's just a fancy letter of marque for a highwayman, Carl. Your community is a licence for those who have spent their lives idling to ride up to the farmer breaking his back in the field and demand a *fair* share of the harvest at the point of a sabre.'

'I'm wasting my time with you, Purist,' shouted Carl.

'Give me back my debating stick, sir, and I'll give you the lesson your people didn't have the guts to learn at the ballot in 1566.'

Oliver interposed himself between the two quarrelling men, his pistols back in his hands – the outlaw who had been holding them along with Hoggstone's debating stick incredulous that the brace of guns had disappeared out of his grasp. Two of the crossbow men loosed their bolts; Oliver tossed a pistol in the air, turned and watched one bolt thud into a bookcase – he caught the other bolt and slammed its metal head into the desk, the quarrel quivering, before catching the pistol and filling the room with his demon's laugh.

'Time for that cup of caffeel, Ben Carl,' said Oliver. 'You haven't gone to the trouble of bringing the First Guardian here to discuss political philosophy.'

'Who are you, compatriot?'

'I am the *people* you two buffoons claim to be working for.'

'And you don't want to be upsetting the people, now,' pointed out the commodore.

'Perish the thought,' agreed Carl. 'It hasn't escaped my notice that the parties have put aside their differences and are working together now. I thought you might consider a . . . wider alliance?'

'With you?' said Hoggstone. 'Dear Circle, man, I thought you would be cock-a-hoop – in case you haven't noticed, it's your people strutting about up on the surface now.'

'Jacob Walwyn was a brilliant scholar, Hoggstone. The best student I ever lectured. When I first knew him he was a gentle man who spent his Circledays teaching poorhouse foundlings how to read. After sixty-six he endured two weeks of beatings and torture from the political police. Not in official custody, mind. He was in the hands of one of your patriot squads. After he escaped the price on his head was second only to mine. Which of us, I wonder, taught the man who now calls himself Tzlayloc his lessons best?'

'Your agitators nearly started a civil war in Jackals,' said Hoggstone. 'Across the border Quatérshift has been bathing in the blood of your legacy for a decade. Why, sir, should I sign a pact with the devil?'

Carl filled one of the porcelain cups and offered it to the

473

First Guardian. 'For the same reason I must, compatriot Purist. I would not suffer your tyranny, but Tzlayloc's is infinitely crueller – the more repugnant to me that he seeks to dress it up with his twisted rendering of the communityist truth. Neither of us on our own is strong enough to overthrow them, but perhaps together . . . did you ever really read my book, Hoggstone, before you threw it on the fire?'

'Your damn philosophy has been nothing but a plague on my house,' said the First Guardian. 'Of course I did.'

'Do you remember the last line of it?'

Commodore Black lifted up the tome from the table and turned the pages to the end. 'Strength has no meaning unless it is used in the service of the weak. One stick may be snapped but the bundle is a community, and the community will never break.'

'An alliance with a Carlist,' said Hoggstone. 'The House of Guardians will have me impeached after this. How many loyalists do you have?'

'I have a whole city full of them, First Guardian. It is time for the voice of the people to be heard again.'

Hoggstone lifted his cup. 'To the people, you communityist dog.'

'To the people then, you Purist slave master.'

Oliver nodded in approval and holstered his two belt pistols. Hoggstone looked at him as he made ready to leave.

'Shootist, this is a historic moment. Where are you going?'

'Where else when the lunatics have taken over? I am going to pay a visit to the asylum.'

Molly was beginning to wish that she had drunk more water when she'd had the opportunity. Every hour they travelled the heat seemed to get more oppressive, sapping her ability to keep up the pace. It was only the increasing strength being channelled by her proximity to the Hexmachina that was allowing her to continue. She had tried riding on the back of Slowstack's hull but the metal of his surface had become scalding; she could have fried a side of ham across the steamman's body if she had one.

There was water somewhere, still being drawn through hidden cooling channels by the Chimecan crystals that survived this far down. She could tell by the haze of mist that filled some of the rooms. The extra burden of functioning this deep meant the crystals had fared far worse than the ones in the Duitzilopochtli Deeps. Many had melted or fractured under the strain of the heat, entire chains of the devices split open like hatched eggs. Bony glass splinters littered the floors of the passages where they had exploded.

Molly slowed down. On the passage wall were lines etched in stone, oblong shapes with stone circles inside them. She imagined a reservoir behind the wall, as cold and as cool as the irrigation waters that had fed the people crops in the higher cities.

'Let's stop, Slowstack.' She hit the wall. 'We need water before we drop.'

Slowstack came back to her, his stack spotted a fierce orange where the metal was overheating. 'We understand, Molly softbody, but we must continue. We are so close now.'

She hit the wall again. 'There's water behind here.'

'No, Molly.' He traced his manipulator arm over the sigils carved in the stone. 'This is not a coolant pipe. This is a sink for draining away the pressure of the magma that the earth passes this deep within her body – liquid fire and earth, Molly softbody. These are escape vents in case the channels overload.'

Molly groaned and sunk to her knees to rest. 'How could the Chimecans bear to live down here?'

'Their coolant mechanisms had not suffered from a thousand years of neglect, Molly softbody. And the heat was valuable; it could be passed through exchangers and used to help keep the nations of the surface subservient to the empire during the harshest years of the coldtime. They needed their cattle – their slaves and food stock – kept alive.'

Reluctantly Molly continued to follow the steamman. The caverns they passed through were smaller now, some of the ziggurats and stalactite towers unfinished, abandoned during the Chimecans' twilight years. A twilight her ancestor had helped inflict on them. Increasingly their passage was blocked – halls where stone fire doors had been triggered by magma breaches ahead, corridors that ended in unfinished caves.

In one of the dead-end caves there was a pile of bones so old they crumbled to dust when she tried to pick them up. There was no armour, Chimecan jewellery or scraps of clothes as with the other skeletons she had seen, but there were some links from an old leg chain. 'A work gang,' said Molly. 'Digging out a new city for their masters, poor souls.'

'We suspect not,' said Slowstack. 'There is no way forward here, we must go back.'

Molly trudged after the steamman as he reversed his tracks. 'But there are chains back there?'

'Only the upper cities were dug with slave labour, Molly softbody, when life on the skin of the world was more populous and there were millions to be discarded digging out the caverns. The bones you saw were not tunnellers; they were a tribute of food, minerals in their body a delicacy for a whitegnaw, created by the flesh mages of Chimeca. The whitegnaw was the miner. Those poor softbodies were merely a plate of sweetmeats sacrificed to her.'

'You have seen this thing, Slowstack, back when you were Silver Onestack?'

'All the great rock tunnellers are female, Molly softbody. They split in two before they die; the aged self expires and the daughter self burrows on. You need not be concerned, the Hexmachina has hunted down most of them for her lover, the Earth.'

'Most of them?'

'There is one whitegnaw that attacked Grimhope – she is old and canny and has evaded the Hexmachina; it is believed she was a Chimecan noblewoman who murdered her family and was sentenced to transformation into a rock worm for her crime. The outlaws' legend says she decided she would never die and would keep her hunger alive long enough to outlast the empire and all its works.'

Molly wiped the condensation off the steamman's vision plate with the sleeve of her tattered dress. 'She has certainly done that.'

'Hunger is a terrible thing, Molly softbody. A hungry creature will forget its intellect, its morality and its gods – in its desperation, a hungry creature is capable of almost anything. The Chimecans were once not so different from your people. Such a life is to be pitied. Mass starvation drove them to terrible crimes, to worship terrible things.'

'When the Hexmachina showed you how to fuse your two bodies together I think she left a little of her essence with you, Slowstack.'

'She was with us, Molly softbody. Even when we were Silver Onestack, only once a desecration, a leper among the people of the metal. Now we are twice a desecration and she is still inside us. If we live through this the people of the metal will not believe it. That the holiest of machines has made a twisted desecration its instrument.'

'They will believe it,' said Molly. 'I'll have our part in this written into a Dock Street penny dreadful and send copies of it to King Steam until they sing your name in their hymns.'

'And what will you call your fiction?'

'"The Terror of the Crystal Caves",' said Molly. 'Except they'll get my feelings wrong. They'll have me being brave and valiant all the way through the story. Not scared and tired and so hot I might throw the whole thing away for a glass of cold water. Everything I do in the story will be because I planned it, not because I had no choice.'

'You *have* had a choice, Molly softbody,' said the steamman, 'and you have followed your path and stayed true to it. There is no greater bravery than that. The Hexmachina showed us glimpses of a world where you did not – and it was a dark, cold, quiet, terrible place. Sometimes the fate of the land turns on the common actions of a common individual.'

'I am not sure it should have been me, Slowstack. Out of everyone in Jackals, I keep on asking why this has fallen upon me. I'm just a Sun Gate scruff that everyone predicted would end up running the streets with the flash mob. Better this duty had fallen to an adventurer like Amelia Harsh or a handsome deck officer on an aerostat. I don't have a family; I don't even have a living. Out of everyone in the world, why me?'

'The great pattern has woven your place in its fabric better than you know, Molly softbody,' said Slowstack. 'The blood of Vindex runs in your veins, not just in a literal sense – you are a true heir to his legacy. Out of all his descendants with the blood-song singing within their veins we can imagine no other we would rather have at our side.'

The last syllable of the steamman's words was lost in the howl that echoed off the walls of the passage.

'That is a softbody throat,' said Slowstack.

'Not merely the race of man,' said Molly. 'Those things are ridden by dirty Loas.'

She extended her senses, felt the rush of the Hexmachina's voyage through the magma. The Hexmachina was at least an hour away from their position.

They started speeding away from the noise, but Molly was reluctant to flee, checking the path with her hands, looking for something.

'Molly softbody?'

'They are too near, Slowstack. They'll run us down in minutes.'

'I have no weapon capable of harming the Wildcaotyl,' said the steamman. 'Even a pair of minor entities. Are you joined yet with the Hexmachina?'

Molly shook her head. 'We should save our strength, stand here and face them down.'

'You can smell another pack of wild pecks?'

'The only thing worth hunting down here is *us*, old steamer.' She pulled him towards her. 'By my side, Slowstack. Don't try and throw yourself in front of me. No heroic sacrifices.'

Down the passage the two convicts rounded the corner, rolling in two spheres of black light suspended above the ground, their hands crackling with an incinerating fire. They sighted their prey and accelerated towards Molly and Slowstack with a howl which was a roar of triumph channelled through burning human throats.

'This is chaos,' shouted Oliver.

Third Brigade soldiers were falling back at the other end of the street in a disciplined line, one rank firing, while the troops who had retreated a couple of steps behind them reloaded from their bandoliers. On Nagcross Bridge equalized revolutionaries were being picked up by their iron legs by rebels and tossed into the Gambleflowers, political fighters running along the shops on the bridge and brandishing their debating sticks.

Commodore Black had one of the dead shifties' carbines and he shot it with the accuracy of a long rifle, Third Brigade troops dropping with each charge he broke. 'Use the cover, lad. Your fey skull will stop a bullet the same as any other.'

One of Benjamin Carl's officers ran up to them, his only mark of rank a red band of cloth bound around his arm. 'They've started putting pickets on the sewer gates, we can't get our people behind them.'

'The other bridges?' asked Oliver.

'Even better defended than this one.'

Nagcross Bridge had to fall. Oliver looked at the ranks of soldiers at the other end of the bridge. They were sheltering behind an interlocking wooden rampart – one of the mobile barricades they erected to seal off troublesome districts back in the Quatérshiftian cities. As he watched a column of soldiers came into view marching in quickstep, reinforcing the position to the north of the bridge.

'Different uniforms,' said the commodore. 'Look, caps, not shakos. The marshal has swallowed his pride and is bringing in another brigade to help crush the city.'

On their side of the lines an old steamman came into sight, supported by a couple of young political fighters from the party of the Levellers.

'Guardian Tinfold,' said the Carlist officer.

Tinfold made a weary whistle as steam escaped out from beneath his metal plates. 'I told Hoggstone our forces were not prepared for an all-out assault. I counselled for a guerrilla campaign.'

Oliver pointed to the Quatérshiftian soldiers blocking the north end of the bridge. 'Time is their ally, old steamer, not ours. If we don't free Middlesteel before the cursewall is lowered you'll have your guerrilla war – generation after generation of fighting from caves in the uplands.'

'Fastbloods are so hasty,' sighed the politician. 'Well then, we must save Jackals from the folly of our alacrity. Our people in the city are cut off now; we must open a passage to the pocket or suffer encirclement and defeat. Nagcross Bridge must fall.'

At the shiftie end of the bridge fresh ammunition boxes had been brought up and the troops felt emboldened enough to start a volley of fire that started cutting down the rioting street fighters. Debating sticks smashed aside doors as the ragtag army took cover.

A couple of fast-bowlers with glass grenades tried running out onto the bridge and pitching the explosives towards the north end, but the range was too far even for the two four-poles fanatics, the explosions showering flames at the foot of the barricade as the Third Brigade cut down the two players. From the rebels a traditional flutter of applause sounded as they honoured the dead men's fatal innings.

Oliver turned as a clatter of hooves reverberated behind them, half expecting to face a charge of exomounts. But instead of heavy cavalry, Oliver saw a line of horses with a collection of riders as motley as the city fighters' own forces. There were huntsmen from the villages wearing red tunics that could almost pass for redcoat uniforms, the black great-coats of mail coachmen, the blue uniforms of the county constabulary, and, by far the greater number, hundreds of roamers – wild gypsies in a flurry of colours, their fire witches riding without saddles and naked, war paint swirled around lithe muscles. At their head was a riding officer of the House Horse Guards, parliament's oldest cavalry regiment.

'Jack Dibnah,' shouted the riding officer, adjusting his roundhead-style helmet. 'Mad Jack to m'friends. Late of the House's own. Been out hunting any shifties foolish enough to stick their heads into the royal county of Stainfolk. Heard there were some of the buggers in Middlesteel needing stringing up too.'

He pointed at the hundreds of horses behind him, sixers mostly, whippet-thin and panting from the thrill of the ride. 'Dibnah's irregulars. Not much for parade turns but handy enough with a sabre or a lance.'

One of the fire witches kicked her horse up to the front of the column. 'Enough of your prattle, we were promised the blood of the *beng* that drove us from the plains of Natsia.'

Mad Jack winked at Oliver and the commodore. 'Not much for the niceties of command either, but they're spirited fillies, eh?' He looked over at the steamman politician. 'You with that lot camped out east?'

'I am the honourable member for Workbarrows, young softbody,' said Guardian Tinfold. 'Which lot are you referring to?'

'Good Circle, man, there's a whole army of your people camped east of the Gambleflowers.'

'King Steam has honoured the ancient treaty,' said Tinfold.

Bullets whistled past Mad Jack's helmet, but he just swatted at the air, as if horseflies drawn to the sweat of his sixer were bothering him.

'We need the steammen here,' said the Carlist officer. 'Why aren't they marching to our relief?'

'King Steam is bound by the treaty,' whistled Tinfold. 'No army from the Free State will cross the Gambleflowers unless it is invited to do so by the House of Guardians.

'Is King Steam mortal insane?' said Commodore Black. 'The Third Brigade is murdering us down here. If we can't break through soon their gallopers will be hauled up and they'll be giving us the whiff of their cannon.'

'I must go to them,' said Tinfold. 'They must accept my

command as a Guardian to traverse the river.' He turned to Mad Jack. 'Will your horse carry me?'

'On the flat of a cart maybe, old steamer. Don't you see how you're spooking her?'

Oliver indicated the fast flowing waters of the Gambleflowers. 'That will carry you fast enough.'

'Would you have us drift the Guardian down the Gambleflowers like a barrel?' asked the commodore. 'The refugees floated away on every skiff that could hold out the mortal river.'

'Not quite everything.'

Commodore Black looked with horror to where Oliver was pointing, at a boat converted into a tavern moored to the banks of the river. 'A jinn house, lad? You'd risk our fate to an old tub that hasn't been cast off the banks of Middlesteel for a decade or more?'

'With an experienced skipper at the wheel, commodore.'

'No, lad. Don't ask that of me. Haven't I been put in harm's way enough? My fine house filled with wicked shifties, my friends and companions slaughtered underground with half the armies of the Commonshare trying to see us off the same way. Those troops on the bridge would fill the tub full of holes as soon as they saw us making off with her.'

'Let's see if we can't throw their aim for you,' said Oliver. He looked up at the cavalry. 'I heard that horses won't jump a line with bayonets.'

The gypsy witch looked at him with contempt. 'These are not *salahori* horses, little *gadje*.'

'Have you never been blooded, dear boy?' said Mad Jack. 'Jump a hedge, jump some shifties with a little cutlery on the end of their rifles. All the same to me.'

Oliver leapt onto the back of the gypsy's mare and flourished his witch-blade. 'Good luck commodore, you've just been promoted to what's left of the Jackelian navy.'

'Ah, lad, when you get to that asylum of yours, have them warm up a cell for you. You'll put poor old Blacky in his grave yet.'

'How does a man who does not know horses ride bareback?' demanded the gypsy woman.

'My memory comes and goes.'

Mad Jack spun his horse around and pointed his sabre down the bridge. 'All those who would ride as free men, all those who would ride for Jackals – then ride with me *now*!'

Their trot became a canter became a gallop, the thunder of their hooves and the screams of the gypsies filling the long run of the bridge. At the other end of the bridge the glass-crack of charges sounded as the order to fire at will rippled down the enemy line. Horses fell, the easiest target to hit and as fatal to their rider as if the bullets had found their hearts, lost beneath the storm of the charge.

Oliver risked a quick glance away from the rapidly approaching barricade and the frantically reloading Third Brigade men. Commodore Black was scurrying down to the moored jinn palace, a handful of Ben Carl's loyalists carrying Tinfold down the steps behind him.

Streamers of fire twisted around the gypsy witch's painted arms in front of Oliver. '*Kris, kris, kris,*' she yelled. They were no longer a charge of cavalry – they were thunder taken mortal form and hurtling towards the Quatérshiftian line, the din of their hooves and cries painful to hear.

In front of them the bayonet-tipped rifles of the Quatérshiftian line rose like the spines on a hedgehog.

'The wall,' shouted Molly to her steamman friend as the two possessed convicts flew towards them. 'Use your voice on the wall.'

Slowstack swivelled to face the stone passage and his voicebox shook as he used the fighting frequency of the knights steammen, a spider web of cracks forming along the wall under the violence of his voice.

Dark energy rolled down the passage, the inhuman banshee howls of the Wildcaotyl channelled through corporeal throats. On the wall the cracks spread, slow at first, then rippling out as the pressure of the magma-drain behind the wall widened the fissure, the earth's fury forcing its way out. Shards of the green stone favoured by the Chimecans blew off, followed by a geyser of molten rock.

Molly caught sight of the two convicts pushing back at the magma with their black light as they tried to retreat. Then her view was cut off as the slab of stone in the ceiling smashed down an inch in front of their position. She felt the rumble of the second door sealing the breach out of sight. Magma caught under the edge of the door began to cool, hissing by their feet.

'Molly softbody, that was *reckless*. What if the trigger on the fire door had malfunctioned?'

'Then at least we would have had the pleasure of the company of those two jiggers as we moved along the Circle.' She pointed at one of the crystal growths on the stone floor. 'That fire sensor is broken, I can feel it. It just looks wrong. But the one on the other side looked good.'

Slowstack let out a whistle – part relief, part frustration. 'Let us see if your senses can lead us towards the Hexmachina.'

'You have a good voice, Slowstack. You should have been a steamman knight.'

Slowstack ignored the teasing. The passages they travelled changed from rough-hewn stone to more intricate paths – false pillars and Doric columns supporting the ceilings, as if the craftsmen of the fallen empire had been drafted in to expend one last burst of vigour at their deepest levels. What did not change was the energy-sapping heat, the rubble of shattered crystal machines that would have regulated the temperature littering their path. Occasionally they came across a cooling crystal still working, glowing like a sun and humming and vibrating from the strain of trying to keep the oven-like temperatures in check.

The two friends passed across a drawbridge that lay suspended over a bubbling channel of magma into a chamber with dark oily walls stretching up high into the darkness. Molly peered at the statues of the Wildcaotyl gods lining the cavern, carved out of a black diamond material, dark stone that seemed to swallow the light of the wall crystals still flickering in their mounts.

'She's close, Slowstack. My body is trembling with the power of her.'

'This is as deep as the cities of Chimeca extend,' said the steamman. 'There are passages that could take us further out underneath the seabed, but none deeper. This is the limit of their territory, the depth of their wound upon the body of the earth.'

At the far end of the vault were piles of bones, not food for a whitegnaw this time, but legionnaires of the old empire. They lay in ordered rows in front of four massive doors – gates large enough to have accommodated the bulk of a Jackelian aerostat. Among the dust and shards of bone lay black plates of armour sewn together with a cable mesh, odd rifles, a mixture of stone and crystal that looked like something a child might cobble together as a toy.

'They were guarding this entrance, Molly softbody, to the very end. They died from starvation still standing here rather than abandon their post.'

Molly shivered as she stepped through the dust that had

once been the hearts of such men; capable of holding their position even as their comrades dropped dying from thirst and hunger around them. Fanatics. Picking a path through the ancient remains she laid a palm on one of the doors, metal and peculiarly cold in the febrile air.

Her blood moved to its own secret tides and she gasped as her body wrenched to one side of its own volition. Molly tried to say something to Slowstack but her voice came out as a gargling hymn of machine noise, a golden light warming her palm, spreading out along the surface of the door and glowing so bright Molly had to shut her eyes. The burning radiance seemed to seep through her eyelids, so painful she cried out. Then it was gone, leaving a headache dancing in her forehead. Molly opened her eyes. The doors had vanished as if they had never existed and the two of them were standing at the rim of a polished crater filled with a coral-growth of black complexity. Threads of glass, millions of them, grown into shapes that pulsed and moved with their own simulacrum of life.

'A machine,' said Slowstack in awe. 'But not of the metal.'

Molly realized it was cold in the room. After days of furnace-like heat, dreaming of the cool autumns of Middlesteel, she was actually shivering.

'No, old steamer. Not of the metal. Those threads are crystallised blood, drawn from the bodies of the Chimecan lords' own children. The ultimate sacrifice that their gods called upon them to make.'

Molly's body fizzed with revulsion at this sly abomination, her proximity to it triggering her relationship with the Hexmachina. Her blood was changing, the structures of her body rebuilding themselves into something new. She was the daughter of Vindex and the philosopher slave had seen this thing, she knew that. He had stood exactly where she stood now and felt the same emotions, passions that had pushed him into leading the revolt of the slave nations.

'Molly softbody, what is the function of this artefact?'

'Nothing yet,' said Molly. She felt the echo of the words in her head before she said them. The Hexmachina was so close now. 'It is only half built. But had its construction been finalized, then it would have been a pipe, a pipe to play a tune for the Wildcaotyl, to crack the substance of the great pattern and allow the Wildcaotyl to call down their own gods. Meta-gods! Beings far beyond the frail substance of our universe.'

'By Steelbhalah-Waldo's beard,' hissed Slowstack, 'there are hymns among the people that are never sung. Names that are never said for fear of what power they might allow into the world. For the Wildcaotyl to do such a thing! The Circle would be closed, the great pattern dissolved. We believed that all the Wildcaotyl desired was to encase the earth in ice again, to return the Chimecan Empire to its ancient glory and control our life force as food for their table.'

Molly shook her head. 'Poor mad Tzlayloc. He thought he was preparing the way for a perfect order, but the order was never his. It is to be his Wildcaotyl masters', a perfect cold eternity of complete method . . . no chaos, no warmth, no gravity or movement or change. Everything subservient to the meta-gods' inert dominion and the will of the Wildcaotyl. We would all be equal in a way – equal in our non-existence, equal in our living death within a circle of time without end. That is the future my ancestor glimpsed. Why he dared rebel against the Chimecan Empire.'

'Molly softbody, you are changing,' said Slowstack, his voicebox disturbed.

He tracked back; the same golden nimbus that had disintegrated the door was now lifting off Molly's skin in waves, an aurora borealis that made the Wildcaotyl's instrument of ultimate destruction glitter like a million crimson stars in a dark firmament. Slowstack's own hull lit up with the glow, the golden energy making his body feel as hale as Slowcogs once had, before Onestack had fused their bodies together in a desecration.

Molly groaned and leant on the railing around the crater's rim, collapsing to her knees with the strain of her body's changes.

As the glow faded Slowstack's vision plate cleared and he saw the dark figure standing three feet behind Molly, black fire leaking from his eyes, the sound of his malevolent laughter an echo from the pits of a nightmare.

Damson Davenport found it hard to keep up with the others – they had been equalized longer than she had and were used to the flat, dull way everything looked in their new bodies. She was continually reaching for things on the mill bench and missing them, or knocking them onto the floor. It was the nice cup of caffeel at the end of the day she missed most. The coke they fed into their boiler chutes might burn for days in their sorcerous new forms but she still remembered what it was like to taste things, to have an appetite. The work leaders boasted that they had eliminated hunger – well, that was true, in a way. And she missed the peace of sleep too. She could only rest for an hour or so in this new body and when she woke up from the dreamless respite she hardly felt refreshed at all.

'Keep up with the line,' shouted their company's work leader, banging her iron back with his punishment wand. 'Compatriot Davenport, you are slowing the column. Can you not take Compatriot Carker as your example? What a fine worker she is, what a fine example to the people she serves.'

Compatriot Carker had found the measure of how to trot in her new body. But then Harriet Carker was a Grimhope loyalist, one of the first to be equalized – the daft fool had volunteered for this existence, had been one of the subterranean renegades who had set up the flesh mills down below in the outlaw realm.

It was so hard to tell the equalized apart – the loyalists from the conscripts. You learned to watch what you said and to whom. Damson Davenport had only tasted the pain stick once and it was enough to cow her tongue. The rumours of a resistance, the rumours of a counter-revolution, had been denied by the company leaders. But then they had interrupted the evening reading of *Community and the Commons* to deny them. They might have sliced her up and stuffed her into this shambling new body of metal and flesh, but they had not cut away her common sense. She could see the fear in the eyes of the brilliant men. She could see the upside down Vs – the lion's teeth – that had been scrawled on the walls of the streets; she could see the distant smoke and hear the fighting.

'Halt,' shouted the company leader. They were outside the Circlist cathedral on the Lilburne road, Third Brigade troops lined up and guarding the doors. What could be inside, wondered Damson Davenport? The practice of Circlist worship was a pain-rod offence now; the company leaders had made that clear. Wagons were drawn up outside, dozens of them with canvas covers concealing their valuable cargo.

'Form up,' shouted the company leader to the column of equalized workers. 'Eight each to a wagon. Then we pull them to Parliament Square. After we have delivered the wagons we will return to this street – there will be more wagons waiting for us. This will be our duty until we are reassigned back to the cannon works.'

The royal *we*, thought Damson Davenport, as the company

leader climbed up to the top of one of the wagons while his equalized compatriots did as they were bid.

'These wagons are meant for horses,' said Damson Davenport. It came out before she realized she had spoken.

'They've been eating them,' whispered the metal-flesher behind her, voicebox set on low. 'I heard the brilliant men complaining that it is the only meat left in Middlesteel now.'

Damson Davenport glanced around. Thank the Circle the company leader had not heard the uncommunityist exchange. To gossip was to steal exertion from the cause – they had been warned against that too. A mixture of Third Brigade troops and brilliant men escorted the large convoy, holding their rifles ready as they marched. A small glimmer of hope rose in her. If they were being guarded, then there was still something to guard against in Middlesteel.

Gates on a barricade with the muzzles of galloper cannons protruding out were heaved back outside Parliament Square. A squat black building had been raised in the centre of the square, its stacks venting oily black smoke into the snow-pregnant sky. Damson Davenport noticed the rubble of the statues that had been smashed to make way for this new structure. Something else had been added recently too – a tall stone cross which had been driven into the ground outside the entrance to the House of Guardians, a figure strapped to it howling like a banshee, his screams carrying across the cold space of the square. Above the figure being punished a crimson-filled jewel boiled as snowflakes fell across it and turned to steam.

Third Brigade soldiers pulled the canvas covers off the wagons, revealing the cages underneath. In Damson Davenport's chest the calculation drums ground in shock. The cages were filled with people, once-fine clothes ripped and soiled by confinement in a space a Jackelian would not have wished to keep a street hound in. There were old men, families and children, the school uniforms of the private academies ruined by weeks of sleeping and living in them. The strangest thing of all was how quiet they were. They were just standing there, resigned. Why weren't they angry? These were the city's quality – they were used to the finest food and the finest accommodation Middlesteel had to offer. Now they had been reduced to gaunt figures without enough spark to spill even a tear for their own predicament.

Soldiers unlocked the cage walls and pushed the dirty prisoners to form a line leading towards the squat structure. Behind her the company leader was talking to one of the brilliant men. After the conversation was over, the leader came over to Damson Davenport and cut her out of the team pulling the wagon. 'You are slowing the wagons down, compatriot. You are not yet used to your beautiful new form, so I have decided to show compassion to you. You will be working on the Collar's boiler for the rest of today.'

The Collar? So, that is what a Gideon's Collar looked like. He led her to the middle of the square, over to the furnace being stoked on the back of the construction. Inside the building she could hear the crack of the bolts as they fired. One every five seconds. Quick, painless, humane. Clearly the product of an advanced society. Damson Davenport looked down at the fuel being fed into the furnace by the equalized workers. 'These are books, Compatriot Coordinator.'

'Supplies of coal have run low, Compatriot Davenport,' said the company leader, indicating the snow. 'Your concern does you credit – but the books are an adequate fuel source and you will not find any copies of *Community and the Commons* among them.'

Of course, there was only one book for the land now. She took a shovel from the company leader and joined the others digging out piles of books and tossing them into the flames of the furnace. She did not feel the heat from the furnace, but then she did not feel the cold either; she knew what the temperature was, her body could tell her that. She just did not feel it. Piercing screams from the figure on the cross nearly made her spill a blade full of tomes onto the snow. 'Who is that?'

One of her co-workers turned his voicebox in her direction. 'The King.'

'The King? But he is dead, isn't he?'

'The *new* King.'

'Oh dear.' She looked at the distant figure writhing on the cross. She must have missed the coronation festival. Everyone back home had so been looking forward to that – she had been building up a little store of rotten fruit for weeks in her room, just so she could throw it on coronation day. Bitterly disappointed, she went back to feeding the fires of the Gideon's Collar.

Chapter Twenty-Four

Glass grenades hurled by the riders blew apart the barricade on the bridge, horses arrowing through the cordon to join those who had already leapt the line of bayonets. Oliver slashed down with his blade, the hex-heavy knife forming itself into the perfect simulacrum of a curved sabre. In front of him the gypsy witch twirled a whip of fire across the nearest Third. Brigade trooper. Oliver ducked the rifle bullet coming towards his skull, pulling a belt pistol out and killing the marksman. To his left he deflected a bayonet with the flat of his sabre, and then turned a boot to kick the soldier down to the ground.

It was strange fighting on horseback, the weight of the sixer striking fear into the hearts of the soldiers on the ground, the height making it easy for him to slice down, but raising him into the line of fire at the same time. With a cry of vengeance the gypsy witch launched herself off the mount and fell into the melee like a flaming comet. The Commonshare had driven her off her lands in Quatérshift and the invaders would pay a blood price for trying to repeat their purges in Jackals.

Oliver looked over the bridge rail and saw the commodore's

tub floating down the watery green surf of the Gambleflowers unmolested by the troops on the bridge. He did not hesitate but pulled himself forward on the horse and took control, kicking its flanks forward and surging out of the scrum. Oliver galloped past a knot of wounded Third Brigade men being pulled back by their compatriots, abandoning the fight behind him for the city. Soon he was into the heart of Middlesteel, windows iced over and dark, the few people out scrabbling for food disappearing as he charged past.

Oliver whispered to the horse using gypsy words that came to him – and the mare increased her speed. He smelled Hawklam Asylum before he saw it, the bonfire smell of the cursewall on the hill, the air shimmering as flecks of snow drifted into its shield. There was a normal wall first, to protect the citizens of Middlesteel from blundering through the worldsinger's barrier. Not entirely necessary. Anyone who was not put off by the evil whine it made was probably past caring. Oliver let his perception extend through the asylum gatehouse, his senses spreading and diffusing across Hawklam Hill; but lacking control he started being pulled part, diffusing himself too wide. With a wrench of concentration he pulled himself back together again, reassembling the jigsaw of his consciousness. He had touched the worldsingers inside and he had tasted their minds, noted the subtle differences. The Jackelian order had been reinforced with Quatérshiftian sorcerers. Their mastery of the worldsong had created more in common between them than any differences of nation, politics and race. All over Middlesteel the Jackelians were fighting for their freedom, but up here it was business as usual. The wild fey had to be contained, that was something both sides agreed on.

In his anger Oliver had not noticed that he had climbed the boundary fence and wandered through the cursewall, leaving a hole in the shimmering barrier. He felt the thrum of the leylines in the bones of the earth, six great currents of power crossing at the top of Hawklam Hill. The mound had been a place of power and superstition for as long as Jackelians had lived in these lands. Ancient religions had raised standing stones here, spilt blood here, tracked the dance of the stars and buried war chiefs here. So much earthflow, so much power.

The front door of the asylum was a steel barrier as thick as the hull on a submarine war craft; they had sealed Hawklam when the invasion started. No fey to escape during the fighting.

Oliver rapped on the door with the hilt of his witch-blade and a viewing slot opened, the grooves of a man-sized portal visible within the larger black barrier.

'How did you get up the hill?' a voice demanded. 'The gatehouse has not admitted anyone.'

'Who do you serve?' asked Oliver.

'What?' The voice on the other side sounded confused.

'I would like to know,' said Oliver. 'The order of worldsingers served the old kings, then it served the House of Guardians. In Quatérshift it served the monarchy then the Commonshare. So I would like to know, is there anyone you jiggers won't whore yourselves out to, to protect your privileges and station?'

A jailer pushed the worldsinger on door duty away and looked through the sally port. 'Clear off you young idiot. If you make me open this door I'll beat you to within an inch of your life and toss you back in the street.'

'I will give you one chance,' said Oliver. 'Bring the feybreed Nathaniel Harwood to me. Bring him to me now or I will take him from you.'

'You'll take the back of my hand from me, boy.' The jailer shouted back to his colleagues, calling for reinforcements. 'You think we're bloody Bonegate? We don't have a visiting day – we don't let gawpers in to see the prisoners dance in their cages for a penny a poke.'

'I haven't come to see him dance,' said Oliver, cutting out a circle in the barrier with his witch-blade, the black steel hissing. The metal fell back before the kick of his boot with a clang like a cathedral bell. 'I have come to see *you* dance.'

He dipped through and into a firestorm of spells, chants and curses, a fury of energy tossed at him by a semi-circle of worldsingers. Oliver let them throw their sorceries at him, the leylines throbbing as the power of the land was manipulated and twisted against his body. The energies grew thinner as their assault expended its force, the anger and confidence the sorcerers felt slipping away to be replaced by surprise, changing to fear as he filled the entrance hall of the asylum with his laughter. Their attack faltered and stopped.

'Oliver Brooks!'

Oliver saw the figure at the other end of the hall. 'Inspector Pullinger. Here I was visiting one old friend and instead I find two.'

'I was right,' spat Edwin Pullinger. 'I was right all the time about you.'

'I took your advice, Inspector. I came to Middlesteel to join the Special Guard. But they seem to be collaborating with the shifties, as do you. Does that make me the last honest guardsman?'

Jailers in hex-covered armour were running up behind Pullinger, tugging out toxin clubs from their belts. 'I always knew you were a dirty little fey boy,' said the worldsinger. 'One of the ones who would never let themselves be controlled.'

'My father was a wolftaker, my mother was a demigod and my fate is my own. For you I am the hand of justice.'

'You are too dangerous to have a torc burned around your neck,' said the sorcerer. He pulled out a snuffbox and inhaled a pinch of purpletwist. 'And now Jackals is operating under the laws of a Commonshare we no longer have to adhere to the tedious restrictions of the charter the House of Guardians forced on us.'

'The law of the mailed fist,' said Oliver in disgust. 'The rule of do as you will. Then we are both free of the laws that used to bind us. Your worldsong can't touch me. That is my power, inspector. I am not touched by the feymist. I *am* the feymist.'

'And for that you will die.'

Pullinger's jailers had their toxin clubs ready. There must have been fifty of them in the hall now. The witch-blade trembled in Oliver's right hand, the metal at the tip of the sabre flowing out and down on both sides of the blade; the hilt reforming and cracking upwards with the noise of breaking bone. The weapon was still unnaturally light – even as a double-headed axe. The part of his father's soul that had been imprinted on the weapon was satisfied with the choice. Oliver tried to shut out the wickedness in the jailers' souls; he felt their sins as an ache – the beatings, the sorcerous experiments, the fights they would make the fey enact just so they could gamble on the outcome, whole lifetimes of casual cruelties.

Twisting and squirming in his hand, the witch-blade knew a way to shut out the evil. 'Come then, proud men of Hawklam Asylum. Show me how I might die.'

'More power to the boilers,' cried the locust priest.

In front of Damson Davenport the Gideon's Collar was shaking on its platform's legs, the processing machine's engine working beyond its tolerances. Every few minutes a shiftie worker in a leather apron would toss out a sack that would slap down on the snow, leaving a puddle of blood behind when one of the brilliant men hauled it off to the palace.

Damson Davenport had stopped hearing the cries of the young king on the cross. By focusing on the work of tending the furnace she could avert her eyes from the wagons and cages being hauled into Parliament Square and emptied of soiled families, the fine-dressed prisoners pushed into line with rifle butts and sabres and pikes.

The important man – the one they called Tzlayloc – came out of the gates of parliament, a phalanx of guards and locust priests in his wake. He had been in and out of the House of Guardians all day like an excited child waiting for his Midwinter gift-giving. Distracted, Compatriot Davenport nearly tripped up over one of the other equalized workers stoking the boiler furnace. There were six of them now feeding the Gideon's Collar.

Tzlayloc walked over to one of the sacks of hearts. 'Faster, compatriots. We are so close now.'

Close to what? she wondered. Their overseer hurried over to the leader, and from all the nodding Damson Davenport knew their service in the shadow of the collar was going to get even more frantic. A Third Brigade riding officer galloping out of the snowstorm interrupted their overseer's act of obsequiousness. She heard snatches of the report. Counter-revolutionaries, steammen knights, First Brigade reinforcements.

Tzlayloc howled with rage. She had no trouble hearing his instructions. 'Cancel the Special Guard's orders to march south. Have them form for battle and bring me Flare.'

His retinue closed in and there was a flurry of commands in the wake of the cavalryman's departure, the leader's minions rushing off to do their master's bidding. Suddenly Tzlayloc dropped to the ground, screaming. Damson Davenport thought he must be having a stroke. All that shouting and hurrying about. It was no wonder. But then she realized his cries sounded more like an exclamation of ecstasy.

A tearing noise sounded and in the air above Parliament Square a fissure appeared, colours she had never seen before leaking out of the rip.

'Xam-ku,' shouted Tzlayloc. 'Xam-ku!'

Black tendrils snaked out of the fissure, snowflakes turning to steam as they touched the arms waving and flexing in the air, moving like the legs of a spider emerging from its hunting hole. Two of the tendrils reached down to Tzlayloc, stroking him gently as he moaned in pleasure. His body was changing, swelling and rippling as the darkness from the fissure slithered its way into his form, leaving Tzlayloc trembling – and not from the cold of the strange winter that had frozen Middlesteel. Around the head of the First Committee his locust priests had fallen to their knees and were chanting in a language she did not recognize.

Tzlayloc's eyes leaked black fire as his gaze swept Parliament Square, a clicking laughter like the rattle of a mandible filling the emptiness of the cold air. Damson Davenport did not know what product of mechomancy they had traded her beating heart for inside her metal-flesher frame, but whatever it was, she realized the organ could still curl in terror.

Commodore Black climbed from the makeshift raft and pushed it through the reeds and the freezing water the remaining foot to the bank of the Gambleflowers. Clutching the debating stick that had made such an excellent punting pole, Guardian Tinfold stepped onto dry land. Smoke from the burning tavern boat chased after them as their makeshift ferry finally sank into the brown waters of the river.

A line of knights from the encamped steammen army had ridden over to meet these new refugees. 'Dear mammal, your circulation will freeze with the temperature of the river.'

Commodore Black looked up from the snowy bank. 'Coppertracks! Blessed Circle, you escaped Tock House.'

'Quite clearly,' said the steamman. War mu-bodies surrounded the slipthinker, giant fighting mechanisms slaved to his consciousness, twice the size of Sharparms, with fiercely glowing vision plates. 'Could you not have found a more river-worthy craft to flee the environs of Middlesteel?'

'Flee! We've come for you, you daft old steamer. Poor old Blacky's been dragged along the length of the Gambleflowers while those devils from the Third Brigade used us as a floating target for their cannons and their rifles. Do you not recognize Guardian Tinfold?'

The mu-bodies around Coppertracks bowed to the politician. 'Guardian Tinfold, I heard rumours you had perished when the Quatérshiftian forces sealed off Steamside and lay siege to our people inside the steammen quarter.'

'I was in Workbarrows on business. Fortunately our party fighters have been able to move around using the sewers,' said Tinfold. 'I come bearing the writ of parliament – where is King Steam?'

'We shall take you to him.'

The knights made way for one of the Free State's gun-boxes to walk up to the riverbank, both iron feet ploughing through the snow. It dipped down like a war elephant and the commodore and Tinfold climbed up next to its mortar mouth. Clutching the bombard they moved out across the steammen army's encampment, Coppertracks and a column of steammen knights at their head. Instead of the tents of a campaigning Jackelian army, the people of the metal had brought iron rods that connected together to make hexagonal skeletons sealed with panels of gutta-percha. It was as if the white meadows of the east bank had been transformed into a bed of coral.

It was not just the orders militant that had marched down

from the mountain kingdom; the boiler trails of ten thousand steammen rose through the falling snow. Steammen who had never served in a fighting regiment had the barrels of pressure repeaters fixed to their arms, pipes coiled back to their boilers, drums rattling with steel balls while they used every precious minute to practise battle manoeuvres under the supervision of their new officers.

Tinfold and the submariner were taken to the centre of the camp where colourful streamers on a field of lances crackled like burning logs with the energy of the wind. There, sixty feet tall, stood King Steam's war body – a thing of functional terror, two claw-like legs bearing a spherical mass of cannons, gun barrels and spiked impaling apparatus. The frame drew closer to the gun-box and the Commodore saw that caged inside it was a small, golden, child-like steamman, twisting and turning the bulk of the machine with control levers.

'King Steam,' called Tinfold, his ancient voicebox straining to carry above the sound of the wind. 'I bear the writ of the House of Guardians of the Kingdom of Jackals. I represent the will of the emergency government of all parties, the army of resistance, the party of the Levellers, and the people of the electorship of Workbarrows. Do you recognize my writ?'

'I DO.' King Steam's voice boomed across the entire riverbank, shaking the organs inside Commodore Black's chest. Loud enough to issue orders to the very mountains they had left behind.

'Then I invoke the treaty of 980, as signed by the Lord First Guardian Isambard Kirkhill and yourself on the Fulven Fields and duly ratified by the House of Guardians. The parliament of Jackals calls upon the force of arms of the Steammen Free State and grants you the dispensation of the House to cross the waters of the Gambleflowers and enter the environs of the royal capital of Jackals.'

King Steam's war machine pistoned closer to the gun-box so the monarch could speak from his golden pilot body. 'You have prospered in this land, Tinfold. You are a true citizen of Jackals, but the Steamo Loas could not be prouder of your achievements if Steelbhalah-Waldo himself had been elected to the Guardianship of Workbarrows.'

'I have often reflected that the spirit of freedom is like a Loa itself, Your Majesty. It rides many within this land.'

'Then let us ride with it,' said King Steam. He swivelled to address his officers and the orders militant, to command the whole army. 'TO WAR. TO WAR! WE MARCH ON MIDDLESTEEL.'

In the House of Guardians the members of the First Committee looked on with horror as Tzlayloc picked up the messenger – an equalized revolutionary – and propelled him through the stained-glass window of the gallery, the herald's components smashed apart in the courtyard outside.

'Machines,' said Tzlayloc. 'Filthy machines.'

At first the committee members thought he must be talking of the equalized messenger, but then they realized he was referring to the news the messenger had brought – the army of the Steammen Free State was advancing. Tzlayloc felt like ripping apart the round table and scattering the maps of Middlesteel and her environs. He had never been stronger, but things were crumbling around him, the ungrateful wretches of Middlesteel joining the counter-revolutionary uprising. Half the city fighting, and now the people of the metal had finally found the guts to interfere in Jackals' affairs. The crafty king of the steammen was rushing to rescue his corrupt allies now their snouts had been pulled from the feeding trough and made into bacon. Had he not fed the people? Had he not fed their masters into the Gideon's Collars raised in their name?

Judging Tzlayloc's fury had subsided, one of the locust priests approached the chairman, almost close enough to touch the black nimbus that now leaked from the leader's body. Tzlayloc's heart lifted. It was the ex-transaction engine man from Greenhall. He always brought good news. The leader was oblivious to the fact that after dealing with the petty mandarins of Greenhall, the priest was well versed in the art of timing good tidings. Husbanding them and squir-relling them away for the right moment to offer them up like tribute.

Tzlayloc nodded as the priest whispered to him, then he raised his head and made that awful clicking laugh. Soon the revolution would feed, feed so well and so long that the Hexmachina would never bind their cause with its web of polluted machine sorcery. Tzlayloc gave his orders to the priest, waiting as the loyal fellow hurried off to return with Marshal Arinze and his retinue, joined a minute later by Captain Flare. The Special Guardsman looked haggard. How ironic that someone so powerful could be so soft. The Wildcaotyl in Tzlayloc sensed the discomfort the captain felt passing the square outside. He had fought on a battlefield; he knew the butcher's bill that war demanded. And the revolution demanded that this last war be fought and won at any cost. The enemy should suffer. It was the way of things.

'The armies of the Free State march on us from the east,' said Tzlayloc. 'What news from our brothers in Quatérshift, compatriot marshal?'

'Our compatriot worldsingers have almost translated the hex on the cursewall,' said Arinze. 'The worldsingers have promised to have the wall lowered within the week. Our compatriots found a labourer in one of the camps who had worked on it, and he was able to provide insight into—'

'We do not have a week!' interrupted Tzlayloc. 'We will

have steammen knights on the outskirts of Middlesteel within four hours.'

'The First Brigade has almost finished arriving through the atmospheric. We can hold the capital until the cursewall is lowered. Compatriot Tzlayloc, we have twenty divisions on the other side of the border. Enough troopers to seize every town, village and city in Jackals.'

'And if the cursewall takes longer to fall?'

'We have miners digging tunnels deep enough to pass underneath the cursewall. Jackelian sappers are not opposing them now. The dregs in the border forts have already fled, there is not a redcoat or frontier company left on the border. The upland regiments are still in the field but they dare not march on us in strength for fear they will return to their crofts and find the caliph's soldiers bedded down in their clansman's halls. Compatriot Flare and his guardsmen have forces enough to secure the south.'

'The Special Guard may earn their city by the feymist later,' said Tzlayloc. 'First they will assist us in breaking the forces of King Steam.'

'Breaking?' The marshal looked at Tzlayloc with incredulity. 'We are dug in, we hold Middlesteel. Let the enemy storm our fortifications and bleed oil on them.'

Tzlayloc stabbed a finger on the map. 'We shall march out and break them here.'

Marshal Arinze looked at where the Chairman of the First Committee was pointing. 'Rivermarsh? There's nothing there but hills, bogs and farmland. Please, Compatriot Tzlayloc. With two brigades I can hold the capital until Midwinter. But you do not fight the armies of Mechancia on open ground. Their knights are better than cavalry, faster, stronger, more heavily armoured; their gun-boxes outclass my light cannon. I could not guarantee victory with a dozen brigades behind me.'

Tzlayloc reached out and seized the marshal's face, applying enough pressure to his skull to make him drop to his knees. 'You have the gods of revolution behind you! The Wildcaotyl are strong and grow stronger with each enemy of the people that is fed to the cause. What does the malevolent life metal have? Loas as thin as the foul smoke they expel from their stacks. That is why Jackals fell so easily to the revolution – because she had forgotten her faith. Do not make me doubt your faith in our communityist principles again, little man.'

Marshal Arinze scrambled back as Tzlayloc released him. Like all natural bullies the officer recognized a superior predator. 'It shall be as you say, compatriot chairman.'

Tzlayloc turned to Flare. 'What of you, compatriot captain? Do you have any counsel to offer on the order of battle?'

Flare stared grimly at the Commonshare worldsingers that were helping Marshal Arinze to his feet. 'We will go to the uplands. We will go to Rivermarsh. You tell us where to go and we will obey. We will march there. We will fight at the other end.'

'An admirable attitude, Compatriot Flare. The First Brigade will fall back to Gallowhill and Spouthall. The Third Brigade and the Special Guard will march out immediately with our equalized companies of the revolutionary army and meet the Free State's invaders at Rivermarsh.'

Captain Flare could not let his air of melancholy detachment override his military judgement. The chairman's plan was madness. 'You are ceding more than two thirds of Middlesteel to the parties' militia. Even if we beat off King Steam's forces, we will be coming back to a city largely occupied by the enemy. The Third Brigade will not have the advantage of surprise, of appearing at night in the heart of the capital. We'll see a terrible cost in the surgeon's tent for every street we take back.'

'Do not worry about the mill masters' private armies of thugs,' said Tzlayloc. 'They will reap their reward for opposing the people.'

A terrible feeling struck Flare. Tzlayloc's order of battle made no sense at all, except in one circumstance. But surely even the Chairman of the First Committee of the newly proclaimed Commonshare of Jackals was not capable of *that*?

'Prince Alpheus,' said Flare. 'Are you leaving him in the city?'

'Compatriot Alpheus is serving the revolution in so many ways,' said Tzlayloc. 'Your attention to duty does you credit compatriot captain, but protecting the people from the monarchy is no longer the Guard's responsibility. What is it that the mob used to shout outside the palace on stoning day? No republic with a king? If it makes you feel better we shall take the cross with us and the King's pain will give succour to the revolutionary hearts and spur them to great acts of valour against the people of the metal.'

Tzlayloc's fingers pawed the maps on the table, his fingers leaving dark trails across the neighbouring nations. 'Yes compatriot captain. You may leave the vermin in the royal breeding house to the care of the Gideon's Collar. Our energies will be focused outward, not inward. Victory after victory for the people, the standard of equality planted across every state in the world.'

Tears of dark energy struck the oak floor of the House of Guardians, burning like acid by his feet. Every society an ordered nest, its equalized citizens working together, indistinguishable as brothers and sisters. Perfect and content in their endless toil. It would be glorious.

In front of Oliver the last remaining cursewall of cell eight-zero-nine shrieked like a dying swine on the abattoir table, the energy of the sorcerers twisted and distorted around his fey body, wrapped and folded in ways that could never have been conceived by the worldsingers who invoked it. Inside, the Whisperer lay propped up against the wall, surrounded by the dirt of his own excrement and the bones of vermin.

'Oliver,' hissed the Whisperer. 'Your perfect body, it's covered in blood.'

'I had to stop a while and negotiate your release upstairs.' Oliver turned his nose away at the smell.

'They stopped taking the bucket away when they stopped bringing me the slop,' said the Whisperer. 'How did you get to Hawklam?'

'Get here? By horse.'

'Good, because I could jigging eat one.'

Outside, the inhabitants of the other cells howled in rage and frustration. Oliver pulled the Whisperer to his feet and gave him one of the dead jailer's rifles to use as a crutch.

'I could break their hexes,' said Oliver, looking at the line of cells.

'You still planning to lead us to the Promised Land, Oliver? Into the feymist for the Lady of the Lights' private menagerie?'

Oliver shook his head. 'She's gone, Nathaniel. The thing that has replaced her, it is – well, it is not as pleasant.'

'I told you the time would come when you'd need my help, boy. Glad to see you've come around to my way of thinking. You can leave the ones on this floor locked up. Anyone capable of thinking straight has already been taken away by the Special Guard for their land of the free fey. The ones this far down are wild and dangerous.'

'And you are not?'

'You tell me, Oliver. You just waded through the blood of a hundred jailers to get to me.'

'They killed themselves by their choices,' said Oliver. 'And I wanted to see why they buried you this deep.'

The Whisperer laughed. 'You're going hunting, aren't you? You crazy bastard. You're going hunting gods.'

'That was your plan, was it not?'

'I just never thought you would agree. The way things have fallen apart in Jackals in the last few weeks, I might have settled for the Lady of the Lights' troll bridge and the feymist.'

As the Whisperer left the cell his deformed appearance seemed to swell in the air of the asylum corridor, growing stronger as the sorcerous fields that cut him off from the earth's power, the bones of the earth, were left behind. 'Now that's better. They'll never catch me again, Oliver. I'm not the boy my father sold down the river for the price of a jinn bottle. I have grown in ways they could never imagine.'

Oliver stepped through the ripples in the air, the cell walls flexing and twisting as the Whisperer drew the power of the leylines into his abnormal form. 'You have your freedom, Nathaniel. Now let's make sure you have a world left to enjoy it in.'

'We'll settle it in the east, boy,' hissed the Whisperer. 'Last night I walked the dreams of a thousand steammen. The army of Mechancia is in the field. It was the life metal that cast down the dark gods last time around and there are some extraordinarily ancient scores waiting to be settled.'

Oliver recalled the people of the mountain cities, images from his journey and of Steamswipe blurring with shadow memories of other journeys through the Free State – some as an enemy, hunted down, others as a friend – standing on the deck of an aerostat, the peaks of the mountains lancing out of the clouds.

'Are you well?' asked the Whisperer.

'My head is so full, sometimes it's difficult to think.'

'That's how I first learnt to walk dreams, the nightmares of half the county leaking into my sleep. You have to learn how to use it.'

'I'll try, Nathaniel.'

The two of them retraced Oliver's passage through the dark and dirty asylum corridors, Oliver's existence sensed by the inhuman beings behind the cursewalls, some pure living fury battering the walls of their cell with their minds, others dark brooding presences, waiting silent and cold like spiders for something to blunder into their web. He could almost see why the order of worldsingers insisted the fey be torced or imprisoned. Some of these feybreed were more like a force of nature, the human part of their minds eaten away by the mist, left in a body half-evolved for the strangeness of a life beyond the feymist curtain; barely conscious of the violence of their existence here in Jackals. Then Oliver remembered that the order had tried to have him committed here; had wanted to pick his mind and body apart, to crack him open like the left-over carcass of a Circleday meal at Seventy Star Hall. His sympathy for the order's endeavours disappeared.

As they walked the Whisperer's body started to change, arms sucked inside the mass of his flesh, bubbles of bone flattening out and becoming smooth skin, fur-like hide crawling up his scalp. The Whisperer had vanished and in his place was a tall warrior with short-cropped golden hair, wearing a strangely archaic uniform with a brown pelisse hanging down his left side.

'I'm still here, Oliver. This is how I would have looked if the feymist had not risen in my village.' The Whisperer touched his new hair. Even his voice sounded normal now, no longer the sibilant hiss produced by the twisted fey gash that had served him as a mouth. 'Perception is all in the mind, and thoughts are such a fluid thing.'

'Your uniform is noticeably out of date.'

'It's from the only book I owned before they buried me down in here. *Duellists of the Court of Quatérshift* – it was my most precious possession. My father bought it for me during one of his sober weeks and there weren't many of those. This uniform is the best, don't you think?'

'By far. The Third Brigade will think their king has come back from the grave to punish them for running him through a Gideon's Collar.'

Snow was drifting in through the open doors of Hawklam's entrance hall. The Whisperer nodded in satisfaction at the corpses littering the marble floor, his tormenters for decades laid out just as he had always imagined them. Oliver looked down the rocky hill at his horse, waiting beyond the gap in the wrecked cursewall. He was about to point it out, but the Whisperer was distracted. Oliver followed the direction of the fey creature's gaze. The southern sky was filled with a fleet of aerostats, chequerboard hulls nosing through the almost luminescent snow clouds.

Wind whipped up Hawklam hill and the Whisperer had to shout to be heard. 'The high fleet has been floated! But by—'

'—whom?' said Oliver. His senses extended out, through the rigid hulls, through the canvas gas spheres – into the newly equalized bodies of Jackals' jack cloudies. Metal-fleshers, bent to Tzlayloc's will by brilliant men and Quatérshiftian officers with button-encrusted pain wands. Liberal doses of nerve fire flaying them for any perceived shirking or reluctance to attend to their orders; a pain more terrible than even the discipline of the RAN's cat-o'-nine-tails.

Oliver did not need to answer the Whisperer – the whistle of tumbling fire-fins on Middlesteel's towers and rookeries spoke for the intentions of those who were now masters of

511

Jackals' great navy, masters of the sky. Flowers of flame blossomed beneath the vessels, pneumatic towers to the south collapsing in clouds of steam as the heat boiled away their stability. Middlesteel was paying the price for its defiance, the ancient guarantor of their freedoms now turned against them to extinguish those same liberties.

'By damn, they're emptying their fin bays on Middlesteel,' said the Whisperer.

'Not emptying,' said Oliver, looking to the east. 'They need to save just enough bombs to stop King Steam's army.'

The two of them scurried down the hill as Middlesteel burned at their feet.

Chapter Twenty-Five

The Whineside Strangler's laugh of triumph turned to a howl of pain as a golden nimbus flared up around Molly's body, the field of darkness surrounding his hands boiling away as his fingers recoiled from her neck.

The second convict entered the chamber on hearing the strangler's screams and Slowstack headed the man off using his steamman voice. Shards of the Chimecan weapon blew off under the impact of the steamman's attack, but the convict only staggered back, then extended a fist, tendrils of black energy lashing out and whipping off Slowstack's chest. Slowstack was knocked over on his tracks, a fizz of dark energy chasing around a tear in his chest hull, exposed crystals black with oil leaking from fibrous pipes as the steamman moaned in agony.

'Slowstack!' Molly was caught off guard as the Whineside Strangler threw himself at her golden nimbus, his black field blending in a dance of colours, clawed fingers piercing and trying to penetrate the golden energy swirling around her form.

'The things I am going to do you,' snarled the strangler,

his words mangled by the fact his tongue had split into two bony mandibles, the smell of burning meat from his throat making Molly want to gag.

She bunched up the energy within her body, collecting it in a golden coil inside her as she rolled with the strangler on the floor.

'Help me,' shouted the strangler back to his partner. 'Help me hold her legs down.'

His compatriot left Slowstack's body and drifted over on eight black lances of energy, a spider's crawl. Molly detonated the charge that had been building inside her. The strangler was blown off her body and thrown down into the pit of the Chimecan death instrument. He rolled down into the body of the thing, blood-red crystals raining onto him as he collided with the instrument.

Detecting the energy of the Wildcaotyl entity, the weapon started to hum, a bone-grinding noise that made the walls of the chamber shake, showers of masonry falling from the ceiling. It was a song the earth had not heard for a thousand years, the music of insects, dreadful shortened notes that surfaced as if they were dying. Molly could see the glow from the machine where it was missing components, where the Chimecans had run out of beloved family members to sacrifice to complete the monstrous thing.

Molly did not need Slowstack's faintly exclaimed warning; she turned and twisted the tendrils of black throbbing energy from the second convict, using them like the reins on a horse to toss the killer after his friend. Inside the pit the two convicts' Wildcaotyl masters tempered the violence of their possession, fearful of damaging the instrument that when completed could summon their meta-gods.

She had no such compulsion. Watching the convicts floating and clawing their way up towards her, she reached inside the death instrument – its workings as cold and alien as the dreams of a locust. But even a device to crack the walls of reality had to be bound by the processes of this universe, the laws of mechanics. Her blood boiled inside her as she formed patterns, rolling through thousands of combinations of the hex-like keys that would unlock the weapon. She adjusted the pattern with each minor success, getting closer and closer to its activation cycle. The two killers were almost at the pit rim, their eyes dark and infinite, the human beasts within their hearts tempered now by the Wildcaotyl. They knew what she was trying to do – realigning the instrument, re-engineering the delicate forces within it. The wasps would protect the nest. *Don't look at them, focus on the task.* She had a tune of her own to play.

The two killers cleared the rim and raised their hands to unleash a hell-storm at her, but she changed the pitch of the instrument, tuned the vibration to the Wildcaotyl riding these executioners. Behind them unearthly notes throbbed in the Chimecan device and the sheath of ebony energy that surrounded the killers was suddenly as insubstantial as meadow mist, wisps of force sucked towards the instrument. The Wildcaotyl spirits had consumed their host bodies. Without the black force feeding their muscles and reinforcing their frames the two convicts convulsed and fitted, the pain of the immortals' withdrawal overwhelming.

Molly repeated the tune, watching the disruption of the apparitions with grim satisfaction. 'You want to meet your gods, you filthy cockroaches? Tell the evil sods that Molly Templar says hello when you see them.'

The Chimecan engine vibrated wildly in its holding arm, the cloud of Wildcaotyl drawn into the blood-made mechanism. It changed its ethereal pitch and finished with an almost human sigh. By the rim of the pit the two convicts lay sprawled, their bones turned to dust inside their skin, streaked black where the Wildcaotyl had burned them out. The Whineside Strangler would circle his fingers around the necks of no more victims in Middlesteel.

A warm breeze blew into the chilly chamber from the open door and Molly ran over to Slowstack, heaving his iron frame back onto his tracks. 'Slowstack, can you hear me?'

'We can,' whispered his voicebox, the grill caved in and crumpled by the force of the convict's attack. 'We heard the song you played too. It was hideous.'

'The Wildcaotyl thought so,' said Molly. She looked around for anything she might use as a tool to work on the damage. There was nothing. She was stuck in the centre of the earth with the greatest engine of destruction the corrupt heart of the race of man had ever created, with not even a hammer to hand. 'Stay with me, Slowstack. Don't leave me down here in these halls alone. Please, not again.'

'It is time for us to walk a different hall,' said the steamman. 'Our thread on the great pattern is coming to an end.'

Molly clasped the iron manipulator fingers of her friend. 'I won't watch you die again.'

'We have been deactivate twice before, Molly softbody. It is easy. It is living as part of the great pattern that is hard. Do not mourn for us overlong.'

'I am afraid, Slowcogs, Silver Onestack.'

'Do not be afraid for us, young fastblood. We do not fear the darkness before we are made activate, why should we fear what may come after? We are notes in a song. The notes are played out and the song of the great pattern goes on forever.'

A pool of water was forming where Slowstack's boiler was leaking and the light of his vision plate was fading. Molly was not sure how long she sat by his metal shell, empty of life now, before she felt the heat behind her. A white sphere hovered above the ground, the size of a bathysphere, a single silver eye sitting on its top. The face of a child appeared on the featureless white metal, like a real-box picture projected through a magic lantern.

'Can you not save him again?' Molly asked the Hexmachina.

<Where there is life and will, I can show the way for the life metal. But he has passed beyond my reach. Slowstack is in the hymns of the people and the toss of the Gear-gi-ju cogs now.>

Molly wept, adding her tears to the pool of water from Slowstack's boiler.

<There are two soul boards inside his chest cavity fused together as one. Break them out, Molly Templar. Slowstack would wish them returned to the halls of Mechancia.>

She did as she was bid, the crystal boards as light as air. Had they weighed more when he was alive?

<Stand in front of me now, child of Vindex. There is work to be done.>

Radiant with a golden luminosity, Molly stepped forward, two rivers of light flowing away from her chest, the beams joining together in a helix that slowly rotated between herself and the Hexmachina. From the sphere a similar golden beam extended out and encircled the helix, joining with it, twisting in joy before retreating back inside the Hexmachina.

<Operator, you are recognized.>

Flowing back like quicksilver the front of the sphere formed an opening, a dazzling white space inside moulded like a hand-made glove for Molly.

'The enemy is powerful,' said Molly, hesitating. 'And there were seven of us before. Seven operators, seven Hexmachina.'

<That is so,> said the Hexmachina. <But the Wildcaotyl have not changed in a thousand years, Molly. They believe they are so perfect that they would freeze us alongside themselves for

cold eternity in amber. But we are capable of change, you and I, and the enemy fear that most of all. I have spent a millennium listening to the secrets of the earth whispered to me by my lover. Growing stronger, cleverer and wiser. And you, Molly, you are remarkable. Perhaps one Hexmachina and one operator will be enough this time.>

Molly pulled herself into the Hexmachina and the door reformed behind her. It was like floating in a sphere of water and she felt the surge of her blood as their two bodies merged, her senses extending in ways her mind could never have imagined, the taste of sounds, the colour of the throbbing veins of the earth, tiny details in the walls of the chamber opening up as if the stone had been placed under a microscope. It was all vibrations, all music, the song of the great pattern that Slowstack had talked of. There was something else. Great pain. The Hexmachina was trying to shield her from it, but their link was too strong – their body was being stressed by a shocking agony.

'What is that?'

<There is another operator, Molly. Tzlayloc is torturing him as he tortured you, to weaken me, to goad me into the Wildcaotyl's trap. But I still have two operators to distribute my consciousness over. His work is agony, but it shall not incapacitate my function.>

'There's an anthill rising in my lawn, old girl. Let's go and step on it.'

A lance of light speared into the ceiling of the chamber from their body and the Hexmachina rose into the sea of fiery earth that began pouring down over the Chimecan's apocalypse trumpet. The malign device collapsed as the sea of magma filled the pit, brimming over and sliding across the two dead convicts, melting the shell of the steamman that had been Slowcogs and Silver Onestack.

Iron and liquid earth joined with a hiss and the Hexmachina's lover reclaimed the scar that had been driven into her heart.

The streets that had been so empty under the occupation were now packed with Middlesteel's inhabitants, the rookeries and towers emptied of their panicked residents as the aerostat bombardment levelled the capital. The Third Brigade and Grimhope's revolutionaries had withdrawn, leaving the roads to the hysterical refugees. Oliver was glad that the Whisperer was maintaining his human form; the true sight of him riding on the back of Oliver's gypsy mare would have caused a panic all of its own. At the other end of the street a group of riders appeared, Mad Jack and a company of his irregulars. Oliver urged the sixer through the crowds, the press of panicked Middlesteelians making her difficult to control.

'Major Dibnah,' shouted Oliver. 'Where's our army?'

'Falling back,' called the riding officer. 'Old Guardian Tinfold must have delivered his invite. The Free State's army has forded the Gambleflowers and is joining up with parliament's forces. We're going too. There's nothing to do in Middlesteel but hide inside the atmospheric stations and take a drubbing.'

Reinforcing his words the shadow of an aerostat passed overhead, causing a stampede among the refugees for the cover of the street's buildings. Screams sounded from the crush by the doors, people scrambling and slipping over the litter of looting.

'Dirt-gas,' shouted a refugee. 'Dirt-gas!'

Mad Jack turned his steed and delivered a kick to the man's head, knocking his stovepipe hat to the ground and sending him sprawling. 'Bloody fool. They're not loaded with gas-fins. Can't kill a steammen regiment with dirt-gas.'

Oliver spurred his horse through the gap in the crowds in the middle of the street. 'This way, major.'

'Good fellow. The First Guardian has sent word for everyone remaining to follow the Third Brigade out to the east. If we can make a scrum of it with their troopers, the aerostats won't be able to target us without killing their own regiments.'

'Yes,' said Oliver. 'When the aerostats finish here they'll head east.'

Mad Jack looked up at the sky. 'They're not handling well at all today. Must be shifties on deck. All the same, it'll be a bloody business when they catch us out on the field. Our regiments aren't used to sitting under the sharp end of the RAN.'

After the shadow of the airship passed, the throng of citizens returned to the streets as thick as ever. Oliver despaired of clearing the city. He could feel the dense pressure of the Wildcaotyl and the heavy mass of evil that moved across the land as the Third Brigade marched to war with the steammen.

Sitting behind him on the horse the Whisperer growled in frustration. 'Now I know why you didn't bring a saddle; you weren't going fast enough to need one.' He shut his eyes and imagined an aerostat floating above the streets, dark creatures like devils capering across the fin bays, flying so low that its weapon hatches barely cleared the spires of the Circlist church behind them. With terrified shrieks the refugees stampeded for cover. The cavalry company looked around them in confusion. The Whisperer had not extended the illusion into the riders' minds, but they understood well enough to take advantage of the space that he had cleared.

'I have a feeling this aerostat is going to follow us all the way out of Middlesteel,' said Oliver, their horse galloping after Mad Jack and his irregulars.

With their way cleared by the escaped feybreed they managed excellent time to reach the city markers – the marble globes carved with the portcullis of the House of Guardians. Oliver could see trails of smoke out beyond the low hills of the east downs, towards Rivermarsh. King Steam's assault on the Quatérshiftian legions had begun.

'They've abandoned their lines,' said Oliver, pointing to fresh ramparts and trenches that had been dug outside the city, now lying empty and unmanned in the snow.

Mad Jack frowned. 'Then it's true, the Special Guard have gone over to the shifties to fight. Those fellas fight better in the open than in the confines of the rookeries. Circle, this is a damn bad turn. Now the Commonshare has the two things that have always swung victory our way: our stats and the guard.'

Mad Jack saw the faces of his riders and realized he had voiced the doubts that they felt themselves in this unequal war – their resolve was crumbling.

'We have something they don't,' said Oliver, raising his voice loud enough that everyone in the irregulars could hear. 'We fight as free citizens of Jackals, not slaves of a king or a first committee or a caliph.' He pulled one of his belt pistols out and the lion of Jackals on the handle seemed to suck in the light of the afternoon, drawing down rays of sunlight that rotated, blinding the troops with a brilliance they had never known before. 'We will not suffer the heel of tyranny, we will not bend our knee to unworthy gods, we will not see an evil without striking it down, and we will not pass meekly into the long face of darkness that is endangering our land. Because we are Jackelians – and our soul of freedom can never, never be conquered. Not as long as one free Jackelian has the heart to say, "No! I think my own thoughts. I choose my own leaders. I select my own book of worship and my law shall be the law of the people, not the whimsy of any bully with a sabre sharp enough to slice a crown off the previous brute's head."'

At the back of the column a lone voice started singing, the words trembling and slight in the cold wind. Then a second voice picked up the tune, and a third, the song rising in intensity as it rippled through the company. 'Lion of Jackals'. The song grew louder, louder than the wind of the land; loud enough to drown out the thunder of falling fin-bombs behind them and the cannon clap in front.

'I can make women see a god-given human form when they look at me, twist dreams like clay,' said the Whisperer, 'but you put something in their soul. That's not a talent that came out of the feymist.'

'Run your hands through the soil,' said Oliver. 'You'll find your answer in the dirt.'

Another sound drifted in from the south, an unholy wailing like a wolf pack pleading to the moon. Out of the falling snow a line appeared, soldiers in the lobster-coloured uniforms of the regiments, kilts in garish tartan billowing in the cold. With bag-like sashes strapped around their tunics the front line played sackpipes, an unnatural noise, its fierce melody flaying the wind.

'Uplanders!' said Mad Jack. 'By the Circle, I was never so glad to hear a cat being strangled.'

A woman from the head of the column rode up to meet them, the back of her brown coat strapped with three loaded rifles. Not fancy fowling pieces, but workaday Brown Janes, the standard rifle of the Jackelian redcoat. 'Bel McConnell. Guardian McConnell. I have stripped out every bonnie boy and lass with a taste for a scrap from all the acres from Braxney to Lethness. We're holding the caliph's border with nothing but bairns and companies from the clan MacHoakumchild, and I'd rather trust a weasel in a henhouse than rely on a MacHoakumchild.'

'Wanted to see the capital, eh?' said Mad Jack. 'Place ain't what it used to be. Shifties have got the picnic blankets out for King Steam over at Rivermarsh.'

'We were following the smoke of it ourselves, laddie,' said Guardian McConnell. 'We've been marching for days and have got a hunger on.'

'Let's inspect the shifties' spread, then,' said Mad Jack. 'Your pipes can play us a merry tune as we ride out.'

'Are you daft, man?' said the uplander Guardian. 'Sackpipes are the music of lament. We'll play a dirge for the Commonshare and their shiftie-loving downlander friends. No offence meant.'

'None taken, I am sure.'

It took half an hour to cross the downs, and by the time they crested the hill to Rivermarsh the dark leviathans of the air were moving after them, scudding across an ocean of black smoke where Middlesteel burnt beneath their hulls. Oliver's sixer whinnied with fright as the vista of battle opened up before them. The Third Brigade and Tzlayloc's revolutionary army held the west side of the field, King Steam and the remaining forces of parliament the east. Shrouds of smoke surrounded the clashing armies, the crackle of fire from Tzlayloc's rifles answered by the saw-like whine of steammen pressure repeaters. On the higher ground at the rear of both armies steammen gun-boxes and Quatérshiftian artillery fought their own duel, great gobs of earth erupting from the frozen ground and scattering troops as fire licked out from the opposing cannonry.

A fizz of energies punctured the shroud of war as worldsingers and the Special Guard traded blows, the leylines throbbing in Oliver's sight as the land's power was leeched out from the bones of the earth. At the far end of the plain gusts of snow moved like phantoms, shapes appearing and whirling around each other, then vanishing into white. The Steamo Loas were losing to the Wildcaotyl, Oliver could feel their fatigue, the presence of Tzlayloc at the rear of his army like the stab of a migraine. The leader of the revolution was different now, fused with his masters, an ant flattened on the boot of giants, his hate for Jackals amplified under their possession and leaking across the battlefield in waves of pure loathing.

Oliver could see Tzlayloc was channelling in the souls of the dead. Drawing strength from the screaming Jackelian on the plain with his leg torn off by a rolling cannon ball; drawing strength from the equalized revolutionary limping in circles, his head caved in by a steamman knight's hammer; drawing strength from the two laughing Third Brigade troopers spearing a parliamentarian as he slipped on the blood of his comrade; drawing strength from the confused refugees running away from collapsing steaming towers in Middlesteel; drawing strength from the tears of Benjamin Carl and Hoggstone as they shouted orders that would send more of their people to the slaughter; drawing strength from the agony in Captain Flare's heart as his guardsmen tore apart their own countrymen, Prince Alpheus hanging like a banner behind him on Tzlayloc's cross of pain. Tzlayloc was feeding, growing stronger from the harvest of evil, and after the aerostats arrived and decimated the Jackelians and their allies, he would rip open the walls of the world and spill a sea of hungry insects into the land.

'We're losing,' said the Whisperer. 'They have the numbers and they have the guns.'

Oliver reached out to grab the reigns of a riderless horse that was galloping away from the skirmish, jumping over to the blood-splattered saddle and leaving the gypsy steed to the Whisperer. 'You know where the bridge is, Nathaniel.'

'Aye, there's our spread alright,' called Guardian McConnell back to her forces. She slipped a claymore out of her saddle and pointed it towards the enemy's right flank. 'That's where we'll take them. Strike up a tune, my bonnie boys and lovely lasses. Play "The Scouring of Clan McMaylie" for your Bel.'

Mad Jack's company formed into two columns, one on either side of the uplanders, trotting along amid the howl of the sackpipes. The uplander troops pulled leather hoods out from the sash-like instruments, raising them up and covering their heads. They were meant to protect from the poison that rose from the feymist curtain, but the hoods also gave them a hideous bird-like appearance, striking terror into enemy hearts. They were marching to their deaths and they knew it, but the mountain people of the south lived freer than any other Jackelian, by their lochs and their glens, and it was only the toss of dirt on their coffins that could tame them.

On the battlefield the plumes of smoke solidified, slowly freezing as a silence fell over the plain.

'Still not taken the rat tunnel, I see.'

Oliver dismounted from his frozen horse to face the Shadow Bear, the creature watching the battle from his bubble of suspended time. 'That would be too easy.'

'There never was any point in saving even a handful of you,' said the Shadow Bear. 'Look at you people. Look at the mess you've made of things. Even when everything is lined up for you, you won't do what is expected. Tell you to run and you stay. Tell you to stay and you run. Frankly, the other side of the curtain doesn't need vermin like your kind breeding and fighting and squabbling.'

'I have been there,' said Oliver. 'And that is something we can agree on.'

The Shadow Bear pointed down towards the heavy weight

of Tzlayloc, the pressure of his Wildcaotyl masters pushing into the world. 'See that. That is what your race is. Condensed and packaged into a tight little ball of destruction and hate and pointlessness. My predecessor cleans out the weeds and your kind just let them grow back.'

'That's not us,' said Oliver. 'That's not us at all.'

The thin slash of red that was the Shadow Bear's eye turned away from Oliver. 'They're pretty furious, the Wildcaotyl. You've kept those wasps trapped in a jar for a thousand years, and now they want to re-paint the canvas without you in the picture. I might almost agree with them, except for the fact they don't plan on leaving us in the canvas either, and that is something that is not negotiable.'

'I thought it might be something that basic,' said Oliver. 'You handle the level of detail down here a lot better than my mother, but I suppose your function is rather basic too. And I would really rather you didn't lecture me about the violence of my people. How many times have you destroyed everything, killed everyone?'

'I do not kill all that is,' said the Shadow Bear. 'That is the job of entropy. How can you kill something that is not immortal? You are all going to die anyway; one day later, one week later, one star death later. No, I *reset* all that is. The same way your foresters burn out an overgrown copse to renew it. Your people are dead wood, Observer child, time to move along and make way for something more worthy.'

'Ah,' said Oliver, remounting his time-frozen horse. 'Rules, rules. You do so hate to be broken. I wonder how you feel about being bent out of shape a little?'

'You are so righteous,' snarled the Shadow Bear. 'But the rule-set is there for a reason. Without the rules to set a trajectory for growth all you have is the perfect tick of the perfectly empty clock, going round and round and going nowhere to the random froth and fizz of the universe. But it is within my power to save you. I could leave time suspended for you; you could still reach the feymist curtain with a few of your twisted half-breed friends.'

'As you said, the more you try and get me to run, the more I seem to want to stay,' said Oliver.

'Where are you going, Observer child?'

'I'm going to ask the Wildcaotyl to leave. And when I am done with them, I'll be asking you the same.'

The Shadow Bear snorted. 'It will be amusing watching you try. After you have rogered things up, I shall let you live just long enough to see how things really end.'

Time jumped forward to the whine of cannon balls scratched across the sky. Oliver kicked his sixer down after the Whisperer.

'Lad,' shouted the commodore. 'You're alive.'

Oliver caught sight of the submariner on the other side of a square of steammen, soldiers moving in tight formation singing a hymn of battle in their machine voices. A cloud of acrid smoke from the battlefront briefly enveloped them, and then Oliver was through it. 'Commodore, where's King Steam's command frame?'

'This way, lad, I'll take you.'

Oliver checked the Whisperer was still following and fell in with Commodore Black. 'You did it, Commodore. They listened to you and Guardian Tinfold.'

'Ah, much good has it done us, Oliver. That devil Tzlayloc has had years to plan his campaign, while parliament's forces are in disarray. These rag-tag companies have never fought beside each other, or followed the leaders that now ask them to die. I would not trust these green-legs to help me lift a harpoon at a slipsharp, let alone crew the guns of

527

a man-o'-war. They're fine fellows when it comes to cracking a debating stick over the head of a rival, but they have never faced a charge of exomounts, or been asked to hold a square for an hour while the Third Brigade's six-pounders give them a broadside.'

Oliver moved aside to make way for a column of steammen knights, their bright banners crackling like whips as they raced past. Then they were at the command post. Riding officers galloped into King Steam's command position, shouting reports to the Jackelian officers there before riding out to their units with fresh orders. In one of the hexagonal frame domes the Free State's own command staff sat cross-legged and track-still, slipthinker brains co-ordinating their mu-bodies, allowing the conscript army and orders militant to move as a single entity. It was a formidable advantage – a collapsing line would be rapidly reinforced from the rear, a sudden enemy advance countered by knights that always appeared out of the snow like sorcery, cannon fire on their lines answered by counter-battery fire from the gun-boxes in the hills behind.

Oliver rode past the giant war body of the King and spotting the child-like form of the Free State's leader, dismounted. Hoggstone was there, and Ben Carl in his bath chair, still being pushed by the girl who had led them through Middlesteel's sewers. The conservative dark jacket of the First Guardian was at odds with the medley of brilliantly coloured uniforms of the surviving officers of the regiments.

'Oliver softbody,' said King Steam. 'So, you have chosen to stay and fight with us. Well met.' He looked over towards the Whisperer. 'And you come with one who is not what he seems. You choose dangerous allies, Oliver softbody. You have unleashed the weaver of dreams.'

'These are dangerous times, Your Majesty,' said Oliver. 'And I seem to be running short of allies. Steamswipe and Lord

Wireburn are dead. They died to protect me ... they died well.'

'Do not mourn for them, child of Jackals. The Keeper of the Eternal Flame now walks with the Loas and Steamswipe's honour is restored. There is no better end for a warrior. They gave their lives to preserve the great pattern and I can feel their harmonics powerful and proud in the hymns of the people.'

'Ah, Your Majesty,' interrupted Commodore Black. 'We are all going to end up in your mortal hymns now. Look!' He pointed towards the hill Oliver had ridden down, the beak of an aerostat nosing over the snow-covered downs, then another and another.

'Prepare to receive fire from the air,' commanded Hoggstone, his officers running to give an order that up to a month ago would have been unthinkable for a Jackelian army.

'It is time,' said King Steam, relaying his orders to the slip-thinkers in the command dome. 'Give the command to load the gun-boxes.'

From the dome Coppertracks emerged and bowed before the King. 'Loading has already begun, Your Majesty.'

'Gravity is on the shifties' side, Aliquot Coppertracks,' said the commodore. 'I've seen boats trade fire with stats, and their ballonets take a fierce beating before they sink.'

Coppertracks' transparent brain crackled with blue fire. 'Dear mammal, Jackals has held a monopoly on celgas for generations, but we have always planned for the worst – that one of the other nations might discover their own supply. We are not loading with mere ball or grapeshot.'

Gangs of steammen pulled long silver shells on flatbed carts past their position, smoke from their stacks steaming in the cold with the exertion of dragging the heavy load. Oliver watched with curiosity, a memory of a siege jumping unbidden into his mind, giant mortars like bloated toads thumping out rounds as large as these – surely they weren't going to use shrapnel against the coerced vessels of the RAN?

Oliver pointed to the pinned-down maps on the collapsible command table. 'When I was coming down here, I saw our forces being rolled back on the eastern flank.'

'That is where the Special Guard are fighting for the Commonshare,' said Hoggstone. 'Most of the Free State's knights have been committed here, but they are being badly punished. Flare's guard are holding back, but they are crawling with worldsingers from the Commonshare. A few of the guard refused to fight at the start of the battle and the shifties executed them by torc in front of us.'

'What of Jackals' worldsingers?' asked Oliver.

'We have a few,' said Ben Carl from his chair. 'But most of the order fled Middlesteel when the capital was invaded. I hate to say it, but we are out-gunned – those that have passed through the flesh-mills are slow, but they carry their own armour with them. The Third Brigade are veterans and—' Carl's words were interrupted by the thunder of the aerostats' fin bays emptying their cargo on the body of the Free State's forces.

'—they have our navy,' said Oliver. He shut his eyes as the ground trembled. The leylines were being sucked dry by the Commonshare's worldsingers. Once pregnant with the land's power, they were thin and barren now. He could feel the weather witches in the Jackelian lines trying to whip up the snowstorm to push the aerostats back, but the bones of the earth under their feet was too thin.

Oliver looked up to the brow of the downs. The mocking presence of the Shadow Bear was there, watching the advance of the Third Brigade troops, gloating as the Jackelian fighters wavered in panic at the shadows of the passing aerostats. It would not take much now to cause a rout. He could feel how close their soldiers were to breaking and running.

'They're about to run,' said the Whisperer.

'I know.' Oliver turned his horse to the east and nodded at King Steam. 'You hold the line against the aerostats, I'll try my luck with the fey.'

Oliver flew across the Free State's lines, the Whisperer's steed hard-pressed to keep up. Nathaniel Harwood could convince the troops he was a six-foot fighting god – even convince his steed – but the illusion of a horseman's skill was not the actuality.

Commodore Black watched the two riders disappear through the ranks of steammen auxiliaries, swallowed by snow and the swirling flags of the army.

'That shootist has spirit,' said Hoggstone.

'He's riding with the devil,' said the commodore. 'I'm just glad he's riding for us.'

Black pulled his undersized greatcoat in tighter – it had belonged to old Loade before he pulled it off its peg back in Middlesteel and the blessed fellow must have been a grasper of a man. But it was warm Jackelian wool and helped shield a poor fellow from the biting cold of this perverse summer. On the command table the maps started shaking, a brass telescope rattling until it fell over. Gun-boxes jolted forward on their stubby legs. The house-sized artillery pieces had abandoned their position on the high ground and were settling down alongside the steammen formations. Rolling the strange-looking shells onto loading cradles, steammen conscripts heaved them into the loading position behind the gun-boxes. Sucked into the breach, the shells vanished, followed by the clank-clank-clank of crystal charges of blow-barrel sap being lowered into position to propel the missiles on their way.

Commodore Black covered his ears. Their barrage had been deafening enough when they had been in the hills duelling with the Third Brigade's artillery.

With the crack of a titan's hammer on the earth the barrels of the gun-boxes flowered flame and flung their shells towards the chequerboard hulls of the aerostats. Some of the shells struck the airship's gondola structures, smashing wood and metal, others tore holes in the hulls, the fabric of their catenary curtains left flapping in the wind. A few ballonets spilled into the air, the gas cells floating out of sight. Not even slowed, the aerostats continued to glide across the fields of Rivermarsh.

Black nodded sadly. History was repeating itself. It was just the same as when the RAN had raided his fleet of royalist privateers. You could pierce their hulls with ball, with shrapnel, hit them with fire, but the cursed vessels were almost indestructible. Celgas did not burn, and each aerostat was filled with thousands of ballonets, each man-sized canvas sphere swelled fat with the precious lighter-than-air substance. Puncture one with shrapnel and they still had a hundred more to lift them out of the range of enemy guns.

King Steam's monster shells had failed and now their forces would be flattened, crushed without the option of slipping away beneath the deep waters of the ocean. The Duke of Ferniethian cursed his luck.

On the bridge of the *RAN Hotspur*, the revolutionary commander of the vessel pointed a discipline rod accusingly at the metal-flesher who had once been a first mate of the Royal Aerostatical Navy. 'It is as I said, we should be running higher, Compatriot Ewart. We should be dropping our fin-bombs from a greater altitude.'

Ewart flinched as the pain stick passed his iron chest. 'We need line of sight for the fin bay crew. A turn of the wind and we would be dropping fins on your people – this snow is working against us.'

'This is more of your defeatist whining and sabotage. I do not want to listen to excuses, compatriot. I have had a bellyful of them from your crew.' The revolutionary officer turned to one of his soldiers. There were as many shiftie marines and brilliant men on the *RAN Hotspur* as equalized sailors, getting in the way and issuing contradictory orders. It was a wonder the aerostat could hold a true course with the skeleton crew that had been assigned to each ship, let alone clear for action. 'Take Compatriot Ewart and a crew of patchers to the larboard hull. I want full lift – any damage from the Free State's gun-boxes must be repaired at once or there will be consequences.'

With four shiftie marines in tow, wet navy lubbers who didn't know one end of a stat from another, Ewart followed the howl of the wind to the breech in the aerostat's curtain. He tethered a holding line around his iron waist so he could climb securely around the ballonets and inspect the damage.

'How many patchers are needed?' shouted up one of the marines.

'The netting is torn,' said Ewart. 'We need to—' he stopped as he found the shell still buried in the ballonets, its metal buckled against one of the larboard girder stays.

It had not detonated and Ewart tapped it. This was his *chance*. If he could detonate it he could bring down the *Hotspur* and take some of these dirty shifties down with him. But it was not crystal-fashioned, so how could it be filled with blow-barrel sap? As Ewart felt the lines of the weld on the shell, metal plates sprung out and he fell back towards the torn curtain flapping in the gust from outside, a garbled cry issuing from his voicebox as he jerked on his support line and hung helplessly in the air.

The Quatérshiftian marines laughed at him, thinking he

had tumbled clumsily off the aerostat's hull frame, still unused to the quirks of his new equalized body. Their laughter was cut short when the steamman dropped down to the repair gantry, a round sphere sporting six pincer-sharp legs and an armoured dome for a head with a pressure repeater protruding from it like a mosquito proboscis. With their rifles slung around their shoulders the marines did not stand a chance – the six barrels of the steamman's nose spun around and a whining blizzard of small iron balls tore the soldiers to pieces, their corpses flopping off the gantry and into the ballonets. The steamman turned its attention to the ballonets, unleashing a wave of fire into the leather gas sacks. The lift bags exploded, deflating and leaking sweet-smelling gas into the cold air of the airship's interior. Then the steamman – actually a mu-body of one of the slipthinkers below – swivelled its pressure repeater in the direction of the laughing metal-flesher.

'Sharply done, mate,' said Ewart. 'I don't mean to knock the gilt off the gingerbread, but you'll be here all day if you're trying to sink the *Hotspur* that way.'

On the ground the steamman slipthinker evaluated the facts in a fraction of a second. Equalized Jackelians were heavy, weight an aerostat could ill afford. Their presence indicated sailors captured at Shadowclock rather than revolutionaries. The slipthinker translated what the metal-flesher had said – knock the gilt off the gingerbread, an expression of nautical origin meaning to cut a tale short. The slipthinker controlling the mu-body made a snap decision and a pincer snaked out and cut down the iron body.

'That's it, mate. Now let me give you a black dog for a white monkey and show you where the *Hotspur's* rudder lines are,' said Ewart, picking himself up from the gantry. 'And then we can visit the fin bay and drop a few shifties down onto their friends below.'

The information raced across the slipthinker council, fleeting from mind to mind like lightning before passing back into the mu-bodies already on the airships as well as those being loaded into the gun-boxes.

Metal-flesher and steamman warrior vanished together into the bowels of the aerostat. There was work to be done.

Earth and flame spouted across the snowy plain as Oliver's sixer held to the direction he was urging her; the new steed he had stolen was raised in a Jackelian cavalry regiment and thought little of the thunder and chaos of war, while the Whisperer's gypsy horse just followed because there was a friendly tail in front.

Riding through the confusion of the aerostat bombardment it was hard to tell which way to head. It was only the press of the fey – the concentration of the Special Guard – that allowed him to home in on the eastern flank of the battlefield.

A Jackelian soldier bearing a standard showing the parliamentary colours staggered past, shouting encouragement to a body of troops that was no longer following him. Two of Ben Carl's rebels dragged a third man through the snow, shouting for the surgeon's tent. Oliver pointed to the way he had come but they ignored him and blundered forward towards the Third Brigade's guns. The man they were dragging was dead. Oliver tried to call out to the pair but cannon smoke had swallowed them.

A square of Jackelian infantry emerged from the carnage, their myriad shakos and tunics bearing testament to the fact that theirs was a motley assemblage of soldiers thrown together from the fall of Middlesteel.

An officer in the centre of the square called out to them. 'Have you seen the shiftie exomounts?'

'We haven't come across them,' Oliver called back.

'Watch out, there's a squadron of them riding around here. Lancers.'

The officer started to say something else but a bullet took him from the front and felled him to the ground in the centre of the square – the Jackelians looking in horror at their crumpled lieutenant. From out of the snow a banshee howl preceded a mob of fleeing soldiers, not a charge, but a retreating tumult. Jackelians. The aerostat bombardment had finally broken the army's spirit. Some of the men on the edge of their square peeled off the formation and sprinted away with the deserters, their red tunics easy prey for any passing lancer.

'Hold the line!' Oliver shouted. 'Hold the line!'

They ignored him, hardly hearing his shouts in their terror and desperation.

'The sky,' shouted the Whisperer. 'Look at the sky.'

Many of the aerostats had fallen silent, drifting higher as if their control lines had been severed, but it was what lay beneath them that stopped the routed soldiers in their tracks. Long trails of smoke and snow cloud had formed into sword-carrying spectres, flowing around the aerostats with the elongated outlines of lions running by their sides. It was as if the heavens had opened and the soul of Jackals had spilled from the sky.

'The first kings!' roared the Whisperer. 'The first kings have returned.'

All over the battlefield heads looked up and saw the ghostly army passing across the sky. Riding officers slipped in their saddles, brawling soldiers caught a glimpse of the sight and stumbled, sackpipers drew breath and their fierce sad music was stilled.

* * *

Next to Marshal Arinze, Tzlayloc raged at the Third Brigade's troopers who had stopped loading their cannons to gawp at the sight. 'It's not real, compatriots. It's not real. You fools, it's not real!' He clawed at his skull. 'Get out of my head, get out of my head now.'

'Our airships have been silenced,' said Marshal Arinze staring upwards at the dark shapes gliding through the snow clouds. Stunned by the sudden hush he did not notice that Tzlayloc's body was growing larger, the skin of the Chairman of the First Committee of Jackals swelling in uneven lumps as if beetles were breeding under his skin.

Arinze clicked his fingers for a telescope from one of the staff officers. The aerostats had been holed by the steammen gun-boxes, but it was damage they could shrug off – how many times had he seen Jackals' airships take their own weight in lead ball from his guns and still continue to wreak destruction on the ground? Too many to count. Aerostats were invincible, the floating angels of death of Jackals. Every time Quatérshift had clashed with its neighbour to the west the RAN had devastated their ambitions, and every time it was the terrible floating wall of Jackals that had laid waste to their place as the rightful masters of the continent. You could not lose with the aerial armada of Jackals behind you – that was an immutable law of warfare, of nature itself.

Arinze turned to Major Wildrake, whose beautiful muscles filled out his Third Brigade greatcoat like rocks. 'What can silence our aerostats, major? Nothing in the world can silence them!'

Wildrake did not hear. He was hypnotised by the lions running through the sky, just like he had imagined as a boy, just like he had drawn so many times in pencil on his mother's table.

*　　*　　*

To the east Oliver turned on his horse to look at the Whisperer.

'So many minds,' hissed the fey creature, the illusion of his human warrior's body flickering. 'Steammen, shifties, Jackelians. So different.'

Around them many of the Jackelian soldiers had dropped to their knees, tears in their eyes at having allowed their fear to overcome them and turn them coward long enough to flee the front.

'For the land,' shouted Oliver. 'For Jackals!'

All around them the cry was taken up and the soldiers picked up their rifles and turned back towards the Third Brigade's guns. Near the Whisperer the energy of the land had become inverted in an invisible vortex as his fey power disrupted the natural harmony of the leylines. Oliver grabbed the reins of the gypsy sixer and led them both away from the carnage and towards the press of fey he sensed.

'No,' said the Whisperer. 'Leave me here. I need to concentrate. Everyone must see, everyone must see.'

Oliver nodded and rode off. If the fortunes of war turned again and the Jackelians were driven back the Whisperer would as like be speared by some passing lancer or bayoneted by pursuing Third Brigade troopers.

The eastern flank of the battlefield had lost any vestige of order – there were no columns, lines or formations manoeuvring for advantage in the intricate dance of infantry, artillery and cavalry; instead a sea of steammen knights fought, dotted with islands of Special Guardsmen, centaur-like warriors of the metal trading blows with the onetime protectors of Jackals. Away from the slaughter, a line of elite Third Brigade troops protected the worldsingers of Quatérshift. Like their brethren in Jackals they showed no taste for getting their hands dirty while their fey slaves could be marched into battle to die for them. They stood ready to activate the suicide torc of any guardsmen tempted to flee the battlefield.

In front of them: the cruel theatre of the war. Voiceboxes vibrated with anger, the fighting screams of the orders militant breaking across fey bones where the knights could pin down the guardsmen. Standard-bearers lifted the Special Guard's colours through the sea of deadly steammen, drawing attacks in wave after wave as the knights tried to seize the colours for their mountain halls. A steamman knight that could have been Steamswipe's twin pulled himself past Oliver's horse, his flank torn in half by a fey attack. Used to facing their enemies alongside each other, neither force had any strategies for fighting their former friends to fall back upon. It was the raw power of the feymist pitted against the physical strength of warriors who had been forged for battle. It was not warfare. It was murder being done here.

Oliver knew what to do. It came to him without thinking, a remembrance of the people of the fast-time, the strange shades of the land beyond the feymist curtain. His human vessel vibrated with the power of that other realm, the part of him that belonged to his mother turning and recycling the building force. It grew and grew, the strain of it building dangerously high. Shouts sounded from the worldsingers minding the Special Guard who could see the ripples in the natural fabric of the world. They were pointing in Oliver's direction. Every inch of his flesh was on fire, dimensions that could not exist on Jackals folding around his body, spinning, circling in impossible ways.

By Oliver's feet the damaged steamman was shaking, blue energy electrifying his juddering body, the unfortunate half-dead knight too close to the maelstrom. Bullets from Third Brigade marksmen passed through Oliver, lacking the match of reality to harm him. Oliver yelled in agony as the shockwave of ethereal energy lashed out, radiating across the fields of Rivermarsh in a blast that hammered over the steammen host, hurling fey guardsmen off their feet, sabres and pistols sent turning through the air. Steammen and Special Guardsmen staggered back to their feet, searching for the cause of the blast.

Something *had* changed. Hands reached for throats, feeling the pale skin of their windpipes for the first time in years. Their torcs had disappeared, the hexed collars of slavery gone from the Special Guardsmen's necks. They were free – the freedom that Tzlayloc had promised them and the Commonshare had stolen was their own at last . . . the freedom to choose, to decide who to fight for. Like hounds that had been beaten by a brutal master they turned on the Quatérshiftian line, the startled worldsingers still trying to activate the hexes that would slay the fey before they realized their slaves were no longer melded with the horrendous devices.

The steammen knights seemed as bewildered as the Commonshare's ranks by the sudden about-turn of the Jackelian feybreed. Oliver watched as a general was hefted skyward on a walking platform. It was Master Saw, his weapon limbs dirtier than they had been in the mountain halls of Mechancia, covered in blood and stack soot. He pointed northwest towards the heart of the Third Brigade's formations and his hymn voice carried across the armoured heads of the orders militant, the song picked up by voicebox after voicebox. The steammen host veered off and arrowed towards the centre of the Third Brigade's lines.

'Our advance is stalled,' reported the riding officer to Marshal Arinze. 'The Special Guard have broken their torcs and fight against us.'

Arinze glanced up nervously towards the chequerboard hulls of the fleet drifting uselessly in the wind, the rain of fire-fins replaced by a downpour of dead Quatérshiftian marines and officers. A corpse had actually plummeted down onto one of the cannons in front of him, the body's uniform obviously torn apart by balls from a pressure repeater.

Marshal Arinze tired to indicate to the scout that he should keep his voice down but it was too late. Tzlayloc had heard and stormed over, lifting the soldier from his saddle and crushing his skull as if it were a soft fruit.

'There will be no retreat,' Tzlayloc howled, dropping the limp corpse. 'Victory is ours this day. It is written on the face of the earth.'

With each piece of bad news the leader of the First Committee of Jackals grew larger, as if he was feeding off their despair. He was as tall as an oak tree now, his muscles unnatural and multiplying like the growths of a sickness.

'It shall be as you say, compatriot chairman,' said Arinze, staring up at the creature. And to think he had regarded the labyrinthine politics of Quatérshiftian revolutionary affairs of state as dangerous. A superstitious dread seized the marshal. It was one thing to call on the help of the deities – how many of his troopers still offered furtive prayers to the sun god while the political officers looked the other way? – but to *become* a god, that was something else again. Tzlayloc's obsession was possessing him until it was hard to see where the man began and the Wildcaotyl ended.

'Prepare the book,' said Tzlayloc to his retinue of locust priests. 'The book of Stinghueteotl.'

'Is Xam-ku strong enough to be called?' asked one of the priests.

'I *am* Xam-ku!' shouted Tzlayloc. 'Do you not see how I am swelled by her grace? It is time for the Wildcaotyl to prove their fidelity to the cause. To seal the fate of these mill-master maggots and their Free State lackeys. Not a servant or minor calling, but the *great* ones – let them walk the halls of Chimeca again with their communityist brethren.'

In the shadow of the command dome, King Steam turned to Coppertracks and his warrior mu-bodies standing sentry. 'Prepare my war body, the time has come.'

'The seers have thrown the cogs of Gear-gi-ju, Your Majesty,' said Coppertracks. 'The auguries are unclear, poor at best. The Loas are exhausted, many are withdrawing. We feed on light and order and I fear today is a dark day.'

'Thousands of the people lay deactivate, Coppertracks, in the aberrant snow of our friends' land. I will not abandon the light. I will not abandon a millennium of harmony and evolution to the laws of superstition and the malicious will of the enemy. I will not ask the knights steammen to support a cause I would not myself fight for. The old enemy prepares to walk our earth again and by the beard of Zaka of the Cylinders, I will meet him.'

The child-like monarch of the Free State watched the slip-thinkers and courtiers fall away as a platform raised him into the heart of his war body. A clatter of steel cage walls enveloped the King. Mu-bodies of a dozen slipthinkers swarmed over his frame, checking the pressure systems, filling the ammunition bins and oiling the joints of numerous fighting arms.

'Bring me my arms,' called the King. 'Bring me my sword and shield.'

It took three knights apiece to carry the sovereign's weapons to him, his shield made of transparent blue crystal with a rim of spiked metal that crackled with the power electric; his sword as tall as four steammen with a cluster of stubby barrels around the buckler. King Steam's manipulator arms lifted the

ancient weapons away from his retainers, and he tested the
air with his blade, the fanned air blowing snow powder across
the command post. Their service done, the steammen flowed
away from his hull, leaving the monarch to face the mass of
the enemy, metal feet juddering the ground as he turned.

Hoggstone and the Jackelian officers came running up to
King Steam. 'Your Majesty, what are you doing? Your place
is here, coordinating your army.'

'First Guardian, I was a warrior before I was a king,' said
the steamman, the spheres of his voicebox shaking in their
mounts. 'And a warrior defends his people.'

Commodore Black turned to Coppertracks as the King
thumped away. 'Sweet Circle! Aliquot Coppertracks, where
is the big fellow heading off to?'

'Where, commodore? I believe he is going to die.'

Oliver found the Whisperer collapsed in the snow, the warrior
illusion replaced by the reality of malformed muscles and flesh
without form. Of his gypsy sixer there was no sign.

'Nathaniel?' asked Oliver. Oliver had to shake the body
before the feybreed started to come to.

'Something pulled the ground from under me,' hissed the
Whisperer. 'I felt it in the earth, in the bones of the world. It
smelled like the Lady of the Lights, but she was stronger, far
stronger.'

'It was not the Lady of the Lights,' said Oliver.

This was dangerous. The Shadow Bear was making
unauthorized interventions of his own. The thing had become
so desperate to finish the job he was designed for, he was
tipping the balance in favour of the very forces he was intended
to sterilize. He wanted the Wildcaotyl to win the day – to
begin the work of birthing their own gods into a realm too
small to contain them – to give him his mandate for total war.

'I told you, she's been replaced by something else, something fierce and wicked that wants us to fail.'

'Whatever it is I hurt the bastard thing,' said the Whisperer. 'It's not much good on detail, just like the Lady of the Lights. That is its weakness: you become the detail and it gets confused, like a slipsharp being attacked by a school of shrimp.'

'Nathaniel,' said Oliver. 'If you have been unconscious, just who in the Circle's name is doing that?'

The Whisperer looked to where Oliver was pointing. The sky was still full of the ghostly lions and ancient warrior-chieftains the fey convict had conjured across the armies' minds, banshees whipped on the wind and riding the sky underneath the drifting aerostats.

'Well I *will* be jiggered,' hissed the Whisperer. His body rippled and transformed back into the ancient duellist from his storybook.

Oliver remounted and helped the Whisperer onto the back of his saddle when Captain Flare stumbled into sight, his guardsman's tunic torn to pieces where the steammen knights had tried to pierce him with lance and repeater ball. There was a red weal around his neck where the torc had once been.

He looked at Oliver with a glimmer of recognition, his eyes widening when he noticed the Whisperer. In some way he saw straight through the feybreed's illusion, his eyes as true as his demigod-like strength. 'That is fey? Dear Circle, I have never seen a body so changed by the mist that wasn't killed by it.'

'You should have spent less time at the palace and visited the lower levels of Hawklam Asylum, pretty boy.'

Oliver touched his neck. 'No more collars, captain. No more orders.'

'You?' said Flare, astonished. 'There isn't enough power in the world to remove the hex that binds.'

'Not enough power in this one, perhaps. Yet here you stand, free – but free to do what?'

'My son,' said Flare. 'I want my son.'

'Son?' said Oliver. 'But you're not married, man, the penny dreadfuls always made a big thing about what a marvellous bachelor you were!'

'Oliver, you turnip – it's Prince Alpheus,' hissed the Whisperer. 'That's his son, flapping like a flag on a standard by Tzlayloc's side.'

'Only a few in the Special Guard know that!'

'I am in your guard, pretty boy. You might say I am the night watch.'

'We'll ride with you,' said Oliver. 'It's about time Tzlayloc stepped down from the First Committee.'

'Three fey boys to save Jackals,' sighed Flare. 'We're not much.'

'I reckon we'll do,' said Oliver.

Tzlayloc and King Steam closed on the battlefield, the armies of the Third Brigade and parliament breaking around their feet as the two titans clashed. The Chairman of the First Committee of Jackals was half again as tall as King Steam's war frame now. His body had become a mass of writhing flesh, creatures with compound eyes and bones as sharp as craynarbian sword arms sprouting from his muscles, leaping off to decapitate Jackelian soldiers and feast on the corpses of the dead scattered across the snow. The two leaders fought inside a surf of two opposing mists, the monarch of the Free State supported by his weakening Loas – as insubstantial as stack steam under the assault of the Wildcaotyl – clouds of dark droning wasps which swung around the steamman, exploding then reforming like schools of black fish. Where they swarmed over the soldiers fighting in the titans' shadows the warriors collapsed clutching their ears, the whine of the Wildcaotyl staying in their brains, intensifying and warping until their eardrums exploded, parliamentarians smashing their heads against rocks and rolling in the snow, as if the ice could cool the pain of the unholy song.

A thing with four clawed feet, hardly a body at all, erupted from Tzlayloc's shoulder and leapt across the gap between the chairman and King Steam. The Wildcaotyl manifestation locked onto the pilot frame and tried to drive a claw into the skull of the King's golden child-form. King Steam dodged the claw, twisting left and right as the razor bone plunged past him. One of the King's chest-mounted pressure repeaters managed to find the right angle and depressed its barrel, hurling the clawing beast off in a storm of pellets.

Slipping the grip of one of Tzlayloc's tentacle limbs King Steam arced his sword arm around, severing the branch of thrashing flesh. The limb fell onto the snow, crushing a Third Brigade trooper and growing millipede-like legs of bone, then rushing towards the King's leg and wrapping itself around the steel in a circle of maddened, slathering tissue. A locust head with rotating jaws forced itself out of the stump where Tzlayloc's tentacle had been severed, looking around and hissing at the monarch.

'This is my time,' jeered Tzlayloc. 'Your reign is over. I have no need for the whir and tick of iron toys, of clockwork slaves.'

King Steam backed away from Tzlayloc, a rotating lantern viewer in front of his pilot cage showing him multiple perspectives of the Chairman of Jackals. 'And I have no need for your stillborn vision for the world. You have become a sickness, Tzlayloc. You have made yourself a cancer on the belly of the world and to save my people, I will cut you out.'

Tzlayloc menaced the war frame with his tentacles and

tilted his head back to laugh, shiny dark things like beetles spilling from his mouth as he did so. 'I will place your soul board on top of the stack of broken components I shall build of your people, little toy. Your race's very existence offends me – you are nothing but a conjurer's trick of crafty mathematics slipping through ore and crystal.'

King Steam shut down his olfactory senses as the heat and stench from Tzlayloc's throat carried across on the wind. 'You shall not hunt my kind again. Never!'

The Free State's ruler pistoned to the side as Tzlayloc hurled a ball of pulp and snapping claws at him. Tzlayloc made an obscene gesture with the fronds that used to be a hand. 'Rust has not yet addled your memory then, I see, king of the toys. After the mountains of Mechancia have been buried under the advancing glaciers, I shall enjoy watching your children cannibalizing each other for food again and scrabbling to avoid my cull.'

Warding off the chairman's swinging arms with his shield, King Steam riddled the trunk-like flesh with a line of soft eruptions from his repeater shells. 'Listen to me, Tzlayloc; listen to me with the softbody heart that is still buried somewhere in that monstrosity of a body you have grown. Your allies plan to freeze our realm with more than ice this time. They would breach the walls of the world and forever silence the dance of time and energy. Whatever philosophies you hold to, whatever dreams you have for Jackals, the Wildcaotyl do not plan to honour them. They will betray you! Your movement is nothing more to them than a host body to lay their eggs inside – they will consume you and make dust of your plans.'

'LIAR!' Tzlayloc's body writhed as if it were on fire, every inch of his bulk pulsing and coming alive. The Chairman of Jackals lurched forward, trying to break through the royal war frame's defences. 'They lifted the Chimecans to supremacy for a thousand years, saved them from the coldtime. Without their succour the race of man would be extinct. How much longer will the Wildcaotyl support our flawless Commonshare where we live in perfect cooperation, a precise mirror of their selfless association? There will be no slave revolt this time, little toy, no clever machines hiding under the ice to pour poison and sedition into the minds of the people.'

King Steam said nothing, but let his sword speak for him, the four barrels around its hilt detonating and carrying cannon balls filled with chemical poison, toxins from the Hall of Architects, into Tzlayloc's chest. Screaming creatures fell out of the craters where the balls had struck and two enraged tentacles coiled out of Tzlayloc, one seizing the King's sword arm while the other smashed into his pilot frame and sent him reeling.

The King looked down in revulsion as the centipede-like limb wrapped around his ankle started burning its way through the leg of his war body, clouds of molten metal spitting out as the Wildcaotyl sweated an acid of appalling complexity. King Steam fired a manipulator arm like a trident, spearing the burning thing, but it was too late. His leg parted, the armour foot-tread left burning in the snow as the King's body started to topple backwards.

In desperation the falling king pitched his shield like a discus at Tzlayloc, the energy bleed from the spikes of the rim tearing at Tzlayloc's face as he swayed back. The shield sailed past and embedded itself in the high ground behind him, Tzlayloc exultant as he looked down at the fallen monarch. King Steam's body-mounted weapons were emptying their ammunition drums at the swarm of Wildcaotyl flowing off Tzlayloc, but it was to no avail – the chairman howled a victory scream. Loas swirled down, forming a shield that started to crumple as the black arrows of the Wildcaotyl broke against it.

Tzlayloc's devils halted in confusion. Behind the wounded monarch, stamping across the battlefield and making the ground tremble, came a wave of war bodies, each piloted by a child-like steamman. Following the war frames a wave of steammen knights charged to the aid of their collapsed monarch, Tzlayloc's demon creatures leaping and crawling to meet the attack.

'How many mu-bodies do you have, little toy?' hissed Tzlayloc, looking down at the fallen monarch. 'It does not matter. I shall rip them all apart and cast your melted slag into images of the Wildcaotyl for the temples of the people.'

'You shall not triumph, Tzlayloc.'

'Have you glimpsed the future, little toy?' laughed Tzlayloc. 'I shall set a new future for you and your people. For all of Jackals and the world beyond. Did the roll of the cogs in the filthy puddle of your own juices show you your death?'

'They did,' groaned King Steam.

Tzlayloc watched in amusement as the weakening Loas faltered around the royal war frame and glanced across at the advancing drone bodies. 'Then I shall leave you to it. You may live just long enough to see the last of your army trodden into the mud.'

Inside the pilot cage King Steam's golden hand fell limply off the control levers. He had to stay alive a little longer yet. There was something he had to wait for before he departed the field of battle, before he moved along the great pattern. Tzlayloc had to be kept distracted. He dare not shut down his pain receptors, in case the lack of sensation carried him away. His time here was ended, but he had to suffer the pain a little longer. Each second became an eternity of torture for the monarch.

*   *   *

To the rear of Tzlayloc, Marshal Arinze's trumpeters sounded new orders. The disciplined lines of the Third Brigade closed into a defensive formation, the equalized outlaws of Grimhope that had been held in reserve at last marching down in columns to lend support. Arinze had fought the Free State both under the flag of the old regime and for the Commonshare – he knew what to expect, as did his soldiers. Canisters of harpoon-like barbs were unloaded from the ammunition train and rolled towards their artillery.

A riding officer galloped up to the marshal. 'Gun-boxes, compatriot marshal. Advancing from the east.'

'Ride to the battery,' ordered Arinze. 'Tell the artillery captains to concentrate their fire on those royal war bodies. Halt them before they get to our lines.'

After the artillery crews had resighted their cannons and fired the first ranging shots it would have taken an observant eye on a telescope to notice that the four war frames seemed surprisingly resilient to the barbs of their canister fire. Or that explosions on the downs to the east were mirroring the explosions around the giant steammen – exactly where they would be falling if they were passing unhindered through the war frames.

Captain Flare jumped onto the dying monarch's chest, the steel plates flexing under the impact of his dense fey bones. Oliver was quick behind him, climbing up handholds in the metal. The Whisperer stayed in the lee of the broken war body, muttering with the effort of creating the living illusion of steammen war bodies, a slightly different angle of view needed for every bystander in Rivermarsh. A roar of fury behind them indicated that the mountain of flesh that was now Tzlayloc had finally discovered the trick that had been played on him.

Flare gazed across at the terrible creature. He did not see the Chairman of the First Committee, or Jacob Walwyn, or any threat to Jackals worthy of his guardsman's oath, he did not even see the betrayer of his fey people's hopes for freedom. He saw the monster that had strung up his son like a rabbit to be skinned and used as a lure. Flare leapt down from the wrecked war frame and met Tzlayloc's charge – Oliver swore the ground shook as the Special Guardsman ran.

'Oliver.'

The Whisperer was climbing up the war body, his shape flickering back and forth from bronzed warrior to his true form.

'Oliver.' It was not the Whisperer speaking – it was King Steam. The steamman looked in a bad way, the right side of his body crushed underneath the crumpled pilot guard, the left pierced by bone-sword strikes and scarred by acid trails.

'Your Majesty, your knights are coming for you.'

'The hardest part of being a monarch is knowing the time of your own death,' said King Steam.

'Your people can save you.'

The King had barely heard Oliver. 'How else can a route for the new king be prepared?'

Oliver pulled at the frame but it was too badly mangled; removing it by violence would tear the steamman apart.

'Stop trying to save me, young softbody,' whispered King Steam. 'Instead, save both our races. The Wildcaotyl feed on souls and the worship of their kind, on the very life of the earth. The souls are of Jackals and the Free State and the Wildcaotyl need the bones of the earth to drain them; when you move along the Circle you move through the bones of the earth. We are the songs of stardust, Oliver, and like all insects the Wildcaotyl are drawn to our flame. Snuff out the flame. . .'

Snuff out the flame!

Captain Flare was surrounded by a sea of Tzlayloc's devils, more and more of them emerging from that deformed body. Flare smashed and crushed the creatures, so covered in blood and the insects' perverted pulp that he looked like a crimson golem come out of the kiln. Broken Wildcaotyl littered the field, swarms of their brethren climbing the wall of corpses to hurl themselves at the Special Guardsman.

Captain Flare was just one man. Soon his fey flesh began to weaken. His rain of punches slowed as more and more of the Wildcaotyl impaled and scraped at his iron body with their claws.

Snuff out the flame.

Oliver extended his senses over the battlefield, reaching for the bones of the earth, but there was so much evil to ignore. Parliament's forces were wavering as they clashed against the disciplined ranks of the Third Brigade, too few professional soldiers and too many amateur street fighters and Carlist rebels filling out their companies' lists. The steammen knights were bogged down amidst the Wildcaotyl horde while ranks of metal-fleshers and First Brigade reinforcements pinned down any scattered Special Guardsmen who had not fled Rivermarsh for freedom. But underneath all the confusion the lattice of the earth's leylines still throbbed, weak and thin after being drained and tapped by worldsingers on both sides.

Around Tzlayloc's misshapen form the lines were distorted and diffuse, the power of the Wildcaotyl a weight on the surface of the world that she could barely support. Now Oliver saw it, the pain and horror of the battlefield being channelled through the bones of the world, the earth a sponge soaking up the blood and souls for the Wildcaotyl to sup on, each new morsel allowing more of them to uncoil through the cracks in the world. The essence of the Jackelians was being destroyed like coke thrown into a furnace, with the world the insects' boiler, an engine to power their insane mission for calling down their unholy high gods.

'Oliver,' hissed the Whisperer. 'Ware the enemy.'

At the foot of the fallen war frame a wave of Wildcaotyl demons were clambering up the steamman weapon, but Oliver did not hear the Whisperer's warning – his attention was spreading out along the lattice of leylines, travelling along the bones of the world.

The Whisperer swore. These things were hard to fool, inhuman, their minds warped flesh that had been unnaturally multiplied from the hive of Tzlayloc's body. Their dreams were cold alien things. He focused. With snarls of anger the creatures fell upon each other, seeing Special Guardsmen rather than their own foul forms, tearing into each other.

Oblivious to the carnage being inflicted at the foot of the King's war body, Oliver started to realign the leylines around him, reforming and re-knitting the strength of the land, drawing the power into himself, a trickle at first – then a stream, then a torrent. Worldsingers on both sides of the battlefield fainted as the source of their wizardry disappeared, their hexes and spells falling apart even as they called them. There seemed an endless reservoir inside Oliver now, a well without an end to soak away the earth's power. At the edge of the battlefield he could feel the Shadow Bear's rage simmering at the intervention. Legitimate though, thought Oliver. The poor little fey boy was making good.

Below, the Wildcaotyl fighting each other were weakening, their mosquito barb into the repast of Jackals blocked. Tzlayloc realized the source of the threat as the shapes breeding inside his skin dried up, cracking and halting in stillbirth. Roaring he turned, wading through steammen knights and his own Wildcaotyl children without care, the mass of his horde heeding his call and breaking away from the steammen, flooding towards the fallen monarch's shell. Captain Flare's body lay in the snow behind them, his clothes ripped to pieces, his muscles scarred and purple. The Captain of the Guard was no more.

Above Rivermarsh the snow clouds had partially cleared, revealing a blue sky filled with drifting aerostats, their control lines cut and helpless before the whims of wind and weather. The Wildcaotyl were losing their ability to reshape the land now, to impose the cold perfection of the hive on Jackals. The false shadows of the steammen war frames flickered out of existence as the Whisperer turned his attention towards the wave of creatures heading towards him. Wildcaotyl stumbled and scrambled as they felt themselves plunged back into the icy angleless realm they had been exiled to, but there were too many for the feybreed's illusion to hold.

Beneath his boots Oliver felt the King's war body tremble. Had his interference with the earth's power caused a floatquake? Surely not. What he was doing was only a variation of what the worldsingers did, tempering the earth's passion to control the land that could be pushed towards the heavens on her temper. Earth fountained up in front of Tzlayloc, a geyser of molten worldstuff rising as tall as the chairman of the First Committee and showering burning rocks across the Wildcaotyl. The shambling mountain of flesh that had been Jacob Walwyn fell back, the spray flaming across the children of Xam-ku that had been birthed out of his tissue.

Something else was coming, surfing a wave of the earth's fury. Oliver felt the bones of the world vibrate, his reformed lattice swept away as a tsunami of earthflow poured out of the hole, sweeping him aside, shattering against the feeding Wildcaotyl.

Leylines reformed around the battlefield, impossible complex shapes, swirling around a white sphere hovering before Tzlayloc.

'Sweet Circle,' hissed the Whisperer.

Oliver felt a burning on his hip. His two belt pistols were glowing, pulsing to the rhythm of the sphere. 'The Hexmachina.'

'Not that. Its twice-jiggered *friends*!' said the Whisperer, pointing up towards a cloud of dark spheres plummeting towards them from the firmament. Aerospheres, a rain of aerospheres. The Court of the Air had emerged out of myth; the wolftakers were protecting their flock at last.

Oliver drew his witch-blade as the first wave of Wildcaotyl demons mounted the King's war body, eager to devour the feybreed who had interrupted their feeding. The Wildcaotyl had been driven into apoplexy by the appearance of the Hexmachina, and now they were boiling towards Oliver and his fey companion.

'It's time for Judgement,' said Oliver.

United with the Hexmachina, Molly Templar felt the battle joined across a myriad levels, the Wildcaotyl immediately trying to subvert her modification of the leylines. *They* had already been weakened, the enemy starved. She recognized the presence of the strange fey boy from Tzlayloc's cells. The unnatural barrenness of the earth around them was his doing. He had put a choke hold on the enemy's windpipe, she could feel the souls of the dead moving uncertainly through the bones of the earth, and with a push of her will she created a puncture for them to escape to where they belonged.

Ignoring the pain of the other operator still burning across the Hexmachina, she pushed back the Wildcaotyl attacks, as if severing the strands of a spider's web one by one. Memories of the previous conflict between the Wildcaotyl and the seven

Hexmachina kept on passing through Molly's mind, the other operators – the other races – the grasper, the craynarbian, the lashlite, the – she pushed them out, leaving just the memory of Vindex to advise her.

Xam-ku, most powerful deity of the Wildcaotyl pantheon, wrapped itself around her, trying to burn through the Hexmachina's shields. So, it was still fighting the last war. A millennium of exile had taught the Wildcaotyl nothing. That was their weakness. The perfect order of the hive craved stasis. All end to the bubbling chaotic growth of the tree of life, the world remade in amber in their image.

<I have learnt,> whispered the Hexmachina. <A thousand years of lessons from my lover, a thousand years of progression. Let me show you.>

Molly learnt too. She changed the set of the bones of the world, changed it again and again. Faster and faster. The Wildcaotyl howled as she transformed the great pattern faster than they could adapt to it. Pushing them a little further back into the abyss they had crawled from with each shift.

The thing that did not belong, the dark angel on the corner of Rivermarsh, bayed across inhuman frequencies as it saw its opportunity for total war disappearing before its senses. She – or was it the Hexmachina? – felt a twinge of sympathy for the Shadow Bear. It was intended for only one thing, and what was the point of a bomb that could not explode?

Now the Wildcaotyl strained for their life in this realm – feeling the cold depths of the angleless realm open up behind them – an eternity of hunger, an eternity of waiting, dreaming of nourishment. They flailed desperately, trying to find the souls in the bones of the world, trying to find the life of the land, but the ground around them was barren – it was the young feybreed from the cells, stealing their energy out from underneath their perverted weight on the world.

<The sword,> whispered Molly.

Oliver ducked underneath the wavering tentacles of one of Tzlayloc's demons, slicing out with his witch-blade. 'The shield.'

Weighted cable lines whirled down between Oliver and the Whisperer, three soldiers riding the lines from their aerosphere towards King Steam's war body.

Nathaniel's body had changed; he wore the illusion of the incrementals landing around them, a black leather cape and menacing rubber tubes hanging at either side of his hood. Now the Whisperer looked identical to the Court of the Air's fighting order, but he had plucked an officer's insignia from their minds for his chest. The soldiers opened fire as they landed, steel boilers strapped on their backs hissing steam as they drew power for their odd-looking guns: thin metal lances connected to rubber belts implanted with crystal shells. No suicide guns these, they fired like a thousand windows being shattered simultaneously, as the shells were pulled through their lances.

They fanned out, firing down into the horde of Wildcaotyl devils trying to scramble up the corpse of King Steam, clouds of rotten flesh and demon-grown blood showering the snow and the side of the collapsed steamman war frame.

In front of them Tzlayloc's flesh had hived off into a swarm of dark insects, attempting to enclose the golden halo of the Hexmachina, but the Wildcaotyl had entered Jackals too early and the seething mass was tiring, slowing, blinking out of existence as they expended the unholy energy they needed to survive. Jacob Walwyn was growing smaller and smaller, collapsing back into his man-shape as rolls of his giant's flesh peeled off and cavorted in agony around him, being pushed and assailed from all sides: drained by their fey assailant, impaled on the steammen knights' battle arms, shot to pieces by the black-clad soldiers landing in their midst. Behind the Wildcaotyl the disciplined lines of the Third Brigade were disintegrating as the aerospheres of the Court hovered over the battlefield, emptying fin-bombs into the shiftie ranks.

Marshal Arinze was shouting orders to his artillery to elevate their cannons, but it was too late. The only aerostats in this battle should have been on his side and the Court of the Air was blowing his batteries apart. His skirmishers were trying to meet the black-clad soldiers that had been dropped down around Rivermarsh, but the troopers were falling to the enemy snipers' long guns and the impossibly fast rate of fire from the interloper's weapons.

He was about to give the order to the forward companies to fight a rearguard cover while the rest of the Third Brigade withdrew to Middlesteel – the defensive plan they should have stuck with from the start – when one of the Free State's advancing gun-boxes found the range of the Quatérshiftian general staff. Shells thumped into the hard snowy ground and the issue of whether Arinze's positions around Middlesteel would hold or not became academic.

On the royal war frame Oliver stood up from the buckled pilot cage. King Steam was deactivate, his body still and empty. Somewhere in Mechancia the seers of the mountain kingdom would be throwing the Gear-gi-ju cogs to locate the steamman child that would be the latest incarnation of their monarch. Across the field Oliver watched the Hexmachina swooping over Tzlayloc's remaining demons, the golden halo burning their skin, beetles scrambling for the darkness of the cracks.

Oliver glanced across to the enemy lines shrouded in smoke from gun-box fire. The cross that had held the crucified prince was empty! There was no life left in Flare's body, but his son had disappeared; had one of the Special Guard honoured their commander's dying wish and rescued the young noble?

At Oliver's side one of the Court's warriors pulled down his leather hood, the rubber air tubes dangling around his gloves. It was the disreputable Stave! Somehow Oliver was not surprised. But if this figure was Harry, where was the Whisperer? Nathaniel had disappeared into the confusion of the battle. He had plans, and they did not include the Court of the Air or the worldsingers scooping him up for his cell back in Hawklam.

'Damson Griggs always said you turned up like a bad penny, Harry.'

'A bad penny with good timing,' said Harry. 'The shifties are being routed.'

'Looks like they're retreating back to the deep atmospheric line.'

'Bloody good luck to them, then, old stick. The incrementals have already paid it a little visit. The only way back home for them now is a long trek to the border and a prayer to their sun god that their worldsingers have found the key to their cursewall.'

'They're all going to die, aren't they?'

Harry shrugged. 'A message, Oliver. You don't poke your nose in Jackals' affairs and expect to keep it on your face.'

'Your people arranged for the worldsingers who knew how to take down the cursewall to be fingered in the purges, didn't they? You were never in danger, Harry.'

'A wall protects both ways, and I was *always* in danger,' said Stave. 'The hunt for us was real. We knew the Court had been infiltrated. The only way for us to find out how wide and deep it went was for me to act as bait. Make the shifties think I knew about their plans and go on the run, see who would come after us. It was far worse than we feared or suspected. The radicals had people in the Court of the Air, in the whistler network, in Ham Yard, in Greenhall, in the regiments and the navy. They called in all their favours to track us down and we followed the chain all the way back.'

'A few more bodies floating down the Gambleflowers,' said Oliver. 'A few more prisoners for the cells of the Court.'

'That's the way the great game is played.'

Oliver looked out across the battlefield. It was twilight now. Had they really been fighting all day? He was exhausted; his body still aching with the power of the earth that had flowed through his fey bones. 'My family paid the price. Our allies, our people, the people in Middlesteel. They all paid the price.'

'Dear Circle, lad. We would have stopped this if we could,' spat Harry. 'That's what we do. We didn't know about Shadowclock or the Special Guard or Tzlayloc's plans for a return to the old ways. When I volunteered to be the bait I just thought this was going to be 1581 all over again – a bunch of Carlist extremists with Commonshare gold jingling in their pockets who wanted Hoggstone's head on the end of a pike. We watch, Oliver. But we are not omnipotent, we are not gods.'

Oliver stared at the remaining Wildcaotyl fleeing from the radiance of the Hexmachina and nodded. 'No, Harry, you are right. No gods for Jackals. Never again.'

'Your uncle knew the risks, Oliver. I'm sorry about Titus, I really am. But you know the man he was. He would have given his life twenty times over to save Jackals.'

The sound of sackpipes floated across the fields of Rivermarsh and Oliver heard a sixer whinny. It was Mad Jack, in the shadow of the steamman war frame. 'Good hunting, young fellow?'

'Yes, major. Where's Guardian McConnell?'

'There's a bit of her over there, and a bit more over that way. Damn bloody shiftie cannon took her head off. Met that gypsy filly by the way, mad as hell at you. Wants her horse back.'

Oliver looked around. 'I believe it ran off.'

'Ah well, she's a witch – she'll call it back to her.' Mad Jack stared up at Harry and the incremental soldiers. 'You bally navy types took your time. Marine regiment?'

Harry tapped the gold lion on his leather tunic. 'Political.'

Mad Jack tapped the side of his nose. 'Ah yes, enough said.'

'I would say the Commonshare are losing, major,' said Oliver.

Mad Jack turned his sixer towards the fleeing Third Brigade troopers. 'Of course. We're Jackelians, and this is our land, eh? Best be back at it, there's plenty of trees between here and Quatérshift and a lot of rope for stringing them up.'

'Good hunting, major.'

Harry watched the cavalryman kick his horse after the retreating Third Brigade companies. 'We need to talk, Oliver.'

Oliver nodded. 'Somehow I thought we might.'

The Court of the Air had weapon-smiths. Mother Loade had been right.

Chapter Twenty-Six

Commodore Black stepped out in front of the two figures fleeing the battlefield, one of them so weak he was staggering – practically being carried by the other. 'Ah now, Jamie, it seems like you are in the same pickle as I.'

Jamie Wildrake looked up. 'Well, well, the Duke of Ferniethian.'

The submariner pointed to the semi-conscious body the agent was hauling behind him. 'Thinking of becoming a royalist, now your wolftaker friends are after you?'

Wildrake dropped Prince Alpheus's body in the snow. 'The House of Guardians will pay to get him back. I'll share the reward with you.'

'What's a king worth, Jamie? As much as the reward that was on my head, for the sea boots of poor old Samson Dark? As much as the blood money they paid you for the fleet in exile? A king must be a rare old thing these days – how many of the royal breeding house did your compatriots push into a Gideon's Collar?'

Wildrake put his hand on his sabre's hilt. 'One too few, it seems. Let's just say noble pedigrees will be at a premium once the Guardians discover how many royals were processed inside the collars. Now get out of my way, fat man.'

The commodore pulled his sabre out. 'You're right to be blessed worried, Jamie. There are worldsingers lying comatose all over Rivermarsh with faces like they're sucking on a berry with no juice. You're duelling on barren ground, Jamie, but even without your witch fighting tricks you've still got those fine muscles of yours. Why don't you show me what they're worth?'

Wildrake thrust out with no warning, his steel springing off the commodore's sword.

'Not bad for a fat man, eh?' said the commodore. 'The royal fleet wasn't fussy, we couldn't afford to be, could we? Our boats took crew from all over. You remember, don't you?'

Wildrake stamped down and feinted, following through with a slashing cut, but the commodore turned it with hardly a movement. It was the kind of spare duelling style that would serve a fighter well in the confined corridors of a submarine vessel.

'Concorzia, the Catosian League, the Holy Kikkosico Empire of – all those different fighting styles, you pick up a little bit here, a little bit there.'

Wildrake moved his sword from side to side, trying to batter his way through the commodore's guard with his superior strength.

'I would say the Court's duelling masters were heavily influenced by the east.'

Wildrake switched the sabre to his left hand and darted in, the ring of steel unheard except by the prone form of Prince Alpheus.

'One cut, one kill,' said the commodore. 'Fast, deadly, versatile. Everything they admire out Thar way. You're good, Jamie.'

'Shut up!' shouted Wildrake. 'Stop talking and fight me!'

'Be careful of what you wish for, lad.' The commodore's sword nipped out and Wildrake caught and turned it, but not before Black nicked the corner of the wolftaker's shirtsleeve, a line of red blood traced across the white silk.

'You should have kept your jacket for protection, Jamie,' said Black. 'But I can see why you chose to throw it away. Commonshare uniforms have never been popular in Jackals and it's the poor that are going to be wearing them in Middlesteel now, after the looters have stripped the corpses of all your friends – and the uniforms have been dyed a decent Jackelian green and brown by the ladies down Handsome Lane.'

Wildrake thrust forward, feinting, changing sword hand from left to right then slicing out at the commodore's arm, drawing blood in a mirror of the submariner's strike.

'A duke's blood looks the same as mine,' spat Wildrake, circling the commodore slowly.

'So they trained you to fight as a secret lefty,' coughed the commodore, giving ground by a couple of steps. 'They're a sharp crew, alright, your clever friends above the clouds. Still dreaming Kirkhill's visions after all these years.'

Wildrake snarled, flipping the sabre between his hands. 'Sharp enough to take you, Samson Dark.'

Wildrake stamped forward, sending a flurry of muddy snow spraying over the commodore's trousers, the clatter of steel floating hollow in the silence of the twilight battlefield. Black curved his opponent's blade away twice, diverting the agent's thrusts with small turns. There was a dull ache in the commodore's arm, the pain of having to hold the weight of the sabre telling now. Wildrake's unnatural shine-stimulated muscles gave him the edge in a contest of endurance. The popinjay probably spent hours in front of a mirror holding a sword out straight, relishing the pain of the weight. Admiring himself.

'Just how much would parliament pay for Prince Alpheus's return?' wheezed the commodore, swaying his sword defensively.

Wildrake grinned. 'Trying to buy time to recover, fat man? You should have spent less time feeding your face in the pantry and more time down the muscle pits.'

'I should have, Jamie. I should have. But maybe the old pirate in me wonders how much I could get for the boy's head.'

Wildrake tried to cut under the commodore's guard. Black barely managed to parry the attack. It was like being battered by a windmill. Relentless vigour without end. Only his defensive fighting style was keeping him alive.

'Sell out one of your own? No, duke. I don't think you're ready for that. You are a sentimentalist, pining for an age that was buried by history long before either of us was born.'

The commodore stamped left but swung right, slipping his blade beneath Wildrake's sabre, trapping it, then with a deft twist spinning the weapon out of the wolftaker's hand and onto the ground. The blade impaled itself in the snow and stood there quivering.

'I should give you the same chance you gave the fleet when you blew us out to the RAN's airships,' said the commodore. 'But maybe I am a sentimentalist, Jamie.' He stepped back and bowed slightly, pointing to the fallen sword with the tip of his sabre.

Wildrake shook his head and grinned ferociously, retrieving his blade without taking his eyes off the commodore. 'You have to be joking! Dark, you are a piece of work and no mistake. You never would have made a wolftaker in a thousand years.'

'You're as cold as your friends, Jamie. The Court and the Commonshare both. You never understood; that piece of metal in your hand is only as good as the heart of the man behind it. You've got the moves and you've got the sinews, but they couldn't give you the heart. You're just a weapon, Jamie, a shiny sabre all bent out of shape and dirty from the hands of the bludgers and assassins who have used you.'

'And you're a relic, Dark. The last of the royal privateers. The last of a dead age. They should stuff you and put you in the museum back in Middlesteel next to one of the old monarchs.'

'That they haven't is not for want of trying. You broke my heart, Jamie, when I found out it was you that was the Court's man on the boats, that it was you that blew on the fleet. You would have made a fine fleet-man if we could have fixed your soul – one of the best.'

Wildrake roared and thrust forward, but the submariner turned sideways and with a – snap – snap – snap – Commodore Black parried past Wildrake's cuts using short controlled butterfly strokes that almost seemed too slight to be effective. But with each snap of metal Black pressed his sabre a little closer until – almost gently – he pushed the blade into the turncoat's chest, sliding it right through Wildrake's heart. 'For old time's sake, Jamie, for old time's sake.'

Wildrake looked at the blade impaled into his body with incredulity. 'I am tight – my muscles – so tight – your body – so flabby.'

Black shoved Wildrake off his sabre with his boot. 'You're all piss and wind, Jamie.'

Wildrake collapsed, falling on the snow, watching disbelievingly as the commodore staggered back and lifted up the prone form of Prince Alpheus.

Black pointed to the smoke of the battlefield rising behind

them. 'You're one of us, Jamie. A Jackelian with the blood of kings running through your veins. Why did you do it?'

'I just got tired – old man. Of the dirt and the pain. The Court was too weak. The Commonshare had what is required to change things. I could have – made – our country perfect.'

'We're a blessed weak people, Jamie, for a perfect idea. Well now, it looks like I've saved the Court the trouble of hunting you down, so I think I shall take the lad as my payment and be saying my goodbyes to you.'

'They will – find – you.'

Black winked before he limped away, hauling the prince behind him. 'You killed Samson Dark, remember? And poor old Blacky, well, he is a hero of the war of 1596 – fought alongside the First Guardian at Rivermarsh, so he did. You killed Samson Dark and now I have returned the favour. I believe that rounds things out nicely.'

When the wolftakers found Wildrake's body, the bloody message of accusation against Samson Dark that he had written in the snow had long since melted away into the meadow grass.

Molly was not sure how long she had been standing on the downs of Rivermarsh when she realized the melting snow was soaking her feet. Despite the fall of night it was warmer now than it had been earlier, the seasons of Jackals returning to normal. Her body felt strange, as if she was not sure where she began and the Hexmachina ended. The land seemed part of her still.

A pile of burrowed dirt in front of her was the only clue that the events of the day had not been a dream. Once more the Hexmachina had returned to her lover's embrace. The Wildcaotyl had faded away like an echo in a well. Down the hill a few torches moved around the dark plain – scavengers looking for boots and coins to strip from the corpses, soldiers calling out for comrades, wives and children calling for fathers who had not returned, a few medical company orderlies moving between the bodies, trying to locate the increasingly weak cries of the wounded.

The stars were in the east, partially covered by smoke still rising from Middlesteel. No glow of fire though – the water must have been restored and the fires put out. For the first time in her life Molly did not know what to do. She had felt the heat of familiar souls when she had been joined with the Hexmachina – the commodore and the fey boy, Coppertracks too. They might be back at Tock House now if the folly had not been smashed apart by the Commonshare's aerial assault. She could join them. She could do . . . anything. Nobody was hunting her blood now, the poor house was gone – Circle, the very records of her existence might lie in a broken transaction engine smouldering in the ruins of Greenhall for all she knew.

But she was a Middlesteel girl at heart; she headed in the direction of the moon, across the battlefield towards the capital.

Molly wandered through the downs of Rivermarsh like a wraith. After being joined with the Hexmachina everything seemed flat and dull, denied the sight beyond sight the ancient machine possessed. It was a surreal nightmare. The wailing of a wife who had just discovered her dead husband on the ground, his face sliced by a Commonshare sabre. The multi-armed steamman she found walking through a field of deactivate knights and mounds of dead metal-fleshers, the water from his boiler leaking out as tears for the warriors he had commanded. She pressed on him the fused soul boards of Slowstack in return for a promise her friend would be taken back to the Free State. She doubted they would inter a desecration in their hall of the dead, but perhaps the board would be scrubbed and returned to a new body, as was their way. Circle knows, there would be enough parts to be returned to the mountain kingdom over the next few weeks, caravans of deactivate. Parts enough for a new generation of steammen to replace the fallen of the last.

She was trudging up a slope when she noticed a figure in a bath chair slowly pushing itself up the hill in front of her. The ground was damp and his wheels were grinding through the slippery mud.

Molly took the handles on the chair and helped persuade it to the top of the rise. 'You want to be careful, old fellow. The steammen have pickets out here to stop mechomancers robbing their graves, they won't care if you're after a Commonshare sabre to sell at the market or a Free State voicebox.'

'Thank you, compatriot, but I'm not with the crows,' said the man. 'I was looking for a friend of mine, an old student.'

'Did you find him?'

'What was left of him. He died during the battle. It helps to see the body sometimes, to remember the man.'

Molly pushed the chair around a collapsed exomount, a circle of dead Jackelians surrounding the beast, testament to the power of its pincers. 'A lot of people died here today.'

'Is that not the truth?' He slowed the chair and they listened together to the cries of the dying and the wounded still out on the field. 'What is it they say about Jackals? Every valley has a battle and every lake has a song. I wonder what they will say about this place in a hundred years?'

'They'll talk about the lions in the sky and the shifties dead in the snow. But you won't have to wait a hundred years; there'll be penny ballads on sale outside Rottonbow by the end of the week.'

'You're a true Jackelian,' laughed the man. 'You should write some of those ballads yourself and approach a printer; you would have the market to yourself if you got in early enough.'

'You know, I think I might just do that,' said Molly. 'And are you going back to teaching?'

'I have an invite,' said the man. 'From a Guardian called Tinfold, to run for parliament.'

Molly snorted. 'That old whistler? He's a radical – the Levellers haven't held the majority for a hundred years.'

'Do you think so? I always thought they were a bit middling. Still, I like to tilt for lost causes.' He indicated one of the corpses Molly was pushing him past. 'And after this I don't think Jackals will be quite as complacent about our position in the natural order of things. Middlesteel will need rebuilding and the fleet will need rebuilding; most of the Special Guard are torcless and on the run; there'll be calls to firebomb Quatérshift to rubble that will need to be fought. Thousands of our people have been turned into metal-fleshers – they will need to be helped. I think a change might be just what we need. How about you? Are you old enough to hold the franchise?'

'Greenhall took my blood code earlier this year,' said Molly. 'Maybe I'll even vote for you, though I don't know if I'd be doing you any favours if I did.'

'I can still hold a debating stick.' He slapped the side of his bath chair. 'And I can strike low, where it hurts.'

'To Middlesteel then?'

'Yes,' said Benjamin Carl. 'Home.'

Harry pushed the dead Third Brigade officer off the chair. The rear guard had made a valiant stand at the little farmhouse north of Rivermarsh. But the vengeful survivors of parliament's new pattern army pursing them had chewed them up.

'Well, he wasn't going to need it,' said Harry, seeing Oliver's look.

'You had an offer for me, Harry.'

'What makes you think that?' asked the disreputable Stave.

'The fact that you're here. If I had to guess, I would say you've been talking to someone who knows their weapons. Or their history. Or both.'

Harry sighed. 'Yes. It's those two pistols, Oliver. They come with a provenance of trouble. That bloody preacher, I should have known he was up to no good.'

'They're part of the earth, Harry, part of the land.'

'That's strange, Oliver, because I was going to propose taking them up there.' He pointed up to the ceiling.

'With or without me?'

Harry winked. 'Either will be acceptable.'

'I don't think I would make a good wolftaker, Harry.'

'I don't think the Court cares. That old preacher gave us the run-around, Oliver. Like no one else has ever done before. At the time I thought he was the man behind the trouble, but I was wrong. It's not often I admit that.'

'That's what I mean. You've got a plan. You're systemized. All that watching and peeping and planning, all those games, all those little intercessions, the small shuffles of pieces across the board, the feints and bluffs.'

'Your father played the great game, Oliver.'

'I am not my father.'

'The Court doesn't like free agents. It pollutes their ability to predict things, having chaotic elements running around down here freelancing.'

'You're right, Harry, these two pistols don't have a plan or an agenda. But when you wear them you can see evil, see it like a colour, feel it like a physical force.'

'We need the rule of law. Have you ever considered that those belt guns understand evil because they *are* evil? The things the preacher did when he was running around Jackals . . . he was operating without any boundaries. He was becoming what he hunted.'

'You think because a king-killer wrote a charter on a piece of bloodstained note paper he stole from the palace and gave it to the Court of the Air that what you do is justice?' said Oliver. 'The Court recruited you from prison. Just like the Third Brigade recruited their soldiers. Does the Court want wolftakers, or does it want killers who will take orders?'

'You can be both.'

'Were you both, Harry, when my father came to see you?'

'Oliver?'

'I can feel evil, Harry. But I don't need the guns to see the guilt you feel.'

'What do you mean, old stick?'

In Oliver's belt the two pistols began to glow. 'The *Chaunting Lay*, your pension. How many canal boats do you own now, Harry? How easy is it to operate a flash mob of smugglers when you have all the resources of the Court of the Air to smooth over the wrinkles? It must have been easy to justify when you started, just cultivating old contacts for the whistler network, a little more like a real gang each year. That was your price for protecting the preacher, for not turning him in. He was working for you in Shadowclock, Harry, wasn't he? It wasn't his smuggling operation, it was *yours*. But when my father found out about your operation he gave you a chance. He didn't go to the Court, he told you to shut it down.'

'Life isn't all black and white,' said Harry. 'Look at me. I just saved Jackals. I rolled up the Carlists that burrowed into the Court and Greenhall and every bloody corridor of the great and the good. How many times have I saved your life? I led the incremental companies that turned the war, for Circle's sake. I'm a bloody hero.'

'The hero who knew enough about aerostats to ensure that my father's vessel took a dive into the feymist curtain.'

'My little enterprise serves Jackals,' said Harry. 'It turns a crust on the side but it wouldn't last long if it didn't.'

Oliver placed the two pistols on the table. 'Then maybe we are both fated to become what we hunt. The Court of the Air gave you three choices. Bring the guns, bring me and the guns, or. . .'

'Don't make me do it, Oliver.'

'The incrementals who followed us were very good; it was almost impossible to know that they were there. But they have the weight of their own sins to carry. No level of worldsinger tricks can hide that.'

'Even if I ordered them, Oliver, they won't just let you walk off.'

Oliver laughed and the sound of it filled Harry Stave with fear. 'I'm not terribly clubbable, Harry. I don't take orders, I don't ask permission, and with my wild blood I don't think the Court has much interest in doing anything except keeping me in a cell.'

'Oliver, the Court will have half a dozen surveillants watching this farmhouse, marksmen with long rifles, a couple of companies of incrementals waiting to storm the building.'

Oliver leant forward. 'You were there for me when it counted, Harry, for Jackals. So I'm going to let you live this time. But don't let them send you after me.'

'You're not listening to me, boy. Unless you surrender those two pistols to me there's not going to be any *after*.'

'I've got a message for the Court. If they want the pistols—'

'Yes?'

'—they will have to come and take them.'

Oliver's laugh remained as he faded from view; the echoes of his cackle left lingering in the room as the black-uniformed soldiers shattered down the door.

The Whisperer pulled his attention from the surveillants in the Court at the same time as he left Harry's mind. Damn but it was cold that high – and the peculiar watchers were hard to influence – their minds changed by all those potions they took to remain awake and vigilant.

'The old sod was right about one thing,' said Nathaniel. 'They're not going to rest until they catch you or kill you.'

Oliver shrugged and spun one of the pistols around before holstering it. 'On the run for being fey – on the run for these. You can slip a piece of paper between the difference. How about you?'

The Whisperer had shifted back to his natural form, leaving the pretence of humanity behind. 'I'm going to find myself a forest and a cave, Oliver. I'm going to live life as a hermit, far, far away from all the hamblins. Roger everyone. I just want the peace that comes from being alone.'

'Is that any different from how you were held at Hawklam?' asked Oliver.

'I will be where I choose to be. That's all the difference in the world – you should understand that. But Oliver, do me a favour. . .'

'I owe you at least that.'

'I saved myself first, you second, the feybreed third, and Jackals last of all. I don't want any part of your mischief, Oliver Brooks.'

'You will have your solitude, Nathaniel. If things get too

hairy here I can always slip somewhere they can't follow. You don't need to worry about me.'

The Whisperer hissed in laughter. 'Worry about you? Dear Circle, and they thought I was a menace to the realm. Goodbye Oliver. Don't sell your life too cheaply.'

Oliver watched the Whisperer head through the trees, his shuffling footsteps through the brambles disappearing, followed only by the hoot of an owl. 'Goodbye Whisperer. Goodbye, old friend.'

As the Whisperer left, the Lady of the Lights materialized into view by Oliver's side. 'I can remove the stain on your soul, Oliver, if you wish it to be so.'

'No more fuse, mother?'

'His time has gone. I am afraid he rather over-reached himself.'

'My fault no doubt, I did rather goad him. As for my soul, I am who I am. Part of you was briefly human once – human enough to take a lover from the race of man – you must remember change, evolution.'

The Lady of the Lights drew a circle in the air, sparkling motes that faded beside the miniature stars that revolved around her orbit. 'The system exists to accommodate change. Change, even at the end of all things, is the only real constant.'

'I hope I did not disappoint you.'

'No Oliver.' She smiled. 'Quite the opposite. You *astonished* me.'

'Will I see you again?'

She was fading away, the trees and moonlight visible through her white robes. 'In another thousand years, perhaps. Your people are always running into trouble, always choosing to believe in the wrong things.'

Oliver sighed. He would not be around in a thousand years.

But Jackals would, and the guns would, and they, they would remember.

Master Saw walked with the leader of the council of seers, their conversation echoing down the corridors of Mechancia. They were almost at the chambers of education; the playful sound of the young steammen's nursery bodies a cheerful counterpoint to the endless stream of business which being regent brought.

'There is no margin for error in this decision,' said Master Saw.

'Nor would the Loas allow it,' said the council leader. 'The cogs of Gear-gi-ju have fallen the same way for weeks – I myself have been ridden by Zaka of the Cylinders and Adjasou-Rust, and they both concur. It has been obvious for a while which body King Steam has settled in. You must see it, Master Saw, even a venerable old fighter like yourself.'

'Yes,' said Master Saw. 'The ancients in the hall of the dead whisper his name; the slipthinkers find it scattered in the great pattern when they grow ill from information sickness. It is a wonder his name does not spontaneously slip into the hymns of the people.'

He nodded to the educator who greeted them at the doors to the level. Two children in nursery bodies raced past them, their tracks skidding along the marble floor, oblivious to the presence of the three adults.

'Delay long enough and I am sure that too will happen,' said the council leader. 'Ah, there he is. Such a serious child.'

The seer, the educator and Master Saw stopped. The young steamman was at a table, paper spread out in front of him, concentrating so hard he had not noticed the adults or the other nursery bodies at play.

Master Saw had his suspicions. The cracked soul board

that had been passed to him by the softbody girl four years ago on the bloody battlefield of Rivermarsh, the soul board that had belonged to the desecration, the one that would have been scrubbed and recycled by the birthing chamber. By the beard of Zaka of the Cylinders, he would dearly love to know where that particular soul board had ended up.

'What is that thing he is doing called?' asked Master Saw.

'It is a form of visual representation,' said the educator. 'Like writing or the plans schema of an architect. You need to stare at it for quite a while, but if you look long enough it starts to make sense. You can see a picture among the strokes and marks. He has been teaching the other children how to do it, too.'

Well, King Steam had always been different, eccentric in many little ways.

'The softbodies do this, do they not?'

'Yes, master,' said the educator, passing the steamman knight one of the sheets of paper. 'They call it painting.'

Master Saw looked at the paper, trying to resolve the mass of colours and detail into an image. There was something there, something elusive. He tried to think of the script of writing, of the steamman iconography that might bring meaning to the representation. It was hard work indeed.

'The slipthinkers are very impressed,' said the educator proudly. 'Especially our people in Jackals who have more familiarity with such things. We have noticed similar representations on some of the walls and floors of the palace; we may have had such an art in the past ourselves but lost it during the coldtime.'

The child looked up at the adults, noticing them for the first time. 'My pictures are in colour.'

Master Saw patted the child's head. 'That much I can see, young person.'

Master Saw took the sheet of paper away with him. He would look at it a little each day. The steamman knight would follow the advice he so often dispensed on the floor of the dojo – with enough time and practice you could master any challenge, any puzzle. Things would become clear in time.

Fladdock stepped over the body of the old man to gaze out of the barred window at the passing boots of the citizens of New Albans. The recently installed Leveller government in Jackals had not made much of a dent in the flow of convicts sentenced to the boat, or for that matter to his own fate – a month on a rotting prison hulk bobbing in the waters of the Gambleflowers, followed by the long transportation to Concorzia in the stinking holds of a merchant steamship.

Most of the convicts were half Fladdock's age, street children who had only stolen to stay alive. Far easier prey for Middlesteel's crushers than the slicker professional criminals that ran with the flash mob. With the exception of the crooked old corn-chandler sleeping at his feet, Fladdock was now the oldest transportee in the cell awaiting the appearance of a colonist farmer to purchase his papers. Fladdock had certainly had his eyes opened since being sentenced for his admittedly incompetent attempt to dip that swell's wallet on Haggswood Field. Eight years' labour and transportation for touching the smooth leather of some quality's wallet – hardly a fair exchange.

'Tell us a story again?' asked Gallon, hopefully.

Fladdock nodded kindly to the young boy. Who would have thought the mere ability to read would see him appointed as the official librarian of the motley group of convicts? He picked up the torn penny sheet which one of the passing settlers – probably an ex-convict – had passed through the bars, and brushed down its front cover. *The Middlesteel*

Illustrated. Four weeks old, the saltwater stains showing where it had been carried over as ballast in one of the clippers lying off the bay of New Albans.

Fladdock would have preferred one of the more relevant local news sheets, but beggars could not be choosers – and transportees had to be even less selective, it seemed.

'Which story would you like me to read, Gallon?'

'Something from the pages with dancing and rich people!' piped up Louisa the Dipper. 'Like the one about the ball at Sun Gate.'

'Boring,' said Gallon. 'Give it a rest, girl. The crime and punishment pages. They're the best!'

'There's a real story in here at the back,' said Fladdock. 'Not just news, but a piece of fiction. It's called a serial. Just like the kind of tale you would find inside a penny dreadful.'

'I know what a chuffing serial is,' said Louisa the Dipper. 'But that's no bleeding good, is it? We'll have missed the start of the tale and none of us will ever know how the story ends up either; we'll be stuck on a farm on the plains sweating in some nob's field.'

'That's a pity,' said Fladdock. 'I read it myself yesterday and it's rather good, something completely new in fact. People are calling it celestial fiction. It's all about a group of aeronauts who travel by airship to one of our moons and find very different creatures living up there. It's all the go back in Jackals; it's written by a woman too.'

'A woman?' said Louisa the Dipper. 'Can I see a picture of her?'

'There's no line illustration of the author,' explained Fladdock, showing the girl the pages. 'But the name reads M.W. Templar. When you find a story where the writer is using initials instead of a first name, the chances are the author is a female . . . you see the stories often sell better if the readership don't know the novelist is a woman.'

Fladdock failed to mention the fact that he knew the author personally. And she was definitely a woman.

'Read the real stories. With the murders and the stealing,' demanded Gallon.

'Again?' sighed Fladdock. 'Alright, we'll stick with the real murders and stealing for now, but only if I can read Louisa the serial afterwards. What story do you want me to start with?'

'The broadsman who took a knife in the gut after they found him cheating at cards,' suggested one of the other convicts, a craynarbian youngling with a missing arm.

'No,' said Gallon, a serious look settling on his gaunt face. 'The Hood-o'-the-marsh story. The one where the Hood-o'-the-marsh escapes twenty crushers after hanging the mine owner, the jigger that left his workers to die in the cave-in because it cost too much to save 'em.'

'You are a turnip, Gallon,' said Louisa the Dipper. 'There's no Hood-o'-the-marsh. It's just a name radicals use when they want to put a scare into the quality.'

'He is bleeding real!' shouted back Gallon. 'His stories are always in the sheets. They say he has two pistols that shine like devil fire and he only kills at night when he becomes invisible; they say that he can whistle down lashlites from the sky to rescue him when the crushers have him cornered!'

'My granddad used to tell me stories about the Hood-o'-the-marsh that he was told by *his* granddad,' said Louisa the Dipper. 'Leaaf addict is this Hood? Ghost is he? You still waiting for your Midwinter presents from Mother White Horse? Maybe they'll be delivered here tomorrow, Gallon.'

Their impromptu reading was interrupted by a clanking at the door of the cell, followed by a colonial guard admitting a gust of fresh air into the fetid holding chamber. 'On your feet now my lovely boys – you've got some respectable visitors.' He glanced at the old craynarbian waiting in the doorway behind him. 'Well, fairly respectable anyway. Two gentlemen farmers after extra hands. Prisoner Fladdock, you in here?'

Fladdock stood up.

'Your lucky day, young fellow my lad. One of the cattle owners scanning the transport list spotted your blood code and reckons you're her second cousin twice removed or some such tosh. She's bought out your contract.'

'Lucky jigger,' someone muttered.

Fladdock nodded, feeling the scrubby beard on his cheeks. About time. The blood code was no more real than his name, no more real than his face – which still felt distorted and swollen when he touched it. He was constantly amazed that the other convicts could not see through the results of his visit to the back-street worldsinger. The farmer picking up his paper could conceivably be his second cousin twice removed, though. Royalists had been finding the wide-open plains and deep forests of Concorzia more than accommodating for generations.

Did Commodore Black's face still feel like this after all the years since his own trip to the worldsinger? Fladdock might have asked if he had known what the effects were going to be like. The cunning old sea dog had been right on the money about one thing. With the forces of the old country still unrelentingly shaking trees to try and turn up Prince Alpheus, the easiest way out of Jackals was with a bona fide prison record turning on the drums of a transaction engine at Greenhall and a free transportation under the crushers' noses courtesy of the office of the colonies. They had declared the former king dead. They could *never* afford to be proved wrong.

The guard turned to the old craynarbian. 'And how many hands will you be requiring today, Mister Ka'oard?'

'Just the ones in this chamber,' said Ka'oard.

The guard groaned. 'Not again. You can't keep on doing this, sir. It is causing tensions among the other landowners. These jacks are meant to be serving labour, not rolling for fish in the waters of one of your streams. Someone in town told me you've even engaged a couple of tutors for these scruffs out at Vauxtion Valley. My lovely boys need to be taught how to harvest and cut down lumber, not master their letters. You realize there's a shortage of labour here now? Just how much money have you got to be spending, driving up the price of convict contracts?'

'Oh, there's a few of your very fine Jackelian pennies left yet, I think,' replied Ka'oard.

The guard sighed in exasperation and waved Fladdock out, passing him over to the cart driver that had been sent to collect the young man.

Fladdock stepped forward, handing the battered news sheet down to Gallon. 'Keep it, Gallon. Keep it for when you've mastered your letters.'

The colonial guard pocketed the customary tip sent by Fladdock's new master and looked over at the craynarbian. 'It's not like the old days anymore, Mister Ka'oard, when you could ride for months without bumping into one of your neighbours. You could breathe back then, you could really feel alive. Those are the times I was born with and they were damn good years too. But those days are gone out here.'

Blinking in the sunlight, Fladdock glanced back at the remaining convicts, flexed his two perfect arms and grinned. Then he was gone.

'Yes,' said Ka'oard. 'You are quite correct. I don't believe these are the old days any more. But they will do.'

Turn the page for a preview of

The Kingdom
Beyond the Waves

Stephen Hunt

Available July 2009 from Tor

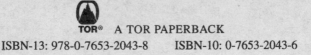
TOR® A TOR PAPERBACK

ISBN-13: 978-0-7653-2043-8   ISBN-10: 0-7653-2043-6

Chapter One

Amelia Harsh wiped the sweat from her hands across her leather trousers, then thrust her fingers up into Mombiko's vice-tight grip. The ex-slave hauled her onto the ledge, the veins on his arms bulging as he lifted her up the final few feet to the summit. Bickering voices chased Amelia up the face of the blisteringly hot mountainside like the chattering of sand beetles.

'You climb better than them, even with your poisoned arm,' said Mombiko.

Amelia rubbed at the raw wound on her right shoulder – like her left, as large as that of a gorilla. Not due to the stinging scorpion that had crept into her tent two nights earlier, but the result of a worldsinger's sorcery. Large sculpted biceps muscles that could rip a door apart or cave in the skull of a camel; a physique that was rendered near useless by that bloody insect's barbed tail. The scorpion had to have stung her gun arm, too.

Mombiko passed the professor a blessedly cool canteen and she took a greedy swig of water before checking the progress of the Macanalie brothers. They were a minute away from the ledge, cursing each other and squabbling over the best footholds and grips to reach the summit.

'The brothers got us through the Northern Desert,' said Amelia. 'There are not many uplanders who could have done that.'

'You know where those three scum developed their knowledge of the sands, mma,' said Mombiko, accusingly. 'The brothers guide traders over the border in both directions – avoiding the kingdom's revenue men to the north and the caliph's tax collectors to the south.'

Amelia pointed to the sea of wind-scoured dunes stretched out beneath them. 'It's not much of a border. Besides, I know about their side-trade as well as you do, capturing escaped slaves who make it to the uplands and dragging them back for the caliph's bounty on the slaves' heads.'

'They are not good men, professor.'

Amelia checked the sling of the rifle strapped to her back. 'They were as good as we were going to get without the university's help.'

Mombiko nodded and clipped the precious water canteen back onto his belt.

Damn the pedants on the High Table. A pocket airship could have crossed the desert in a day rather than the weeks of sun-scorched marching Amelia's expedition had endured. But the college at Saint Vines did not want the technology of an airship falling into the caliph's hands. And it was a fine excuse for the college authorities to drop another barrier in front of her studies, her obsession.

'You wait here,' Amelia said to Mombiko. 'Help them up.'

'If they try anything?'

She pointed to his pistol and the bandolier of crystal charges strapped over his white robes. 'Why do you think I made sure we were climbing at the front? I wouldn't trust a Macanalie to hold my guide rope.'

A sound like a crow screeched in the distance. Shielding her eyes, Amelia scanned the sky. Blue, cloudless. Clear of any tell-tale dots around the sun that would indicate the presence of the lizard-things that the caliph's scouts flew. No match for an airship's guns, but the unnatural creatures could fall upon the five of them easily enough; rip their spines out in a dive and carry their shredded remains back to one of Cassarabia's military garrisons. Again, the screech. She saw a dark shape shuffling higher up the mountainside – a sand hawk – and relaxed. It was eying up one of the small salamanders on the dunes beneath them, no doubt.

Professor Harsh returned her attention to the wall on the ledge, following the trail of stone sigils worn away to near-indecipherability by Cassarabia's sandstorms over the millennia. Mombiko's contact had been right after all; a miracle the deserter from the caliph's army had made it this far, had spotted the carving in the rocks below. Had possessed enough education to know what the carving might signify and the sand-craft to reach the uplands of Jackals and the safety of the clans. The path between the crags led to a wall of boulders with a circular stone slab embedded in it. A door! Shielded from the worst of the storm abrasions, the sigils on the portal had fared better than the worn iconography that had led her up here.

Amelia marvelled at the ancient calligraphy. So primitive, yet so beautiful. There were illustrations too, a swarm of brutal-looking vehicles ridden by fierce barbarians – horseless carriages, but not powered by the high-tension clockwork milled by her own nation of Jackals. Engines from a darker time.

Her revelry at the discovery was interrupted by the snarling voices behind her.

'Is this it, then, lassie?'

Amelia looked at the three upland smugglers, practically drooling at the thought of the treasures they were imagining behind the door. 'Roll the door back, but *carefully*,' she ordered.

Dipping into her backpack she pulled out five cotton masks with string ties. 'Put these on before you go in.'

'Are you daft, lassie?' spat the oldest of the brothers. 'There's no sandstorm coming.'

'These are not sand masks,' Amelia said, tapping a thumb on the door. 'You are standing outside the tomb of a powerful chieftain. He would have owned worldsingers as part of his slave-clan and would not have been above having them leave a sprinkling of curse-dust in his tomb to kill grave robbers, bandits and any of his rivals tempted to desecrate his grave.' She slipped the mask over her mouth, the chemicals in the fabric filling her nose with a honey-sweet smell. 'But you are free to go in without protection.'

The brothers each gave her a foul look, but pulled on the masks all the same, then got to work rolling the door back with all the vigour that only greed could generate. Mombiko drew out a gas spike and ignited the lantern. 'I shall go first, mma.'

Amelia signalled her agreement. Mombiko had been raised in the great forests of the far south and possessed an uncanny sixth sense. Curse-dust aside, there should only be a single trap in this ancient tomb – the mausoleum's creators were an unsubtle brutish people – but it was best to be sure.

The door rolled back. Mombiko held the gas spike in front of him, shadows dancing in the dark tunnel that lay revealed behind the stone slab. It was cool inside after the heat of the desert. Crude stone-hewn steps led downward, iron brackets in the wall where lanterns would once have hung.

'Did you hear something?' asked one of the brothers.

'Put your gun down, you fool,' said Amelia. 'It's just an echo. You fire your pistol in here and the ricochet of your ball will be what kills you.'

'If there's a treasure, there will be something to guard it,' insisted one of the brothers. 'A wee beastie.'

'Nothing that could survive over two thousand years trapped down here without any food,' said Amelia.

'Holster your pistol,' ordered the oldest brother, 'the lass is right. Besides, it's her laddie-boy that's going in first, right?'

Followed by the cold echoes of their own steps, the five interlopers walked down the carved passage; at the bottom of the sloping cut was a foreboding stone door, a copper panel in a wall-niche by its side, the space filled with levers, nobs and handles.

'I've got a casket of blow-barrel sap back with the camels,' said one of the Macanalie brothers.

Amelia wiped the cobwebs off the copper panel. 'You got enough to blow up *all* the treasure, clansman? Leave the archaeology to me.'

Amelia touched the levers, tracing the ancient script with her fingers. Like most of the Black-oil Horde's legacy to history, their language was stolen, looted from one of the many non-nomadic nations the barbarians had over-run during their age. The script was a riddle – filled with jokes and black humour.

'The wrong choice . . .' whispered Mombiko behind her.

'I know, I know,' said Amelia, eyeing the impressions along the wall where the tomb builders had buried their compressed oil explosives. Surely the passage of time would have spoiled their potency? 'Now, let's see. In their legends the sun rises when the petrol-gods sleep, but sleeping is a play on words, so—' she grabbed two levers, sliding one up while shoving another into a side channel and down, then clicked one of the nobs clockwise to face the symbol of the sun.

Ancient counter-weights shifted and the door drew upwards into the ceiling of the passage with a *rack-rack-rack*. Mombiko let out his breath.

The oldest of the smuggler brothers nodded in approval. 'Clever lass. I knew there was a reason we brought you along.'

The professor flicked back her mane of dark hair. 'I'm not paying you extra for your poor sense of humour, Macanalie. Let's see what's down here.'

They walked into the burial chamber. With its rough, jagged walls, it might almost have been mistaken for a natural cavern were it not for the statues holding up the vaulted roof – squat totem-poles of granite carved with smirking goblin faces. Mombiko's gas spike was barely powerful enough to reveal the eight-wheeled carriage that rose on a dais in the centre of the chamber, spiral lines of gold rivets studding its armoured sides and exhaust stacks. The nearest of the smugglers gasped, scurrying over to the boat-sized machine to run his hand over the lance points protruding from the vehicle's prow. They were silver-plated, but Amelia knew that reinforced steel would lie hidden beneath each deadly lance head.

'It's true, after all this time,' said Amelia, as if she did not really believe it herself. 'A war chief of the Black-oil Horde, perhaps even the great Diesela-Khan himself.'

'This is a horseless carriage?' asked one of the Macanalies. 'I can't see the clockwork. Where's the clockwork?'

He was elbowed aside by his excited elder. 'What matters that? It's a wee fortune, man! Look at the gems on the thing – her hood here, is this beaten out of solid gold?'

'Oil,' said Amelia, distracted. 'They burnt oil in their engines, they hadn't mastered high-tension clockwork.'

'Slipsharp oil?' queried the smuggler. Surely there were not enough of the great beasts of the ocean swimming the world's seas to bleed blubber to fuel such a beautiful, deadly vehicle?

'Do you not know anything?' said Mombiko, waving the gas spike over the massive engine at the carriage's rear. 'Black water from the ground. This beautiful thing would have drunk it like a horse.'

Amelia nodded. One of the many devices that stopped functioning many thousands of years ago if the ancient sagas were to be believed – overwhelmed by the power of the worldsong and the changing universe. Mombiko pointed to a silver sarcophagus in the middle of the wagon and Amelia climbed in, pulling out her knife to lever open the ancient wax-sealed coffin.

'They must have taken the wagon to pieces outside,' laughed the youngest brother. 'Put it back together down here.'

'Obviously,' said Amelia, grunting as she pressed her knife under the coffin lid. Her shoulder burned with the effort. Damn that scorpion.

'Oh, you're a sly one, Professor Harsh,' spat the eldest brother. 'All your talk of science and the nobility of ancient history and all of the past's lessons. All those fine-sounding lectures back in the desert. And here you are, scrabbling for jewels in some quality's coffin. You almost had me believing you, lassie.'

She shot a glare at the smuggler, ignoring his taunts. She deserved it. Perhaps she was no better than these three gutter-scrapings of the kingdom's border towns.

'Her wheels weren't built to run on sand,' mused one of the Macanalies. He ran his hand covetously along the shining spikes of gold on the vehicle's rim.

Amelia was nearly done, the last piece of wax seal giving way. It was a desecration really. No wonder the eight great universities had denied her tenure, kept her begging for expedition funds like a hound kept underneath the High Table. But there might be treasure inside. *Her* treasure.

'There wasn't a desert outside when our chieftain here was buried,' said Amelia. 'It was all steppes and grassland. This mountain once stretched all the way back to the uplands, before the glaciers came and crushed the range to dust.'

At last the lid shifted and Amelia pushed the sarcophagus open. There were weapons in there alongside the bones, bags of coins too – looted from towns the ancient nomads had sacked, no doubt, given that the Black-oil Horde either wore or drove their wealth around. But might there be something else hidden amongst their looted booty? Amelia's hands pushed aside the diamond-encrusted ignition keys and the black-powder guns of the barbarian chief – torn between scrabbling among the find like a looter and honouring her archaeologist's pledge. There! Among the burial spoils, the hexagonal crystal-books she had crossed a desert for.

Professor Amelia Harsh lifted them out and then she sobbed. Each crystal-book was veined with information sickness, black lines threading out as if a cancer had infected the hard purple glass. Had the barbarians of the Black-oil Horde unknowingly spoiled the ancient information blocks? Or had their final guardian cursed the books even as the nomads smashed their way into the library of the ancient civilization that had created them? They were useless. Good for nothing except bookends for a rich merchant with a taste for antiques.

The oldest of the brothers mistook her sobs for tears of joy. 'There's enough trinkets in that dead lord's chest to pay for a mansion in Middlesteel.'

Amelia looked up at the ugly faces of the nomad gods on the columns. They stared back at her. Chubba-Gearshift. Tartar of the Axles. Useless deities that had not been worshipped for millennia, leering granite faces that seemed to be mocking her flesh-locked desires.

'The crystal-books are broken,' said Mombiko, climbing up on the wagon to spill his light down over the contents of the coffin. 'That is too bad, mma. But with these other things here, you can finance a second expedition – there will be more chances, later . . .'

'I fear you have been misinformed.'

Amelia turned to see a company of black-clad desert warriors standing by the entrance to the tomb, gauze sand masks pushed up under their hoods. The three Macanalie brothers had moved to stand next to them, out of the line of fire of the soldiers' long spindly rifles.

'Never trust a Macanalie,' Amelia swore.

'Finding this hoard was never a sure thing,' said the eldest brother. 'But the price on your head, lassie, now that's filed away in the drawer of every garrison commander from here to Bladetenbul.'

'The caliph remembers those who promise much and do not keep their word,' said the captain of the company of soldiers. 'But not, I fear for you, with much fondness.'

Amelia saw the small desert hawk sitting on his leather glove. Just the right size to carry a message. Damn. She had let her excitement at finding the tomb blind her to the Macanalie brothers' treachery; they had sent for the scout patrol. She and Mombiko were royally betrayed.

'The caliph is still cross about Zal-Rashid's vase?' Amelia eyed the soldiers. At least five of them. 'I told him it was nothing but a myth.'

'Far more equitable then, Professor Harsh, if you had given the vase to his excellency *after* you had dug it out of his dunes,' said the soldier. 'Just as you had agreed. Rather than stealing it and taking it back to Jackals with you.'

'Oh, that. I can explain that,' said Amelia. 'There's an explanation, really. What is it that your people say, the sand has many secrets?'

'You will have much time to debate the sayings of the hundred prophets with his exulted highness,' said the officer. 'Much time.'

Mombiko looked at Amelia with real fear in his eyes and she bit her lip. His fate as an escaped slave of a Cassarabian nobleman would be no kinder than her own. It would be little consolation for Mombiko that he did not have a womb as Amelia did, that could be twisted into a breeding tank for Cassarabia's dark sorcerers to nurture their pets and monstrosities inside. One of the Macanalie brothers sniggered at the thought of the fates awaiting the haughty Jackelian professor and her colleague, but when the smuggler tried to move towards the ancient vehicle, a desert warrior shoved him back with his bone-like rifle butt.

'What's this, laddie?' spat the eldest of the brothers. 'We had a deal. You get these two. We get the reward and all of this.'

'And so you shall receive your reward,' said the caliph's officer. He waved at the ancient wagon. 'But *this* was not part of our arrangement.'

'You have to be joking me, laddie. Listen to me, you swindling jiggers, there's enough down here to share out for all of us.'

The caliph's man pointed to the leering bodies on the totem-pole columns. 'There will be nothing left to share, effendi. These bloated infidel toads are not of the Hundred Ways, they are idols of darkness and shall be cast down.' He gestured to one of the sand warriors. 'Go back to the saddlebags and bring enough charges to bury this unholy place under rock for another thousand years.'

'Are you out of your skull, laddie? There's wealth enough here to make us all rich! We can live like kings, you could live like an emir.'

The officer laughed with contempt. 'The caliph has lived two-score of your miserable lifetimes and if the hundred prophets be blessed, he shall live two-score more. What need does he have for the unclean gold of infidel gods when he has countless servants in every province of Cassarabia labouring to offer him their tribute for eternity?'

Amelia looked at Mombiko and understanding flashed between them. Mombiko would never again be a slave, and Amelia was jiggered if she would be used as a breeder, or allow herself to be handed over to a Cassarabian torture-sculptor to twist and mutate her bones until she was left stretched out like a human oak tree in the caliph's scented punishment gardens.

'He may be hundreds of years old,' said Amelia, 'but let me tell you a few home truths about your ruler. One, the caliph is too boring for me to listen to for a single hour, let alone a lifetime of agonized captivity. Two, he's not even a man. He's a woman dressed up as a male, and a damned ugly one at that. How she continues to fool all of you desert lads is beyond me.'

There was an intake of breath at her blasphemy.

'And three – next time you try and sneak up on me, bring your *own* damn lamp!'

Mombiko killed the gas spike. With a hissing sputter the chamber was plunged into absolute darkness. Amelia kicked down the lever alongside the carriage's steering wheel and the hisses from the spring-mounted spears decorating the wagon's prow were followed by screams and shouts and sickening thuds as the steel heads found their mark. This was followed by a crack of snapping glass. One of the collapsing desert soldier's spindly rifles splintering its charge, providing a brief gun-fire illumination of the carnage in which all the professor noticed was Mombiko sprinting before her towards the exit. Someone tried to grab Amelia and she heard the rustle of a dagger being slid from its hilt. She used her left arm to shove out towards where her assailant's throat should be, and was rewarded by a snap and a body falling limp against her own. Amelia vaulted the corpse and found the stairs out of the tomb, nearly tripping over a speared soldier.

One of their treacherous guides was screaming for his brothers, something about trying to scrape up the gems inside the sarcophagus. Groping inside the panel-niche Amelia reversed the levers and the door started to lower itself with its *rack-rack-rack* rasp. She had brought herself and Mombiko a couple of minutes as the caliph's survivors, left in the dark, tried to locate the door release wheel she had spotted back inside the burial chamber. Amelia panted, taking the stairs three treads at a time. Damn, the steps had not seemed so long nor so steep on the way down. And her rifle – a trusty Jackelian Brown Bess – was not going to be much good to her one-armed.

'Professor!'

'Keep going, Mombiko. Beware the ledge. The caliph's boys might have left sentries outside.'

She pulled out a glass charge from her bandolier, cracking it against the wall so the two chambers of blow-barrel sap nearly mixed, then, still sprinting, bent down to roll the shell along the stone floor behind her. A wall of searing heat greeted Amelia as she left the tomb, the sun raised to its midday zenith. Thank the Circle, the ledge was clear of desert warriors.

Mombiko peered over the cliff. 'There are their mounts. No soldiers that I can see.'

Amelia glanced down; sandpedes tethered together, long leathery hides and a hundred insect-like legs: the ingenuity of this hear-blasted land's womb mages unrestrained by ethics or her own nation's Circlist teachings. Amelia let her good arm take the strain of the downward climb, aided by gravity and the rush of blood thumping through her heart. Crumbling dust from the scramble down coated her hair, making her cough. Her gun arm was burning in agony. She had accidentally thumped it into one of the cliff's outcrops and the scorpion-poisoned flesh felt like the caliph's torturers were already extracting their revenge from her body. They were near the bottom of the cliff face when an explosion sounded. Someone had stepped on her half-shattered shell, mixed the explosive sap in the firing chamber.

Amelia dropped the remaining few feet onto the warm orange sands. 'I do hope that was one of the Macanalies.'

'Better it was one of the soldiers, professor.' Mombiko had his knife out and advanced to where the caliph's men had picketed their sandpedes. The creatures' legs fluttered nervously as he approached them and reached out to slice their tethers free. Mandibles chattered, the sandpedes exchanging nervous glances, only the green human eyes in their beetle-black faces betraying their origins in some slave's sorcery-twisted womb. Too well trained, they were failing to escape. Amelia picked up a rock with her left hand and lobbed it hard at the creatures, the mounts exploding in an eruption of bony feet as they fled the shadow of the mountains.

Cracks sounded from the top of the peak, spouts of sand spewing up where the lead balls struck close to Mombiko and Amelia. The caliph's bullyboys had found the chamber's door release faster than she had hoped. Sand spilled down Amelia's boots as the two of them scrambled for their camels, the creatures whining as the soldiers' bullets whistled past their ears. There was a grunt from Mombiko, and he clutched his side in pain with one hand, but he spurred his camel after the retreating sandpedes, waving at her to ride on. Amelia urged her camel into an uncustomarily fast pace for the heat of the day. Luckily, the ornery beasts were skittish after seeing the unnatural sandpedes and only too glad to gallop away from the mountainside's shade.

Once the pursuit was lost behind the boundless dunes, Amelia drew to a halt, Mombiko sagging in his saddle. She pulled him off his camel and laid him down in the sand, turning aside his robes to find the wound.

'It's not too deep, Mombiko.'

'Poisoned,' hissed Mombiko. 'The soldiers hollow out their balls and fill them with the potions of their garrison mages. Look at my camel.'

His steed was groaning, sinking to its stomach on the sands

while Amelia's camel tried to nuzzle it back to its feet. The creature had been struck on its flanks by one of the soldier's parting shots. Mombiko pointed to a protruding wooden handle strapped under his saddlebags. 'For the sun.'

She took it down and passed it to Mombiko. The umbrella had been her gift to him when he had started working at their university. Such a small thing in return for his prodigious talents. He could learn a new language in a week, quote verbatim from books he had read a year before. He had told her once that his seemingly unnatural memory was a common trait among many of his caste.

'The forest way,' said Mombiko.

Amelia nodded, tears in her eyes, understanding his request. No burial. From nature you have emerged, to nature so you shall return. The desert would blow over his unburied bones.

Mombiko reached out for Amelia's hand and when she opened her palm there was a cut diamond pressed inside it, the image of one of the Black-oil Horde's gods etched across the jewel's glittering prism.

'Sell it,' rasped Mombiko. 'Use the money to find the city – for both of us.'

'Are you an archaeologist's assistant or a crypt-robber, man?'

'I am Mombiko Tibar-Wellking,' said the ex-slave, raising his voice. Sweat was flooding down his face now. He was so wet he looked as if he had been pulled from the sea rather than stretched out across a sand dune. 'I am a lance lord of the Red Forest and I shall take my leave of my enemies – a – free – man.'

Amelia held him as he shuddered, each jolt arriving a little further apart, until he had stopped moving. His spirit was blowing south, back to the vast ruby forests of his home. But her path lay north to Jackals, the republic with a king. Her green and blessed land. A home she would in all likelihood never see again now.

Amelia closed his eyes. 'I shall be with you in a little while, Mombiko Tibar-Wellking.' She took the water canteen from the dead camel and left her friend's body behind, his umbrella held to his still chest for a lance.

The stars of the night sky would guide her true north, but not past the water holes that the Macanalie brothers had known about, not past the dozens of fractious tribes that feuded across the treacherous sands. Amelia Harsh kicked her camel forward and tried to fill her mind with the dream of the lost city.

The city in the air.